AMERICAN
TABLOID

AMERICAN TABLOID

a novel by

JAMES ELLROY

ALFRED A. KNOPF
New York
1995

Castro ousted the democratically elected anti-Communist Cuban Premier Fulgencio Batista last New Year's Day. The bombastic bushy-bearded beatnik bard promised land reforms, social justice and tackled plantocrats on every—the standard stipends of welfare-warfed Commie commissars. He took over a small bastion of freedom 90 miles off U.S. shores, pathologically picked the pocket of patriotic patriarchs, nauseously "nationalized" U.S.-owned hotel-casinos, fried the friendly fragrant fields of the United Fruit Company and generally absconded with astronomical sums—nonetheless the most peon-protecting, Commie-constraining export: money!!!

Yes, kats and kittens, it all comes down to divinely deigned dollops of dollars—U.S., of course, those gorgeously garlanded greenbacks replete with pulsatingly powerful Presidential portraits, caricatures captivating in their corrosive condemnation of Communism!!!

Item: the beatnik bard bamboozled beleaguered bellhops at the formerly swank Nacional and Capri hotels in Havana, nastily nationalized their tips and rapidly replaced them with a regiment of rowdy Red regulators—bandy-legged bantamweight bandidos who also serve as crucifyingly-corrupt craps croupiers!

Item: fruit fields frantically french-fried! Peons passionately protected by America's altruistically-altered egalitarian economy are now welfare-wilted, pauper-periled Red Recidivists grubbing for Commie compensation!

Item: Raul "The Tool" Castro has flamboyantly flooded Florida with hellishly horrific, hophead-hazarding amounts of demonically deadly "Big H": Heroin!!! He's bent on needle-notching vast legions of Cuban immigrant slaves: zorched-out zombies to spread the cancerous Castro gospel between bouts of Heroin-hiatus junkie junketeered euphoria!

Item: there's a growing number of Cuban exiles and home-grown American patriots who take a regious exception to the beatnik brothers' broadside of bamboozlement. Right now they're recruiting in Miami and South Florida. These men are tantalizingly tough tigers who have earned their stripes in the jungles of Castro's jam-packed, jerry-rigged jails. Every day, more and more men like them are arriving on America's shores, anxious to sing the mellifluous messages of "My Country 'Tis of Thee."

This reporter talked to an American named "Big Pete," a dedicated anti-Communist currently training anti-Castro guerrillas. "It all comes down to patriotism," Big Pete said. "Do you want a Communist dictatorship 90 miles off our shores or not? I don't, so I've joined the Cuban Freedom Cause. And I'd like to extend an invitation to all Cuban exiles and native-born men of Cuban descent. Join us. If you're in Miami, ask around. Local Cubans will tell you we mean business."

Item: with men like Big Pete on the job, Castro should be considering a new career. Hey! I know a few coffeehouses in L.A.'s own Venice West who could use a gone beatnik poet like Fidel! Hey, Fidel! Can you dig it, Daddy-O?

THIS IS A BORZOI BOOK
PUBLISHED BY ALFRED A. KNOPF, INC.

Copyright © 1995 by James Ellroy
All rights reserved under International and Pan-American Copyright
Conventions. Published in the United States by Alfred A. Knopf,
Inc., New York, and simultaneously in Canada by Random House of Canada
Limited, Toronto. Distributed by Random House, Inc., New York.

Library of Congress Cataloging-in-Publication Data

Ellroy, James, [date]
American tabloid : a novel by / James Ellroy. — 1st ed.
p. cm.
ISBN 0-679-40391-4
I. Title.
PS3555.L6274A8   1995
813'.54—dc20   94-42898
                              CIP

Published February 27, 1995
Reprinted Twice
Fourth Printing, March 1995

To

NAT SOBEL

AMERICAN
TABLOID

America was never innocent. We popped our cherry on the boat over and looked back with no regrets. You can't ascribe our fall from grace to any single event or set of circumstances. You can't lose what you lacked at conception.

Mass-market nostalgia gets you hopped up for a past that never existed. Hagiography sanctifies shuck-and-jive politicians and reinvents their expedient gestures as moments of great moral weight. Our continuing narrative line is blurred past truth and hindsight. Only a reckless verisimilitude can set that line straight.

The real Trinity of Camelot was Look Good, Kick Ass, Get Laid. Jack Kennedy was the mythological front man for a particularly juicy slice of our history. He talked a slick line and wore a world-class haircut. He was Bill Clinton minus pervasive media scrutiny and a few rolls of flab.

Jack got whacked at the optimum moment to assure his sainthood. Lies continue to swirl around his eternal flame. It's time to dislodge his urn and cast light on a few men who attended his ascent and facilitated his fall.

They were rogue cops and shakedown artists. They were wiretappers and soldiers of fortune and faggot lounge entertainers. Had one second of their lives deviated off course, American History would not exist as we know it.

It's time to demythologize an era and build a new myth from the gutter to the stars. It's time to embrace bad men and the price they paid to secretly define their time.

Here's to them.

Part I

SHAKEDOWNS

November–December 1958

Part I

SHAKEDOWNS

November–December 1958

Pete Bondurant

(Beverly Hills, 11/22/58)

He always shot up by TV light. Some spics waved guns. The head spic plucked bugs from his beard and fomented. Black & white footage; CBS geeks in jungle fatigues. A newsman said, Cuba, bad juju—Fidel Castro's rebels vs. Fulgencio Batista's standing army.

Howard Hughes found a vein and mainlined codeine. Pete watched on the sly—Hughes left his bedroom door ajar.

The dope hit home. Big Howard went slack-faced.

Room service carts clattered outside. Hughes wiped off his spike and flipped channels. The "Howdy Doody" show replaced the news—standard Beverly Hills Hotel business.

Pete walked out to the patio—pool view, a good bird-dog spot. Crappy weather today: no starlet types in bikinis.

He checked his watch, antsy.

He had a divorce gig at noon—the husband drank lunch alone and dug young cooze. Get *quality* flashbulbs: blurry photos looked like spiders fucking. On Hughes' timecard: find out who's hawking subpoenas for the TWA antitrust divestment case and bribe them into reporting that Big Howard blasted off for Mars.

Crafty Howard put it this way: "I'm not going to fight this divestment, Pete. I'm simply going to stay incommunicado indefinitely and force the price up until I *have* to sell. I'm tired of TWA anyway, and I'm not going to sell until I can realize *at least* five hundred million dollars."

He'd said it pouty: Lord Fauntleroy, aging junkie.

Ava Gardner cruised by the pool. Pete waved; Ava flipped him the bird. They went back: he got her an abortion in exchange for a weekend with Hughes. Renaissance Man Pete: pimp, dope procurer, licensed PI goon.

Hughes and him went *waaay* back.

June '52. L.A. County Deputy Sheriff Pete Bondurant—night watch commander at the San Dimas Substation. That one shitty night: a nigger rape-o at large, the drunk tank packed with howling juiceheads.

This wino gave him grief. "I know you, tough guy. You kill innocent women and your own—"

He beat the man to death barefisted.

The Sheriff's hushed it up. An eyeball witness squealed to the Feds. The L.A. agent-in-charge tagged Joe Wino "Joe Civil Rights Victim."

Two agents leaned on him: Kemper Boyd and Ward J. Littell. Howard Hughes saw his picture in the paper and sensed strongarm potential. Hughes got the beef quashed and offered him a job: fixer, pimp, dope conduit.

Howard married Jean Peters and installed her in a mansion by herself. Add "watchdog" to his duties; add the world's greatest rent-free doghouse: the mansion next door.

Howard Hughes on marriage: "I find it a delightful institution, Pete, but I also find cohabitation stressful. Explain that to Jean periodically, won't you? And if she gets lonely, tell her that she's in my thoughts, even though I'm very busy."

Pete lit a cigarette. Clouds passed over—pool loungers shivered. The intercom crackled—Hughes was beckoning.

He walked into the bedroom. "Captain Kangaroo" was on TV, the volume down low.

Dim black & white lighting—and Big Howard in deep-focus shadows.

"Sir?"

"It's 'Howard' when we're alone. You know that."

"I'm feeling subservient today."

"You mean you're feeling your oats with your paramour, Miss Gail Hendee. Tell me, is she enjoying the surveillance house?"

"She likes it. She's as hinky of shack jobs as you are, and she says twenty-four rooms for two people smooths things out."

"I like independent women."

"No you don't."

Hughes plumped up his pillows. "You're correct. But I do like the *idea* of independent women, which I have always tried to exploit in my movies. And I'm sure Miss Hendee is both a wonderful extortion partner *and* mistress. Now, Pete, about the TWA divestment . . ."

Pete pulled a chair up. "The process servers won't get to you. I've got every employee at this hotel bribed, and I've got an actor set up in a bungalow two rows over. He looks like you and dresses like you, and I've got call girls going in at all hours, to perpetuate the myth that you still fuck women. I check every man and woman who applies for work here, to make sure the Justice Department doesn't slip a ringer in. All the shift bosses here play the stock market, and for every month you go unfucking-subpoenaed I give them twenty shares of Hughes Tool Company stock apiece. As long as you stay in this bungalow, you won't be served and you won't have to appear in court."

Hughes plucked at his robe—little palsied fidgets. "You're a very cruel man."

"No, I'm *your* very cruel man, which is why you let me talk back to you."

"You're 'my man,' but you still retain your somewhat tawdry private investigator sideline."

"That's because you crowd me. That's because I'm not so good at cohabitation either."

"Despite what I pay you?"

"No, *because* of it."

"For instance?"

"For instance, I've got a mansion in Holmby Hills, but you've got the deed. I've got a '58 Pontiac coupe, but you've got the pink slip. I've got a—"

"This is getting us nowhere."

"Howard, you want something. Tell me what it is and I'll do it."

Hughes tapped his remote-control gizmo. "Captain Kangaroo" blipped off. "I've purchased *Hush-Hush* magazine. My reasons for acquiring a scurrilous scandal rag are twofold. One, I've been corresponding with J. Edgar Hoover, and I want to solidify my friendship with him. We both love the type of Hollywood gossip that *Hush-Hush* purveys, so owning the magazine would be both pleasurable and a smart political move. Second, there's politics itself. To be blunt, I want to be able to smear politicians that I dislike, especially profligate playboys like Senator John Kennedy, who might be running for President against my good friend Dick Nixon in 1960. As you undoubtedly know, Kennedy's father and I were business rivals back in the '20s, and frankly, I hate the entire family."

Pete said, "And?"

"And I know that you've worked for *Hush-Hush* as a 'story verifier,' so I know you understand that aspect of the business. It's a quasi-extortion aspect, so I know it's something you'll be good at."

Pete popped his knuckles. " 'Story verification' means 'Don't sue the magazine or I'll hurt you.' If you want me to help out that way, fine."

"Good. That's a start."

"Wrap it up, Howard. I know the people there, so tell me who's going and who's staying."

Hughes flinched—just a tad. "The receptionist was a Negro woman with dandruff, so I fired her. The stringer and so-called 'dirt digger' quit, and I want you to find me a new one. I'm keeping Sol Maltzman on. He's been writing all the articles, under a pseudonym, for years, so I'm prone to retaining him, even though he's a blacklisted Commie known to belong to no less than twenty-nine left-wing organizations, and—"

"And that's all the staff you need. Sol does a good job, and if worse comes to worse, Gail can fill in for him—she's written for *Hush-Hush* on and off for a couple of years. You've got your lawyer Dick Steisel for the legal stuff, and I can get you Fred Turentine for bug work. I'll find you a good dirt digger. I'll keep my nose down and ask around, but it might take a while."

"I trust you. You'll do your usual superb job."

Pete worked his knuckles. The joints ached—a sure sign that rain was coming. Hughes said, "Is that necessary?"

"These hands of mine brought us together, Boss. I'm just letting you know they're still here."

The watchdog house living room was 84′ by 80′.

The foyer walls were gold-flecked marble.

Nine bedrooms. Walk-in freezers thirty feet deep. Hughes had the carpets cleaned monthly—a jigaboo walked across them once.

Surveillance cameras were mounted on the roof and the upstairs landings—aimed at Mrs. Hughes' bedroom next door.

Pete found Gail in the kitchen. She had these great curves and long brown hair—her looks still got to him.

She said, "You usually hear people walk into houses, but our front door's a half-mile away."

"We've been here a year, and you're still cracking jokes."

"I live in the Taj Mahal. That takes some getting used to."

Pete straddled a chair. "You're nervous."

Gail slid her chair away from him. "Well . . . as extortionists go, I'm the nervous type. What's the man's name today?"

"Walter P. Kinnard. He's forty-seven years old, and he's been cheating on his wife since their honeymoon. He's got kids he dotes on, and the wife says he'll fold if I squeeze him with pictures and threaten to show them to the kids. He's a juicer, and he always gets a load on at lunchtime."

Gail crossed herself—half shtick, half for real. "Where?"

"You meet him at Dale's Secret Harbor. He's got a fuck pad a few blocks away where he bangs his secretary, but you insist on the Ambassador. You're in town for a convention, and you've got a snazzy room with a wet bar."

Gail shivered. Early a.m. chills—a sure sign that she had the yips.

Pete slipped her a key. "I rented the room next door to yours, so you can lock up and make it look good. I picked the lock on the connecting door, so I don't think this one will be noisy."

Gail lit a cigarette. Steady hands—good. "Distract me. Tell me what Howard the Recluse wanted."

"He bought *Hush-Hush*. He wants me to find him a stringer, so he can pull his pud over Hollywood gossip and share it with his pal J. Edgar Hoover. He wants to smear his political enemies, like your old boyfriend Jack Kennedy."

Gail smiled toasty warm. "A few weekends didn't make him my boyfriend."

"That fucking smile made him something."

"He flew me down to Acapulco once. That's a Howard the Recluse kind of gesture, so it makes you jealous."

"He flew you down on his honeymoon."

"So? He got married for political reasons, and politics makes for strange bedfellows. And my God, you are *suuuch* a voyeur."

Pete unholstered his piece and checked the clip—so fast that he didn't know why. Gail said, "Don't you think our lives are strange?"

They took separate cars downtown. Gail sat at the bar; Pete grabbed a booth close by and nursed a highball.

The restaurant was crowded—Dale's did a solid lunch biz. Pete got choice seating—he broke up a fag squeeze on the owner once.

Lots of women circulating: mid-Wilshire office stuff mostly. Gail stuck out: beaucoup more je ne sais quoi. Pete wolfed cocktail nuts—he forgot to eat breakfast.

Kinnard was late. Pete scanned the room, X-ray-eye-style.

There's Jack Whalen by the pay phones—L.A.'s #1 bookie collector. There's some LAPD brass two booths down. They're fucking whispering: "Bondurant" . . . "Right, that Cressmeyer woman."

There's Ruth Mildred Cressmeyer's ghost at the bar: this sad old girl with the shakes.

Pete slid down Memory Lane.

Late '49. He had some good sidelines going: card-game guard and abortion procurer. The scrape doctor was his kid brother, Frank.

Pete joined the U.S. Marines to bag a green card. Frank stayed with the family in Quebec and went to medical school.

Pete got hip early. Frank got hip late.

Don't speak French, speak English. Lose your accent and go to America.

Frank hit L.A. with a hard-on for money. He passed his medical boards and hung out his shingle: abortions and morphine for sale.

Frank loved showgirls and cards. Frank loved hoodlums. Frank loved Mickey Cohen's Thursday-night poker game.

Frank made friends with a stickup guy named Huey Cressmeyer. Huey's mom ran a Niggertown scrape clinic. Huey got his girlfriend pregnant and asked Mom and Frank for help. Huey got stupid and heisted the Thursday-night game—Pete was off guard duty with the flu.

Mickey gave Pete the contract.

Pete got a tip: Huey was holed up at a pad in El Segundo. The house belonged to a Jack Dragna trigger.

Mickey hated Jack Dragna. Mickey doubled the price and told him to kill everyone in the house.

December 14, 1949—overcast and chilly.

Pete torched the hideout with a Molotov cocktail. Four shapes ran out the back door swatting at flames. Pete shot them and left them to burn.

The papers ID'd them:

Hubert John Cressmeyer, 24.

Ruth Mildred Cressmeyer, 56.

Linda Jane Camrose, 20, four months pregnant.

François Bondurant, 27, a physician and French-Canadian émigré.

The snuffs stayed officially unsolved. The story filtered out to insiders.

Somebody called his father in Quebec and ratted him. The old man called him and begged him to deny it.

He must have faltered or oozed guilt. The old man and old lady sucked down monoxide fumes the same day.

That old babe at the bar was fucking Ruth Mildred's twin.

Time dragged. He sent the old girl an on-the-house refill. Walter P. Kinnard walked in and sat down next to Gail.

The poetry commenced.

Gail signaled the bartender. Attentive Walter caught the gesture and whistled. Joe Barman zoomed over with his martini shaker—regular boozer Walt packed some weight here.

Helpless Gail searched her purse for matches. Helpful Walt flicked his lighter and smiled. Sexy Walt was dripping scalp flakes all over the back of his jacket.

Gail smiled. Sexy Walt smiled. Well-dressed Walt wore white socks with a three-piece chalk-stripe suit.

The lovebirds settled in for martinis and small talk. Pete eyeballed the pre-bed warmup. Gail guzzled her drink for courage—her jaggedy nerves showed through plain.

She touched Walt's arm. Her guilty heart showed plain—except for the money, she hates it.

Pete walked over to the Ambassador and went up to his room. The setup was perfect: his room, Gail's room, one connecting door for a slick covert entrance.

He loaded his camera and attached a flashbulb strip. He greased the connecting doorjamb. He framed angles for some face shots.

Ten minutes crawled by. Pete listened for next-door sounds. There, Gail's signal—"Damn, where's my key?" a beat too loud.

Pete pressed up to the wall. He heard Lonely Walt pitch some boo-hoo: my wife and kids don't know a man has certain needs. Gail said, Why'd you have *seven* kids then? Walt said, It keeps my wife at home, where a woman belongs.

Their voices faded out bed-bound. Shoes went thunk. Gail kicked a high-heeled pump at the wall—her three-minutes-to-blastoff signal.

Pete laughed—thirty-dollar-a-night rooms with goddamn wafer-thin walls.

Zippers snagged. Bedsprings creaked. Seconds tick-tick-ticked. Walter P. Kinnard started groaning—Pete clocked him saddled in at 2:44.

He waited for 3:00 even. He eeeeased the door open—that doorjamb grease lubed out every little scriiich.

There: Gail and Walter P. Kinnard fucking.

In the missionary style, with their heads close together—courtroom adultery evidence. Walt was loving it. Gail was feigning ecstasy and picking at a hangnail.

Pete got closeup close and let fly.

One, two, three—flashbulb blips Tommy-gun fast. The whole goddamn room went glare bright.

Kinnard shrieked and pulled out dishrag limp. Gail tumbled off the bed and ran for the bathroom.

Sexy buck-naked Walt: 5'9", 210, pudgy.

Pete dropped his camera and picked him up by the neck. Pete laid his pitch out nice and slow.

"Your wife wants a divorce. She wants eight hundred a month, the house, the '56 Buick and orthodontic treatments for your son Timmy. You give her everything she wants, or I'll find you and kill you."

Kinnard popped spit bubbles. Pete admired his color: half shock-blue, half cardiac-red.

Steam whooshed out the bathroom door—Gail's standard postfuck shower always went down quick.

Pete dropped Walt on the floor. His arm fluttered from the lift: two hundred pounds plus, not bad.

Kinnard grabbed his clothes and stumbled out the door. Pete saw him tripping down the hallway, trying to get his trousers on right.

Gail walked out of a steam cloud. Her "I can't take much more of this" was no big surprise.

Walter P. Kinnard settled non-litigiously. Pete's shutout string jumped to Wives 23, Husbands 0. Mrs. Kinnard paid off: five grand up front, with 25% of her alimony promised in perpetuity.

Next: three days on Howard Hughes' time clock.

The TWA suit was spooking Big Howard. Pete stepped up his diversions.

He paid hookers to spiel to the papers: Hughes was holed up in numerous fuck pads. He bombarded process servers with phone tips: Hughes was in Bangkok, Maracaibo, Seoul. He set up a second Hughes double at the Biltmore: an old stag-movie vet, beaucoup hung. Pops was priapic for real—he sent Barbara Payton over to service him. Booze-addled Babs thought the old geek really *was* Hughes. She dished far and wide: Little Howard grew six inches.

J. Edgar Hoover could stall the suit easy. Hughes refused to ask him for help.

"Not yet, Pete. I need to cement my friendship with Mr. Hoover first.

I see my ownership of *Hush-Hush* as the key, but I need you to find me a new scandal man first. You *know* how much Mr. Hoover loves to accrue titillating information. . . ."

Pete put the word out on the grapevine:

New *Hush-Hush* dirt digger needed. Interested bottom-feeders—call Pete B.

Pete stuck by the watchdog house phone. Geeks called. Pete said, Give me a hot dirt tidbit to prove your credibility.

The geeks complied. Dig the sampling:

Pat Nixon just hatched Nat "King" Cole's baby. Lawrence Welk ran male prosties. A hot duo: Patti Page and Francis the Talking Mule.

Eisenhower had certified spook blood. Rin Tin Tin got Lassie pregnant. Jesus Christ ran a coon whorehouse in Watts.

It got worse. Pete logged in nineteen applicants—all fucking strange-o's.

The phone rang—Strange-O #20 loomed. Pete heard crackle on the line—the call was probably long distance.

"Who's this?"

"Pete? It's Jimmy."

HOFFA.

"Jimmy, how are you?"

"Right now I'm cold. It's cold in Chicago. I'm calling from a pal's house, and the heater's on the blink. Are you sure *your* phone's not tapped?"

"I'm sure. Freddy Turentine runs tap checks on all of Mr. Hughes' phones once a month."

"I can talk then?"

"You can talk."

Hoffa cut loose. Pete held the phone at arm's length and heard him juuuust fine.

"The McClellan Committee's on me like flies on shit. That little weasel cocksucker Bobby Kennedy's got half the country convinced the Teamsters are worse than the goddamn Commies, and he's fucking hounding me and my people with subpoenas, and he's got investigators crawling all over my union like—"

"Jimmy—"

"—fleas on a dog. First he chases Dave Beck out, and now he wants *me*. Bobby Kennedy is a fucking avalanche of dogshit. I'm building this resort in Florida called Sun Valley, and Bobby's trying to trace the three million that bankrolled it. He figures I took it from the Central States Pension Fund—"

"Jimmy—"

"—and he thinks he can use me to get his pussy-hound brother elected President. He thinks James Riddle Hoffa's a fucking political steppingstone. He thinks I'm gonna bend over and take it in the keester like some goddamn homosexual queer. He thinks—"

"Jimmy—"

"—I'm some pansy like him and his brother. He thinks I'm gonna roll over like Dave Beck. As if all this ain't enough, I own this cabstand in Miami. I've got these hothead Cuban refugees working there, and all they do is debate fucking Castro versus fucking Batista like like like . . ."

Hoffa gasped out hoarse. Pete said, "What do you want?"

Jimmy caught some breath. "I've got a job for you in Miami."

"How much?"

"Ten thousand."

Pete said, "I'll take it."

He booked a midnight flight. He used a fake passenger name and charged a first-class seat to Hughes Aircraft. The plane landed at 8:00 a.m., on time.

Miami was balmy working on hot.

Pete cabbed over to a Teamster-owned U-Drive and picked up a new Caddy Eldo. Jimmy pulled strings: no deposit or ID was required.

A note was taped under the dashboard.

"Go by cabstand: Flagler at N.W. 46th. Talk to Fulo Machado." Directions followed: causeways to surface streets marked on a little map.

Pete drove over. The scenery evaporated quick.

Big houses got smaller and smaller. White squares went to white trash, jigs and spics. Flagler was wall-to-wall low-rent storefronts.

The cabstand was tiger-striped stucco. The cabs in the lot had tiger-stripe paint jobs. Dig those tiger-shirted spics on the curb—snarfing doughnuts and T-Bird wine.

A sign above the door read: Tiger Kab. Se Habla Español.

Pete parked directly in front. Tiger men scoped him out and jabbered. He stretched to six-five-plus and let his shirttail hike. The spics saw his piece and jabbered on overdrive.

He walked in to the dispatch hut. Nice wallpaper: tiger photos taped floor to ceiling. *National Geographic* stock—Pete almost howled.

The dispatcher waved him over. Dig his face: scarred by tic-tac-toe knife cuts.

Pete pulled a chair up. Butt-Ugly said, "I'm Fulo Machado. Batista's secret police did this to me, so take your free introductory look now and forget about it, all right?"

"You speak English pretty well."

"I used to work at the Nacional Hotel in Havana. An American crou-pier guy taught me. It turned out he was a *maricón* trying to corrupt me."

"What did you do to him?"

"The *maricón* had a shack on a pork farm outside of Havana, where he brought little Cuban boys to corrupt them. I found him there with an-other *maricón* and murdered them with my machete. I stole all the pigs' food from their troughs and left the door of the shack open. You see, I had read in the *National Geographic* that starving pigs found decompos-ing human flesh irresistible."

Pete said, "Fulo, I like you."

"Please reserve judgment. I can be volatile where the enemies of Je-sus Christ and Fidel Castro are concerned."

Pete stifled a yuk. "Did one of Jimmy's guys leave an envelope for me?"

Fulo forked it over. Pete ripped it open, itchy to roll.

Nice—a simple note and a photo.

"Anton Gretzler, 114 Hibiscus, Lake Weir, Fla. (near Sun Valley). OL4-8812." The pic showed a tall guy almost too fat to live.

Pete said, "Jimmy must trust you."

"He does. He sponsored my green card, so he knows that I will re-main loyal."

"What's this Sun Valley place?"

"It is what I think is called a 'sub-division.' Jimmy is selling lots to Teamster members."

Pete said, "So who do you think's got more juice these days—Jesus or Castro?"

"I would say it is currently a toss-up."

Pete checked in at the Eden Roc and buzzed Anton Gretzler from a pay phone. The fat man agreed to a meet: 3:00, outside Sun Valley.

Pete took a snooze and drove out early. Sun Valley was the shits: three dirt roads gouged from swampland forty yards off the Interstate.

It was "sub-divided"—into matchbook-size lots piled with junk sid-ing. Marshland formed the perimeter—Pete saw gators out sunning.

It was hot and humid. A wicked sun cooked greenery dry brown.

Pete leaned against the car and stretched some kinks out. A truck crawled down the highway belching steam; the man in the passenger seat waved for help. Pete turned his back and let the geeks pass by.

A breeze kicked dust clouds up. The access road hazed over. A big sedan turned off the Interstate and barreled in blind.

Pete stood aside. The car brodied to a stop. Fat Anton Gretzler got out.

Pete walked over to him. Gretzler said, "Mr. Peterson?"

"That's me. Mr. Gretzler?"

Fats stuck his hand out. Pete ignored it.

"Is something wrong? You said you wanted to see a lot."

Pete steered Fat Boy down to a marsh glade. Gretzler caught on quick: Don't resist. Gator eyes poked out of the water.

Pete said, "Look at my car. Do I look like some union schmuck in the market for a do-it-yourself house?"

"Well . . . no."

"Then don't you think you're doing Jimmy raw by showing me these piece-of-shit pads?"

"Well . . ."

"Jimmy told me he's got a nice block of houses around here just about ready to go. You're supposed to wait and show *them* to the Teamsters."

"Well . . . I thought I—"

"Jimmy says you're an impetuous guy. He says he shouldn't have made you a partner in this thing. He says you've told people he borrowed money from the Teamsters' Pension Fund and skimmed some off the top. He's says you've been talking up the Fund like you're a made guy."

Gretzler squirmed. Pete grabbed his wrist and snapped it—bones sheared and poked out through his skin. Gretzler tried to scream and choked up mute.

"Has the McClellan Committee subpoenaed you?"

Gretzler made "yes" nods, frantic.

"Have you talked to Robert Kennedy or his investigators?"

Gretzler made "no" nods, shit-your-pants scared.

Pete checked the highway. No cars in view, no witnesses—

Gretzler said, "PLEASE."

Pete blew his brains out halfway through a rosary.

Kemper Boyd

(Philadelphia, 11/27/58)

The car: a Jaguar XK-140, British racing green/tan leather. The garage: subterranean and dead quiet. The job: steal the Jag for the FBI and entrap the fool who paid you to do it.

The man pried the driver's-side door open and hot-wired the ignition. The upholstery smelled rich: full leather boosted the "resale" price into the stratosphere.

He eased the car up to the street and waited for traffic to pass. Cold air fogged the windshield.

His buyer was standing at the corner. He was a Walter Mitty crime-voyeur type who had to get close.

The man pulled out. A squad car cut him off. His buyer saw what was happening—and ran.

Philly cops packing shotguns swooped down. They shouted standard auto-theft commands: "Get out of the car with your hands up!"/ "Out—now!"/"Down on the ground!"

He obeyed them. The cops threw on full armor: cuffs, manacles and drag chains.

They frisked him and jerked him to his feet. His head hit a prowl car cherry light—

The cell looked familiar. He swung his legs off the bunk and got his identity straight.

I'm Special Agent Kemper C. Boyd, FBI, interstate car theft infiltrator.

I'm *not* Bob Aiken, freelance car thief.

I'm forty-two years old. I'm a Yale Law School grad. I'm a seventeen-year Bureau veteran, divorced, with a daughter in college—and a long-time FBI-sanctioned car booster.

He placed his cell: tier B at the Philly Fed Building.

His head throbbed. His wrists and ankles ached. He tamped down his identity a last notch.

I've rigged auto-job evidence and skimmed money off of it for years. IS THIS AN INTERNAL BUREAU ROUST?

He saw empty cells down both sides of the catwalk. He spotted some papers on his sink: newspaper mock-ups topped by banner headlines:

"Car Thief Suffers Heart Attack in Federal Custody"/"Car Thief Expires in Federal Building Cell."

The text was typed out below.

> This afternoon, Philadelphia Police enacted a daring arrest in the shadow of picturesque Rittenhouse Square.
>
> Acting on information supplied by an unnamed informant, Sergeant Gerald P. Griffen and four other officers captured Robert Henry Aiken, 42, in the act of stealing an expensive Jaguar automobile. Aiken meekly let the officers restrain him and—

Someone coughed and said, "Sir?"

Kemper looked up. A clerk type unlocked the cell and held the door open for him.

"You can go out the back way, sir. There's a car waiting for you."

Kemper brushed off his clothes and combed his hair. He walked out the freight exit and saw a government limo blocking the alley.

His limo.

Kemper got in the back. J. Edgar Hoover said, "Hello, Mr. Boyd."

"Good afternoon, Sir."

A partition slid up and closed the backseat off. The driver pulled out.

Hoover coughed. "Your infiltration assignment was terminated rather precipitously. The Philadelphia Police were somewhat rough, but they have a reputation for that, and anything less would have lacked verisimilitude."

"I've learned to stay in character in situations like that. I'm sure the arrest was believable."

"Did you affect an East Coast accent for your role?"

"No, a midwestern drawl. I learned the accent and speech patterns when I worked the St. Louis office, and I thought they'd complement my physical appearance more effectively."

"You're correct, of course. And personally, I would not want to second-guess you on anything pertaining to criminal role-playing. That sports jacket you're wearing, for instance. I would not appreciate it as standard Bureau attire, but it's quite appropriate for a Philadelphia car thief."

Get to it, you officious little—

"In fact, you've always dressed distinctly. Perhaps 'expensively' is more apt. To be blunt, there have been times when I wondered how your salary could sustain your wardrobe."

"Sir, you should see my apartment. What my wardrobe possesses, it lacks."

Hoover chuckled. "Be that as it may, I doubt if I've seen you in the same suit twice. I'm sure the women you're so fond of appreciate your sartorial flair."

"Sir, I hope so."

"You endure my amenities with considerable flair, Mr. Boyd. Most men squirm. You express both your inimitable personal panache and a concurrent respect for me that is quite alluring. Do you know what this means?"

"No, Sir. I don't."

"It means that I like you and am prone to forgive indiscretions that I would crucify other agents for. You're a dangerous and ruthless man, but you possess a certain beguiling charm. This balance of attributes outweighs your profligate tendencies and allows me to be fond of you."

DON'T SAY "WHAT INDISCRETIONS?"—HE'LL TELL YOU AND MAIM YOU.

"Sir, I greatly appreciate your respect, and I reciprocate it fully."

"You didn't include 'fondness' in your reciprocity, but I won't press the point. Now, business. I have an opportunity for you to earn two regular paychecks, which should delight you no end."

Hoover leaned back coax-me style. Kemper said, "Sir?"

The limo accelerated. Hoover flexed his hands and straightened his necktie. "The Kennedy brothers' recent actions have distressed me. Bobby seems to be using the McClellan Committee's labor racketeering mandate as a means to upstage the Bureau and advance his brother's presidential aspirations. This displeases me. I've been running the Bureau since before Bobby was born. Jack Kennedy is a desiccated liberal playboy with the moral convictions of a crotch-sniffing hound dog. He's playing crimefighter on the McClellan Committee, and the very existence of the committee is an implicit slap in the Bureau's face. Old Joe Kennedy is determined to buy his son the White House, and I want to possess information to help mitigate the boy's more degenerately egalitarian policies, should he succeed."

Kemper caught his cue. "Sir?"

"I want you to infiltrate the Kennedy organization. The McClellan Committee's labor-racketeering mandate ends next spring, but Bobby Kennedy is still hiring lawyer-investigators. As of now you are retired from the FBI, although you will continue to draw full pay until July 1961, the date you reach twenty years of Bureau service. You are to prepare a convincing FBI retirement story and secure an attorney's job with the McClellan Committee. I know that both you and Jack Kennedy have been intimate with a Senate aide named Sally Lefferts. Miss Lefferts is a talkative woman, so I'm sure young Jack has heard about you. Young Jack is on the McClellan Committee, and young Jack loves sexual gossip and dangerous friends. Mr. Boyd, I am sure that you will fit in with the Kennedys. I'm sure that this will be both a salutary opportunity for you to practice your skills of dissembling and duplicity, *and* the chance to exercise your more promiscuous tastes."

Kemper felt weightless. The limo cruised on thin air.

Hoover said, "Your reaction delights me. Rest now. We'll arrive in Washington in an hour, and I'll drop you at your apartment."

Hoover supplied up-to-date study notes—in a leather binder stamped "CONFIDENTIAL." Kemper mixed a pitcher of extra-dry martinis and pulled up his favorite chair to read through them.

The notes boiled down to one thing: Bobby Kennedy vs. Jimmy Hoffa.

Senator John McClellan chaired the U.S. Senate's Select Committee on Improper Activities in the Labor and Management Field, established in January 1957. Its subsidiary members: Senators Ives, Kennedy, McNamara, McCarthy, Ervin, Mundt, Goldwater. Its chief counsel and investigative boss: Robert F. Kennedy.

Current personnel: thirty-five investigators, forty-five accountants, twenty-five stenographers and clerks. Its current housing: the Senate Office Building, suite 101.

The Committee's stated goals:

To expose corrupt labor practices; to expose labor unions collusively linked to organized crime. The Committee's methods: witness subpoenas, document subpoenas, and the charting of union funds diverted and misused in organized crime activities.

The Committee's de facto target: the International Brotherhood of Teamsters, the most powerful transportation union on earth, arguably the most corrupt and powerful labor union ever.

Its president: James Riddle Hoffa, age 45.

Hoffa: mob bought-and-paid-for. The suborner of: extortion, wholesale bribery, beatings, bombings, management side deals and epic abuse of union funds.

Hoffa's suspected holdings, in violation of fourteen antitrust statutes:

Trucking firms, used car lots, a dog track, a car-rental chain, a Miami cabstand staffed by Cuban refugees with extensive criminal records.

Hoffa's close friends:

Mr. Sam Giancana, the Mafia boss of Chicago; Mr. Santo Trafficante Jr., the Mafia boss of Tampa, Florida; Mr. Carlos Marcello, the Mafia boss of New Orleans.

Jimmy Hoffa:

Who lends his "friends" millions of dollars, put to use illegally.

Who owns percentages of mob-run casinos in Havana, Cuba.

Who illegally funnels cash to Cuban strongman Fulgencio Batista *and* rebel firebrand Fidel Castro.

Who rapes the Teamsters' Central States Pension Fund, a cash-rich watering hole rumored to be administered by Sam Giancana's Chicago mob—a loan-shark scheme wherein gangsters and crooked entrepreneurs borrow large sums at usurious interest rates, with nonpayment penalties up to and including torture and death.

Kemper caught the gist: Hoover's jealous. He always said the Mob didn't exist—because he knew he couldn't prosecute it successfully. Now Bobby Kennedy begs to differ. . . .

A chronology followed.

Early '57: the Committee targets Teamster president Dave Beck. Beck testifies five times; Bobby Kennedy's relentless goading breaks the man. A Seattle grand jury indicts him for larceny and income tax evasion.

Spring '57: Jimmy Hoffa assumes complete control of the Teamsters.

August '57: Hoffa vows to rid his union of gangster influence—a large lie.

September '57: Hoffa goes to trial in Detroit. The charge: tapping the phones of Teamster subordinates. A hung jury—Hoffa escapes sentencing.

October '57: Hoffa is elected International Teamster president. A persistent rumor: 70% of his delegates were illegally selected.

July '58: the Committee begins to investigate direct links between the Teamsters and organized crime. Closely scrutinized: the November '57 Apalachin Conclave.

Fifty-nine high-ranking mobsters meet at the upstate New York home of a "civilian" friend. A state trooper named *Edgar* Croswell runs their license plates. A raid ensues—and Mr. Hoover's longstanding "there is no Mafia" stance becomes untenable.

July '58: Bobby Kennedy proves that Hoffa resolves strikes through management bribes—this practice dating back to '49.

August '58: Hoffa appears before the Committee. Bobby Kennedy goes at him—and traps him in numerous lies.

The notes concluded.

The Committee was currently probing Hoffa's Sun Valley resort outside Lake Weir, Florida. Bobby Kennedy subpoenaed the Central States Pension Fund books and saw that three million dollars went into the project—much more than reasonable building costs. Kennedy's theory: Hoffa skimmed at least a million dollars off the top and was selling his union brothers defective prefab material and alligator-infested swampland.

Ergo: felony land fraud.

A closing addendum:

"Hoffa has a Sun Valley front man: Anton William Gretzler, 46, a Florida resident with three previous bunco convictions. Gretzler was subpoenaed 10/29/58, but now appears to be missing."

Kemper checked the Hoffa "Known Associates" list. One name sizzled:

Pete Bondurant, W.M., 6'5", 230, DOB 7/16/20, Montreal, Canada.

No criminal convictions. Licensed private investigator/former Los Angeles County deputy sheriff.

Big Pete: shakedown man and Howard Hughes' pet goon. He and Ward Littell arrested him once—he beat a Sheriff's inmate to death. Littell's comment: "Perhaps the most fearsome and competent rogue cop of our era."

Kemper poured a fresh drink and let his mind drift. The impersonation took shape: heroic aristocrats form a common bond.

He liked women, and cheated on his wife throughout their marriage. Jack Kennedy liked women—and held his marriage vows expedient and whimsical. Bobby liked his wife and kept her pregnant—insider talk tagged him faithful.

Yale for him; Harvard for the Kennedys. Filthy-rich Irish Catholics; filthy-rich Tennessee Anglicans gone bankrupt. Their family was large and photogenic; his family was broke and dead. Someday he might tell Jack and Bobby how his father shot himself and took a month to die.

Southerners and Boston Irish: both afflicted with incongruous accents. He'd resurrect the drawl it took so long to lose.

Kemper prowled his clothes closet. Impersonation details clicked in.

The charcoal worsted for the interview. A holstered .38 to impress tough guy Bobby. No Yale cuff links—Bobby might possess a proletarian streak.

His closet was twelve feet deep. The back wall was offset by framed photographs.

His ex-wife, Katherine—the best-looking woman who ever breathed. They debuted at the Nashville Cotillion—a society scribe called them "southern grace personified." He married her for sex and her father's money. She divorced him when the Boyd fortune evaporated and Hoover addressed his law school class and *personally* invited him to join the FBI.

Katherine, in November 1940:

"You watch out for that prissy little fussbudget, do you hear me, Kemper? I think he has carnal designs on you."

She didn't know that Mr. Hoover only fucked power.

In matching frames: his daughter, Claire, Susan Littell and Helen Agee—three FBI daughters hell-bent on law careers.

The girls were best friends split up by studies at Tulane and Notre Dame. Helen was disfigured—he kept the pictures in his closet to quash pitying comments.

Tom Agee was sitting in his car—working a routine stakeout for some bank heisters outside a whorehouse. His wife had just left him— Tom couldn't find a sitter for nine-year-old Helen. She was sleeping in the backseat when the heisters came up shooting.

Tom was killed. Helen was muzzle-burned and left for dead. Help arrived—six hours later. Flash particles had scorched Helen's cheeks and scarred her for life.

Kemper laid out his interview clothes. He got some lies straight and called Sally Lefferts.

The phone rang twice. "Uh, hello?"—Sally's little boy picked up.

"Son, get your mother. Tell her it's a friend from the office."

"Uh . . . yessir."

Sally came on the line. "Who's this from the U.S. Senate clerical pool bothering this poor overworked aide?"

"It's me. Kemper."

"Kemper, what are you doing calling me with my husband in the backyard right now as we speak!"

"Ssssh. I'm calling you for a job referral."

"What are you saying? Are you saying Mr. Hoover got wise to your evil ways with women and showed you the gate?"

"I retired, Sally. I utilized a dangerous-duty dispensation clause and retired three years early."

"Well, my heavens, Kemper Cathcart Boyd!"

"Are you still seeing Jack Kennedy, Sally?"

"Occasionally, dear heart, since *you* gave *me* the gate. Is this about trading little black books and evil tales out of school, or—?"

"I'm thinking of applying for a job with the McClellan Committee."

Sally whooped. "Well, I think you *should*! I think I should put a note on Robert Kennedy's desk recommending you, and you should send me a dozen long-stemmed Southern Beauty roses for the effort!"

"You're the southern beauty, Sally."

"I was too much woman for De Ridder, Louisiana, and that is a fact!"

Kemper hung up with kisses. Sally would spread the word: ex-FBI car thief now seeking work.

He'd tell Bobby how he crashed the Corvette theft ring. He wouldn't mention the Vettes he stripped for parts.

He moved the next day. He walked right in to the Senate Office Building and suite 101.

The receptionist heard him out and tapped her intercom. "Mr. Kennedy, there's a man here who wants to apply for an investigator's position. He has FBI retirement credentials."

The office spread out unpartitioned behind her—all cabinet rows, cubicles and conference rooms. Men worked elbow-to-elbow tight—the place hummed.

The woman smiled. "Mr. Kennedy will see you. Take this first little aisle straight back."

Kemper walked into the hum. The office had a scavenged look: mismatched desks and filing bins, and corkboards top-heavy with paper.

"Mr. Boyd?"

Robert Kennedy stepped out of his cubicle. It was the standard size, the standard desk and two chairs.

He offered the standard too-hard handshake—totally predictable.

Kemper sat down. Kennedy pointed to his holster bulge. "I didn't know that retired FBI men were allowed to carry guns."

"I've incurred enemies through the years. My retirement won't stop them from hating me."

"Senate investigators don't wear sidearms."

"If you hire me, I'll put mine in a drawer."

Kennedy smiled and leaned against his desk. "You're from the South?"

"Nashville, Tennessee."

"Sally Lefferts said you were with the FBI for what, fifteen years?"

"Seventeen."

"Why did you retire early?"

"I worked auto-theft infiltration assignments for the past nine years, and it had gotten to the point where I was too well known to car thieves to go undercover convincingly. The Bureau bylaws contain an early-retirement clause for agents who have engaged in prolonged stints of hazardous duty, and I utilized it."

" 'Utilized'? Did those assignments debilitate you in some way?"

"I applied for a position with the Top Hoodlum Program first. Mr. Hoover rejected my application personally, although he knew full well that I had desired organized crime work for some time. No, I wasn't debilitated. I was frustrated."

Kennedy brushed hair from his forehead. "So you quit."

"Is that an accusation?"

"No, it's an observation. And frankly, I'm surprised. The FBI is a tight-knit organization that inspires great loyalty, and agents do not tend to retire out of pique."

Kemper raised his voice—just barely. "A great many agents realize that organized crime, not domestic Communism, poses the greatest threat to America. The Apalachin revelations forced Mr. Hoover to form the Top Hoodlum Program, which of course he did with some reluctance. The program is accruing antimob intelligence, but not seeking hard evidence to build toward Federal prosecution, but at least that's something, and I wanted to be part of it."

Kennedy smiled. "I understand your frustration, and I agree with your critique of Mr. Hoover's priorities. But I'm still surprised that you quit."

Kemper smiled. "Before I 'quit,' I snuck a look at Mr. Hoover's private file on the McClellan Committee. I'm up-to-date on the Committee's work, up to and including Sun Valley and your missing witness Anton

Gretzler. I 'quit' because Mr. Hoover has the Bureau neurotically focused on harmless leftists, while the McClellan Committee is going after the real bad guys. I 'quit' because given my choice of monomaniacs, I'd rather work for you."

Kennedy grinned. "Our mandate ends in five months. You'll be out of work."

"I have an FBI pension, and you'll have forwarded so much evidence to municipal grand juries that they'll be begging your investigators to work for them ad hoc."

Kennedy tapped a stack of papers. "We work hard here. We plod. We subpoena and trace money and litigate. We don't risk our lives stealing sports cars or dawdle over lunch or take women to the Willard Hotel for quickies. Our idea of a good time is to talk about how much we hate Jimmy Hoffa and the Mob."

Kemper stood up. "I hate Hoffa and the Mob like Mr. Hoover hates you and your brother."

Bobby laughed. "I'll let you know within a few days."

Kemper strolled by Sally Lefferts' office. It was 2:30—Sally might be up for a quickie at the Willard.

Her door was open. Sally was at her desk fretting tissues—with a man straddling a chair up close to her.

She said, "Oh, hello, Kemper."

Her color was up: rosy verging on flushed. She had that too-bright I've-lost-at-love-again glow on.

"Are you busy? I can come back."

The man swiveled his chair around. Kemper said, "Hello, Senator."

John Kennedy smiled. Sally dabbed at her eyes. "Jack, this is my friend Kemper Boyd."

They shook hands. Kennedy did a little half-bow.

"Mr. Boyd, a pleasure."

"My pleasure entirely, sir."

Sally forced a smile. Her rouge was streaked—she'd been crying.

"Kemper, how did your interview go?"

"It went well, I think. Sally, I have to go. I just wanted to thank you for the referral."

Little nods went around. Nobody's eyes met. Kennedy handed Sally a fresh tissue.

Kemper walked downstairs and outside. A storm had fired up—he ducked under a statue ledge and let the rain graze him.

The Kennedy coincidence felt strange. He walked straight from an interview with Bobby into a chance meeting with Jack. It felt like he was gently pushed in that direction.

Kemper thought it through.

Mr. Hoover mentioned Sally—as his most specific link to Jack Kennedy. Mr. Hoover knew that he and Jack shared a fondness for women. Mr. Hoover sensed that he'd visit Sally after his interview with Bobby.

Mr. Hoover *sensed* that he'd call Sally for an interview referral immediately. Mr. Hoover knew that Bobby needed investigators and interviewed walk-in prospects at whim.

Kemper took the logical leap—

Mr. Hoover has Capitol Hill hot-wired. He knew that you broke up with Sally at her office—to forestall a big public scene. He picked up a tip that Jack Kennedy was planning the same thing—and took a stab at maneuvering you into a position to witness it.

It felt logically sound. It felt quintessentially Hoover.

Mr. Hoover doesn't entirely trust you to forge a bond with Bobby. He took a shot at placing you in a symbiotic context with Jack.

The rain felt good. Lightning crackled down and backlit the Capitol dome. It felt like he could stand here and let the whole world come to him.

Kemper heard foot scrapes behind him. He knew who it was instantly.

"Mr. Boyd?"

He turned around. John Kennedy was cinching up his overcoat.

"Senator."

"Call me Jack."

"All right, Jack."

Kennedy shivered. "Why the hell are we standing here?"

"We can run for the Mayflower bar when this lets up a bit."

"We can, and I think we should. You know, Sally's told me about you. She told me I should work on losing my accent the way you lost yours, so I was surprised to hear you speak."

Kemper dropped his drawl. "Southerners make the best cops. You lay on the cornpone and people tend to underestimate you and let their secrets slip. I thought your brother might know that, so I acted accordingly. You're on the McClellan Committee, so I figured I should go for uniformity."

Kennedy laughed. "Your secret's safe with me."

"Thanks. And don't worry about Sally. She likes men the way we like women, and she gets over the attendant heartaches pretty fast."

"I knew you figured it out. Sally told me you cut her off in a similar fashion."

Kemper smiled. "You can always go back occasionally. Sally appreciates an occasional afternoon at a good hotel."

"I'll remember that. A man with my aspirations has to be conscious of his entanglements."

Kemper stepped closer to "Jack." He could almost see Mr. Hoover grinning.

"I know a fair number of women who know how to keep things unentangled."

Kennedy smiled and steered him into the rain. "Let's go get a drink and talk about it. I've got an hour to kill before I meet my wife."

3

Ward J. Littell

(Chicago, 11/30/58)

Black bag work—a classic FBI Commie crib prowl.

Littell snapped the lock with a ruler. His hands dripped sweat—apartment-house break-ins always played risky.

Neighbors heard B&E noise. Hallway sounds muffled incoming footsteps.

He closed the door behind him. The living room took shape: ratty furniture, bookshelves, labor protest posters. It was a typical CPUSA member's dwelling—he'd find documents in the dinette cupboard.

He did. Ditto the standard wall photos: Sad old "Free the Rosenbergs" shots.

Pathos.

He'd surveilled Morton Katzenbach for months. He'd heard scads of leftist invective. He knew one thing: Morty posed no threat to America.

A Commie cell met at Morty's doughnut stand. Their big-time "treason": feeding bear claws to striking auto workers.

Littell got out his Minox and snapped "documents." He blew three rolls of film on donation tallies—all short of fifty dollars a month.

It was boring, shitty work. His old refrain kicked in automatically.

You're forty-five years old. You're an expert bug/wire man. You're an ex–Jesuit seminarian with a law degree, two years and two months shy of retirement. You've got an alimony-fat ex-wife and a daughter at Notre Dame, and if you pass the Illinois Bar exam and quit the FBI, your gross earnings over the next X-number of years will more than compensate for your forfeited pension.

He shot two lists of "political expenses." Morty annotated his dough-nut handouts: "Plain," "Chocolate," "Glazed."

He heard key-in-the-lock noise. He saw the door open ten feet in front of him.

Faye Katzenbach lugged groceries in. She saw him and shook her head like he was the saddest thing on earth.

"So you people are common thieves now?"

Littell knocked over a lamp running past her.

The squadroom was noontime quiet—just a few agents standing around clipping teletypes. Littell found a note on his desk.

K. Boyd called. In town en route to Florida. Pump Room, 7:00?

Kemper—yes!

Chick Leahy walked up, waving file carbons. "I'll need the complete Katzenbach folder, with photo attachments, by December 11th. Mr. Tolson's coming in for an inspection tour, and he wants a CPUSA presentation."

"You'll have it."

"Good. Complete with documents?"

"Some. Mrs. Katzenbach caught me before I finished."

"Jesus. Did she—?"

"She did *not* call the Chicago PD, because she knew who I was and what I was doing. Mr. Leahy, half the Commies on earth know the term 'black bag job.' "

Leahy sighed. "Say it, Ward. I'm going to turn you down, but you'll feel better if you say it."

"All right. I want a Mob assignment. I want a transfer to the Top Hoodlum Program."

Leahy said, "No. Our THP roster is full. And as special agent-in-charge my assessment of you is that you're best suited for political sur-veillance, which I consider important work. Mr. Hoover considers domestic Communists more dangerous than the Mafia, and I have to say that I agree with him."

They stared at each other. Littell broke it off—Leahy would stand there all day if he didn't.

Leahy walked back to his office. Littell shut his cubicle door and got out his bar texts. Civic statutes went unmemorized—Kemper Boyd memories cut them adrift.

Late '53: they corner a kidnapper in L.A. The man pulls a gun; *he* shakes so hard he drops his. Some LAPD men laugh at him. Kemper doctors the report to make *him* the hero.

They protest the disposition of Tom Agee's pension—Mr. Hoover wants to award it to Tom's floozy wife. Kemper talks him into a surviving-daughter disbursement; Helen now has a handsome sinecure.

They arrest Big Pete Bondurant. *He* makes a gaffe: ribbing Pete in Québecois French. Bondurant snaps his handcuff chain and goes for his throat.

He runs. Big Pete laughs. Kemper bribes Bondurant into silence on the matter—catered cell food does the trick.

Kemper never judged his fearful side. Kemper said, "We both joined the Bureau to avoid the war, so who's to judge?" Kemper taught him how to burglarize—a good fear tamper-downer.

Kemper said, "You're my priest-cop confessor. I'll reciprocate and hear your confessions, but since my secrets are worse than yours, I'll always get the better end of the deal."

Littell closed his textbook. Civil statutes were dead boring.

The Pump Room was packed. A gale blew off the lake—people seemed to whoosh inside.

Littell secured a back booth. The maître d' took his drink order: two martinis, straight up. The restaurant was beautiful: colored waiters and a pre-symphony crowd had the place sparkling.

The drinks arrived. Littell arranged them for a quick toast. Boyd walked in, via the hotel lobby.

Littell laughed. "Don't tell me you're staying here."

"My plane doesn't leave until two a.m., and I needed a place to stretch my legs. Hello, Ward."

"Hello, Kemper. A valedictory?"

Boyd raised his glass. "To my daughter Claire, your daughter Susan and Helen Agee. May they do well in school and become better attorneys than their fathers."

They clicked goblets. "Neither of whom ever practiced law."

"You clerked, though. And I heard you wrote deportation writs that saw litigation."

"We're not doing so badly. At least you're not. So who's putting you up here?"

"My new temporary employer booked me a room out by Midway, but I decided to splurge and make up the difference out of my pocket.

And the difference between the Skyliner Motel and the Ambassador-East is pretty steep."

Littell smiled. "What new temporary employer? Are you working Cointelpro?"

"No, it's something a good deal more interesting. I'll tell you a few drinks down the line, when you're more likely to get blasphemous and say, 'Jesus Fucking Christ.' "

"I'll say it now. You've just effectively killed small talk, so I will say it *fucking* now."

Boyd sipped his martini. "Not yet. You just hit the jackpot on the wayward-daughter front, though. That should cheer you up."

"Let me guess. Claire's transferring from Tulane to Notre Dame."

"No. Helen graduated Tulane a semester early. She's been accepted at the University of Chicago law school, and she'll be moving here next month."

"Jesus!"

"I knew you'd be pleased."

"Helen's a courageous girl. She'll make a damn fine lawyer."

"She will. And she'll make some man a damn fine consort, if we haven't ruined her for young men her own age."

"It would take a—"

"Special young man to get by her affliction?"

"Yes."

Boyd winked. "Well, she's twenty-one. Think of how the two of you would upset Margaret."

Littell killed his drink. "And upset my own daughter. Susan, by the way, says Margaret is spending weekends with a man in Charlevoix. But she'll never marry him as long as she has my paycheck attached."

"You're her devil. You're the seminarian boy who got her pregnant. And in the religious terms you're so fond of, your marriage was purgatory."

"No, my job is. I black-bagged a Commie's apartment today and photographed an entire ledger page devoted to doughnuts. I honestly don't know how much longer I can do this kind of thing."

Fresh drinks arrived. The waiter bowed—Kemper inspired subservience. Littell said, "I figured something out in the process, right between the chocolate and the glazed."

"What?"

"That Mr. Hoover hates left-wingers because their philosophy is based on human frailty, while his own is based on an excruciating rectitude that denies such things."

Boyd held his glass up. "You never disappoint me."

"Kemper—"

Waiters swooped past. Candlelight bounced off gold flatware. Crêpe suzettes ignited—an old woman squealed.

"Kemper—"

"Mr. Hoover had me infiltrate the McClellan Committee. He hates Bobby Kennedy and his brother Jack, and he's afraid their father will buy Jack the White House in '60. I'm now a fake FBI retiree on an indefinite assignment to cozy up to both brothers. I applied for a job as a temporary Committee investigator, and I got the word today that Bobby hired me. I'm flying to Miami in a few hours to look for a missing witness."

Littell said, "Jesus Fucking Christ."

Boyd said, "You never disappoint me."

"I suppose you're drawing two salaries?"

"You know I love money."

"Yes, but do you like the brothers?"

"Yes, I do. Bobby's a vindictive little bulldog, and Jack's charming and not as smart as he thinks he is. Bobby's the stronger man, and he hates organized crime like you do."

Littell shook his head. "You don't hate anything."

"I can't afford to."

"I've never understood your loyalties."

"Let's just say they're ambiguous."

DOCUMENT INSERT: 12/2/58. Official FBI telephone call transcript: "Recorded at the Director's Request"/"Classified Confidential 1-A: Director's Eyes Only." Speaking: Director Hoover, Special Agent Kemper Boyd.

JEH: Mr. Boyd?

KB: Sir, good morning.

JEH: Yes, it is a good morning. Are you calling from a secure phone?

KB: Yes. I'm at a coin phone. If the connection seems weak, it's because I'm calling from Miami.

JEH: Little Brother has put you to work already?

KB: Little Brother doesn't waste time.

JEH: Interpret your rapid hiring. Use names if you must.

KB: Little Brother was initially suspicious of me, and I think it will take time to win him over. I ran into Big Brother at Sally Lefferts' office, and circumstances forced us into a private conversation. We went out for a drink and developed a rapport. Like many charming men, Big Brother is also easily charmed. We hit it off quite well, and I'm certain he told Little Brother to hire me.

JEH: Describe the "circumstances" you mentioned.

KB: We discovered that we shared an interest in sophisticated and provocative women, and we went to the Mayflower bar to discuss related matters. Big Brother confirmed that he is going to run in 1960, and that Little Brother will begin the campaign groundwork when the McClellan Committee mandate ends this coming April.

JEH: Continue.

KB: Big Brother and I discussed politics. I portrayed myself as incongruously liberal by Bureau standards, which Big Brother—

JEH: You have no political convictions, which adds to your efficacy in situations like this. Continue.

KB: Big Brother found my feigned political convictions interesting and opened up. He said that he considers Little Brother's hatred of Mr. H. somewhat untoward, although justified. Both Big Brother and their father have urged Little Brother to strategically retreat and offer Mr. H. a deal if he cleans up his organization, but Little Brother has refused. My personal opinion is that Mr. H. is legally inviolate at this time. Big Brother shares that opinion, as do a number of Committee investigators. Sir, I think Little Brother is ferociously dedicated and competent. My feeling is that he will take Mr. H. down, but not in the foreseeable future. I think it will take years and most likely many indictments, and that it certainly won't happen within the Committee mandate time frame.

JEH: You're saying the Committee will hand the ball to municipal grand juries once their mandate expires?

KB: Yes. I think it will take years for the Brothers to reap real political benefit from Mr. H. And I think a backlash might set in and hurt Big Brother. Democratic candidates can't afford to be viewed as antiunion.

JEH: Your assessments seem quite astute.

KB: Thank you, Sir.

JEH: Did Big Brother bring my name up?

KB: Yes. He knows about your extensive files on politicians and movie stars you deem subversive, and he's afraid you have a file on him. I told him your file on his family ran to a thousand pages.

JEH: Good. You would have lost credibility had you been less candid. What else did you and Big Brother discuss?

KB: Chiefly women. Big Brother mentioned a trip to Los Angeles on December 9th. I gave him the phone number of a promiscuous woman named Darleen Shoftel and urged him to call her.

JEH: Do you think he has called her?

KB: No, Sir. But I think he will.

JEH: Describe your duties for the Committee thus far.

KB: I've been looking for a subpoenaed witness named Anton Gretzler here in Florida. Little Brother wanted me to serve him a backup summons. There's an aspect of this we should discuss, since Gretzler's disappearance may tie in to a friend of yours.

JEH: Continue.

KB: Gretzler was Mr. H.'s partner in the alleged Sun Valley land fraud. He—

JEH: You said "was." You're assuming Gretzler is dead?

KB: I'm certain he's dead.

JEH: Continue.

KB: He disappeared on the afternoon of November 26th. He told his secretary he was going to meet a "sales prospect" at Sun Valley and never returned. The Lake Weir Police found his car in a swamp marsh nearby, but they haven't been able to locate a body. They canvassed for witnesses and turned up a man who was driving by Sun Valley on the Interstate at the same time the "sales prospect" was to meet Gretzler. The man said he saw a man parked

on the Sun Valley access road. He said the man averted his face
when he drove by, so it's doubtful he could identify him. He did describe him, however. Six foot four or five, "huge," two hundred
and forty pounds. Dark hair, thirty-five to forty. I'm thinking it—

JEH: Your old friend Peter Bondurant. He's singularly outsized,
and he's on that list of Mr. H.'s known associates that I gave you.

KB: Yes, Sir. I checked airline and car rental records in Los
Angeles and Miami and turned up a Hughes Aircraft charge that
I'm certain Bondurant made. I know he was in Florida on November 26th, and I'm circumstantially certain that Mr. H. hired him
to kill Gretzler. I know that you and Howard Hughes are friends,
so I thought I'd inform you of this before I told Little Brother.

JEH: Do not inform Little Brother under any circumstances.
The status of your investigation should remain thus: Gretzler is
missing, perhaps dead. There are no leads and no suspects. Pete
Bondurant is invaluable to Howard Hughes, who is a valuable
friend of the Bureau. Mr. Hughes recently purchased a scandal
magazine to help disseminate political information favorable to
the Bureau, and I do not want his feathers ruffled. Do you
understand?

KB: Yes, Sir.

JEH: I want you to fly to Los Angeles on a Bureau charge and
tweak Pete Bondurant with your suspicions. Get a favor from him,
and cloak your friendly overtures with the knowledge that you can
hurt him. And when your Committee duties permit, go back to
Florida and clean up potential loose ends on the Gretzler front.

KB: I'll wrap up here and fly to L.A. late tomorrow.

JEH: Good. And while you're in Los Angeles, I want you to
bug and wire Miss Darleen Shoftel's home. If Big Brother contacts her, I want to know.

KB: She won't voluntarily assent, so I'll have to rig her apartment sub rosa. Can I bring in Ward Littell? He's a great wire man.

JEH: Yes, bring him in. This reminds me that Littell has been
coveting a Top Hoodlum Squad spot for some time. Do you think
he'd like a transfer as a reward for this job?

KB: He'd love it.

JEH: Good, but let me be the one to inform him. Goodbye, Mr.
Boyd. I commend you for work well done.

KB: Thank you, Sir. Goodbye.

4

(Beverly Hills, 12/4/58)

Howard Hughes cranked his bed up a notch. "I can't tell you how lackluster the last two issues have been. *Hush-Hush* is a weekly now, which increases the need for interesting gossip incrementally. *We need a new dirt digger.* We've got you for story verification, Dick Steisel for legal vetting and Sol Maltzman to write the pieces, but we're only as good as our scandals, and our scandals have been chaste and ridiculously dull."

Pete slouched in a chair and thumbed last week's issue. On the cover: "Migrant Workers Carry VD Plague!" A co-feature: "Hollywood Ranch Market—Homo Heaven!"

"I'll keep at it. We're looking for a guy with unique fucking qualifications, and that takes time."

Hughes said, "You do it. And tell Sol Maltzman that I want a piece entitled 'Negroes: Overbreeding Creates TB Epidemic' on next week's cover."

"That sounds pretty far-fetched."

"Facts can be bent to conform to any thesis."

"I'll tell him, Boss."

"Good. And while you're out ..."

"Will I get you some more dope and disposable hypos? *Yes, sir!*"

Hughes flinched and turned the TV on. "Sheriff John's Lunch Brigade" hit the bedroom—squealing tots and cartoon mice the size of Lassie.

Pete strolled out to the parking lot. Lounging upside his car like he owned it: Special Agent Kemper Fucking Boyd.

Six years older and still too handsome to live. That dark gray suit had to run four hundred clams easy.

"What is this?"

Boyd folded his arms over his chest. "This is a friendly errand for Mr. Hoover. He's concerned about your extracurricular work for Jimmy Hoffa."

"What are you talking about?"

"I've got an 'in' on the McClellan Committee. They've got some pay phones near Hoffa's house in Virginia rigged to register slug calls. That cheap fuck Hoffa makes his business calls from public booths and uses slugs."

"Keep going. Your slug call pitch is bullshit, but let's see where you're taking it."

Boyd winked—brass-balled motherfucker.

"One, Hoffa called you twice late last month. Two, you bought a round-trip L.A.-to-Miami ticket under an assumed name and charged it to Hughes Aircraft. Three, you rented a car at a Teamster-owned rent-a-car outlet and were *maybe* seen waiting for a man named Anton Gretzler. I think Gretzler's dead, and I think Hoffa hired you to clip him."

They'd never find a corpse: he tossed Gretzler in a swamp and watched gators eat him.

"So arrest me."

"No. Mr. Hoover doesn't like Bobby Kennedy, and I'm sure he wouldn't want to upset Mr. Hughes. He can live with you and Jimmy on the loose, and so can I."

"So?"

"So let's do something nice for Mr. Hoover."

"Give me a hint. I'm just dying to roll over."

Boyd smiled. "The head writer at *Hush-Hush* is a Commie. I know Mr. Hughes appreciates cheap help, but I still think you should fire him immediately."

Pete said, "I'll do that. And you tell Mr. Hoover that I'm a patriotic guy who knows how friendship works."

Boyd waltzed off—no nod, no wink, suspect dismissed. He walked two car rows over and bagged a blue Ford with a Hertz bumper sticker.

The car pulled out. Boyd fucking waved.

Pete ran to the hotel phone bank and called information. An operator shot him the main Hertz number.

He dialed it. A woman answered: "Good morning, Hertz Rent-a-Car."

"Good morning. This is Officer Peterson, LAPD. I need a current customer listing on one of your cars."

"Has there been an accident?"

"No, it's just routine. The car is a blue '56 Ford Fairlane, license V as in 'Victor,' D as in 'dog,' H as in 'Henry,' four-nine-zero."

"One minute, Officer."

Pete held the line. Boyd's McClellan pitch danced around in his head.

"I have your listing, Officer."

"Shoot."

"The car was rented to a Mr. Kemper C. Boyd, whose current Los Angeles address is the Miramar Hotel in Santa Monica. The invoice says the charge is to be billed to the U.S. Senate Select Committee on Investigations. Does that help?—"

Pete hung up. His head dance went stereophonic.

Strange: Boyd in a Committee-rented car. Strange because: Hoover and Bobby Kennedy were rivals. Boyd as FBI man *and* Committee cop?—Hoover would never allow him to moonlight.

Boyd was stylish working on slick—and a good man to front friendly warnings.

A good man to spy on Bobby?—"Maybe" working on "Yes."

Sol Maltzman lived in Silverlake—a dive above a tux rental joint.

Pete knocked. Sol opened up, pissed—this knock-kneed geek in Bermuda shorts and a T-shirt.

"What is it, Bondurant? I'm very busy."

"Bohn-dew-rahn"—the little Commie prick said it French-style.

The pad reeked of cigarettes and cat litter. Manila folders dripped off every stick of furniture; a wooden cabinet blocked the one window.

He's got Hollywood dirt files. He's just the type to hoard scandal skank.

"Bohn-dew-rahn, what *is* it?"

Pete grabbed a folder off a lamp stand. Press clippings on Ike and Dick Nixon—snoresville.

"Put that down and tell me what you want!"

Pete grabbed his neck. "You're fired from *Hush-Hush*. I'm sure you've got some dirt files we can use, and if you point them out and save me trouble, I'll tell Mr. Hughes to shoot you some severance pay."

Sol flipped him off—the double bird, twirling at eye level.

Pete let him go. Dig his neck: 360'd by a jumbo hand print.

"I'll bet you keep the good stuff in that cabinet."

"No! There's nothing in there you'd want!"

"Open it for me, then."

"No! It's locked, and I'm not giving you the combination!"

Pete kneed him in the balls. Maltzman hit the floor gasping. Pete tore his shirt off and stuffed a wad of fabric in his mouth.

Check that TV by the couch—gooood audial cover.

Pete turned it on full blast. A car huckster hit the screen, screaming shit about the new Buick line. Pete pulled his piece and shot the padlock off the cabinet—wood chips sprayed out craaaazy.

Three files fell out—maybe thirty skank pages total.

Sol Maltzman shrieked through his gag. Pete kicked him unconscious and turned the TV down.

He had three files and a bad case of the post-strongarm hungries. The ticket was Mike Lyman's and the Steak Lunch De-Luxe.

Dirt De-Luxe pending: Sol wouldn't hoard bum information.

Pete took a back booth and noshed a T-bone and hash browns. He laid the folders out for easy perusal.

The first file featured document photos and typed notes. No Hollywood gossip; no *Hush-Hush* feature ammo.

The pix detailed bankbook tallies and an income tax return. The tax filer's name came off familiar: Mr. Hughes' pal George Killebrew, some Tricky Dick Nixon flunky.

The name on the bankbook was "George Kill*ington*." The 1957 deposit total was $87,416.04. George Kill*ebrew*'s reported income for the year: $16,850.00.

A two-syllable name change—hiding over seventy grand.

Sol Maltzman wrote: "Bank employees confirm that Killebrew deposited the entire $87,000 in five to ten thousand dollar cash increments. They also confirm that the tax identification number that he gave was false. He withdrew the entire amount in cash, along with six thousand odd dollars in interest, closing out the account before the bank sent out its standard notification of interest income to the Federal tax authorities."

Unreported income and unreported bank interest. Bingo: felony tax fraud.

Pete made a late snap-connection.

The House Committee on Un-American Activists fucked Sol Maltzman. Dick Nixon was a HUAC member; George Killebrew worked for him.

File #2 featured blow-job pix galore. The suckee: a teenage pansy. The sucker, Sol Maltzman identified: "HUAC counsel Leonard Hosney, 43, of Grand Rapids, Michigan. My soul-debilitating work for *Hush-Hush* finally paid off in the form of a tip proffered by a bouncer at a male brothel in Hermosa Beach. He took the photos and assured me that the boy is a minor. He will be supplying additional documentation photos in the near future."

Pete chained a cigarette butt to tip. The Big Picture came into focus.

The files were Sol's revenge against HUAC. It was some kind of fucked-up penance: Sol wrote right-wing-slanted smears and stashed this shit for belated payback.

File #3 packed more photos: of canceled checks, deposit slips and bank notes. Pete shoved his food aside—*this* was smear bait supreme.

Sol Maltzman wrote: "The political implications of Howard Hughes' 1956 loan of $200,000 to Richard Nixon's brother Donald are staggering, especially since Nixon is expected to be the 1960 Republican Presidential nominee. This is a clear-cut case of an immensely wealthy industrialist buying political influence. It can be circumstantially supported by serving up many verifiable examples of Nixon-initiated policy directly beneficial to Hughes."

Pete rechecked the evidence pix. The verification was solid— straight down the line.

His food was cold. He'd sweated his shirt starched to wilted.

Insider knowledge was a big fucking blast.

His day was all aces and 8's—some dead man's hand he couldn't play or fold.

He could hold onto the Hughes/Nixon dirt. He could let Gail take Sol's job at *Hush-Hush*—she'd done magazine work before—she was tired of divorce shakedowns anyway.

The HUAC staff was aces flush, but MONEY angles eluded him. Kemper Boyd's walk-on had his antenna feelers perk-perk-perking.

Pete drove to the Miramar Hotel and staked out the parking lot. Boyd's car was stashed back by the pool. Lots of women in swimsuits were out sunning—surveillance conditions could be worse.

Hours dragged by. The women came and went. Dusk hampered and shut down the view.

Miami crossed his mind—tiger-striped cabs and hungry gators.

6:00 p.m., 6:30, 7:00. 7:22: Boyd and Ward Fucking Littell walking by the pool.

They got into Boyd's rent-a-car. They pulled out onto Wilshire eastbound.

Littell was Joe Scaredy Cat to Boyd's Cool Cat. Memory Lane: those Feds and him shared a history.

Pete eased into traffic behind them. They did a two-car rollout: east on Wilshire, Barrington north to Sunset. Pete dawdled back and leap-frogged lanes—mobile bird-dog jobs jazzed him.

He was good. Boyd was unhip to the tail—he could tell.

They cruised east on Sunset: Beverly Hills, the Strip, Hollywood. Boyd turned north on Alta Vista and parked—midway down a block of small stucco houses.

Pete slid to the curb three doors up. Boyd and Littell got out; a streetlamp lit their moves.

They put on gloves. They grabbed flashlights. Littell unlocked the trunk and picked up a tool box.

They walked up to a pink stucco house, picked the lock and entered.

Flashlight beams crisscrossed the windows. Pete U-turned and spotted the curb plate: 1541 North.

It had to be a bug/wire job. FBI men called B&E's "black baggers."

The living-room lights snapped on. The fuckers were going at it brazen.

Pete grabbed his reverse book off the backseat. He skimmed it by the dashboard light.

1541 North Alta Vista matched to: Darleen Shoftel, HO3-6811.

Bug jobs took about an hour—he could run her through R&I. He saw a phone booth back at the corner—he could call and watch the house simultaneous.

He walked down and buzzed the County line. Karen Hiltscher picked up—he recognized her voice immediately.

"Records and Information."

"Karen, it's Pete Bondurant."

"You knew it was me after all this time?"

"I guess it's just one of those voices. Look, can you run somebody for me?"

"I suppose, even though you're not a deputy sheriff anymore, and I really shouldn't."

"You're a pal."

"I sure am, especially after the way you—"

"The name's Darleen Shoftel. That's D-A-R-L-E-E-N, S-H-O-F-T-E-L. The last known address I have is 1541 North Alta Vista, Los Angeles. Check all—"

"I know what to do, Pete. You just hold the line."

Pete held. House lights blinked up the block—covert Feds at work.

Karen came back on. "Darleen Shoftel, white female, DOB 3/9/32. No wants, no warrants, no criminal record. She's clean with the DMV, but West Hollywood Vice has a blue sheet on her. There's one notation, dated 8/14/57. It says that a complaint was filed against her by the management at Dino's Lodge. She was soliciting for acts of prostitution at the bar. She was questioned and released, and the investigating detective described her as a 'high-class call girl.' "

"That's all?"

"That's not bad for one phone call."

Pete hung up. He saw the house lights blip off and checked his watch.

Boyd and Littell walked out and loaded their car. Sixteen minutes flat—a black-bag world record.

They drove away. Pete leaned against the booth and worked up a scenario.

Sol Maltzman was working up his own scheme, unknown to the Feds. Boyd was in town to warn him on the Gretzler hit and hot-wire a call girl's pad. Boyd was a glib liar: "I've got an 'in' on the McClellan Committee."

Boyd knew he clipped Gretzler—a McClellan Committee witness. Boyd told Hoover he clipped Gretzler. Hoover said, That's no skin off my ass.

Boyd's car: McClellan Committee–vouchered. Hoover: well-known Bobby Kennedy hater and subterfuge king. Boyd, smooth and educated: probably a good infiltration man.

Question #1: Did the infiltration tie in to the wire job? Question #2: If this turns into money, who signs *my* paycheck?

Maybe Jimmy Hoffa—the McClellan Committee's chief target. Fred Turentine could piggyback the Fed wiring and pick up every word the Feds did.

Pete saw $$$'s—like a 3-across slot-machine jackpot.

He drove home to the watchdog pad. Gail was on the portico—her cigarette tip bobbed and dipped, like she was pacing.

He parked and walked up. He kicked an overflowing ashtray and spilled butts on some prize rosebushes.

Gail backed away from him. Pete kept his voice soft and low.

"How long have you been out here?"

"For hours. Sol was calling every ten minutes, begging for his files. He said you stole some files of his and pushed him around."

"It was business."

"He was frantic. I couldn't listen."

Pete reached for her arms. "It's cold out. Let's go inside."

"No. I don't want to."

"Gail—"

She pulled away. "No! I don't want to go back in that big awful house!"

Pete cracked some knuckles. "I'll take care of Sol. He won't bother you anymore."

Gail laughed—shrill and weird and something else. "I know he won't."

"What do you mean?"

"I mean he's dead. I called him back to try to calm him down, and a policeman answered the phone. He said Sol shot himself."

Pete shrugged. He didn't know what to do with his hands.

Gail ran to her car. She stripped gears pulling out of the driveway—and almost plowed a woman pushing a baby carriage.

5

(Washington, D.C., 12/7/58)

Ward was scared. Kemper knew why: Mr. Hoover's private briefings spawned legends.

They waited in his outer office. Ward sat hold-your-breath still. Kemper knew: he'll be twenty minutes late exactly.

He wants Ward cowed. He wants *me* here to buttress the effect.

He'd already phoned in his report: The Shoftel job went perfectly. A Los Angeles–based agent was assigned to monitor the bug and wiretap recordings from a listening post and forward the salient tapes to Littell in Chicago. Ace wire man Ward would cull them—and send the best excerpts to Mr. Hoover.

Jack wasn't due in L.A. until December 9th. Darleen Shoftel was servicing four tricks a night—the listening-post man praised her stamina. The L.A. *Times* ran a brief mention of Sol Maltzman's suicide. Mr. Hoover said Pete Bondurant probably "fired him" rather harshly.

Ward crossed his legs and straightened his necktie. Don't: Mr. Hoover hates fidgeters. He ordered us here to reward you—so please do not fidget.

Hoover walked in. Kemper and Littell stood up.

"Gentlemen, good morning."

They said, "Good morning, Sir"—in unison, with no overlap.

"I'm afraid this will have to be brief. I'm meeting Vice-President Nixon shortly."

Littell said, "I'm very pleased to be here, Sir."

Kemper almost winced: Do not interject comments, however servile.

"My schedule forces me to effect brevity. Mr. Littell, I appreciate the job you and Mr. Boyd did in Los Angeles. I'm rewarding you with a position on the Chicago Top Hoodlum Squad. I'm doing this at the displeasure of SAC Leahy, who considers you best suited for political surveillance work. I realize, Mr. Littell, that you consider the CPUSA ineffectual, if not moribund. I deem this attitude dangerously fatuous, and sincerely hope you'll outgrow it. You're a personal colleague of mine now, but I warn you not to be seduced by the dangerous life. You can't possibly be as good at it as Kemper Boyd is."

6

(Washington, D.C., 12/8/58)

Littell did paperwork in his bathrobe.

He did it exultantly hung over: they celebrated with Cordon Rouge and Glenlivet. The damage showed: empty bottles and room-service carts piled with untouched food.

Kemper showed restraint. He didn't. Hoover's "brevity" stung; champagne and scotch let him make fun of it. Coffee and aspirin hardly dented his hangover.

A snowstorm closed the airport—he was stuck in his hotel room. Hoover sent up a mimeo file for him to study.

CHICAGO TOP HOODLUM SQUAD CONFIDENTIAL: CRIME FIGURES, LOCATIONS, METHODS OF OPERATION AND RELATED OBSERVATIONS.

It ran sixty detail-padded pages. Littell popped two more aspirin and underlined salient facts.

The current stated goal of the Top Hoodlum Program (outlined in Bureau Directive #3401, 12/19/57) is the gathering of organized crime intelligence. At this date, and until direct notice of a superseding policy, any and all criminal intelligence gathered is to be retained solely for future use. The Top Hoodlum Program is not mandated to gather intelligence to be employed in the process of directly building cases for Federal prosecution. Criminal intelligence obtained through electronic surveillance methods may be, at the discretion of the Regional SAC, transmitted to municipal police agencies and prosecuting bodies.

The elliptical gist: Hoover knows you can't prosecute the Mob and consistently win. He won't sacrifice Bureau prestige for occasional convictions.

Top Hoodlum Program squads may employ electronic surveillance methods on their own autonomy. Verbatim tape and transcription logs are to be rigorously kept and transmitted to the Regional SAC for periodic review.

Bug-and-tap carte blanche—good.

The Chicago THP Squad has effected an electronic surveillance penetration (microphone placements only) at Celano's Custom Tailors, 620 North Michigan Avenue. Both the U.S. Attorney's Office (Northern Illinois Region) and the Cook County Sheriff's Intelligence Division consider this location to be the informal headquarters of ranking Chicago mobsters, their chief lieutenants and selected underlings. A comprehensive tape and stenographer-transcribed intelligence library has been established on the listening post premises.

The suborning of informants should be considered a priority of all THP agents. As of this (12/19/57) date, no informants with intimate knowledge of the Chicago Crime Syndicate have been activated. Note: All transactions involving the exchange of informant intelligence for Bureau-vouchered monies must first be approved by the Regional SAC.

Translation: FIND YOUR OWN SNITCH.

The Top Hoodlum Program mandate currently allows for the assignment of six agents and one secretary/stenographer per regional office. Yearly budgets are not to exceed the guidelines established in Bureau directive #3403, 12/19/57.

Budget stats droned on. Littell flipped to CRIME FIGURES.

Sam Giancana, born 1908. AKA "Mo," "Momo," "Mooney."
Giancana is the Chicago Mob "Boss of Bosses." He follows Al

Capone, Paul "The Waiter" Ricca and Anthony "Joe Batters"/"Big Tuna" Accardo as the Chicago overlord of all gambling, loan-sharking, numbers, vending machine, prostitution and labor rackets. Giancana has been personally involved in numerous Mob-related killings. He was rejected for World War II service as a "constitutional psychopath." Giancana lives in suburban Oak Park. He is frequently seen in the company of his personal body-guard Dominic Michael Montalvo, AKA "Butch Montrose," born 1919. Giancana is a close personal associate of International Brotherhood of Teamsters President James Riddle Hoffa. He is ru-mored to have a voice in the loan selection process of the Team-sters' Central States Pension Fund, an exceedingly rich and dubiously administered union trust believed to have financed many illegal ventures.

Gus Alex, born 1916. (Numerous AKA's.) Alex is the former North Side rackets boss now deployed as the Chicago Mob's po-litical "fixer" and liaison to corrupt elements within the Chicago Police Department and the Cook County Sheriff's Office. He is a closely allied associate of Murray Llewellyn Humphreys, AKA "Hump" and "The Camel," born 1899. Humphreys is the Chicago Mob's "elder statesman." He is semi-retired, but is sometimes consulted on Chicago Mob policy decisions.

John "Johnny" Rosselli, born 1905. Rosselli is a closely allied associate of Sam Giancana and serves as the front man of the Chicago Mob–owned Stardust Hotel and Casino in Las Vegas. Rosselli is rumored to have substantial casino-hotel holdings in Havana, Cuba, along with Cuban gambling magnates Santo Traf-ficante Jr. and Carlos Marcello, the Mob bosses of Tampa, Florida, and New Orleans, Louisiana, respectively.

Known-associate and investment lists followed. Staggering: Gianca-na/Hoffa/Rosselli/Trafficante/Marcello et al. knew every major hoodlum in every major U.S. city and owned legitimate interests in trucking firms, nightclubs, factories, race horses, banks, movie theaters, amusement parks and over three hundred Italian restaurants. Their collective indictment-to-conviction ratio: 308 to 14.

Littell skimmed an appendix: MINOR CRIME FIGURES. Mob bosses wouldn't snitch—but the little fish might.

Jacob Rubenstein, born 1911. AKA "Jack Ruby." This man op-erates a striptease club in Dallas, Texas, and is known to dabble in small-time loansharking. He is rumored to occasionally transmit Chicago Mob money to Cuban politicians, including President Fulgencio Batista and rebel leader Fidel Castro. Rubenstein/Ruby is Chicago-born and has maintained extensive ties within the Chicago Mob. He is a frequent Chicago visitor.

Herschel Meyer Ryskind, born 1901. AKA "Hersh," "Hesh," "Heshie." This man is a former (circa 1930s) member of the Detroit-based 'Purple Gang.' He resides in Arizona and Texas, but maintains strong Chicago Mob ties. He is rumored to be active in the Gulf Coast heroin trade. He is alleged to be a close friend of Sam Giancana and James Riddle Hoffa and is said to have mediated labor disputes for the Chicago Mob.

"Alleged to be"/"rumored to have"/"believed to be." Key phrases revealing a key truth: the file read noncommittal and equivocal. Hoover didn't really hate the Mob—the THP was his response to Apalachin.

Lenny Sands, born 1924. (Formerly Leonard Joseph Seidelwitz), AKA "Jewboy Lenny." This man is considered to be a mascot to the Chicago Mob. His nominal occupation is lounge entertainer. He frequently entertains at Chicago Mob and Cook County Teamster gatherings. Sands is said to have occasionally delivered Chicago Mob funds to Cuban police officials as part of the Chicago Mob's efforts to maintain a friendly political climate in Cuba and insure the continued success of their Havana casinos. Sands has a vending machine pick-up route and is a salaried employee of the Chicago Mob's quasi-legitimate "Vendo-King" business front. (Note: Sands is a well-established Las Vegas/Los Angeles entertainment business "fringe character." He is also rumored to have given U.S. Senator John Kennedy (D–Massachusetts) speech lessons during his 1946 Congressional campaign.)

A Mob flunky knew Jack Kennedy. And *he* wired a whore's pad to entrap him.

Littell jumped back and forth: MINOR CRIME FIGURES to RELATED OBSERVATIONS.

Chicago Mob territories are geographically divided. The North Side, Near North Side, West Side, South Side, Loop, Lakefront and northern suburb areas are run by underbosses who report directly to Sam Giancana.

Mario Salvatore D'Onofrio, born 1912. AKA "Mad Sal." This man is an independent loan shark and bookmaker. He is allowed to operate because he pays Sam Giancana a large operating tribute. D'Onofrio was convicted of 2nd Degree Manslaughter in 1951 and served a five-year sentence at the Illinois State Penitentiary at Joliet. A prison psychiatrist described him as a "Psychopathically-derived criminal sadist with uncontrollable psycho-sexual urges to inflict pain." He was recently a suspect in the torture-murders of two Bob O'Link Country Club golf professionals rumored to owe him money.

Independent bookmaker-loansharks flourish in Chicago. This is due to Sam Giancana's policy of extracting high-percentage operating tributes. One of Giancana's most fearsome underbosses, Anthony "Icepick Tony" Iannone (born 1917), serves as the Chicago Mob's liaison to independent bookmaker-loanshark factions. Iannone is strongly believed to be responsible for the mutilation murders of no less than nine heavily indebted loanshark customers.

Names jumped out. Odd appellations made him laugh.

Tony "the Ant" Spilotro, Felix "Milwaukee Phil" Alderisio, Frank "Franky Strongy" Ferraro.

Joe Amato, Joseph Cesar Di Varco, Jackie "Jackie the Lackey" Cerone.

The Teamsters' Central States Pension Fund remains a source of constant law enforcement speculation. Does Sam Giancana have final Fund loan approval? What is the established protocol for granting loans to criminals, quasi-legitimate businessmen and labor racketeers seeking capital?

Jimmy "Turk" Torello, Louie "the Mooch" Eboli.

The Miami PD Intelligence Squad believes that Sam Giancana is a silent partner in the Tiger Kab Kompany, a Teamster-owned taxi service run by Cuban refugees believed to possess extensive criminal records.

Daniel "Donkey Dan" Versace, "Fat Bob" Paolucci—

The phone rang. Littell fumbled for it—eyestrain had him seeing double.

"Hello?"

"It's me."

"Kemper, hi."

"What have you been doing? When I left you were two sheets to the wind."

Littell laughed. "I've been reading the THP file. And so far, I'm not too impressed with Mr. Hoover's anti-Mob mandate."

"Watch your mouth, he might have bugged your room."

"That's a cruel thought."

"Yes, if not far-fetched. Ward, look, it's still snowing, and you'll never be able to fly out today. Why don't you meet me at the Committee office? Bobby and I are grilling a witness. He's a Chicago man, and you might learn something."

"I could use some air. You're at the old Senate Office Building?"

"Right, suite 101. I'll be in interview room A. It's got an observation corridor, so you'll be able to watch. And remember my cover. I'm retired from the FBI."

"You're a glib dissembler, Kemper. It's rather sad."

"Don't get lost in the snow."

The setup was perfect: a closed hallway with one-way glass access and wall-mounted speakers. Partitioned off in cubicle A: the Kennedy brothers, Kemper, and a blond man.

Cubicles B, C and D were vacant. He had the watching gallery to himself—the snowstorm must have scared people home.

Littell hit the speaker switch. Voices crackled out with minimum static.

The men sat around a desk. Robert Kennedy played host and worked the tape recorder.

"Take your time, Mr. Kirpaski. You're a voluntary witness, and we're here at your disposal."

The blond man said, "Call me Roland. Nobody calls me Mr. Kirpaski."

Kemper grinned. "Any man who rolls over on Jimmy Hoffa deserves that formality."

Brilliant Kemper—reviving his Tennessee drawl.

Roland Kirpaski said, "That's nice, I guess. But you know, Jimmy Hoffa's Jimmy Hoffa. What I mean is, it's like they say about the elephant. He don't forget."

Robert Kennedy laced his hands behind his head. "Hoffa will have plenty of time in prison to remember everything that put him there."

Kirpaski coughed. "I'd like to say something. And I'd ... uh ... like to read it off when I testify in front of the Committee."

Kemper said, "Go ahead."

Kirpaski leaned his chair back. "I'm a union guy. *I'm a Teamster.* Now, I told you all them stories about Jimmy doing this and doing that, you know, telling his guys to lean on these other guys that wouldn't play ball and so forth. I guess maybe all that stuff is illegal, but you know what? That don't bother me so much. The only reason I'm so-called rolling over on Jimmy is because I can add up two and two and get four, and I heard enough at fucking Chicago Local 2109 to figure out that Jimmy Fucking Hoffa is cutting side deals with management, which means that he is a scab piece of shit, pardon my French, and I want to go on the record as saying that that is my motive for ratting him off."

John Kennedy laughed. Littell flashed on the Shoftel job and winced.

Robert Kennedy said, "Duly noted, Roland. You'll be able to read any statement you like before you testify. And remember, we're saving your testimony for a televised session. Millions of people will see you."

Kemper said, "The more publicity you get, the more unlikely it is that Hoffa will attempt reprisals."

Kirpaski said, "Jimmy don't forget. He's like an elephant that way. You know those gangster pictures you showed me? Those guys I saw Jimmy with?"

Robert Kennedy held up some photos. "Santo Trafficante Jr. and Carlos Marcello."

Kirpaski nodded. "Right. I also want to go on the record as saying that I've heard good things about those guys. I heard they hire union men exclusively. No Mafia guy ever said, 'Roland, you're a dumb Southside Polack' to me. Like I said, they visited Jimmy at his suite at the Drake, and all they talked about was the weather, the Cubs and politics in Cuba. I want to go on the record as saying I got no gripe against the fucking Mafia."

Kemper winked at the one-way. "Neither does J. Edgar Hoover."

Littell laughed. Kirpaski said, "What?"

Robert Kennedy drummed the table. "Mr. Boyd is performing for some unseen colleague of his. Now, Roland, let's get back to Miami and Sun Valley."

Kirpaski said, "I'd like to. Jesus, this snow."

Kemper stood up and stretched his legs. "Walk us through your observations again."

Kirpaski sighed. "I was a Chicago delegate to the convention last year. We stayed at the Deauville in Miami. I was still friendly with Jimmy then, because I hadn't figured out he was a scab cocksucker cutting side deals with—"

Robert Kennedy cut in. "Stick to the point, please."

"The point is I ran some errands for Jimmy. I went by the Tiger Kab stand, which is spelled with a goddamn K, and picked up some cash so Jimmy could take some guys from the Miami locals out on a boat to shoot sharks with Tommy guns, which is one of Jimmy's favorite Florida things to do. I must have picked up three grand easy. The cabstand was like the planet Mars. All these crazy Cuban guys wearing tiger-colored shirts. The boss Cuban was this guy Fulo. He was selling these hot TVs out of the parking lot. The Tiger Kab business is strictly cash-operated. If you want my considered opinion, it's a tax evasion bounce looking to happen."

Static rattled the speaker—Littell tapped the squelch button and smoothed the volume out. John Kennedy looked bored and restless.

Robert Kennedy doodled on a notepad. "Tell us about Anton Gretzler again."

Kirpaski said, "We all went out shark shooting. Gretzler came along. Him and Jimmy were talking by themselves over on one end of the boat away from the shark shooters. I was down in the can, being seasick. I guess they thought they had privacy, because they were talking up this not-too-legal-sounding stuff, which I want to go on the record as stating was no skin off my ass, because it didn't involve collusion with management."

John Kennedy tapped his watch. Kemper prompted Kirpaski. "What exactly did they discuss?"

"Sun Valley. Gretzler said he had land surveys done, and his surveyor said the land wouldn't fall into the swamp for five years or so, which would let them off the hook, legally speaking. Jimmy said he could tap the Pension Fund for three million dollars to purchase the land and prefab material, and maybe they could pocket some cash up front."

Robert Kennedy jumped up. His chair crashed—the one-way glass shimmied. "That is very strong testimony! That is a virtual admission of conspiracy to commit land fraud and intent to defraud the Pension Fund!"

Kemper picked the chair up. "It's only courtroom valid if Gretzler corroborates it or perjures himself denying it. Without Gretzler, it's Roland's word versus Hoffa's. It comes down to credibility, and Roland has two drunk-driving convictions while Hoffa's record is technically clean."

tors will be forwarding our evidence along to other agencies. Whatever we dig up will be acted on."

Jack said, "Eventually?" Littell translated: "Too late to bolster *my* career."

The brothers locked eyes. Kemper leaned across the table between them. "Hoffa's got a block of houses set up at Sun Valley. He's down there himself, giving PR tours. Roland's going down to look around. He runs a Chicago local, so it won't look suspicious. He'll be calling in to report what he sees."

Kirpaski said, "Yeah, and I'm also gonna 'see' this cocktail waitress I met when I went down for the convention. But you know what? I'm not gonna tell my wife she's on the menu."

Jack motioned Kemper in close. Littell caught static-laced whispers:

"I'm flying to L.A. when this snow lets up."/"Call Darleen Shoftel—I'm sure she'd love to meet you."

Kirpaski said, "I'm hungry."

Robert Kennedy packed his briefcase. "Come on, Roland. You can join the family for supper at my house. Try not to say 'fuck' around my children, though. They'll learn the concept soon enough."

The men filed out a back door. Littell hugged the glass for one last look at Bobby.

Bobby fumed. Kemper said, "Bob, Gretzler has to be de
was dumped in a swamp, and the man himself can't be foun
a lot of hours in trying to find him, and I haven't turned up o
lead."

"He could have faked his own death to avoid appearing be
Committee."

"I think that's unlikely."

Bobby straddled his chair and gripped down on the slats. "You
be right. But I may still send you down to Florida to make sure."

Kirpaski said, "I'm hungry."

Jack rolled his eyes. Kemper winked at him.

Kirpaski sighed. "I said I'm hungry."

Kemper checked his watch. "Wrap it up for the senator, Roland. T
us how Gretzler got drunk and shot his mouth off."

"I get the picture. Sing for your supper."

Bobby said, "Goddamnit—"

"All right, all right. It was after the shark shoot. Gretzler was pissed
because Jimmy ridiculed him for holding his Tommy gun like a sissy.
Gretzler started talking up these rumors he'd heard about the Pension
Fund. He said he heard the Fund is a lot fucking richer than people
knew, and nobody could subpoena the books, because the books
weren't real. See, Gretzler said there were these 'real' Teamster Fund
books, probably in code, with fucking tens of millions of dollars ac-
counted for in them. This money gets loaned out at these exorbitant
rates. There's supposed to be some retired Chicago gangster—a real
brain—who's the bookkeeper for the 'real' books and the 'real' money,
and if you're thinking about corroboration, forget it—I'm the only one
Gretzler was talking to."

Bobby Kennedy pushed his hair back. His voice went high, like an
excited child's.

"It's our big wedge, Jack. First we subpoena the front books again
and determine their solvency. We trace the loaned-out money the Teamsters admit to and try to determine the existence of hidden assets
within the Fund and the probability that those 'real' books exist."

Littell pressed up to the glass. He felt magnetized: tousle-haired, passionate Bobby—

Jack Kennedy coughed. "It's strong stuff. *If* you can produce verifiable testimony on those books before the Committee's mandate ends."

Kirpaski applauded. "Hey, he speaks. Hey, Senator, glad you could
join us."

Jack Kennedy cringed, mock-wounded. Bobby said, "My investiga-

7

(Los Angeles, 12/9/58)

Darleen Shoftel faked a mean climax. Darleen Shoftel had whore pals over for shop talk. Darleen was a bigggg name dropper.

She said Franchot Tone dug bondage. She called Dick Contino a champion muff diver. She dubbed B-movie man Steve Cochran "Mr. King Size."

Phone calls came in and went out. Darleen talked to tricks, hooker chums and Mom in Vincennes, Indiana.

Darleen loved to talk. Darleen said nothing to explain why two Feds wired her crib.

They attached the Fed apparatus four days ago. 1541 North Alta Vista was miked up floor to rafters.

Fred Turentine piggybacked the Boyd/Littell setup. He heard everything the FBI heard. The Feds rented a listening-post house down the block; Freddy monitored *his* hookups from a van parked next door and kept Pete supplied with tape copies.

And Pete smelled money and called Jimmy Hoffa—maybe a bit premature.

Jimmy said, "You got a good sense of smell. Come down to Miami on Thursday and tell me what you got. If you got nothing, we can go out on my boat and shoot sharks."

Thursday was tomorrow. Shark shooting was strictly for geeks. Freddy's pay was two hundred a day—steep for a crash course in extraneous sex jive.

Pete moped around the watchdog house. Pete savored the hints he dropped on Mr. Hughes: I know you lent Dick Nixon's brother some coin. Pete kept playing the piggyback tapes out of sheer boredom.

He hit Play. Darleen moaned and groaned. Bedsprings creaked; something headboard-like slammed something wall-like. Dig it: Darleen with a big fat porker in the saddle.

The phone rang—Pete grabbed it fast.

"Who's this?"

"It's Fred. Get over here now—we just hit paydirt."

The van was crammed with contraptions and gadgets. Pete banged his knees climbing in.

Freddy looked all hopped up. His zipper was down, like he'd been choking the chicken.

He said, "I recognized that Boston accent immediately, and I called you the second they started screwing. Listen, this is live."

Pete put on headphones. Darleen Shoftel spoke, loud and clear.

". . . you're a bigger hero than your brother. I read about you in *Time* magazine. Your PT boat got rammed by the Japs or something."

"I'm a better swimmer than Bobby, that's certainly true."

3-cherry jackpot: Gail Hendee's old squeeze, Jack the K.

Darleen: "I saw your brother's picture in *Newsweek* magazine. Doesn't he have like four thousand kids?"

Jack: "At least three thousand, with new ones popping up all the time. When you visit his house the little shits attach themselves to your ankles. My wife finds Bobby's need to breed vulgar."

Darleen: " 'Need to breed'—that's cute."

Jack: "Bobby's a true Catholic. He needs to have children and punish the men that he hates. If his hate instincts weren't so unerring, he'd be a colossal pain in the ass."

Pete clamped his headset down. Jack Kennedy talked, postfuck languid:

"I don't hate like Bobby does. Bobby hates with a fury. Bobby hates Jimmy Hoffa very powerfully and simply, which is why he'll win in the end. I was in Washington with him yesterday. He was taking a deposition from a Teamster man who'd become disgusted with Hoffa and had decided to inform on him. Here's this dumb brave Polack, Roland something from Chicago, and Bobby takes him home for dinner with his family. You see, uh . . ."

"Darleen."

"Right, Darleen. You see, Darleen, Bobby's more heroic than I am because he's truly passionate and generous."

Gadgets blinked. Tape spun. They hit the royal flush/Irish Sweepstakes jackpot—Jimmy Hoffa would SHIT when he heard it.

Darleen: "I still think that PT boat thing was pretty swell."

Jack: "You know, you're a good listener, Arlene."

Fred looked ready to DROOL. His fucking eyes were dollar-sign dilated.

Pete made fists. "This is mine. You just sit tight and do what I tell you to."

Freddy cringed. Pete smiled—his hands put the fear out every time.

A Tiger Kab met his plane. The driver talked Cuban politics nonstop: *El grande* Castro advancing! *El puto* Batista in retreat!

Pancho dropped him off at the cabstand. Jimmy had the dispatch shack commandeered—goons were packing up life jackets and Tommy guns.

Hoffa shooed them out. Pete said, "Jimmy, how are you?"

Hoffa picked up a nail-studded baseball bat. "I'm all right. You like this? Sometimes the sharks get up close to the boat and you can give them a few whacks."

Pete opened up his tape rig and plugged it into a floor outlet. The tiger-stripe wallpaper made his head swim.

"It's cute, but I brought something better."

"You said you smelled money. That's gotta mean my money for your trouble."

"There's a story behind it."

"I don't like stories, unless I'm the hero. And you know I'm a busy—"

Pete put a hand on his arm. "An FBI man braced me. He said he had an 'in' on the McClellan Committee. He said he made me for the Gretzler job, and he said Mr. Hoover didn't care. You know Hoover, Jimmy. He's always left you and the Outfit alone."

Hoffa pulled his arm loose. "So? You think they've got evidence? Is that what that tape's all about?"

"No. I think the Fed's spying on Bobby Kennedy and the Committee for Hoover, or something like that, and I think Hoover's on our side. I tailed the guy and his partner up to a fuck pad in Hollywood. They bugged and wired it, and my guy Freddy Turentine hooked up a piggy-back. Now, listen."

Hoffa tapped his foot like he was bored. Hoffa brushed tiger-striped lint off his shirt.

Pete tapped Play. Tape hissed. Sex groans and mattress squeaks escalated.

Pete timed the fuck. Senator John F. Kennedy: 2.4-minute man.

Darleen Shoftel faked a climax. There, that Boston bray: "My god-damn back gave out."

Darleen said, "It was goooood. Short and sweet's the best."

Jimmy twirled his baseball bat. Goosebumps bristled up his arms.

Pete pushed buttons and cut to the good stuff. Two-Minute Jack rhapsodized:

". . . a Teamster man who'd become disgusted with Hoffa . . . this dumb brave Polack, Roland something from Chicago."

Hoffa popped goose bumps. Hoffa choked up a grip on his bat.

"This Roland something has working-class panache. . . . Bobby's got his teeth in Hoffa. When Bobby bites down he doesn't let go."

Hoffa popped double goose bumps. Hoffa went bug-eyed like a fright-wig nigger.

Pete stood back.

Hoffa let fly—watch that nail-topped Louisville Slugger GO—

Chairs got smashed to kindling. Desks got knocked legless. Walls got spike-gouged down to the baseboard.

Pete stood *way* back. A glowing plastic Jesus doorstop got shattered into eight million pieces.

Paper stacks flew. Wood chips ricocheted. Drivers watched from the sidewalk—Jimmy roundhoused the window and glass-blasted them.

James Riddle Hoffa: heaving and voodoo-eyed stuporous.

His bat snagged on a doorjamb. Jimmy stared at it—say what?

Pete grabbed him in a bear hug. Jimmy's eyes rolled back, catatonic-style.

Hoffa flailed and squirmed. Pete squeezed him close to breathless and baby-talked him.

"I can keep Freddy on the piggyback for two hundred a day. Sooner or later we might get something you can fuck the Kennedys with. I've got some political dirt files, too. They might do us some good someday."

Hoffa focused in half-lucid. His voice came out laughing-gas squeaky.

"What . . . do . . . you . . . want?"

"Mr. Hughes is going nuts. I was thinking I'd get next to you and cover my bets."

Hoffa squirmed free. Pete almost choked on his smell: sweat and bargain-basement cologne.

His color receded. He caught his breath. His voice went down a few octaves.

"I'll give you 5% of this cabstand. You keep the piggyback going in L.A. and show up here once in a while to keep these Cubans in line. Don't try to Jew me up to 10%, or I'll say 'fuck you' and send you back to L.A. on the bus."

Pete said, "It's a deal."

Jimmy said, "I've got a job in Sun Valley. I want you to come with me."

They took a Tiger Kab out. Shark-shoot goodies bulged up the trunk: nail bats, Tommy guns and suntan oil.

Fulo Machado drove. Jimmy wore fresh threads. Pete forgot to bring spare clothes—Hoffa's stink stuck to him.

Nobody talked—Jimmy Hoffa sulking killed chitchat. They passed buses filled with Teamster chumps headed for the sucker-bait tract pads.

Pete did mental arithmetic.

Twelve cab drivers working around-the-clock. Twelve men with Jimmy Hoffa–sponsored green cards—taking short-end taxi-fare splits to stay in America. Twelve moonlighters: stickup men, strikebreakers, pimps. 5% of the top-end money and whatever else he could scrounge— this gig packed potential.

Fulo pulled off the highway. Pete saw the spot where he whacked Anton Gretzler. They followed a bus convoy to the bait cribs—three miles from the Interstate easy.

Movie spotlights gave off this huge glow—extra-bright, like a premiere at Grauman's Chinese. The cosmetic Sun Valley looked good: tidy little houses in a blacktop-paved clearing.

Teamsters were boozing at card tables—at least two hundred men squeezed into the walkways between houses. A gravel parking lot was crammed with cars and buses. A bar-b-que pit stood adjacent—check that spike-impaled steer twirling and basting.

Fulo parked close to the action. Jimmy said, "You two wait here."

Pete got out and stretched. Hoffa zoomed into the crowd—toadies swarmed him right off the bat.

Fulo sharpened his machete on a pumice stone. He packed it in a scabbard strapped to the backseat.

Pete watched Jimmy work the crowd.

He showed off the pads. He gave little speeches and wolfed bar-b-que. He seized up and flushed around a blond Polack type.

Pete chain-smoked. Fulo played the cab radio: some Spanish-language pray-for-Jesus show.

A few buses took off. Two carloads of hookers pulled in—trashy Cuban babes chaperoned by off-duty state troopers.

Jimmy huckstered and hawked Sun Valley applications. Some Teamsters grabbed their cars and fishtailed off drunk and rowdy.

The Polack bagged a U-drive Chevy and burned gravel like he had a hot date somewhere.

Jimmy walked up fast—stubby legs chugging on overdrive. You didn't need a fucking road map: the Polack was Roland Kirpaski.

They piled in to the tiger sled. Fulo gunned it. The radio geek cranked up a donation plea.

Lead-foot Fulo got the picture. Lead-foot Fulo went 0 to 60 inside six seconds.

Pete saw the Chevy's taillights. Fulo floored the gas and rammed them. The car swerved off the road, clipped some trees and stalled dead.

Fulo brodied in close. His headlights strafed Kirpaski—stumbling through a clearing thick with marsh grass.

Jimmy got out and chased him. Jimmy waved Fulo's machete. Kirpaski tripped and stood up flashing two fuck-you fingers.

Hoffa came in swinging. Kirpaski went down flailing wrist stumps gouting blood. Jimmy swung two-handed—scalp flaps flew.

The radio clown jabbered. Kirpaski convulsed head to toe. Jimmy wiped blood from his eyes and kept swinging.

8

(Miami, 12/11/58)

Kemper called the car game Devil's Advocate. It helped him keep his loyalties straight and honed his ability to project the right persona at the right time.

Bobby Kennedy's distrust inspired the game. His southern accent slipped once—Bobby caught it instantly.

Kemper cruised South Miami. He began the game by marking who knew what.

Mr. Hoover knew *everything*. SA Boyd's "retirement" was cloaked in FBI paperwork: if Bobby sought corroboration, he'd find it.

Claire knew everything. She'd never judge his motives or betray him.

Ward Littell knew of the Kennedy incursion. He most likely disapproved of it—Bobby's crimebuster fervor deeply impressed him. Ward was also an ad hoc infiltration partner, compromised by the Darleen Shoftel wire job. The job shamed him—but gratitude for his THP transfer outweighed his guilt pangs. Ward did not know that Pete Bondurant killed Anton Gretzler; Ward did not know that Mr. Hoover condoned the murder. Bondurant terrified Ward—a sane response to Big Pete and the legend he inspired. The Bondurant matter should be kept from Ward at all cost.

Bobby knew that he was pimping for Jack—supplying him with the numbers of especially susceptible old flames.

Questions and answers next: practice for deflecting skepticism.

Kemper braked for a woman lugging groceries. His game snapped to the present tense.

Bobby thinks I'm chasing leads on Anton Gretzler. I'm really protecting Howard Hughes' pet thug.

Q: You seem bent on crashing the Kennedy inner circle.

A: I can spot comers a mile off. Cozying up to Democrats doesn't make me a Communist. Old Joe Kennedy's as far right as Mr. Hoover.

Q: You "cozied up" to Jack rather fast.

A: If circumstances had been different, I could have been Jack.

Kemper checked his notebook.

He had to go by Tiger Kab. He had to go to Sun Valley and show mug shots to the witness who saw the "big man" avert his face off the Interstate.

He'd show him *old* mug shots—bad current Bondurant likenesses. He'd discourage a confirmation: you didn't really see *this* man, did you?

A tiger-striped taxi swerved in front of him. He saw a tiger-striped hut down the block.

Kemper pulled up and parked across the street. Some curbside loungers smelled COP and dispersed.

He walked into the hut. He laughed—the wallpaper was fresh-flocked tiger-striped velveteen.

Four tiger-shirted Cubans stood up and circled him. They wore their shirttails out to cover waistband bulges.

Kemper pulled his mug shots out. The tiger men circled in tighter. A man pulled out a stiletto and scratched his neck with the blade.

The other tiger men laughed. Kemper braced the closest one. "Have you seen him?"

The man passed the mug strip around. Every man flashed recognition and said "No."

Kemper grabbed the strip. He saw a white man on the sidewalk checking his car out.

The knife man sidled up close. The other tiger men giggled. The knife man twirled his blade right upside the gringo's eyes.

Kemper judo-chopped him. Kemper snapped his knees with a side-kick. The man hit the floor prone and dropped his shiv.

Kemper picked it up. The tiger men backed off en masse. Kemper stepped on the knife man's knife hand and slammed the blade through it.

The knife man screamed. The other tiger men gasped and tittered. Kemper exited with a tight little bow.

. . .

He drove out I-95 to Sun Valley. A gray sedan stuck close behind him. He changed lanes, dawdled and accelerated—the car followed from a classic tail distance.

Kemper eased down an off-ramp. A hicktown main street ran perpendicular to it—just four gas stations and a church. He pulled into a Texaco and parked.

He walked to the men's room. He saw the tail car idle up to the pumps. The white man dawdling by Tiger Kab got out and looked around.

Kemper shut the door and pulled his piece. The room was smelly and filthy.

He counted seconds off his watch. He heard foot scuffs at fifty-one.

The man nudged the door open. Kemper yanked him in and pinned him to the wall.

He was fortyish, sandy-haired, and slender. Kemper pat-searched him from the ankles up.

No badge, no gun, no leatherette ID holder.

The man didn't blink. The man ignored the revolver in his face.

The man said, "My name is John Stanton. I'm a representative of a U.S. Government agency, and I want to talk to you."

"About what?"

Stanton said, "Cuba."

9

(Chicago, 12/11/58)

S nitch candidate at work: "Jew-boy Lenny" Sands collecting jukebox cash.

Littell tailed him. They hit six Hyde Park taverns in an hour—Lenny worked fast.

Lenny kibitzed. Lenny cracked jokes. Lenny passed out Johnnie Walker Red Label miniatures. Lenny told the story of Come-San-Chin, the Chinese cocksucker—and bagged his coin receipts inside seven minutes.

Lenny was a deficient tail-spotter. Lenny had unique THP stats: lounge entertainer/Cuban bagman/Mob mascot.

Lenny pulled up to the Tillerman's Lounge. Littell parked and walked in thirty seconds behind him.

The place was overheated. A bar mirror tossed his reflection back: lumberjack coat, chinos, work boots.

He still looked like a college professor.

Teamster regalia lined the walls. A framed glossy stood out: Jimmy Hoffa and Frank Sinatra holding up trophy fish.

Workingmen walked through a hot buffet line. Lenny sat at a back ta-ble, with a stocky man wolfing corned beef.

Littell ID'd him: Jacob Rubenstein/AKA Jack Ruby.

Lenny brought his coin sacks. Ruby brought a suitcase. It was a probable vending cash transfer.

There were no empty tables adjoining them.

Men stood at the bar drinking lunch: rye shots and beer chasers. Littell signaled for the same—nobody laughed or snickered.

The barman served him and took his money. He downed his lunch quick—just like his Teamster brothers.

The rye made him sweat; the beer gave him goose bumps. The combination tamped down his nerves.

He'd had one THP Squad meeting. The men seemed to resent him—Mr. Hoover slotted him in personally. An agent named Court Meade came on friendly; the others welcomed him with nods and perfunctory handshakes.

He had three days in as a THP agent. Including three shifts at the bug post, studying Chi-mob voices.

The barman cruised by. Littell raised two fingers—the same way his Teamster brothers called for refills.

Sands and Ruby kept talking. There was no table space near them—he couldn't get close enough to listen.

He drank and paid up. The rye went straight to his head.

Drinking on duty was a Bureau infraction. Not *strictly* illegal—like wiring fuck pads to entrap politicians.

The agent working the Shoftel post was probably swamped—he hadn't sent a single tape out yet. Mr. Hoover's Kennedy hate seemed insanely misguided.

Robert Kennedy seemed heroic. Bobby's kindness to Roland Kirpaski seemed pure and genuine.

A table opened up. Littell walked through the lunch line and grabbed it. Lenny and Rubenstein/Ruby were less than three feet away.

Ruby was talking. Food dribbled down his bib.

"Heshie always thinks he's got cancer or some farkakte disease. With Hesh a pimple's always a malignant tumor."

Lenny picked at a sandwich. "Heshie's a class guy. When I played the Stardust Lounge in '54 he came every night. Heshie always preferred lounge acts to the main-room guys. Jesus Christ and the Apostles could be playing the big room at the Dunes, and Heshie'd be over at some slot palace checking out some guinea crooner 'cause his cousin's a made guy."

Ruby said, "Heshie loves blow jobs. He gets blow jobs exclusively, 'cause he says it's good for his prostrate. He told me he hasn't dipped the schnitzel since he was with the Purples back in the '30s and some shiksa tried to schlam him with a paternity suit. Heshie told me he's had over ten thousand blow jobs. He likes to watch 'The Lawrence Welk Show' while he gets blown. He's got nine doctors for all these diseases he thinks he's got, and all the nurses blow him. That's how he knows it's good for his prostrate."

"Heshie" was most likely Herschel Meyer Ryskind: "active in the Gulf Coast heroin trade."

Lenny said, "Jack, I hate to stiff you with all these coins, but I didn't have time to go to the bank. Sam was very specific. He said you were making rounds and only had limited time. I'm glad we had time to nosh, though, 'cause I always enjoy watching you eat."

Ruby wiped his bib. "I'm worse when the food's better. There's a deli in Big D that's to die for. Here, my shirt's just spritzed. At that deli it's spray-painted."

"Who's the money for?"

"Batista and the Beard. Santo and Sam are hedging their bets political-wise. I'm flying down next week."

Lenny pushed his plate aside. "I've got this new routine where Castro comes to the States and gets a job as a beatnik poet. He's smoking maryjane and talking like a shvartze."

"You're big-room talent, Lenny. I've always said so."

"Keep saying it, Jack. If you keep saying it, somebody might hear you."

Ruby stood up. "Hey, you never know."

"That's right, you never do. Shalom, Jack. It's always a pleasure watching you eat."

Ruby walked out with his suitcase. Jewboy Lenny lit a cigarette and rolled his eyes up to God.

Lounge acts. Blow jobs. Rye and beer for lunch.

Littell walked back to his car lightheaded.

Lenny left twenty minutes later. Littell tailed him to Lake Shore Drive northbound.

Whitecap spray hit the windshield—booming wind had the lake churning. Littell cranked up his heater—too hot replaced too cold.

The liquor left him cotton-mouthed and just a tad woozy. The road kept dipping—just a little.

Lenny signaled to exit. Littell leaped lanes and eased up behind him. They swung down into the Gold Coast—too upscale to be Vendo-King turf.

Lenny turned west on Rush Street. Littell saw high-toned cocktail spots up ahead: brownstone fronts and low-key neon signs.

Lenny parked and walked into Hernando's Hideaway. Littell cruised by extra-slow.

The door swung back. He saw two men kissing—a little half-second teaser blip.

Littell double-parked and switched jackets: lumberjack to blue blazer. The chinos and boots had to stay.

He walked in bucking wind. The place was dark and mid-afternoon quiet. The decor was discreet: all polished wood and forest-green leather.

A banquette section was roped off. Two duos sat at opposite ends of the bar: older men, Lenny and a college boy.

Littell took a seat between them. The bartender ignored him.

Lenny was talking. His inflections were polished now—devoid of growl and Yiddish patter.

"Larry, you should have seen this wretched man eat."

The bartender came over. Littell said, "Rye and beer." Heads turned his way.

The barman poured a shot. Littell downed it and coughed. The barman said, "My, aren't we thirsty!"

Littell reached for his wallet. His ID holder popped out and landed on the bar badge-up.

He grabbed it and threw some change down. The barman said, "Don't we want our beer?"

Littell drove to the office and typed up a tail report. He chewed a roll of Clorets to kill his liquor breath.

He omitted mention of his beverage intake and his blunder at Hernando's Hideaway. He stressed the basic gist: that Lenny Sands might have a secret homosexual life. This might prove to be a recruitment wedge: he was obviously hiding that life from his Mob associates.

Lenny never noticed him. So far, his tail stood uncompromised.

Court Meade rapped on his cubicle screen. "You've got a long-distance call, Ward. A man named Boyd in Miami on line 2."

Littell picked up. "Kemper, hi. What are you doing back in Florida?"

"Working at cross-purposes for Bobby and Mr. Hoover, but don't tell anyone."

"Are you getting results?"

"Well, people keep approaching me, and Bobby's witnesses keep disappearing, so I'd have to call it a toss-up. Ward . . ."

"You need a favor."

"Actually, two."

Littell leaned his chair back. "I'm listening."

Boyd said, "Helen's flying into Chicago tonight. United flight 84, New Orleans to Midway. She gets in at 5:10. Will you pick her up and take her to her hotel?"

"Of course. And I'll take her to dinner, too. Jesus, that's last-minute but great."

Boyd laughed. "That's our Helen, an impetuous traveler. Ward, do you remember that man Roland Kirpaski?"

"Kemper, I saw him three days ago."

"Yes, you did. In any event, he's allegedly down in Florida, but I can't seem to find him. He was supposed to call Bobby and report on Hoffa's Sun Valley scheme, but he hasn't called, and he left his hotel last night and hasn't returned."

"Do you want me to go by his house and talk to his wife?"

"Yes, if you wouldn't mind. If you get anything pertinent, leave a coded message with Communications in D.C. I haven't found a hotel here yet, but I'll check in with them to see if you've called."

"What's the address?"

"It's 818 South Wabash. Roland's probably off on a toot with some bimbo, but it can't hurt to see if he's called home. And Ward?"

"I know. I'll remember who you're working for and play it close to the vest."

"Thanks."

"You're welcome. And by the way, I saw a man today who's as good a role player as you are."

Boyd said, "That impossible."

Mary Kirpaski rushed him inside. The house was overfurnished and way overheated.

Littell took off his overcoat. The woman almost pushed him into the kitchen.

"Roland always calls home every night. He said if he didn't call on this trip, I should cooperate with the authorities and show them his notebook."

Littell smelled cabbage and boiled meat. "I'm not with the McClellan Committee, Mrs. Kirpaski. I haven't really worked with your husband."

"But you know Mr. Boyd and Mr. Kennedy."

"I know Mr. Boyd. He's the one who asked me to check on you."

She'd chewed her nails bloody. Her lipstick was applied way off-center.

"Roland didn't call last night. He kept this notebook on Mr. Hoffa's doings, and he didn't take it to Washington because he wanted to talk to Mr. Kennedy before he agreed to testify."

"What notebook?"

"It's a list of Mr. Hoffa's Chicago phone calls, with dates and everything like that. Roland said he stole the phone bills of some of Mr. Hoffa's friends because Mr. Hoffa was afraid to call long distance from his hotel, because he thought his phone might be tapped."

"Mrs. Kirpaski . . ."

She grabbed a binder off the breakfast table. "Roland would be so mad if I didn't show it to the authorities."

Littell opened the binder. Page 1 listed names and phone numbers, neatly arranged in columns.

Mary Kirpaski crowded up to him. "Roland called up the phone companies in all the different cities and found out who the numbers belonged to. I think he impersonated policemen or something like that."

Littell flipped pages front to back. Roland Kirpaski printed legibly and neatly.

Several "calls received" names were familiar: Sam Giancana, Carlos Marcello, Anthony Iannone, Santo Trafficante Jr. One name was familiar and scary: Peter Bondurant, 949 Mapleton Drive, Los Angeles.

Hoffa called Big Pete three times recently: 11/25/58, 12/1/58, 12/2/58.

Bondurant snapped manacles bare-handed. He allegedly killed people for ten thousand dollars and plane fare.

Mary Kirpaski was fondling rosary beads. She smelled like Vicks VapoRub and cigarettes.

"Ma'am, could I use the phone?"

She pointed to a wall extension. Littell pulled the cord to the far end of the kitchen.

She left him alone. Littell heard a radio snap on one room over.

He dialed the long-distance operator. She put him through to the security desk at L.A. International Airport.

A man answered. "Sergeant Donaldson, may I help you?"

"This is Special Agent Littell, Chicago FBI. I need an expedite on some reservation information."

"Yes, sir. Tell me what you need."

"I need you to query the airlines that fly Los Angeles to Miami round-trip. I'm looking for reservations going out on either December the eighth, ninth or tenth, and returning any time after that. I'm looking for a reservation under the name Peter Bondurant, spelled B-O-N-D-U-R-A-N-T, or reservations charged to the Hughes Tool Company or Hughes

Aircraft. If you turn up positive on any of that, and the reservation is in a man's name, I need a physical description of the man either picking up his ticket or boarding the airplane."

"Sir, that last part is needle-in-a-haystack stuff."

"I don't think so. My suspect is a male Caucasian in his late thirties, and he's about six-foot-five and very powerfully built. If you see him, you don't forget him."

"I copy. Do you want me to call you back?"

"I'll hold. If you don't get me anything in ten minutes, come back on the line and take my number."

"Yes, sir. You hold now. I'll get right on this."

Littell held the line. An image held him: Big Pete Bondurant crucified. The kitchen cut through it: cramped, hot, saints' days marked on a parish calendar—

Eight minutes crawled by. The sergeant came back on the line, excited.

"Mr. Littell?"

"Yes."

"Sir, we hit. I didn't think we would, but we did."

Littell got out his notebook. "Tell me."

"American Airlines flight 104, Los Angeles to Miami. It left L.A. at 8:00 a.m. yesterday, December 10th, and arrived in Miami at 4:10 p.m. The reservation was made under the name Thomas Peterson and was charged to Hughes Aircraft. I talked to the agent who issued the ticket, and she remembered that man you described. You were right, you don't forget—"

"Is there a return reservation?"

"Yes, sir. American flight 55. It arrives in Los Angeles at 7:00 a.m. tomorrow morning."

Littell felt dizzy. He cracked a window for some air.

"Sir, are you there?"

Littell cut the man off and dialed O. A cold breeze flooded the kitchen.

"Operator."

"I need Washington, D.C. The number is KL4-8801."

"Yes, sir, just one minute."

The call went through fast. A man said, "Communications, Special Agent Reynolds."

"This is Special Agent Littell in Chicago. I need to transmit a message to SA Kemper Boyd in Miami."

"Is he with the Miami office?"

"No, he's on a detached assignment. I need you to transmit the message to the Miami SAC and have him locate SA Boyd. I think it's a matter of a hotel check, and if it wasn't so urgent, I'd do it myself."

"This is irregular, but I don't see why we can't do it. What's your message?"

Littell spoke slowly. "Have circumstantial and suppositional— underline those two words—evidence that J.H. hired our old oversized French confrere to eliminate Committee witness R.K. Our confrere leaves Miami late tonight, American flight 55. Call me in Chicago for details. Urge that you inform Robert K. immediately. Sign it W.J.L."

The agent repeated the message. Littell heard Mary Kirpaski sobbing just outside the kitchen door.

Helen's flight was late. Littell waited in a cocktail lounge near the gate.

He rechecked the phone call list. His instinct held firm: Pete Bondurant killed Roland Kirpaski.

Kemper mentioned a dead witness named Gretzler. If he could connect the man to Bondurant, TWO murder charges might fly.

Littell sipped rye and beer. He kept checking the back wall mirror to gauge his appearance.

His work clothes looked wrong. His glasses and thinning hair didn't jibe with them.

The rye burned; the beer tickled. Two men walked up to his table and grabbed him.

They jerked him upright. They clamped down on his elbows. They steered him back to an enclosed phone bank.

It was swift and sure—no civilian patrons caught it.

The men pinned his arms back. Chick Leahy stepped out of a shadow and got right up in his face.

Littell felt his knees go. The men propped him up on his toes.

Leahy said, "Your message to Kemper Boyd was intercepted. You could have violated his cover on the incursion. Mr. Hoover does not want to see Robert Kennedy aided, and Peter Bondurant is a valued colleague of Howard Hughes, who is a great friend of Mr. Hoover and the Bureau. Do you know what *fully* coded messages are, Mr. Littell?"

Littell blinked. His glasses fell off. Everything went blurry.

Leahy jabbed his chest, hard. "You're off the THP and back on the Red Squad as of now. And I strongly urge you not to protest."

One man grabbed his notebook. The other man said, "You reek of liquor."

They elbowed him aside and walked out. The whole thing took thirty seconds.

His arms hurt. His glasses were scratched and dented. He couldn't quite breathe or stay balanced on his feet.

He swerved back to his table. He choked down rye and beer and leveled his shakes out.

His glasses fit crooked. He checked out his new mirror image: the world's most ineffectual workingman.

An intercom boomed, "United flight 84 from New Orleans is now arriving."

Littell finished his drinks and chased them with two Clorets. He walked over to the gate and bucked passengers up to the jetway.

Helen saw him and dropped her bags. Her hug almost knocked him down.

People stepped around them. Littell said, "Hey, let me see you."

Helen looked up. Her head grazed his chin—she'd grown tall.

"You look wonderful."

"It's Max Factor number-four blush. It does wonders for my scars."

"What scars?"

"Very funny. And what are *you* now, a lumberjack?"

"I was. For a few days, at least."

"Susan says Mr. Hoover's finally letting you chase gangsters."

A man kicked Helen's garment bag and glared at them. Littell said, "Come on, I'll buy you dinner."

They had steaks at the Stockyard Inn. Helen talked a blue streak and got tipsy on red wine.

She'd gone from coltish to rangy; her face had settled in strong. She'd quit smoking—she said she knew it was fake sophistication.

She always wore her hair in a bun to flaunt her scars. She wore it down now—it rendered her disfigurement matter-of-fact.

A waiter pushed the dessert cart by. Helen ordered pecan pie; Littell ordered brandy.

"Ward, you're letting me do all the talking."

"I was waiting to summarize."

"Summarize what?"

"You at age twenty-one."

Helen groaned. "I was starting to feel mature."

Littell smiled. "I was going to say that you've become poised, but not at the expense of your exuberance. You used to trip over your words when you wanted to make a point, but now you think before you talk."

"Now people just trip over my luggage when I'm excited about meeting a man."

"A man? You mean a friend twenty-four years your senior who watched you grow up?"

She touched his hands. "A man. I had a professor at Tulane who said that things change with old friends and students and teachers, so what's a quarter of a century here and there?"

"You're saying he was twenty-five years older than you?"

Helen laughed. "Twenty-six. He was trying to minimize things to make them seem less embarrassing."

"You're saying you had an affair with him?"

"Yes. And I'm saying it wasn't lurid and pathetic, but going out with undergrad boys who thought I'd be easy because I was scarred up was."

Littell said, "Jesus Christ."

Helen waved her fork at him. "Now I know you're upset, because some part of you is still a Jesuit seminarian, and you only invoke our Savior's name when you're flustered."

Littell sipped brandy. "I was going to say, 'Jesus Christ, have Kemper and I ruined you for young men your own age?' Are you going to spend your youth chasing middle-aged men?"

"You should hear Susan and Claire and I talk."

"You mean my daughter and her best friends swear like longshoremen?"

"No, but we've been discussing men in general and you and Kemper in specific for years, in case you've felt your ears burning."

"I can understand Kemper. He's handsome and dangerous."

"Yes, and he's heroic. But he's a tomcat, and even Claire knows it."

Helen squeezed his hands. He felt his pulse racing. He got this Jesus Fucking Christ crazy idea.

Littell took off his glasses. "I'm not so sure Kemper's heroic. I think heroes are truly passionate and generous."

"That sounds like an epigram."

"It is. Senator John F. Kennedy said it."

"Are you enamored of him? Isn't he some terrible liberal?"

"I'm enamored of his brother Robert, who is truly heroic."

Helen pinched herself. "This is the strangest conversation to be having with an old family friend who's known me since before my father died."

That Idea—Jesus Christ.

Littell said, "I'll be heroic for you."

Helen said, "We can't let this be pathetic."

He drove her to her hotel and carried her bags upstairs. Helen kissed him goodbye on the lips. His glasses snagged in her hair and fell to the floor.

Littell drove back to Midway and caught a 2:00 a.m. flight to Los Angeles. A stewardess gawked at his ticket: his return flight left an hour after they landed.

One last brandy let him sleep. He woke up woozy just as the plane touched down.

He made it with fourteen minutes to spare. Flight 55 from Miami was landing at gate 9, on time.

Littell badged a guard and got permission to walk out on the tarmac. A wicked hangover headache started kicking in.

Baggage men cruised by and checked him out. He looked like a middle-aged bum who'd slept in his clothes.

The airplane landed. A ground crew pushed passenger steps out.

Bondurant exited up front. Jimmy Hoffa flew his killers first-class.

Littell walked up to him. His chest hammered and his legs went numb. His voice fluttered and broke.

"Someday I'm going to punish you. For Kirpaski and everything else."

10

(Los Angeles, 12/14/58)

Freddy left a note under the wiper blades:

"I'm getting some lunch. Wait for me."

Pete climbed in the back of the van. Freddy had a cooling system rigged: a fan aimed at a big bowl of ice cubes.

Tape spun. Lights flashed. Graph needles twitched. The place was like the cockpit of a low-rent spaceship.

Pete cracked a side window for some air. A Fed type walked by—probably listening-post personnel.

Air blew in—Santa Ana hot.

Pete dropped an ice cube down his pants and laughed falsetto. He sounded just like SA Ward J. Littell.

Littell squeaked his warning. Littell smelled like stale booze and sweat. Littell had jackshit for evidence.

He could have told him:

I whacked Anton Gretzler, but Hoffa killed Kirpaski. I stuffed shotgun shells in his mouth and glued his lips shut. We torched Roland and his car at a refuse dump. Double-aught buckshot blew his head up—you'll never get a dental-work ID.

Littell doesn't know that Jack's big mouth killed Roland Kirpaski. The listening-post Fed might be sending him tapes—but Littell hasn't put the scenario together.

Freddy climbed in the van. He adjusted some graph gizmo and spritzed grief straight off.

"That Fed that just walked by keeps checking out the van. I'm parked here at all fucking hours, and all he needs to do is sweep me with a fucking Geiger counter to figure out I'm doing the same fucking thing he is. I can't park around the fucking block 'cause I'll lose the fucking signal. I need a fucking house around here to work from, 'cause then I can set up some equipment that's fucking powerful enough to pick up from the Shoftel babe's pad, but that fucking Fed bagged the last fucking For Rent sign in the fucking neighborhood, and the fucking two hundred a day you and Jimmy are paying me ain't enough to make up for the fucking risks I'm taking."

Pete snagged an ice cube and squeezed it into shards. "Are you finished?"

"No. I've also got a fucking boil on my fucking ass from sleeping on the fucking floor here."

Pete popped a few knuckles. "Wrap it up."

"I need some *good* money. I need it for fucking hazardous-duty pay, and to upgrade this operation with. Get me some good money and I'll kick a nice piece of it back to you."

"I'll talk to Mr. Hughes and see what I can do."

Howard Hughes got his dope from a nigger drag queen named Peaches. Pete found the drop pad cleaned out—the queen next door said Peaches went up on a sodomy bounce.

Pete improvised.

He drove to a supermarket, bought a box of Rice Krispies and pinned the toy badge inside to his shirt front. He called Karen Hiltscher at R&I and glommed some prime information: the fry cook at Scrivner's Drive-In sold goofballs and might be extortable. She described him: white, skinny, acne scars and Nazi tattoos.

Pete drove to Scrivner's. The kitchen door was open; the geek was at the deep fryer, dipping spuds.

The geek saw him.

The geek said, "That badge is a fake."

The geek looked at the freezer—a sure sign that he stored his shit there.

Pete said, "How do you want to do this?"

The geek pulled a knife. Pete kicked him in the balls and deep-fried his knife hand. Six seconds only—pill heists didn't rate total mayhem.

The geek screamed. Street noise leveled out the sound. Pete shoved a sandwich in his mouth to muzzle him.

His dope stash was in the freezer next to the ice cream.

. . .

The hotel manager gave Mr. Hughes a Christmas tree. It was fully flocked and decorated—a bellboy left it outside the bungalow.

Pete carried it into the bedroom and plugged it in. Sparkly lights blinked and twinkled.

Hughes blipped off a Webster Webfoot cartoon. "What is this? And why are you carrying a tape recorder?"

Pete dug through his pockets and tossed pill vials under the tree. "Ho, ho, fucking ho. It's Christmas ten days early. Codeine and Dilaudid, ho, ho."

Hughes scrunched himself up on his pillows. "Well . . . I'm delighted. But aren't you supposed to be auditioning stringers for *Hush-Hush*?"

Pete yanked the tree cord and plugged in the tape rig. "Do you still hate Senator John F. Kennedy, Boss?"

"I certainly do. His father screwed me on business deals going back to 1927."

Pete brushed pine needles off his shirt. "I think we've got the means to juke him pretty good in *Hush-Hush*, if you've got the money to keep a certain operation going."

"I've got the money to buy the North American continent, and if you don't quit leading me on I'll put you on a slow boat to the Belgian Congo!"

Pete pressed the Play button. Senator Jack and Darleen Shoftel boned and groaned. Howard Hughes clutched his bedsheets, dead ecstatic.

The fuck crescendoed and diminuendoed. Jack K. said, "My goddamn back gave out."

Darleen said, "It was goooood. Short and sweet's the best."

Pete pressed Stop. Howard Hughes twitched and trembled.

"We can have *Hush-Hush* print this up if we're careful, Boss. But we've got to watch the wording real close."

"Where . . . did . . . you . . . get that?"

"The girl's a prostitute. The FBI had her place wired, and Freddy Turentine hooked up on top of it. So we can't print anything that would tip the Feds off. We can't print anything that only could have come from the bug."

Hughes plucked at his sheets. "Yes, I'll finance your 'operation.' Have Gail Hendee write the story up—something like 'Priapic Senator Dallies with Hollywood Playgirl.' We've got an issue coming out the day after tomorrow, so if Gail writes it today and gets it to the office by this evening, it can make that next issue. Have Gail write it today. The Kennedy family will ignore it, but the legitimate newspapers and wire services might come to us asking for details to enlarge the story, which of course we will give them."

Big Howard beamed kid-at-Christmas-like. Pete plugged his tree back in.

Gail needed convincing. Pete sat her down on the watchdog-house veranda and laid out a line of sweet talk.

"Kennedy's a geek. He had you meet him on his goddamned honeymoon. He dropped you two weeks later, and kissed you off with a goddamn mink coat."

Gail smiled. "He was nice, though. He never said, 'Honey, let's get a divorce racket going.' "

"When your old man's worth a hundred million dollars, you don't have to do things like that."

Gail sighed. "You win, like always. And you know why I haven't been wearing that mink lately?"

"No."

"I gave it to Mrs. Walter P. Kinnard. You took a big cut of her alimony, and I figured she could use some cheering up."

Twenty-four hours zipped by.

Hughes kicked loose thirty grand. Pete pocketed fifteen. If the *Hush-Hush* smear exposed the bug, he'd be covered financially.

Freddy bought a long-range transceiver and started looking for a house.

That Fed kept eyeballing his van. Jack K. didn't call or drop by. Freddy figured Darleen was only worth one poke.

Pete stuck by the watchdog-house phone. Geeks kept interrupting his daydreams.

Two *Hush-Hush* stringer prospects called: ex–vice cops hipped on Hollywood lowdown. They flunked his impromptu pop quiz: Who's Ava Gardner fucking?

He made some calls out—and planted a new Hughes double at the Beverly Hilton. Karen Hiltscher recommended the man: her scabby wino father-in-law. Pops said he'd work for three hots and a cot. Pete booked the Presidential Suite and placed a standing room-service order: T-bird and cheeseburgers for breakfast, lunch and dinner.

Jimmy Hoffa called. He said, The *Hush-Hush* thing sounds good, but I want MORE! Pete neglected to share his basic opinion: Jack and Darleen were just a two-minute mattress ride.

He kept thinking about Miami. The cabstand, colorful spics, tropical sunshine.

Miami felt like adventure. Miami felt like money.

He woke up early publication morning. Gail was gone—she'd taken to avoiding him with aimless drives to the beach.

Pete walked outside. His first-press-run copy was stuffed in the mailbox, per instructions.

Dig the cover lines: "Tomcat Senator Likes Catnip! Ask Nipped-At L.A. Kittens!" Dig the illustration: John Kennedy's face on a cartoon cat's body, the tail wrapped around a blonde in a bikini.

He flipped to the piece. Gail used the pen name Peerless Politicopundit.

U.S. Senate cloakroom wags say he's far from being the most dedicatedly demonic Democrat dallier. No, Senator L.B. (Lover Boy?) Johnson probably tops political polls in that department, with Florida's George F. 'Pass the Smackeroos' Smathers coming in second. No, Senator John F. Kennedy is rather a tenuously tumescent tomcat, with a tantalizingly trenchant taste for those finely-furred and felicitous felines who find him fantastically fetching themselves!

Pete skimmed the rest. Gail played it half-assed—the smear wasn't vicious enough. Jack Kennedy ogled women and "bewitched, bothered and bewildered" them with "baubles, bangles, beads" and "brilliant Boston beatitudes." No heavy-duty skank; no implied fucking; no snide jabs at Two-Minute-Man Jack.

Perk, perk, perk—his all-star feelers started twitching—

Pete drove downtown and cruised by the *Hush-Hush* warehouse. Things looked absolutely first-glance SOP.

Men were wheeling bound stacks out on dollies. Men were loading pallets. A line of newsstand trucks were backed up to the dock.

SOP, but:

Two unmarked prowl cars were parked down the street. That ice cream wagon idling by looked dicey—the driver was talking into a hand mike.

Pete circled the block. The fuzz multiplied: four unmarkeds at the curb and two black & whites around the corner.

He circled again. The shit hit the fan and sprayed out in all directions.

Four units were jammed up to the loading dock—running full lights and siren.

Plainclothesmen piled out. A bluesuit cordon hit the warehouse with cargo hooks.

An LAPD van blocked the distribution trucks off. Swampers dropped their loads and threw their hands up.

It was fucking scandal-rag chaos. It was fucking skank-sheet Armaggedon—

Pete drove to the Beverly Hills Hotel. A Big Ugly Picture formed: some-body ratted off the Kennedy issue.

He parked and ran by the pool. He saw a big crowd outside the Hughes bungalow.

They were peeping in Big Howard's bedroom window. They looked like fucking ghouls at an accident scene.

He ran up and pushed to the front. Billy Eckstine nudged him. "Hey, check this out."

The window was open. Two men were jacking up Mr. Hughes—double-teaming him with Big Verbal Grief.

Robert Kennedy and Joseph P. Kennedy Sr.

Hughes was swaddled in bed quilts. Bobby was waving a hypo. Old Joe was raging.

". . . You're a pathetic lecher and a narcotics addict. I am two sec-onds away from exposing you to the whole wide world, and if you think I'm bluffing please note that I opened the window to let your hotel neighbors have a sneak preview of what the whole world will know if you ever allow your filthy scandal rag to write another word about my family."

Hughes cringed. His head banged the wall and sent a picture frame toppling.

Some all-star voyeurs dug the show: Billy, Mickey Cohen, some fag-got Mouseketeer sporting a jumbo mouse-ear beanie.

Howard Hughes whimpered. Howard Hughes said, "Please don't hurt me."

. . .

Pete drove to the Shoftel pad. The Big Ugly Picture expanded: either Gail snitched or the Feds exposed the piggyback.

He pulled up behind Freddy's van. Freddy was down on his knees in the street—cuffed to the front-bumper housing.

Pete ran over. Freddy yanked at his shackle chain and tried to stand up.

He'd scraped his wrist bloody. He'd ripped his knees raw crawling on the pavement.

Pete knelt down in front of him. "What happened? Quit grabbing at that and look at me."

Freddy did some wrist contortions. Pete slapped him. Freddy snapped to and focused in half-alert.

He said, "The listening-post guy sent his transcripts to some Fed in Chicago and told him he was hinked on my van. Pete, this thing plays wrong to me. There's just one FBI guy working single-o, like he went off half-cocked or some—"

Pete ran across the lawn and bolted the porch. Darleen Shoftel ducked out of his way, snapped a high heel and fell on her ass.

The Big and Ugly Final Picture:

Spackle-coated mikes on the floor. Two tap-gutted phones belly-up on an end table.

And SA Ward J. Littell, standing there in an off-the-rack blue suit.

It was a stalemate. You don't whack FBI men impromptu.

Pete walked up to him. He said, "This is a bullshit roust, or you wouldn't be here alone."

Littell just stood there. His glasses slipped down his nose.

"You keep flying out here to bother me. Next time's the last time."

Littell said, "I've put it together." The words came out all quivery.

"I'm listening."

"Kemper Boyd told me he had an errand at the Beverly Hills Hotel. He talked to you there, and you got suspicious and tailed him. You saw us black-bag this place and got your friend to put in auxiliary wires. Senator Kennedy told Miss Shoftel about Roland Kirpaski testifying, and you heard it and talked Jimmy Hoffa into giving you the contract."

Booze guts. This skinny stringbean cop with 8:00 a.m. liquor breath.

"You've got no proof, and Mr. Hoover doesn't care."

"You're right. I can't arrest you and Turentine."

Pete smiled. "I'll bet Mr. Hoover liked the tapes. I'll bet he won't be too pleased that you blew this operation."

Littell slapped his face. Littell said, "That's for the blood on John Kennedy's hands."

The slap was weak. Most women slapped harder.

He knew she'd leave a note. He found it on their bed, next to her house keys.

I know you figured out I soft-soaped the article. When the editor didn't question it I realized it wasn't enough and called Bob Kennedy. He said he would probably be able to pull strings and get the issue pulled. Jack is sort of callous in some ways, but he doesn't deserve what you planned. I don't want to be with you any more. Please don't try to find me.

She left the clothes he bought her. Pete dumped them out in the street and watched cars drive over them.

11

(Washington, D.C., 12/18/58)

"To say that I am furious belittles the concept of fury. To say that I consider your actions outrageous demeans the notion of outrage."

Mr. Hoover paused. The pillow on his chair made him tower over two tall men.

Kemper looked at Littell. They sat flush in front of Hoover's desk.

Littell said, "I understand your position, Sir."

Hoover patted his lips with a handkerchief. "I do not believe you. And I do not rate the value of objective awareness nearly as high as I rate the virtue of loyalty."

Littell said, "I acted impetuously, Sir. I apologize for that."

" 'Impetuous' describes your attempt to contact Mr. Boyd and foist your preposterous Bondurant suspicions on him and Robert Kennedy. 'Duplicitous' and 'treacherous' describe your unauthorized flight to Los Angeles to uproot an official Bureau operation."

"I considered Bondurant a murder suspect, Sir. I thought that he had implemented a piggyback on the surveillance equipment that Mr. Boyd and I had installed, and I was correct."

Hoover said nothing. Kemper knew he'd let the silence build.

The operation blew from two flanks. Bondurant's girlfriend tipped Bobby to a smear piece; Ward logicked out the Kirpaski hit himself. That logic held a certain validity: Pete was in Miami concurrent with Roland.

Hoover fondled a paperweight. "Is murder a Federal offense, Mr. Littell?"

"No, Sir."

"Are Robert Kennedy and the McClellan Committee direct rivals of the Bureau?"

"I don't consider them that, Sir."

"Then you are a confused and naive man, which your recent actions more than confirm."

Littell sat perfectly still. Kemper saw his pulse hammer his shirt front.

Hoover folded his hands. "January 16, 1961, marks the twentieth anniversary of your Bureau appointment. You are to retire on that day. You are to work at the Chicago office until then. You are to remain on the CPUSA Surveillance Squad until the day you retire."

Littell said, "Yes, Sir."

Hoover stood up. Kemper stood a beat later, per protocol. Littell stood up too fast—his chair teetered.

"You owe your continued career and pension to Mr. Boyd, who was most persuasive in convincing me to be lenient. I expect you to repay my generosity by promising to maintain absolute silence regarding Mr. Boyd's McClellan Committee and Kennedy family incursion. *Do you promise that, Mr. Littell?*"

"Yes, Sir. I do."

Hoover walked out.

Kemper put his drawl on. "You can breathe now, son."

The Mayflower bar featured wraparound banquettes. Kemper sat Littell down and thawed him out with a double scotch-on-the-rocks.

They bucked sleet walking over—there was no chance to talk. Ward took the thrashing better than he expected.

Kemper said, "Any regrets?"

"Not really. I was going to retire at twenty years, and the THP is a half-measure at best."

"Are you rationalizing?"

"I don't think so. I've had a . . ."

"Finish the thought. Don't let me explicate for you."

"Well . . . I've had a . . . taste of something very dangerous and good."

"And you like it."

"Yes. It's almost as if I've touched a new world."

Kemper stirred his martini. "Do you know why Mr. Hoover allowed you to remain with the Bureau?"

"Not exactly."

"I convinced him that you were volatile, irrational and addicted to taking heedless risks. The element of truth in that convinced him that you were better off inside the barn pissing out than outside the barn pissing in. He wanted me there to buttress the intimidation, and if he had signaled me I would have laced into you myself."

Littell smiled. "Kemper, you're leading me. You're like an attorney drawing out a witness."

"Yes, and you're a provocative witness. Now, let me ask you a question. What do you think Pete Bondurant has planned for you?"

"My death?"

"Your postretirement death, more likely. He murdered his own brother, Ward. And his parents killed themselves when they found out. It's a Bondurant rumor that I've chosen to believe."

Littell said, "Jesus Christ."

He was awed. It was a perfectly lucid response.

Kemper speared the olive in his glass. "Are you going to continue the work you started without Bureau sanction?"

"Yes. I've got a good informant prospect now, and—"

"I don't want to know specifics just yet. I just want you to convince me that you understand the risks from both within and outside the Bureau, and that you won't behave foolishly."

Littell smiled—and *almost* looked bold. "Hoover would crucify me. If the Chicago Mob knew I was investigating them without sanction, they'd torture and kill me. Kemper, I've got a wild notion about where you're leading me."

"Tell me."

"You're thinking of working for Robert Kennedy for real. He's gotten to you, and you respect the work he's doing. You're going to turn things over a notch and start feeding Hoover a minimum of information and selected misinformation."

Lyndon Johnson waltzed a redhead by the back booths. He'd seen her before—Jack said he could arrange an introduction.

"You're right, but it's the senator I want to work for. Bobby's more your type. He's as Catholic as you are, and the Mob is just as much his raison d'être."

"And you'll feed Hoover as much information as you deem fit."

"Yes."

"The inherent duplicities won't bother you?"

"Don't judge me, Ward."

Littell laughed. "You enjoy my judgments. You enjoy it that someone besides Mr. Hoover has your number. So *I'll* warn *you*. Be careful with the Kennedys."

Kemper raised his glass. "I will be. And you should know that Jack might damn well be elected President two years from now. If he is, Bobby will have carte blanche to fight organized crime. A Kennedy administration might mean considerable opportunities for both of us."

Littell raised his glass. "An opportunist like you would know."

"*Salud.* Can I tell Bobby that you'll share your intelligence with the Committee? Anonymously?"

"Yes. And it just hit me that I retire four days before the next presidential inauguration. Should your profligate friend Jack be the one taking office, you might mention a worthy lawyer-cop who needs a job."

Kemper pulled out an envelope. "You were always a quick study. And you forget that Claire has both our numbers."

"You're smirking, Kemper. Read me what you've got there."

Kemper unrolled a sheet of notebook paper. "Quote, 'And Dad, you wouldn't believe this one a.m. phone call I got from Helen. Are you sitting down? She had a hot date with Uncle Ward (date of birth March 8, 1913, to Helen's October 29, 1937) and necked with him in her room. Wait until Susan finds out! Helen's always sideswiped older men, but this is like Snow White attacking Walt Disney! And I always thought you were the one she had eyes for,' unquote."

Littell stood up, blushing. "She's meeting me later, at my hotel. I told her men liked women who traveled for them. And she's been the pursuer so far."

"Helen Agee is a college girl in the guise of a Mack truck. Remember that if things get complicated."

Littell laughed, and walked off primping. His posture was good, but those dented glasses had to go.

Idealists disdained appearances. Ward had no flair for nice things.

Kemper ordered a second martini and watched the back booths. Echoes drifted his way—congressmen were talking up Cuba.

John Stanton called Cuba a potential Agency hotspot. He said, I might have work for you.

Jack Kennedy walked in. Lyndon Johnson's redhead passed him a napkin note.

Jack saw Kemper and winked.

Part II

COLLUSION

January 1959–January 1961

12

(Chicago, 1/1/59)

Unidentified Male #1: "Beard, schmeard. All I know is Mo's real fuckin' nervous."

Unidentified Male #2: "The Outfit's always covered its bets Cuba-wise. Santo T. is Batista's best fuckin' friend. I talked to Mo maybe an hour ago. He goes out for the paper and comes back to watch the fuckin' Rose Bowl on TV. The paper says Happy fuckin' New Year, Castro has just taken over Cuba and who knows if he's pro-U.S., pro-Russian or pro-Man-from-Mars."

Littell tilted his seat back and adjusted his headphones. It was 4:00 p.m. and snowing—but the Celano's Tailor Shop talkfest talked on.

He was alone at the THP bug post. He was violating Bureau regs and Mr. Hoover's direct orders.

Man #1: "Santo and Sam got to be sweating the casinos down there. The gross profit's supposed to run half a million a day."

Man #2: "Mo told me Santo called him right before the kickoff. The crazy fuckin' Cubans down in Miami are pitching a fit. Mo's got a piece of that cabstand, you know the one?"

Man #1: "Yeah, the Tiger Kabs. I went down there for the Teamster convention last year and rode in one of those cabs, and I was picking orange and black fuzz out of my ass for the next six fuckin' months."

Man #2: "Half those Cuban humps are pro-Beard, and half of them are pro-Batista. Santo told Sam it's nuts at the stand, like niggers when their welfare checks don't arrive."

Laughter hit the feed box—static-laced and overamplified. Littell unhooked his headset and stretched.

He had two hours left on his shift. He'd gleaned no salient intelligence so far: Cuban politics didn't interest him. He'd logged in ten days of covert listening—and accrued no hard evidence.

He cut a deal with SA Court Meade—a surreptitious work trade. Meade's mistress lived in Rogers Park; some Commie cell leaders lived nearby. They worked out an agreement: I take your job, you take mine.

They spent cosmetic time working their real assignments and flip-flopped all report writing. Meade chased Reds and an insurance-rich widow. He listened to hoodlums colloquialize.

Court was lazy and pension-secure. Court had twenty-seven years with the Bureau.

He was careful. *He* hoarded insider knowledge of Kemper Boyd's Kennedy incursion. *He* filed detailed Red Squad reports and forged Meade's signature on all THP memoranda.

He always watched the street for approaching agents. He always entered and exited the bug post surreptitiously.

The plan would work—for a while. The lackluster bug talk was vexing—he needed to recruit an informant.

He'd tailed Lenny Sands for ten consecutive nights. Sands did not habituate homosexual meeting spots. His sexual bent might not prove exploitable—Sands might belittle the threat of exposure.

Snow swirled up Michigan Avenue. Littell studied his one wallet photo.

It was a laminated snapshot of Helen. Her hairdo made her burn scars stand out.

The first time he kissed her scars she wept. Kemper called her "the Mack Truck Girl." He gave her a Mack truck bulldog hood hanger for Christmas.

Claire Boyd told Susan they were lovers. Susan said, "When the shock wears off, I'll tell Dad what I think."

She still hadn't called him.

Littell put on his headset. He heard the tailor shop door slam.

Unknown Man #1: "Sal, Sal D. Sal, do you believe this weather? Don't you wish you were down in Havana shooting dice with the Beard?"

"Sal D.": most likely Mario Salvatore D'Onofrio, AKA "Mad Sal." Key THP stats:

Independent bookmaker/loan shark. One manslaughter conviction in 1951. Labeled "a psychopathically-derived criminal sadist with uncontrollable psycho-sexual urges to inflict pain."

Unknown Man #2: "*Che se dice*, Salvatore? Tell us what's new and unusual."

Sal D.: "The news is I lost a bundle on the Colts over the Giants, and I had to tap Sam for a fucking loan."

Unknown Man #1: "You still got the church thing, Sal? Where you take the paisan groups out to Tahoe and Vegas?"

Static hit the line. Littell slapped the feed box and cleared the air flow.

Sal D.: ". . . and Gardena and L.A. We catch Sinatra and Dino, and the casinos set us up in these private slot rooms and kick back a percentage. It's what you call a junket—you know, entertainment and gambling and shit. Hey, Lou, you know Lenny the Jew?"

Lou/Man #1: "Yeah, Sands. Lenny Sands."

Man #2: "Jewboy Lenny. Sam G.'s fuckin' court jester."

Squelch noise drowned out the incoming voices. Littell slapped the console and untangled some feeder cords.

Sal D.: ". . . So I said, 'Lenny, I need a guy to travel with me. I need a guy to keep my junketeers lubed up and laughing, so they'll lose more money and juke up my kickbacks.' He said, 'Sal, I don't audition, but catch me at the North Side Elks on January 1st. I'm doing a Teamster smoker, and if you don't dig—' "

The heat needle started twitching. Littell hit the kill switch and felt the feed box go cool to the touch.

The D'Onofrio/Sands connection was interesting.

He checked Sal D.'s on-post file. The agent's summary read horrific.

D'Onofrio lives in a South Side Italian enclave surrounded by Negro-inhabited housing projects. The majority of his bettors and loan customers live within that enclave and D'Onofrio makes his collection rounds on foot, rarely missing a day. D'Onofrio considers himself to be a guiding light within his community, and the Cook County Sheriff's Gangster Squad believes that he plays the role of "protector"—i.e., protecting Italian-Americans against Negro criminal elements, and that this role and his strongarm collection and intimidation tactics have helped to insure his long bookmaker/loanshark reign. It should also be noted that D'Onofrio was a suspect in the unsolved 12/19/57 torture-murder of Maurice Theodore Wilkins, a Negro youth suspected of burglarizing a church rectory in his neighborhood.

A mug shot was clipped to the folder. Mad Sal was cyst-scarred and gargoyle ugly.

. . .

Littell drove to the South Side and circled D'Onofrio's loan turf. He spotted him on 59th and Prairie.

The man was walking. Littell ditched his car and foot-tailed him from thirty yards back.

Mad Sal entered apartment buildings and exited counting money. Mad Sal tabulated transactions in a prayer book. Mad Sal picked his nose compulsively and wore low-top tennis shoes in a blizzard.

Littell stuck close behind him. Wind claps covered his footsteps.

Mad Sal peeped in windows. Mad Sal took a beat cop's money: $5 on the Moore/Durelle rematch.

The streets were near-deserted. The tail felt like a sustained hallucination.

A deli clerk tried to stiff Mad Sal. Mad Sal plugged in a portable stapler and riveted his hands to the counter.

Mad Sal entered a church rectory. Littell stopped at the pay phone outside and called Helen.

She picked up on the second ring. "Hello?"

"It's me, Helen."

"What's that noise?"

"It's the wind. I'm calling from a phone booth."

"You're outside in this?"

"Yes. Are you studying?"

"I'm studying torts and welcoming this distraction. Susan called, by the way."

"Oh, shit. And?"

"And she said I'm of age, and you're free, white and forty-five. She said, 'I'm going to wait and see if you two last before I tell my mother.' Ward, are you coming over tonight?"

Mad Sal walked out and slipped on the rectory steps. A priest helped him up and waved goodbye.

Littell took his gloves off and blew on his hands. "I'll be by late. There's a lounge act I have to catch."

"You're being cryptic. You act like Mr. Hoover's looking over your shoulder every second. Kemper tells *his* daughter everything about his work."

Littell laughed. "I want you to analyze the Freudian slip you just made."

Helen whooped. "Oh, God, you're right!"

A Negro boy walked by. Mad Sal bolted after him.

Littell said, "I have to go."

"Come by later."

"I will."

Mad Sal chased the kid. Snowdrifts and low-cut sneakers slowed him down.

The Elks Hall steps were jammed. Non-Teamster admittance looked dicey: goons were running an ID checkpoint at the door.

Men filed in with bottle bags and six-packs. They had union badges pinned to their topcoats—about the same size as Bureau shields.

A fresh swarm hit the steps. Littell held up his FBI badge and pushed to the middle. The stampede jostled him inside.

A blonde in G-string and pasties ran the coat-check concession. The foyer walls were lined with bootleg slot machines. Every pull hit a jackpot—Teamsters scooped up coins and yelled.

Littell pocketed his badge. The crowd whooshed him into a big rec hall.

Card tables faced a raised bandstand. Every table was set up with whisky bottles, paper cups and ice.

Strippers dispensed cigars. Tips bought unlimited fondling.

Littell grabbed a ringside seat. A redhead dodged hands, naked—cash wads had popped her G-string.

The lights went down. A baby spot hit the bandstand. Littell built a quick scotch-on-the-rocks.

Three other men sat at his table. Total strangers pounded his back.

Lenny Sands walked on stage, twirling a mike cord à la Sinatra. Lenny mimicked Sinatra—straight down to his spitcurl and voice:

"Fly me to the moon in my souped-up Teamster rig! I'll put skidmarks on management's ass, 'cause my union contract's big! In other words, Teamsters are kings!!"

The audience hooted and yelled. A man grabbed a stripper and forced her into some dirty-dog dance steps.

Lenny Sands bowed. "Thank you thank you thank you! And ring-a-ding, men of the Northern Illinois Council of the International Brotherhood of Teamsters!"

The crowd applauded. A stripper brought ice refills by—Littell caught a breast in the face.

Lenny said, "It sure is hot up here!"

The stripper hopped on stage and dropped ice cubes down his pants. The audience howled; the man beside Littell squealed and spat bourbon.

Lenny made ecstatic faces. Lenny shook his trouser legs until the ice dropped out.

The crowd wolf-whistled and shrieked and thumped their tables—

The stripper ducked behind a curtain. Lenny put on a Boston accent—Bobby Kennedy's voice pushed into soprano range.

"Now you listen to me, Mr. Hoffa! You quit associating with those nasty gangsters and nasty truck drivers and snitch off all your friends or I'll tell my daddy on you!"

The room rocked. The room rolled. Foot stomps had the floor shaking.

"Mr. Hoffa, you're a no-goodnik and a nasty man! You quit trying to unionize my six children or I'll tell my daddy and my big brother Jack on you! You be nice or I'll tell my daddy to buy your union and make all your nasty truck drivers servants at our family compound in Hyannis Port!"

The room roared. Littell felt queasy-hot and lightheaded.

Lenny minced. Lenny preened. Lenny DID Robert F. Kennedy, faggot crusader.

"Mr. Hoffa, you stop that nasty forced bargaining this instant!"

"Mr. Hoffa, stop yelling, you're wilting my hairdo!"

"Mr. Hoffa, be NIIICE!"

Lenny squeezed the room dry. Lenny wrung it out from the basement to the roof.

"Mr. Hoffa, you're just SOOOOO butch!"

"Mr. Hoffa, quit scratching—you'll ruin my nylons!"

"Mr. Hoffa, your Teamsters are just TOOOOO sexy! They've got the McClellan Committee and me in such a TIZZY!"

Lenny kept it cranking. Littell caught something three drinks in: he never ridiculed *John* Kennedy. Kemper called it the Bobby/Jack dichotomy: if you liked one man, you disliked the other.

"Mr. Hoffa, stop confusing me with facts!"

"Mr. Hoffa, stop berating me, or I won't share my hairdressing secrets with your wife!"

The Elks Hall broiled. Open windows laced in freezing air. The drink ice ran out—strippers filled bowls with fresh snow.

Mob men table-hopped. Littell spotted file-photo faces.

Sam "Mo"/"Momo"/"Mooney" Giancana. Icepick Tony Iannone, Chi-mob underboss. Donkey Dan Versace, Fat Bob Paolucci, Mad Sal D'Onofrio himself.

Lenny wrapped it up. The strippers shimmied on stage and took bows.

"So fly me to the stars, union paycheck fat! Jimmy Hoffa is our tiger now—Bobby's just a scrawny rat! In other words, Teamsters are kings!!!!"

Table thumps, claps, cheers, yells, whistles, howls—

Littell ran out a back exit and sucked air in. His sweat froze; his legs fluttered; his scotch dinner stayed down.

He checked the door. A conga line snaked through the rec hall—strippers and Teamsters linked up hands-to-hips. Mad Sal joined them—his tennis shoes squished and leaked snow.

Littell caught his breath and slow-walked around to the parking lot. Lenny Sands was cooling off by his car, scooping ice packs from a snow drift.

Mad Sal walked up and hugged him. Lenny made a face and pulled free.

Littell crouched behind a limousine. Their voices carried his way.

"Lenny, what can I say? You were stupendous."

"Insider crowds are easy, Sal. You just gotta know what switches to flip."

"Lenny, a crowd's a crowd. These Teamsters are working Joes, just like my junket guys. You lay off the politics and pour on the Italian stuff. I fuckin' guarantee, every time you lay on the paisan stuff you'll have a roomful of hyenas on your hands."

"I don't know, Sal. I might have a Vegas gig coming up."

"I am fuckin' begging you, Lenny. And my fuckin' junketeers are well known as the biggest casino losers in fuckin' captivity. Va-va-voom, Lenny. The more they lose, the more we make."

"I don't know, Sal. I might have a chance to open for Tony Bennett at the Dunes."

"Lenny, I am begging. On all fours like a fuckin' dog I am begging."

Lenny laughed. "Before you start barking, go to fifteen percent."

"Fifteen? . . . fuck . . . You Jew me up, you fuckin' Jew hump."

"Twenty percent, then. I only associate with Jew haters for a price."

"Fuck you, Lenny. You said fifteen."

"Fuck *you*, Sal. I changed my mind."

Silence stretched—Littell visualized a long staredown.

"Okay okay okay. Okay for fuckin' twenty, you fuckin' Jew bandit."

"Sal, I like you. Just don't shake my hand, you're too greasy to touch."

Car doors slammed. Littell saw Mad Sal snag his Caddy and slalom out to the street.

Lenny turned on his headlights and idled the engine. Cigarette smoke blew out the driver's-side window.

Littell walked to his car. Lenny was parked two rows over—he'd spot his departure.

Lenny just sat there. Drunks careened in front of his beams and took pratfalls on ice.

Littell wiped ice off his windshield. The car sat in snow up to its bumpers.

Lenny pulled out. Littell cut him a full minute's slack and followed his tracks in the slush.

They led straight to Lake Shore Drive northbound. Littell caught up with him just short of the ramp.

Lenny swung on. Littell stayed four car lengths behind him.

It was a crawl tail—tire chains on crusted blacktop—two cars and one deserted expressway.

Lenny passed the Gold Coast off-ramps. Littell dawdled back and fixed on his taillights.

They crawled past Chicago proper. They crawled past Glencoe, Evanston and Wilmette.

Signs marked the Winnetka town limits. Lenny spun right and pulled off the highway at the very last second.

There was no way to follow him—he'd spin out or clip a guardrail.

Littell took the next off-ramp down. Winnetka was 1:00 a.m. quiet and beautiful—all Tudor mansions and freshly plowed streets.

He grid-cruised and hit a business thoroughfare. A stretch of cars were parked outside a cocktail lounge: Perry's Little Log Cabin.

Lenny's Packard Caribbean was nosed up to the curb.

Littell parked and walked in. A ceiling banner brushed his face: "Welcome 1959!" in silver spangles.

The place was cold-weather cozy. The decor was rustic: mock-timber walls, hardwood bar, Naugahyde lounging sofas.

The clientele was all male. The bar was standing room only. Two men sat on a lounge sofa, fondling—Littell looked away.

He stared straight ahead. He felt eyes strafe him. He spotted phone booths near the rear exit—enclosed and safe.

He walked back. Nobody approached him. His holster rig had

rubbed his shoulders raw—he'd spent the whole night sweating and fidgeting.

He sat down in the first booth. He cracked the door and caught a full view of the bar.

There's Lenny, drinking Pernod. There's Lenny and a blond man rubbing legs.

Littell watched them. The blond man slipped Lenny a note and waltzed off. A Platters medley hit the jukebox.

The room thinned out a few couples at a time. The sofa couple stood up, unzipped. The bartender announced last call.

Lenny ordered Cointreau. The front door opened. Icepick Tony Iannone walked in.

"One of Giancana's most feared underbosses" started French-kissing the barman. The Chicago Mob killer suspected of nine mutilation murders was sucking and biting on the barman's ear.

Littell went dizzy. Littell went dry-mouthed. Littell felt his pulse go crazy.

Tony/Lenny/Lenny/Tony—who knows who's QUEER?

Tony saw Lenny. Lenny saw Tony. Lenny ran out the rear exit.

Tony chased Lenny. Littell froze. The phone booth went airless and sucked all the breath out of him.

He got the door open. He stumbled outside. Cold air slammed him.

An alley ran behind the bar. He heard noise down and left, by the back of the adjoining building.

Tony had Lenny pinned down on a snowdrift. Lenny was biting and kicking and gouging.

Tony pulled out two switchblades. Littell pulled his gun, fumbled it and dropped it. His warning scream choked out mute.

Lenny kneed Tony. Tony pitched sideways. Lenny bit his nose off.

Littell slid on ice and fell. Soft-packed snow muffled the sound. Fifteen yards between him and them—they couldn't see him or hear him.

Tony tried to scream. Lenny spat his nose out and jammed snow in his mouth. Tony dropped his knives; Lenny grabbed them.

They couldn't see him. He slid on his knees and crawled for his gun.

Tony pawed at the snow. Lenny stabbed him two-handed—in his eyes, in his cheeks, in his throat.

Littell crawled for his gun.

Lenny ran.

Tony died coughing up bloody snow.

Music drifted outside: a soft last-call ballad.

The exit door never opened. Jukebox noise covered the whole—

Littell crawled over to Tony. Littell picked the corpse clean: watch, wallet, key ring. Print-sustaining switchblades shoved in hilt-deep—yes, do it.

He pulled them free. He got his legs. He ran down the alley until his lungs gave out.

13

(Miami, 1/3/59)

Pete pulled up to the cabstand. A mango splattered on his windshield.

The street was void of tiger cars and tiger riffraff. Placard wavers prowled the sidewalk, armed with bags full of too-ripe fruit.

Jimmy called him in L.A. yesterday. He said, "Earn your five fucking percent. The Kennedy bug went down, but you still owe me. My Cubans have been batshit since Castro took over. You go to Miami and restore fucking order and you can keep your five fucking—"

Somebody yelled, *"Viva Fidel!"* Somebody yelled, *"Castro, el grande puto communisto!"* A garbage war erupted two doors down: kids tossing fat red pomegranates.

Pete locked his car and ran into the hut. A redneck type was working the switchboard, solo.

Pete said, "Where's Fulo?"

The geek yuk-yuk-yukked. "The trouble with this operation is half the guys are pro-Batista and half the guys are pro-Castro. You just can't get guys like that to show up for work when there's a nifty riot in progress, so here I am all by myself."

"I said, 'Where's Fulo?' "

"Working this switchboard is an education. I've been getting these calls asking me where the action is and 'What should I bring?' I like Cubans, but I think they're prone to untoward displays of violence."

The geek was cadaver thin. He had a bad Texas drawl and the world's worst set of teeth.

Pete cracked his knuckles. "Why don't you tell me where Fulo is."

"Fulo went looking for action, and my guess is he brought his machete. And you're Pete Bondurant, and I'm Chuck Rogers. I'm a good friend of Jimmy and some boys in the Outfit, and I am a *dedicated* opponent of the worldwide Communist conspiracy."

A garbage bomb wobbled the front window. Two lines of placard wavers squared off outside.

The phone rang. Rogers plugged the call in. Pete wiped pomegranate seeds off his shirt.

Rogers unhooked his headset. "That was Fulo. He said if '*el jefe* Big Pete' got in, he should go by his place and give him a hand with something. I think it's 917 Northwest 49th. That's three blocks to the left, two to the right."

Pete dropped his suitcase. Rogers said, "So who do you like, the Beard or Batista?"

The address was a peach stucco shack. A Tiger Kab with four slashed tires blocked the porch.

Pete climbed over it and knocked. Fulo cracked the door and slid a chain off.

Pete shoved his way in. He saw the damage straight off: two spics wearing party hats, *muerto* on the living-room floor.

Fulo locked up. "We were celebrating, Pedro. They called my beloved Fidel a true Marxist, and I took offense at this slander."

He shot them in the back at point-blank range. Small-bore exit wounds—the cleanup wouldn't be that big a deal.

Pete said, "Let's get going on this."

Fulo smashed their teeth to powder. Pete burned their fingerprints off on a hot plate.

Fulo dug the spent rounds out of the wall and flushed them down the toilet. Pete quick-scorched the floor stains—spectograph tests would read negative.

Fulo pulled down the living-room drapes and wrapped them around the bodies. The exit wounds had congealed—no blood seeped through.

Chuck Rogers showed up. Fulo said he was competent and trustworthy. They dumped the stiffs into the trunk of his car.

Pete said, "Who are you?"

Chuck said, "I'm a petroleum geologist. I'm also a licensed pilot and a professional anti-Communist."

"So who foots the bill?"

Chuck said, "The United States of America."

Chuck felt like cruising. Pete co-signed the notion—Miami grabbed his gonads like L.A. used to.

They cruised. Fulo tossed the bodies off a deserted stretch of the Bal Harbor Causeway. Pete chain-smoked and dug the scenery.

He liked the big white houses and the big white sky—Miami as one big shiny bleach job. He liked the breathing room between swank districts and slums. He liked the shitkicker cops out prowling—they looked like they'd be hell on rambunctious niggers.

Chuck said, "Castro's ideological beliefs are up in the air. He's made statements that can be construed as very pro-U.S. and very pro-Red. My friends in the intelligence community are working on plans to cornhole him if he goes Commie."

They drove back to Flagler. Armed men were guarding the cab-stand—off-duty fuzz with that fat-and-sassy look.

Chuck waved to them. "Jimmy takes good care of the police contingent around here. He's got this phantom union set up, and half the cops working this sector have got nice no-show jobs and nice paychecks."

A kid slammed a leaflet on their windshield. Fulo translated odd slogans—Commie-type platitudes all.

Rocks hit the car. Pete said, "This is too crazy. Let's go stash Fulo someplace."

Rogers leased a room in an all-spic boardinghouse. Radio gear and hate leaflets covered every spare inch of floor space.

Fulo and Chuck relaxed with beers. Pete skimmed pamphlet titles and got a good laugh mojo going.

"Kikes Kontrol Kremlin!" "Fluoridation: Vatican Plot?" "Red Storm-clouds Brewing—One Patriot's Response." "Why Non-Caucasians Overbreed: A Scientist Explains." "Pro-American Checklist: Do You Score RED or Red, White and Blue?"

Fulo said, "Chuck, it is rather crowded in here."

Rogers futzed with a short-wave receiver. A hate tirade kicked in: Jew bankers, blah blah.

Pete hit a few switches. The rant sputtered out cold.

Chuck smiled. "Politics is something you come around to slow. You can't expect to understand the world situation immediately."

"I should introduce you to Howard Hughes. He's as crazy as you are."

"You think anticommunism is crazy?"

"I think it's good for business, and anything that's good for business is okay with me."

"I don't think that's a very enlightened attitude."

"Think what you like."

"I will. And I know you're thinking, 'Holy Hannah, who is this guy that's my fellow murder-one accessory, because we sure have shared some unusual experiences in our short acquaintance."

Pete leaned against the window. He caught a little blip of a prowl car half a block down.

"My guess is you're a CIA contract hand. You're supposed to get next to the Cubans at the stand while everybody waits to see how Castro jumps."

Fulo came on indignant. "Fidel will jump toward the United States of America."

Chuck laughed. "Immigrants make the best Americans. You should know, huh, Pete? Aren't you some kind of frog?"

Pete popped his thumbs. Rogers flinched.

"You just make like I'm a 100% American who knows what's good for business."

"Whoa now. I never doubted your patriotism."

Pete heard whispers outside the door. Looks circulated—Chuck and Fulo caught the gist quick. Pete heard shotgun announcement noise: three loud and clear breach-to-barrel pumps.

He dropped his piece behind some pamphlets. Fulo and Chuck put their hands up.

Plainclothesmen kicked the door down. They ran in with shotgun butts at high port arms.

Pete went down behind a powder-puff shot. Fulo and Chuck played it rugged and got beaten skull-cracking senseless.

A cop said, "The big guy's faking." A cop said, "We can fix that."

Rubber-padded gun butts slammed him. Pete curled up his tongue so he wouldn't bite it off.

. . .

He came to cuffed and shackled. Chair slats gouged his back; percussion bopped him upside his brain.

Light hit his eyes. One eye only—tissue flaps cut his sight in half. He made out three cops sitting around a bolted-down table.

Snare drums popped behind his ears. A-bombs ignited up and down his spine.

Pete flexed his arms and snapped his handcuff chain.

Two cops whistled. One cop applauded.

They'd *double*-manacled his ankles—he couldn't give them an encore.

The senior cop crossed his legs. "We got an anonymous tip, Mr. Bondurant. One of Mr. Machado's neighbors saw Mr. Adolfo Herendon and Mr. Armando Cruz-Martín enter Mr. Machado's house, and he heard what might have been shots several hours later. Now, a few hours after that, you and Mr. Rogers arrive separately. The two of you and Mr. Machado leave carrying two large bundles wrapped in window curtains, and the neighbor gets Mr. Rogers' license number. We checked Mr. Rogers' car, and we noticed some debris that looks like skin fragments, and we certainly would like to hear your comments on all of this."

Pete stuck his eyebrow back in place. "Charge me or release me. You know who I am and who I know."

"We know you know Jimmy Hoffa. We know you're pals with Mr. Rogers, Mr. Machado and some other Tiger Kab drivers."

Pete said, "Charge me or release me." The cop tossed cigarettes and matches on his lap.

Cop #2 leaned in close. "You probably think Jimmy Hoffa's bought off every policeman in this town, but son, I'm here to tell you that simply ain't the case."

"Charge me or release me."

"Son, you are trying my patience."

"I'm not your son, you cracker faggot."

"Boy, that kind of talk will get your face slapped."

"If you slap me, I'll go for your eyes. Don't make me prove it."

Cop #3 came on soft. "Whoa, now, whoa. Mr. Bondurant, you know we can hold you for seventy-two hours without charging you. You know you've probably got a concussion and could use some medical attention. Now, why don't you—"

"Give me my phone call, then charge me or release me."

The senior cop laced his hands behind his head. "We let your friend Rogers make a call. He fed the jailer some cock-and-bull story about having government connections and called a Mr. Stanton. Now, who are you gonna call—Jimmy Hoffa? You think Uncle Jimmy's gonna go your bail on a double-homicide charge and maybe engender all kinds of bad publicity that he doesn't need?"

An A-bomb blast hit his neck. Pete almost blacked out.

Cop #2 sighed. "This boy's too woozy to cooperate. Let's let him rest up a bit."

He passed out, woke up, passed out. His headache subsided from A-bomb to nitroglycerine.

He read wall scratchings. He swiveled his neck to stay limber. He broke the world's record for holding a piss.

He broke down the situation.

Fulo cracks or Fulo doesn't crack. Chuck cracks or Chuck doesn't. Jimmy buys them bail or lets them swing. Maybe the DA gets smart: spic-on-spic homicides rate bubkes.

He could call Mr. Hughes. Mr. Hughes could nudge Mr. Hoover— which meant case fucking closed.

He told Hughes he'd be gone three days. Hughes agreed to the trip, no questions asked. Hughes agreed because the Kennedy shakedown backfired. Joe and Bobby shrunk his balls down to peanut size.

And Ward J. Littell slapped *him*.

Which decreed the cocksucker's death sentence.

Gail was gone. The Jack K. gig went pfffft. Hoffa's Kennedy hate sizzled—hot, hot, hot. Hughes was still gossip/smear crazed and hot to find a new *Hush-Hush* stringer.

Pete read wall musings. The Academy Award winner: "Miami PD Sucks Rhino Dick."

Two men walked in and pulled chairs up. A jailer unshackled his legs and walked out fast.

Pete stood up and stretched. The interrogation room dipped and swayed.

The younger man said, "I'm John Stanton, and this is Guy Banister. Mr. Banister is retired FBI, and he was assistant superintendent of the New Orleans Police for a spell."

Stanton was slight and sandy-haired. Banister was big and booze-flushed.

Pete lit a cigarette. Inhaling torqued his headache. "I'm listening."

Banister grinned. "I remember that civil rights trouble of yours. Kemper Boyd and Ward Littell arrested you, didn't they?"

"You know they did."

"I used to be the Chicago SAC, and I always thought Littell was a weak sister."

Stanton straddled his chair. "But Kemper Boyd's another matter. You know, Pete, he went by the Tiger stand and showed your mug shot around. One of the men pulled a knife, and Boyd disarmed him in a rather spectacular fashion."

Pete said, "Boyd's a stylish guy. And this is starting to play like some kind of audition, so I'll tell you that I'd recommend him for just about any kind of law-enforcement work."

Stanton smiled. "You're not a bad audition prospect yourself."

Banister smiled. "You're a licensed private investigator. You're a former deputy sheriff. You're Howard Hughes' man, and you know Jimmy Hoffa, Fulo Machado and Chuck Rogers. Those are stylish credentials."

Pete stubbed his cigarette out on the wall. "The CIA's not so bad, as credentials go. That's who you are, right?"

Stanton stood up. "You're free to go. No charges will be filed on you, Rogers or Machado."

"But you'll be keeping in touch?"

"Not exactly. But I may ask a favor of you one day. And of course, you'll be well paid for it."

14

(New York City, 1/5/59)

The suite was magnificent. Joe Kennedy bought it from the hotel outright.

A hundred people left the main room only half-filled. The picture window gave you the breadth of Central Park in a snowstorm.

Jack invited him. He said his father's Carlyle bashes were not to be missed—and besides, Bobby needs to talk to you.

Jack said there might be women. Jack said Lyndon Johnson's redhead might appear.

Kemper watched cliques constellate and dissolve. The party swirled all around him.

Old Joe stood with his horsy daughters. Peter Lawford ruled an all-male group. Jack speared cocktail shrimp with Nelson Rockefeller.

Lawford prophesied the Kennedy cabinet. Frank Sinatra was considered a shoo-in for Prime Minister of Pussy.

Bobby was late. The redhead hadn't arrived—Jack would have signaled him if he saw her first.

Kemper sipped eggnog. His tuxedo jacket fit loose—he'd had it cut to cover a shoulder holster. Bobby enforced a strict no-sidearms policy—*his* men were lawyers, not cops.

He was *twice* a cop—double-salaried and double-dutied.

He told Mr. Hoover that Anton Gretzler and Roland Kirpaski were dead—but their "presumed dead" status had not demoralized Bobby Kennedy. Bobby was determined to chase Hoffa, the Teamsters and the

Mob WAY past the McClellan Committee's expiration date. Municipal PD racket squads and grand jury investigators armed with Committee-gathered evidence would then become the Get Hoffa spearhead. Bobby would soon be preparing the groundwork for Jack's 1960 campaign—but Jimmy Hoffa would remain his personal target.

Hoover demanded investigatory specifics. He told him that Bobby wanted to trace the "spooky" three million dollars that financed Hoffa's Sun Valley development—Bobby was convinced that Hoffa skimmed cash off the top and that Sun Valley itself constituted land fraud. Bobby instinctively believed in the existence of separate, perhaps coded, Teamster Central States Pension Fund books—ledgers detailing tens of millions of dollars in hidden assets—money lent to gangsters and crooked businessmen at gargantuan interest rates. An elusive rumor: A retired Chicago hoodlum managed the Fund. Bobby's personal instinct: The total Fund package was his most viable Get Hoffa wedge.

He had two salaries now. He had two sets of conflicting duties. He had John Stanton hinting at offers—if the CIA's Cuban plans stabilized.

It would give him a third salary. It would give him enough income to sustain his own pied-à-terre.

Peter Lawford cornered Leonard Bernstein. Mayor Wagner chatted up Maria Callas.

A waiter refilled Kemper's tankard. Joe Kennedy walked an old man up.

"Kemper, this is Jules Schiffrin. Jules, Kemper Boyd. You two should talk. The two of you are rascals from way back."

They shook hands. Joe slid off to talk to Bennett Cerf.

"How are you, Mr. Schiffrin?"

"I'm fine, thank you. And I know why I'm a rascal. But you? You're too young."

"I'm a year older than Jack Kennedy."

"And I'm four years younger than Joe, so things even out. Is that your occupation, rascal?"

"I'm retired from the FBI. Right now, I'm working for the McClellan Committee."

"You're an ex-G-man? And retired so young?"

Kemper winked. "I got tired of FBI-sanctioned car theft."

Schiffrin mimicked the wink. "Tired, schmired. How bad could it be if it bought you custom mohair tuxedos like you're wearing? I should own such a tux."

Kemper smiled. "What do you do?"

" 'Did do' is more like it. And what I did do was serve as a financier and a labor consultant. Those are euphemisms, in case you're wondering. What I *didn't* do was have lots of lovely children to enjoy in my old age. Such lovely children Joe has. Look at them."

Kemper said, "You're from Chicago?"

Schiffrin beamed. "How did you know that?"

"I've studied regional accents. It's something I'm good at."

"Good doesn't describe it. And that drawl of yours, is that Alabama?"

"Tennessee."

"Aah, the Volunteer State. It's too bad my friend Heshie isn't here. He's a Detroit-born gonif who's lived in the Southwest for years. He's got an accent that would baffle you."

Bobby walked into the foyer. Schiffrin saw him and rolled his eyes. "There's your boss. Pardon my French, but don't you think he's a bit of a shitheel?"

"In his way, yes."

"Now *you're* euphemizing. I remember Joe and I were yakking once, about how we fucked Howard Hughes on a deal thirty years ago. Bobby objected to the word 'fuck' because his kids were in the next room. They couldn't even hear, but—"

Bobby signaled. Kemper caught the gesture and nodded.

"Excuse me, Mr. Schiffrin."

"Go. Your boss beckons. Nine kids Joe had, so one shitbird isn't such a bad average."

Kemper walked over. Bobby steered him straight into the cloakroom. Fur coats and evening capes brushed up against them.

"Jack said you wanted to see me."

"I did. I need you to collate some evidence briefs and write out a summary of everything the Committee's done, so that we can send out a standardized report to all the grand juries who'll be taking over for us. I realize that paperwork isn't your style, but this is imperative."

"I'll start in the morning."

"Good."

Kemper cleared his throat. "Bob, there's something I wanted to run by you."

"What?"

"I have a close friend. He's an agent in the Chicago office. I can't tell you his name just yet, but he's a very capable and intelligent man."

Bobby wiped snow off his topcoat. "Kemper, you're leading me. I realize that you're used to having your way with people, but please get to the point."

"The point is he was transferred off the Top Hoodlum Program against his will. He hates Mr. Hoover and Mr. Hoover's 'There is no Mob' stance, and he wants to conduit anti-Mob intelligence through me to you. He understands the risks, and he's willing to take them. And for what it's worth, he's an ex–Jesuit seminarian."

Bobby hung his coat up. "Can we trust him?"

"Absolutely."

"He wouldn't be a conduit to Hoover?"

Kemper laughed. "Hardly."

Bobby looked at him. Bobby gave him his witness-intimidation stare.

"All right. But I want you to tell the man not to do anything illegal. I don't want a zealot out there wiretapping and God knows what else because he thinks I'll back him up on it."

"I'll tell him. Now, what areas do you—?"

"Tell him I'm interested in the possibility that secret Pension Fund books exist. Tell him that if they do, it's likely that the Chicago Mob administers them. Have him work off that supposition, and see if he can come up with any general Hoffa intelligence while he's at it."

Guests filed past the cloakroom. A woman trailed her mink coat on the floor. Dean Acheson almost tripped over it.

Bobby winced. Kemper saw his eyes slip out of focus.

"What is it?"

"It's nothing."

"Is there anything else you'd—?"

"No, there isn't. Now, if you'll excuse me . . ."

Kemper smiled and walked back to the party. The main room was crowded now—maneuvering was a chore.

The mink woman had heads turning.

She made a butler pet her coat. She insisted that Leonard Bernstein try it on. She mambo-stepped through the crowd and snatched Joe Kennedy's drink.

Joe gave her a small, gift-wrapped box. The woman tucked it in her purse. Three Kennedy sisters walked off in a huff.

Peter Lawford ogled the woman. Bennett Cerf slid by and peeked down her dress. Vladimir Horowitz waved her over to the piano.

Kemper took a private elevator down to the lobby. He picked up a courtesy phone and badged the switchboard girl for a straight patch to Chicago.

She put him through. Helen answered on the second ring. "Hello?"

"It's me, sweetheart. The one you used to have a crush on."

"Kemper! What are you doing with that syrupy southern accent!"

"I'm engaged in subterfuge."

"Well, *I'm* engaged in law school and looking for an apartment, and it is *so* difficult!"

"All good things are. Ask your middle-aged boyfriend, he'll tell you."

Helen whispered. "Ward's been moody and secretive lately. Will you try to—?"

Littell came on the line. "Kemper, hi."

Helen blew kisses and put her extension down. Kemper said, "Hello, son."

"Hello yourself. I hate to be abrupt, but have you—?"

"Yes, I have."

"And?"

"And Bobby said yes. He said he wants you to work for us sub rosa, and he wants you to follow up on that lead Roland Kirpaski gave us, and try to determine if there really are secret Pension Fund books hiding untold zillions of dollars."

"Good. This is . . . very good."

Kemper lowered his voice. "Bobby reiterated what I told you. Don't take unnecessary risks. You remember that. Bobby's more of a stickler for legalities than I am, so you just remember to be careful, and remember who you have to look out for."

Littell said, "I'll be careful. I may have a Mob man compromised on a homicide, and I think I might be able to turn him as an informant."

The mink woman walked through the lobby. A slew of bellboys rushed to get the door for her.

"Ward, I have to go."

"God bless you for this, Kemper. And tell Mr. Kennedy that I won't disappoint him."

Kemper hung up and walked outside. Wind roared down 76th Street and toppled trashcans set out on the curb.

The mink woman was standing under the hotel canopy. She was unwrapping Joe Kennedy's gift.

Kemper stood a few feet away from her. The gift was a diamond broach tucked inside a roll of thousand-dollar bills.

A wino stumbled by. The mink woman gave him the broach. Wind fanned the roll and showed off at least fifty grand.

The wino giggled and looked at his broach. Kemper laughed out loud.

A cab pulled up. The mink woman leaned in and said, "881 Fifth Avenue."

Kemper opened the door for her.

She said, "Aren't the Kennedys vulgar?"

Her eyes were drop-dead translucent green.

15

(Chicago, 1/6/59)

ne jiggle snapped the lock. Littell pulled his pick out and closed the door behind him.

Passing headlights strafed the windows. The front room was small and filled with antiques and art deco gewgaws.

His eyes adjusted to the dark. There was good outside light—he didn't need to risk turning lamps on.

Lenny Sands' apartment was tidy and midwinter stuffy.

The Icepick Tony killing was five days old and unsolved. The TV and papers omitted one fact: that Iannone died outside a queer tryst spot. Court Meade said Giancana put the fix in: he didn't want Tony slandered as a homo, and refused to believe it himself. Meade quoted some scary bug-post talk: "Sam's got scouts out rousting known fruit rollers"; "Mo said Tony's killer is gonna get castrated."

Giancana couldn't believe a self-evident fact. Giancana thought Tony walked into Perry's Little Log Cabin by mistake.

Littell got out his pen flash and Minox. Lenny's recent schedule included Vendo-King pickups until midnight. It was 9:20 now—he had time to work.

Lenny's address book was tucked under the living-room phone. Littell skimmed through it and noted auspicious names.

Eclectic Lenny knew Rock Hudson and Carlos Marcello. Hollywood Lenny knew Gail Russell and Johnnie Ray. Gangland Lenny knew Giancana, Butch Montrose and Rocco Malvaso.

One strange thing: His Mob address/numbers didn't match the on-file THP listings.

Littell flipped pages. Odd names hit him.

Senator John Kennedy, Hyannis Port, Mass.; Spike Knode, 114 Gardenia, Mobile, Alabama; Laura Hughes, 881 5th Ave., New York City; Paul Bogaards, 1489 Fountain, Milwaukee.

He shot through the book alphabetically. He held the pen flash in his teeth and snapped one photograph per page. He notched thirty-two exposures up to the M's.

His legs ached from squatting down to shoot. The flash kept slipping out of his mouth.

He heard key/lock noise. He heard door rattles—NINETY MINUTES AHEAD OF SCHED—

Littell hugged the wall by the door. He replayed every judo move Kemper taught him.

Lenny Sands walked in. Littell grabbed him from behind and cupped his mouth shut. Remember—"Jam one thumb to the suspect's carotid and take him down supine."

He did it Kemper-pure. Lenny went prone with no resistance. Littell pulled his muzzle hand free and kicked the door shut.

Lenny didn't scream or yell. His face was jammed into a wad of scrunched-up carpet.

Littell eased off the carotid. Lenny coughed and retched.

Littell knelt beside him. Littell pulled out his revolver and cocked it.

"I'm with the Chicago FBI. I've got you for the Tony Iannone killing, and if you don't work for me I'll hand you up to Giancana and the Chicago PD. I'm not asking you to inform on your friends. What I'm interested in is the Teamsters' Pension Fund."

Lenny heaved for breath. Littell stood up and hit a wall switch—the room went bright with glare.

He saw a liquor tray by the couch. Cut-glass decanters full of scotch, bourbon and brandy.

Lenny pulled his knees up and hugged them. Littell tucked his gun in his waistband and pulled out a glassine bag.

It held two blood-crusted switchblades.

He showed them to Lenny. He said, "I dusted them for prints and got four latents that matched your DMV set."

It was a bluff. All he got were smears.

"You've got no choice in this, Lenny. You know what Sam would do to you."

Lenny broke a sweat. Littell poured him a scotch—the smell made him salivate.

Lenny sipped his drink two-handed. His tough-guy voice didn't quite work.

"I know bubkes about the Fund. What I know is that connected guys and certain businessman types apply for these large-interest loans and get pushed up some kind of loan ladder."

"To Sam Giancana?"

"That's one theory."

"Then elaborate on it."

"The theory is that Giancana consults with Jimmy Hoffa on all the big-money loan applications. Then they get accepted or refused."

"Are there alternative Pension Fund books? What I'm thinking of is coded books hiding secret assets."

"I don't know."

Kemper Boyd always said COW YOUR INFORMANTS.

Lenny hauled himself into a chair. Schizophrenic Lenny knew that tough Jewboys don't cringe on the floor.

Littell poured himself a double scotch. Lounge-Act Lenny said, "Make yourself at home."

Littell tucked the switchblades in his pocket. "I checked your address book, and I noticed that your addresses don't match the addresses that the Top Hoodlum Program has on file."

"What addresses?"

"The addresses of members of the Chicago Crime Cartel."

"Oh, *those* addresses."

"Why don't they match?"

Lenny said, "Because they're fuck pads. They're pads where guys go to cheat on their wives. I've got keys to some of the pads, because I drop off jukebox receipts to them. In fact, I was bagging receipts at that fucking queer bar when that fucking faggot Iannone came on to me."

Littell downed his drink. "I *saw* you kill Iannone. I *know* why you were at Perry's Little Log Cabin, and *why* you frequent Hernando's Hideaway. I *know* you've got two lives and two voices and two sets of God knows what else. I *know* that Iannone went after you because he didn't want you knowing that he did, too."

Lenny SQUEEEZED his glass, two-handed. Thick-cut crystal snapped and shattered—

Whisky sprayed out. Blood mixed with it. Lenny did not yelp or flinch or move.

Littell tossed his glass on the couch. "I know you made a deal with Sal D'Onofrio."

No response.

"I know you're going to travel with his gambling junkets."

No response.

"Sal's a loan shark. Could he refer prospects up the Pension Fund ladder?"

No response.

Littell said, "Come on, talk to me. I'm not going to leave until I have what I came for."

Lenny wiped blood off his hands. "I don't know. Maybe, maybe not. As sharks go, Sal's small fry."

"What about Jack Ruby? He sharks part-time down in Dallas."

"Jack's a clown. He knows people, but he's a clown."

Littell lowered his voice. "Do the Chicago boys know you're a homosexual?"

Lenny choked sobs back. Littell said, "Answer the question and admit what you are."

Lenny shut his eyes and nodded, no no no.

"Then answer this question. *Will you be my informant?*"

Lenny shut his eyes and nodded, yes yes yes.

"The papers said Iannone was married."

No response.

"Lenny . . ."

"Yes. He was married."

"Did he have a fuck pad?"

"He must have."

Littell buttoned up his overcoat. "I might do you a solid, Lenny."

No response.

"I'll be in touch. You know what I'm interested in, so get on it."

Lenny ignored him. Lenny started picking glass out of his hands.

He took a key ring off Iannone's body. It contained four keys on a fob marked "Di Giorgio's Locksmith's, 947 Hudnut Drive, Evanston."

Two car keys and one assumed house key. The remaining key might be for a fuck-pad door.

Littell drove up to Evanston. He hit on some dumb late-night luck: the locksmith lived in back of his shop.

The unexpected FBI roust scared the man. He identified the keys as his work. He said he installed all of Iannone's door locks—at two addresses.

2409 Kenilworth in Oak Park. 84 Wolverton in Evanston.

Iannone lived in Oak Park—that fact made the papers. The Evanston address was a strong fuck-pad possibility.

The locksmith supplied easy-to-follow directions. Littell found the address in just a few minutes.

It was a garage apartment behind a Northwestern U frat house. The neighborhood was dark and dead quiet.

The key fit the door. Littell let himself in, gun first. The place was uninhabited and musty.

He turned on the lights in both rooms. He tossed every cupboard, drawer, shelf, cubbyhole and crawl space. He found dildoes, whips, spiked dog collars, amyl nitrite ampules, twelve jars of K-Y Jelly, a bag of marijuana, a brass-studded motorcycle jacket, a sawed-off shotgun, nine rolls of Benzedrine, a Nazi armband, oil paintings depicting all-male sodomy and soixante-neuf and a snapshot of Icepick Tony Iannone and a college boy nude cheek-to-cheek.

Kemper Boyd always said PROTECT YOUR INFORMANTS.

Littell called Celano's Tailor Shop. A man answered—"Yeah?"—unmistakably Butch Montrose.

Littell disguised his voice. "Don't worry about Tony Iannone. He was a fucking faggot. Go to 84 Wolverton in Evanston and see for yourself."

"Hey, what are you say—?"

Littell hung up. He nailed the snapshot to the wall for the whole world to see.

16

(Los Angeles, 1/11/59)

Hush-Hush was cramming toward deadline. The office staff was buzzing on Benzedrine-spiked coffee.

"Artists" were pasting up a cover: "Paul Robeson—Royal Red Recidivist." A "correspondent" was typing copy: "Wife Beater Spade Cooley— Will the Country Stomper Stomp Too Far?" A "researcher" was browsing pamphlets, trying to link nigger hygiene to cancer.

Pete watched.

Pete was bored.

MIAMI bopped through his head. Hush-Hush felt like a giant cactus shoved up his ass.

Sol Maltzman was dead. Gail Hendee was long gone. The new Hush-Hush staff was 100% geek. Howard Hughes was frantic to find a dirt digger.

His prospects all said NO. Everybody knew the L.A. fuzz seized the Kennedy smear issue. Hush-Hush was the leper colony of scandal-sheet journalism.

Hughes CRAVED dirt. Hughes CRAVED slander skank to share with Mr. Hoover. What Hughes CRAVED, Hughes BOUGHT.

Pete bought an issue's worth of dirt. His cop contacts supplied him with a one-week load of lackluster skank.

"Spade Cooley, Boozefried Misogynist!" "Marijuana Shack Raid Nets Sal Mineo!" "Beatnik Arrests Shock Hermosa Beach!"

It was pure bullshit. It was very un-Miami.

Miami was goood. Miami was this drug he got withdrawals from. He left Miami with a mild concussion—not bad for the pounding he took.

Jimmy Hoffa called him in to restore order. He got out of jail and did it.

The cabstand demanded order—political rifts had business fucked six ways from Sunday. The riots sputtered out, but Tiger Kab still simmered with factional jive. He had pro-Batista and pro-Castro guys to deal with—left- and right-wing ideologue thugs who needed to be toilet-trained and broken in to the White Man's Rule of Order.

He laid down laws.

No drinking and placard waving on the job. No guns or knives—check your weapons with the dispatcher. No political fraternizing—rival factions must remain segregated.

One Batistaite challenged the rules. Pete beat him half-dead.

He laid down more laws.

No pimping on duty—leave your whores at home. No B&Es or stick-ups on duty.

He made Chuck Rogers the new day dispatcher. He considered it a political appointment.

Rogers was a CIA contract goon. Co-dispatcher Fulo Machado was CIA-linked.

John Stanton was a mid-level CIA agent—and a new cabstand habitué. He got Fulo's murder-one beef squelched with a snap of his fingers.

Stanton's pal Guy Banister hated Ward Littell. Banister and Stanton were hipped on Kemper Boyd.

Jimmy Hoffa owned Tiger Kab. Jimmy Hoffa had points in two Havana casinos.

Littell and Boyd made *him* for two killings. Stanton and Banister probably didn't know that. Stanton fed him that little teaser: "I may ask a favor of you one day."

Things were dovetailing tight and cozy. His feelers started perk-perk-perking.

Pete buzzed the receptionist. "Donna, get me long distance person-to-person. I want to talk to a man named Kemper Boyd at the McClellan Committee office in Washington, D.C. Tell the operator to try the Senate Office Building, and if you get through, say I'm the caller."

"Yes, sir."

Pete hung up and waited. The call was a longshot—Boyd was probably out somewhere, conniving.

His intercom light flashed. Pete picked up the phone.

"Boyd?"

"Speaking. And surprised."

"Well, I owe you one, so I thought I'd deliver."

"Keep going."

"I was in Miami last week. I ran into two men named John Stanton and Guy Banister, and they seemed real interested in you."

"Mr. Stanton and I have already spoken. But thanks. It's nice to know they're still interested."

"I gave you a good reference."

"You're a sport. Is there anything I can do for you?"

"You can find me a new dirt digger for *Hush-Hush*."

Boyd hung up, laughing.

17

(Miami, 1/13/59)

The Committee booked him into a Howard Johnson's. Kemper upgraded to a two-room suite at the Fontainebleau.

He made up the difference out of his own pocket. He was closing in on three salaries—it wasn't that big an extravagance.

Bobby sent him back to Miami. He instigated the trip himself—and promised to return with some key Sun Valley depositions. He didn't tell Bobby that the CIA was thinking about recruiting him.

The trip was a little vacation. If Stanton was good, they'd connect.

Kemper carried a chair out to the balcony. Ward Littell had mailed him a report—he needed to edit it before sending it on to Bobby.

The report was twelve typed pages. Ward included a longhand preface.

K.B.,

Since we're partners in this gentle subterfuge, I'm giving you a verbatim account of my activities. Of course, you'll want to omit mention of my more flagrant illegalities, given Mr. Kennedy's proviso. As you'll note, I have made substantial progress. And believe me, given the extreme circumstances, I have been very careful.

Kemper read the report. "Extreme circumstances" didn't quite cover it.

Littell witnessed a homosexual murder. The victim was a Chicago

Mob underboss. The killer was a Mob fringe dweller named Lenny Sands.

Sands was now Littell's snitch. Sands had recently partnered up with a bookie/loanshark named "Mad Sal" D'Onofrio. D'Onofrio shepherded gambling junkets to Las Vegas and Lake Tahoe—Sands was to accompany the groups as their "traveling lounge act." Sands had keys to mobster "fuck pads." Littell coerced him into making duplicates and surreptitiously entered three fuck pads to look for evidence. Littell observed and left untouched: weapons, narcotics, and $14,000 in cash—hidden in a golf bag at the fuck pad of one Butch Montrose.

Littell located Tony Iannone's fuck pad: a garage apartment littered with homosexual paraphernalia. Littell was determined to protect his informant from potential reprisals. Littell disclosed the fuck pad's location to Chicago Mob members and staked it out to see if they followed up on his anonymous tip. They did: Sam Giancana and two other men broke down the fuck pad door an hour later. They undoubtedly saw Iannone's homosexual contraband.

Amazing. Fully emblematic of the Ward Littell Trinity: luck, instinct, naive courage.

Littell concluded:

My ultimate goal is to facilitate a loan seeker "up the ladder" to the Teamsters' Central States Pension Fund. This loan seeker will be, ideally, my own legally compromised informant. Lenny Sands (and potentially "Mad Sal" D'Onofrio) may prove to be valuable allies in recruiting such an informant. My ideal loan seeker would be a crooked businessman with Organized Crime connections, a man susceptible to physical intimidation and threats of Federal prosecution. Such an informant could help us determine the existence of alternative Pension Fund books containing hidden, thus illegal, assets. This avenue of approach presents Robert Kennedy with unlimited opportunities at prosecution. If such books do exist, the administrators of the hidden assets will be indictable on numerous counts of Grand Larceny and Federal Tax Fraud. I agree with Mr. Kennedy: this may prove to be the way to link Jimmy Hoffa and the Teamsters to the Chicago Mob and break their collective power. If monetary collusion on such a rich and pervasive scale can be proven, heads will roll.

The plan was ambitious and stratospherically risky. Kemper snapped to a possible glitch straight off.

Littell exposed Icepick Tony's sexual bent. Did he consider *all* the potential ramifications?

Kemper called the Miami airport and altered his D.C. flight for a Chicago stopover. The move felt sound: if his hunch proved right, he'd need to give Ward a good thrashing.

Dusk came on. Room service brought his standing order up—punctual to the minute.

He sipped Beefeater's and picked at smoked salmon. Collins Avenue glowed; twinkling lights bracketed the beachfront.

Kemper got a mild glow on. He reprised his moments with the mink woman and thought of a dozen lines he could have used.

Chimes rang. Kemper ran a comb through his hair and opened the door.

John Stanton said, "Hello, Mr. Boyd."

Kemper ushered him in. Stanton walked around and admired the suite.

"Robert Kennedy treats you well."

"You're being disingenuous, Mr. Stanton."

"I'll be blunt, then. You grew up wealthy and lost your family. Now you've adopted the Kennedys. You're in the practice of reclaiming your wealth in small increments, and this really is quite a handsome room."

Kemper smiled. "Would you like a martini?"

"Martinis taste like lighter fluid. I've always judged hotels by their wine list."

"I can send down for whatever you like."

"I won't be here long enough."

"What's on your mind?"

Stanton pointed to the balcony. "Cuba's out there."

"I know that."

"We think Castro will go Communist. He's set to come to America in April and offer his friendship, but we think he'll behave badly and force an official rejection. He's going to deport some 'politically undesirable' Cubans soon, and they'll be granted asylum here in Florida. We need men to train them and form them into an anti-Castro resistance. The pay is two thousand dollars a month, in cash, plus the chance to purchase discount-priced stock in Agency-backed front companies. This is a firm offer, and you have my personal assurance that we won't let your Agency work interfere with your other affiliations."

" 'Affiliations'? Plural?"

Stanton stepped out on the balcony. Kemper followed him up to the railing.

"You 'retired' from the FBI rather precipitously. You were close to Mr. Hoover, who hates and fears the Kennedy brothers. *Post hoc, propter ergo hoc.* You were an FBI agent on Tuesday, a prospective pimp for Jack Kennedy on Wednesday, and a McClellan Committee investigator on Thursday. I can follow logical—"

"What's the standard pay rate for CIA contract recruits?"

"Eight-fifty a month."

"But my 'affiliations' make me a special case?"

"Yes. We know you're getting close to the Kennedys, and we think Jack Kennedy might be elected President next year. If the Castro problem extends, we'll need someone to help influence his Cuban policy."

"As a lobbyist?"

"No. As a very subtle agent provocateur."

Kemper checked the view. Lights seemed to shimmer way past Cuba.

"I'll consider your offer."

18

(Chicago, 1/14/59)

Littell ran into the morgue. Kemper called him from the airport and said MEET ME THERE NOW.

He called half an hour ago. He didn't elaborate. He said just those four words and slammed the phone down.

A row of autopsy rooms extended off the foyer. Sheet-covered gurneys blocked the hallway.

Littell pushed through them. Kemper stood by the far wall, next to a row of freezer slabs.

Littell caught his breath. "What the fuck is—?"

Kemper pulled a slab out. The tray held a male Caucasian dead body.

The boy was torture slashed and cigarette burned. His penis was severed and stuffed in his mouth.

Littell recognized him: the kid in Icepick Tony's nude snapshot.

Kemper grabbed his neck and forced him down close. "This is on you, Ward. You should have destroyed every bit of evidence pointing to Iannone's known associates *before* you tipped off those Mob guys. Guilty or not, they had to kill someone, so they decided to kill the boy in the picture *you* left for them to see."

Littell jerked backward. He smelled stomach bile and blood and forensic dental abrasive.

Kemper shoved him down closer.

"You're working for Bobby Kennedy, and *I* set it up, and Mr. Hoover will destroy me if he finds out. You're damn lucky I decided to check some missing-persons reports, and you had damn well better convince me you won't fuck up like this again."

Littell closed his eyes. Tears spilled out. Kemper shoved him in cheek to cheek with the dead boy.

"Meet me at Lenny Sands' apartment at ten. We'll shore things up."

Work didn't help.

He tailed Commies and wrote out a surveillance log. His hands shook; his printing was near-illegible.

Helen didn't help.

He called her just to hear her voice. Her law school chitchat brought him close to screaming.

Court Meade didn't help.

They met for coffee and exchanged reports. Court told him he looked lousy. Court said his report looked threadbare—like he wasn't spending much time at the listening post.

He couldn't say, I'm slacking off because I found a snitch. He couldn't say, I fucked up and got a boy killed.

Church helped a little.

He lit a candle for the dead boy. He prayed for competence and courage. He cleaned up in the bathroom and remembered something Lenny said: Sal D. was recruiting junketeers at Saint Vibiana's this evening.

A tavern stop helped.

Soup and crackers settled his stomach. Three rye-and-beers cleared his head.

Sal and Lenny had the Saint Vib's rec hall all to themselves. A dozen K of C men took in their pitch.

The group sat at a clump of bingo tables near the stage. The Knights looked like drunks and wife beaters.

Littell loitered outside a fire exit. He cracked the door to watch and listen.

Sal said, "We leave in two days. Lots of my regulars couldn't get away from their jobs, so I'm lowering my price to nine-fifty, airfare included. First we go to Lake Tahoe, then Vegas and Gardena, outside L.A. Sinatra's playing the Cal-Neva Lodge in Tahoe, and you'll be front row center to catch his show. Now, Lenny Sands, formerly Lenny Sanducci, and a Vegas star in his own right, will give you a Sinatra that out-Sinatras Sinatra. Go, Lenny! Go, paisan!"

Lenny blew smoke rings Sinatra-style. The K of C men clapped. Lenny flicked his cigarette above their heads and glared at them.

"Don't applaud until I finish! What kind of Rat Pack Auxiliary are you! Dino, go get me a couple of blondes! Sammy, go get me a case of gin and ten cartons of cigarettes or I'll put your other eye out! Hop to it, Sammy! When the Chicago Knights of Columbus Chapter 384 snaps its fingers, Frank Sinatra jumps!"

The Knights haw-haw-hawed. A nun pushed a broom by the group and never looked up. Lenny sang, "Fly me to the Coast with Big Sal's junket tour! He's the swingin' gambling junket king, so dig his sweet allure! In other words, Vegas beware!"

The Knights applauded. Sal dumped a paper bag out on a table in front of them.

They sifted through the clutter and grabbed knickknacks. Littell saw poker chips, French ticklers, and Playboy rabbit key chains.

Lenny held up a novelty pen shaped like a penis. "Which one of you big-dick gavones wants to be the first one to sign up?"

A line formed. Littell felt his stomach turn over.

He walked to the curb and vomited. The rye and beer burned his throat. He hunched over and puked himself dry.

Some junket men walked past him twirling key chains. A few laughed at him.

Littell braced himself against a lamppost. He saw Sal and Lenny in the rec hall doorway.

Sal backed Lenny into the wall and jabbed at his chest. Lenny mimed a single word: "Okay."

The door stood ajar. Littell pushed it all the way open.

Kemper was going through Lenny's address book. He'd turned on all the living-room lights.

"Easy, son."

Littell shut the door. "Who let you in?"

"I taught you how to B&E, remember?"

Littell shook his head. "I want him to trust me. Another man showing up like this might frighten him."

Kemper said, "You need to frighten him. Don't underestimate him just because he's queer."

"I saw what he did to Iannone."

"He panicked, Ward. If he panics again, we could get hurt. I want to establish a certain tone tonight."

Littell heard footsteps outside the door. There was no time to kill the lights for surprise.

Lenny walked in. He did a broad stage actor's double-take.

"Who's he?"

"This is Mr. Boyd. He's a friend of mine."

"And you were in the neighborhood, so you thought you'd break in and ask me a few questions."

"Let's not go at things this way."

"*What* way? You said we'd talk on the phone, and you told me you were in this by yourself."

"Lenny—"

Kemper said, "I did have a question."

Lenny hooked his thumbs through his belt loops. "Then ask it. And help yourself to a drink. Mr. Littell always does."

Kemper looked amused. "I glanced through your address book, Lenny."

"I'm not surprised. Mr. Littell always does that, too."

"You know Jack Kennedy and a lot of Hollywood people."

"Yes. And I know you and Mr. Littell, which proves I'm not immune to slumming."

"Who's this woman Laura Hughes? This address of hers—881 Fifth Avenue—interests me."

"Laura interests lots of men."

"You're trembling, Lenny. Your whole manner just changed."

Littell said, "What are you talk—?"

Kemper cut him off. "Is she in her early thirties? Tall, brunette, freckles?"

"That sounds like Laura, yes."

"I saw Joe Kennedy give her a diamond broach and at least fifty thousand dollars. That looks to me like he's sleeping with her."

Lenny laughed. His smile said, Oh, you heathen.

Kemper said, "Tell me about her."

"No. She's got nothing to do with the Teamsters' Pension Fund or anything illegal."

"You're reverting, Lenny. You're not coming off like the hard boy that took out Tony Iannone. You're starting to sound like a little fairy with a squeaky voice."

Lenny went instant baritone. "Is this better, Mr. Boyd?"

"Save the wit for your lounge engagements. Who is she?"

"I don't have to tell you that."

Kemper smiled. "You're a homosexual and a murderer. You have no rights. You're a Federal informant, and the Chicago FBI owns you."

Littell felt queasy. His heartbeat did funny little things.

Kemper said, *"Who is she?"*

Lenny came on hard butch. "This is not FBI-approved. If it was there'd be stenographers and paperwork. This is some sort of private thing with you two. And I won't say a goddamned thing that might hurt Jack Kennedy."

Kemper pulled out a morgue glossy and forced it on Lenny. Littell saw the dead boy with his mouth stuffed full.

Lenny shuddered. Lenny put on an instant rough-trade face.

"So? So this is supposed to scare me?"

"Giancana did this, Lenny. He thought this man killed Tony Iannone. One word from us, and this will be you."

Littell grabbed the snapshot. "Let's hold back a second. You've made your point."

Kemper steered him into the dining room. Kemper pressed him into a cabinet with his fingertips.

"Don't ever contradict me in front of a suspect."

"Kemper . . ."

"Hit him."

"Kemper—"

"*Hit him.* Make him afraid of you."

Littell said, "I can't. Goddamnit, don't do this to me."

"Hit him, or I'll call Giancana and rat him off right now."

"No. Come on . . . please."

Kemper handed him brass knuckles. Kemper made him lace his fingers in.

"Hit him, Ward. Hit him, or I'll let Giancana kill him."

Littell trembled. Kemper slapped him. Littell stumbled over to Lenny and weaved in front of him.

Lenny smiled this preposterous pseudo-tough-guy smile. Littell balled his fist and hit him.

Lenny clipped an end table and went down spitting teeth. Kemper threw a sofa cushion at him.

"Who's Laura Hughes? Tell me in detail."

Littell dropped the knucks. His hand throbbed and went numb.

"I said, 'Who's Laura Hughes?' "

Lenny nuzzled the cushion. Lenny spat out a chunk of gold bridgework.

"He panicked, Ward. If he panics again, we could get hurt. I want to establish a certain tone tonight."

Littell heard footsteps outside the door. There was no time to kill the lights for surprise.

Lenny walked in. He did a broad stage actor's double-take.

"Who's he?"

"This is Mr. Boyd. He's a friend of mine."

"And you were in the neighborhood, so you thought you'd break in and ask me a few questions."

"Let's not go at things this way."

"*What* way? You said we'd talk on the phone, and you told me you were in this by yourself."

"Lenny—"

Kemper said, "I did have a question."

Lenny hooked his thumbs through his belt loops. "Then ask it. And help yourself to a drink. Mr. Littell always does."

Kemper looked amused. "I glanced through your address book, Lenny."

"I'm not surprised. Mr. Littell always does that, too."

"You know Jack Kennedy and a lot of Hollywood people."

"Yes. And I know you and Mr. Littell, which proves I'm not immune to slumming."

"Who's this woman Laura Hughes? This address of hers—881 Fifth Avenue—interests me."

"Laura interests lots of men."

"You're trembling, Lenny. Your whole manner just changed."

Littell said, "What are you talk—?"

Kemper cut him off. "Is she in her early thirties? Tall, brunette, freckles?"

"That sounds like Laura, yes."

"I saw Joe Kennedy give her a diamond broach and at least fifty thousand dollars. That looks to me like he's sleeping with her."

Lenny laughed. His smile said, Oh, you heathen.

Kemper said, "Tell me about her."

"No. She's got nothing to do with the Teamsters' Pension Fund or anything illegal."

"You're reverting, Lenny. You're not coming off like the hard boy that took out Tony Iannone. You're starting to sound like a little fairy with a squeaky voice."

Lenny went instant baritone. "Is this better, Mr. Boyd?"

"Save the wit for your lounge engagements. Who is she?"

"I don't have to tell you that."

Kemper smiled. "You're a homosexual and a murderer. You have no rights. You're a Federal informant, and the Chicago FBI owns you."

Littell felt queasy. His heartbeat did funny little things.

Kemper said, *"Who is she?"*

Lenny came on hard butch. "This is not FBI-approved. If it was there'd be stenographers and paperwork. This is some sort of private thing with you two. And I won't say a goddamned thing that might hurt Jack Kennedy."

Kemper pulled out a morgue glossy and forced it on Lenny. Littell saw the dead boy with his mouth stuffed full.

Lenny shuddered. Lenny put on an instant rough-trade face.

"So? So this is supposed to scare me?"

"Giancana did this, Lenny. He thought this man killed Tony Iannone. One word from us, and this will be you."

Littell grabbed the snapshot. "Let's hold back a second. You've made your point."

Kemper steered him into the dining room. Kemper pressed him into a cabinet with his fingertips.

"Don't ever contradict me in front of a suspect."

"Kemper . . ."

"Hit him."

"Kemper—"

"*Hit him.* Make him afraid of you."

Littell said, "I can't. Goddamnit, don't do this to me."

"Hit him, or I'll call Giancana and rat him off right now."

"No. Come on . . . please."

Kemper handed him brass knuckles. Kemper made him lace his fingers in.

"Hit him, Ward. Hit him, or I'll let Giancana kill him."

Littell trembled. Kemper slapped him. Littell stumbled over to Lenny and weaved in front of him.

Lenny smiled this preposterous pseudo-tough-guy smile. Littell balled his fist and hit him.

Lenny clipped an end table and went down spitting teeth. Kemper threw a sofa cushion at him.

"Who's Laura Hughes? Tell me in detail."

Littell dropped the knucks. His hand throbbed and went numb.

"I said, 'Who's Laura Hughes?' "

Lenny nuzzled the cushion. Lenny spat out a chunk of gold bridgework.

"I said, 'Who's Laura Hughes?' "

Lenny coughed and cleared his throat. Lenny took a big let's-get-this-over-with breath.

He said, "She's Joe Kennedy's daughter. Her mother's Gloria Swanson."

Littell shut his eyes. The Q&A made absolutely no—

Kemper said, "Keep going."

"How far? I'm the only one outside the family who knows."

Kemper said, "Keep going."

Lenny took another breath. His lip was split up to his nostrils.

"Mr. Kennedy supports Laura. Laura loves him and hates him. Gloria Swanson hates Mr. Kennedy because he cheated her out of lots of money when he was a movie producer. She disowned Laura years ago, and that's all the 'keep going' I've got, goddamn you."

Littell opened his eyes. Lenny picked up the end table and flopped into a chair.

Kemper twirled the knucks on one finger. "Where did she get the name Hughes?"

"From Howard Hughes. Mr. Kennedy hates Hughes, so Laura took the name to annoy him."

Littell closed his eyes. He started seeing things he wasn't conjuring up.

"Ask Mr. Sands a question, Ward."

An image flickered out—Lenny with his phallus-shaped pen.

"Ward, open your eyes and ask Mr. Sands a—"

Littell opened his eyes and took his glasses off. The room went soft and blurry.

"I saw you arguing with Mad Sal outside the church. What was that about?"

Lenny worked a tooth loose. "I tried to quit the junket gig."

"Why?"

"Because Sal's poison. Because he's poison like you are."

He sounded I'm-a-snitch-now resigned.

"But he didn't let you quit?"

"No. I told him I'd work with him for six months tops, if he's still . . ."

Kemper twirled his knucks. "If he's still what?"

"Still fucking alive."

He sounded calm. He sounded like an actor who just figured out his role.

"Why wouldn't he be?"

"Because he's a degenerate gambler. Because he owes Sam G. twelve grand, and a contract's going out if he doesn't pay it back."

Littell put his glasses on. "I want you to stick with Sal, and let me worry about his debts."

Lenny wiped his mouth on the cushion. That one knuck shot cut him a brand-new harelip.

Kemper said, "Answer Mr. Littell."

Lenny said, "Oh yes, yes, Mr. Littell, sir"—arch-ugly-faggot inflected.

Kemper slipped the knucks into his waistband. "Don't tell Laura Hughes about this. And don't tell anybody about our arrangement."

Lenny stood up, knock-kneed. "I wouldn't dream of it."

Kemper winked. "You've got panache, son. And I know a magazine man in L.A. who could use an insider like you."

Lenny pushed his lip flaps together. Littell sent up a prayer: Please let me sleep through this night with no dreams.

DOCUMENT INSERT: 1/16/59. Official FBI telephone call transcript: "Recorded at the Director's Request"/"Classified Confidential 1-A: Director's Eyes Only." Speaking: Director Hoover, Special Agent Kemper Boyd.

JEH: Good morning, Mr. Boyd.

KB: Sir, good morning.

JEH: We have an excellent connection. Are you nearby?

KB: I'm at a restaurant on Northeast "I" Street.

JEH: I see. The Committee offices are close by, so I imagine you're hard at work for Little Brother.

KB: I am, Sir. At least cosmetically.

JEH: Update me, please.

KB: I convinced Little Brother to send me back to Miami. I told him that I could depose some Sun Valley land fraud witnesses, and in fact I did bring back some inconclusive depositions.

JEH: Continue.

KB: My real motive in traveling to Florida was to accrue information for you on the Gretzler and Kirpaski matters. You'll be pleased to know that I checked in with both the Miami and Lake Weir Police Departments and learned that both cases have been moved to open file status. I consider that a tacit admission that both homicides will remain unsolved.

JEH: Excellent. Now update me on the brothers.

KB: The Committee's labor racketeering mandate expires in ninety days. The paperwork forwarding process is now in the compilation stage, and I'll be sending you carbons of every piece of salient memoranda sent to our target grand juries. And, again, Sir, my opinion is that Jimmy Hoffa is legally inviolate at this time.

JEH: Continue.

KB: Big Brother has been calling legitimate labor leaders allied with the Democratic Party, to assure them that the trouble that Little Brother has stirred up with Hoffa does not mean that he is anti-labor overall. My understanding is that he will announce his candidacy in early January of next year.

JEH: And you remain certain that the brothers do not suspect the Bureau of collusion in the Darleen Shoftel matter?

KB: I'm certain, Sir. Pete Bondurant's girlfriend informed Little Brother of the Hush-Hush piece, and Ward Littell exposed both our primary bug and Bondurant's secondary bug independent of her.

JEH: I heard the Brothers' father made Howard Hughes eat crow.

KB: That's true, Sir.

JEH: Hush-Hush has been lackluster lately. The advance peeks that Mr. Hughes has been sending me have been quite tame.

KB: I've been staying in touch with Pete Bondurant on general principles, and I think I've found him a Hollywood-connected man he could use as a stringer.

JEH: If my bedtime reading improves, I'll know you've succeeded.

KB: Yes, Sir.

JEH: We have Ward Littell to thank for that entire Big Brother snafu.

KB: I passed through Chicago and saw Littell two days ago, Sir.

JEH: Continue.

KB: I had initially thought that his THP expulsion might push him toward taking anti-Mob actions on his own, so I decided to check up on him.

JEH: And?

KB: And my concerns were groundless. Littell seems to be suffering his Red Squad work in silence, and the only change of habit that I could detect was that he's begun an affair with Tom Agee's daughter Helen.

JEH: An affair of a sexual nature?

KB: Yes, Sir.

JEH: Is the girl of age?

KB: She's twenty-one, Sir.

JEH: I want you to keep an eye on Littell.

KB: I will, Sir. And while I have you, could I bring up a tangential matter?

JEH: Certainly.

KB: It involves the Cuban political situation.

JEH: Continue.

KB: In the course of my Florida visits I've met several pro-Batista and pro-Castro Cuban refugees. Now, apparently Castro is going Communist. I've learned that undesirables of varying political stripes will be expelled from Cuba and granted asylum in the

U.S., with most of them settling in Miami. Would you like information on them?

JEH: Do you have an information source?

KB: Yes, Sir.

JEH: But you'd rather not reveal it?

KB: Yes, Sir.

JEH: I hope they're paying you.

KB: It's an ambiguous situation, Sir.

JEH: You're an ambiguous man. And yes, any and all Cuban emigre intelligence would be appreciated. Have you anything to add? I'm due at a meeting.

KB: One last thing, Sir. Did you know that the brothers' father had an illegitimate daughter with Gloria Swanson?

JEH: No, I did not know that. You're certain?

KB: Reasonably. Should I follow up on it?

JEH: Yes. But avoid any personal entanglements that might upset your incursion.

KB: Yes, Sir.

JEH: Forewarned is forearmed. You have a tendency to adopt people, such as the morally-impaired Ward Littell. Don't extend that tendency toward the Kennedys. I suspect that their powers of seduction exceed even your own.

KB: I'll be careful, Sir.

JEH: Good day, Mr. Boyd.

KB: Good day, Sir.

19

(Los Angeles, 1/18/59)

Dick Steisel said, "If Mr. Hughes is so tight with J. Edgar Hoover, have *him* call off the goddamn process servers."

Pete scoped out his office. The client photos were boffo—Hughes shared a wall with some South American dictators and bongo player Preston Epps.

"He won't ask Hoover for favors. He figures he hasn't kissed his ass enough yet."

"He can't keep dodging subpoenas forever. He should simply divest TWA, earn his three or four hundred million and get on to his next conquest."

Pete rocked his chair and put his feet up on Steisel's desk. "He doesn't see things that way."

"And how do you see things?"

"The way he pays me to."

"Which means, in this instance?"

"Which means I'm going to call Central Casting, bag a half-dozen actors and have them made up as Mr. Hughes, then send them out in Hughes Aircraft limos. I'm going to tell them to hit some night spots, throw some cash around and talk up their travel plans. Timbuktu, Nairobi—who gives a shit? It'll buy us some time."

Steisel sifted through desk clutter. "TWA aside, you should know that most of the *Hush-Hush* articles you've sent over for vetting are libelous. Here's an example from that Spade Cooley piece. 'Does Ella Mae Cooley have 'Everlast' stamped across her chest? She should, because

Spade's been bopping bluegrass ballads on her already dangerously dented decolletage! It seems that Ella Mae told Spade she wanted to join a free love cult! Spade responded with fiddle-honed fisticuffs, and now Ella Mae has been sporting brutally black-and-blue blistered bosomage.' You see, Pete, there's no loophole rhetoric or—"

Steisel moaned and droned. Pete shut him out and daydreamed.

Kemper Boyd called him yesterday. He said, "I've got you a lead on a magazine stringer. His name's Lenny Sands, and he's playing a junket engagement at the Cal-Neva Lodge in Lake Tahoe. Go talk to him—I think he'd be perfect for *Hush-Hush*. But—he's tight with Ward Littell, and I know you'll figure out he's FBI-connected. And you should also know that Littell has an eyeball witness on the Gretzler job. Mr. Hoover told him to forget about it, but Littell's the volatile type. I don't want you to even mention Littell to Lenny."

Lenny Sands sounded good. The "eyeball witness" line was horseshit.

Pete said, "I'll go see Sands. But let's talk turkey about something else, too."

"Cuba?"

"Yeah, Cuba. I'm starting to think it's a gravy train for us law-enforcement retirees."

"You're right. And I'm thinking of buying in myself."

"I want in. Howard Hughes is driving me nuts."

"Do something nice, then. Do something John Stanton would like."

"For instance?"

"Look me up in the Washington, D.C. white pages, and send me some goodies."

Steisel jerked him out of his daydream. "Get these college kids to insert 'alleged' and 'supposed,' and make the pieces more hypothetical. Pete, are you listening to me?"

Pete said, "Dick, I'll see you. I've got things to do."

He drove to a pay phone and dialed favors. He called a cop buddy, Mickey Cohen, and Fred Otash, "Private Eye to the Stars." They said they could glom some "goodies," with D.C. delivery guaranteed pronto.

Pete called Spade Cooley. He said, I just kiboshed a new smear on you. Grateful Spade said, "What can *I* do for *you*?"

Pete said, I need six girls from your band. Have them meet me at Central Casting in an hour.

Spade said, Yes, Big-Daddy-O!

Pete called Central Casting and Hughes Aircraft. Two clerks promised satisfaction: six Howard Hughes look-alikes and six limousines would be waiting at Central in one hour.

Pete rendezvoused with his shills and paired them off: six Howards, six women, six limos. The Howards got specific instructions: Live it up through to dawn and spread the word that you're blasting off for Rio!

The limos hauled ass. Spade dropped Pete off at the Burbank airport.

He caught a puddle jumper to Tahoe. The pilot started his downswing right over the Cal-Neva Lodge.

Be good, Lenny.

The casino featured slots, craps, roulette, blackjack, poker, keno, and the world's thickest deep-pile carpets. The lobby featured a panoply of jumbo cardboard Frank Sinatras.

Dig that one by the door—somebody drew a dick in Frankie's mouth.

Dig that tiny cardboard cutout by the bar: "Lenny Sands at the Swingeroo Lounge!"

Somebody yelled, "Pete! Pete the Frenchman!" It had to be somebody Outfit—or somebody suicide prone.

Pete looked around. He saw Johnny Rosselli, waving from a booth just inside the bar enclosure.

He walked over. The booth was all-star: Rosselli, Sam G., Heshie Ryskind, Carlos Marcello.

Rosselli winked. "Frenchman Pete, *che se dice*?"

"Good, Johnny. You?"

"*Ça va*, Pete, *ça va*. You know the boys here? Carlos, Mo and Heshie?"

"Just by reputation."

Handshakes went around. Pete stayed standing—per Outfit protocol.

Rosselli said, "Pete's French-Canadian, but he don't like to be reminded of it."

Giancana said, "Everybody's gotta come from somewhere."

Marcello said, "Except me. I got no fucking birth certificate. I was either born in fucking Tunis, North Africa, or fucking Guatemala. My parents were Sicilian greenhorns with no fucking passports. I shoulda asked them, 'Hey, where was I born?' when I had the chance."

Ryskind said, "Yeah, but I'm a Jew with a finicky prostate. My people came from Russia. And if you don't think that's a handicap in this crowd . . ."

Marcello said, "Pete's been helping Jimmy out in Miami lately. You know, at the cabstand."

Rosselli said, "And don't think we don't appreciate it."

Giancana said, "Cuba has to get worse before it gets better. Now the fucking Beard has 'nationalized' our fucking casinos. He's got Santo T. in custody down there, and he's costing us hundreds of thousands a day."

Rosselli said, "It's like Castro just shoved an atom bomb up the ass of every made guy in America."

Nobody said, "Sit down."

Sam G. pointed out a lowlife walking by counting nickels. "D'Onofrio brings these chumps here. They stink up my room and don't lose enough to compensate. Me and Frank have got forty percent of the Lodge between us. This is a top-line room, not a resort for the lunchpail crowd."

Rosselli laughed. "Your boy Lenny's working with Sal now."

Giancana took a bead on the lowlife and pulled a make-believe trigger. "Somebody's gonna put a new part in Mad Sal D'Onofrio's hair. Bookies that owe more than they take in are like fucking Communists sucking the welfare tit."

Rosselli sipped his highball. "So, Pete, what brings you to the Cal-Neva?"

"I'm interviewing Lenny Sands for a job. I thought he might make a good stringer for *Hush-Hush.*"

Sam G. passed him some play chips. "Here, Frenchman, lose a grand on me. But don't move Lenny out of Chicago, all right? I like having him around."

Pete smiled. The "boys" smiled. Get the picture? They've tossed you all the crumbs they think you're worth.

Pete walked. He got caught up in the tail end of a stampede—low rollers heading for the low-rent lounge.

He followed them in. The room was SRO: every table full, latecomers holding up the walls.

Lenny Sands was on stage, backed by a piano and drums.

The keyboard man tickled some blues. Lenny bopped him on the head with his microphone.

"Lew, Lew, Lew. What are we, a bunch of moolies? What are you playing? 'Pass me the Watermelon, Mama, 'Cause My Spareribs are Double-Parked'?"

The audience yukked. Lenny said, "Lew, give me some Frankie."

Lew Piano laid down an intro. Lenny sang, half Sinatra/half fag falsetto:

"I've got you under my skin. I've got you, keestered deep inside of me. So deep, my hemorrhoids are riding me. I've got you—WHOA!—under my skin."

The junket chumps howled. Lenny cranked up his lisp:

"I've got you, chained to my bed. I've got you, and extra K-Y now! So deep, you can't really say why now! I've got you under my skin!"

The geeks yuk-yuk-yukked and tee-hee-heed. Peter Lawford walked in and checked the action—Frank Sinatra's #1 toady.

The drummer popped a rim shot. Lenny stroked his mike at crotch level.

"You gorgeous he-men from the Chicago Knights of Columbus, I just adore you!"

The audience cheered—

"And I want you to know that all my womanizing and chasing ring-a-ding cooze is just subterfuge to hide my overweening lust for YOU, the men of K of C Chapter 384, you gorgeous hunks of manicotti with your king-sized braciolas that I just can't wait to sautee and fricassee and take deep into my tantalizing Tetrazzini!"

Lawford looked hot to trot. It was common insider knowledge that he'd kill to suck up to Sinatra.

The junketeers roared. Some clown waved a K of C flag.

"I just love you love you love you! I can't wait to dress up in drag and invite all of you to sleep over at my Rat Pack slumber party!"

Lawford bolted toward the stage.

Pete tripped him.

Dig the toady's pratfall—an instant all-time classic.

Frank Sinatra shoved his way into the lounge. The junketeers went stone fucking nuts.

Sam G. intercepted him. Sam G. whispered to him, nice and gentle and FIRM.

Pete caught the gist.

Lenny's with the Outfit. Lenny's not a guy you rough up for sport.

Sam was smiling. Sam dug Lenny's act.

Sinatra about-faced. Ass-kissers surrounded him.

Lenny cranked his lisp waaaaay up. "Frankie, come back! Peter, get up off the floor, you gorgeous nincompoop!"

Lenny Sands was one cute shitbird.

. . .

He slipped the head blackjack dealer a note to forward to Sands. Lenny showed up at the coffee shop, on-the-dot punctual.

Pete said, "Thanks for coming."

Lenny sat down. "Your note mentioned money. That's something that always gets my attention."

A waitress brought them coffee. Jackpot gongs went off—baby slots were bolted to every table.

"Kemper Boyd recommended you. He said you'd be perfect for the job."

"Are you working for him?"

"No. He's just an acquaintance."

Lenny rubbed a scar above his lips. "What is the job exactly?"

"You'd be the stringer for *Hush-Hush*. You'd be digging up the stories and scandal bits and feeding them to the writers."

"So I'd be a snitch."

"Sort of. You keep your nose down in L.A., Chicago and Nevada, and report back."

"For how much?"

"A grand a month, cash."

"Movie-star dirt, that's what you want. You want the skank on entertainment people."

"Right. And liberal-type politicians."

Lenny poured cream in his coffee. "I've got no beef with that, except for the Kennedys. Bobby I can do without, but Jack I like."

"You were pretty tough on Sinatra. He's pals with Jack, isn't he?"

"He pimps for Jack and brown-noses the whole family. Peter Lawford's married to one of Jack's sisters, and he's Frank's brown-nose contact. Jack thinks Frank's good for chuckles and not much else, and you didn't hear any of this from me."

Pete sipped coffee. "Tell me more."

"No, you ask."

"Okay. I'm on the Sunset Strip and I want to get laid for a C-note. What do I do?"

"You see Mel, the parking-lot man at Dino's Lodge. For a dime, he'll send you to a pad on Havenhurst and Fountain."

"Suppose I want nigger stuff?"

"Go to the drive-in at Washington and La Brea and talk to the colored carhops."

"Suppose I dig boys?"

Lenny flinched. Pete said, "I know you hate fags, but answer the question."

"Shit, I don't . . . wait . . . the doorman at the Largo runs a string of male prosties."

"Good. Now, what's the story on Mickey Cohen's sex life?"

Lenny smiled. "It's cosmetic. He doesn't really dig cooze, but he likes to be seen with beautiful women. His current quasi-girlfriend is named Sandy Hashhagen. Sometimes he goes out with Candy Barr and Liz Renay."

"Who clipped Tony Trombino and Tony Brancato?"

"Either Jimmy Frattiano or a cop named Dave Klein."

"Who's got the biggest dick in Hollywood?"

"Steve Cochran or John Ireland."

"What's Spade Cooley do for kicks?"

"Pop bennies and beat up his wife."

"Who'd Ava Gardner cheat on Sinatra with?"

"Everybody."

"Who do you see for a quick abortion?"

"I'd go see Freddy Otash."

"Jayne Mansfield?"

"Nympho."

"Dick Contino?"

"Muff diver supreme."

"Gail Russell?"

"Drinking herself to death at a cheap pad in West L.A."

"Lex Barker?"

"Pussy hound with jailbait tendencies."

"Johnnie Ray?"

"Homo."

"Art Pepper?"

"Junkie."

"Lizabeth Scott?"

"Dyke."

"Billy Eckstine?"

"Cunt man."

"Tom Neal?"

"On the skids in Palm Springs."

"Anita O'Day?"

"Hophead."

"Cary Grant?"

"Homo."

"Randolph Scott?"

"Homo."

"Senator William F. Knowland?"

"Drunk."

"Chief Parker?"

"Drunk."

"Bing Crosby?"

"Drunk wife-beater."

"Sergeant John O'Grady?"

"LAPD guy known for planting dope on jazz musicians."

"Desi Arnaz?"

"Whore chaser."

"Scott Brady?"

"Grasshopper."

"Grace Kelly?"

"Frigid. I popped her once myself, and I almost froze my shvantze off."

Pete laughed. "Me?"

Lenny grinned. "Shakedown king. Pimp. Killer. And in case you're wondering, I'm much too smart to ever fuck with you."

Pete said, "You've got the job."

They shook hands.

Mad Sal D. walked in the door, waving two cups spilling nickels.

20

(Washington, D.C., 1/20/59)

United Parcel dropped off three big boxes. Kemper carried them into his kitchen and opened them.

Bondurant wrapped the stuff in oilcloth. Bondurant understood the concept of "goodies."

Bondurant sent him two submachine guns, two hand grenades and nine silencer-fitted .45 automatics.

Bondurant included a succinct, unsigned note:

"Your move and Stanton's."

The machine guns came with fully loaded drums and a maintenance manual. The .45s fit his shoulder rig perfectly.

Kemper strapped one on and drove to the airport. He caught the 1:00 p.m. New York shuttle with time to spare.

881 Fifth Avenue was a high-line Tudor fortress. Kemper ducked past the doorman and pushed the "L. Hughes" lobby buzzer.

A woman's voice came on the intercom. "Take the second lift on the left, please. You can leave the groceries in the foyer."

He elevatored up twelve floors. The doors opened straight into an apartment vestibule.

The vestibule was the size of his living room. The mink woman was leaning against a full-sized Greek column, wearing a tartan robe and slippers.

Her hair was tied back. She was juuust starting to smile.

"I remember you from the Kennedys' party. Jack said you're one of Bobby's policemen."

"My name's Kemper Boyd, Miss Hughes."

"From Lexington, Kentucky?"

"You're close. Nashville, Tennessee."

She folded her arms. "You heard me give the cab driver my address, and you described me to the doorman downstairs. He told you my name, and you rang my bell."

"You're close."

"You saw me give that vulgar diamond broach away. Any man as elegantly dressed as you are would appreciate a gesture like that."

"Only a well-taken-care-of woman would make that kind of gesture."

She shook her head. "That's not a very sharp perception."

Kemper stepped toward her. "Then let's try this. You did it because you knew you had an audience. It was a Kennedy kind of thing to do, and I'm not criticizing you for it."

Laura cinched her robe. "Don't get presumptuous with the Kennedys. Don't even talk presumptuously about them, because when you least expect it they'll cut you off at the knees."

"You've seen it happen?"

"Yes, I have."

"Did it happen to you?"

"No."

"Because you can't expel what you haven't admitted?"

Laura pulled out a cigarette case. "I started smoking because most of the sisters did. They had cases like this, so Mr. Kennedy gave me one."

"Mr. Kennedy?"

"Or Joe. Or Uncle Joe."

Kemper smiled. "My father went broke and killed himself. He willed me ninety-one dollars and the gun he did it with."

"Uncle Joe will leave me a good deal more than that."

"What's the current stipend?"

"A hundred thousand dollars a year and expenses."

"Did you decorate this apartment to resemble the Kennedys' suite at the Carlyle?"

"Yes."

"It's beautiful. Sometimes I think I could live in hotel suites forever."

She walked away from him. She turned on her heels and disappeared down a museum-width hallway.

Kemper let five minutes pass. The apartment was huge and quiet—he couldn't get his bearings.

He worked his way left and got lost. Three corridors led him back to the same pantry; the four entrances to the dining room had him spinning in circles. He hit intersecting hallways, a library, *wings*—

Traffic sounds straightened him out. He heard foot scuffs on the terrace behind the grand piano.

He walked over. The terrace would swallow up his kitchen at least twice.

Laura was leaning against the railing. A breeze ruffled her robe.

She said, "Did Jack tell you?"

"No. I figured it out myself."

"You're lying. The Kennedys and a friend of mine in Chicago are the only ones who know. Did Mr. Hoover tell you? Bobby says he doesn't know, but I've never believed him."

Kemper shook his head. "Mr. Hoover doesn't know. Lenny Sands told a Chicago FBI man who's a friend of mine."

Laura lit a cigarette. Kemper cupped his hands around the match.

"I never thought Lenny would tell a soul."

"He didn't have much choice. If it's any consol—"

"*No*, I don't want to know. Lenny knows bad people, and bad people can make you say things you don't want to."

Kemper touched her arm. "Please don't tell Lenny you met me."

"Why, Mr. Boyd?"

"Because he's embarrassingly well connected."

"No, you don't understand. I'm asking you what you're doing here."

"I saw you at Joe Kennedy's party. I'm sure you can fill in the rest yourself."

"That's not an answer."

"I couldn't very well ask Jack or Bobby for your number."

"Why not?"

"Because Uncle Joe wouldn't approve, and Bobby doesn't entirely trust me."

"Why?"

"Because I'm embarrassingly well connected."

Laura shivered. Kemper draped his suitcoat around her shoulders.

She pointed to his holster. "Bobby told me the McClellan people don't carry guns."

"I'm off duty."

"Did you think I'd be so bored and indolent that you could just ring my bell and seduce me?"

"No, I thought I'd buy you dinner first."

Laura laughed and coughed smoke. "Is Kemper your mother's maiden name?"

"Yes."

"Is she alive?"

"She died in a nursing home in '49."

"What did you do with the gun your father left you?"

"I sold it to a classmate in law school."

"Does he carry it?"

"He died on Iwo Jima."

Laura dropped her cigarette in a coffee cup. "I know so many orphans."

"So do I. You're sort of one your—"

"*No.* That's not true. You're just saying it to make points with me."

"I don't think it's much of a stretch."

She snuggled into his suitcoat. The sleeves flopped in the wind.

"Repartee is one thing, Mr. Boyd, and the truth is another. The truth is my robber-baron father fucked my movie-star mother and got her pregnant. My movie-star mother had already had three abortions and didn't want to risk a fourth. My movie-star mom disowned me, but my father enjoys flaunting me in front of his legitimate family once a year. The boys like me because I'm provocative, and they think I'm nifty because they can't fuck me, because I'm their half-sister. The girls hate me because I'm a coded message from their father that says men can fuck around, but women can't. Do you get the picture, Mr. Boyd? I have a family. My father put me through boarding school and several colleges. My father supports me. My father informed his family of my existence when Jack brought me home from a Harvard alumni mixer as the unwitting pawn in a rather vicious ploy I had initiated to assert myself into the family. Imagine his surprise when Father said, 'Jack, you can't fuck her, she's your half-sister.' Little Bobby, twenty and Calvinistic, overheard the conversation and spread the word. My father figured what the hell, the word's out, and invited me to stay for dinner. Mrs. Kennedy had a rather traumatic reaction to all of this. Our 'embarrassingly well connected' friend Lenny Sands was giving Jack speech lessons for his first congressional campaign, and was at the house for dinner. He stopped Rose from making a scene, and we've been sharing secrets ever since. *I have a family*, Mr. Boyd. My father is evil and grasping and ruthless and willing to destroy anybody who so much as looks the wrong way at the children he publicly acknowledges. And I hate everything about him except the money he gives me and the fact that he would probably destroy anybody who tried to hurt me as well."

Car horns bleeped long and shrill. Laura pointed down at a line of taxis. "They perch there like vultures. They always make the most noise when I'm playing Rachmaninoff."

Kemper unholstered his piece. He honed in on a sign marked Yellow Cabs Only.

He braced his arm on the railing and fired. Two shots sheared the sign off the signpost. The silencer went *thwack*—Pete was a good ordnance supplier.

Laura whooped. Cabbies gestured up, spooked and bewildered.

Kemper said, "I like your hair."

Laura untied it. The wind made it dance.

They talked.

He told her how the Boyd fortune evaporated. She told him how she flunked out of Juilliard and flopped as a socialite.

She called herself a musical dilettante. He called himself an ambitious cop. She recorded Chopin on a vanity label. He sent Christmas cards to car thieves he arrested.

He said he loved Jack but couldn't stand Bobby. She called Bobby deep Beethoven and Jack Mozart most glib. She called Lenny Sands her one true friend and didn't mention his betrayal. He said his daughter, Claire, shared all his secrets.

Devil's Advocate snapped on automatically. He knew exactly what to say and what to omit.

He called Mr. Hoover a vindictive old queen. He portrayed himself as a liberal pragmatist hitched to the Kennedy star.

She revived the orphanhood theme. He described the three-daughter combine.

Susan Littell was judgmental and shrill. Helen Agee was courageous and impetuous. His Claire was too close to know just yet.

He told her about his friendship with Ward. He said he wanted a younger brother for keeps—and the Bureau gave him one. He said Ward worshiped Bobby. She said Bobby sensed that Uncle Joe was evil and chased gangsters to compensate for his patrimony.

He hinted at his own lost brother. He said the loss made him push Ward in odd ways.

They talked themselves exhausted. Laura called "21" and had dinner sent up. The chateaubriand and wine made her drowsy.

They left it unspoken.

Not tonight—next time.

Laura fell asleep. Kemper walked through the apartment.

Two circuits taught him the layout. Laura told him the maid needed a map. The dining room could feed a small army.

He called the Agency's Miami Ops number. John Stanton picked up immediately.

"Yes?"

"It's Kemper Boyd. I'm calling to accept your offer."

"I'm very pleased to hear that. I'll be in touch, Mr. Boyd. We'll have lots to discuss."

"Good night, then."

"Good night."

Kemper walked back to the drawing room. He left the terrace curtains open—skyscrapers across the park threw light on Laura.

He watched her sleep.

21

(Chicago, 1/22/59)

Lenny's spare fuck-pad key unlocked the door. Littell hacked the jamb down to the bolt to fake a forensically valid burglar entry.

He broke the blade off his pen knife. The B&E shakes had him hacking too hard.

His trial break-in taught him the floor plan. He knew where everything was.

Littell shut the door and went straight for the golf bag. The $14,000 was still tucked inside the ball pocket.

He put his gloves on. He allotted seven minutes for cosmetic thievery.

He unplugged the hi-fi.

He emptied drawers and ransacked the medicine cabinet.

He dumped a TV, a toaster and the golf bag by the door.

It looked like a classic junkie-pad boost. Butch Montrose would never suspect anything else.

Kemper Boyd always said PROTECT YOUR INFORMANTS.

He pocketed the money. He carried the swag to his car, drove it to the lake and dumped it in a garbage-strewn tide pool.

Littell got home late. Helen was asleep on his side of the bed.

Her side was cold. Sleep wouldn't come—he kept replaying the break-in for errors.

He drifted off around dawn. He dreamed he was choking on a dildo.

He woke up late. Helen left him a note.

> School bodes. What time did you get home? For a (dismayingly) liberal FBI man you certainly are a zealous Communist chaser. What do Communists do at midnight?
>
> Love, love, love,
> H

Littell forced down coffee and toast. He wrote his note on plain bond paper.

> Mr. D'Onofrio,
> Sam Giancana has issued a contract on you. You will be killed unless you repay the $12,000 you owe him. I have a way for you to avoid this. Meet me this afternoon at 4:00. The Kollege Klub, 1281 58th, Hyde Park.

Littell put the note in an envelope and added five hundred dollars. Lenny said the junket tour had concluded—Sal should be back at home.

Kemper Boyd always said SEDUCE YOUR INFORMANTS WITH MONEY.

Littell called the Speedy-King Messenger Service. The dispatcher said he'd send a courier right over.

Mad Sal was prompt. Littell pushed his rye and beer aside.

They had the whole row of tables to themselves. The college kids at the bar wouldn't be able to hear them.

Sal sat down across from him. His flab rolls jiggled and hiked his shirt up over his belly button.

He said, "So?"

Littell pulled his gun and held it in his lap. The table covered him.

"So what did you do with that five hundred?"

Sal picked his nose. "I got down on the Blackhawks versus the Canadiens. Ten o'clock tonight that five hundred is a thousand."

"You owe Giancana eleven thousand more than that."

"So who the fuck told you?"

"A reliable source."

"You mean some Fed snitch cocksucker. You're a Fed, right? You're too candy-ass looking to be anything else, and if you was CPD or the Cook County Sheriff's, I'd've bought you off by now, and I'd be fucking your wife and cornholing your snotnose little boy while you was off at work."

"You owe Giancana twelve thousand dollars that you don't have. He's going to kill you."

"Tell me something I don't know."

"You killed a colored boy named Maurice Theodore Wilkins."

"That accusation is stale bread. It is fucking rebop you got out of some file."

"I just turned an eyeball witness."

Sal dug into his ears with a paper clip. "That is horse pucky. Feds don't investigate nigger homicides, and a little birdie told me that that kid was killed by an unknown assailant in the basement of the church rectory he stole from. The birdie said the assailant waited for the priests to go to a ball game, and then he cut the nigger boy up with a chainsaw after he made the nigger boy blow him. The birdie said there was lots of blood, and the assailant took care of the stink with altar wine."

Kemper Boyd always said NEVER SHOW FEAR OR DISGUST.

Littell laid a thousand dollars on the table. "I'm prepared to pay off your debt. In two or three installments, so Giancana won't suspect anything."

Sal grabbed the money. "So I take it, so I don't take it. For all I know, Mo might decide to whack me 'cause he's jealous of my good looks."

Littell cocked his gun. "Put the money down."

Sal did it. "So?"

"So are you interested?"

"So if I'm not?"

"So Giancana clips you. So I put out the word that you killed Tony Iannone. You've heard the rumors—Tony got whacked outside a homo joint. Sal, you're an open book. Jesus, 'blow' and 'cornhole.' I think you developed a few habits in Joliet."

Sal ogled the cash. Sal smelled like tobacco sweat and Aqua Velva lotion.

"You're a loan shark, Sal. What I'm asking for won't be too far out of line."

"S-s-so?"

"So I want to get at the Teamsters' Pension Fund. I want you to help me push somebody up the ladder. I'll find a man with a pedigree looking for a loan, and you help me set him up with Sam and the Fund. It's that simple. And I'm not asking you to snitch anybody."

Sal ogled the money.

Sal popped sweat.

Littell dropped three thousand dollars on the pile.

Sal said, "Okay."

Littell said, "Take it to Giancana. Don't gamble with it."

Sal gave him the bah-fungoo sign. "Stow the lecture. And remember I fucked your mother, which makes me your daddy."

Littell stood up and roundhoused his revolver. Mad Sal caught the barrel square in the teeth.

Kemper Boyd always said COW YOUR INFORMANTS.

Sal coughed up blood and gold fillings. Some kids at the bar watched the whole thing, bug-eyed.

Littell stared them down.

22

(Miami, 2/4/59)

The boat was late.

U.S. Customs agents crowded the dock. The U.S. Health Service had a tent pitched in the parking lot behind it.

The refugees would be X-rayed and blood-tested. The contagious ones would be shipped to a state hospital outside Pensacola.

Stanton checked his passenger manifest. "One of our on-island contacts leaked us a list. All the deportees are male."

Waves hit the pilings. Guy Banister flicked a cigarette butt at them.

"Which implies that they're criminals. Castro's getting rid of plain old 'undesirables' under the 'politically undesirable' blanket."

Debriefing huts flanked the dock. U.S. Border Patrol marksmen crouched behind them. They had first-hint-of-trouble/shoot-to-kill orders.

Kemper stood above the front pilings. Waves smashed up and sprayed his trouser legs.

His specific job was to interview Teofilio Paez, the ex–security boss for the United Fruit Company. A CIA briefing pouch defined UF: "America's largest, most long-established and profitable in-Cuba corporation and the largest on-island employer of unskilled and semi-skilled Cuban National workers. A long-standing bastion of Cuban anti-Communism. Cuban National security aides, working for the company, have long been effective in recruiting anti-Communist youth eager to infiltrate left-wing worker's groups and Cuban educational institutions."

Banister and Stanton watched the skyline. Kemper stepped into a breeze and let it ruffle his hair.

He had ten days in as a contract agent—two briefings at Langley and this. He had ten days in with Laura Hughes—the La Guardia shuttle made trysting easy.

Laura felt legitimate. Laura went crazy when he touched her. Laura said brilliant things and played Chopin *con brio*.

Laura was a Kennedy. Laura spun Kennedy tales with great verve.

He hid those stories from Mr. Hoover.

It felt like near-loyalty. It felt near-poignant—and Hoover-compromised.

He needed Mr. Hoover. He continued to feed him phone reports, but limited them to McClellan Committee intelligence.

He rented a suite at the St. Regis Hotel, not far from Laura's apartment. The monthly rate was brutal.

Manhattan got in your blood. His three paychecks totaled fifty-nine thousand a year—nowhere near enough to sustain the life he wanted.

Bobby kept him busy with boring Committee paperwork. Jack had dropped hints that the family might have post-Committee work for him. His most likely position would be campaign security boss.

Jack enjoyed having him around. Bobby continued to vaguely distrust him.

Bobby wasn't up for grabs—and Ward Littell knew it.

He talked to Ward twice a week. Ward was ballyhooing his new snitch—a bookie/loan shark named Sal D'Onofrio.

Cautious Ward said he had Mad Sal cowed. Angry Ward said Lenny Sands was now working for Pete Bondurant.

Angry Ward knew that *he* set it up.

Ward sent him intelligence reports. He edited out the illegalities and forwarded them to Bobby Kennedy. Bobby knew Littell solely as "The Phantom." Bobby prayed for him and marveled at his courage.

Hopefully, that courage was tinged with circumspection. Hopefully, that boy on the morgue slab taught Ward a few things.

Ward was adaptable and willing to listen. Ward was another orphan—raised in Jesuit foster homes.

Ward had good instincts. Ward believed that "alternative" Pension Fund books existed.

Lenny Sands thought the books were administered by a Mob elder statesman. He'd heard that cash was paid for loan referrals that resulted in large profits.

Littell might be stalking *big* money. It was potential knowledge to hide from Bobby.

He did hide it. He cut every Fund reference from the Phantom's reports.

Littell was malleable for a zealot. The Big Question was this: Could his covert work be hidden from Mr. Hoover?

A dark speck bobbed on the water. Banister held up binoculars. "They don't look wholesome. There's a crap game going on at the back of the barge."

Customs men hit the dock. They packed revolvers, billy clubs and shackle chains.

Stanton showed Kemper a photograph. "This is Paez. We'll grab him right off, so Customs can't requisition him."

Paez looked like a skinny Xavier Cugat. Banister said, "I can see him now. He's up front, and he's cut and bruised."

Stanton winced. "Castro hates United Fruit. Our propaganda section picked up a polemic he wrote on it nine months ago. It was an early indication that he might go Commie."

Whitecaps pushed the barge in close. The men were kicking and clawing to be first off.

Kemper flicked the safety off his piece. "Where are we detaining them?"

Banister pointed north. "The Agency owns a motel in Boynton Beach. They concocted a cover story about fumigation and evicted all the tenants. We'll pack these beaners in six to a room and see who we can use."

The refugees yelled and waved little flags on sticks. Teo Paez was crouched to sprint.

The Customs boss yelled, "On ready!"

The barge tapped the dock. Paez jumped off. Kemper and Stanton grabbed him and bear-hugged him.

They picked him up and ran with him. Banister ran interference—"CIA custody! He's ours!"

The riflemen fired warning shots. The refugees ducked and covered. Customs men grappled the barge in and cinched it to the pilings.

Kemper hustled Paez through the crowd. Stanton ran ahead and unlocked a debriefing hut.

Somebody yelled, "There's a body on the boat!"

They got their man inside. Banister locked the door. Paez hit the floor and smothered it with kisses.

Cigars fell out of his pockets. Banister picked one up and sniffed the wrapper.

Stanton caught his breath. "Welcome to America, Mr. Paez. We've heard very good things about you, and we're very glad you're here."

Kemper cracked a window. The dead man passed by on a gurney—blade-punctured from head to toe. Customs agents lined up the exiles—maybe fifty men total.

Banister set up his tape recorder on a table. Stanton said, "You had a death on the boat?"

Paez slumped into a chair. "No. It was a political execution. We surmised that the man had been deported to serve as an anti-American spy. Under interrogation he revealed that this was true. We acted accordingly."

Kemper sat down. "You speak excellent English, Teo."

"I speak the slow and exaggeratedly formal English of the laboriously self-taught. Native speakers tell me that I sometimes lapse into hilarious malapropisms and mutilations of their language."

Stanton pulled a chair up. "Would you mind talking with us now? We've got a nice apartment ready for you, and Mr. Boyd will drive you there in a little while."

Paez bowed. "I am at your disposable."

"Excellent. I'm John Stanton, by the way. And these are my colleagues, Kemper Boyd and Guy Banister."

Paez shook hands all around. Banister pocketed the rest of the cigars and turned on the tape machine.

"Can we get you anything before we start?"

"No. I would like my first American meal to be a sandwich at Wolfie's Delicatessen in Miami Beach."

Kemper smiled. Banister laughed outright. Stanton said, "Teo, is Fidel Castro a Communist?"

Paez nodded. "Yes. Indubitably so. He is a Communist in both thought and practice, and my old network of student informants have told me that airplanes carrying Russian diplomats have flown in to Havana late at night on several occasions recently. My friend Wilfredo Olmos Delsol, who was on the boat with me, has the flight numbers memorized."

Banister lit a cigarette. "Che Guevara's been Red since way back."

"Yes. And Fidel's brother Raúl is a Communisto pig himself. Moreover, he is a hypocriticize. My friend Tomás Obregón says that Raúl is selling confiscated heroin to rich drug addicts and hypocriticizingly spewing Communist rhetoric at the same time."

Kemper checked his custody list. "Tomás Obregón was on the boat with you."

"Yes."

"How would he have information on the Cuban heroin trade?"

"Because, Mr. Boyd, he was involved in the heroin trade himself. You see, my fellow boat passengers are mostly criminal scum. Fidel wanted to be rid of them and foisted them on America in hopes that they would practice their trades on your shores. What he failed to realize was that Communism is a bigger crime than dope peddling or robbery or murder, and that even criminals might possess the patriotic desire to reclaim their homeland."

Stanton rocked his chair back. "We've heard that Castro has taken over the Mafia-owned hotels and casinos."

"It is true. Fidel calls it 'nationalization.' He has stolen the casinos and millions of dollars from the Mafia. Tomás Obregón told me that the illustrious American gangster Santo Trafficante Jr. is currently in custody at the Nacional Hotel."

Banister sighed. "That cocksucker Castro has a death wish. He is fucking with both the United States of America *and* the Mafia."

"There is no Mafia, Guy. At least Mr. Hoover has always said so."

"Kemper, even God can make mistakes."

Stanton said, "Enough of that. Teo, what's the status of the American citizens remaining inside Cuba?"

Paez scratched and stretched. "Fidel wants to appear humane. He is coddling the influential Americans still in Cuba and allowing them to see only the alleged good his revolution has done. He is going to release them slowly, to return to America as duped tools to dispense communistic propaganda. And in the meantime, Fidel has burned many of the cane fields of my beloved United Fruit, and has tortured and killed many of my student informants under the indictment that they are spies for the *'imperialisto y fascisto'* La United."

Stanton checked his watch. "Guy, take Teo over for his medical. Teo, go with Mr. Banister. Mr. Boyd will drive you into Miami in a little while."

Banister hustled Paez out. Kemper watched them walk to the X-ray shack.

Stanton shut the door. "Dump the dead man somewhere, Kemper. I'll debrief all the personnel who've seen him. And don't rattle Guy's cage, he can be volatile."

"I've heard. Rumor has it that he was assistant superintendent of the New Orleans Police for about ten minutes, until he got drunk and shot off his gun in a crowded restaurant."

Stanton smiled. "And rumor has it that you've fenced a few hot Corvettes in your day."

"Touché. And parenthetically, what did you think of Pete Bondurant's gun donation?"

"I was impressed. We're thinking of making Pete an offer, and I'll be bringing it up the next time I talk to the deputy director."

Kemper said, "Pete's a good man. He's good at keeping rowdies in line."

"Yes, he is. Jimmy Hoffa uses him to good effect at that Tiger Kab place. Keep going, Kemper. I can tell that you've got your thinking cap on."

Kemper turned off the tape recorder. "John, you're going to find that a sizable percentage of those men out there are uncontrollably psychopathic. Your notion of indoctrinating them and training them as potential anti-Castro guerrillas may not work. If you house them with stable Cuban immigrant families and find them work, per your existing plan, you'll find them reverting to their former criminal predilections as soon as the novelty of being in this country wears off."

"You're saying we should screen them more thoroughly."

"No, I'm saying *I* should. I'm saying we should extend the detention period at the Agency's motel, and I should be the one with final authority as to who we recruit."

Stanton laughed. "May I ask what qualifies you for this?"

Kemper ticked off points on his fingers. "I worked undercover for nine years. I know criminals, and I like them. I infiltrated car theft rings, arrested the members and worked with the U.S. Attorney's Office in building their cases for prosecution. I understand the need certain criminals have to acquiesce to authority. John, I got so close to some of those car thieves that they insisted on deposing their confessions to me only—the agent who betrayed them and arrested them."

Stanton whistled—out-of-character for him. "Are you suggesting that you expand your duties and remain with the men you select as their field officer? That seems unrealistic to me, given your other entanglements."

Kemper slapped the table. "*No.* I'm strongly proposing Pete Bondurant for that job. What I'm saying is this: A hardcore criminal contingent, properly indoctrinated and supervised, could be very effective. Let's assume that the Castro problem extends. I think that even at this early date, it's safe to assume that the Agency will have a large pool of future deportees and legally emigrated Cubans to choose from. Let's make this first cadre an elite one. It's *ours*, John. Let's make it the best."

Stanton tapped his chin. "Mr. Dulles was ready to request green cards for all the men. He'd be pleased to know that we're being so selective early on. He hates begging the INS for favors."

Kemper put a hand up. "Don't deport the men we reject. Banister knows some Cubans in New Orleans, doesn't he?"

"Yes. There's a large Batistaite community there."

"Then let Guy have the men we reject. Let them find jobs or not find jobs, and have them file for visas on their own in Louisiana."

"How many men do you think will meet your qualifications?"

"I have no idea."

Stanton looked eager. "Mr. Dulles has approved the purchase of some cheap south Florida land for our initial training site. I think I could convince him to keep our permanent cadre there small and contained, if you think the men you select can also train future arrivals before we disperse them to the other camps that I'm certain will be springing up."

Kemper nodded. "I'll make training skills one of my criteria. Where is this land?"

"It's on the coast, outside a small town named Blessington."

"Is it accessible to Miami?"

"Yes. Why?"

"I was thinking of the Tiger Kab stand as a recruiting hub."

Stanton looked almost hot and bothered. "Gangster connotations aside, I think the Tiger Kab place could be utilized. Chuck Rogers is working there already, so we've already got an in."

Kemper said, "John"—very slowly.

Stanton looked dead ecstatic. "The answer to all your suggestions is yes, pending the deputy director's approval. And bravo, Kemper. You're more than fulfilling my expectations."

Kemper stood up and bowed. "Thanks. And I think we'll make Castro rue the day he sent that boat off."

"From your mouth to God's ears. And by the way, what do you think your friend Jack would say about our little freedom barge?"

Kemper laughed. "Jack would say, 'Where's the women?' "

Paez talked a blue streak. Kemper rolled down his window for relief.

They hit Miami at rush hour. Paez kept jabbering. Kemper drummed the dashboard and tried to replay his talk with Stanton.

". . . and Mr. Thomas Gordean was my *patrón* at La United. He loved pussy until his fondness for I. W. Harper bonded bourbon inappropriated him. Most of the executives at La United got out after Castro took over, but Mr. Gordean has remained behind. Now, he is drinking even more heavily. He has several thousand shares of United Fruit stock with him, and refuses to leave. He has bought off militiamen to be his private bodyguards and is beginning to sprout the Communist line himself. My great fear is that Mr. Gordean will go Communisto like the Fidel I loved long ago. I fear that he will become a propaganda tool par eccentricity and . . ."

"Stock shares"—

"Thomas Gordean"—

A light bulb popped on and nearly blinded him. Kemper almost ran his car off the road.

DOCUMENT INSERT: 2/10/59. Hush-Hush stringer report: Lenny Sands to Pete Bondurant.

Pete,

Here's a lead I've picked up. 1.—Mickey Cohen's diving for crumbs. He's got two goons (George Piscatelli & Sam Lo Cigno) set to maybe work a sex shakedown racket. I got this from Dick Contino, in Chicago for some accordion soiree. Mickey got the idea when he read Lana Turner's love letters to Johnny Stompanato after Lana's daughter shanked Johnny. Johnny used to screw rich widows and had some out-of-work cameraman film it. Mickey's got some choice film clips. Tell Mr. Hughes he'll sell them for 3 grand.

Cheers,
Lenny

DOCUMENT INSERT: 2/24/59. Hush-Hush stringer report: Lenny Sands to Pete Bondurant.

Pete,

I've been on the road with Sal D'Onofrio's junket gig. Here's some tidbits. 1.—All the midnight shift cocktail waitresses at the Dunes Hotel in Vegas are hookers. They serviced President Eisenhower's Secret Service crew when Ike addressed the Nevada State Legislature. 2.—Rock Hudson's banging the maitre d' at the Cal-Neva restaurant. 3.—Lenny Bruce is hooked on dilaudid. There's a whole squad of L.A. County Sheriff's set to entrap him the next time he appears on the Strip. 4.—Freddy Otash got Jayne Mansfield an abortion. The daddy was a shvartze dishwasher with a 16" schlong. Peter Lawford's got pictures of the guy stroking it. I bought one off Freddy O. I'll send it to you to forward to Mr. Hughes. 5.—Bing Crosby's drying out at a Catholic Church retreat for alcoholic priests and nuns outside 29 Palms. Cardinal Spellman visited him there. They went on a bender and drove to L.A. blotto. Spellman sideswiped a car filled with wetbacks and sent 3 of them to the hospital. Bing bought them off with autographed pictures and a few hundred dollars.

Spellman flew back to New York with the DT's. Bing stayed in L.A. long enough to beat up his wife and then went back to the dry-out farm.

Cheers,
Lenny

DOCUMENT INSERT: 3/4/59. Personal note: J. Edgar Hoover to Howard Hughes.

Dear Howard,

I thought I would drop you a line to tell you how much I think Hush-Hush has improved since Mr. Bondurant hired your new stringer. Now there's a man who would make an excellent FBI agent! I so look forward to the verbatim reports that you send me! Should you wish to expedite their delivery, have Mr. Bondurant contact Special Agent Rice at the Los Angeles Office. Many thanks also for the Stompanato home movie and the snapshot of the prodigiously endowed negro. Forewarned is forearmed: you have to know your enemy before you can combat him.

All best,
Edgar

DOCUMENT INSERT: 3/19/59. Personal letter: Kemper Boyd to J. Edgar Hoover. Marked: EXTREMELY CONFIDENTIAL.

Sir:

Per our previous conversation, I'm passing on salient Kennedy family information gleaned from Laura (Swanson) Hughes.

I've gained a degree of Miss Hughes' confidence in the course of establishing a casual friendship with her. My relationship with the Kennedys gives me credibility, and Miss Hughes was impressed with the fact that I determined the secret of her parentage without actually broaching the topic to Kennedy family members or her other knowledgeable friends.

Miss Hughes loves to talk about the family, but she only discusses John, Robert, Edward, Rose and the sisters in bland terms. She reserves considerable wrath for Joseph P. Kennedy Sr., cites his ties to Boston mobster Raymond L.S. Patriarca and a retired Chicago "bootlegger-financier" named Jules Schiffrin, and delights in telling stories of Mr. Kennedy's business rivalry with Howard Hughes. (Miss Hughes adopted the name "Hughes" on her eighteenth birthday, replacing the Kennedy-Swanson proffered "Johnson" in an effort to somehow fluster her father, one of Howard Hughes' most auspicious enemies.)

Miss Hughes contends that Joseph P. Kennedy's gangster ties run considerably deeper than the "he was a bootlegger" tag foisted upon him by the press in reference to his highly successful scotch whisky import business pre-prohibition. She cannot cite specific gangster intimates or recall incidents that she has witnessed or heard of second-hand; nevertheless, her sense of Joseph P. Kennedy as "deeply gangster connected" remains inchoately strong.

I will continue my friendship with Miss Hughes and report all salient Kennedy family intelligence to you.

Respectfully,
Kemper Boyd

DOCUMENT INSERT: 4/21/59. Summary report: SA Ward J. Littell to Kemper Boyd. "For editing and forwarding to Robert F. Kennedy."

Dear Kemper,

Things continue apace here in Chicago. I'm continuing to pursue domestic Communists per my regular Bureau assignment, although they impress me as more pathetic and less dangerous by the day. That said, I'll move to our real concerns.

Sal D'Onofrio and Lenny Sands continue, unknown to each other, to serve as my informants. Sal, of course, paid back the $12,000 he owed Sam Giancana; Giancana let him off with a beating. Apparently, my theft of Butch Montrose's $14,000 was never connected to Sal's $12,000 windfall. I ordered Sal to repay Giancana in three increments and he followed that order. My initial violence directed at Sal proved to be far-sighted: I seem to have the man thoroughly cowed. In the course of casual conversation I told him that I had been a Jesuit seminarian. D'Onofrio, a self-described "Devout Catholic," was impressed by this and now considers me something of a father-confessor. He has confessed to six torture-murders, and of course I now have those (gruesomely detailed) confessions to hold over him. Aside from the occasional nightmares the confessions have induced, Sal and I seem to be proceeding on an even keel. I told him I would appreciate it if he would refrain from killing and self-destructive gambling while under my stewardship, and so far he seems to be doing that. Sal has provided me with rather tame pieces of anti-Mob intelligence (not worth forwarding to you or Mr. Kennedy) but has not been of help in steering me toward a loan seeker to hoist up the Teamster Pension Fund ladder. This was the sole reason I suborned him as my informant, and he has failed me in that capacity. I suspect that proving the existence of "alternative" Pension Fund books will be a gruesomely attenuated process.

Lenny Sands continues to wear almost as many hats as you. He's the Hush-Hush stringer (God, what ugly work that must be!), Sal's junket partner and a general Chicago Mob drone. He says he's actively engaged in attempting to accrue information on the workings of the Pension Fund and says that he believes the rumor that Sam Giancana pays bonuses for Fund loan referrals is true. He also believes that "alternative," perhaps coded, Pension Fund books detailing hidden assets do exist. In conclusion, I've yet to glean hard information from either Sands or D'Onofrio.

On another front, Mr. Hoover seems to be dodging a potential opportunity to impede Chicago Mob members. Court Meade picked up an (elliptically worded) mention of a robbery on the tailor shop bug. Chicago Mob soldiers Rocco Malvaso and Dewey Di Pasquale apparently clouted $80,000 from a (non-Chicago Mob) high-stakes crap game in Kenilworth. THP agents airteled this information to Mr. Hoover, who told them not to forward it to the applicable agencies for follow-up investigation. My God, that man's twisted priorities!

I'll close now. By way of farewell: you continue to amaze me, Kemper. God, you as a CIA man! And with the McClellan Committee disbanded, what will you be doing for the Kennedys?

Godspeed,
WJL

DOCUMENT INSERT: 4/26/59. Personal note: Kemper Boyd to J. Edgar Hoover. Marked: EXTREMELY CONFIDENTIAL.

Sir:

I thought I would drop you a line and update you on the Ward Littell front. Littell and I continue to speak regularly on the telephone, and I remain convinced that he is not undertaking overt or covert anti-Mob actions on his own authority.

You mentioned that Littell was spotted near Celano's Tailor Shop and the Top Hoodlum Program listening post. I subtly queried Littell on this and am satisfied with his answer: that he was meeting SA Court Meade for lunch.

Littell's personal life seems to revolve around his affair with Helen Agee. This affair has put a strain on his relationship with his daughter, Susan, who disapproves of the liaison. Normally, Helen is in close contact with my daughter Claire, but now that they attend different colleges the frequency of that contact has been curtailed. The Littell-Agee romance seems to be comprised of three or four nights a week of domestic get-togethers. Both retain separate residences, and I think they will continue to do so. I'll continue to keep an eye on Littell.

> Respectfully,
> Kemper Boyd

DOCUMENT INSERT: 4/30/59. Personal note: Kemper Boyd to Ward J. Littell.

Ward:

I strongly urge that you stay away from Celano's Tailor Shop and the listening post area, and avoid being seen with Court Meade. I think I've eased some mild suspicions Mr. Hoover might have had, but you cannot be too careful. I strongly advise you to stop your assignment trade with Meade. Destroy this letter immediately.

> KB

DOCUMENT INSERT: 5/4/59. Summary report: Kemper Boyd to John Stanton. Marked: CONFIDENTIAL/HAND POUCH DELIVER.

John:

Here's the update you requested in your last pouch. I apologize for the delay, but as you've pointed out, I'm "multiply-employed."

1.—Yes, the McClellan Committee's labor racketeering mandate has terminated. No, the Kennedys haven't offered me a permanent job yet. I think they will soon. There are numerous possibilities, since I'm both an attorney and a cop. Yes, I have discussed Cuba with Jack. He has no opinion on its viability as a 1960 campaign issue yet. He is strongly anti-Communist, despite his reputation as a liberal. I'm optimistic.

2.—I've concluded my "auditions" at the Boynton Beach Motel. Today marks the end of the 90-day sequestering period prescribed by Deputy Director Bissell, and tomorrow the bulk of our men will be sent to Louisiana. Guy Banister has a network of legally emigrated Cubans ready to receive them. They will be providing housing, employment and references aimed at procuring them visas. Guy will funnel the men into his own indoctrination/training program.

I have selected four men to form the nucleus of our Blessington Cadre. I consider them to be the best of the fifty-three men on the 2/4/59 "Banana Boat." Since I am "multiply-employed," I was not present for much of the sequestering, but capable case officers followed the indoctrination and psychological testing guidelines I set down.

Those guidelines were exceedingly rigorous. I personally supervised polygraph tests to determine the presence of Castro-planted informants. All fifty-three men passed (I think the man they killed on the boat was the ringer). Backup Sodium Pentothal tests were administered. Again, all the men passed.

Interrogations followed. As I suspected, all fifty-three men possessed extensive criminal records inside Cuba. Their offenses included armed robbery, burglary, arson, rape, heroin smuggling, murder and various "political crimes." One man was revealed to be a deviate who had molested and decapitated six small children in Havana. Another man was a homosexual procurer despised by the other exiles. I deemed both men to be dangerously unstable and terminated them under the indoctrination guidelines set down by the Deputy Director.

All the men were subjected to hard interrogation verging on torture. Most resisted with great courage. All the men were physically drilled and verbally abused in the manner of Marine Corps boot camp. Most responded with the perfect mixture of anger and subservience. The four men I selected are intelligent, violent in a controlled manner, physically skilled, garrulous (they'll be good Miami recruiters), acquiescent to authority and resoundingly pro-American, anti-Communist and anti-Castro. The men are:

A)—TEOFILIO PAEZ himself. DOB 8/6/21. Former Security Chief for United Fruit. Skilled in weaponry and interrogation techniques. Former Cuban Navy frogman. Adept at political recruitment.

B)—TOMAS OBREGON. DOB 1/17/30. Former Castro guerrilla. Former Havana dope courier and bank robber. Skilled in Jujitsu and the manufacture of explosives.

C)—WILFREDO OLMOS DELSOL. DOB 4/9/27. OBREGON's cousin. Former leftist firebrand turned rightist zealot when his bank accounts were "Nationalized." Former Cuban Army drill instructor. Small arms weaponry expert.

D)—RAMON GUTIERREZ. DOB 10/24/19. Pilot. Skilled propaganda pamphleteer. Former torturer for Batista's Secret Police. Expert in counterinsurgency techniques.

3.—I've toured the area surrounding the land the Agency purchased for the Blessington campsite. It is impoverished and inhabited by poor white trash, a fair number of them Ku Klux Klan members. I think we need an impressive white man to run the campsite, a man capable of instilling fear in any local rednecks who become perturbed at the notion of Cuban emigres squatting in their bailiwick. I recommend Pete Bondurant. I checked his World War II Marine Corps record and was impressed: he survived fourteen hand-to-hand combat charges on Saipan, won the Navy Cross and rose from buck private to captain via field commission. I strongly urge you to hire Bondurant on an Agency contract basis.

That's all for now. I'll be at the St. Regis in New York if you need me.

Yours,
KB

PS: You were right about Castro's U.S. trip. He refused to register in a hotel that didn't admit Negroes, then went up to Harlem and began issuing anti-U.S. statements. His behavior at the U.N. was deplorable. I salute your prescience: the man <u>was</u> "forcing a rejection."

<u>DOCUMENT INSERT</u>: 5/12/59. Memo: John Stanton to Kemper Boyd.

Kemper,

The Deputy Director has approved the hiring of Pete Bondurant. I have minor qualms, and I want you to send him on a trial run of some sort before we approach him. Use your own discretion.

JS

23

(Chicago, 5/18/59)

Helen buttered a slice of toast. "Susan's slow burn is getting to me. I don't think we've spoken more than three or four times since she heard about us."

Mad Sal was due to call. Littell pushed his breakfast aside—he had absolutely no appetite.

"I've spoken to her exactly twice. Sometimes I think it's a pure tradeoff—I gained a girlfriend and lost a daughter."

"You don't seem too bothered by the loss."

"Susan feeds on resentment. She's like her mother that way."

"Claire told me Kemper's having an affair with some rich New York City woman, but she won't divulge details."

Laura Hughes was one-half Kennedy. Kemper's Kennedy incursion was now a two-front campaign.

"Ward, you're very remote this morning."

"It's work. It preoccupies me."

"I'm not so sure."

It was almost 9:00—7:00 a.m. Gardena time. Sal was an inveterate early-bird gambler.

Helen waved her napkin at him. "Yoo-hoo, Ward! Are you listening to—?"

"What are you saying? What do you mean, 'I'm not so sure'?"

"I mean your Red Squad work bores and vexes you. You always describe it with contempt, but for months you've been engrossed in it."

"And?"

"And you've been having nightmares and mumbling in Latin in your sleep."

"And?"

"And you're starting to hide out from me when we're in the same room. You're starting to act like you're forty-six and I'm twenty-one, and there's things you can't tell me, because I just wouldn't understand."

Littell took her hands. Helen pulled them away and knocked a napkin holder off the table.

"Kemper tells Claire everything. I would think that you'd try to emulate him that way."

"Kemper is Claire's father. I'm not yours."

Helen stood up and grabbed her purse. "I'll think about that on my way home."

"What happened to your 9:30 class?"

"It's Saturday, Ward. You're so 'preoccupied' that you don't know what day it is."

Sal called at 9:35. He sounded agitated.

Littell made nice to calm him down. Sal enjoyed sweet talk.

"How's the tour going?"

"A junket's a junket. Gardena's good 'cause it's close to L.A., but fuckin' Jewboy Lenny keeps taking off to dig up shit for *Hush-Hush* and keeps showing up late for his gigs. You think I should slice him like I did that guy who—"

"Don't confess over the phone, Sal."

"Forgive me, Father, for I have sinned."

"Stop it. You know what I'm interested in, so if you have anything, tell me."

"Okay, okay. I was in Vegas and heard Heshie Ryskind talking. Hesh said the boys are worried on the Cuban front. He said the Outfit paid the Beard a shitload of money in exchange for his word the fuckin' casinos could keep operating if he took over the fuckin' country. But now he's gone Commie and fuckin' nationalized the casinos. Hesh said the Beard's got Santo T. in jail in Havana. The boys don't like the Beard so much these days. Hesh said the Beard's like the low man in a Mongolian cluster fuck. You know, sooner or later he'll get *really* fucked."

Littell said, "And?"

"And before I left Chicago I talked on the phone to Jack Ruby. Jack had a case of the shorts, so I lent him a wad to unload this one strip club and buy himself another one, the Carousel or something. Jack's always good on the payback, 'cause he sharks on the side himself down in Dallas, and—"

"Sal, you're building up to something. Tell me what it is."

"Whoa whoa whoa—I thought cops liked that corroboration stuff."

"Sal—"

"Whoa, listen now. Jack corroborated what Heshie said. He said he'd talked to Carlos Marcello and Johnny Rosselli, and they both said the Beard is costing the Outfit seventy-five thousand a day in bank interest on top of their daily fucking casino profit nut. Think about it, Padre. Think of what the Church could do with seventy-five grand a day."

Littell sighed. "Cuba doesn't interest me. Did Ruby give you anything on the Pension Fund?"

Mad Sal said, "Weeeeel . . ."

"Sal, goddamnit—"

"Naughty, naughty, Padre. Now say ten Hail Marys and check this. Jack told me he forwarded this Texas oil guy straight to Sam G. for a Pension Fund loan, like maybe a year ago. Now this is a class-A tip, and I deserve a reward for it, and I need some fuckin' money to cover bets with, because bookies and shylocks with no bankroll get hurt and can't snitch to candy-ass Fed cocksuckers like you."

Ruby's THP designation: bagman/small-time loan shark.

"Padre Padre Padre. Forgive me because I have bet. Forgive me because—"

"I'll try to get you some money, Sal. If I can find a borrower for you to introduce to Giancana. I'm talking about a direct referral, from you to Sam."

"Padre . . . Jesus."

"Sal . . ."

"Padre, you're fucking me so hard it hurts."

"I saved your life, Sal. And this is the only way you'll ever get another dime out of me."

"Okay okay okay. Forgive me, Father, for I have taken it up the dirt road from this ex-seminarian Fed who—"

Littell hung up.

The squadroom was weekend quiet. The agent manning the phone lines ignored him.

Littell cadged the teletype machine and queried the Dallas office.

The reply would take at least ten minutes. He called Midway for flight information—and hit lucky.

A Pan-Am connector departed for Dallas at noon. A return flight would have him home shortly after midnight.

The kickback rolled off the wire: Jacob Rubenstein/AKA Jack Ruby, DOB 3/25/11.

The man had three extortion arrests and no convictions: in '47, '49 and '53.

The man was a suspected pimp and Dallas PD informant.

The man was the subject of a 1956 ASPCA investigation. The man was strongly suspected of sexually molesting dogs. The man was known to occasionally shylock to businessmen and desperate oil wildcatters.

Littell ripped up the teletype. Jack Ruby was worth the trip.

Airplane hum and three scotches lulled him to sleep. Mad Sal's confessions merged like a Hit Parade medley.

Sal makes the Negro boy beg. Sal feeds the bet welcher Drano. Sal decapitates two kids who wolf-whistle at a nun.

He'd verified those deaths. All four stood "Unsolved." All four victims were rectal-raped postmortem.

Littell woke up sweaty. The stewardess handed him a drink unsolicited.

The Carousel Club was a striptease-row dive. The sign out front featured zaftig girls in bikinis.

Another sign said, Open 6:00 P.M.

Littell parked behind the building and waited. His rental car reeked of recent sex and hair pomade.

A few cops cruised by. One man waved. Littell caught on: They think you're a brother cop with your hand in Jack's pocket.

Ruby drove up at 5:15, alone.

He was a dog fucker and a pimp. This would have to be ugly.

Ruby got out and unlocked the back door. Littell ran up and intercepted him.

He said, "FBI. Let's see your hands." He said it in the classic Kemper Boyd style.

Ruby looked skeptical. He was wearing a ridiculous porkpie hat.

Littell said, "Empty your pockets." Ruby obeyed him. A cash roll, dog biscuits, and a .38 snub-nose hit the ground.

Ruby spat on them. "I know out-of-town shakedowns on an intimate level. I know how to deal with cops in cheap blue suits with liquor breath. Now take what you want and leave me the fuck alone."

Littell picked up a dog biscuit. "Eat it, Jack."

Ruby got up on his toes—some kind of lighter-weight boxer's stance. Littell flashed his gun and handcuffs.

"I want you to eat that dog biscuit."

"Now look . . ."

" 'Now look, *sir*.' "

"Now look, *sir*, who the fuck do you—?"

Littell jammed the biscuit in his mouth. Ruby chewed on it to keep from gagging.

"I'm going to make demands of you, Jack. If you don't comply, the IRS will audit you, Federal agents will pat-search your customers every night and the Dallas *Morning News* will expose your sexual bent for dogs."

Ruby chewed. Ruby sprayed crumbs. Littell kicked his legs out from under him.

Ruby went down on his knees. Littell kicked the door open and kicked him inside.

Ruby tried to stand up. Littell kicked him back down. The room was ten-by-ten and littered with piles of striptease gowns.

Littell kicked a pile in Ruby's face. Littell dropped a fresh dog biscuit in his lap.

Ruby put it in his mouth. Ruby made horrible choking sounds.

Littell said, "Answer this question. *Have you ever referred borrowers to higher-end loan sharks than yourself?*"

Ruby nodded—yes yes yes yes yes.

"Sal D'Onofrio lent you the money to buy this place. Nod if that's true."

Ruby nodded. His feet were snagged up in soiled brassieres.

"Sal kills people routinely. Did you know that?"

Ruby nodded. Dogs started barking one room over.

"He tortures people, Jack. He enjoys inflicting pain."

Ruby thrashed his head. His cheeks bulged like that dead boy on the morgue slab.

"Sal burned a man to death with a blowtorch. The man's wife came home unexpectedly. Sal shoved a gasoline-soaked rag in her mouth and ignited it. He said she died shooting flames like a dragon."

Ruby pissed in his pants. Littell saw the lap stain spread.

"Sal wants you to know a few things. One, your debt to him is erased. Two, if you don't cooperate with me or you rat me to the Outfit or any of your cop friends, he'll come to Dallas and rape you and kill you. Do you understand?"

Ruby nodded—yes yes yes. Biscuit crumbs shot out of his nostrils.

Kemper Boyd always said DON'T FALTER.

"You're not to contact Sal. You're not to know my name. You're not to tell anyone about this. You're to contact me every Tuesday at 11:00 a.m. at a pay phone in Chicago. I'll call you and give you the number. Do you understand?"

Ruby nodded—yes yes yes yes yes yes. The dogs keened and clawed at a door just a few feet in front of him.

"I want you to find a high-end borrower for Sal. Somebody Sal can send up to Giancana and the Pension Fund. Nod if you agree to do it, and nod twice if you understand the whole situation."

Ruby nodded three times.

Littell walked out.

The dog noise went cacophonous.

His return flight landed at midnight. He drove home, keyed up and exhausted.

Helen's car was parked out front. She'd be up; she'd be earnest; she'd be eager to reconcile.

Littell drove to a liquor store and bought a half-pint. A wino panhandled him. He gave him a dollar—the poor shit looked sort of like Jack Ruby.

It was 1:00 a.m. Sunday morning. Court Meade might be working the listening post.

He called. No one answered. Some THP man was ditching his shift.

Kemper urged him to avoid the post. Kemper might not consider one last visit too risky.

Littell drove over and let himself in. The bug transmitter was unplugged; the room was freshly cleaned and tidied up. A note taped to the main console box explained why.

Memo:

Celano's Tailor Shop is undergoing fumigation 5/17–5/20/59.

All on-premises shifts will be suspended during that time.

Littell cracked his bottle. A few drinks revitalized him and sent his thoughts scattergunning out in a million directions.

Some brain wires crackled and crossed.

Sal needed money. Court Meade was talking up a dice-game heist. Mr. Hoover said to let the matter rest.

Littell checked the bug transcript logs. He found a colloquy on the job, filed by SA Russ Davis last month.

4/18/59. 2200 hrs. Alone at tailor shop: Rocco Malvaso & Dewey "The Duck" Di Pasquale. What sounded like drinking toasts was obscured by jackhammer and general construction noise outside on Michigan Ave. Two minutes passed while both men apparently used the bathroom. Then this conversation occurred.

Malvaso: Te salud, Duck.

Di Pasquale: Quack, quack. The nice thing is, you know, they can't report it.

Malvaso: The Kenilworth cops would shit. That is the squarejohn town to end all squarejohn towns. The last time two handsome big dick guys like us took down eighty grand in a crap game there was the twelfth of fucking never.

Di Pasquale: Quack, quack. I say they're independent guys who had it coming. I say if you're not mobbed-up with Momo you're duck shit. Hey, we wore masks and disguised our voices. To boot, those Indy cocksuckers don't know we're connected. I felt like Super Duck. I'm thinking I should get a Super Duck costume and wear it the next time I take my kids to Disneyland.

Malvaso: Quack, fucking quack, you web-footed cocksucker. You had to shoot your gun off, though. Like no fucking getaway is fucking complete without some duck-billed cocksucker shooting off his gun.

(Note: the Kenilworth Police report unexplained shots fired on the 2600 block of Westmoreland Ave., 2340 hrs., 4/16/59).

Di Pasquale: Hey, quack, quack. It worked. We've got it stashed nice and safe and

Malvaso: And too fucking public for my taste.

Di Pasquale: Quack, quack. Sixty days ain't too long to wait for the split. Donald's been waiting fucking twenty years to bang Daisy, 'cause Walt Disney won't let him. Hey, remember last year? Jewboy Lenny did my birthday party? He did that routine where Daisy's sucking Donald off with her beak, what a fucking roar.

Malvaso: Quack, quack, you cocksucker.

(Note: construction noise obscured the rest of this conversation. Door slam sounds at 2310 hrs.)

Littell checked the THP ID file. Malvaso and Di Pasquale lived in Evanston.

He played the 4/18/59 tape and compared it to the typed transcript. Russ Davis forgot to include departing shtick.

The Duck hummed "Chattanooga Choo Choo."

Malvaso sang, "I got the key to your heart."

"Too public," "key" and "choo choo." Two *suburban-situated* robbers waiting sixty days for their split.

There were forty-odd *suburban* train stations linked to Chicago.

With forty-odd waiting rooms lined with storage lockers.

The lockers were rented by the month. For cash only, with no records kept, with no-name receipts issued.

Two robbers. Two *separate* key locks per locker door.

The locks were changed every ninety days—per Illinois TA law.

Thousands of lockers. Unmarked keys. Sixty days until the split—with thirty-three already elapsed.

The lockers were steel-plated. The waiting rooms were guarded 24 hours.

Littell spent two full days thinking it through. It came down to this:

He could tail them. But when they picked up the money, he'd be helpless.

He could only tail them one at a time. It came down to this: pre-existing bad odds doubled against him.

He decided to try anyway. He decided to pad his Red Squad reports and tail the men on alternate days for one week.

Day one: He tails Rocco Malvaso from 8:00 a.m. to midnight. Rocco drives to his numbers dens, his union shops and his girlfriend's place in Glencoe.

Rocco goes nowhere near a train station.

Day two: He tails Dewey the Duck from 8:00 a.m. to midnight. Dewey drives to numerous prostitution collections.

Dewey goes nowhere near a train station.

Day three: He tails Rocco Malvaso from 8:00 a.m. to midnight. Rocco drives to Milwaukee and pistol-whips recalcitrant pimps.

Rocco goes nowhere near a train station.

Day four: He tails Dewey the Duck from 8:00 a.m. to midnight. Dewey entertains at Dewey Junior's outdoor birthday party, dressed up as Donald Duck.

Dewey goes nowhere near a train station.

Day five: He tails Rocco Malvaso from 8:00 a.m. to midnight. Rocco spends said time with a call girl at the Blackhawk Hotel in Chicago.

Rocco goes nowhere near a train station.

Day six, 8:00 a.m.: He picks up his tail on Dewey the Duck. 9:40 a.m.: Dewey's car won't start. Mrs. Duck drives Dewey to the Evanston train station.

Dewey loiters in the waiting room.

Dewey eyes the lockers.

Locker #19 is affixed with a Donald Duck decal.

Littell almost swoons.

Nights six, seven and eight: He stakes out the station. He learns that the watchman leaves for his coffee break at 3:10 a.m.

The man walks down the street to an all-night diner. The waiting room is left unguarded for at least eighteen minutes.

Night nine: He hits the station. He's armed with a crowbar, tin snips, a mallet and a chisel. He snaps the door off locker 19 and steals the four grocery bags full of money inside.

It totals $81,492.

He now has an informant fund. The bills are old and well circulated.

He gives Mad Sal ten thousand dollars for starters.

He finds the Jack Ruby look-alike wino and gives him five hundred.

The Cook County Morgue supplies him with a name. Icepick Tony Iannone's lover was one Bruce William Sifakis. He sends the boy's parents ten thousand dollars anonymously.

He drops five thousand in the poor box at Saint Anatole's and stays to pray.

He asks forgiveness for his hubris. He tells God that he has gained his selfhood at great cost to other people. He tells God that he loves danger now, and it thrills him much more than it frightens him.

24

(Havana, 5/28/59)

The plane taxied in. Pete got out his passport and a fat roll of ten-spots.

The passport was Canadian, and CIA-forged.

Militiamen hit the runway. The Cuban fuzz tapped all the Key West flights for handouts.

Boyd called him two days ago. He said John Stanton and Guy Banister dug that old Big Pete panache. Boyd had just signed on with the Agency. He said he had a tailor-made Big Pete job, which might prove to be a CIA audition run.

He said, "You fly from Key West to Havana under a Canadian passport. You speak French-accented English. You find out where Santo Trafficante is and take delivery of a note from him. The note should be addressed to Carlos Marcello, Johnny Rosselli and Sam Giancana, et al. It should state that Trafficante advises no Mob retaliation against Castro for nationalizing the casinos. You're also to locate a very frightened United Fruit executive named Thomas Gordean and bring him back with you for debriefing. This has to be accomplished very soon—Castro and Ike are set to permanently cancel all commercial flights running from the U.S. to Cuba."

Pete said, "Why me?"

Boyd said, "Because you can handle yourself. Because the cabstand gave you a crash course in Cubans. Because you're not a known Mob man that Castro's secret police might have a file on."

Pete said, "What's the pay?"

Boyd said, "Five thousand dollars. And if you're detained, the same diplomatic courier who's trying to get Trafficante and some other Americans out will arrange for your release. It's just a matter of time before Castro releases all foreign nationals."

Pete wavered. Boyd said, "You'll also receive my personal promise that Ward Littell—a very disturbed and dangerous man—will never touch you. In fact, I set you up with Lenny Sands to buffer the two of you."

Pete laughed.

Boyd said, "If the Cuban cops roust you, tell the truth."

The doors opened. Pete stuck a ten-dollar bill inside his passport. Militiamen climbed into the plane.

They wore mismatched gun belts and carried odd pistols. Their shirt-front regalia was straight out of some Kellogg's Corn Flakes box.

Pete squeezed up toward the cockpit. Arc lights strafed the doorways and windows. He walked down the ramp ducking blinding goddamn glare.

A guard snatched his passport. The ten-spot disappeared. The guard bowed and handed him a beer.

The other passengers filed out. Militia geeks checked their passports for tips and came up empty.

The boss guard shook his head. His minions confiscated purses and wallets. A man protested and tried to hold on to his billfold.

The spics laid him out prone on the runway. They cut his trousers off with razor blades and picked his pockets clean.

The other passengers quit squawking. The boss guard rifled through their stuff.

Pete sipped beer. Some guards walked up with their hands out.

He greased them, one ten-spot per hand. He goofed on their uniforms: lots of frayed khaki and epaulets like the ushers at Grauman's Chinese.

A little spic waved a camera. "You play futbol, hombre? Hey, big man, you play futbol?"

Somebody lobbed a football. Pete caught it one-handed. A flashbulb popped right upside his face.

Get the picture? They want you to pose.

He crouched low and waved the ball like Johnny Unitas. He went deep for a pass, blocked an invisible lineman and bounced the ball off his head like a nigger soccer ace he saw on TV once.

The spics clapped. The spics cheered. Flashbulbs pop-pop-popped.

24

(Havana, 5/28/59)

The plane taxied in. Pete got out his passport and a fat roll of ten-spots.

The passport was Canadian, and CIA-forged.

Militiamen hit the runway. The Cuban fuzz tapped all the Key West flights for handouts.

Boyd called him two days ago. He said John Stanton and Guy Banister dug that old Big Pete panache. Boyd had just signed on with the Agency. He said he had a tailor-made Big Pete job, which might prove to be a CIA audition run.

He said, "You fly from Key West to Havana under a Canadian passport. You speak French-accented English. You find out where Santo Trafficante is and take delivery of a note from him. The note should be addressed to Carlos Marcello, Johnny Rosselli and Sam Giancana, et al. It should state that Trafficante advises no Mob retaliation against Castro for nationalizing the casinos. You're also to locate a very frightened United Fruit executive named Thomas Gordean and bring him back with you for debriefing. This has to be accomplished very soon—Castro and Ike are set to permanently cancel all commercial flights running from the U.S. to Cuba."

Pete said, "Why me?"

Boyd said, "Because you can handle yourself. Because the cabstand gave you a crash course in Cubans. Because you're not a known Mob man that Castro's secret police might have a file on."

Pete said, "What's the pay?"

Boyd said, "Five thousand dollars. And if you're detained, the same diplomatic courier who's trying to get Trafficante and some other Americans out will arrange for your release. It's just a matter of time before Castro releases all foreign nationals."

Pete wavered. Boyd said, "You'll also receive my personal promise that Ward Littell—a very disturbed and dangerous man—will never touch you. In fact, I set you up with Lenny Sands to buffer the two of you."

Pete laughed.

Boyd said, "If the Cuban cops roust you, tell the truth."

The doors opened. Pete stuck a ten-dollar bill inside his passport. Militiamen climbed into the plane.

They wore mismatched gun belts and carried odd pistols. Their shirt-front regalia was straight out of some Kellogg's Corn Flakes box.

Pete squeezed up toward the cockpit. Arc lights strafed the doorways and windows. He walked down the ramp ducking blinding goddamn glare.

A guard snatched his passport. The ten-spot disappeared. The guard bowed and handed him a beer.

The other passengers filed out. Militia geeks checked their passports for tips and came up empty.

The boss guard shook his head. His minions confiscated purses and wallets. A man protested and tried to hold on to his billfold.

The spics laid him out prone on the runway. They cut his trousers off with razor blades and picked his pockets clean.

The other passengers quit squawking. The boss guard rifled through their stuff.

Pete sipped beer. Some guards walked up with their hands out.

He greased them, one ten-spot per hand. He goofed on their uniforms: lots of frayed khaki and epaulets like the ushers at Grauman's Chinese.

A little spic waved a camera. "You play futbol, hombre? Hey, big man, you play futbol?"

Somebody lobbed a football. Pete caught it one-handed. A flashbulb popped right upside his face.

Get the picture? They want you to pose.

He crouched low and waved the ball like Johnny Unitas. He went deep for a pass, blocked an invisible lineman and bounced the ball off his head like a nigger soccer ace he saw on TV once.

The spics clapped. The spics cheered. Flashbulbs pop-pop-popped.

Somebody yelled, "Hey, eees Robert Mitchum!"

Peasant types ran out on the runway, waving autograph books. Pete ran for a taxi stand by the gate.

Little kids urged him on. Cab doors opened, presto chango.

Pete dodged an oxcart and piled into an old Chevy. The driver said, "Joo are not Robert Mitchum."

They cruised Havana. Animals and street riffraff clogged traffic. They never got above ten miles an hour.

It was 92 degrees at 10:00 p.m. Half the geeks out on the stroll wore fatigues and full Jesus Christ beards.

Dig those whitewashed Spanish-style buildings. Dig the posters on every facade: Fidel Castro smiling, Fidel Castro shouting, Fidel Castro waving a cigar.

Pete flashed the snapshot Boyd gave him. "Do you know this man?"

The driver said, "*Sí.* It is Mr. Santo Junior. He is in custody at the Nacional Hotel."

"Why don't you take me there."

Pancho hung a U-turn. Pete saw hotel row up ahead—a line of half-assed skyscrapers facing the beach.

Lights sparkled down on the water. A big stretch of glow lit the waves up turquoise blue.

The cab pulled up to the Nacional. Bellboys swooped down—clowns in threadbare tuxedos. Pete whipped a ten-spot on the driver—the fuck almost wept.

The bellboys stuck their hands out. Pete lubed them at the rate of ten scoots per. A cordon pushed him into the casino.

The joint was packed. Commies dug capitalisto-style gambling.

The croupiers wore shoulder holsters. Militia geeks ran the black-jack table. The clientele was 100% beaner.

Goats roamed free. Dogs splashed in a crap table filled with water. Dig the floorshow back by the slot machines: an Airedale and a Chihuahua fucking.

Pete grabbed a bellboy and yelled in his ear. "Santo Trafficante. You know him?"

Three hands appeared. Three tens went out. Somebody pushed him into an elevator.

Fidel Castro's Cuba should be renamed Nigger Heaven.

The elevator zoomed up. A militiaman opened the door gun first.

Dollar bills dripped out of his pockets. Pete added a ten-spot. The gun disappeared, *rápidamente.*

"Did you wish to enter custody, *señor?* The fee is fifty dollars a day."

"What does that include?"

"It includes a room with a television, gourmet food, gambling and women. You see, American passport holders are being temporarily detained here in Cuba, and Havana itself is momentarily unsafe. Why not enjoy your detention in luxury?"

Pete flashed his passport. "I'm Canadian."

"Yes. And of French distraction, I can tell."

Steam trays lined the hallway. Bellboys pushed cocktail carts by. A goat was taking a shit on the carpet two doors down.

Pete laughed. "Your guy Castro's some innkeeper."

"Yes. Even Mr. Santo Trafficante Jr. concedes that there are no four-star jails in America."

"I'd like to see Mr. Trafficante."

"Please follow me, then."

Pete fell in step. Boozed-out gringo fat cats careened down the hallway. The guard pointed out custody high spots.

Suite 2314 featured stag films screened on a bedsheet. Suite 2319 featured roulette, craps and baccarat. Suite 2329 featured naked hookers on call. Suite 2333 featured a live lesbian peep show. Suite 2341 featured suckling pigs broiled on a spit. Suites 2350 through 2390 comprised a full-size golf driving range.

A spic caddy squeezed by them schlepping clubs. The guard clicked his heels outside 2394.

"Mr. Santo, you have a visitor!"

Santo Trafficante Jr. opened the door.

He was fortyish and pudgy. He wore nubby-silk Bermuda shorts and glasses.

The guard scooted off. Trafficante said, "The two things I hate most are Communists and chaos."

"Mr. Trafficante, I'm—"

"I've got eyes. Four, in fact. You're Pete Bondurant, who clips guys for Jimmy. Some six-foot-six gorilla knocks on my door and acts servile, I put two and two together."

Pete walked into the room. Trafficante smiled.

"Did you come to bring me back?"

"No."

"Jimmy sent you, right?"

"No."

"Mo? Carlos? I'm so fucking bored I'm playing guessing games with a six-foot-six gorilla. Hey, what's the difference between a gorilla and a nigger?"

Pete said, "Nothing?"

Trafficante sighed. "You heard it already, you hump. My father killed a guy once who spoiled one of his punch lines. Maybe you've heard of my father?"

"Santo Trafficante *Senior*?"

"*Salud*, Frenchman. Jesus, I'm so fucking bored I'm playing one-up with a gorilla."

Pig grease spattered out a cooling vent. The pad was furnished modern-ugly—lots of fucked-up color combos.

Trafficante scratched his balls. "So who sent you?"

"A CIA man named Boyd."

"The only CIA guy I know is a redneck named Chuck Rogers."

"I know Rogers."

Trafficante shut the door. "I know you know him. I know the whole story of you and the cabstand, and you and Fulo and Rogers, and I know stories about you that I bet you wished I didn't know. You know *how* I know? I know because everybody in this life of ours likes to talk. And the only fucking saving grace is that none of us talks to people outside the life."

Pete looked out the window. The ocean glowed turquoise blue way past the buoy line.

"Boyd wants you to write a note to Carlos Marcello, Sam Giancana and Johnny Rosselli. The note's supposed to say that you recommend no reprisals against Castro for nationalizing the casinos. I think the Agency's afraid the Outfit will go off half-cocked and screw up their own Cuban plans."

Trafficante grabbed a scratch pad and pen off the TV. He wrote fast and enunciated clearly.

"Dear Premier Castro, you Commie dog turd. Your revolution is a crock of Commie shit. We paid you good money to let us keep our casinos running if you took over, but you took our money and fucked us up the brown trail until we bled. You are a bigger piece of shit than that faggot Bobby Kennedy and his faggot McClellan Committee. May you personally get syphillis of the brain and the dick, you Commie cocksucker, for fucking up our beautiful Nacional Hotel."

Golf balls ricocheted down the hallway. Trafficante flinched and held the note up.

Pete read it. Santo Junior delivered—nice, neat, grammatical.

Pete tucked the note in his pocket. "Thanks, Mr. Trafficante."

"You're fucking welcome, and I can tell you're surprised that I can write and say two different things at the same time. Now, you tell your Mr. Boyd that that promise is good for one year and no more. Tell him we're all swimming in the same stream as far as Cuba goes, so it's in our best interest not to piss in his face."

"He'll appreciate it."

"Appreciate, shit. If you appreciated, you'd take me back with you."

Pete checked his watch. "I've only got two Canadian passports, and I'm supposed to bring back a United Fruit man."

Trafficante picked up a golf club. "Then I can't complain. Money's money, and United Fruit's tapped more out of Cuba than the Outfit ever did."

"You'll get out soon. Some courier's working on getting all the Americans out."

Trafficante lined up a make-believe putt. "Good. And I'll set you up with a guide. He'll drive you around and take you and the UF man to the airport. He'll rob you before he drops you off, but that's as good as the help gets with these fucking Reds in power."

A croupier supplied directions to the house—Tom Gordean threw a torch party there just last week. Jesús the guide said Mr. Tom burned a mean cane field—he was hot to revamp his *fascisto* image.

Jesús wore jungle fatigues and a baseball cap. He drove a Volkswagen with a hood-mounted machine gun.

They took dirt roads out of Havana. Jesús steered with one hand and blasted palm trees simultaneous. Sizzling cane fields lit the sky up orange-pink—torch parties were a big deal in post-Batista Cuba.

Phone poles blipped by. Fidel Castro's face adorned every one.

Pete saw house lights in the distance—two hundred yards or so up. Jesús pulled into a clearing dotted with palm stumps.

He eased in like he knew where he was going. He didn't gesture or say one fucking word.

It felt wrong. It felt *prearranged.*

Jesús braked and doused his headlights. A torch whooshed the second they snapped off.

Light spread out over the clearing. Pete saw a Cadillac ragtop, six spics, and a white man reeling drunk.

Jesús said, "That is Señor Tom."

The spics had sawed-off shotguns. The Caddy was stuffed with luggage and mink coats.

Jesús jumped out and jabbered spic to the spics. The spics waved to the gringo in the Volkswagen.

The minks were piled above the door line. U.S. currency was bulging out of a suitcase.

Pete caught on, dead solid perfect.

Thomas Gordean was weaving. He was waving a bottle of Demerara rum. He was putting out a line of pro-Commie jive talk.

He was slurring his words. He was dead drunk working on dead.

Pete saw torches ready to light. Pete saw a gas can sitting on a tree stump.

Gordean kept spritzing. He got up a fucking A-#1 Commie cliché head of steam.

Jesús huddled with the spics. They waved at the gringo again. Gordean puked on the hood of the Caddy.

Pete slid next to the machine gun. The spics turned away and went for their waistbands.

Pete fired. One tight swivel at their backs cut them down. The *ack-ack* sent a flock of birds up squawking.

Gordean hit the ground and curled himself up fetal-tight. The bullet spread missed him by inches.

The spics died screaming. Pete strafed their bodies into pulp. Cordite and muzzle-scorched entrails formed one putrid smell combination.

Pete poured gas on the stiffs and the Volkswagen and torched them. A box of .50-caliber ammo exploded.

Señor Tom Gordean was passed out cold.

Pete tossed him in the backseat of the Caddy. The mink coats made a cozy little bed.

He checked the luggage. He saw a shitload of money and stock certificates.

Their flight left at dawn. Pete found a road map in the glove compartment and marked a route back to Havana.

He got in the Caddy and punched it. French-fried palm trees provided a glow to drive by.

He made the airport before first light. Friendly militiamen swamped El Señor Mitchum.

Tom Gordean woke up with the shakes. Pete fed him rum-and-Cokes to keep him docile. The spics nationalized the money and furs—no big surprise.

Pete signed Robert Mitchum autographs. Some Commie commissar escorted them to the plane.

The pilot said, "You're not Robert Mitchum."

Pete said, "No shit, Sherlock."

Gordean dozed off. The other passengers eyeballed them—they reeked of gasoline and liquor.

The plane landed at 7:00 a.m. Kemper Boyd met them. He handed Pete an envelope containing five thousand dollars.

Boyd was juuuuust a tad nervous. Boyd was more than just a tad dismissive.

He said, "Thanks, Pete. Take that jitney into town with the other people, all right? I'll call you in L.A. in a few days."

He got five grand. Boyd got Gordean and a suitcase full of stock shares. Gordean looked bewildered. Boyd looked quintessentially un-Boyd.

Pete hopped on the jitney. He saw Boyd steer Gordean to a storage hut.

Here's this deserted hick-town airfield. Here's this CIA man and this drunk, alone.

His feelers started twitching in high fucking gear.

25

(Key West, 5/29/59)

The hut was matchbook-size. He had to cram the table and two chairs in.

Kemper handled Gordean with kid gloves. The interrogation dragged—his subject had the DTs.

"Does your family know that you possess this United Fruit stock?"

"What 'family'? I've been married and divorced more than Artie Shaw *and* Mickey Rooney. I've got a few cousins in Seattle, but all they know is the way to the bar at the Woodhaven Country Club."

"Who else in Cuba knows that you own this stock?"

"My bodyguards know. But one minute we're drinking and getting ready to expunge a few imperialist cane fields, and the next thing I know I'm in the backseat of my car with that buddy of yours at the wheel. I'm not ashamed to admit that I've been on a toot, and things are pretty dim. That buddy of yours, does he carry a machine gun?"

"I don't think so."

"What about a Volkswagen?"

"Mr. Gordean . . ."

"Mr. Boyce, or whatever your name is, what's going on? You sit me down in this shack and ransack my suitcase. You ask me these questions. You think because I'm a rich American businessman that I'm on your side. You think I don't know how you CIA fuckers rigged the elections in Guatemala? I was on my way to cocktails with Premier Castro when your buddy shanghaied me. That's *Fidel Castro*. He's the liberator of Cuba. He's a nice man and a wonderful basketball player."

Kemper laid down his stock release forms. They were superbly forged—a counterfeiter friend did the job.

"Sign these please, Mr. Gordean. They're reimbursement vouchers for your airfare."

Gordean signed in triplicate. Kemper signed the notary statement and seal-stamped all three signatures.

His friend rigged the seal, at no extra charge.

Gordean laughed. "CIA man/notary public. What a combo."

Kemper pulled his .45 and shot him in the head.

Gordean flew off his chair. Blood sprayed out one ear. Kemper stepped on his head to stanch the spritz.

Something rustled outside. Kemper pushed the door open with his gun.

It was Pete Bondurant, standing there with his hands in his pockets.

They both smiled.

Pete drew "50/50" in the air.

DOCUMENT INSERT: 6/11/59. Summary Report: Kemper Boyd to John Stanton. Marked: CONFIDENTIAL/HAND POUCH DELIVER.

John:

I delayed the writing of this communique for two reasons. One, I wanted to see a botched incident through to its conclusion before contacting you. Two, this note details a mission that I (quite frankly) blew.

You had asked me to use my own discretion and send Pete Bondurant on a trial run to help determine his suitability for Agency contract employment. I did this, and sent Bondurant into Cuba to pull out a United Fruit executive named Thomas Gordean, a man whom Teofilio Paez described as "volatile" and "espousing the Communist line." Bondurant succeeded in the first part of his mission. We installed Mr. Gordean at the Rusty Scupper Motel in Key West for de-briefing, and made the mistake of leaving him alone to rest. Gordean committed suicide with a .45 automatic he had secreted on his person. I summoned the Key West Police, and Bondurant and I de-briefed them. A coroner's jury ruled Gordean's death a suicide. Bondurant testified as to Gordean's apparent alcoholism and depressive behavior. An autopsy confirmed that Gordean showed signs of advanced liver damage. His body was shipped to a distant cousin in Seattle (Gordean had no immediate family).

Should you require verification, please contact Captain Hildreth of the Key West Police. Of course, I apologize for this boondoggle. And I assure you that nothing like this will happen again.

Sincerely,
Kemper Boyd

DOCUMENT INSERT: 6/19/59. Personal note: John Stanton to Kemper Boyd.

Dear Kemper,

Of course, I am furious. And of course you should have informed me of this snafu immediately. Thank God Gordean had no immediate family capable of causing trouble for the Agency. That expressed, I'll state that most likely you were to some degree a victim of mitigating circumstances. After all, as you once said, you are an attorney and a cop, not a spy.

You'll be pleased to know that Deputy Director Bissell is quite taken with your idea of creating an elite cadre to run the Blessington campsite. The campsite is currently under construction; your four personally selected recruits (Paez, Obregon, Delsol, Gutierrez) are undergoing further training at Langley and doing quite well. As previously stated, the Deputy Director has approved the hiring of Pete Bondurant to run the campsite. That, of course, was before the Gordean snafu. Right now, I want to wait and reconsider Bondurant.

In conclusion, the Gordean incident sits poorly with me, but my enthusiasm for you as a contract agent remains strong. Until I tell you otherwise, undertake no more missions on your own authority.

John Stanton

DOCUMENT INSERT: 6/28/59. Personal note: Ward J. Littell to Kemper Boyd. "For editing and forwarding to Robert F. Kennedy."

Kemper,

My anti-Mob intelligence gathering continues apace. I now have several independently gleaned indications that alternative (most likely coded) Teamster Pension Fund books do exist. Lenny Sands believes they exist. Sal D'Onofrio has heard rumors to that effect. Other sources have supplied rumors: a retired Chicago Mob man administers the books; Sam Giancana serves as the Pension Fund's "Chief Loan Approval Officer." As pervasive as these rumors are, I have nothing resembling corroboration. And of course I won't, until I can suborn a cosmetic borrower and gain some kind of literal access to the Fund itself.

And (on May 18th) I coerced a third informant into my stable. This man (a Dallas-based strip club operator/loanshark) is searching for a borrower to refer to Sal D'Onofrio and thence to Sam Giancana. I consider this man to be a major informant, because he previously referred a loan seeker to Giancana and the Pension Fund. He calls me at a pay phone near my apartment every Tuesday morning; I have given him money on several occasions. He fears me and respects me to just the right degree. Like Sal D'Onofrio, he has perpetual money troubles. I believe that, sooner or later, he will supply me with a potentially subornable borrower.

I also now have a fund of my own, i.e., an informant fund. In late May I secured an $81,000 robbery stash, one unreported to any police agency. I have paid Sal D'Onofrio $32,000 from this fund, strengthening my hold over him. Strange, but I had originally thought that Lenny Sands would be my most valued informant, but both Sal and the Dallas man have proven themselves more competent (or is it more desperate for money)? I blame you, Kemper. Setting Lenny up with Pete Bondurant and Hush-Hush was detrimental to my purposes. Lenny has seemed abstracted lately. He travels with Sal's junket tours and moonlights for Hush-Hush, and seems to have forgotten what I hold over him. Does he talk to your friend Miss Hughes? I'd be curious to know.

Per your instructions, I'm avoiding Court Meade and the listening post. Court and I have also formally ceased our assignment trade. I'm being careful, but I can't help dreaming utopian dreams. My essential dream? A John F. Kennedy Presidential Administration, with Robert Kennedy fulfilling his brother's anti-Mob mandate. God, Kemper, wouldn't that be heaven? Tell Mr. Kennedy he's in my prayers.

Yours,
WJL

DOCUMENT INSERT: 7/3/59. Personal note: Kemper Boyd to Robert F. Kennedy.

Dear Bob,

Just a short note to update you on the work of your anonymous colleague the "Chicago Phantom."

He's working hard, and I hope you find it gratifying that there's at least one human being on earth who hates Organized Crime as much as you do. But, as hard as he is working—and always within the legal guidelines you set down to me—he's getting scant results pursuing the possibility that alternative Pension Fund books exist. The Chicago Mob is a closed circle, and he hasn't been able to gain the inside information he hoped he would.

Moving along. Aren't you and Jack going to offer me some post–McClellan Committee employment?

Yours,
Kemper

DOCUMENT INSERT: 7/9/59. Personal Letter: Robert F. Kennedy to Kemper Boyd.

Dear Kemper,

Thanks for your note on the Phantom. It is good to know that an ex-seminarian FBI man shares my anti-Mob fervor, and what most impresses me about him is that he doesn't seem to want anything. (Jesuit sem boys are schooled in self-denial.) You, however, want everything. So, yes, Jack and I have an offer for you. (We'll discuss details and money later.)

We want you to stay with our organization and fill two positions. The first: traffic manager for the McClellan Committee's legal paperwork. We've disbanded, but like the Phantom, I'm still afire. Let's keep our anti-Mob and anti-Hoffa momentum going. You could be very helpful in seeing that our evidence gets into the proper investigatory hands. Secondly, Jack's going to announce his candidacy in January. He wants you to manage security for his primary campaigns and hopefully through to November. How about it?

Bob

DOCUMENT INSERT: 7/13/59. Personal note: Kemper Boyd to Robert F. Kennedy.

Dear Bob,

I accept. Yes, unlike the Phantom I want everything. Let's nail Jimmy Hoffa and elect Jack President.

Kemper

DOCUMENT INSERT: 7/27/59. Official FBI telephone call transcript: "Recorded at the Director's Request"/"Classified Confidential 1-A: Director's Eyes Only." Speaking: Director Hoover, Special Agent Kemper Boyd.

JEH: Good morning, Mr. Boyd.

KB: Good morning, Sir.

JEH: Your message mentioned good news.

KB: Excellent news, Sir. The brothers have hired me on a more or less permanent basis.

JEH: In what capacity?

KB: I'm to supervise the routing of McClellan Committee evidence to various grand juries and investigative agencies, and run security for Big Brother's campaign.

JEH: Little Brother remains persistent on the Hoffa front, then.

KB: He'll crucify the man sooner or later.

JEH: Catholics have been known to go overboard with the concept of crucifixion.

KB: Yes, Sir.

JEH: Let's continue on the Catholic recidivist front. Is Mr. Littell continuing to walk the straight and narrow?

KB: Yes, Sir.

JEH: SAC Leahy has airtelled me his Red Squad reports. He appears to be doing a satisfactory job.

KB: You frightened him last year, Sir. He just wants to make it through to his retirement. As I've told you, he's drinking quite a bit and is quite caught up in his affair with Helen Agee.

JEH: Allow me to use "affair" as a segue point. How is your liaison with Miss Laura Hughes progressing?

KB: I'd hardly call it a liaison, Sir.

JEH: Mr. Boyd, you are talking to the world's nonpareil bullshit artist and master of subterfuge. As good as you are at it, and you are brilliantly good, I am better. You are fucking Laura Hughes, and I'm sure you would fuck all the acknowledged Kennedy sisters and old Rose Kennedy herself if you thought it would ingratiate you with Jack. There. That said, what does Miss Hughes have to say about the family?

KB: She limits her anecdotes to her father, Sir. She's quite vitriolic on the topic of her father and his friends.

JEH: Continue.

KB: Apparently Joe and his old friend Jules Schiffrin secreted

Mexican illegals across the border during the '20s. They used the men as set construction help when Joe owned the RKO Studio. Joe and Schiffrin used the women sexually, hired them out as domestics, took half their pay for room-and-board, then turned them over to the Border Patrol and had them deported. Schiffrin took a number of the women back to Chicago with him and opened up a whorehouse that catered to mobsters and politicians exclusively. Laura says Joe made a movie surreptitiously at the whorehouse. It's Huey Long and two Mexican midgets with over-sized breasts.

JEH: Miss Hughes is a vivid anecdotist. What does she say about the brothers?

KB: She's guarded about them.

JEH: As you yourself are.

KB: I'm fond of them, yes.

JEH: I think you've set limits to your betrayal. I think you're unaware of how deeply enthralled you are with that family.

KB: I keep things compartmentalized, Sir.

JEH: Yes, I'll credit you with that. Now, let's move to your Cuban emigre compartment. Do you recall telling me that you had access to Cuban exile intelligence?

KB: Of course, Sir. I'll be sending a detailed summary report along soon.

JEH: Laura Hughes must be quite expensive.

KB: Sir?

JEH: Don't act disingenuous, Kemper. It's quite obvious the CIA has recruited you. Three paychecks, my lord.

KB: Sir, I keep things compartmentalized.

JEH: You certainly do, and far be it from me to upset those compartments. Good day, Mr. Boyd.

KB: Good day, Sir.

DOCUMENT INSERT: 8/4/59. Hush-Hush stringer report: Lenny Sands to Pete Bondurant.

Pete,

It's strange, but every homo in captivity seems to want to bite my tush these days, which is unusual because I've been playing some pretty square rooms. As you know, I've been working my wop gig with Sal D'Onofrio. We've been playing Reno, Vegas, Ta-

DOCUMENT INSERT: 7/27/59. Official FBI telephone call transcript: "Recorded at the Director's Request"/"Classified Confidential 1-A: Director's Eyes Only." Speaking: Director Hoover, Special Agent Kemper Boyd.

JEH: Good morning, Mr. Boyd.

KB: Good morning, Sir.

JEH: Your message mentioned good news.

KB: Excellent news, Sir. The brothers have hired me on a more or less permanent basis.

JEH: In what capacity?

KB: I'm to supervise the routing of McClellan Committee evidence to various grand juries and investigative agencies, and run security for Big Brother's campaign.

JEH: Little Brother remains persistent on the Hoffa front, then.

KB: He'll crucify the man sooner or later.

JEH: Catholics have been known to go overboard with the concept of crucifixion.

KB: Yes, Sir.

JEH: Let's continue on the Catholic recidivist front. Is Mr. Littell continuing to walk the straight and narrow?

KB: Yes, Sir.

JEH: SAC Leahy has airtelled me his Red Squad reports. He appears to be doing a satisfactory job.

KB: You frightened him last year, Sir. He just wants to make it through to his retirement. As I've told you, he's drinking quite a bit and is quite caught up in his affair with Helen Agee.

JEH: Allow me to use "affair" as a segue point. How is your liaison with Miss Laura Hughes progressing?

KB: I'd hardly call it a liaison, Sir.

JEH: Mr. Boyd, you are talking to the world's nonpareil bullshit artist and master of subterfuge. As good as you are at it, and you are brilliantly good, I am better. You are fucking Laura Hughes, and I'm sure you would fuck all the acknowledged Kennedy sisters and old Rose Kennedy herself if you thought it would ingratiate you with Jack. There. That said, what does Miss Hughes have to say about the family?

KB: She limits her anecdotes to her father, Sir. She's quite vitriolic on the topic of her father and his friends.

JEH: Continue.

KB: Apparently Joe and his old friend Jules Schiffrin secreted

Mexican illegals across the border during the '20s. They used the
men as set construction help when Joe owned the RKO Studio.
Joe and Schiffrin used the women sexually, hired them out as domestics, took half their pay for room-and-board, then turned
them over to the Border Patrol and had them deported. Schiffrin
took a number of the women back to Chicago with him and
opened up a whorehouse that catered to mobsters and politicians
exclusively. Laura says Joe made a movie surreptitiously at the
whorehouse. It's Huey Long and two Mexican midgets with over-
sized breasts.

JEH: Miss Hughes is a vivid anecdotist. What does she say
about the brothers?

KB: She's guarded about them.

JEH: As you yourself are.

KB: I'm fond of them, yes.

JEH: I think you've set limits to your betrayal. I think you're
unaware of how deeply enthralled you are with that family.

KB: I keep things compartmentalized, Sir.

JEH: Yes, I'll credit you with that. Now, let's move to your Cuban emigre compartment. Do you recall telling me that you had
access to Cuban exile intelligence?

KB: Of course, Sir. I'll be sending a detailed summary report
along soon.

JEH: Laura Hughes must be quite expensive.

KB: Sir?

JEH: Don't act disingenuous, Kemper. It's quite obvious the
CIA has recruited you. Three paychecks, my lord.

KB: Sir, I keep things compartmentalized.

JEH: You certainly do, and far be it from me to upset those
compartments. Good day, Mr. Boyd.

KB: Good day, Sir.

DOCUMENT INSERT: 8/4/59. Hush-Hush stringer report:
Lenny Sands to Pete Bondurant.

Pete,

It's strange, but every homo in captivity seems to want to bite
my tush these days, which is unusual because I've been playing
some pretty square rooms. As you know, I've been working my
wop gig with Sal D'Onofrio. We've been playing Reno, Vegas, Ta-

hoe, Gardena and some Lake Michigan cruise boats that feature gambling. I've been running into fruits galore, a regular Layfayette Escad (butt) drill of fruitness. 1)—Delores' Drive-In on Wilshire & La Cienega in L.A. employs all fruit carhops moon-lighting as male prosties. A frequent customer: Adlai (Lay?) Stevenson, 2-time prez'l candidate with pinko (Lavender?) lean-ings Mr. Hughes probably disapproves of. 2)—Dave Garroway of TV's Today Show was recently popped for honking young boys in NYC's Times Square. It was (hush?) hushed up, but "Dave the Slave" as he's known on the fag circuit was recently spotted at an all-male tomcat house outside Vegas. 3)—I ran into an off-duty Marine Corps lance-corporal in Tahoe. He said he knows a gunnery-sergeant running a fruit roller ring out of Camp Pendleton. It works this way: handsome young jarheads prowl Silverlake (The <u>Swish</u> Alps?) & the Sunset Strip & entrap homos. They don't put out & shake the fruits down for $. I called the gunnery sgt & wired him a C-note. He spilled on some celebrity fruitcakes the fruit roller ring glommed onto. Dig this: Walter Pidgeon (12" wang) bangs boys at a plushly-furnished fag crib in the Los Feliz district. Also, British matinee idol Larry (the Fairy?) Olivier recently took the law into his own hands when he groped a Marine MP at the Wiltern Theatre. Other homos ID'd by the Fruit Roller Corps include Danny Kaye, Liberace (big sur-prise), Monty Clift & conductor Leonard Bernstein. Hey, have you noticed I'm starting to write in the Hush-Hush style? More later.

Cheers,
Lenny

<u>DOCUMENT INSERT</u>: 8/12/59. Personal memorandum: Kemper Boyd to John Stanton. Marked: <u>CONFIDENTIAL/HAND POUCH DELIVER</u>.

John:

Some further thoughts on Pete Bondurant, the Tiger Kab stand and our elite Cadre.

The more I think about it, the more I see Tiger Kab as the po-tential hub for our Miami activities. I broached this thought to Fulo Machado (a former Castroite now bristlingly anti-Castro), the cabstand co-dispatcher and a close friend of contract agent Chuck Rogers. Machado shared my enthusiasm. He agreed to let Rogers take over as permanent cabstand dispatcher-boss. Fulo got approval from Jimmy Hoffa, who frankly prefers white men in supervisory positions. Fulo is now recruiting for us, on the cabstand payroll. Hoffa knows that cooperating with the Agency is smart business. He sees Cuba as our common cause, far-sighted for such a brutal and single-minded man.

I would like to propose Fulo Machado as the fifth member of our cadre. I would also like you to allow Rogers to hire Tomas Obregon, Wilfredo Olmos Delsol, Teofilio Paez and Ramon Gutierrez as full-time drivers. Although construction of the Blessington campsite is almost complete, we do not have exile re-cruits to train there. Until more deportees arrive, I think our men can be best utilized recruiting in Miami's Cuban community.

Per Bondurant. Yes, he (and I) screwed up on the Thomas Gordean matter. But, Bondurant is already employed as Jimmy Hoffa's ad hoc cabstand enforcer. He also secured a note from Santo Trafficante personally requesting that no Mafia reprisals be launched against Castro for nationalizing the Havana casinos. Bondurant forwarded this note to S. Giancana, C. Marcello and J. Rosselli. All three agree with Trafficante's reasoning. Again, brutal, short-sighted men are cooperating with the Agency out of a sense of common cause.

Bondurant is also the de-facto editor of a scandal magazine we can use as a counterintelligence organ. And, finally, I think he's the best man alive to run the campsite. They don't come any tougher, as I think any local rednecks who toy with him will discover.

What do you think of my proposals?

Kemper Boyd

DOCUMENT INSERT: 8/19/59. Personal memo: John Stanton to Kemper Boyd.

Kemper,

You batted 1000%. Yes, Machado can join the Cadre. Yes, Rog-ers can hire Delsol, Obregon, Paez and Gutierrez as drivers. Yes, have them recruit in Miami. Yes, hire Pete Bondurant to run Blessington, but have him retain his job with Howard Hughes as

hoe, Gardena and some Lake Michigan cruise boats that feature
gambling. I've been running into fruits galore, a regular
Layfayette Escad (butt) drill of fruitness. 1)—Delores' Drive-In
on Wilshire & La Cienega in L.A. employs all fruit carhops moon-
lighting as male prosties. A frequent customer: Adlai (Lay?)
Stevenson, 2-time prez'l candidate with pinko (Lavender?) lean-
ings Mr. Hughes probably disapproves of. 2)—Dave Garroway of
TV's Today Show was recently popped for honking young boys in
NYC's Times Square. It was (hush?) hushed up, but "Dave the
Slave" as he's known on the fag circuit was recently spotted at
an all-male tomcat house outside Vegas. 3)—I ran into an off-duty
Marine Corps lance-corporal in Tahoe. He said he knows a
gunnery-sergeant running a fruit roller ring out of Camp
Pendleton. It works this way: handsome young jarheads prowl
Silverlake (The Swish Alps?) & the Sunset Strip & entrap homos.
They don't put out & shake the fruits down for $. I called the
gunnery sgt & wired him a C-note. He spilled on some celebrity
fruitcakes the fruit roller ring glommed onto. Dig this: Walter
Pidgeon (12" wang) bangs boys at a plushly-furnished fag crib in
the Los Feliz district. Also, British matinee idol Larry (the
Fairy?) Olivier recently took the law into his own hands when he
groped a Marine MP at the Wiltern Theatre. Other homos ID'd by
the Fruit Roller Corps include Danny Kaye, Liberace (big surprise), Monty Clift & conductor Leonard Bernstein. Hey, have
you noticed I'm starting to write in the Hush-Hush style? More
later.

Cheers,
Lenny

DOCUMENT INSERT: 8/12/59. Personal memorandum:
Kemper Boyd to John Stanton. Marked: CONFIDENTIAL/HAND
POUCH DELIVER.

John:

Some further thoughts on Pete Bondurant, the Tiger Kab·
stand and our elite Cadre.
The more I think about it, the more I see Tiger Kab as the potential hub for our Miami activities. I broached this thought to
Fulo Machado (a former Castroite now bristlingly anti-Castro),

the cabstand co-dispatcher and a close friend of contract agent
Chuck Rogers. Machado shared my enthusiasm. He agreed to let
Rogers take over as permanent cabstand dispatcher-boss. Fulo
got approval from Jimmy Hoffa, who frankly prefers white men
in supervisory positions. Fulo is now recruiting for us, on the
cabstand payroll. Hoffa knows that cooperating with the Agency
is smart business. He sees Cuba as our common cause, far-
sighted for such a brutal and single-minded man.

I would like to propose Fulo Machado as the fifth member of
our cadre. I would also like you to allow Rogers to hire Tomas
Obregon, Wilfredo Olmos Delsol, Teofilio Paez and Ramon
Gutierrez as full-time drivers. Although construction of the
Blessington campsite is almost complete, we do not have exile recruits to train there. Until more deportees arrive, I think our
men can be best utilized recruiting in Miami's Cuban community.

Per Bondurant. Yes, he (and I) screwed up on the Thomas
Gordean matter. But, Bondurant is already employed as Jimmy
Hoffa's ad hoc cabstand enforcer. He also secured a note from
Santo Trafficante personally requesting that no Mafia reprisals
be launched against Castro for nationalizing the Havana casinos.
Bondurant forwarded this note to S. Giancana, C. Marcello and
J. Rosselli. All three agree with Trafficante's reasoning. Again,
brutal, short-sighted men are cooperating with the Agency out of
a sense of common cause.

Bondurant is also the de-facto editor of a scandal magazine we
can use as a counterintelligence organ. And, finally, I think he's
the best man alive to run the campsite. They don't come any
tougher, as I think any local rednecks who toy with him will
discover.

What do you think of my proposals?

Kemper Boyd

DOCUMENT INSERT: 8/19/59. Personal memo: John Stanton
to Kemper Boyd.

Kemper,

You batted 1000%. Yes, Machado can join the Cadre. Yes, Rogers can hire Delsol, Obregon, Paez and Gutierrez as drivers. Yes,
have them recruit in Miami. Yes, hire Pete Bondurant to run
Blessington, but have him retain his job with Howard Hughes as

well. Hughes is a potentially valuable ally, and we don't want him estranged from the Agency.

Good work, Kemper.

John

DOCUMENT INSERT: 8/21/59. Teletype report: Intelligence Division, Los Angeles Police Department, to SA Ward J. Littell, Chicago FBI. Sent "Private Mail Closure" to SA Littell's home address.

Mr. Littell,

Per your: telephone query on Salvatore D'Onofrio's recent Los Angeles activities. Be advised that:

The subject was spot-surveilled as a known underworld figure.

He was seen borrowing money from independent shylocks. Subsequent questioning of said shylocks revealed that the subject told them he would give them "big kickbacks" for referring "high-ticket" loan-seekers to him. The subject was also seen betting heavily at Santa Anita Racetrack. Surveilling officers heard the subject tell a just-met acquaintance: "I've blown half the wad my sugar daddy-o gave me already."

The subject was observed behaving in an erratic fashion during his gambling junket engagement at the Lucky Nugget Casino in Gardena. His junket companion, Leonard Joseph Seidelwitz (AKA Lenny Sands), also a known underworld figure, was seen entering various homosexual cocktail lounges. It should be noted that Seidelwitz's junket skits have become increasingly obscene and violently anti-homosexual.

Should you require further information, please let me know.

James E. Hamilton
Captain, Intelligence Division, Los Angeles Police Department

26

(Chicago, 8/23/59)

The amp made small talk boom. Littell picked up mobster amenities.

He wire-linked Mad Sal's parlor to his back bedroom closet. He overmiked the walls and got excessive voice vibrato.

The closet was hot and cramped. Littell sweated up his headset.

Talking: Mad Sal and "movie producer" Sid Kabikoff.

Sal went on a gambling binge. Littell confronted him with an LAPD teletype describing his actions. Sal said he blew the fifty-odd grand Littell gave him.

The train-locker heist stood unsolved—Sal didn't know where the cash came from. The tailor-shop bug blasted scuttlebutt on the topic— but Malvaso and the Duck remained clueless.

Then Jack Ruby called him.

And said, "I finally got a guy for Sal D. to goose up to the Pension Fund."

His informants were in sync—except for Lenny Sands.

Littell wiped off his headset. Kabikoff spoke, overamp loud: ". . . and Heshie says his blow-job tally's closing in on twenty thousand."

Mad Sal: "Sid, Sid the Yid. You didn't fly up from bumfuck Texas to schmooze the grapevine with me."

Kabikoff: "You're right, Sal. I was passing through Dallas and had a schmooze with Jack Ruby. Jack said, 'See Sal D. In Chicago. Sal's the man to see for a big vigorish loan from the Pension Fund.' Jack said,

'Sal's the middleman. He can fix you up with Momo and above. Sal's the man with access to the money.' "

Mad Sal: "You say 'Momo' like you think you're some kind of made guy."

Kabikoff: "It's like you talking Yiddish. Everybody wants to think they're connected. Everybody wants to be in the loop."

Mad Sal: "The Loop's downtown, you fat bagel bender."

Kabikoff: "Sal, Sal."

Mad Sal: "Sal, my big fat braciola, you lox jockey. Now you tell me the scheme, 'cause there's gotta be a scheme, 'cause you ain't tapping the Fund for your little bagel biter's bar mitzvah."

Kabikoff: "The scheme is smut movies, Sal. I've been shooting smut down in Mexico for a year now. T.J., Juarez, you can get talent cheap down there."

Mad Sal: "Get to it. Cut the fucking travelogue."

Kabikoff: "Hey, I'm setting a mood."

Mad Sal: "I'll mood you, you mameluke."

Kabikoff: "Sal, Sal. I've been shooting smut. I'm good at it. In fact, I'm shooting a picture down in Mexico in a couple of days. I'm using some strippers from Jack's club. It's going to be great—Jack's got some gorgeous gash working for him. Sal, Sal, don't look at me that way. What I want to do is this. I want to make legit horror and action pictures with smut-movie casts. I want to book the legit pictures into the bottom half of double features and film the pornographic shit to help defer costs. Sal, Sal, don't frown like that. It's a moneymaker. I'll cut Sam and the Pension Fund in for 50% of my profits *plus* my payback and vigorish. Sal, listen to me. This deal has got 'Moneymaker' scrawled across the fucking stars in fucking neon."

Silence—twenty-six seconds worth.

Kabikoff: "Sal, quit giving me the evil eye and listen. This deal is a moneymaker, and I want to keep it in the loop. You know, in a way, the Fund and me go way back. See, I heard Jules Schiffrin's the bookkeeper for the Fund. You know, for the real books that people outside the loop don't know about. See, I knew Jules way back when. Like feature back in the '20s even, when he was selling dope and using the profits to finance movies with RKO back when Joe Kennedy owned it. Tell Sam to remember me to Jules, okay? Just to remind him that I'm a trustworthy guy and I'm still in the loop."

Littell clamped down on his headphones. Jesus Fucking—

"Jules Schiffrin"/"Fund bookkeeper"/"real books."

Sweat seeped into the phones—voices fizzed out incoherent. Littell wrote the quotes down verbatim on the closet wall.

Kabikoff: "... so I'm flying back to Texas in a few days. Take my card, Sal. No, take two and give one to Momo. Business cards always make a good impression."

Littell heard goodbyes and a door slamming. He took off his headset and stared at the words on the wall.

Mad Sal walked up. Fat jiggled under his T-shirt.

"How'd I do? I had to give him some shit or he wouldn't've believed it was the real me."

"You were good. Now just watch your money. You won't get another dime from me until I've tapped into the Fund."

"What do I do about Kabikoff?"

"I'll call you inside a week and tell you whether or not to refer him to Giancana."

Sal belched. "Call me in L.A. I'm taking another junket out to Gardena."

Littell stared at the wall. He memorized each and every word and copied them over into his notebook.

27

(Gardena, 8/25/59)

L enny preened and smacked kisses. The junketeers ate it up—go Lenny, go, go, go.

Lenny hated fags. Lenny ate fags like Godzilla ate Tokyo. Lenny ate up the Lucky Nugget lounge.

Pete watched. Lenny spritzed shtick—fag Castro gropes fag Ike at the All-Fag Summit!!!!

"Fidel! Get your beard out of my crotch this instant! Fidel! What a biiiig Havana cigar you have!"

The junketeers loved it. The junketeers thought it was high-tone political satire.

Pete was bored. Stale shtick and stale beer—the Lucky Nugget was an armpit.

Dick Steisel sent him down. Dick had a grievance: Lenny's recent shit was too coarse to print. Hughes and Hoover loved it—but random homo slurs could deep-six *Hush-Hush*.

"Fidel! Pass me the K-Y, and we'll renew diplomatic relations! Fidel! My hemorrhoids are burning up like a United Fruit cane field!"

Kemper Boyd thought Lenny had talent. Kemper had a brainstorm: Let's dispense anti-Castro rage through *Hush-Hush*!

Lenny could write the stuff up. Lenny used to run bag to Batista—he knew the turf and the style, and Cuban Commies couldn't sue.

Lenny cranked shtick. Pete screened 10:00 p.m. daydreams. THAT MOMENT flashed by in Technicolor.

There's Tom Gordean, dead. There's Boyd, smiling. There's the suitcase full of UF stock.

They cut their deal right there beside the body. They rented a motel room, popped a shot off and rigged Gordean in a suicide pose. The stupid Key West cops bought the charade.

Boyd sold the stock. They made $131,000 apiece.

They met in D.C. for the split. Boyd said, "I can get you in on the Cuban thing, but it will probably take months. I'll have to explain the Gordean mission as a fuck-up."

Pete said, "Tell me more."

Boyd said, "Go back to L.A., do your *Hush-Hush* work and baby-sit Howard Hughes. I think Cuba and our combined connections can make us both rich."

He flew back and did it. He told Hughes he might have to go on leave soon.

Hughes was pissed. He unpissed him with a shitload of codeine.

The Cuban Cause had him drooling. He wanted in wicked bad. Santo Trafficante got booted out of Cuba last month, and spread the word that Castro should get butt-fucked for his Crimes Against Casino Profiteering.

Boyd called the cabstand a "potential launching pad." Boyd had this big throbbing wet dream: Jimmy Hoffa sells Tiger Kab to the Agency.

Chuck Rogers called him once a week. He said the cabstand was running trouble-free. Jimmy Hoffa sent him his monthly 5%—and he wasn't doing jackshit to earn it.

Boyd had Rogers hire his pet Cubans: Obregón, Delsol, Paez and Gutiérrez. Chuck fired the six *pro*-Castro geeks on the payroll—the fucks drove off hurling death threats.

Tiger Kab was now 100% anti-Castro.

Lenny ended his routine—with a riff on Ad*lay* Stevenson, King of the Turd Burglars. Pete ducked out behind a standing ovation.

The junketeers loved their Lenny. Lenny brushed through them like a prima diva slumming.

Perk-perk-perk—his feelers kicked in strong. He got this feeler-verified idea: Let's tail the little hump.

They drove north, with three cars between them. Lenny's Packard had a big whip antenna—Pete used it as a tracking device.

They took Western Avenue up to L.A. proper. Lenny swung west on Wilshire and north on Doheny. Traffic had thinned out—Pete hung back and cut the boy some slack.

Lenny turned east on Santa Monica. Pete grooved on the string of fruit bars—the 4-Star, the Klondike, some new ones. It was Memory Lane turf—he extorted every joint on the row back in his Sheriff's days.

Lenny hugged the curb, slooow cruising. He passed the Tropics, the Orchid and Larry's Lasso Room.

Lenny, don't wear your hate so fucking outré and naked.

Pete dawdled two car lengths back. Lenny pulled into the parking lot behind Nat's Nest.

Big Pete's got X-ray eyes. Big Pete's like Superman and the Green Hornet.

Pete circled the block and cruised through the lot. Lenny's car was parked by the back door.

Pete wrote out a note.

If you get lucky, send him home. Meet me at Stan's Drive-In at Sunset & Highland. I'll stay there until after bar closing time.

Pete B.

He stuck the note to Lenny's windshield. A fruit swished by and checked him out head-to-toe.

Pete ate in his car. He had two chili burgers, French fries and coffee.

Carhops skated by. They wore leotards, push-up bras and tights.

Gail Hendee used to call him a voyeur. It always jazzed him when women nailed his shit.

The carhops looked good. Hauling trays on skates kept them trim. The blonde lugging hot fudge sundaes looked like good shakedown bait.

Pete ordered peach pie à la mode. The blonde brought it to him. He saw Lenny walking up to the car.

He opened the passenger door and slid in.

He looked stoic. The prima diva was one tough little fruitfly.

Pete lit a cigarette. "You told me you were too smart to fuck with me. Does that still hold?"

"Yes."

"Is this what Kemper Boyd and Ward Littell have on you?"

" 'This'? Yeah, 'this' is."

"I don't buy it, Lenny, and I don't think Sam Giancana would care in the long run. I think I could call Sam right now and say, 'Lenny Sands fucks boys,' and he'd be shocked for a couple of minutes, then sit on the information. If Boyd and Littell tried to bluff you with that, I think you'd have the brains and the stones to call them on it."

Lenny shrugged. "Littell said he'd spill to Sam *and* the cops."

Pete dropped his cigarette in his water glass. "I'm not buying. Now, you see that brunette on skates over there?"

"I see her."

"I want you to tell me what Boyd and Littell squeezed you with by the time she gets over to that blue Chevy."

"Suppose I can't remember?"

"Then figure everything you've heard about me is true, and take it from there."

Lenny smiled, prima-diva-style. "I killed Tony Iannone, and Littell made me for it."

Pete whistled. "I'm impressed. Tony was a rough boy."

"Don't string me along, Pete. Just tell me what you're going to do about it."

"The answer's nothing. All this secret shit of yours goes no further."

"I'll try to believe it."

"You can believe that Littell and I go back awhile, and I don't like him. Boyd and me are friendly, but Littell's something else. I can't lean on him without pissing off Boyd, but if he ever gets too rowdy with you, let me know."

Lenny bristled and clenched up. "I don't need a protector. I'm not that kind of . . ."

Carhops zigzagged by. Pete rolled down his back window for some air.

"You've got credentials, Lenny. What you do in your spare time is your business."

"You're an enlightened guy."

"Thanks. Now, do you feel like telling me who or what you're snitching for Littell?"

"No."

"Just plain 'No'?"

"I want to keep working for you. Let me out of here with something, all right?"

Pete popped the passenger door latch. "No more fag stuff for *Hush-Hush*. From now on you write anti-Castro, anti-Commie stuff exclusively. I want you to write the pieces directly for the magazine. I'll get you some information, and you can make the rest of the shit up. You've been to Cuba, and you know Mr. Hughes' politics. Take it from there."

"Is that all?"

"Unless you want pie and coffee."

. . .

Lenny Sands fucks boys. Howard Hughes lends Dick Nixon's brother money.

Secret shit.

Big Pete wants a woman. Extortion experience preferred, but not mandatory.

The phone rang too fucking early.

Pete picked up. "Yeah?"

"It's Kemper."

"Kemper, shit, what time is it?"

"You're hired, Pete. Stanton's putting you on immediate contract status. You're going to be running the Blessington campsite."

Pete rubbed his eyes. "That's the official gig, but what's ours?"

"We're going to facilitate a collaboration between the CIA and organized crime."

28

(New York City, 8/26/59)

Joe Kennedy handed out presidential-sealed tie pins. The Carlyle suite took on a fake-presidential glow.

Bobby looked bored. Jack looked amused. Kemper pinned his necktie to his shirt.

Jack said, "Kemper's a thief."

Bobby said, "We came here to discuss the campaign, remember?"

Kemper brushed lint off his trousers. He wore a seersucker suit and white bucks—Joe called him an ice-cream jockey out of work.

Laura loved the outfit. He bought it with his stock-theft money. It was good summertime wedding attire.

Joe said, "FDR gave me those pins. I kept them because I knew I'd host a meeting like this one day."

Joe wanted an event. The butler had arranged hors d'oeuvres on a sideboard near their chairs.

Bobby pulled off his necktie. "My book will be published in hardback in February, about a month after Jack announces. The paperback edition will come out in July, right around the time of the convention. I'm hoping it will put the whole Hoffa crusade in perspective. We don't want Jack's association with the McClellan Committee to hurt him with labor."

Jack laughed. "That goddamn book's eating up all your time. You should get a ghost writer. I did, and I won the Pulitzer Prize."

Joe smeared caviar on a cracker. "I heard Kemper wanted his name deleted from the text. That's too bad, because then you could have titled it *The Ice Cream Jockey Within*."

Kemper toyed with his tie pin. "There's a million car thieves out there who hate me, Mr. Kennedy. I'd prefer that they not know what I'm doing."

Jack said, "Kemper's the furtive type."

Joe said, "Yes, and Bobby could learn from him. I've said it a thousand times before, and I'll say it a thousand times again. This hard-on for Jimmy Hoffa and the Mafia is horseshit. You may need those people to help you get out the vote one day, and now you're adding insult to injury by writing a book on top of chasing them via the goddamn Committee. Kemper plays his cards close to the vest, Bobby. You could learn from him."

Bobby chuckled. "Enjoy the moment, Kemper. Dad sides against his kids with outsiders present once in a decade."

Jack lit a cigar. "Sinatra's pals with those gangster guys. If we need them, we could use him as a go-between."

Bobby punched a chair cushion. "Frank Sinatra is a cowardly, finger-popping lowlife, and I will never make deals with gangster scum."

Jack rolled his eyes. Kemper took it as a cue to play middleman.

"I think the book has possibilities. I think we can distribute copies to union members during the primaries and notch some points that way. I've made a lot of law-enforcement connections working for the Committee, and I think we can forge an alliance of nominally Republican DAs by pushing Jack's anticrime credentials."

Jack blew smoke rings. "Bobby's the gangbuster, not me."

Kemper said, "You were on the Committee."

Bobby smiled. "I'll portray you heroically, Jack. I won't say that you and Dad were soft on Hoffa from the gate."

They all laughed. Bobby grabbed a handful of canapes.

Joe cleared his throat. "Kemper, we invited you to this session chiefly to discuss J. Edgar Hoover. We should discuss the situation now, because I'm hosting a dinner at Pavillon tonight, and I need to get ready."

"Do you mean the files that Hoover has on all of you?"

Jack nodded. "I was thinking specifically of a romance I had during the war. I've heard that Hoover's convinced himself that the woman was a Nazi spy."

"Do you mean Inga Arvad?"

"That's right."

Kemper snatched one of Bobby's canapes. "Mr. Hoover has that documented, yes. He bragged about it to me years ago. May I make a suggestion and clear the air about something?"

Joe nodded. Jack and Bobby pushed up to the edge of their chairs.

Kemper leaned toward them. "I'm sure Mr. Hoover knows that I went to work for the Committee. I'm sure he's disappointed that I haven't been in touch with him. Let me re-establish contact and tell him that I'm working for you. Let me assure him that Jack won't replace him as FBI director if he's elected."

Joe nodded. Jack and Bobby nodded.

"I think it's a smart, cautious move. And while I've got the floor, I'd like to bring up the Cuban issue. Eisenhower and Nixon have declared themselves anti-Castro, and I've been thinking that Jack should establish some anti-Fidel credentials."

Joe fiddled with his tie pin. "Everybody's starting to hate Castro. I don't see Cuba as a partisan issue."

Jack said, "Dad's right. But I've been thinking that I might send some Marines down if I'm elected."

Joe said, "*When* you're elected."

"Right. I'll send some Marines down to liberate the whorehouses. Kemper can lead the troops. I'll have him establish a spearhead in Havana."

Joe winked. "Don't forget your spear, Kemper."

"I won't. And seriously, I'll keep you posted on the Cuban front. I know some ex-FBI men with good anti-Castro intelligence."

Bobby brushed hair off his forehead. "Speaking of FBI men, how's the Phantom?"

"In a word, he's persistent. He's chasing those Pension Fund books, but he's not making much headway."

"He's starting to impress me as pathetic."

"Believe me, he's not."

"Can I meet him?"

"Not until he retires. He's afraid of Mr. Hoover."

Joe said, "We all are."

Everybody laughed.

The St. Regis was a slightly downscale Carlyle. Kemper's suite was a third the size of the Kennedys'. He kept a room at a modest hotel in the West 40s—Jack and Bobby contacted him there.

It was stifling hot outside. The suite was a perfect 68 degrees.

Kemper wrote a note to Mr. Hoover. He said, It's confirmed—if elected, Jack Kennedy won't fire you. He played a game of Devil's Advocate next—his standard post-Kennedy-conference ritual.

Doubters questioned his travels. Doubters questioned his complex allegiances.

He sprang logical traps on himself and evaded them brilliantly.

He was seeing Laura tonight—for dinner and a recital at Carnegie Hall. She'd ridicule the pianist's style and practice his showstopper piece endlessly. It was the Kennedy quintessence: Compete, but don't go public unless you can win. Laura was half-Kennedy and a woman— she possessed competitive spirit but no family sanction. Her half-sisters married skirt chasers and stayed faithful; Laura had affairs. Laura said Joe loved his girls but deep down considered them niggers.

He'd been with Laura for seven months now. The Kennedys had no inkling of the liaison. When an engagement was formalized, he'd tell them.

They would be shocked, then relieved. They considered him trustworthy and knew that he kept things compartmentalized.

Laura loved ballsy men and the arts. She was a solitary woman— with no real friends except Lenny Sands. She exemplified the pervasive Kennedy orbit: A mobbed-up lounge lizard gave Jack speech lessons and forged a bond with his half-sister.

That bond was borderline scary. Lenny might tell Laura things. Lenny might tell her grisly stories.

Laura never mentioned Lenny—despite the fact that he facilitated their meeting.

She probably talked to Lenny long-distance.

Lenny was volatile. An angry or frightened Lenny might say:

Mr. Boyd made Mr. Littell hit me. Mr. Boyd and Mr. Littell are nasty extortionists. Mr. Boyd got me my *Hush-Hush* job—which is very nasty employment.

His Lenny fears peaked in late April.

The Boynton Beach auditions revealed two security risks: a child molester and a homosexual pimp. CIA guidelines mandated termination. He took them out to the Everglades and shot them.

The pimp saw it coming and begged. He shot him in the mouth to cut his squeals off.

He told Claire he killed two men in cold blood. She responded with anti-Communist platitudes.

The pimp reminded him of Lenny. The pimp sparked Devil's Advocate impromptus that he couldn't lie his way out of.

Lenny could ruin him with Laura. Further coercion might backfire—Lenny was volatile.

There was no cut-and-dried Lenny solution. Easing Laura's loneliness might help—she'd be less inclined to contact Lenny.

He brought Claire up from Tulane and introduced her to Laura in mid-May. She was wowed by Laura—a big-city sophisticate ten years her senior. A friendship clicked—the two became great phone chums. Claire joined Laura for occasional weekends, full of concerts and museum tours.

He traveled to earn his three paychecks. His daughter kept his future fiancée company.

Laura told Claire her whole story. Claire inspired full disclosure. Claire was wowed—My Dad might be the President's secret brother-in-law someday.

He pimped for the maybe future President. Jack went through his little black book and sideswiped a hundred women inside six months. Sally Lefferts called Jack a de facto rapist. "He backs you into a corner and charms you until you're plain bushed. He convinces you that turning him down would make you just about the most worthless female who ever lived."

His little black book was near-depleted. Mr. Hoover might tell him to fix Jack up with FBI-plant call girls.

It might happen. If Jack's campaign flourished, Mr. Hoover might simply say, "DO IT."

The phone rang. Kemper caught it on the second ring.

"Yes?"

A long-distance line crackled. "Kemper? It's Chuck Rogers. I'm at the stand, and something happened I figured you should know about."

"What?"

"Those pro-Castro guys I fired cruised by last night and shot up the parking lot. We were damn lucky nobody got hurt. Fulo says he thinks they've got a hole-up someplace close."

Kemper stretched out on the couch. "I'll be down in a few days. We'll fix things up."

"Fix things how?"

"I want to convince Jimmy to sell the stand to the Agency. You'll see. We'll work something out with him."

"I say let's be decisive. I say we can't lose face in the Cuban community by letting Commie shitheads shoot at us."

"We'll send them a message, Chuck. You won't be disappointed."

. . .

Kemper let himself in with his key. Laura left the terrace doors open—concert lights had Central Park sparkling.

It was too simple and too pretty. He'd seen some Cuban reconnaissance shots that put it to shame.

They showed United Fruit buildings torched against a night sky. The pictures were pure raw spellbinding—

Something said:

Check Laura's phone bills.

He rifled her study drawers and found them. She'd called Lenny Sands eleven times within the past three months.

Something said, *Convince yourself decisively.*

It was most likely nothing. Laura never mentioned Lenny or acted in any way suspicious.

Something said, *Make her tell you.*

They sat down to martinis. Laura was sunburned from a long day shopping.

She said, "How long were you waiting?"

Kemper said, "About an hour."

"I called you at the St. Regis, but the switchboard man said you'd left already."

"I felt like a walk."

"When it's so grisly hot out?"

"I had to check my messages at the other hotel."

"You could have called the desk and asked for them."

"I like to show myself every so often."

Laura laughed. "My lover's a spy."

"Not really."

"What would my ersatz family think if they knew you had a suite at the St. Regis?"

Kemper laughed. "They'd consider it imitative, and wonder how I could afford it."

"I've wondered myself. Your FBI pension and salary from the family aren't that generous."

Kemper put a hand on her knees. "I've been lucky in the stock market. I've said it before, Laura. If you're curious, ask."

"All right, I will. You've never mentioned taking walks before, so why did you take a walk on the hottest day of the year?"

Kemper made his eyes mist over. "I was thinking of my friend Ward, and these walks we'd take along the lakefront in Chicago. I've been missing him lately, and I think I confused the Chicago lakefront climate with Manhattan's. What's the matter, you look sad."

"Oh, nothing."

She took the bait. His Chicago/friend talk nailed her.

"Horseshit, 'Oh, nothing.' Laura . . ."

"No, really, it's nothing."

"Laura . . ."

She pulled away from him. "Kemper, *it's nothing.*"

Kemper sighed. Kemper feigned perfect chagrined exasperation.

"No, it's not, it's Lenny Sands. Something I said reminded you of him."

She relaxed. She was buying the whole verbal package.

"Well, when you said you knew Lenny you were evasive, and I haven't brought him up because I thought it might bother you."

"Did Lenny tell you that he knew me?"

"Yes, and some other nameless FBI man. He wouldn't give me any details, but I could tell that he was afraid of you both."

"We helped him out of trouble, Laura. There was a price. Do you want me to tell you what that price was?"

"No. I don't want to know. It's an ugly world that Lenny lives in . . . and . . . well, it's just that *you* live in hotel suites and work for my quasi-family and God knows who else. I just wish we could be more open somehow."

Her eyes convinced him to do it. It was dead risky but the stuff of legends.

Kemper said, "Put on that green dress I gave you."

Pavillon was all silk brocade and candlelight. A pre-theater crowd came dressed to the nines.

Kemper slipped the maître d' a hundred dollars. A waiter led them back to the family's private room.

Time stood still. Kemper posed Laura beside him and opened the door.

Joe and Bobby looked up and froze. Ava Gardner put her glass down in slow motion.

Jack smiled.

Joe dropped his fork. His soufflé exploded. Ava Gardner caught chocolate sauce on the bodice.

Bobby stood up and balled his fists. Jack grabbed his cummerbund and pulled him back into his chair.

Jack laughed.

Jack said something like, "More balls than brains."

Joe and Bobby glowed—radioactively pissed.

Time stood still. Ava Gardner looked smaller than life.

29

(Dallas, 8/27/59)

He rented a suite at the Adolphus Hotel. His bedroom faced the south side of Commerce Street and Jack Ruby's Carousel Club.

Kemper Boyd always said DON'T SCRIMP ON SURVEILLANCE LODGING.

Littell watched the door with binoculars. It was 4:00 p.m. now, with no Live Striptease Girls until 6:00.

He'd checked Chicago-to-Dallas flight reservations. Sid Kabikoff flew in to Big D yesterday. His itinerary included a rent-a-car pickup.

His final destination was McAllen, Texas—smack on the Mexican border.

He flew down to make a smut film. He told Mad Sal that he was shooting it with Jack Ruby strippers.

Littell called in some sick time. He coughed when he talked to SAC Leahy. He purchased his airplane ticket under a pseudonym—Kemper Boyd always said COVER YOUR TRACKS.

Kabikoff told Mad Sal that "real" Fund books existed. Kabikoff told Mad Sal that Jules Schiffrin kept them. Kabikoff told Mad Sal that Jules Schiffrin knew Joe Kennedy.

It had to be a benign business acquaintance. Joe Kennedy cut a wide business swath.

Littell watched the door. An eyestrain headache slammed him. A crowd formed outside the Carousel Club.

Three muscular young men and three cheap-looking women. Sid Kabikoff himself—fat and sweaty.

They said hellos and lit cigarettes. Kabikoff waved his hands, effusive.

Jack Ruby opened the door. A dachshund ran out and took a shit on the sidewalk. Ruby kicked turds into the gutter.

The crowd moved inside. Littell visualized a rear-entry reconnaissance.

The back door was hook-and-eye latched, with slack at the door-doorjamb juncture. A dressing room connected to the club proper.

He walked across the street and hooked around to the parking lot. He saw one car only: a '56 Ford convertible with the top down.

The registration was strapped to the steering column. The owner was one Jefferson Davis Tippit.

Dogs yapped. Ruby should rename his dive the Carousel Kennel Club. Littell walked up to the door and popped the latch with his penknife.

It was dark. A crack of light cut through the dressing room.

He tiptoed up to the source. He smelled perfume and dog effluvia. The crack was a connecting door left ajar.

He heard overlapping voices. He made out Ruby, Kabikoff and a man with a deep Texas twang.

He squinted into the light. He saw Ruby, Kabikoff and a uniformed Dallas cop—standing by a striptease runway.

Littell craned his neck. His view expanded.

The runway was packed. He saw four girls and four boys, all buck naked.

Ruby said, "J.D., are they not gorgeous?"

The cop said, "I'm partial to women exclusively, but all in all I got to agree."

The boys stroked erections. The girls oohed and aahed. Three dachshunds cavorted on the runway.

Kabikoff giggled. "Jack, you're a better talent scout than Major Bowes and Ted Mack combined. 100%, Jack. I'm talking no rejections for these lovelies."

J.D. said, "When do we meet?"

Kabikoff said, "Tomorrow afternoon, say 2:00. We'll meet at the coffee shop at the Sagebrush Motel in McAllen, and drive across to the shoot from there. What an audition! All auditions should go so smooth!"

One boy had a tattooed penis. Two girls were knife-scarred and bruised. A dogfight erupted—Ruby yelled, "No, children, no!"

Littell ordered a room-service dinner: steak, Caesar salad and Glenlivet. It was a robbery-stash splurge—and more Kemper's style than his.

Three drinks honed his instincts. A fourth made him certain. A night-cap made him call Mad Sal in L.A.

Sal pitched a tantrum: I need money, money, money.

Littell said, I'll try to get you some.

Sal said, Try hard.

Littell said, It's on. I want you to refer Kabikoff for a Fund loan. Call Giancana and set up a meeting. Call Sid in thirty-six hours and con-firm it.

Sal gulped. Sal oozed fear. Littell said, I'll try to get you some money.

Sal agreed to do it. Littell hung up before he started begging again.

He didn't tell Sal that his robbery stash was down to eight hundred dollars.

Littell left a 2:00 a.m. wake-up call. His prayers ran long—Bobby Ken-nedy had a large family.

The drive took eleven hours. He hit McAllen with sixteen minutes to spare.

South Texas was pure hot and humid. Littell pulled off the highway and inventoried his backseat.

He had one blank-paged scrapbook, twelve rolls of Scotch tape and a Polaroid Land Camera with a long-range Rolliflex zoom lens. He had forty rolls of color film, a ski mask and a contraband FBI flashing roof light.

It was a complete mobile evidence kit.

Littell eased back into traffic. He spotted the Sagebrush Motel: a horseshoe-shaped bungalow court right on the main drag.

He pulled in and parked in front of the coffee shop. He put the car in neutral and idled with the air conditioner on.

J.D. Tippit pulled in at 2:06. His convertible was overloaded: six smut kids up front and camera gear bulging out of the trunk.

They entered the coffee shop. Littell snapped a zoom-lens shot to capture the moment.

The camera whirred. A picture popped out and developed in his hand in less than a minute.

Amazing—

Kabikoff pulled up and beeped his horn. Littell snapped a shot of his rear license plate.

Tippit and the kids walked out with soft drinks. They divided up between the cars and headed out southbound.

Littell counted to twenty and followed them. Traffic was light—they drove surface streets for five minutes and hit the border crossing one-two-three.

A guard waved them through. Littell popped a location-setting snapshot: two cars en route to Federal violations.

Mexico was a dusty extension of Texas. They drove through a long string of tin-shack villages.

A car squeezed in behind Tippit. Littell used it for protective cover.

They drove up into scrub hills. Littell fixed on J.D.'s foxtail-tipped antenna. The road was half dirt and half blacktop—gravel chunks snapped under his tires.

Kabikoff turned right at a sign: Domicilio de Estado Policía. "State Police Barracks"—an easy translation.

Tippit followed Kabikoff. The road was all dirt—the cars sent dust clouds swirling. They fishtailed up a little rock-clustered mountain.

Littell stayed on the main road and kept going. He saw some tree cover fifty yards up the mountainside—a thick clump of scrub pines to shoot from.

He pulled over and parked off the road. He packed his gear into a duffel bag and covered his car with scrub branches and tumbleweeds.

Echoes bounced his way. The "shoot" was just over the top of the hill.

He followed the sounds. He lugged his gear up a 90-degree grade.

The crest looked down on a dirt-packed clearing. His vantage point was goddamn superb.

The "barracks" was a tin-roofed shack. State Police cars were parked beside it—Chevys and old Hudson Hornets.

Tippit was lugging film cans. Fat Sid was bribing Mexican cops. The smut kids were checking out some handcuffed women.

Littell crouched behind a bush and laid out his gear. His zoom lens brought him into close-up range.

He saw wide-open barracks windows and mattresses set up inside. He saw black shirts and armbands on the cops.

The cop cars had leopard-skin seat covers. The women wore prison ID bracelets.

The crowd dispersed. The blackshirts uncuffed the women. Kabikoff hauled equipment inside the barracks.

Littell went to work. The heat had him weaving on his knees. His zoom lens got him in very close.

He snapped pictures and watched them develop. He placed them in neat rows inside his duffel bag.

He snapped smut girls entwined on a mattress. He snapped Sid Kabikoff coercing lesbian action.

He snapped obscene insertions. He snapped dildo gang bangs. He snapped smut boys whipping Mexican women bloody.

The Polaroid cranked out instant closeups. Fat Sid was color-glossy indicted:

For Suborning Lewd Conduct. For Felony Assault. For Filming Pornography for Interstate Sales, in violation of nine Federal statutes.

Littell shot his way through forty rolls of film. Sweat soaked the ground all around him.

Sid Kabikoff was evidence-snapped:

White slaving. Violating the Mann Act. Serving as an accessory to kidnapping and sexual battery.

Snap!—a snack break—cops baking tortillas on a prowl-car roof.

Snap!—a prisoner tries to escape. Snap!/snap!/snap!—two cops catch her and rape her.

Littell walked back to his car. He started sobbing just over the border.

He taped the pictures into his scrapbook and calmed down with prayers and a half-pint. He found a good spot to perch: the access-road curb, a half-mile north of the border.

The road ran one way. It was the only route to the Interstate. It was nicely lit—you could almost read license plate numbers.

Littell waited. Air-conditioner blasts kept him from dozing. Midnight came and went.

Cars drove by law-abidingly slow—the Border Patrol gave tickets all the way to McAllen.

Headlights swept by. Littell kept scanning rear plates. The air-conditioner freeze was making him sick.

Kabikoff's Cadillac passed—

Littell slid out behind him. He slapped the cherry light to his roof and pulled on his ski mask.

The light swirled bright red. Littell hit his high beams and tapped the horn.

Kabikoff pulled over. Littell boxed him in and walked up to his door.

Kabikoff screamed—the mask was bright red with white devil's horns.

Littell remembered making threats.

Littell remembered his final pitch: YOU'RE GOING TO TALK TO GIANCANA WIRED UP.

He remembered a tire iron.

He remembered blood on the dashboard.

He remembered begging God PLEASE DON'T LET ME KILL HIM.

30

(Miami, 8/29/59)

"**C**ocksucking Commie fuckers shoot up my cabstand! First it's Bobby Kennedy, now it's these Red Cuban shitheels!"

Heads turned their way—Jimmy Hoffa talked loud. Lunch with Jimmy was risky—the hump sprayed food and coffee routinely.

Pete had a headache. The Tiger Kab hut stood catty-corner from the diner—the fucking tiger stripes were giving him eyestrain.

He turned away from the window. "Jimmy, let's talk—"

Hoffa cut him off. "Bobby Kennedy's got every shithead grand jury in America chasing me. Every shithead prosecutor in creation wants to go the rump route with James Riddle Hoffa."

Pete yawned. The red-eye from L.A. was brutal.

Boyd gave him marching orders. Boyd said, Make a deal for the cabstand—I want an intelligence/recruiting hub in Miami. More banana boats are due. When the Blessington campsite flies, we'll need more driver spots for our boys.

A waitress brought fresh coffee—Hoffa had spritzed his cup empty. Pete said, "Jimmy, let's talk business."

Hoffa dumped in cream and sugar. "I didn't think you flew in for that roast-beef sandwich."

Pete lit a cigarette. "The Agency wants to lease a half-interest in the cabstand. There's lots of Agency and Outfit guys that are starting to feel pretty strongly about Cuba, and the Agency thinks the stand would be a good place to recruit out of. And there'll be shitloads of Cuban exiles coming into Miami, which means big business if the stand goes anti-Castro in a big way."

Hoffa belched. "What do you mean, 'lease'?"

"I mean you get a guaranteed $5,000 a month, in cash, plus half the gross profits, plus an Agency freeze with the IRS, just in case. My 5% comes off the top, you'll still have Chuck Rogers and Fulo running the stand, and I'll be coming by to check in regularly, once I start my contract job down in Blessington."

Jimmy's eyes flashed—$$$$$. "I like it. But Fulo said Kemper Boyd's tight with the Kennedys, which I do not like one iota."

Pete shrugged. "Fulo's right."

"Could Boyd get me off the hook with Bobby?"

"I'd say his loyalties are stretched too thin to try it. With Boyd, you take the bitter with the sweet."

Hoffa dabbed a stain off his necktie. "The bitter is those Commie humps who shot up my cabstand. The sweet is that if you took care of them, I'd be inclined to accept that offer."

Pete huddled up a crew at the dispatch hut. Solid guys: Chuck, Fulo, Boyd's man Teo Paez.

They pulled chairs up in front of the air conditioner. Chuck passed a bottle around.

Fulo sharpened his machete on a rock. "I understand that all six of the traitors have vacated their apartments. I have been told that they have moved into a place called a 'safe house.' It is near here, and I believe it is Communisto-financed."

Chuck wiped spit off the bottle. "I saw Rolando Cruz checking out the stand yesterday, so I think it's safe to say we're under surveillance. A cop friend of mine got me their license numbers, so if you say we go trawling, that'll help."

Paez said, "Death to traitors."

Pete ripped the air conditioner off the wall. Steam billowed out.

Chuck said, "I get it. You want to give them a target."

Pete closed down the stand—in full public view. Fulo called an air-conditioner repairman. Chuck radioed his drivers and told them to return their cabs *now.*

The repairman came and removed the wall unit. The drivers

dropped off their taxis and went home. Fulo put a sign on the door: Tiger Kab Temporarily Closed.

Teo, Chuck and Fulo went trawling. They drove their radio-rigged off-duty cars, devoid of tiger stripes and Tiger Kab regalia.

Pete snuck back to the hut. He kept the lights off and the windows locked. The dump was brutal hot.

A four-way link hooked in: the three cars to the Tiger Kab switchboard. Fulo prowled Coral Gables; Chuck and Teo prowled Miami. Pete connected in to them via headset and hand microphone.

It was ass-scratching, sit-still duty. Chuck hogged the airwaves with a long rant on the Jew-Nigger Pantheon.

Three hours slogged by. The trawl cars kept a line of chatter up. They did not see hide-nor-fucking-hair of the pro-Castro guys.

Pete dozed with his headset on. The thick air had him wheezing. Crosstalk gibberish sparked these little two-second nightmares.

His *standard* nightmares: charging Jap infantry and Ruth Mildred Cressmeyer's face.

Pete dozed to radio fuzz and wah-wah feedback. He thought he heard Fulo's voice: "Two Car to base, urgent, over."

He jerked awake and snapped his mike on. "Yeah, Fulo."

Fulo clicked on. Traffic noise filtered in behind his voice.

"I have Rolando Cruz and César Salcido in sight. They stopped at a Texaco station and filled up two Coca-Cola bottles with gasoline. They are driving toward the stand rapidly."

"Flagler or 46th?"

"46th Street. Pete, I think they—"

"*They're going to torch the cabs.* Fulo, you stay behind them, and when they turn into the lot, you box them in. *And no shooting, do you understand?*"

"*Sí,* I comprende. Ten-four, over."

Pete dumped his headset. He saw Jimmy's nail-topped baseball bat on a shelf above the switchboard.

He grabbed it and ran out to the parking lot. The sky was pitch black and the air oooozed moisture.

Pete swung the bat and worked out some kinks. Headlights bounced down 46th—low, like your classic Cubano hot rod.

Pete crouched by a tiger-striped Merc.

The taco wagon swung into the lot.

Fulo's Chevy glided in sans lights and engine, right behind it.

Rolando Cruz got out. He was packing a Molotov cocktail and matches. He didn't notice Fulo's car—

Pete came up behind him. Fulo flashed his brights and backlit Cruz plain as day.

Pete swung the bat full-force. It ripped into Cruz and snagged on his ribs.

Cruz screamed.

Fulo piled out of his car. His high beams strafed Cruz, spitting blood and bone chips. César Salcido piled out of the spicmobile, wet-your-pants scared.

Pete yanked the bat free. The Molotov hit the pavement AND DID NOT SHATTER.

Fulo charged Salcido. The taco wagon idled at a high pitch—good cover noise.

Pete pulled his piece and shot Cruz in the back. The high beams caught Fulo's part of the show.

He's duct-taping Salcido upside the face. He's got the taco-wagon trunk wide open. There's dervish-quick Fulo, uncoiling the parking-lot hose.

Pete dumped Cruz in the trunk. Fulo nozzle-sprayed his entrails down a sewer hole.

It was dark. Cars cruised up and down Flagler, oblivious to the whole fucking thing.

Pete grabbed the Molotov. Fulo parked his Chevy. He was lip-syncing numbers over and over—Salcido probably spilled the safe-house address.

The taco wagon was metal-flake purple and fur-upholstered—a cherry '58 Impala niggered up.

Fulo took the wheel. Pete got in back. Salcido tried to scream through his gag.

They hauled down Flagler. Fulo yelled an address: 1809 Northwest 53rd. Pete turned on the radio full-blast.

Bobby Darin sang "Dream Lover," earsplitting loud. Pete shot Salcido in the back of the head—exploding teeth ripped the tape off his mouth.

Fulo drove VERY VERY SLOW. Blood dripped off the dashboard and seats.

They gagged on muzzle smoke. They kept the windows up to seal the smell in.

Fulo made left turns and right turns. Fulo made nice directional signals. They drove their coffin wagon out to the Coral Gables Causeway—VERY VERY SLOW.

They found an abandoned mooring dock. It ran thirty yards out into the bay.

It was deserted. No winos, no lovebirds, no late-night fly casters.

They got out. Fulo put the car in neutral and pushed it up on the planks. Pete lit the Molotov and tossed it inside.

They ran.

Flames hit the tank. The Impala exploded. The planking ignited kindling-quick.

The dock whoooshed into one long fireball. Waves lapped up and fizzed against it.

Pete coughed his lungs out. He tasted gunsmoke and swallowed blood off the dead men.

The dock caved in. The Impala sunk down on some reef rocks. Steam hissed off the water for a solid minute.

Fulo caught his breath. "Chuck lives nearby. I have a key to his room, and I know he has equipment we can use."

They found suppressor-rigged revolvers and bulletproof vests. They found Chuck's Tiger Kab parked at the curb.

They grabbed the guns and vested up. Pete hot-wired the cab.

Fulo drove a hair too fast. Pete thought of old Ruth Mildred all the way.

The house looked decrepit. The door looked un-breakdownable. The place was bracketed by palm groves—the only crib on the block.

The front room lights were on. Gauze curtains covered the window. Shadows stood out well defined.

They crouched beside the porch, just below the windowsill. Pete made out four shadow shapes and four voices. He pictured four men boozing on a couch FACING THE WINDOW.

Fulo seemed to pick up on his brainwaves. They checked their vests and their guns—four revolvers and twenty-four rounds total.

Pete counted off. They stood up and fired on "three"—straight through the window.

Glass exploded. Silencer thunks faded into screams.

The window went down. The curtains went down. They had *real* targets now—Commie spics up against a blood-spattered wall.

The spics were flailing for guns. The spics were wearing shoulder holsters and cross-draw hip rigs.

Pete vaulted the sill. Return fire hit his vest and spun him backward.

Fulo charged. The Commies fired wide; the Commies fired near-

death erratic. They got off un-suppressed big-bore pistol shots—
tremendously goddamn loud.

A vest deflection sent Fulo spinning. Pete stumbled up to the couch
and emptied both his guns at ultraclose range. He notched head hits
and neck hits and chest hits, and took in a big gasping breath of gray
viscous something—

A diamond ring rolled across the floor. Fulo grabbed it and kissed it.

Pete wiped blood from his eyes. He saw a stack of plastic-wrapped
bricks by the TV set.

White powder was leaking out. He knew it was heroin.

31

(Miami, 8/30/59)

Kemper read by the Eden Roc pool. A waiter freshened his coffee every few minutes.

The *Herald* ran it in banner print: "Four Dead in Cuban Dope War."

The paper reported no witnesses and no leads. The assumed perpetrators were "Rival Cuban Gangs."

Kemper linked events.

John Stanton sends him a report three days ago. It states that President Eisenhower's Cuban-Ops budget has come in way below the requested amount. It states that Raúl Castro is funding a Miami propaganda drive through heroin sales. It states that a distribution shack/safe house has already been established. It states that the heroin gang includes two ex-Tiger Kab men: César Salcido and Rolando Cruz.

He tells Pete to clear an Agency/cabstand lease deal. He assumes that Jimmy Hoffa will stipulate vengeance on the men who shot up the stand. He knows that Pete will wreak that vengeance with considerable flair.

He has dinner with John Stanton. They discuss his report at length.

John says, Heroin-pushing Commies are tough competition. Ike will kick loose more money later on, but now is now.

More banana boats are due. Anti-Castro zealots will swarm Florida. Hothead ideologues will join the Cause and demand action.

Rampant factionalism might reign. The Blessington campsite is still short of operational and their Elite Cadre is still untested. The dope clique might usurp their strategic edge and financial hegemony.

Kemper said, Heroin-pushing Commies *are* tough. You can't compete with men who'll go that far.

He made Stanton say it himself. He made Stanton say, Unless we exceed their limits.

Talk went ambiguous. Abstractions passed as facts. A euphemistic language asserted itself.

"Self-budgeted," "autonomous" and "compartmentalized." "Need-to-know basis" and "Ad hoc utilization of Agency resources."

"Co-opting of Agency-aligned pharmacological sources on a cash-and-carry basis."

"Without divulging the destination of the merchandise."

They sealed the deal with elliptical rhetoric. He let Stanton think he devised most of the plan.

Kemper skimmed his newspaper. He noticed a page-four banner: "Grisly Causeway Discovery."

An arsoned Chevy collapses a rickety wooden dock. Rolando Cruz and César Salcido are along for the dip.

"Authorities believe the killings of Cruz and Salcido may be connected to the slayings of four other Cubans in Coral Gables late last night."

Kemper flipped back to page one. A single paragraph stood out.

"Although the dead men were rumored to be heroin traffickers, no narcotics were found on the premises."

Be prompt, Pete. And be as smart and farsighted as I think you are.

Pete showed up early, carrying a large paper bag. He didn't check out the women by the pool or walk up with his usual swagger.

Kemper slid a chair out. Pete saw the *Herald* on the table, folded to the page-one headline.

Kemper said, "You?"

Pete put the bag on the table. "Fulo and me."

"Both jobs?"

"That's right."

"What's in the bag?"

"Fourteen point six pounds of uncut heroin and a diamond ring."

Kemper fished the ring out. The stones and gold setting were beautiful.

Pete poured a cup of coffee. "Keep it. To consecrate my marriage to the Agency."

"Thanks. I may be popping a question with it soon."

"I hope she says yes."

"Did Hoffa?"

"Yeah, he did. He put a condition on the deal, which I fucking fulfilled, as I'm sure you already know."

Kemper nudged the bag. "You could have unloaded it yourself. I wouldn't have said anything."

"I'm along for the ride. And for now, I'm enjoying it too much to fuck with your agenda."

"Which is?"

"Compartmentalization."

Kemper smiled. "That's the biggest word I've ever heard you use."

"I read books to teach myself English. I must have read the Webster's Unabridged Dictionary at least ten times."

"You're an immigrant success story."

"Go fuck yourself. But before you do it, tell me my official CIA duties."

Kemper twirled the ring. Sunlight made the diamonds twinkle.

"You'll be nominally running the Blessington campsite. There's some additional buildings and a landing strip going up, and you'll be supervising the construction. Your assignment is to train Cuban refugees for amphibious sabotage runs into Cuba, and to funnel them to other training sites, the cabstand and Miami for general gainful employment."

Pete said, "It sounds too legal."

Pool water splashed at their feet. His suite upstairs was almost Kennedy-sized.

"Boyd—"

"Eisenhower has given the Agency a tacit mandate to covertly undermine Castro. The Outfit wants their casinos back. Nobody wants a Communist dictatorship ninety miles off the Florida coast."

"Tell me something I don't know."

"Ike's budget allocation came in a little low."

"Tell me something interesting."

Kemper poked the bag. A tiny trace of white powder puffed out.

"I have a plan to refinance our part of the Cuban Cause. It's *implicitly* Agency-vetted, and I think it will work."

"I'm getting the picture, but I want to hear you say it."

Kemper lowered his voice. "We link up with Santo Trafficante. We utilize his narcotics connections and my Cadre as pushers, and sell this dope, Santo's dope and all the other dope we can get our hands on in Miami. The Agency has access to a poppy farm in Mexico, and we can buy some fresh-processed stuff there and have Chuck Rogers fly it in. We finance the Cause with the bulk of the money, give Trafficante a percentage as operating tribute and send a small percentage of the dope into Cuba with our Blessington men. They'll distribute it to our on-island contacts, who will sell it and use the money to purchase weapons. Your specific job is to supervise my Cadre and make sure they sell only to Negroes. You make sure my men don't use the dope themselves, and keep their profit skim at a minimum."

Pete said, "What's our percentage?" Pete's response was utterly predictable.

"We don't take one. If Trafficante approves my plan, we'll get something much sweeter."

"Which you're not going to talk about now."

"I'm meeting Trafficante in Tampa this afternoon. I'll let you know what he says."

"And in the meantime?"

"If Trafficante says yes, we'll get going in a week or so. In the meantime, you drive down to Blessington and check things out, meet the Cadre and tell Mr. Hughes that you'll be taking some prolonged Florida vacations."

Pete smiled. "He'll be pissed."

"You know how to get around that."

"If I'm working up in Miami, who's going to run the campsite?"

Kemper got out his address book. "Go see Guy Banister in New Orleans. Tell him we need a tough white man to run the camp, a shitkicker type who can handle the crackers around Blessington. Guy knows every right-wing hardcase on the Gulf Coast. Tell him we need a man who's not too insane and willing to move to South Florida."

Pete wrote Banister's number on a napkin. "You're convinced all this is going to work?"

"I'm certain. Just pray that Castro doesn't go pro-U.S."

"That's a nice sentiment from a Kennedy man."

"Jack would appreciate the irony."

Pete cracked his knuckles. "Jimmy thinks you should tell Jack to put a leash on Bobby."

"Never. And I want to see Jack elected President, and I will not intercede with the Kennedys to help Hoffa. I keep—"

"—things compartmentalized, I know."

Kemper held the ring up. "Stanton wants me to help influence Jack's Cuban policy. We want the Cuban problem to extend, Pete. Hopefully into a Kennedy administration."

Pete cracked his thumbs. "Jack's got a nice head of hair, but I don't see him as President of the United States."

"Qualifications don't count. All Ike did was invade Europe and look like your uncle."

Pete stretched. His shirttail slid up over two revolvers.

"Whatever happens, I'm in. This is too fucking big to pass up."

His rent-a-car came with a discreet dashboard Jesus. Kemper slipped the ring over its head.

The air conditioner died outside Miami. A radio concert kept his mind off the heat.

A virtuoso played Chopin. Kemper replayed the scene at Pavillon.

Jack played peacemaker and smoothed things out. Old Joe's freeze thawed out nicely. They stayed for one awkward drink.

Bobby sulked. Ava Gardner was plain flummoxed. She had no idea what the scene meant.

Joe sent him a note the next day. It closed with, "Laura deserves a man with balls."

Laura said "I love you" that night. He made up his mind to propose to her at Christmas.

He could afford Laura now. He had three paychecks and two full-time hotel suites. He had a low six-figure bank-account balance.

And if Trafficante says yes . . .

Trafficante understood abstract concepts.

"Self-budgeted," "autonomous" and "compartmentalized" amused him.

"Agency-aligned pharmacological sources" made him laugh outright.

He wore a nubby-weave silk suit. His office was turned out in blond-wood Danish modern.

He loved Kemper's plan. He grasped its political thrust immediately.

The meeting extended. A yes-man served anisette and pastry.

Their conversation veered in odd directions. Trafficante critiqued the Big Pete Bondurant myth. The paper bag by Kemper's feet went unmentioned.

The yes-man served espresso and Courvoisier VSOP. Kemper marked the moment with a bow.

"Raúl Castro sent this in, Mr. Trafficante. Pete and I want you to have it, as a symbol of our good faith."

Trafficante picked up the bag. He smiled at the weight and gave it a few little squeezes.

Kemper swirled his brandy. "If Castro is eliminated as a direct or indirect result of our efforts, Pete and I will insure that your contribution is recognized. More importantly, we'll try to convince the new Cuban ruler to allow you, Mr. Giancana, Mr. Marcello and Mr. Rosselli to regain control of your casinos and build new ones."

"And if he refuses?"

"We'll kill him."

"And what do you and Pete want for all your hard work?"

"If Cuba is liberated, we want to split 5% of the profits from the Capri and Nacional Hotel casinos in perpetuity."

"Suppose Cuba stays Communist?"

"Then we get nothing."

Trafficante bowed. "I'll talk to the other boys, and of course, my vote is 'Yes.' "

32

(Chicago, 9/4/59)

Littell picked up static interference. House-to-car bug feeds always ran rough.

The signal fed in from fifty yards out. Sid Kabikoff wore the microphone taped to his chest.

Mad Sal had arranged the meet. Sam G. insisted on his apartment—take it or leave it. Butch Montrose met Sid on the stoop and walked him up to the left-rear unit.

The car was broiling. Littell kept his windows up as a sound filter.

Kabikoff: "You've got a nice place, Sam. Really, what a choice pad-à-terre."

Littell heard scratching noise—flush on the mike. He visualized the at-the-source cause.

Sid's stretching the tape. He's rubbing those bruises I inflicted down in Texas.

Giancana's voice came in garbled. Littell thought he heard Mad Sal mentioned.

He tried to find Sal this morning. He cruised his collection turf and couldn't locate him.

Montrose: "We know you knew Jules Schiffrin back in the old days. We know you know some of the boys, so it's like you're recommended from the gate."

Kabikoff: "It's like a loop. If you're in the loop you're in the loop."

Cars boomed by. Windowpanes rattled close to the feed-in.

Kabikoff: "Everybody in the loop knows I'm the best smut man in the West. Everybody knows Sid the Yid's got the best-looking cunt and the boys with the putzes down to their knees."

Giancana: "Did Sal tell you to ask for a Pension Fund loan specific?"

Kabikoff: "Yeah, he did."

Montrose: "Is Sal in some kind of money trouble, Sid?"

Traffic noise covered the signal. Littell timed it at six seconds even.

Montrose: "I know Sal's in the loop, and I know the loop's the loop, but I'm also saying my own little love shack got burglarized in January, and I got rammed for fourteen Gs out of my fucking golf bag."

Giancana: "And in April some friends of ours got clouted for eighty grand they had stashed in a locker. You see, right after these hits Sal started spending new money. Butch and me just put it together, sort of circumstantially."

Littell went lightheaded. His pulse went haywire.

Kabikoff: "No. Sal wouldn't do something like that. No ... he wouldn't. . . ."

Montrose: "The loop's the loop and the Fund's the Fund, but the two ain't necessarily the same thing. Jules Schiffrin's with the Fund, but that don't mean he'd roll over for a loan for you, just because you shared spit way back when."

Giancana: "We sort of think somebody's trying to get at Jimmy Hoffa and the Fund through a goddamn fake loan referral. We talked to Sal about it, but he didn't have nothing to say."

Littell hyperventilated. Spots blipped in front of his eyes.

Montrose: "So, did somebody approach you? Like the Feds or the Cook County Sheriff's?"

Thumps hit the mike. It had to be Sid's pulse racing. Fizzing noise overlapped the thumps—Sid's sweat was clogging up the feeder ducts.

The feed sputtered and died. Littell hit his volume switch and got nothing but a static-fuzzed void.

He rolled down the windows and counted off forty-six seconds. Fresh air cleared his head.

He can't rat me. I wore that ski mask both times that we talked.

Kabikoff stumbled out to the sidewalk. Wires dangled from the back of his shirt. He got his car and punched it straight through a red light.

Littell hit the ignition. The car wouldn't start—his bug feed ran down the battery.

．　．　．

He knew what he'd find at Sal's house. Four rye-and-beers prepared him to break in and see it.

They tortured Sal in his basement. They stripped him and tied him to a ceiling pipe. They hosed him and scorched him with jumper cables.

Sal didn't talk. Giancana didn't know the name Littell. Fat Sid didn't know his name or what he looked like.

They might let Sid go back to Texas. They might or might not kill him somewhere down the line.

They left a cable clamped to Sal's tongue. Voltage burned his face shiny black.

Littell called Fat Sid's hotel. The desk clerk said Mr. Kabikoff was in—he had two visitors just an hour ago.

Littell said, "Don't ring his room." He stopped for two more rye-and-beers and drove over to see for himself.

They left the door unlocked. They left Sid in an overflowing bathtub. They tossed a plugged-in TV set on top of him.

The water was still bubbling. Electric shock had burned Kabikoff bald.

Littell tried to weep. The rye-and-beers left him too anesthetized.

Kemper Boyd always said DON'T LOOK BACK.

33

(New Orleans, 9/20/59)

Banister supplied files and pedigree notes. Pete narrowed his prospects down to three men.

His hotel room was file-inundated. He was deluged with rap sheets and FBI reports—the far-right South captured on paper.

He got the scoop on Ku Klux Klan klowns and neo-Nazis. He learned about the National States Rights Party. He marveled at the pointy-heads on the FBI payroll—half the Klans in Dixie were Fed-saturated.

Fed snitches were out castrating and lynching. Hoover's only real concern was KKK mail-fraud minutiae.

A fan ruffled loose file papers. Pete stretched out on the bed and blew smoke rings.

Memo to Kemper Boyd:

The Agency should bankroll a Blessington KKK Klavern. Dirt-poor crackers surrounded the campsite—spic haters all. Klan hijinks would help keep them diverted.

Pete skimmed rap sheets. His instinct held—his prospects were the least rabid of the bunch.

Said prospects:

The Reverend Wilton Tompkins Evans, ex-con radio messiah. Pastor of the "Anti-Communist Crusade of the Air," a weekly short-wave tirade. Spanish-fluent; ex-paratrooper; three convictions for statutory rape. Banister's assessment: "Capable and tough, but perhaps too anti-papist to work with Cubans. He'd be a great training officer and I'm sure he'd relocate, because he can broadcast his radio program from anywhere. Close friend of Chuck Rogers."

Douglas Frank Lockhart, FBI informant/Klansman. Ex–Tank Corps sergeant; ex–Dallas cop; ex–gun runner to rightist dictator Rafael Trujillo. Banister's assessment: "Probably the premier Klan informant in the South and a true Klan zealot in his own right. Tough and brave, but easily led and somewhat volatile. Seems to bear no grudge against Latins, especially if they are strongly anti-Communist."

Henry Davis Hudspeth, the South's #1 purveyor of hate propaganda. Spanish fluent; expert in Hapkido jujitsu. World War II fighter ace, with thirteen Pacific Theater kills. Banister's assessment: "I like Hank, but he can be stubborn and untowardedly vitriolic. He's currently working for me as liaison between my exile camp near Lake Pontchartrain and Dougie Frank Lockhart's nearby Klan Klavern. (I own the property both are situated on.) Hank's a good man, but maybe not suited for second banana status."

All three men were close by. All three had party plans tonight—the Klan was torching a cross out by Guy's camp.

Pete tried to notch a pre-cross-burn nap. He was running on a sleep deficit—his past three weeks were hectic and exhausting.

Boyd glommed some morphine from that CIA-friendly dope ranch. He flew it out to L.A. and gave it to Mr. Hughes.

Mr. Hughes appreciated the gift. Mr. Hughes said, Go back to Miami with my best wishes.

He didn't tell him, I'm an anti-Red crusader now. With 5% of two casinos forever—if Cuba trades Red for Red, White and Blue.

Boyd sold the deal to Trafficante. Marcello, Giancana and Rosselli agreed to it. Boyd figured they'd make at least fifteen million dollars per year per man.

He told Lenny to swamp *Hush-Hush* with anti-Castro propaganda. He told him to shitcan the sex jive that Hughes and Hoover drooled for. He told him to make up some skank to keep them happy.

L.A. was prison camp. Florida was summer camp.

He flew back to Miami quicksville. Boyd had signed on the Mexican dope farm as the Cadre's chief supplier. Chuck flew the initial fourteen pounds down for cutting and brought it back at six times the weight. Trafficante kicked loose bonuses for all Cadre personnel.

He gave them sawed-offs and magnums. He gave them bulletproof vests and cherry-new dopemobiles.

Fulo chose a '59 Eldo. Chuck picked out a sweet Ford Vicky. Delsol,

Obregón, Paez and Gutiérrez were all Chevy men. Spics will be spics—they tacoized their sleds from stem to stern.

He met the men and got to know them.

Gutiérrez was solid and quiet. Delsol was calculating and smart. His cousin Obregón seemed borderline dicey—Boyd was starting to think he might run light on balls.

Santo Junior retooled his Miami dope biz. The Cadre took over the nigger trade exclusively.

Boyd decreed free tastes for all local junkies. The Cadre dispensed a shitload of shit totally gratis. Chuck renamed Niggertown Cloud Nine.

They segued from philanthropy to business. They prowled and sold their shit in two-man cars—with shotguns in plain sight. A junkie tried to rob Ramón Gutiérrez. Teo Paez cut him down with rat-poison-laced buckshot.

Santo Junior was pleased so far. Santo proffered the #1 Cadre Commandment: You may not sample the merchandise. Pete proffered Commandment #2: If you use Big "H," I will kill you.

Miami was Crime Heaven. Blessington was the Pearly Gates To.

The campsite took up fourteen acres. The installation included two bunkhouses, a weapons shed, an operations hut, a drill field and a landing strip. A dock and speedboat launch site were still in construction.

Cadre recruiters jumped the gun and sent some training prospects down. Local crackers took offense at the spic squatters on their turf. Pete hired some unemployed Klansmen to work on the dock. The move facilitated a temporary peace—Klavernites and exiles were toiling together.

Fourteen squatters were now in residence. More exiles were fleeing Cuba every day. There were more CIA campsites pending—with forty-odd projected by mid-1960.

Castro would survive—just long enough to make Boyd and him rich.

The cross burned high and wide. Pete caught the glow from half a mile out.

A dirt road veered off the highway. Signs pointed the way: "Nigger stay out!" "KKK—White Man Unite!"

Bugs popped in through his air vents. Pete swatted them off. He saw a barbed-wire fence and Klansmen at parade rest.

They wore white robes and hoods with purple piping. Dig their kanine kompanions: sheet-swaddled Doberman pinschers.

Pete flashed Banister's gate pass. The pointy-heads checked him out and waved him in.

He parked beside some trucks and went strolling. The cross lit up a segregated pine-forest clearing.

Cubans milled around on one side. Whites boogie-woogied on the other. A row of sign-plastered trailers divided them.

On his left: Klan bake sale, Klan rifle range, vendors hawking Klan regalia. On his right: the Blessington campsite duplicated.

Pete strolled the redneck side. Pointy-hoods bobbed his way—Hey, man, where's your sheet?

Bugs buzz-bombed the cross. Rifle shots and target pings overlapped. The humidity was close to 100%.

Nazi armbands went for $2.99. Jew rabbi voodoo dolls—a steal at 3 for $5.00.

Pete walked by the trailers. He saw a sandwich board propped up against an old Airstream: "WKKK—Rev. Evans Anti-Communist Crusade."

A hi-fi speaker was bolted to the axle. Sound sputtered out—pure crackpot gibberish.

He looked in the window. He saw twenty-odd cats pissing, shitting and fucking. A tall geek was screaming into a microphone. A cat was clawing some short-wave wires, about to get French-fried to kingdom come.

Pete scratched one prospect and kept walking. All the Caucasoids wore hoods—he couldn't match Hudspeth or Lockhart to their mug shots.

"Bondurant! Down here!"

It was Guy Banister's voice, booming up from below ground level.

A hatch snapped out of the dirt. A periscope thingamajig popped up and wiggled.

Guy had rigged himself a fucking bomb shelter.

Pete dropped down into it. Banister pulled the hatch shut behind him.

The space was twelve-by-twelve square. *Playboy* pinups covered the walls. Guy had socked in a shitload of Van Camp's pork & beans and bourbon.

Banister retracted the telescope. "You looked lonesome all by yourself with no sheet."

Pete stretched. His head grazed the ceiling.

"It's sweet, Guy."

"I thought you might like it."

"Who's paying for it?"

"Everybody."

"Which means?"

"Which means I own the land, and the Agency put up the buildings. Carlos Marcello donated three hundred thousand for guns, and Sam Giancana put up some money to buy off the State Police. The Klan folks pay to enter and sell their wares, and the exiles work four hours a day on a road crew and kick back half their pay to the Cause."

An air cooler hummed full-blast. The shelter was a goddamn igloo.

Pete shivered. "You said Hudspeth and Lockhart would be here."

"Hudspeth was arrested for grand theft auto this morning. It's his third offense, so there's no bail. Evans is here, though. And he's not a bad fellow, if you stay off the topic of religion."

Pete said, "He's got to be psycho. And Boyd and I don't want psychos working for us."

"But you'll employ more presentable psychos."

"Have it your way. And if it's Lockhart by default, I want a few minutes alone with him."

"Why?"

"Any man who parades around in a sheet has got to be able to convince me he can keep things compartmentalized."

Banister laughed. "That's a big word for a guy like you, Pete."

"People keep telling me that."

"That's because you're dealing with a higher type of person now that you're Agency."

"Like Evans?"

"Point taken. But offhand, I'd say that that man has stronger anti-Communist credentials than you do."

"Communism's bad for business. Don't pretend it's anything more than that."

Banister hooked his thumbs in his belt. "If you think that makes you sound worldly, you're sadly mistaken."

"Yeah?"

Banister smiled, too smug to live. "Accepting Communism is synonymous with promoting Communism. Your old nemesis Ward Littell accepts Communism, and a friend of mine in Chicago told me that Mr. Hoover is building a pro-Communist profile on him, based on his inactions more than his actions. You see where being worldly and accepting gets you when the chips are down?"

Pete cracked some knuckles. "Go get Lockhart. You know what Boyd wants, so explain it to him. And from here on in, shitcan the lectures."

Banister flinched. Banister started to open his mouth.

Pete went "Boo!"

Banister scurried out the hatch, double-time quick.

The silence and cold air felt sweet. The canned goods and liquor looked tasty. The wallpaper looked sweet—Miss July, especially.

Say the Russians drop the A-bomb. Say you hole up here. Cabin fever might set in and convince you the women were real.

Lockhart dropped down the hatch. He wore a soot-flecked sheet, cinched by a gunbelt and two revolvers.

He had bright red hair and freckles. His drawl was deep Mississippi.

"The money I like, and the move to Florida don't bother me. But that no-lynching rule has gotta go."

Pete backhanded him. Dougie Frank stayed upright—give him an A-plus for balance.

"Man, I have killed oversized white trash for less than what you just did!"

Punk bravura: Give him a C-minus.

Pete slapped him again. Lockhart pulled his right-hand piece—but didn't aim it.

Nerves: A-plus. Sense of caution: B-minus.

Lockhart wiped blood off his chin. "I like Cubans. I might stretch my racial-exclusion policy and let your guys into my Klavern."

Sense of humor: A-plus.

Lockhart spit a tooth out. "Give *me* something. Let me know that I'm more than just some punching bag."

Pete winked. "Mr. Boyd and I might put you on a bonus plan. And the Agency just might give you your own Ku Klux Klan."

Lockhart did a Stepin Fetchit shuffle. "Thank you, massah! If you was pro-Klan like a real white man, I'd kiss the hem of your sheet!"

Pete kicked him in the balls.

He went down—but didn't yelp or whimper. He cocked his gun—but didn't fire.

The man got passing marks overall.

34

(New York City, 9/29/59)

The cab crawled uptown. Kemper balanced paperwork on his briefcase.

A graph showed primary-election states divided by county. Intersecting columns listed his law-enforcement contacts.

He checkmarked the presumed Democrats. He crossed out the presumed GOP hardcases.

It was boring work. Joe should simply buy Jack the White House.

Traffic slogged. The cabbie rode his horn. Kemper played a game of Devil's Advocate—dissembling practice never hurt.

Bobby questioned his constant Florida sojourns. His response verged on indignation.

"I'm in charge of forwarding McClellan Committee evidence, aren't I? Well, the Sun Valley case sticks in my craw, and Florida's a state that Jack needs to carry in the general election. I've been down there talking to some disaffected Teamsters."

The cab passed through slums. Ward Littell crashed his thoughts.

They hadn't talked or corresponded in a month. The D'Onofrio killing made a brief news splash and stayed unsolved. Ward didn't call or write to comment.

He should contact Ward. He should find out if Mad Sal's death derived from his work as Ward's informant.

The driver stopped at the St. Regis. Kemper paid him and quick-walked to the desk.

A clerk hovered. Kemper said, "Would you buzz my suite and ask Miss Hughes to come down?"

The clerk slipped on a headset and punched his switchboard. Kemper checked his watch—they were running way late for dinner.

"She's on the phone, Mr. Boyd. There's a conversation in progress."

Kemper smiled. "It's probably Miss Hughes and my daughter. They talk for hours at hotel rates."

"It's Miss Hughes and a man, actually."

Kemper caught himself clenching. "Let me have your headset, would you?"

"Wellllll . . ."

Kemper slipped him ten dollars.

"Wellllll . . ."

Kemper went to fifty. The clerk palmed it and handed him his earphones.

Kemper slipped them on. Lenny Sands was talking, very high-pitched and fey.

". . . As terrible as he was he's dead, and he worked for the drunk just like me. There's the drunk and the brute, and now the brute has me writing these preposterous articles about Cuba. I can't name names, but Laura, my God . . ."

"You don't mean my friend Kemper Boyd?"

"He's not the one I'm afraid of. It's the brute and the drunk. You never know what the drunk will do, and I haven't heard from him since Sal was killed, which is driving me absolutely stark raving . . ."

It was compartmental turbulence. It would have to be contained.

35

(Chicago, 10/1/59)

aves pushed litter up on the shore. Paper cups and cruise-boat programs shredded at his feet.

Littell kicked them out of his way. He passed the spot where he dumped the Montrose B&E swag.

Garbage then, garbage now.

He had three dead men to light candles for. Jack Ruby seemed to be safe—he called the Carousel Club once a week to hear his voice.

Sal resisted torture. Sal never said "Littell" or "Ruby." Kabikoff knew him only as a cop in a ski mask.

"Mad Sal" and "Sid the Yid"—the nomenclature used to amuse him. Bobby Kennedy allegedly loved Mob nicknames.

He was sloughing off his Phantom reports. He was sloughing off his Red Squad work. He told SAC Leahy that God and Jesus Christ were leftists.

He cut Helen down to one night a week. He quit calling Lenny Sands. He had two constant companions: Old Overholt and Pabst Blue Ribbon.

A sodden magazine washed in. He saw a picture of Jack Kennedy and Jackie.

Kemper said the senator had hound blood. Kemper said Bobby held his marriage vows sacred.

Fat Sid said their dad knew Jules Schiffrin. Schiffrin kept the real Pension Fund books—liquor couldn't numb that one fact.

Littell cut over to Lake Shore Drive. His feet ached and his trouser cuffs spilled sand.

It was dusk. He'd been walking due south for hours.

His bearings clicked in. He saw that he was three blocks away from a real live destination.

He walked over and knocked on Lenny Sands' door. Lenny opened up and just stood there.

Littell said, "It's over. I won't ask anything else of you."

Lenny stepped closer. Words roared out in one long string.

Littell heard "stupid" and "worthless" and "coward." He looked Lenny in the eyes and stood there while he roared himself breathless.

36

(Chicago, 10/2/59)

Kemper snapped the lock with his Diners Club card. Lenny didn't learn that it takes deadbolts to keep rogue cops out.

Littell never learned that INFORMANTS DON'T RETIRE. He observed the retirement gala from the street—and saw Ward soak up abuse like a true flagellant.

Kemper closed the door and stood in the dark. Lenny walked to the A&P ten minutes ago, and should return within half an hour.

Laura learned not to press embarrassing topics. She never mentioned that call at the St. Regis.

Kemper heard footsteps and key sounds. He moved toward the light switch and screwed the silencer to his piece.

Lenny walked in. Kemper said, "It's not over."

A shopping bag fell. Glass broke.

"You don't talk to Laura or Littell again. You work *Hush-Hush* for Pete. You find out everything you can about the Pension Fund books and report exclusively to me."

Lenny said, "No."

Kemper hit the switch. The living room lit up—antique-overfurnished and *très, très* effete.

Lenny blinked. Kemper shot the legs off an armoire. The crash shattered bone china and crystal.

He shot up a bookcase. He shot a Louis Fourteen couch into stuffing wads and wood chips. He shot up a hand-painted Chippendale wardrobe.

Sawdust and muzzle smoke swirled. Kemper got out a fresh clip.

Lenny said, "Yes."

DOCUMENT INSERT: 10/5/59. Hush-Hush magazine article. Written by Lenny Sands, under the pseudonym Peerless Politicopundit.

CANCEROUS CASTRO COMMUNISTICALLY CALCIFIES CUBA WHILE HEROIC HERMANOS HUNGER FOR HOMELAND!

He's been in power a scant ten months, but the Free World already has the number of that slogan-slamming, stogie-stinking strongman Fidel Castro!

Castro ousted the democratically-elected anti-Communist Cuban Premier Fulgencio Batista last New Year's day. The bombastic bushy-bearded beatnik bard promised land reforms, social justice and pickled plantains on every plate—the standard stipends of welfare-waffled Commie commissars. He took over a small bastion of freedom 90 miles off U.S. shores, pathologically picked the pockets of patriotic patriarchs, nauseously "nationalized" U.S.-owned hotel-casinos, fried the friendly fragrant fields of the United Fruit Company and generally absconded with astronomical amounts of America's most peon-protecting, Commie-constraining export: money!!!

Yes, kats and kittens, it all comes down to divinely-deigned dollops of dollars—U.S., of course, those gorgeously garlanded greenbacks replete with pulsatingly powerful Presidential portraits, caricatures captivating in their corrosive condemnation of Communism!!!

Item: the beatnik bard bamboozled beleaguered bellhops at the formerly swank Nacional and Capri hotels in Havana, nastily nationalized their tips and rapidly replaced them with a regiment of rowdy Red regulators—bandy-legged bantamweight bandidos who also serve as crucifyingly-corrupt craps croupiers!

Item: fruit fields frantically french-fried! Peons passionately protected by America's altruistically-altered egalitarian economy are now welfare-wilted, pauper-periled Red Recidivists grubbing for Commie compensation!

Item: Raul "The Tool" Castro has flamboyantly flooded Florida with hellishly horrific, hophead-hazarding amounts of the demonically deadly "Big H": Heroin!!! He's bent on needle-notching vast legions of Cuban immigrant slaves: zorched-out zombies to spread the cancerous Castro gospel between bouts of Heroin-hiatused, junkie-junketeered euphoria!

Item: there's a growing number of Cuban exiles and home-grown American patriots who take egregious exception to the beatnik brothers' broadside of bamboozlement. Right now they're recruiting in Miami and South Florida. These men are tantaliz-ingly tough tigers who have earned their orange-and-black—not Red—stripes in the jungles of Castro's jam-packed, jerry-rigged jails. Every day, more and more men like them are arriving on America's shores, anxious to sing the mellifluous melodies of "My Country 'Tis of Thee."

This reporter talked to an American named "Big Pete," a dedi-cated anti-Communist currently training anti-Castro guerrillas. "It all comes down to patriotism," Big Pete said. "Do you want a Communist dictatorship 90 miles off our shores or not? I don't, so I've joined the Cuban Freedom Cause. And I'd like to extend an invitation to all Cuban exiles and native-born men of Cuban descent. Join us. If you're in Miami, ask around. Local Cubans will tell you we mean business."

Item: with men like Big Pete on the job, Castro should be con-sidering a new career. Hey! I know a few coffeehouses in L.A.'s way-out Venice West who could use a gone beatnik poet like Fidel! Hey, Fidel! Can you dig it, Daddy-O?

Remember, dear reader, you heard it first here: off the rec-ord, on the Q.T. and very Hush-Hush.

DOCUMENT INSERT: 10/19/59. Personal Note: J. Edgar Hoo-ver to Howard Hughes.

Dear Howard,

I greatly enjoyed Peerless Politicopundit's piece in the October 5th issue of Hush-Hush. It was, of course, far-fetched, but sub-tract the purple prose and what remains is politically substantive.

Lenny Sands has certainly adapted to the Hush-Hush style. And as a fledgling propagandist he shows promise. I found the subliminally-planted plugs for the Tiger Kab Kompany to be a nice little aside to the cognoscenti, and especially enjoyed the lofty sentiments expressed by our pragmatist friend Pierre Bondurant.

All in all, a most salutary issue.

Warmest regards,
Edgar

DOCUMENT INSERT: 10/30/59. Summary Report: John Stanton to Kemper Boyd. Marked: <u>CONFIDENTIAL/HAND POUCH DELIVER</u>.

Dear Kemper,

A short note to keep you advised of some recent policy decisions. You remain hard to reach, so I'm sending this to you via courier.

First off, our superiors are now more than ever convinced that the Castro problem will extend. Although the President's latest allocation came in low, we have every hope that Castro's powers of persistence will loosen up the White House pursestrings. To paraphrase our friend Peerless Politicopundit: "Nobody wants a Communist dictatorship ninety miles from our shores." (I wish I could write reports like he writes yellow journalism).

Mr. Dulles, Deputy Director Bissell and selected Cuban-expert case officers are beginning to plan for an exile invasion in late 1960 or early 1961. It is assumed that by that date the Agency will have a pool of at least ten thousand well-trained U.S.-based exile troops to draw from, and that public opinion will be strongly on our side. The general idea is to launch an amphibious assault force, backed by air cover, from Gulf Coast campsite-launch sites. I'll keep you abreast as plans develop further. And you keep at our friend Jack. If this plan stays on hold until after January 20, 1961, there's a chance he'll be the man to approve it or scrap it.

Since we last spoke, eleven more "Banana Barges" have landed in Florida and Louisiana. Regional case officers have been assigned immigrant caseloads and are dispersing the men to various campsites. Many who decline regular Agency assistance will be heading to Miami. I'll be curious to see if our Cadre latches on to any of them. As I'm sure you know, the Blessington site is now ready to house troops formally. I have approved the hiring of Douglas Frank Lockhart to run the camp, and I think it is time to rotate our Cadre on a Miami-business, Blessington-training axis. Put Pete Bondurant and Chuck Rogers on this immediately, and have Bondurant pouch deliver a report to me inside six weeks.

Per our Cadre's Miami "business," and in keeping with our elliptical way of discussing it, I'll state that I'm glad profits seem to be growing and that the agreement you reached with our Agency-friendly source in Mexico seems to be flourishing. I envision a time when our superiors will vet this "business" as good common sense, but until anti-Castro rancor or whatever reaches that point I must stress absolute compartmentalization and secrecy. Mr. Trafficante's participation must remain secret, and I would not want it generally known that Mr. S. Giancana and Mr. C. Marcello have also contributed to the Cause.

Keep me posted, and burn this communique.

All best,
John

DOCUMENT INSERT: 11/1/59. Summary Report: Kemper Boyd to Robert F. Kennedy.

Dear Bob,

I had a talk with James Dowd, the head of the Organized Crime Section at the Department of Justice. (I knew him when he was with the U.S. Attorney's Office.) As a courtesy, I had sent Mr. Dowd carbons of the paperwork I forwarded to various grand juries seeking Hoffa evidence, and now that courtesy seems to be bringing results.

As you know, the Landrum-Griffin Labor Reform Bill passed Congress, so now the Republican-dominated Justice Department has a clear "Get Hoffa" mandate. Dowd has deployed investigators and assistant-counsels to grand jury investigatory bodies in Ohio, Louisiana and Florida. The McClellan Committee spawned Landrum-Griffin; everyone knows it. Dowd has seen the political light and has decided to concentrate his energy on our Sun Valley evidence. (He thinks the two missing witnesses—Gretzler and Kirpaski—give it a moral weight.) As of 10/25/59, he had assigned six men to serve with three south Florida grand juries. They are actively seeking disgruntled Teamsters who had purchased Sun Valley property. Dowd thinks the "Get Hoffa" process will be grindingly attenuated, which suits our political purposes to a degree.

My strongest sense is that we do not want "Get Hoffa" rancor to go too bi-partisan, and we do want Jack to stand out as the anti-labor corruption candidate. Dowd told me that he expects Hoffa to barnstorm primary election states and deluge voters with anti-Kennedy sentiment, and I think this may play into our hands. As hard as he sometimes tries to hide it, under duress Hoffa always comes off as a psychopathic thug. We want the Teamsters to endorse the Republican candidate. We want Richard Nixon to take Hoffa's money and sidestep labor corruption as an issue in the general election. That said, I think it is imperative that Jack redouble his efforts to woo legitimate labor leaders and convince them that he differentiates them from Hoffaites.

I'm shifting my emphasis now to the primaries. The Kennedy crime fighter image has impressed many of my normally-Republican law enforcement acquaintances, and I'm working my way through Wisconsin, New Hampshire and West Virginia county by county. Your local organizations seem sound, and I've told each and every volunteer I've met to keep their ears down for Hoffa barnstorming scuttlebutt.

More later. Write your book; I think it could be a valuable campaign tool.

Yours,
Kemper

DOCUMENT INSERT: 11/9/59. Memorandum: Robert F. Kennedy to Kemper Boyd.

Kemper,

Thanks for the note. You're starting to think politically, and I think your Hoffa-Republican observations were quite astute. I'm glad the Justice Department has focused on Sun Valley, which I have always considered our strongest Hoffa case.

I've always believed that illegally-procured Pension Fund money (the "Spooky" 3 million) financed Hoffa's Sun Valley investment, and that Hoffa skimmed a large amount off the top. Some Pension Fund leads and/or intelligence on the possibility of "Real" Pension Fund books would do us a lot of good now. What's the Chicago Phantom been doing? You've always portrayed this anonymous Jesuit crusader as quite a worker, but you haven't forwarded a Phantom report to me in months.

Bob

DOCUMENT INSERT: 11/17/59. Note: Kemper Boyd to Robert F. Kennedy.

Dear Bob,

I agree. We certainly could use some Pension Fund leads now. The Phantom is working hard, but he's run up against one brick wall after another. And keep in mind, he's an FBI agent with a full load of regular duties. He's persisting, but as I've said before, it's very slow going.

Kemper

DOCUMENT INSERT: 12/4/59. FBI Field Surveillance Report: Chicago Special Agent-in-Charge Charles Leahy to J. Edgar Hoover. Marked: EXTREMELY CONFIDENTIAL/DIRECTOR'S EYES ONLY.

Sir,

Per your request, agents co-opted from the Sioux City Office have kept SA Ward J. Littell under spot surveillance since 9/15/59. He has not been observed in the vicinity of Celano's Tailor Shop, and he has apparently refrained from covert anti-Organized Crime activity. He has not been seen with SA Kemper Boyd, and the (11/20/59 initiated) tap on his home telephone indicates that he speaks only to Helen Agee, with occasional calls to his ex-wife Margaret. He does not call or receive calls from his daughter Susan, and since the 11/20/59 tap initiation date SA Boyd has not called him.

Littell's work performance has steadily deteriorated. This decline was in effect before the spot tails were initiated. Assigned to surveil CPUSA members in Hyde Park and Rogers Park, Littell frequently abandons his surveillance positions to drink in taverns or visit various Catholic churches.

Littell's Red Squad reports have been slipshod. He regularly misrepresents the hours he spends on his assignments and his comments on CPUSA members can only be considered overly charitable.

On 11/26/59, SA W.R. Hinckle observed CPUSA cell leader Malcolm Chamales accost Littell outside his apartment building. Chamales accused Littell of "FBI black bag chicanery" and challenged him to respond. Littell invited Chamales to a tavern. SA Hinckle observed them engaged in a political discussion. They met again on 11/29 and 12/1. SA Hinckle observed both meetings and believes the two men are becoming friends or at least drinking companions.

Bureau-friendly University of Chicago sources have reported that SA Littell and Helen Agee have been seen on campus arguing heatedly. Their affair appears to be strained and Miss Agee was overheard urging Littell to seek help for his drinking problem. On 11/3/59, SA J.S. Burtler observed Littell and Miss Agee engage in a political discussion. Miss Agee expressed admiration for Vice-President Richard Nixon. Littell referred to Mr. Nixon as "Tricky Dick" and called him a "Red-baiting, slush-fund financed crypto-fascist."

In conclusion: a pro-Communist profile of Littell is now being compiled. I believe that his subversive statements, treasonous Red Squad omissions and friendship with Malcolm Chamales will continue and comprise a damaging security risk portrait.

Respectfully,
Charles Leahy
SAC, Chicago Office

DOCUMENT INSERT: 12/21/59. Field Report: Pete Bondurant to Kemper Boyd, "For Forwarding to John Stanton." Marked: KB—BE CAREFUL HOW YOU TRANSMIT THIS.

KB,

Sorry this report Stanton wanted is late. I don't like writing things down, so cross out what you want and get it to him. Make sure Stanton destroys it. I know he thinks the Agency will go along with what we're doing 100% somewhere down the line, but that might be a long time.

1.—My Klan workers finished up the dock and the speedboat launch-site. Blessington's now 100% operational.

2.—Dougie Frank Lockhart is solid. He's got the usual crazy

ideas that guys in his line of work have, but that's just the way things are & I don't think it's too bad if it doesn't interfere with his job. His FBI contact was pissed that he won't be snitching those rival KKK's in Louisiana, but he changed his tune when Lockhart told him you were heading up the operation. My guess is that he checked with Hoover, who told him you have carte blanche. Lockhart has done a good job so far. I got some $ from Trafficante for him & he's used it to start up his own Klan outside Blessington. He handed out signing bonuses and all the local Klan guys quit their old Klans to sign on with Dougie Frank. I've told him you want no lynchings, church bombings or beatings. He's disappointed, but going along. Lockhart gets along with Cubans & has told his Klan guys not to stir up any racial trouble with the Cadre or our trainees. So far, the guys have gone along with his orders.

3.—Our Miami business is good and getting better. Last month's gross at the Booker T. Washington Housing Project was 14% higher than the Trafficante organization's best month ever. The October gross at the George Washington Carver Project was 9% higher than ST's best. Chuck Rogers says the men at the Mexican ranch are solid. They set up a deal where he can fly in & out without filing flight logs with the Mex. State Police. We've got a landing strip at Blessington now, so Chuck can make the pick-up runs that much safer. I've been driving the split money to ST in Tampa every week. He's pleased with his profits and has been dishing out bonus $ to the Cadre regularly. He's been kicking back 15% directly to me to funnel into the Cause and 5% to a gun fund that Guy Banister has set up in New Orleans. So far, Fulo, Chuck, Paez, Obregon, Delsol & Gutierrez have been completely honest. There have been no shortages of merchandise or $.

4.—Stanton wanted fitness reports on the men. My feeling is that until somebody steals merchandise or $ or punks out on a job they all deserve A+ ratings. Obregon's a little gunshy about speedboat runs into Cuba & his cousin Delsol is a little shifty, but so far this is just minor stuff. What matters is that these are pro-U.S., anti-Castro diehards who don't steal from Trafficante. I say let them bootjack fares at the cabstand and blow off steam with booze and whores. I say you can't snap their leashes too hard or they'll get antsy.

5.—As recruiters, they're not bad. We've got 44 bunks at Blessington & they've been keeping them filled up. Chuck, Fulo,

Lockhart & me have been training the men in 15 day cycles. We
teach small arms, riflery, hand-to-hand combat & speedboat sabotage techniques, then funnel the men to Miami with job leads.
The men recruit there & send their own prospects to a case officer codenamed HK/Cougar, who sends them to one of the Agcy-
backed resident training camps according to bunk-availability. If
this invasion you told me about ever comes off we should have a
surplus of well-trained soldiers to pick from.

6.—Paez, Obregon, Delsol, Gutierrez, Fulo & me have all made
night speedboat runs into Cuba. We've dropped off merchandise
with our on-island contacts & gunned down some militia patrol
boats. Fulo & Gutierrez made a run & saw some militiamen
sleeping on the beach. They killed all 30 with Tommy guns. Fulo
scalped the ranking officer & now flies the scalp on the radio antenna of our lead boat.

7.—Like you wanted, I'm spreading myself between
Blessington, our Miami business & the cabstand. Jimmy Hoffa is
sort of pissed that you're pals with the Kennedys, but he's
pleased with the lease deal, & the more Cuban immigrants that
hit Miami the more $ Tiger Kab makes. And thanks for the mer-
chandise you gave me for H.H. Since I'm in Florida all the time I
guess that that stuff is what's keeping me on his payroll. I'd
quit, but I know you want to cultivate some kind of Agcy. connection with him. I call him once a week to keep my hand in. H.H.
says he's got Mormons looking after him now. They're helping
him dodge the TWA process servers & doing the work I used to,
except for procuring merchandise. I think that as long as I can
supply that I'll draw an L.A. paycheck.

8.—Lenny Sands is editing Hush-Hush singlehandedly. I
thought that Cuban piece he wrote was pretty good & got some
good plugs in for the Cause.

That's it. I don't like writing things down, so tell Stanton to
destroy this.

Viva La Causa!

PB

37

(Blessington, 12/24/59)

Lockhart put his feet up on the dashboard. His fiber-fill Santa Claus suit had him sweating.

"You won't let me bomb churches or kill niggers. Now, what about enforcing the Klan Moral Kode?"

Pete played in—Dougie Frank was good for yuks. "What's that?"

"Well, you get word Joe Redneck's sister Sally has eyes for Leroy with the rumored 12-inch hog leg, and you catch them at it. You heat up your KKK branding iron and mark Sally as a race mixer."

"What about Leroy?"

"You ask him where he got his, and do they make them that size in white."

Pete laughed. Dougie Frank blew his nose out the window.

"I'm serious, Pete. I'm the Imperial Wizard of the South Florida Royal Knights of the Ku Klux Klan, and so far all I've done is hand out CIA bonus money and start up a softball team to play your goddamn crypto-jigaboo exiles."

Pete swerved around a stray dog. The truck hit a pothole; the gift-wrapped turkeys in the back bounced and slid.

"Don't tell me your FBI operator let you do lynchings."

"No, he didn't. But he also didn't say, 'Dougie Frank, don't kill no niggers while you're on the U.S. Government payroll, now.' You see the difference? You're *tellin'* me I can't do it, and you mean it."

Pete saw shacks up ahead—good turkey drop-off spots. Santo Junior

said to lube the locals—he had excess poultry stock off a hijack and figured free Christmas birds would promote goodwill.

"Do your job. This is big stuff we're involved in, so treat it
seriously."

Lockhart said, "I am. I am doing my job and keeping my mouth shut
about Chuck Rogers flying white powder airlines into the Fort
Blessington airstrip, yessir. What I'm also sayin' is my boys need some
recreation."

Pete swung around a turn. "I'll talk to Jimmy Hoffa. Maybe he can
take your guys out shark shooting."

"What I had in mind was enforcing Moral Kode Bylaw Number
3Ixty-nine."

"What's that?"

"That's where you catch Leroy's brothers Tyrone and Rufus knockin'
on Sally's door."

"What do you do?"

"Tar and feather Sally."

"What about Tyrone and Rufus?"

"You make them pull down their pants to see if it runs in the family."

Pete laughed. Dougie Frank scratched his snowy-white beard. "How
come I'm the one who had to dress up like Santa Claus?"

"I couldn't find a red suit my size."

"You could have dressed up one of the Cubans."

"Come on. A spic Santa Claus?"

"I think this job is degrading."

Pete pulled into a ratty dirt playground. Some colored kids saw
Santa and went gaga.

Dougie Frank got out and lobbed turkeys at them. The kids ran up
and tugged at his beard.

The local whites got turkeys. The local jigs got turkeys. The Blessington
cops got turkeys and hijack Jim Beam.

The trainees got turkey dinners and Trojan prophylactics. Santo Junior sent down a Christmas treat: a busload of Tampa whores. Forty-four
men and forty-four hookers made for squeaks off forty-four bunks.

Pete sent the girls home at midnight. Lockhart burned a Yuletide
cross out in the boonies. Pete got an urge to hit Cuba and kill Commies.

He called Fulo in Miami. Fulo dug the idea. Fulo said, I'll round up
some guys and drive down.

Chuck Rogers flew a load of dope in. Pete gassed up the lead speedboat.

Lockhart cruised by with some moonshine. Pete and Chuck traded chugs. Nobody smoked—the shit might ignite.

They sat on the dock. Floodlights lit up the whole campsite.

A trainee screamed in his sleep. Embers blew down off the cross. Pete remembered Xmas '45: The L.A. Sheriff's signed him on fresh out of the Marine Corps.

Fulo's car dipsy-doodled across the runway. Chuck stacked Tommy guns and ammo by the dock moorings.

Dougie Frank said, "Can I go?"

Pete said, "Sure."

Delsol, Obregón and Fulo piled out of the Chevy. They walked sway-bellied—blitzed by too much beer and turkey.

They waddled over to the dock. Tomás Obregón wore shades—at 2:00 a.m. Shades *and* long sleeves—on a half-assed balmy night.

A dog barked out in the sticks. Chuck Rogers mimicked hound yelps like this late-nite cracker deejay he grooved on. Everybody traded holiday back slaps.

Pete slapped Obregón's shades off. The fuck had dope-pinned eyes—floodlight glare nailed them clean.

Obregón froze. Rogers threw a choke hold on him.

Nobody talked. Nobody had to—the picture spread *rápidamente.*

Obregón squirmed. Fulo jerked his sleeves up. Skin-pop tracks ran down his arms, red and ugly.

Everybody looked at Delsol—Obregón's fucking cousin. The picture spread: Let *him* do it.

Chuck let Obregón go. Pete handed his gun to Delsol.

Obregón trembled and almost teetered off the dock. Delsol shot him six times in the chest.

He spun into the water. Steam hissed out his exit wounds.

Fulo dove in and scalped him.

Delsol looked away.

38

(Hyannis Port, 12/25/59)

 Christmas tree grazed the ceiling. Spray-on snowflakes dusted a huge pile of gifts.

Kemper sipped eggnog.

Jack said, "Holidays make you sad, I can tell."

"Not exactly."

"My parents overdid having children, but yours should have had the foresight to give you a sibling or two."

"I had a younger brother. He died in a hunting accident."

"I didn't know that."

"My father and I were stalking deer near our summer place. We kept getting glimpses, and kept firing through brush. One of the glimpses was Compton Wickwire Boyd, age eight. He was wearing a tan jacket and a hat with white ear flaps. It was October 19, 1934."

Jack looked away. "Kemper, I'm sorry."

"I shouldn't have mentioned it. You said you wanted to talk, and I have to leave for New York in an hour. That story is a guaranteed conversation-stopper."

The den was overheated. Jack inched his chair away from the fireplace.

"You're meeting Laura?"

"Yes. My daughter's having Christmas dinner with some friends in South Bend, then going on a ski trip. She'll be joining Laura and I in New York."

Pete's ring was buffed and polished. He was set to pop the question tonight.

"You and Laura were a hell of a shock."

"But you're getting used to it?"

"I think everyone is, to one degree or another."

"You're nervous, Jack."

"I'm announcing in eight days. Obstacles keep popping up in my mind, and I keep wondering how to deal with them."

"For instance?"

"West Virginia. What do I say to a coal miner who says, 'Son, I heard your daddy's one of the richest men in America, and you never had to work a day in your life?' "

Kemper smiled. "You say, 'That's true.' And a grizzled old character actor that we plant in the crowd says, 'And son, you ain't missed a damn thing.' "

Jack roared. Kemper snapped to a connection: Giancana and Trafficante ran big blocks of West Virginia.

"I know some people down there who might be able to help you."

"Then indebt me to them in unconscionable ways, so I can embrace my genetic fate as a corrupt Irish politician."

Kemper laughed. "You're still nervous. And you said you wanted to talk to me, which implied a serious discussion."

Jack rocked his chair back and brushed fake snow off his sweater. "We've been thinking of Mr. Hoover. We were thinking he knows the story of Laura's parentage."

Devil's Advocate clicked in, automatically. "He's known for years. He knows I'm seeing Laura, and he told me the facts of her parentage before she did."

Bobby's kids romped through the room. Jack shooed them out and toed the door shut.

"That voyeuristic little faggot cocksucker."

Kemper ad-libbed. "He also knows about all your paternity buyouts, and most of your sustained affairs. Jack, I'm your best hedge against Hoover. He likes me and trusts me, and all he wants is to keep his job if you're elected."

Jack tapped a humidor on his chin. "Dad's got himself half-convinced that Hoover sent you over to spy on us."

"Your dad's no dummy."

"What?"

"Hoover caught me skimming off a car-theft investigation and retired me early. I applied for the McClellan Committee job on my own, and Hoover started keeping tabs on me. He learned I was seeing Laura and asked me for information on you. I said no, and Hoover said, 'You owe me one.' "

Jack nodded. His look said: Yes, I'll buy that.

"Dad had a private detective follow you around Manhattan. The man said you keep a suite at the St. Regis."

Kemper winked. "The way you live rubs off, Jack. I've got a pension, a salary and stock dividends, and I'm courting an expensive woman."

"You're in Florida a good deal."

"Hoover has me spying on pro-Castro groups. It's that 'one' I owe him."

"That's why you're so hipped on Cuba as a campaign issue."

"Right. I think Castro's a goddamned menace, and I think you should take a hard line against him."

Jack lit his cigar. His look said: Thank God this is over.

"I'll tell Dad it's all okay. He wants a promise, though."

"Which is?"

"That you won't marry Laura any time soon. He's afraid reporters might get nosy."

Kemper handed him the ring. "Keep this for me. I was planning to ask Laura tonight, but I guess I'll have to wait until you're elected."

Jack slipped it in his pocket. "Thanks. Does this mean you're out a Christmas gift?"

"I'll pick something up in New York."

"There's an emerald pin under the tree there. Laura looks good in green, and Jackie won't miss it."

39

(South Bend, 12/25/59)

Littell got off the train and checked for tails.

The arrivals and departures looked normal—just Notre Dame kids and anxious parents. Some cheerleaders shivered—short-skirted pompom girls out in ten-degree weather.

The crowd dispersed. No platform loiterers stuck close to him. In a phrase: The Phantom sees phantoms.

Tail sightings were a probable booze by-product. The clicks on his phone line were most likely overactive nerves.

He'd dismantled his two phones. He found no wiretap apparatus. The Mob couldn't rig *outside* taps—only police agencies could. That man watching him and Mal Chamales last week—probably just a barfly tweaked by their left-of-center conversation.

Littell hit the station lounge and knocked back three rye-and-beers. Christmas dinner with Susan mandated fortification.

Amenities dragged. Talk bounced between safe topics.

Susan tensed when he hugged her. Helen steered clear of his hands. Claire had grown into a distaff Kemper—the resemblance had solidified amazingly.

Susan never addressed him by name. Claire called him "Ward baby"—Helen said she was in a Rat Pack phase. Susan smoked like her mother now—straight down to match flicks and exhales.

Her apartment mimicked Margaret's: too many porcelain knick-knacks and too much stiff furniture.

Claire played Sinatra records. Susan served diluted eggnog—Helen must have told her that her father drank to excess.

He said he hadn't heard from Kemper in months. Claire smiled—she knew all her father's secrets. Susan laid out dinner: Margaret's boring glazed ham and sweet potatoes.

They sat down. Littell bowed his head and offered a prayer.

"O heavenly Father, we ask thy blessing on all of us, and on our absent friends. I commend to you the souls of three men recently departed, whose deaths were caused by arrogant if heartfelt attempts to facilitate justice. I ask you to bless all of us on this sacred day and in the year to come."

Susan rolled her eyes and said "Amen." Claire carved the ham; Helen poured wine.

The girls got full glasses. He got a splash. It was cheap Cabernet Sauvignon.

Claire said, "My Dad's proposing to his mistress tonight. Let's hear it for my Dad and my nifty new mom, who's only nine and a half years older than me."

Littell almost gagged. Social climber Kemper as secret Kennedy in-law—

Susan said, "Claire, really. 'Mistress' and 'nifty' in the same sentence?"

Claire made cat claws. "You forgot to mention the age difference. How could you? We both know that age gaps are your pet peeve."

Helen groaned. Susan pushed her plate aside and lit a cigarette.

Littell filled his glass. Claire said, "Ward baby, assess the three of us as attorneys."

Littell smiled. "It's not hard. Susan prosecutes misdemeanors, Helen defends wayward FBI men, and Claire goes into corporate law to finance her father's expensive tastes in his old age."

Helen and Claire laughed. Susan said, "I don't appreciate being defined by pettiness."

Littell gulped wine. "You can join the Bureau, Susie. I'll be retiring in a year and twenty-one days, and you can take my place and torment pathetic leftists for Mr. Hoover."

"I wouldn't characterize Communists as pathetic, Father. And I don't think you could support your bar tab on a twenty-year pension."

Claire flinched. Helen said, "Susan, please."

Littell grabbed the bottle. "Maybe I'll go to work for John F. Kennedy. Maybe he'll be elected President. His brother hates organized crime more than Communists, so maybe it runs in the family."

Susan said, "I can't believe you place common hoodlums in the same league as a political system that has enslaved half the world. I can't believe that you could be hoodwinked by a fatuous liberal politician whose father intends to buy him the presidency."

"Kemper Boyd likes him."

"Excuse me, Father, and excuse me, Claire, but Kemper Boyd worships money, and we all know that John F. Kennedy has plenty of that."

Claire ran out of the room. Littell flat-guzzled wine.

"Communists don't castrate innocent men. Communists don't hook up car batteries to people's genitals and electrocute them. Communists don't drop TV sets into bathtubs or—"

Helen ran out. Susan said, "Father, goddamn you for your weakness."

He called in accumulated sick leave and holed up through New Year's. The A&P delivered food and liquor.

Law school finals kept Helen away. They talked on the phone—mostly petty chitchat and sighs. He heard occasional clicks on the line and wrote them off to nerves.

Kemper didn't call or write. The man was ignoring him.

He read Bobby Kennedy's book about the Hoffa wars. The story thrilled him. Kemper Boyd did not appear in the text.

He watched the Rose Bowl and Cotton Bowl on TV. He eulogized Icepick Tony Iannone—dead one year ago exactly.

Exactly four rye-and-beers induced euphoria. He fantasized an exact form of courage: the will to move on Jules Schiffrin and the Fund books.

More liquor killed the notion. To move meant to sacrifice lives. His courage was weakness pushed into grandiosity.

He watched John Kennedy announce his Presidential candidacy. The Senate Caucus Room was packed with his supporters.

Cameras cut to a picket line outside. Teamsters chanted: "Hey, hey, ho, ho, Kennedy says 'Labor NO!' "

A reporter spoke voice-over: "A Florida grand jury has Teamster president James R. Hoffa under close scrutiny. He is suspected of felony land fraud in matters pertaining to the Teamsters' Sun Valley development."

An insert shot caught Hoffa laughing off Sun Valley.

Littell juxtaposed words:

Pete, kill some men for me, will ya?

Father, goddamn you for your weakness.

40

(Tampa, 2/1/60)

Jack Ruby said, "I am desperate. That well-known indigent Sal D. owed me a bundle when he died, and the IRS is climbing up my you-know-what for back payments I ain't got. I'm overextended on my club, Sam already turned me down, and you know I am a great friend to the Cuban Cause. A pal and me brought strippers down to entertain the boys in Blessington, which was strictly voluntary on my part and has nothing to do with the request I just made."

Santo Junior sat at his desk. Ruby stood in front of it. Three fat German shepherds drooped off the couch.

Pete watched Ruby grovel. The office stunk: Santo gave his dogs free run of the furniture.

Ruby said, "I am desperate. I am here before you like a supplicant before his local pontiff."

Trafficante said, "No. You brought some girls down when I was locked up in Havana, but that is not ten grand's worth of collateral. I can let you have a thousand out of my pocket, but that's it."

Ruby stuck his hand out. Santo greased him with C-notes off a flash roll. Pete got up and opened the door.

Ruby walked out fondling the money. Santo spritzed cologne on the spot where he stood groveling.

"That man is rumored to have strange sexual tastes. He could give you diseases that would put cancer to shame. Now, tell me some good things, because I don't like to start my day with beggars."

Pete said, "Profits went up 2% in December and January. I think Wilfredo Delsol's okay on his cousin, and I don't think he'd ever rat off the Cadre. Nobody's stealing from us, and I think the Obregón thing put a good little scare out."

"Somebody's fucking up, or you wouldn't've asked to see me."

"Fulo's been running whores. He's got them turning tricks for five-dollar pops and candy bars. He's turning over all the money, but I still think it's bad business."

Trafficante said, "Make him stop."

Pete sat on the edge of the couch. King Tut put out a cursory growl.

"Lockhart and his Klan buddies built a social club down the road from the campsite, and now they're talking about lynching spooks. On top of that, Lockhart's pals with that Dallas cop guy J.D. that drove down here with Ruby. Chuck Rogers wants to take J.D. up in his plane and drop some hate leaflets. He's talking about saturation-bombing South Florida."

Trafficante slapped his desk blotter. "Make this foolishness stop."

"I will."

"You didn't have to run this by me."

"Kemper thinks all discipline should initiate with you. He wants the men to think we're labor as opposed to management."

"Kemper's a subtle guy."

Pete stroked King Farouk and King Arthur. Fucking King Tut evil-eyed him.

"He's every bit of subtle."

"Castro turned my casinos into pigsties. He lets goats shit on the carpets my wife picked out personally."

Pete said, "He'll pay."

He drove back to Miami. The cabstand was packed with loafers: Lockhart, Fulo, and the whole fucking Cadre.

Minus Chuck Rogers—up in his airplane dropping hate bombs.

Pete shut down the stand and laid down The Law. He called it the Declaration of Cadre Non-Independence and the New KKK Bill of Non-Rights.

No pimping. No robbery. No flim-flam. No B&E. No extortion. No hijacking.

No lynching. No nigger assaults. No church bombings. No racial shit directed at Cubans.

The Blessington Klan's specific mandate:

Love all Cubans. Leave them alone. Fuck up anybody who fucks with your new Cuban brethren.

Lockhart called the mandate quasi-genocidal. Pete cracked his knuckles. Lockhart shut his mouth.

The huddle broke up. Jack Ruby came by and begged a ride—his carburetor blew, and he needed to run his girls down to Blessington.

Pete said okay. The girls wore capris and halter tops—things could be worse.

Ruby rode up front. J.D. Tippit and the strippers rode in the back of the truck. Rain clouds were brewing—if a storm hit, they were screwed.

Pete took two-lane roadways south. He played the radio to keep Ruby quiet. Chuck Rogers flew down from deep nowhere and spun tree-level backflips.

The girls cheered. Chuck dropped a six-pack; J.D. caught it. Hate leaflets blew down—Pete plucked one out of the air.

"Six Reasons Why Jesus Was Pro-Klan." #1 set the tone: because Commies fluoridated the Red Sea.

Ruby eyeballed the scenery. Tippit and the girls guzzled beer. Chuck blew off his flight pattern and brick-bombed a nigger church.

The radio signal faded. Ruby started whining.

"Santo don't possess the world's longest memory. Santo stiffs me with one-tenth of what I asked him for 'cause his memory's nine-tenths on the blink. Santo don't understand the tsuris I went through bringing those ladies down to Havana. Sure the Beard was giving him grief. But he didn't have no crazy Fed from Chicago leeching onto him."

Pete snapped to. "What Fed from Chicago?"

"I don't know his name. I only met him in the flesh once, praise Allah."

"Describe him."

"Maybe six foot one, maybe forty-six or -seven years of age. Glasses, thin gray hair, and a boozer in my considered opinion, since the one time I met him face-to-face he had whisky on his breath."

The road dipped. Pete hit the brakes and almost stalled the truck out.

"Tell me how he leeched onto you."

"Why? Give me one good reason why I should share this abuse with you."

"I'll give you a thousand dollars to tell me the story. If I like the story, I'll give you four more."

Ruby counted on his fingers—one to five a half dozen times.
Pete tapped a little tune on the wheel. The beat ran 1-2-3-4-5.
Ruby lip-synched numbers: 1-2-3-4-5, 1-2-3-4-5.
Pete held up five fingers. Ruby counted them out loud.

"Five thousand if you like it?"

"That's right, Jack. And a thousand if I don't."

"I am taking a tremendous risk in telling you this."

"Then don't."

Ruby fretted his Jew-star necklace. Pete splayed five fingers out on the dashboard. Ruby kissed the star and took a bigggg breath.

"Last May this farkakte Fed braces me down in Dallas. He makes every conceivable threat on God's green earth, and I believe him, 'cause I know he's this crazy goyishe zealot with nothing to lose. He knows I've sharked in Big D and up in Chicago, and he knows I've sent people looking for high-end loans to Sam Giancana. That's what he's got this colossal hard one for. He wants to trace the money that gets loaned out from the Teamsters' Pension Fund."

It was vintage Littell: bold *and* stupid.

"He gets me to call him at a pay phone in Chicago once a week. He gives me a few dollars when I tell him I'm running on fumes. He gets me to tell him about this movie guy I know, Sid Kabikoff, who's interested in seeing this loan shark named Sal D'Onofrio, who's gonna shoot him up to Momo for a Pension Fund loan. What happened after that I don't know. But I read in the Chicago papers that both Kabikoff and D'Onofrio have been murdered, so-called 'torture-style,' and that both cases are unsolved. I'm not no Einstein, but 'torture' in Chicago means Sam G. And I also know that Sam don't know I was involved, or I'd have been visited. And it don't take an Einstein to figure out the crazy Fed was at the root of all this pain."

Littell was working outlaw. Littell was Boyd's best friend. Lenny Sands worked with Littell *and* D'Onofrio.

Ruby plucked a dog hair off his lap. "Is that five thousand dollars' worth of story?"

The road blurred. Pete damn near plowed a gator.

"Has the Fed called you since Sal D. and Kabikoff died?"

"No, praise Allah. Now what about my five—?"

"You'll get it. And I'll pay you three thousand extra if he calls you again and you get back to me on it. And if you end up helping me out with him, I'll make it another five."

Ruby went apoplectic. "Why? Why the fuck do you care to the extent of all this money?"

Pete smiled. "Let's keep this between the two of us, all right?"

"You want secret, I'll give you secret. I'm a well-known secret type of guy who knows how to keep his mouth shut."

Pete pulled his magnum and drove with his knees. Ruby smiled—ho, ho—What's this?

Pete popped the cylinder, dumped five rounds and spun it.

Ruby smiled—ho, ho—Kid, you're too much.

Pete shot him in the head. The five-to-one odds held: the hammer hit an empty chamber.

Ruby went Klan-sheet white.

Pete said, "Ask around. See what people say about me."

They hit Blessington at dusk. Ruby and Tippit got their strip show ready.

Pete called Midway Airport and impersonated a police officer. A clerk confirmed Ruby's story: A Ward J. Littell flew to Dallas and back last May 18.

He hung up and called the Eden Roc Hotel. The switchboard girl said Kemper Boyd was "out for the day."

Pete left him a message: "10:00 tonight, the Luau Lounge—urgent."

Boyd took it casual. He said, "I know Ward's been chasing the Fund," like he was too bored to breathe.

Pete blew smoke rings. Boyd's tone pissed him off—he drove eighty miles for a display of fucking ennui.

"It doesn't seem to bother you."

"I'm a bit overextended on Littell, but other than that, I don't think it's anything to be concerned about. Do you feel like divulging your source?"

"No. He doesn't know Littell's name, and I've got him cowed pretty good."

A tiki torch lit their table. Boyd flickered in and out of this weird little glow.

"I don't see how this concerns you, Pete."

"It concerns Jimmy Hoffa. He's tied to us on the Cuban thing, and Jimmy *is* the fucking Pension Fund."

Boyd drummed the table. "Littell is fixated on the Chicago Mob and the Fund. It doesn't touch on our Cuban work, and I don't think we owe Jimmy a warning. And I don't want you to talk to Lenny Sands about this. He's not conversant on the topic, and you don't need to trouble him with it."

It was vintage Boyd: "need-to-know basis" straight down the line.

"We don't have to warn Jimmy, but I'll say this loud and clear. Jimmy hired me to clip Anton Gretzler, and I don't want Littell to burn me for it. He's already made me for the job, and he's just crazy enough to go public with it, Mr. Hoover or no Mr. Hoover."

Boyd twirled his martini stick. "You clipped Roland Kirpaski, too."

"No. Jimmy clipped him himself."

Boyd whistled—très, très casual.

Pete got up in his face. "You cut Littell too much slack. You make fucking allowances for him that you shouldn't."

"We both lost brothers, Pete. Let it go at that."

The line didn't compute. Boyd talked on these weird levels sometimes.

Pete leaned back. "Are you watchdogging Littell? How tight a leash are you keeping on him?"

"I haven't been in touch with him in months. I've been distancing myself from him and Mr. Hoover."

"Why?"

"Just an instinct."

"Like an instinct for survival?"

"More of a homing instinct. You move away from some people, and you move toward the people of the moment."

"Like the Kennedys."

"Yes."

Pete laughed. "I've hardly seen you since Jack hit the trail."

"You won't be seeing me at all until after the election. Stanton knows I can't be dividing my time."

"He *should* know. He hired you to get next to the Kennedys."

"He won't regret it."

"I don't. It means I get to run the Cadre solo."

"Can you handle it?"

"Can niggers dance?"

"They surely can."

Pete sipped his beer. It was flat—he forgot he ordered it.

"You said 'election' like you think the job's going through to November."

"I'm reasonably certain it will. Jack's ahead in New Hampshire and Wisconsin, and if we get past West Virginia I think he'll go all the way."

"Then I hope he's anti-Castro."

"He is. He's not as voluble as Richard Nixon, but then Dick's a Red-baiter from way back."

"President Jack. Jesus Christ."

Boyd signaled a waiter. A fresh martini hit the table quick.

"It's seduction, Pete. He'll back the country into a corner with his charm, like it's a woman. When America sees that it's a choice between Jack and twitchy old Dick Nixon, who do you think they'll get between the sheets with?"

Pete raised his beer. "Viva La Causa. Viva Bad-Back Jack."

They clinked glasses. Boyd said, "He'll get behind the Cause. And if the invasion goes, we want it to be in his administration."

Pete lit a cigarette. "I'm not worried about that. Put Littell aside, and there's only one thing to be worried about."

"You're concerned that the Agency at large will find out about our Cadre business."

"That's right."

Boyd said, "I want them to find out. In fact, I'm going to inform them some time before November. It's inevitable that they will find out, and by the time they do my Kennedy connection will make me too valuable to dismiss. The Cadre will have recruited too many good men and have made too much money, and as far as morality goes, how does selling heroin to Negroes rate when compared to illegally invading an island?"

More vintage Boyd: "self-budgeted," "autonomous"—

"And don't worry about Littell. He's trying to accrue evidence to send to Bobby Kennedy, but I monitor all the information that Bobby sees, and I will not let Littell hurt you at all, or hurt Jimmy for the Kirpaski killing or anything else related to you or the Cause. But sooner or later Bobby *will* take Hoffa down, and I do not want you to meddle in it."

Pete felt his head swim. "I can't argue with any of that. But I've got a pipeline to Littell now, and if I think your boy needs a scare, I'm going to scare him."

"And I can't argue with that. You can do whatever you have to do, as long as you don't kill him."

They shook hands. Boyd said, *"Les gens que l'on comprend—ce sont eux que l'on domine."*

En français, Pierre, souviens-toi:

Those we understand are those we control.

41

(New York City/Hyannis Port/
New Hampshire/Wisconsin/Illinois/West Virginia
2/4/60–5/4/60)

Christmas Day made him certain. Every day since built on it.

Jack kept Laura's ring. Kemper took Jackie's emerald pin. His car wouldn't start—a Kennedy chauffeur checked it out for him. Kemper strolled the compound and caught Jack in mid-transformation.

He was standing on the beach, alone. He was rehearsing his public persona in full voice.

Kemper stood out of sight and watched him.

Jack went from tallish to tall. He brayed less and rumbled more. His stabbing gestures hit some mark he'd always missed before.

Jack laughed. Jack cocked his head to listen. Jack masterfully summarized Russia, civil rights, the race for space, Cuba, Catholicism, his perceived youth and Richard Nixon as a duplicitous, do-nothing reactionary unfit to lead the greatest country on earth into perilous times.

He looked heroic. Claiming the moment drained all the boy out of him.

The self-possession was always there. He'd postponed the claim until it could give him the world.

Jack knew he'd win. Kemper knew he'd impersonate greatness with the force of an enigma granted form. This new freedom would make people love him.

Laura loved the pin.

Jack took New Hampshire and Wisconsin.

Jimmy Hoffa barnstormed both states. Jimmy mobilized Teamsters and ranted on national TV. Jimmy betrayed his essential lunacy every time he opened his mouth.

Kemper mobilized the backlash. Pro-Jack pickets scuffled with Teamster pickets. The pro-Jack boys were good shouters and good placard swingers.

Bobby's book hit the best-seller lists. Kemper distributed free copies at union halls. The consensus four months in: Jimmy Hoffa was nullified.

Jack was spellbindingly handsome. Hoffa was bloated and harried. All his anti-Kennedy broadsides carried a footnote: "Currently under investigation for land fraud."

People loved Jack. People wanted to touch him. Kemper let the people get non-security close.

Kemper let photographers get close. He wanted people to think Jack's amusement was really love beaming back.

They were running unopposed in Nebraska. The West Virginia primary was six days off—Jack should knock Hubert Humphrey out of the race.

Frank Sinatra was wowing hillbilly voters. A Rat Pack stooge composed a ring-a-ding Jack Anthem. Payola got it constant airplay.

Laura called Sinatra a small penis with a big voice.

Jack's ascent enraged her. She was blood kin and an outcast. Kemper Boyd was a stranger granted insider status.

He called her from the road every night. Laura considered the contact pro forma.

He knew that she missed Lenny Sands. She didn't know that he'd banished him.

Lenny changed his Chicago number—there was no way that Laura could call him. Kemper put a trace on his phone bills and confirmed that he hadn't called her.

Bobby remembered "voice coach" Lenny. Some staffers decreed a brush-up course and invited Lenny to New Hampshire.

Jack "introduced" Lenny to Kemper. Lenny played along and did not display an ounce of rancor or fear.

Lenny worked Jack's speaking voice into top shape. Bobby put him on the Wisconsin payroll—as a crowd-building front man. Lenny built up big crowds on a small budget—Bobby was thrilled.

Claire spent most weekends with Laura. She said Jack's half-sister was a rabid Nixon fan.

Like Mr. Hoover.

They talked in mid-February. Mr. Hoover made the call. He said, "My, it's been a long time!" in a purely disingenuous tone.

Kemper updated his allegiances and detailed Joe Kennedy's old suspicions. Hoover said, "I'll build up a file to buttress your dissemblings. We'll make it appear that all your Florida trips were solely on my behalf. I'll anoint you the Bureau's ace pro-Castro-group monitor."

Kemper supplied key Florida dates. Hoover sent him mock itineraries to memorize.

Hoover never mentioned the campaign. Kemper knew that he sensed a Kennedy victory.

Hoover did not mention Jack and women. Hoover did not suggest hot-wiring prostitutes. Hoover did not nail the reason why Kemper Boyd had stayed distant.

He didn't want to implement another sex shakedown. He wanted to retain one strong loyalty compartment.

Pimp shakedowns?—no. Pimp *service*?—certainly.

He got Jack one call girl per night. He called his local vice squad contacts for referrals—and skin-searched every girl that Jack fucked.

The girls loved Jack.

So did SA Ward Littell.

They hadn't spoken in over six months. Ward showed up at Jack's big Milwaukee rally—the old Chicago Phantom as the new Chicago Wraith.

He looked frail and unkempt. He did not look like anyone's notion of a G-man.

Ward refused to talk Mob scuttlebutt or Pension Fund strategy. Ward refused to discuss the D'Onofrio homicide.

Ward said he was neglecting his Red Squad assignment. He said he'd struck up a friendship with a leftist he was tailing.

The Kennedy campaign thrilled him. He wore Kennedy buttons to work and made a scene when SAC Leahy told him to stop it.

Littell's anti-Mob crusade was dead. Mr. Hoover couldn't touch them now: the Boyd/Littell collusion was null and void.

Kemper told Bobby the Phantom was still plugging. Bobby said, Don't bother me with trifles.

Littell was set to retire in eight months. His drunken dream was a Kennedy appointment.

Ward loves Jack.

New Hampshire loves Jack.

Wisconsin loves Jack.

West Virginia had its heart up for grabs. Greenbrier County was vote-crucial and totally Mob-run.

He decided not to ask the Boys for help. Why indebt Jack to men that Bobby hated?

America loves Jack.

Sinatra put it best:

"That old Jack Magic has me in its spell!"

42

(Blessington/Miami, 2/4/60–5/4/60)

That "lost brothers" line kept zinging him. Pete couldn't get it out of his head.

John Stanton toured the campsite in mid-March. Pete quizzed him on Kemper Boyd's background.

Stanton said the CIA researched the man. The hunting-accident story earned him high marks—Kemper didn't let shit weigh him down.

Boyd spoke French. Boyd made big words come alive. Boyd made his whole world go whoosh—

His last three months: "autonomous," straight from Webster's Unabridged.

Kemper's timecard read strictly KENNEDY. Pete's timecard now read strictly CUBA.

Fulo quit running whores. Lockhart embraced the New Klan Kode. Six two-week cycles worked through Blessington—746 men total.

They learned weaponry, judo, speedboating and demolition fundamentals. Chuck Rogers fed them pro-U.S. doctrine.

The Cadre kept recruiting in Miami. Cuban hotheads kept signing up.

The Agency now had sixty operational campsites. They established an exile "grad school" in Guatemala: a fully equipped military facility.

Ike loosened his pursestrings. Ike approved exile invasion plans. It was a big policy shift—three plots to whack Fidel backfired and scrambled the thinking at Langley.

Shooters couldn't get close. Aides smoked exploding cigars marked for the Beard. Langley figured fuck it—let's invade Cuba.

Maybe early next year. Maybe in Bad-Back Jack's administration.

Boyd said Jack would approve the plan. Boyd was fucking persuasive. Santo Junior spread the word: Kemper Boyd has Jack Kennedy's ear.

The Outfit dropped some coin on Jack's campaign—quietly and anonymously. Big fat compartmentalized donations.

Jimmy Hoffa didn't know. Jack didn't know—and wouldn't be told until the optimum moment to call in the debt.

Sam G. said he could buy Jack Illinois. Lenny Sands said Sam spent a fortune in Wisconsin. West Virginia ditto—Chi-Mob money had the state locked in for Jack.

Pete asked Lenny if Boyd knew about all that finagling. Lenny said, I don't think so. Pete said, Let's keep it that way—Kemper wouldn't like to think that he'd put Jack in hock.

Boyd inspired confidence. Trafficante loved him. Santo passed the Cuban Cause hat—Giancana, Rosselli and Marcello ponied up large.

It was classic compartmentalization.

The CIA high brass condoned the gifts. And they learned about the Cadre dope biz—before Kemper informed them.

They condoned it. They considered it plausibly deniable and told John Stanton to continue. They told Stanton to hide this knowledge from non-CIA personnel.

Like outside police agencies. Like moralistic politicians.

Stanton was relieved. Kemper was amused. He said the issue illustrated the Jack/Bobby dichotomy: dope peddling as divisive moral issue.

Big Brother would wince and try to ignore the alliance. Little Brother would side with God and banish all Mob-CIA contact.

Big Brother was worldly, like his dad. Little Brother was prissy, like a dejuiced Ward Littell with functioning balls.

Bobby had his father's money and his brother's cache. Littell had booze and religion. Jack Ruby had a five-grand pointer's fee—if Littell swerved through his life again, Big Pete would be notified.

Boyd told him not to kill Littell. Boyd co-signed Littell's Pension Fund hard-on—which meant at least an outside chance at co-opting big money.

Littell loved Bad-Back Jack.

Like Darleen Shoftel. Like Gail Hendee.

Like himself.

Hey, Jack—you fucked my old girlfriend. I don't care—Kemper Boyd says you're a white man.

I'm selling dope for you. I'm running cash to a man named Banister—who links YOU to a Jew/papist plot to butt-fuck America.

You'd dig Fort Blessington, Jack. It's a Mob resort now—the Boys come by to catch the anti-Castro floorshow. Santo Junior bought a motel outside town. He'd put you up for free—if you dump your kid brother in the Everglades.

Sam G. drops by. Carlos Marcello visits. Johnny Rosselli brings Dick Contino and his accordion. Lenny Sands puts on shows—his transvestite Fidel shtick brings the house down.

Dope profits were up. Cadre morale was sky-high. Ramón Gutiérrez kept a tally of speedboat-run scalpees. Heshie Ryskind started up a scalp bonus fund.

Lenny Sands was on smear duty: the Beard as scandal-sheet whipping boy. Mr. Hughes dug the political thrust, but preferred to see *Hush-Hush* exposit sex skank exclusively.

Pete called Hughes once a week. The fucker ranted nonstop.

The TWA gig was dragging on. Dick Steisel kept Hughes look-alikes on retainer. Hughes believed that niggers caused cancer—and kept urging Ike to reinstate slavery.

Germ-obsessed Mormon nuts kept Big Howard company. They kept his bungalow sanitized: A-bomb-strength bug spray worked wonders. Some doofus named Duane Spurgeon bossed the crew. He stretched lubricated rubbers over every doorknob spooks might have touched.

Hughes was on a new kick: getting weekly blood transfusions. He sucked in pure Mormon blood exclusively—purchased from a blood bank outside Salt Lake City.

Hughes always said, Thanks for the dope. Pete always said, Thank the Agency.

He still got a Hughes paycheck. He still got twenty-three alimony cuts. He got 5% of Tiger Kab and his contract agent pay.

He used to pimp and pull shakedowns. Now he rode shotgun to History.

Jimmy Hoffa stopped by the cabstand every few days. His standard M.O. was to rave at non-English-speaking drivers. Wilfredo Delsol was running the switchboard now—whacking his cousin killed his appetite for strongarm.

Wilfredo understood English. He said Jimmy teed off on Cubans, but couldn't sustain it. Whoever took the first few "fuckheads" got a reprieve. Hoffa couldn't scream a sentence that didn't end "Kennedy."

Pete saw Jack and Jimmy on TV back-to-back. Kennedy charmed a heckler speechless. Hoffa wore white socks and an egg-spattered necktie.

Hold the tip sheet—I can spot winners and losers.

Sometimes he just couldn't sleep. That big fucking whoooosh was like a hydrogen bomb inside his head.

43

(Greenbrier, 5/8/60)

Flanking cordons jammed up to the rostrum. Pro-Jack and pro-Teamster pickets—hard boys all. The main drag was blocked off to cars. The pre-rally crowd extended back three blocks: at least six thousand people packed in shoulder-to-shoulder tight.

They jabbered and hummed. Placards bobbed ten feet high.

Jack was set to speak first. Humphrey lost a rigged coin toss and spoke last. Jack regalia outgunned Hubert three to one—the West Virginia campaign in a nutshell.

Teamster goons yelled into bullhorns. Some rednecks hoisted a cartoon banner: Jack with fangs and a papal biretta.

Kemper cupped his ears—the crowd roar was painful. Rocks shredded the banner—he paid some kids to crouch down and let fly.

Jack was due. Bad acoustics and Hoffa invective would drown out his speech.

No great loss—people would still *see* him. The crowd would disperse when Humphrey showed up—free liquor was being served at select downtown taverns.

It was Kemper Boyd liquor. An old pal hijacked a Schenley's truck and sold him the contents.

The street was packed. The sidewalks were packed. Peter Lawford was lobbing tie tacks at a gaggle of nuns.

Kemper mingled and watched the rostrum. He saw non-sequitur faces a few yards apart: Lenny Sands and a prototype Mob guy.

The Mob guy flashed Lenny a thumbs-up. Lenny flashed him two thumbs back.

Lenny was *off* the campaign payroll. Lenny had no *official* duties here.

The Mob man veered right. Lenny pushed his way left and ducked down an alley lined with trash cans.

Kemper followed him. Stray elbows and knees slowed him down.

High-school kids jostled him across the sidewalk. Lenny was midway down the alley, huddled with two cops.

The crowd noise leveled out. Kemper crouched behind a trash can and eavesdropped.

Lenny fanned a cash roll. A cop plucked bills off of it. His buddy said, "For two hundred extra we can stall the Humphrey bus and bring in some boys to shout him down."

Lenny said, "Do it. And this is strictly on Mr. G., so don't mention it to anybody with the campaign."

The cops grabbed the whole roll and squeezed through an alleyway door. Lenny leaned against the wall and lit a cigarette.

Kemper walked up to him. Hipster Lenny said, "So?"

"So, tell me about it."

"What's to tell?"

"Fill in the blanks for me, then."

"What's to fill in? We're both Kennedy guys."

Lenny could maneuver. Lenny could outfrost any cool cat on earth.

"Giancana put money into Wisconsin, too. Is that right? You couldn't have performed the way you did on what Bobby gave you."

Lenny shrugged. "Sam and Hesh Ryskind."

"Who told them to? You?"

"My advice don't rate that high. You know that."

"Spill, Lenny. You're playing coy, and it's starting to annoy me."

Lenny stubbed his cigarette on the wall. "Sinatra was bragging up his influence with Jack. He was saying Jack as President wouldn't be the same Jack that sat on the McClellan Committee, if you catch my meaning."

"And Giancana bought the whole package?"

"No. I think you gave Frank a big fucking assist. Everybody's real impressed with what you've been doing on the Cuba front, so they figured if you like Jack he can't be all bad."

Kemper smiled. "I don't want Bobby and Jack to find out about this."

"Nobody does."

"Until the debt gets called in?"

"Sam don't believe in frivolous reminders. And in case you're thinking of reminding me, I'll tell you now. I haven't come up with bubkes on the Pension Fund."

Kemper heard footscrapes. He saw Teamsters left and Teamsters right—chain swingers crouched at both ends of the alley.

They had their sights on Lenny. Tiny Lenny, Jewish Lenny, Kennedy toady Lenny—

Lenny didn't see them. Pissy Lenny was entrenched in his cool cat/ tough guy act.

Kemper said, "I'll be in touch."

Lenny said, "See you in shul."

Kemper backed through the alleyway door and double-locked it behind him. He heard shouts, chain rattles and thuds—the classic labor-goon two-way press.

Lenny never yelled or screamed. Kemper timed the beating at a minute and six seconds.

44

(Chicago, 5/10/60)

The work was driving Littell schizophrenic. He had to satisfy the Bureau *and* his conscience.

Chick Leahy hated Mal Chamales. HUAC had linked Mal to sixteen Commie front groups. Leahy's FBI mentor was former Chicago SAC Guy Banister.

Banister hated Mal. Mal's Red Squad sheet was eighty pages long.

He liked Mal. They had coffee every so often. Mal spent '46 to '48 in Lewisburg—Banister built up a sedition profile and talked the U.S. Attorney into an indictment.

Leahy called him this morning. He said, "I want lockstep surveillance on Mal Chamales, Ward. I want you to go to every meeting he goes to and catch him making inflammatory remarks that we can use."

Littell called Chamales and warned him. Mal said, "I'm addressing an SLP group this afternoon. Let's just pretend we don't know each other."

Littell mixed a rye and soda. It was 5:40—he had time to work before the national news.

He padded his report with useless details. He omitted Mal's anti-Bureau tirade. He closed with noncommital remarks.

"The subject's Socialist Labor Party speech was tepid and filled with nebulous cliches of a decidedly leftist, but non-seditious nature. His comments during the question and answer period were not inflammatory or in any way provocative."

Mal called Mr. Hoover "a limp-wristed Fascist in jackboots and lavender lederhosen." An inflammatory statement?—hardly.

Littell turned on the TV. John Kennedy filled the screen—he just won the West Virginia primary.

The doorbell rang. Littell hit the entry buzzer and got out some money for the A&P kid.

Lenny Sands walked in. His face was scabbed, bruised and sutured. A bandaged splint held his nose in place.

Lenny swayed. Lenny smirked. Lenny twirled his fingers at the TV— "Hello, Jack, you gorgeous slice of Irish roast lamb!"

Littell stood up. Lenny weaved into a bookcase and stiff-armed himself steady.

"Ward, you look marvelous! Those frayed slacks from J.C. Penney's and that cheap white shirt are so YOU!"

Kennedy was addressing civil rights. Littell hit the off switch in mid-discourse.

Lenny waved goodbye. "Ta, Jack, my brother-in-law in the best of all possible worlds if I liked girls and you had the profile in courage to acknowledge my dear friend Laura that that gorgeously cruel Mr. Boyd drove out of my life."

Littell moved toward him. "Lenny . . ."

"Don't you fucking come any closer or try to touch me or try to assuage your pathetic guilt or in any way mess with my gorgeous Percodan high or I won't spill my lead on the Teamster Pension Fund books that I've had all along, you sad excuse for a policeman."

Littell stiff-armed a chair. His fingers ripped through the fabric. He started weaving on his feet just like Lenny.

The bookcase shimmied. Lenny was weaving on his heels—doped up and punch-drunk.

"Jules Schiffrin keeps the books someplace in Lake Geneva. He's got an estate there, and he's got the books in safes or in safe-deposit boxes at some banks around there. I know because I played a gig there and I heard Jules and Johnny Rosselli talking. Don't ask for details because I don't have any and concentrating makes my head hurt."

His arm slid. The chair slid behind it. Littell stumbled up against the TV console.

"Why are you telling me this?"

"Because you're a tiny smidgen better than Mr. Beast and Mr. Boyd and in my opinion Mr. Boyd only wants the information for its profit potential, and besides I took a beating for doing some work for Mr. Sam—"

"Lenny—"

"—and Mr. Sam said he'd make a powerful man crawl for it, but I said please don't do that—"

"Lenny—"

"—and Jules Schiffrin was with him, and they were talking about somebody called 'Irish Joe' back in the '20s, and how they made these movie extra girls crawl—"

"Lenny, come on—"

"—and it all felt so ugly that I popped a few more Percs, and here I am, and if I'm lucky I won't remember all this in the morning."

Littell stepped closer. Lenny slapped and scratched and flailed and kicked him away.

The bookcase fell. Lenny tripped and weaved out the door.

Law texts hit the floor. A framed photograph of Helen Agee shattered.

Littell drove to Lake Geneva. He arrived at midnight and checked in at a motel off the Interstate. He paid cash in advance and registered under a fake name.

The phone book in his room listed Jules Schiffrin. His address was marked "Rural Free Delivery." Littell checked a local map and pegged it: a woodland estate near the lake.

He drove out and parked off the road. Binoculars got him in close.

He saw a stonework mansion on a minimum of ten acres. Trees enclosed the property. There were no walls or fences.

No floodlamps. Two hundred yards from the door to the roadway. Alarm tape bracketing the front windows.

No guard hut and no gate. The Wisconsin State Police probably kept watch on an informal basis.

Lenny said "safes or safe-deposit boxes." Lenny said "Mr. Boyd"/ "information"/"profit potential."

Lenny was drugged up but lucid. His Mr. Boyd line was easy to decode.

Kemper was chasing Fund leads independently.

Littell drove back to his motel. He checked the Yellow Pages and found listings for nine local banks.

Discreet behavior would cloak his lack of sanction. Kemper Boyd always stressed boldness *and* discretion.

Kemper shook down Lenny on his own. The revelation didn't shock him at all.

.   .   .

He slept until 10:00. He checked a map and saw that the banks were all within walking distance.

The first four managers cooperated. Their replies were direct: Mr. Schiffrin does not rent with us. The next two managers shook their heads. Their replies were direct: Our facilities do not include safe-deposit boxes.

Manager number seven asked to see a bank writ. It was no great loss: the name Schiffrin sailed past him, unrecognized.

Banks number eight and nine: no safe-deposit boxes on the premises.

There were several major cities nearby. There were two dozen small towns spread out in a hundred-mile radius. Safe-deposit box access was a pipe dream.

"Safes" meant on-site placement. Safe-alarm companies retained placement diagrams—and did not release them without suit for legal cause.

Lenny played an on-site engagement. He might have seen the safe or safes firsthand.

Lenny was too combustible to approach now.

But—

Jack Ruby was a probable Schiffrin acquaintance. Jack Ruby was bribable and acquiescent.

Littell found a pay phone. A long-distance operator patched him through to Dallas.

Ruby picked up on the third ring. "This is the Carousel Club, where your entertainment dollar goes—"

"It's me, Jack. Your friend from Chicago."

"Fuck ... this is grief I don't ..."

He sounded flummoxed, flabbergasted and dyspeptically peeved.

"How well do you know Jules Schiffrin, Jack?"

"Casual. I know Jules casual at best. Why? Why? Why?"

"I want you to fly up to Wisconsin and drop by his place in Lake Geneva on some pretext. I need to know the interior layout of his house, and I'll give you my life savings if you do it."

"Fuck. You are grief I don't—"

"Four thousand dollars, Jack."

"Fuck. You are grief I don't—"

Dog yaps cut Ruby off.

45

(Blessington, 5/12/60)

Jimmy Hoffa said, "I know how Jesus must have felt. The fucking pharaohs rose to power on his coattails like the fucking Kennedy brothers are rising on mine."

Heshie Ryskind said, "Get your history straight. It was Julius Caesar that did Jesus in."

Santo Junior said, "Joe Kennedy is a man you can reason with. It's strictly Bobby that's the bad seed. Joe will explain certain facts of life to Jack if he makes it."

Johnny Rosselli said, "J. Edgar Hoover hates Bobby. And he knows you can't fight the Outfit and win. If the kid is elected, cooler heads than that little cocksucker Bobby's will prevail."

The Boys were sprawled in deck chairs out on the speedboat dock. Pete kept their drinks fresh and let them run off at the mouth.

Hoffa said, "Fucking Jesus turned fish into bread, and that's about the only thing I haven't tried. I've spent six hundred grand on the primaries and bought every fucking cop and alderman and councilman and mayor and fucking grand juror and senator and judge and DA and fucking prosecutorial investigator who'd let me. I'm like Jesus trying to part the Red Fucking Sea and not getting no further than some motel on the beach."

Ryskind said, "Jimmy, calm down. Go get yourself a nice blow job and relax. I've got some reliable local numbers. These are girls who know their trade and would love to satisfy a famous guy like you."

Rosselli said, "If Jack is elected, Bobby will fade into the woodwork. My bet is he'll run for governor of Massachusetts, and Raymond Patriarca and the Boston boys will have to worry about him."

Santo Junior said, "That will never happen. Old Joe and Raymond go too far back. And when push comes to shove, it's Joe who hands down the law—not Jack or Bobby."

Hoffa said, "It's the handing down of grand jury indictments that bothers me. My lawyer said the Sun Valley thing is unlikely to go my way, which means indictments by the end of the year. So don't make Joe Kennedy sound like Jesus handing God the Ten Commandments on Mount Fucking Vesuvius."

Ryskind said, "Santo was just making a point."

Rosselli said, "It's Mount Ararat, Jimmy. Mount Vesuvius is in fucking Yellowstone Park."

Hoffa said, "You guys don't know Jack Kennedy. Fucking Kemper Boyd's got you convinced he's a gung-ho anti-Castro guy when he's really a pinko, Commie-appeasing, nigger-loving fucking homo masquerading as a cunt man."

Wave spray hit the dock. Cadence counts sounded off fifty yards over—Lockhart was running troops through close-order drill.

Ryskind said, "I could go for a blow job."

Rosselli said, "What's the count at, Hesh?"

Ryskind said, "Somewhere in the vicinity of seventeen thousand."

Santo Junior said, "Don't shit a shitter. I'd say eight thousand tops. Anything more than that and you'd be too fucking occupied to make money."

The dock phone rang. Pete tilted his chair back and grabbed the receiver.

"This is Bondurant."

"I'm glad it's you, but don't you soldier types say hello?"

Jack Ruby—un-fucking-mistakable.

Pete cupped the mouthpiece. "What is it? I told you not to call unless it's important."

"What it is is the crazy Fed. He called me yesterday, and I've been stalling him."

What did he want?

"He offered me four Gs to fly up to Lake Geneva Goddamn Wisconsin and case the layout of Jules Schiffrin's house up there. It seems to me this is part of that farkakte Pension Fund—"

"Tell him you'll do it. Set up a meet someplace quiet forty-eight hours from now and call me back."

Ruby gulped and stammered. Pete hung up and popped his knuckles ten across.

The goddamn phone rang again—

Pete snagged it. "Jack, what are you doing?"

A man said, "This ain't Jack. This is a certain Mr. Giancana looking for a certain Mr. Hoffa, who a little birdie told me is there with you."

Pete waved the phone. "It's for you, Jimmy. It's Mo."

Hoffa belched. "Hit that loudspeaker doohickey on that post there. Sam and me got nothing to hide from you guys."

Pete tapped the switch. Hoffa yelled straight at the mike stand: "Yeah, Sam."

The speaker kicked in loud:

"Your West Virginia guys fucked up my boy Lenny Sands, Jimmy. Don't let anything like that happen again or I'd be inclined to make you apologize in front of an audience. My advice to you is to leave politics the fuck alone and concentrate on staying out of jail."

Giancana slammed his phone down. The sound made the whole dock shimmy. Heshie, Johnny and Santo shared this green-at-the-gills look.

Hoffa blew verbal. Birds shot up out of trees and covered the sky.

46

(Lake Geneva, 5/14/60)

The road bisected two fenced-off pastures. Clouds covered the moon—visibility was close to nil. Littell pulled over and stuffed his money in a grocery bag. It was 10:06—Ruby was late.

Littell turned off his headlights. Clouds skittered by. The moon lit up a huge shape walking toward the car.

The windshield exploded. The dashboard fell on his lap. A steel bar cracked the steering wheel and ripped the gearshift out.

Hands jerked him across the hood. Glass ripped through his cheeks and lodged in his mouth.

Hands dumped him in a ditch.

Hands picked him up and pinioned him against a barbed-wire fence.

He was dangling. Steel barbs pierced his clothes and held him upright.

The monster ripped his holster off. The monster hit him and hit him and hit him.

The fence shook. Twisty metal gouged his backside down to the bone. He coughed up blood and chunks of glass and a big piece of a Chevy hood ornament.

He smelled gasoline. His car exploded. A heat blast singed his hair.

The fence collapsed. He looked up and saw clouds ignite.

DOCUMENT INSERT: 5/19/60. FBI Memorandum: Milwaukee Special Agent-in-Charge John Campion to Director J. Edgar Hoover.

Sir:

Our investigation into the near-fatal assault on SA Ward Littell is proceeding but making scant headway, primarily due to SA Littell's poor attitude and lack of cooperation.

Agents from both the Milwaukee and Chicago Offices canvassed Lake Geneva for eyewitnesses to the assault and for witnesses to Littell's general presence in the area and were unable to locate any. Chicago SAC Leahy informed me that Littell was under loose surveillance for matters pertaining to internal Bureau security and that on two recent occasions (May 10th and May 14th) the agents mobile-tailing Littell lost him on roadways leading north to the Wisconsin border. The nature of Littell's business in the Lake Geneva area is thus far unknown.

Per investigatory specifics:

1)—The assault occurred on a rural access road four miles southeast of Lake Geneva. 2)—Brush marks in the dirt near the remains of Littell's car indicate that the assailant obliterated all traces of his tire tracks, rendering forensic casting impossible. 3)—Littell's car was burned with a highly-flammable nitrous gas compound of the type used in the manufacture of military explosives. Such compounds burn themselves out very quickly and are used because they minimize the risk of decimating the area surrounding the target. The assailant obviously has military experience and/or access to military ordnance. 4)—Forensic analysis revealed the presence of charred U.S. currency laced with paper bag fragments. The aggregate weight of the fragments indicates that Littell was carrying a large amount of money in a grocery sack. 5)—Farmers rescued Littell, who was pinned to a downed section of barbed-wire fence. He was taken to Overlander Hospital near Lake Geneva and treated for a massive series of posterior cuts and lacerations, broken ribs, contusions, a broken nose, broken collarbone, internal hemorrhaging and facial gouges caused by contact with windshield glass. Littell checked out against medical advice fourteen hours later and engaged a taxi

cab to drive him to Chicago. Chicago Office agents assigned to
loose-tail Littell saw him entering his apartment building. He collapsed in the entry hall, and the agents interceded on their own
authority and drove him to Saint Catherine's Hospital. 6)—Littell
remains at the hospital. He is listed in "good condition" and will
most likely be released within a week. A supervising physician
told agents that the scarring on his face and backside will be permanent and that he should slowly recover from his other inju-
ries. 7)—Agents have repeatedly queried Littell on three topics:
his presence in Lake Geneva, the presence of the burned money
and enemies who might want to hurt him. Littell stated that he
was in Lake Geneva scouting retirement property and denied the
presence of the money. He said that he had no enemies and considered the assault a case of mistaken identity. When asked
about CPUSA members who might be seeking vengeance on him
for his Bureau Red Squad work, Littell replied, "Are you kid-
ding? Those Commies are all nice guys." 8)—Agents have surmised that Littell has made at least two trips to Lake Geneva. His
name has not appeared on any hotel or motel ledgers, so we are
assuming he either registered under assumed names or stayed
with friends or acquaintances. Littell's response—that he took
catnaps in his car—was not convincing.

The investigation continues. I respectfully await orders.

John Campion
Special Agent-in-Charge, Milwaukee Office

DOCUMENT INSERT: 6/3/60. FBI Memorandum: Chicago SAC
Charles Leahy to Director J. Edgar Hoover.

Sir,

Per SA Ward J. Littell, please be informed.

SA Littell is now back on light duty and has been assigned to
review Federal deportation briefs in conjunction with the U.S. Attorney's Office, work which utilizes the writ-analysis expertise he
developed in law school. He refuses to discuss the assault with
other agents, and as SAC Campion may have told you, we have
yet to find witnesses to his Lake Geneva visits. Helen Agee told
agents that Littell has not discussed the assault with her. I per-

sonally questioned SA Court Meade, Littell's only friend in the Chicago Office, and have the following to report.

A)—Meade states that in late 1958 and early 1959, following his expulsion from the Top Hoodlum Program, Littell "loitered" near the THP listening post and expressed interest in the squad's work. That interest dissipated, Meade stated, and he further surmised that it is extremely unlikely that Littell engaged in anti-Mob actions on his own. Meade scoffed at the notion that the Chicago Mob was responsible for the assault or that left-wingers surveilled by Littell were seeking vengeance for his Red Squad efforts. Meade thinks that Littell's "marked bent" for young women, as evinced by his continuing affair with Helen Agee, was the motive for the assault. Meade colorfully stated, "Go back up to Wisconsin and look for some idealistically-inclined girl with nasty brothers who didn't take kindly to sis consorting with a forty-seven-year-old boozehound, G-man or no G-man." I find this theory plausible.

B)—Littell's Bureau arrest record going back to 1950 was checked with an eye toward uncovering recently paroled felons perhaps inclined toward vengeance. A list of twelve men was compiled, and all twelve were alibi-cleared. I recalled Littell's 1952 arrest of one Pierre "Pete" Bondurant, and how the man taunted Littell during detainment procedures. Agents checked Bondurant's whereabouts during the assault time frame and confirmed that he was in Florida.

The pro-Communist profile of Littell continues to develop. Littell remains a confirmed friend of long-term subversive Mal Chamales and phone tap logs now pinpoint a total of nine Littell/Chamales telephone conversations, all of which contain lengthy expressions of Littell's sympathy for left-wing causes and expressions of his disdain for FBI "witch hunting." On May 10 I called Littell and ordered him to implement immediate lockstep surveillance on Mal Chamales. Five minutes later Littell called Chamales and warned him. Chamales addressed a Socialist Labor Party meeting that afternoon. Littell and a trusted Bureau informant attended, unknown to each other. The informant presented me with a verbatim transcript of Chamales' seditious, virulently anti-Bureau, anti-Hoover remarks. Littell's May 10th report on the meeting called these remarks non-inflammatory. The report was filled with numerous other outright lies and distortions of a treasonous nature.

Sir, I believe it is now time to confront Littell on both his lack of cooperation in the assault matter and more pertinently on his recent seditious actions. Will you please respond? I think this demands immediate action.

Respectfully,
Charles Leahy

DOCUMENT INSERT: 6/11/60. FBI Memorandum: Director J. Edgar Hoover to Chicago SAC Charles Leahy.

Mr. Leahy,

Per Ward Littell: do nothing yet. Put Littell back on CPUSA surveillance duties, relax the surveillance on him and keep me informed of the assault investigation.

JEH

DOCUMENT INSERT: 7/9/60. Official FBI Telephone Call Transcript: "Recorded at the Director's Request"/"Classified Confidential 1-A: Director's Eyes Only." Speaking: Director Hoover, Special Agent Kemper Boyd.

KB: Good afternoon, Sir.

JEH: Kemper, I'm peeved at you. You've been avoiding me for some time.

KB: I wouldn't put it that way, Sir.

JEH: Of course you wouldn't. You'd put it in a way calculated to minimize my rancor. The question is, would you have contacted me if I hadn't contacted you?

KB: Yes, Sir. I would have.

JEH: Before or after the coronation of King Jack the First?

KB: I wouldn't call the coronation a sure thing, Sir.

JEH: Does he have a delegate majority?

KB: Almost. I think he'll be nominated on the first ballot.

JEH: And you think he'll win.

KB: Yes, I'm reasonably certain.

JEH: I can't dispute that. Big Brother and America have all the earmarks of a fatuous love affair.

KB: He is going to retain you, Sir.

JEH: Of course he is. Every President since Calvin Coolidge has, and you should temper your distancing process with the

knowledge that Prince Jack will be in office for a maximum of
eight years, while I shall remain in office until the Millennium.

KB: I'll keep that in mind, Sir.

JEH: I would advise you to. You should also be advised that
my interest in Big Brother extends beyond the confines of wish-
ing to keep my job. Unlike you, I have altruistic concerns, such
as the internal security of our nation. Unlike you, my primary
concern is not self-preservation and monetary advancement. Unlike you, I do not credit the ability to dissemble as my single
greatest skill.

KB: Yes, Sir.

JEH: Allow me to interpret your reluctance to contact me.
Were you afraid I would ask you to introduce Big Brother to
Bureau-friendly women?

KB: Yes and no, Sir.

JEH: Meaning?

KB: Meaning Little Brother doesn't entirely trust me. Meaning
the primary campaign schedule was hectic and only left me time
to procure local call girls. Meaning I might have been able to
house Big Brother in hotel rooms with standing Bureau bugs, but
Little Brother has been around law enforcement for years, and
he just might know that co-opt bugs like that exist.

JEH: I always reach a certain point with you.

KB: Meaning?

JEH: Meaning I don't know whether or not you're lying, and
to one degree or another I don't care.

KB: Thank you, Sir.

JEH: You're welcome. It was an appalling compliment, but a
sincere one. Now, are you going to Los Angeles for the
convention?

KB: I'm leaving tomorrow. I'll be staying at the downtown
Statler.

JEH: You'll be contacted. King Jack will not want for female
friendship should he find himself bored between accolades.

KB: Electronically-adorned friends?

JEH: No, just good listeners. We'll talk about some co-opt work
during the fall campaign, if Little Brother trusts you with travel
plans.

KB: Yes, Sir.

JEH: Who assaulted Ward Littell?

KB: I'm not sure, Sir.

JEH: Have you spoken to Littell?

KB: Helen Agee called and told me about the beating. I called Ward at the hospital, but he refused to tell me who did it.

JEH: Pete Bondurant comes to mind. He's involved in your Cuban escapades, isn't he?

KB: Yes, he is.

JEH: Yes, he is, and?

KB: And we talk as Agency business dictates.

JEH: The Chicago Office was satisfied with Bondurant's alibi. The alibi-giver was a reputed Heroin trafficker with numerous rape convictions inside Cuba, but as Al Capone once said, an alibi is an alibi.

KB: Yes, Sir. And as you once said, anti-Communism breeds strange bedfellows.

JEH: Goodbye, Kemper. I very much hope that our next communique is at your instigation.

KB: Goodbye, Sir.

47

(Los Angeles, 7/13/60)

The clerk handed him a gold-plated key. "We had a reservations glitch, sir. Your room was inadvertently given away, but we're going to give you a suite at our regular room rate."

Check-ins pushed up to the desk. Kemper said, "Thanks. It's a glitch I can live with."

The clerk shuffled papers. "May I ask you a question?"

"Let me guess. If my room is being charged to the Kennedy campaign, why am I staying here instead of at the Biltmore with the rest of the staff?"

"Yes, sir. That's it exactly."

Kemper winked. "I'm a spy."

The clerk laughed. Some delegate types waved to get his attention.

Kemper brushed past them and elevatored up to the twelfth floor. His suite: the double-doored, gold-sealed, all-antique Presidential.

He walked through it. He savored the appointments and checked out the north-by-northeast view.

Two bedrooms, three TVs and three phones. Complimentary champagne in a pewter ice bucket marked with the U.S. presidential seal.

He deciphered the "glitch" instantly: J. Edgar Hoover at work.

He wants to scare you. He's saying, "I own you." He's satirizing your Kennedy fervor and love of hotel suites.

He wants potential bug/tap intelligence.

Kemper turned on the living-room TV. Convention commentary hit the screen.

He turned on the other sets—and boosted the volume way up.

He grid-searched the suite. He found condensor mikes inside five table lamps and fake panels behind the bathroom mirrors.

He found two auxiliaries spackled into the living-room wainscoting. Tiny perforations served as sound ducts—nonprofessionals would never spot them. He checked out the telephones. All four were tapped.

Kemper thought it through from Hoover's perspective.

We discussed standing bugs a few days ago. He knows I don't want to set Jack up with "Bureau-friendly" women.

He said he thinks Jack is inevitable. He may be dissembling. He may be seeking knowledge of adultery—to aid his good friend Dick Nixon.

He knows you'll see through the "reservations glitch." He thinks you'll make your confidential calls from pay phones. He thinks you'll curtail your in-suite talk or destroy the bug/taps out of pique.

He knows Littell taught you bug/tap fundamentals. He doesn't know Littell taught you some fine points.

He knows you'll uncover the *main bugs*. He thinks you won't uncover the backups—the ones he plans to sucker-punch you with.

Kemper turned off the TVs. Kemper faked a vivid temper tantrum—"Hoover, goddamn you!" and worse expletives.

He ripped out the primary bug/taps.

He grid-searched the suite again—even more diligently.

He found secondary phone taps. He spotted microphone perforations on two mattress labels and three chair cushions.

He went down to the lobby and rented room 808 under a pseudonym. He called John Stanton's service and left his fake name and room number.

Pete was in L.A., meeting with Howard Hughes. He called the watchdog house and left a message with the pool cleaner.

He had free time now. Bobby didn't need him until 5:00.

He walked to a hardware store. He bought wire cutters, pliers, a Phillips-head screwdriver, three rolls of friction tape and two small magnets. He walked back to the Statler and worked.

He rewired the buzzer housings. He recircuited the feeder wires. He muffled the bells with pillow stuffing. He scraped the rubber off the lead cables—incoming talk would register incoherently on all the backup-tapped phones.

He laid the pieces out for easy reassembly. He called room service for Beefeater's and smoked salmon.

■　■　■

Calls came in. His squelch system worked perfectly.

He barely heard the callers. Line crackle would drown out all second-party talk—the taps would only pick up *his* voice.

His LAPD liaison called. As planned: a motorcycle escort would accompany Senator Kennedy to the convention.

Bobby called. Could he get some cabs to shuttle staffers back to the Biltmore?

Kemper called a car service and implemented Bobby's order. He had to strain to hear the dispatcher talk.

Horns blasted down on Wilshire Boulevard. Kemper checked his watch and the living-room window.

His "Protestants for Kennedy" motorcade passed by. On time to the minute—and prepaid at fifty dollars a car.

Kemper turned on the TVs and paced between them. History beamed out in crisp black & white.

CBS called Jack a first ballot shoo-in. ABC flashed panning shots—a big Stevenson demonstration just erupted. NBC featured a prissy Eleanor Roosevelt: "Senator Kennedy is simply too young!"

ABC ballyhooed Jackie Kennedy. NBC showed Frank Sinatra working the delegate floor. Frankie was vain—Jack said he spray-painted his bald spot to cut down camera glare.

Kemper paced and flipped channels. He caught a late-afternoon potpourri.

Convention analysis and a baseball game. Convention interviews and a Marilyn Monroe movie. Convention shots, convention shots, convention shots.

He caught some nice shots of Jack's HQ suite. He saw Ted Sorensen, Kenny O'Donnell and Pierre Salinger.

He met Salinger and O'Donnell once only. Jack pointed out Sorensen—"the guy who wrote *Profiles in Courage* for me."

It was "compartmentalization" classically defined. Jack and Bobby knew him—but no one else really did. He was just that cop who fixed things and got Jack women.

Kemper wheeled the TVs together. He created a tableau: Jack in closeups and mid-shots.

He turned the room lights off and dimmed the volume. He got three images and one homogeneous whisper.

Wind ruffled Jack's hair. Pete called Jack's head of hair his chief attribute.

Pete refused to discuss the Littell assault. Pete sidestepped the issue to talk money.

Pete called him while Littell was still in the hospital. Pete got right to the point.

"You're jazzed on the Pension Fund books, and so's Littell. You're goosing him to find them, so you can work a money angle on it. I say, after the election we *both* brace Littell. Whatever the angle is, we split the profit."

Pete emasculated Ward. Pete delivered the "scare" that he said he would.

He called Littell at the hospital. Ward compartmentalized his response.

"I don't trust you on this, Kemper. You can get the forensic particulars from the Bureau, but I'm not telling you WHO or WHY."

The WHERE was Lake Geneva, Wisconsin. The location *had to be* Pension Fund pertinent. "I don't trust you on this" could only mean one thing: Lenny Sands was talking trash to Littell.

Pete knew compartmentalization. Ward and Lenny knew it. John Stanton said the CIA coined that particular concept.

John called him in D.C. in mid-April. He said Langley just erected a compartmental wall.

"They're cutting us off, Kemper. They know about our Cadre business, and they approve, but they will not budget us one nickel. We're on salary as Blessington campsite staff, but our actual Cadre business has been excommunicated."

It meant no CIA cryptonyms. No CIA acronyms. No CIA code names and no CIA initial/oblique-sign gobbledegook.

The Cadre was purely compartmentalized.

Kemper flipped channels with the sound off. He got a gorgeous juxtaposition: Jack and Marilyn Monroe on adjoining TV screens.

He laughed. He snapped to the ultimate tweak-Hoover embellishment.

He picked up the phone and dialed the daily weather number. He got a monotone buzz—barely audible.

He said, "Kenny? Hi, it's Kemper Boyd." He waited four seconds. "No, I need to talk to the senator."

He waited fourteen seconds. He said, "How are you, Jack?"—bright and cheerful.

He waited five seconds to allow for a plausible reply. He said, "Yes, everything *is* set up with the escort."

Twenty-two seconds. "Yes. Right. I know you're busy."

Eight seconds. "Yes. Tell Bobby I've got the security people at the house all set up."

Twelve seconds. "Right, the purpose of this call *is* to see if you want to get laid, because if you do, I'm expecting calls from a few girls who'd love to meet you."

Twenty-four seconds. "I don't believe it."

Nine seconds. "Lawford set it up?"

Eight seconds. "Come on, Jack. *Marilyn Monroe?*"

Eight seconds. "I'll believe it if you tell me not to send my girls over."

Six seconds. "Jesus Christ."

Eight seconds. "They'll be disappointed, but I'll extend the raincheck."

Eight seconds. "Right. Naturally, I'll want details. Right. Goodbye, Jack."

Kemper hung up. Jack and Marilyn bumped television heads.

He just created Voyeur/Wiretap Heaven. Hoover would cream his jeans and maybe even spawn some crazy myth.

48

(Beverly Hills, 7/14/60)

Wyoming went for Bad-Back Jack. The delegates went stone fucking nuts.

Hughes doused the volume and scrunched up on his pillows. "He's nominated. But that's a far cry from being elected."

Pete said, "Yes, sir."

"You're being deliberately obtuse. 'Yes, sir' is not the proper response, and you're sitting there in that chair being deliberately disrespectful."

A commercial blipped on: Yeakel Oldsmobile, the voters' choice!

"How's this? 'Yes, sir, Jack's got a nice head of hair, but your man Nixon will thrash him soundly in the general election.' "

Hughes said, "It's better, but I detect a certain impertinence."

Pete cracked his thumbs. "I flew out because you said you needed to see me. I brought you a three-month supply of shit. You said you wanted to discuss some subpoena dodging strategy, but all you've done so far is rant about the Kennedys."

Hughes said, "That is *gross* impertinence."

Pete sighed. "Get your Mormons to show me the door, then. Get Duane Spurgeon to score you dope in violation of six trillion fucking state and Federal statutes."

Hughes flinched. His IV tubes stretched; his blood bottle wiggled. Vampire Howard: sucking in transfusions to assure his germ-free longevity.

"You're a very cruel man, Pete."

"No. Like I told you once before, I'm *your* very cruel man."

"Your eyes have gotten smaller and crueler. You keep looking at me strangely."

"I'm waiting for you to bite my neck. I've been around the block a few times, but this new Dracula kick of yours is something to see."

Hughes fucking *smiled*. "It's no more amazing than you fighting Fidel Castro."

Pete smiled. "Was there something important you wanted to talk about?"

The convention flashed back on. Bad-Back Jack supporters whooped and swooned.

"I want you to vet the subpoena-avoidance plans my Mormon colleagues have devised. They've come up with some ingenious—"

"We could have done it over the phone. You've been holding the TWA paperwork off since '57, and I don't think the Justice Department gives a shit anymore."

"Be that as it may, I now have a specific reason to avoid divesting TWA until the most opportune moment."

Pete sighed. Pete said, "I'm listening."

Hughes tapped his drip gizmos. A blood bottle drained red to pink.

"When I finally divest, I want to use the money to buy hotel-casinos in Las Vegas. I want to accumulate large, undetectable cash profits and breathe wholesome, germ-free desert air. I'll have my Mormon colleagues administer the hotels, to insure that Negroes who might pollute the environment are politely but firmly discouraged from entering, and I'll create a cash-flow base that will allow me to diversify into various defense-industry areas without paying taxes on my seed money. I'll—"

Pete tuned him out. Hughes kept spritzing numbers: millions, billions, trillions. Jack the K. was on TV—spritzing "Vote for Me!" with the sound down.

Pete ran numbers in his head.

There's Littell in Lake Geneva—chasing the Pension Fund. There's Jules Schiffrin—a well-respected Chi-Mob graybeard. Jules *just might* have the Pension books stashed at his pad.

Hughes said, "Pete, you're not listening to me. Quit looking at that puerile politician and give me your full attention."

Pete hit the off switch. Jack the Haircut faded out.

Hughes coughed. "That's better. You were looking at that boy with something like admiration."

"It's his hair, Boss. I was wondering how he got it to stand up like that."

"You have a short memory. And I have a short fuse where ironic answers are concerned."

"Yeah?"

"Yes. You might recall that two years ago I gave you thirty thousand dollars to try to compromise that boy with a prostitute."

"I remember."

"That's not a complete answer."

"The complete answer is 'Things change.' And you don't think America's going to get between the sheets with Dick Nixon when they can cozy up to Jack, do you?"

Hughes pushed himself upright. His bed rails shook; his IV rig teetered.

"I own Richard Nixon."

Pete said, "I know you do. And I'm sure he's real grateful for that loan you floated his brother."

Dracula got the shakes. Dracula got his dentures snagged up on the roof of his mouth.

Dracula got some words out. "I—I—I'd forgotten that you knew about that."

"A busy guy like you can't remember everything."

Drac reached for a fresh hypo. "Dick Nixon's a good man, and the entire Kennedy family is rotten down to the core. Joe Kennedy's been lending gangsters money since the '20s, and I know for a fact that the infamous Raymond L. S. Patriarca owes him the very shirt off his back."

He had the Nixon loan documented. He could feed the dope to Boyd and curry big-time favor with Jack.

Pete said, "Like I owe you."

Hughes beamed. "I knew you'd see my point."

49

(Chicago, 7/15/60)

L ittell studied his new face.

His weak jawline was rebuilt with pins and bone chips. His weak chin was smashed into a cleft. The nose he always hated was flattened and ridged.

Helen said he looked dangerous. Helen said his scars put hers to shame.

Littell stepped back from the mirror. Shifting light gave him new angles to savor.

He limped now. His jaw clicked. He put on twenty pounds in the hospital.

Pete Bondurant was a cosmetic surgeon.

He had a bold new face. His old pre-Phantom psyche couldn't live up to it.

He was afraid to move on Jules Schiffrin. He was afraid to confront Kemper. He was afraid to talk on the phone—little line clicks popped in his ears.

The clicks could be jaw-pin malfunctions. The clicks could be audial DTs.

He was six months short of retirement. Mal Chamales said the Party needed lawyers.

A TV boomed next door. John Kennedy's acceptance speech faded into applause.

The Bureau discontinued their assault inquiry. Hoover knew that he could sabotage Boyd's Kennedy incursion.

Littell stepped close to the mirror. The scars above his eyebrows furrowed.

He couldn't stop looking.

50

Pete turned forty on a speedboat run to Cuba. He led a raid on a militia station and took sixteen scalps.

Ramón Gutiérrez sketched up a Cadre mascot: a pit bull with an alligator snout and razor-blade teeth. Ramón's girlfriend sewed up mascot shoulder patches.

A printer fashioned mascot calling cards. "FREE CUBA!" roared out of the Beast's mouth.

Carlos Marcello carried one. Sam G. carried one. Santo Junior handed out dozens to friends and associates.

The Beast craved blood. The Beast craved Castro's beard on a stick.

Training cycles pushed through Blessington. The invasion plan mandated new ordnance. Dougie Frank Lockhart purchased surplus landing craft and "invaded" Alabama once per cycle.

The Gulf Coast simulated Cuba. Trainees hit the beach and scared the shit out of sunbathers.

Dougie Frank trained troops full-time. Pete trained troops part-time. Chuck, Fulo and Wilfredo Delsol ran the cabstand.

Pete led speedboat runs into Cuba. Everybody went along—except Delsol.

The Obregón kill snipped part of his balls. Pete didn't judge him—losing blood kin in a flash was no picnic.

Everybody sold dope.

The Cadre supplied spook junkies exclusively. The Miami PD implicitly approved. Narco Squad payouts served as disapproval insurance.

A redneck gang tried to crash their turf late in August. One geek shot and killed a Dade County deputy.

Pete found the guy—holed up with seventy grand and a case of Wild Turkey. He took him out with Fulo's machete and donated the cash to the deputy's widow.

Profits zoomed. The % system worked slick as shit—fat stipends went to Blessington and Guy Banister. Lenny Sands ran the *Hush-Hush* propaganda war. Purple prose bopped the Beard every week.

Dracula called weekly. He spouted broken-record bullshit: I want to buy up Las Vegas and render it germ-free! Drac was half lucid and half nuts—and only really cagey where coin was concerned.

Boyd called bi-weekly. Boyd was Bad-Back Jack's security boss and head pimp.

Mr. Hoover kept chasing him with phone calls. Kemper kept avoiding them. Hoover wanted him to slip Jack some hot-wired pussy.

Boyd called it a sprint: Avoid The Man until Jack becomes The Man.

Hoover hot-wired Boyd's L.A. hotel suite. Kemper shot him some spicy misinformation: Jack the K is banging Marilyn Monroe!

Hoover bought the lie. An L.A. agent told Boyd that Monroe was now under intense surveillance: bug/taps and six full-time men.

Said agents were baffled. Jack the Haircut and MM have not been in contact.

Pete laughed himself silly. Dracula confirmed the rumor: Marilyn and Jack were one hot item!!!!

Boyd said he skin-searched all Jack's girls.

Boyd said Kennedy and Nixon were running neck-and-neck.

Pete didn't say, *I've* got dirt. I can SELL it to Jimmy Hoffa; I can GIVE it to you to smear Nixon with.

Jimmy's a colleague. Boyd's a partner. Who's more pro-Cause—Jack or Nixon?

Tricky Dick was hotly anti-Beard. Jack was vocal but still short of rabid.

John Stanton called Nixon "Mr. Invasion." Kemper said Jack would green-light all invasion plans.

Boyd's key campaign issue was COMPARTMENTALIZATION.

Ike and Dick knew the Agency and the Mob were Cuba-linked. The Kennedys didn't know—and might or might not be told if Jack bags the White House.

Who decides whether to spill?—Kemper Cathcart Boyd himself. The deciding factor: moralist Bobby's perceived influence on Big Brother.

Bobby could scut all Mob/CIA ties. Bobby could scut the Boyd/ Bondurant casino incentive deal.

Jack or Dick—one very tough call.

The smart bet: Don't smear seasoned Red-baiter Nixon. Not so smart, but sexy: Smear him and put Jack in the White House.

Vote Boyd. Vote the Beast. Vote Fidel Castro's beard on a stick.

DOCUMENT INSERT: 10/13/60. FBI memorandum: Chicago SAC
Charles Leahy to Director J. Edgar Hoover. Marked: CONFIDEN-
TIAL/DIRECTOR'S EYES ONLY.

Sir,

The pro-Communist derogatory profile on SA Ward J. Littell is
now complete. This memo supplants all previous confidential reports pertaining to Littell, with itemized evidence documents to
follow under separate cover.

To briefly update you on recent developments:

1.—Claire Boyd (daughter of SA Kemper C. Boyd and longtime
Littell family friend) was contacted and agreed not to tell her father of the interview. Miss Boyd stated that last Christmas SA
Littell made obscenely disparaging anti-Bureau, anti-Hoover remarks and praised the American Communist Party.

2.—There are no leads in the Littell assault investigation. We
still do not know what Littell was doing in Lake Geneva,
Wisconsin.

3.—SA Littell's mistress, Helen Agee, was spot-surveilled for a
two-week period last month. Several of Miss Agee's University of
Chicago Law School professors were quizzed about her political
statements. We now have four confirmed reports that Miss Agee
has also been publicly critical of the Bureau. One professor (Chicago Office informant #179) stated that Miss Agee railed against
the FBI for their failure to solve a "simple assault case up in
Wisconsin" and went on to call the Bureau "the American Ge-
stapo that got my father killed and turned my lover into a crip-
ple." (A U of C dean is going to recommend that Miss Agee's
graduate school grant funding be rescinded under provisions of a
student loyalty statement that all law school enrollees sign.)

In conclusion:

I think it is now time to approach SA Littell. I await further
orders.

Respectfully,
Charles Leahy
Chicago SAC

DOCUMENT INSERT: 10/15/60. FBI memorandum: Director J. Edgar Hoover to SAC Charles Leahy.

Mr. Leahy,

No approach on SA Littell until I so direct.

JEH

51

(Chicago, 10/16/60)

His hangover was brutal. Bad dreams left him schizy—every man in the diner looked like a cop.

Littell stirred his coffee. His hands shook. Mal Chamales toyed with a sweet roll and shook almost as hard.

"Mal, you're leading up to something."

"I'm in no position to be asking favors."

"If it's an official FBI favor, you should know that I retire exactly three months from today."

Mal laughed. "Like I said, the Party always needs lawyers."

"I'd have to pass the Illinois Bar first. It's either that or move to D.C. and practice Federal law."

"You're not much of a leftist sympathizer."

"Or a Bureau apologist. Mal—"

"I'm up for a teaching job. The word's out that the State Board of Ed's breaking the blacklist. I want to cover my bets, and I was thinking you could edit your reports to show that I quit the Party."

The tall man at the counter looked familiar. The man loitering outside did, too.

"Ward . . ."

"Sure, Mal. I'll write it up in my next report. I'll say you quit the Party to take a job with the Nixon campaign."

Mal dashed some tears back. Mal almost dumped the table trying to hug him.

Littell said, "Get out of here. I don't like embracing Commies in public."

The diner faced his apartment building. Littell hogged a window seat and killed time polling bumper stickers.

Two Nixon cars were parked at the curb. He saw a Nixon-Lodge decal on his landlord's windshield.

Traffic whizzed by. Littell caught glimpses: six Nixons and three Kennedys.

The waitress topped off his coffee. He added two shots from his flask.

Instant straw poll results: Nixon sweeps Chicago!

Sunlight hit the window. Wonderful distortions hit him: his new face and his jagged new hairline.

Helen ran up the steps outside his apartment. She looked harried—no makeup, no overcoat, mismatched skirt and blouse.

She saw his car. She looked across the street and saw him in the window.

She ran over. Notebook paper flew out of her handbag.

Littell walked to the door. Helen *shoved* it open two-handed.

He tried to grab her. She pulled his gun out of his holster and hit him with it.

She hit him in the chest. She hit him in the arms. She tried to pull the trigger with the safety on. She hit him with flailing girl punches—too fast to stop.

Eyeliner ran down her cheeks. Her handbag capsized and spilled books. She shouted odd words: "grant fund rescinding" and "loyalty oath" and "FBI" and "YOU YOU YOU."

Heads bobbed their way. Two men at the counter pulled *their* guns.

Helen stopped hitting him. Helen said, "Goddamnit, this is YOU, I know it is."

He drove to the office. He boxed in Leahy's car and ran up to the squadroom.

Leahy's door was shut. Court Meade saw him and turned away.

Two men walked by in shirtsleeves and shoulder holsters. Littell remembered them: the phone guys rigging lines outside his apartment.

Leahy's door swung open. A man stuck his head out. Littell remembered him: that guy at the post office yesterday.

The door closed. Voices seeped through it: "Littell," "the Agee girl."

He kicked the door off its hinges. He framed the scene à la Mal Chamales.

Four gray-flannel fascists in conference. Four parasitic, exploitative, right-wing—

Littell said, "Remember what I know. Remember how I can hurt the Bureau."

He bought wire cutters, safety goggles, magnetic shielding strips, a glass cutter, rubber gloves, a .10-gauge shotgun, a hundred rounds of double-aught buckshot, a box of industrial dynamite, three hundred yards of acoustical baffling, a hammer, nails and two large duffel bags.

He stored his car in a service garage.

He rented a '57 Ford Victoria—with fake Cointelpro ID.

He bought three quarts of scotch—just enough to wean himself dry.

He drove south to Sioux City, Iowa.

He turned in his rental car and caught a train north to Milwaukee.

<u>DOCUMENT INSERT</u>: 10/17/60. Confidential memorandum: John Stanton to Kemper Boyd.

Kemper,

I got a disquieting phone call from Guy Banister, so I thought I'd pass the information along to you. You're hard to reach these days, so I hope this gets to you within a reasonable length of time.

Guy's friends with the Miami SAC, who's tight with the CO of the Miami PD Intelligence Squad. The Squad keeps suspected pro-Castro Cubans under loose surveillance, with routine license plate checks on all the male Latins they are spotted with. Our man Wilfredo Olmos Delsol was seen on two occasions with <u>Gaspar Ramon Blanco</u>, age 37, a known pro-Communist member of the <u>Committee for Cuban Understanding</u>, a Raul Castro-financed propaganda front. This troubles me, chiefly because of PB's set-to with Delsol's cousin Tomas Obregon. Have PB check this out, would you? Our compartmentalization procedures preclude my contacting him directly.

All best,
John

52

(Miami, 10/20/60)

The pilot announced a late arrival. Kemper checked his watch—Pete's allotted time just evaporated.

Pete caught up with him in Omaha this morning. He said, I've got something for you—something you'll want to *see*.

He promised that the stopover would take no more than twenty minutes. He said, I'll put you on the next plane back to Jack.

Miami twinkled below. He had crucial work in Omaha—postponed by this six-hour detour.

The race was too close to call. Nixon *might* have a slight edge—with eighteen days left to go.

He called Laura from the departure lounge. She lit into his Kennedy ties. Claire kept saying that Laura ached for a Nixon victory.

Claire said FBI men questioned her last month. Their sole topic was Ward Littell's politics.

The agents intimidated her. They cautioned her not to mention the interview to her father.

Claire broke the promise and called him three days ago. He called Ward immediately.

His phone rang and rang. The rings had a distinct wiretap pitch.

He called Court Meade to check on Ward's whereabouts. Meade said Ward kicked the SAC's door down and vanished.

Claire called him in Omaha last night. She said the Bureau got Helen's law school grant revoked.

Mr. Hoover stopped calling him two days ago. It all connected some-how. The campaign had him running too fast to be scared.

Crosswinds roughed up their descent. The plane taxied in with a fishtailing whoosh.

Kemper checked his window. He saw Pete standing outside, with the ground crew. The men were palming cash rolls and fawning at the big guy with the money.

Landing stairs locked in. Kemper crowded up to the door.

The co-pilot cranked it open. There's Pete—with a baggage cart parked on the runway, right below them.

Kemper took the steps three at a time. Pete grabbed him and cupped a yell. "Your plane's delayed! We've got half an hour!"

Kemper jumped on the cart. Pete gunned it. They dodged luggage piles and swung around to a janitor's hut.

A baggage handler got the door. Pete slipped him twenty dollars.

A linen tablecloth was draped over a workbench. On it: gin, ver-mouth, a glass and six sheets of paper.

Pete said, "Read through that."

Kemper skimmed the top page. His hackles jumped immediately.

Howard Hughes lent Dick Nixon's kid brother $200,000. Check photo-stats, bookkeeping notes and bank slips proved it. Somebody compiled an itemized list: Nixon-proffered legislation linked to Hughes govern-ment contracts.

Kemper mixed a drink. His hands shook. He spilled Beefeater's all over the workbench.

He looked at Pete. "You haven't asked for money."

"If I wanted money, I would have called Jimmy."

"I'll tell Jack he's got a friend in Miami."

"Tell him to let us invade Cuba, and I'll call it even."

The martini was gorgeously dry. The janitor's hut glowed like the Carlyle.

"Keep an eye on Wilfredo Delsol. It's anticlimactic now, but I think he might be screwing up."

Pete said, "Call Bobby. I want to hear you put the little fuck in hock to me."

DOCUMENT INSERT: 10/23/60. Cleveland Plain Dealer headline:

HUGHES-NIXON LOAN REVELATIONS ROCK CAMPAIGN

DOCUMENT INSERT: 10/24/60. Chicago Tribune subhead:

KENNEDY BLASTS NIXON-HUGHES "COLLUSION"

DOCUMENT INSERT: 10/25/60. Los Angeles Herald-Express headline and subhead:

NIXON DENIES INFLUENCE-PEDDLING ACCUSATIONS

HUGHES LOAN BROUHAHA CUTS VEEP'S LEAD IN POLLS

DOCUMENT INSERT: 10/26/60. New York Journal-American subhead:

NIXON CALLS LOAN FLAP "TEMPEST IN TEAPOT"

DOCUMENT INSERT: 10/28/60. San Francisco Chronicle headline:

NIXON BROTHER CALLS HUGHES LOAN "NON-POLITICAL"

DOCUMENT INSERT: 10/29/60. Kansas City Star subhead:

KENNEDY BLASTS NIXON FOR HUGHES LOAN

DOCUMENT INSERT: 11/3/60: Boston Globe headline:

GALLUP POLL: PREZ'L RACE DEAD HEAT!

53

(Lake Geneva, 11/5/60)

Littell ran through his checklist.

Goggles, earplugs, wire cutters, glass cutter—check. Magnet strips, gloves, shotgun, ammunition—check.

Waterproof-fuse dynamite—check. Acoustical baffling, hammer, nails—check.

Check: You wiped every print-sustaining surface in this motel room.

Check: You left your check-out cash on the dresser.

Check: You avoided all contact with your fellow motel tenants.

He ran through his three-week precaution list.

You changed motels every other day—in zigzag patterns throughout southern Wisconsin.

You wore fake beards and fake mustaches at all times.

You changed rental cars at odd intervals. You took buses between car-rental pickups. You secured said cars at distant sites: Des Moines, Minneapolis and Green Bay.

You rented said cars with fake ID.

You paid cash.

You parked said cars nowhere near the motels you checked into.

You made no motel-room phone calls. You print-wiped every surface before you checked out.

You employed tail-evasion tactics. You limited your liquor intake: six shots a night to insure steady nerves.

You spotted no tails.

You stared at single men, gauged their reactions and discerned nothing cop- or Mob-like. Most men evinced discomfort: you were rough-looking now.

You cased Jules Schiffrin's estate. You determined that the man had no live-in help or on-site watchmen.

You learned Schiffrin's routine:

Saturday-night dinner and cards at Badger Glen Country Club. Early-Sunday-morning sojourns at the home of one Glenda Rae Mattson.

Jules Schiffrin was gone from 7:05 p.m. to 2:00 a.m. every Saturday into Sunday. His estate was police patrolled every two hours—cursory perimeter road checks.

You secured safe-placement and alarm diagrams. You queried seventeen services to get them. You impersonated a Milwaukee PD lieutenant and buttressed the impersonations with forged documents and credentials purchased from a forger that you arrested years ago.

All your police impersonations were carried out in disguise.

Two steel-plated safes were installed on the premises. They weighed ninety-five pounds apiece. You had their exact location memorized.

Final checks:

Your new motel room outside Beloit: safely rented.

The newspaper piece on Schiffrin's art collection: clipped out to leave at the crime scene.

Littell took a deep breath and downed three quick shots. His nerves fluttered and *almost* leveled out.

He checked his face in the bathroom mirror. One last look for courage—

Low clouds covered the moon. Littell drove to the half-mile-out point.

It was 11:47. He had two hours and thirteen minutes to get clear.

A State Police cruiser passed him eastbound. On time: the standard 11:45 perimeter check.

Littell swung off the pavement. Hard-packed dirt grabbed his tires. He hit his brights and slalomed downhill.

The slope evened out. He brodied his back wheels to obliterate tread marks.

Trees dotted the clearing—his car couldn't be seen from the road.

He killed the lights and grabbed his duffel bag. He saw house lights due west uphill—a faint directional glow to work off of.

He walked toward it. Leaf clumps obscured his footprints. The glow expanded every few seconds.

He hit the driveway adjoining the carport. Schiffrin's Eldorado Brougham was gone.

He ran to the library window and crouched low. An inside lamp provided hazy light to work by.

He got out his tools and snipped two wires taped to a storm drain. An exterior arc light sputtered. He saw alarm tape bracketing the window glass—mounted between two thick panes.

He gauged the circumference.

He cut magnet-tape strips to cover it.

He stuck them to the outside glass in a near-perfect outline.

His legs ached. Cold sweat stung some shaving cuts.

He ran a magnet over the tape. He traced a circle inside the outline with his glass cutter.

The glass was THICK—it took two hands and all his weight to notch a groove.

No alarms went off. No lights flashed.

He gouged circles in the glass. No sirens whirred; no general pursuit noise went down.

His arms burned. His blade went sharp to dull. His sweat froze and made him shiver.

The outside pane broke. He tucked his sleeves inside his gloves and bore down harder.

TWENTY-NINE MINUTES ELAPSED.

Elbow pressure snapped the inside pane. Littell kicked the frame glass out to make a crawl space.

He vaulted inside. The fit was tight—glass shards cut him down to the skin.

The library was oak-paneled and furnished with green leather chairs. The side walls featured artwork: one Matisse, one Cézanne, one van Gogh.

Floor lamps gave him light—just enough to do the job by.

He arranged his tools.

He found the safes: wall-panel-recessed two feet apart.

He covered every inch of wall space with triple-thick acoustical baffling. He hammered it down tight—fivepenny nails into high-varnished oak.

He X-marked the sections covering the safes. He put on his goggles and stuffed in his earplugs. He loaded his shotgun and let fly.

One round, two rounds—huge contained explosions. Three rounds, four rounds—padding chunks and hardwood decomposing.

Littell reloaded and fired, reloaded and fired, reloaded and fired.

Wood chips sliced his face. Muzzle smoke had him retching. Visibility was zero: mulch slammed up against his goggles.

Littell reloaded and fired, reloaded and fired, reloaded and fired. Forty-odd rounds took the wall and rear ceiling beams down.

Wood and plaster crashed. Second-story furniture dropped down and shattered. Two safes fell out of the rubble.

Littell kicked through it—Please, God, let me breathe.

He vomited splinters and scotch. He coughed up gunsmoke and black phlegm. He dug through wood heaps and lugged the safes over to his duffel bag.

SEVENTY-TWO MINUTES ELAPSED.

The library was blasted through to the dining room. Forty-odd explosions toppled the artwork.

The Cézanne was intact. The Matisse bore slight frame damage. The van Gogh was pellet-shredded nothingness.

Littell dropped the newspaper clip.

Littell lashed the duffel to his back with curtain strips.

Littell grabbed the paintings and ran out the front door.

Pure air made him go lightheaded. He gulped it in and ran.

He slid on leaves and bounced off trees. His bladder went—nothing ever felt so good. He stumbled, hunched over double—two hundred pounds of steel kept him plummeting downhill.

He fell. His body went rubber—he couldn't stand up or lift the duffel bag.

He crawled and dragged it the rest of the way. He loaded his car and fishtailed up to the access road, heaving for breath the whole time.

He caught his face in the rearview mirror. The word "heroic" came up short.

He took switchbacks north/northwest. He found his preselected detonation spot: a forest clearing outside Prairie du Chien.

He lit the clearing with three big Coleman lanterns. He burned the paintings and scattered the ashes.

He crimped the butt ends of six sticks of dynamite and slid them up against the safe dial-housings.

He strung fuses a hundred yards out and lit a match.

The safes blew. The doors shot all the way up to the tree line. A breeze scattered scorched piles of currency.

Littell sifted through them. The blast destroyed at least a hundred thousand dollars.

Undamaged:

Three large ledger books wrapped in plastic.

Littell buried the scraps of money and dumped the safe sections in a sewage stream adjoining the clearing. He drove to his new motel and obeyed all speed limits en route.

Three ledgers. Two hundred pages per unit. Cross-column notations on each page, squared off in a standard bookkeeping style.

Huge figures listed left to right.

Littell laid the books out on the bed. His first instinct:

The amounts exceeded all possible compilations of monthly or yearly Pension Fund dues.

The two brown leather ledgers were coded. The number/letter listings in the far left-hand column roughly corresponded in digit length to names.

Thus:

AH795/WZ458YX =

One five-letter first name and one seven-letter last name.

MAYBE.

The black leather ledger was uncoded. It contained similarly large financial tallies—and two-and three-letter listings in the far left-hand column.

The listings *might* be: lender or lendee initials.

The black book was subdivided into vertical columns. They were real-word designated: "Loan %" and "Transfer #."

Littell put the black book aside. His second instinct: code breaking would not be easy.

He went back to the brown books.

He followed symbol names and figures and watched money accrue horizontally. Neatly doubled sums told him the Pension Fund repayment rate: a usurious 50%.

He spotted letter repetitions—in four-to-six-letter increments—most likely a simple date code. A for 1, B for 2—something told him it was just that simple.

He matched letters to numbers and EXTRAPOLATED:

Fund loan profiteering went back thirty years. The letters and numbers ascended left to right—straight up to early 1960.

The average amount lent was $1.6 million. With repayment fees: $2.4 million.

The smallest loan was $425,000. The largest was $8.6 million.

Numbers growing left to right. Multiplications and divisions in the far right-hand columns—odd percentage calculations.

He EXTRAPOLATED:

The odd numbers were loan investment profits, tallied in over and above payback interest.

Eyestrain made him stop. Three quick shots of scotch refueled him.

He got a brainstorm:

Look for Hoffa's Sun Valley skim money.

He scanned columns with a pencil. He linked the dots: mid '56 to mid '57 and ten symbols to spell "Jimmy Hoffa."

He found 1.2 and 1.8—hypothetically Bobby Kennedy's "spooky" three million. He found five symbols, six, and five in a perfectly intersecting column.

5, 6, 5 = James Riddle Hoffa.

Hoffa laughed off the Sun Valley charges. With valid assurance: his chicanery was very well cloaked.

Littell skimmed the books and picked out odd totals. Tiny zeros extended—the Fund was billionaire rich.

Double vision set in. He corrected it with a magnifying glass.

He quick-scanned the books again. Identical numbers kept recurring—in four-figure brackets.

[1408]—over and over.

Littell went through the brown books page by page. He found twenty-one 1408s—including two next to the Spooky Three Million. Quick addition gave him a total: forty-nine million dollars lent out or borrowed. Mr. 1408 was well-heeled either way.

He checked the black book initial column. It was alphabetically arranged and entered in Jules Schiffrin's neat block printing.

It was 9:00 a.m. He had five hours of study in.

The "Loan %" subhead tweaked him. He saw "B-E" straight down the graph—the number/letter code decoded to 25%.

He EXTRAPOLATED:

The initials tagged Pension Fund lenders—*repaid* at a fat but not brutal rate.

He checked the "Transfer #" column. The listings were strictly uniform: initials and six digits, no more.

He EXTRAPOLATED:

The initials were bank account numbers—repaid mobster money laundered clean. Said initials all ended in B—most likely short for the word "branch."

Littell copied over letters on a scratch pad.

BOABHB = Bank of America, Beverly Hills branch. HSALMBB = Home Savings & Loan, Miami Beach branch.

It worked.

He was able to form known bank names out of every set of letters.

He jumped columns tracing 1408. Right there on the money: JPK, SR/SFNBB/811512404.

SFN meant Security–First National. BB could mean Buffalo branch, Boston branch, or other B-city branches.

The SR probably denoted a "Senior." Why the added designation?

Just above JPK, SR: JPK [1693] BOADB. The man was a piker compared to 1408: he lent the Fund a paltry $6.4 million.

The added SR was simply to distinguish the lender from someone with the same initials.

JPK, SR [1408] SFNBB/811512404. One filthy-rich money-lending—

Stop.

Stop right there.

JPK, SR.

Joseph P. Kennedy, Senior.

BB for Boston branch.

August '59—Sid Kabikoff talking to Mad Sal:

"I knew Jules way back when"/"when he was SELLING DOPE and USING THE PROFITS to finance movies with RKO back when JOE KENNEDY owned it."

Stop. Make the call. Impersonate a Bureau hard-on and confirm it or refute it.

Littell dialed O. He dripped sweat all over the telephone.

An operator came on. "What number, please?"

"I want the Security–First National Bank, in Boston, Massachusetts."

"One moment, sir. I'll look the number up and connect you."

Littell held the line. Adrenaline hit: he went dizzy and parched.

A man answered. "Security–First National."

"This is Special Agent Johnson, FBI. Let me speak to the manager, please."

"Please hold. I'll transfer you."

Littell heard connection clicks. A man said, "This is Mr. Carmody. May I help you?"

"Th-this is Special Agent Johnson, FBI. I have an account number at your bank here, and I need to know who it belongs to."

"Is this an *official* request? It's a Sunday, and I'm here overseeing our monthly inventory—"

"This is an official request. I can get a bank writ, but I'd rather not put you to the trouble of an in-person visit."

"I see. Well . . . I guess. . . ."

Littell came on firm. "The number is 811512404."

The man sighed. "Well, uh, the 404 listings denote safe-deposit-box storage accounts, so if you're interested in balance figures, I'm afraid—"

"How many storage boxes are rented out to that account number?"

"Well, that account is quite familiar to me, because of its size. You see—"

"How many boxes?"

"An entire vault now of ninety."

"Can valuables be transferred directly into that vault from outside sources?"

"Certainly. They could be placed in the boxes sight unseen, by second parties with access to the account holder's password."

Ninety stash boxes. Millions in Mob-laundered CASH—

"Who does that account number belong to?"

"Well . . ."

"Shall I get a writ?"

"Well, I . . ."

Littell almost shouted it. *"Is the account holder Joseph P. Kennedy Sr.?"*

"Well . . . uh . . . yes."

"The senator's father?"

"Yes, the senator's—"

The phone slipped out of his hand. Littell kicked it across the room.

The black book. Mr. 1408, millionaire loan shark.

He went back over the numbers and confirmed it. He triple-checked every digit until his vision blurred.

Yes: Joe Kennedy lent the Fund Sun Valley seed money. Yes: The Fund lent the money out to James Riddle Hoffa.

Sun Valley constituted felony land fraud. Sun Valley spawned two Pete Bondurant killings: Anton Gretzler and Roland Kirpaski.

Littell tracked 1408s across paper. He saw continuous commas—and no cash-out bottom-line one-time profit.

Joe only took interest out. Joe's base loan sums stayed liquid inside the Fund.

Growing.

Laundered, hidden, obfuscated, tax-sheltered and funneled—

disbursed to labor thugs, dope pushers, shylocks and mobbed-up fascist dictators.

The all-code books contained specifics. He could crack the code and know exactly where the money went.

My secrets, Bobby—I'll never let you hate your father.

Littell went eight drinks over his limit. He passed out shouting numbers.

54

(Hyannis Port, 11/8/60)

Jack stood a million votes up and way ahead in the electoral. Nixon gouged at his lead—the Midwest looked problematic.

Kemper watched three TVs and juggled four phones. His motel room was one big cable socket—the Secret Service demanded multiple lines in and out.

The red phone was his personal line. The two white phones hooked in direct to the Kennedy compound. The blue phone linked the Secret Service to the almost-President-elect.

It was 11:35 p.m.

CBS called Illinois tight. NBC said "Cliffhanger!" ABC said Jack would win, with 51% of the vote.

Kemper checked the window. Secret Service men mingled outside—they'd booked up the entire motel complex.

White phone #2 rang. It was Bobby, with complaints.

A journalist pole-vaulted into the compound. A hot rod sporting Nixon banners plowed the main house lawn.

Kemper called two off-duty cops and sent them over. He told them to beat up all trespassers and impound their vehicles.

The red phone rang. It was Santo Junior, with Mob scuttlebutt.

He said, Illinois looks dicey. He said, Sam G. threw some weight to help Jack.

Lenny Sands was out stuffing ballot boxes. He had a hundred aldermen helping him. Jack should blitz Cook County and eke out a statewide win by a nun's-cunt-hair margin.

Kemper hung up. The red phone rang again. It was Pete, with more secondhand gossip.

He said Mr. Hoover called Mr. Hughes. Mr. Hughes told Pete that Marilyn Monroe was quite naughty.

The Feds had her hot-wired. During the past two weeks she banged disc jockey Allan Freed, Billy Eckstine, Freddy Otash, Rin Tin Tin's trainer, Jon "Ramar of the Jungle" Hall, her pool cleaner, two pizza delivery boys, talk-show man Tom Duggan and her maid's husband—but no Senator John F. Kennedy.

Kemper laughed and hung up. CBS judged the race "too close to call."

ABC retracted its prediction. The race was now "too close to call."

White phone #1 rang.

Kemper picked up. "Bob?"

"It's me. I just called to say we're way ahead in the electoral, and Illinois and Michigan should put us over. The Hughes loan thing helped, Kemper. Your 'unnamed source' should know that it was a factor."

"You don't sound too elated."

"I won't believe it until it's final. And a friend of Dad's just died. He was younger than him, so he's taking it hard."

"Anybody I know?"

"Jules Schiffrin. I think you met him a few years ago. He had a heart attack in Wisconsin. He came home and found his house burglarized, and just keeled over. A friend of Dad's in Lake Geneva called—"

"Lake Geneva?"

"Right. North of Chicago. Kemper . . ."

The Littell assault location. Schiffrin: a Chicago-based gonif type.

"Kemper . . ."

"I'm sorry. I was distracted."

"I was going to say something . . ."

"About Laura?"

"How did you know that?"

"You never come off hesitant unless it's about Laura."

Bobby cleared his throat. "Call her. Tell her we'd appreciate it if she didn't contact the family for a while. I'm sure she'll understand."

Court Meade said Littell vanished. It was circumstantial, but—

"Kemper, are you listening to me?"

"Yes."

"Call Laura. Be kind, but be firm."

"I'll do it."

Bobby hung up. Kemper placed a red phone call through the switch-board: Chicago, BL8-4908.

It went through. He heard two rings and two very faint tap-clicks.

Littell said, "Hello?"

Kemper covered the mouthpiece.

Littell said, "Is that you, Boyd? Are you coming back into my life be-cause you're scared, or because you think I might have something you want?"

Kemper disconnected.

Ward J. Littell—Jesus Fucking Christ.

55

(Miami, 11/9/60)

uy Banister screeched long-distance. Pete felt an earache coming on.

"We're looking at a new papist hegemony. He loves niggers and Jews, and he's been soft-line on Communism since he was a congressman. I can't believe he won. I can't believe the American people bought his line of bull—"

"Get to it, Guy. You said J.D. Tippit picked up something."

Banister de-throttled his spiel. "I forgot I called you for a reason. And I forgot you were soft-line on Kennedy."

Pete said, "I like his hair. It gets my dick hard."

Banister *re*-throttled. Pete cut him off quick.

"It's 8:00 fucking a.m. I've got cab calls backed up and three drivers out sick. Tell me what you want."

"I want Dick Nixon to demand a recount."

"Guy—"

"All right, then. Boyd was supposed to tell you to talk to Wilfredo Delsol."

"He did."

"*Did* you talk to him?"

"No. I've been busy."

"Tippit said he heard Delsol's been seen with some Castro guys. A bunch of us think he should explain."

"I'll go see him."

"You do that. And while you're at it, try to develop some political brains."

Pete laughed. "Jack's a white man. I've got a big hard-on just thinking about his hair."

Pete drove to Wilfredo's pad and knocked on the door. Delsol opened up in his skivvies.

He was bleary-eyed. He was scrawny. He looked too sleepy to stand upright.

He shivered and plucked at his balls. He shook the cobwebs out of his head and caught on fast.

"Somebody told you something bad about me."

"Keep going."

"You only visit people in order to scare them."

"That's right. Or to ask them to explain some things."

"Ask me, then."

"You were seen talking to some pro-Castro guys."

"That's true."

"So?"

"So they heard how my cousin Tomás died. They thought they could get me to betray the Cadre."

"And?"

"And I told them I hated what happened to Tomás, but I hate Fidel Castro more."

Pete leaned against the door. "You don't much like speedboat runs."

"Killing odd militiamen is futile."

"Suppose you get assigned to an invasion group?"

"I'll go."

"Suppose I tell you to whack one of those guys you were seen talking to?"

"I would say Gaspar Blanco lives two blocks from here."

Pete said, "Kill him."

Pete cruised Niggertown—for the pure time-marking fuck of it. The radio ran election news exclusively.

Nixon conceded. Frau Nixon pitched some boo-hoo. Bad-Back Jack thanked his staff and announced that Frau Bad-Back was pregnant.

Nigger junkies were cliqued up by a shine stand. Fulo and Ramón drove up to service them. Chuck was trading bindles for signed-over welfare checks.

Jack talked up the New Frontier. Fulo dropped off a fat load of shit with the shoeshine man.

A local bulletin flashed on.

Shots fired outside Coral Gables bodega! Police ID dead man as one Gaspar Ramón Blanco!

Pete smiled. November 8, 1960, was an all-time classic day.

He stopped at Tiger Kab after lunch. Teo Paez had a parking-lot sale going: hot TVs for twenty scoots a pop.

The sets were hooked up to a battery pack. Jack the K beamed out of two dozen screens.

Pete mingled with potential buyers. Jimmy Hoffa popped out of the crowd, popping sweat on a nice cool day.

"Hi, Jimmy."

"Don't gloat. I know you and Boyd wanted that cunt-lapping faggot to win."

"Don't worry. He'll put his kid brother on a tight leash."

"As if that's my only worry."

"What do you mean?"

"I mean Jules Schiffrin's dead. His place in Lake Geneva got clouted for some priceless fucking paintings, and some priceless fucking paperwork got lost in the process. Jules had a heart attack, and now our shit has probably been torched in some burglar's fucking basement."

LITTELL. 100% certifiably insane.

Pete started laughing.

Hoffa said, "What's so fucking funny?"

Pete roared.

Hoffa said, "Stop laughing, you frog fuck."

Pete couldn't stop. Hoffa pulled a piece and shot Jack the Haircut six TV screens across.

56

The mailman brought a special-delivery letter. It was postmarked Chicago and sent without a return address. Kemper opened the envelope. The one page inside was neatly typed.

I have the books. They are fail-safed against my death or disappearance in a dozen different ways. I will release them only to Robert Kennedy, if I am given a Kennedy Administration appointment within the next three months. The books are safely hidden. Hidden with them is an 83-page deposition, detailing my knowledge of your McClellan Committee–Kennedy incursion. I will destroy that deposition only if I am given a Kennedy Administration appointment. I remain fond of you, and am grateful for the lessons you taught me. At times, you acted with uncharacteristic selflessness and risked exposure of your many duplicitous relationships in an effort to help me achieve what I must fatuously describe as my manhood. That said, I will also state that I do not trust your motives regarding the books. I still consider you a friend, but I do not trust you one iota.

Kemper jotted a note to Pete Bondurant.

Forget about the Teamster books. Littell finessed us, and I'm beginning to rue the day I taught him some things. I made some discreet queries with the Wisconsin State Police, who are frankly baffled. I'll supply forensic details the next time we talk. I think you'll be grudgingly impressed. Enough pissing and moaning. Let's depose Fidel Castro.

57

(Chicago, 12/8/60)

ind rocked the car. Littell turned up the heat and pushed his seat back to stretch out.

His stakeout was strictly cosmetic. He might join the party himself—Mal would get a huge kick out of it.

It was a Bust the Blacklist bash. The Chicago Board of Ed had hired Mal Chamales to teach remedial math.

Guests walked up to the house. Littell recognized leftists with Red Squad sheets half a mile long.

A few waved to him. Mal said he might send his wife out with coffee and cookies.

Littell watched the house. Mal turned his Christmas lights on—the tree by the porch bloomed all blue and yellow.

He'd stay until 9:30. He'd write the bash up as a routine holiday soiree. Leahy would accept his assessment pro forma—their stalemate precluded direct confrontations.

His door-kicking episode and Lake Geneva time went unquestioned. He had thirty-nine days to go until his retirement. The Bureau's no-confrontation policy would hold and see him through to civilian life.

He had the Fund books stashed in a bank vault in Duluth. He had two dozen cryptography texts at home. He had seventeen days logged in without an ounce of liquor.

He could send the Fund books to Bobby on a moment's notice. He could delete Joe Kennedy's name with a few swipes of a pencil.

Dead leaves strafed the windshield. Littell got out of the car and stretched his legs.

He saw men running up Mal's driveway. He heard metal-on-metal pump-shotgun-slide noise.

He heard footsteps behind him. Hands slammed him across the hood and ripped off his gunbelt.

He gouged his face on a sharp strip of chrome. He saw Chick Leahy and Court Meade kick Mal's door down.

Big men in suits and overcoats swarmed him. His glasses fell off. Everything went claustrophobic and blurry.

Hands dragged him into the street. Hands cuffed and shackled him.

A midnight-blue limo pulled up.

Hands grappled him in. Hands shoved him face-to-face with J. Edgar Hoover.

Hands slapped tape across his mouth.

The limo pulled out. Hoover said, "Mal Chamales is being arrested for sedition and advocating the violent overthrow of the United States of America. Your FBI service is terminated as of this day, your pension has been revoked, and a detailed profile of you as a Communist sympathizer has been sent to the Justice Department, the bar associations of all fifty states and the deans of every university law school in the Continental U.S. Should you go public with information pertaining to Kemper Boyd's clandestine activities, I will guarantee you that your daughter, Susan, and Helen Agee will never practice law, and guarantee that the interesting coincidence of your three-week absence and the destruction of Jules Schiffrin's Lake Geneva estate will be mentioned to key organized-crime figures who might find that coincidence intriguing. In keeping with your leftist sympathies and bleeding-heart concern for the financially wretched and morally impaired, you will now be deposited into a venue where your instincts for self-abnegation, self-flagellation and pinko vicissitudes will be fully appreciated. Driver, stop the car."

The limo decelerated. Hands uncuffed him and unshackled him.

Hands dragged him out the door. Hands dumped him into a South Side gutter.

Colored piss bums walked up and checked him out. Say what, white man?

DOCUMENT INSERT: 12/18/60. Personal note: Kemper Boyd to Attorney General Designate Robert F. Kennedy.

Dear Bob,

Congratulations, first of all. You'll make a splendid Attorney General, and I can envision Jimmy Hoffa and certain others swinging from yardarms already.

Hoffa makes for a good segue point. The purpose of this letter is to recommend former Special Agent Ward J. Littell for a Justice Department counselship. Littell (the Chicago Phantom who has worked for us sub-rosa since early 1959) is a 1940 Summa Cum Laude Notre Dame Law grad, Federal-Bar licensed. He is considered brilliant in the field of Federal Deportation Statutes and will be bringing with him a good deal of recently accrued anti-Mob, anti-Teamster evidence.

I realize that Littell, in his anonymous capacity, has been out of touch with you for some time, and hope that that fact will not dampen your enthusiasm for him. He is a splendid attorney and a dedicated crimefighter.

Yours,
Kemper

DOCUMENT INSERT: 12/21/60. Personal note: Robert F. Kennedy to Kemper Boyd.

Dear Kemper,

Per Ward Littell, my answer is emphatically "No." I have received a report from Mr. Hoover that, though perhaps biased, persuasively paints a portrait of Littell as an alcoholic with ultra left-wing tendencies. Mr. Hoover also included evidence that indicates that Littell was receiving bribes from Chicago Mob members. This, to me, negates the viability of his alleged anti-Mob, anti-Teamster evidence.

I realize that Littell is your friend, and that he did work hard for us at one time. Frankly, though, we cannot afford even the slightest taint on our new appointees.

Let's consider the Littell matter closed. The question of your

Kennedy Administration employment remains, and I think you'll
be pleased with what the President-elect and I have come
up with.

Best,
Bob

DOCUMENT INSERT: 1/17/61. Personal letter: J. Edgar Hoover to Kemper Boyd.

Dear Kemper,

Three-fold congratulations.
One, your recent evasion tactics were superbly efficacious.
Two, your Marilyn Monroe aside had me going for quite some
time. What a myth you have created! With luck, it will enter
what Hush-Hush would call the "Peephole Pantheon!"
Thirdly, bravo for your appointment as roving Justice Department counsel. My contacts tell me you'll be concentrating on voting rights abuse in the south. How fitting! Now you'll be able to
champion left-inclined negroes with the same tenacity that you
embrace right-wing Cubans!
I think you've found your metier. I would be hard-pressed to
conceive of work more suitable for a man with such a lenient
code of loyalty.
I hope we'll get the chance to be colleagues again.

As always,
JEH

58

(New York City, 1/20/61)

She'd been crying. Tear streaks had ruined her makeup.

Kemper stepped into the foyer. Laura cinched her robe and stepped away from him.

He held out a small bouquet. "I'm going down to the Inaugural. I'll be back in a few days."

She ignored the flowers. "I figured that out. I didn't think you put on that tuxedo to impress me."

"Laura . . ."

"I wasn't invited. Some neighbors of mine were, though. They donated ten thousand dollars to Jack's campaign."

Her mascara was running. Her whole face looked off-kilter.

"I'll be back in a few days. We'll talk things over then."

Laura pointed to an armoire. "There's a check for three million dollars in the top drawer. It's mine, if I never contact the family again."

"You could rip it up."

"Would you?"

"I can't answer that question."

Her fingers were cigarette-stained. She'd left overflowing ashtrays out in plain sight.

Laura said, "Them or me?"

Kemper said, "Them."

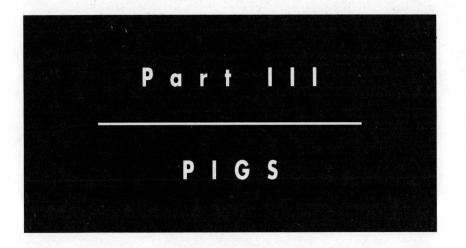

Part III

PIGS

February–November 1961

DOCUMENT INSERT: 2/7/61. Memorandum: Kemper Boyd to John Stanton. Marked: CONFIDENTIAL/HAND POUCH DELIVER.

John,

I've been subtly pressing Little Brother and a few White House aides for information, and I am sad to report that as of this date the President is ambivalent about our invasion plans. The imminent nature of the plans apparently has him waxing indecisive. It's obvious that he doesn't want to deal with something so pressing this early in his administration.

The President and Attorney General Kennedy have been briefed by Director Dulles and Deputy Director Bissell. Little Brother attends many high-level presidential briefings; it is obvious that he is becoming the President's chief advisor on all urgent matters. Little Brother (to the consternation of some friends of ours) remains fixated on Organized Crime and seems to be uninterested in the Cuban issue. My contacts tell me that the President hasn't updated him on the "at-ready" status of our invasion plans.

The Blessington campsite stands pre-invasion ready. Recruit training cycles have been suspended; as of 1/30/61, the forty-four bunks have been filled with graduate troops culled from other induction camps: men specifically trained in amphibious warfare tactics. These men now stand as the Blessington Invasion Force. Pete Bondurant and Douglas Frank Lockhart are putting them through rigorous daily maneuvers and report that their morale is very high.

I visited Blessington last week, to assess its at-ready status prior to Mr. Bissell's 2/10/61 inspection. I'm happy to report that Pete and Lockhart have whipped things into top-flight shape.

Landing crafts are now docked at camouflaged inlets built by laborers recruited from Lockhart's Klan Klavern. Chuck Rogers gave Ramon Gutierrez a refresher flying course as part of a Bondurant-devised plan to have Gutierrez portray a Castro defector and fly into Blessington on Invasion Day with doctored anti-Castro atrocity photographs to be leaked to the press as genuine. Weapons and ammunition stand inventoried and at-ready. An inlet a half mile from the campsite is being prepared to house the troopship that will carry the Blessington invasion force. It should be at-ready by 2/16/61.

I am now free to spend occasional time in Florida, chiefly because the brothers believe the falsehood that I established over a year ago: that Mr. Hoover has coerced me into spying on anti-Castro groups in the Miami area. My current Justice Department assignment (investigating the accusations of Negroes denied voting rights) should have me sequestered in the south for some time. I specifically requested this assignment because of its proximity to Miami and Blessington. My southern background convinced Little Brother to give me the job, and he has allowed me to choose my initial target districts. I picked the area surrounding Anniston, Alabama. There are eight daily commercial flights to Miami, which should make job hopping just a matter of a ninety-minute plane ride. Should you need me, call my service in D.C. or contact me directly at the Wigwam Motel outside Anniston. (Don't say what you're thinking: I know it's beneath me.)

Again, let me stress the importance of obfuscating all Agency-Outfit links to Little Brother. I was as amazed and dismayed as our Sicilian colleagues when Big Brother tapped him for AG. His anti-Outfit fervor has if anything increased, and we do not want him to learn that Messrs. C.M., S.G. and J.R. have donated money to the Cause, or that our Cadre business even exists.

I'll close now. See you in Blessington 2/10.

                                                              KB

DOCUMENT INSERT: 2/9/61. Memorandum: John Stanton to Kemper Boyd. Marked: CONFIDENTIAL/HAND POUCH DELIVER.

Kemper,

I received your memo. Things sound excellent, although I wish Big Brother wasn't waffling. I've developed some new additions to our basic Blessington Invasion Plan. Will you tell me what you think when we meet at the inspection?

1.—I've assigned Pete Bondurant and Chuck Rogers to coordinate on-site Blessington security and communications between Blessington and other launch sites in Nicaragua and Guatemala.

Rogers can fly between sites, and I think Pete will be especially effective as a rover-peacekeeper.

2.—Teo Paez has brought in a new recruit: Nestor Javier Chasco, DOB 4/12/23. Teo knew the man in Havana when he was running a string of informants for United Fruit. Chasco infiltrated numerous left-wing groups and once foiled an assassination attempt on a UF executive.

When Castro took over, Chasco infiltrated Raul Castro's on-island heroin operation and siphoned dope to anti-Castro rebels, who of course sold it and used the money to purchase weapons. Chasco is an experienced dope trafficker, an expert interrogator, and a Cuban Army-trained sharpshooter lent out by President Batista to various South American government leaders. Teo says that Chasco assassinated no less than fourteen leftist insurgents between the years 1951 and 1958.

Chasco, who had been supporting himself by selling marijuana, escaped Cuba by speedboat last month. He contacted Paez in Miami and begged him to find him pro-Cause work. Teo introduced him to Pete Bondurant and later described the meeting to me as "Love at first sight."

You were unreachable, so Pete contacted me and recommended Nestor Chasco for immediate Blessington and Cadre employment. I met Chasco and was very impressed. I hired the man immediately and had Pete introduce him to the other Cadre members. Paez told me that the meetings were amicable. Chasco is learning the Cadre business ropes and doubling as a Blessington drill instructor. He'll be shuffling between Blessington, Miami and our formal facilities in Guatemala and Nicaragua—a case officer passing through Blessington noted his training skills and put in an expedite personnel request directly to Mr. Bissell.

You'll meet Chasco at the inspection. I think you'll be impressed, too.

3.—During the actual invasion time frame, I want you and Chasco to patrol the Cadre's Miami business sites. Our on-island sources expect some invasion plan intelligence to leak to Cuba, and I want to make sure that local pro-Castro groups don't try to hit us when they think we're focusing solely on invasion logistics. It should be easy for you to get away. Miami is Anniston-accessible and you can tell Little Brother that Mr. H. sent you in to monitor pro-Castro activity.

I'll close with an embarrassing request.

Carlos M. gave Guy Banister an additional $300,000 gun

money. The man is a great friend to the Cause, and he has some very great (and I think justified) fears regarding Little Brother. Can you find out what Bobby's plans are regarding Carlos?

Thanks in advance for considering this. See you tomorrow in Blessington.

John

59

(Blessington, 2/10/61)

Eyes left, eyes right. Port arms, snap the bolt—let's see those carbon-free M-1 chambers.

The drill field sparkled. The trainees moved like spic Rockettes—every turn and slapdown was synchronized.

Lockhart called cadence. Néstor Chasco played flag bearer. The Stars & Stripes and Pit Bull Monster fluttered.

Pete lead a white-glove inspection line. Richard Bissell and John Stanton trailed him—civilian squarejohns in worsted wool suits.

The trainees wore starched fatigues and chrome helmets. Fulo, Paez, Delsol, and Gutiérrez stood off in a squad leader flank.

Boyd watched from the dock. He didn't want rank-and-file recruits to know him.

Pete checked weapons and handed them back. Bissell patted shoulders and smiled. Stanton stifled yawns—he knew it was all PR bullshit.

Lockhart yelled, "Shoulderrr arms! Guide-on front and centerrr!"

Forty-four rifles went up. Chasco marched ten paces forward and about-faced.

Chasco saluted. Chasco snapped his flags out at arm's length.

Lockhart yelled, "At ease!" The men hoisted down one by one for a nifty ripple effect.

Bissell gawked. Stanton applauded.

Boyd was eyeballing Chasco. Stanton built the little shitbird up as Jesus Christ sans mercy.

Chasco ate tarantula meat and drank panther piss. Chasco killed Reds from Rangoon to Rio.

Chasco coughed and spat on the pavement. "It is a pleasure to be here with joo in America. It is an honor to be able to fight the tyrant Fidel Castro, and an honor to introduce to joo Señor Richard Bissell."

Locomotive cheers went up—choo-choo-choo fifty voices strong.

Bissell waved the noise down. "Señor Chasco is right. Fidel Castro is a murderous tyrant who needs to be taken down a peg or two. I'm here to tell you that we're going to do it, most likely in the not-too-distant future."

CHOO-CHOO-CHOO-CHOO-CHOO-CHOO—

Bissell stabbed the air Kennedy-style. "Your morale is high, and that's damn good. There's also some pretty damn high morale inside Cuba, and I would have to say that right now that morale is running about three or four brigade's worth. I'm referring to on-island Cubans just waiting for you to establish a beachhead and show them the way to Fidel Castro's parlor."

CHOO-CHOO-CHOO-CHOO-CHOO—

"You men, and many other men, are going to invade and recapture your homeland. You are going to link with anti-Castro forces living on-island and depose Fidel Castro. We have close to sixteen hundred troops now stationed in Guatemala, Nicaragua and along the Gulf Coast, ready to be launched from coastal installations. You are among those troops. You are a crack unit which will see action. You will be backed by surplus B-26s and escorted to your homeland by a task force of U.S. Navy supply boats. You will succeed. You will spend Christmas with your loved ones in a liberated Cuba."

Pete gave the signal. A forty-four-gun salute shocked Bissell speechless.

Stanton threw a lunch at the Breakers Motel. The guest list was White Men Only: Pete, Bissell, Boyd, Chuck Rogers.

Santo Junior owned the place. Blessington men dined and drank on the cuff. The coffee shop served starchy wop food—strictly shitsville.

They hogged a choice window table. Bissell hogged the conversation—nobody could squeeze a word in. Pete sat down next to Boyd and picked at a plate of linguine.

Chuck handed out beers. Boyd passed Pete a note.

I like Chasco. He's got that "Don't underestimate me because I'm puny" look that I associate with W.J. Littell. Can we send him in to shoot Fidel?

Pete scribbled up his napkin.

Let's have him shoot Fidel & WJL. Jimmy's scared & pissed because his Fund books got clouted & we're the only ones who know who did it. Can't we do something about it?

Boyd wrote *NO* on his menu. Pete laughed out loud.

Bissell took offense. "Did I say something funny, Mr. Bondurant?"

"No, sir. You didn't."

"I didn't think so. I was saying that President Kennedy has been briefed several times, but he still won't commit to an invasion date, which I don't find amusing at all."

Pete poured himself a beer. Stanton said, "Mr. Dulles describes the President as 'enthusiastic, but cautious.'"

Bissell smiled. "Our secret weapon is Mr. Boyd here. He's our Kennedy confidante, and I imagine that if push came to shove, he could reveal his covert Agency standing, and then overtly advocate our invasion plan."

Pete froze the moment: Boyd about to lose it six ways from Sunday.

Stanton stepped in. "Mr. Bissell's joking, Kemper."

"I know that. And I know that he understands how complex our alliances have become."

Bissell fingered his napkin. "I do, Mr. Boyd. And I know how generous Mr. Hoffa, Mr. Marcello and a few other Italian gentlemen have been to the Cause, and I know that you possess a certain amount of influence in the Kennedy camp. And as the President's chief Cuban-issue liaison, I also know that Fidel Castro and Communism are a good deal worse than the Mafia, although I wouldn't dream of asking you to intercede on our friends' behalf, because it might cost you credibility with your sacred Kennedys."

Stanton dropped his soup spoon. Pete let a big breath out eeeasy.

Boyd put out a big shit-eating grin. "I'm glad you feel that way, Mr. Bissell. Because if you did ask me, I'd have to tell you to go fuck yourself."

60

(Washington, D.C., 3/6/61)

He took three shots a night—no more, no less.

He switched from whisky to straight gin. The burn compensated for the scant volume.

Three shots tweaked his hatreds. Four shots and up cut those hatreds all the way loose.

Three shots said, You project danger. Four shots or more said, You're ugly and you limp.

He always drank facing his hallway mirror. The glass was chipped and cracked—his new apartment was furnished on the cheap.

Littell knocked the shots back, one-two-three. The glow let him spar with himself.

You're two days shy of forty-eight years old. Helen left you. J. Edgar Hoover fucked you—you fucked him and he fucked you back much more efficaciously.

You risked your life for nothing. Robert F. Kennedy shunned you. You went to hell and back for a form-letter rejection.

You tried to contact Bobby in person. Yes-men showed you out. You sent four notes to Bobby. All four went unanswered.

Kemper tried to get you work at the Justice Department. Bobby nixed it—the alleged Hoover hater kowtowed to Hoover. Hoover put the fix in: No law firm or law school will employ you.

Kemper knows you've got the Fund books. His fear defines your bond now.

You went to a Jesuit retreat in Milwaukee. Newspapers lauded your burglary daring: MYSTERY ART THIEF TEARS LAKE GENEVA ESTATE DOWN! You did odd jobs for the monsignor and imposed your own code of silence.

You boiled the booze out. You put on some muscle. You studied cryptography texts. Prayer told you who to hate and who to forgive.

You read a Chicago *Trib* obit: Court Meade died of a massive heart attack. You toured old haunts. The foster homes you grew up in were still churning out Jesuit robots.

You're licensed to practice in D.C. Hoover left you an escape hatch—in his own backyard.

The move east was invigorating. Washington law firms seeking applicants were shocked by your Commie pedigree.

Kemper comes through. Egalitarian Kemper was still friendly with old car-thief confreres. Car thieves were prone to Federal indictments and always in need of cheap representation.

Car thieves brought you occasional work—enough to sustain an apartment and three shots a night.

Kemper called to chat. He never mentioned the Fund books. You can't hate a man so high up on a ledge. You can't hate a man so immune to hatred himself.

He gave you great gifts. They compensate for his betrayals.

Kemper calls his civil rights work "moving." It's that cheap noblesse oblige the Kennedys evince so condescendingly.

You hate the mass seduction that Joe Kennedy financed. Your foster fathers bought you one cheap toy per Christmas. Joe bought his sons the world with cancerous money.

Prayer taught you to hate falsehood. Prayer gave you insight. Prayer was like a choke hold on mendacity.

You see the President's face and see through it. You see Jimmy Hoffa skate on Sun Valley charges—a newsman cites insufficient evidence.

You hold numbers to reverse that injustice. You hold numbers to indict the Kennedy seduction.

You can break the remaining Fund code. You can expose the Robber Baron and his son the Priapic Boy Führer.

Littell got out his cryptography books. Three shots a night taught him this:

You're down, but you're capable of anything.

61

(Washington, D.C., 3/14/61)

Bobby held the floor. Fourteen lawyers pulled chairs up and balanced notebooks and ashtrays on their knees.

The briefing room was drafty. Kemper leaned against the back wall with his topcoat slung over his shoulders.

The AG brayed—there was no need to get close. He had free time—a storm delayed his flight to Alabama.

Bobby said, "You know why I called you in, and you know what your basic job is. I've been tied up in red tape since the Inauguration, so I haven't been able to get to the applicable case files, and I've decided to let you do that on your own. You're the Organized Crime Unit, and you know what your mandate is. And I'll be damned if I'm going to dawdle any longer."

The men got out pens and pencils. Bobby straddled a chair in front of them.

"We've got lawyers and investigators of our own, and any attorney worth his salt is also a catch-as-catch-can investigator. We've got FBI agents we can utilize as needed, if I can convince Mr. Hoover to shift his priorities a bit. He's still convinced that domestic Communists are more dangerous than organized crime, and I think that making the FBI more cooperative is going to be a major obstacle to overcome."

The men laughed. An ex–McClellan cop said, "We shall overcome."

Bobby loosened his tie. "We shall. And roving counsel Kemper Boyd, who's spying from the peanut gallery, will overcome racial exclusion practices in the South. I won't ask Mr. Boyd to join us, because skulking at the back of the room is very much his modus operandi."

Kemper waved. "I'm a spy."

Bobby waved back. "The President has always contended that."

Kemper laughed. Bobby half-ass liked him now—breaking off with Laura clinched it. Claire and Laura stayed close—he got regular updates from New York.

Bobby said, "Enough bullshit. The McClellan Committee hearings have provided us with a hit list, and at the top we've got Jimmy Hoffa, Sam Giancana, Johnny Rosselli and Carlos Marcello. I want the IRS files on these men pulled, and I want the intelligence files of the Chicago, New York, Los Angeles, Miami, Cleveland and Tampa PDs combed for mention of them. I also want probable-cause briefs written, so that we can subpoena their financial books and personal records."

A man said, "What about Hoffa specifically? He got hung-juried on Sun Valley, but there's got to be other approaches we can use."

Bobby rolled up his sleeves. "A hung jury first time out means an acquittal next time. I've given up hope of tracing the Spooky Three Million, and I'm starting to think that the so-called 'Real' Pension Fund books are nothing but a pipe dream. I think we need to impanel grand juries and deluge them with Hoffa evidence. And while we're at it, I want to pass a Federal law requiring all municipal PDs to obtain Justice Department writs to implement their wiretaps, so that *we* can have access to every bit of wiretap intelligence seized nationwide."

The men cheered. An old McClellanite threw some mock punches.

Bobby stood up. "I found an old deportation order on Carlos Marcello. He was born in Tunis, North Africa, of Italian parents, but he's got a phony Guatemalan birth certificate. I want to deport him to Guatemala, and I want to do it damn soon."

Kemper broke a little lightweight sweat—

62

(Rural Mexico, 3/22/61)

Poppy fields blitzed the horizon. Stalk bulbs oozing dope covered a valley half the size of Rhode Island.

Prison inmates did the plucking. Mexican cops cracked the whip and did all the conversion work.

Heshie Ryskind led the tour. Pete and Chuck Rogers tagged along and let him play MC.

"This farm has supplied me and Santo for years. They convert 'O' into morphine for the Agency, too, 'cause the Agency's always backing some right-wing insurgents that get shot at and wounded a lot, and they always need the morph as medication. Most of the zombies they got working here stay past the end of their sentence 'cause all they want to do is suck a pipe and nosh a few tortillas on the side. I wish I had such simple needs. I wish I didn't have to keep nine fucking doctors on retainer 'cause I'm such a fucking hypochondriac, and I wish I didn't have the chutzpah—which is the same as 'audacity' to you goyim—to try to break the world's record for getting blow jobs, 'cause I think I've reached the point where all that suction is doing my prostate more harm than good. And I'm not the blow-job magnet I used to be. I've got to travel with a good cunt man now to see any action at all. Lately, I've had Dick Contino bird-dogging for me. I catch all his lounge gigs, and Dick shoots me all the surplus suction I can handle."

The sun slammed down. They rode out in rickshaws, with junkie inmates at the helm.

Pete said, "We need ten pounds precut for the Cadre. I won't be able to get back here until after the invasion."

Chuck laughed. "If and when your boy Jack approves it."

Pete flicked a bulb—white shit oozed out. "And I want a substantial morphine supply for the medics at Blessington. Let's just figure this is our last visit for a while."

Heshie leaned against his rickshaw. The pilot wore a loincloth and a Dodger baseball cap.

"All this can be arranged. It's a lot simpler than arranging blow jobs for sixty at some farkakte Teamster convention."

Chuck dabbed bulb goo on a shaving cut. "My jaw's going a little numb. It's a nice effect, but I wouldn't ruin my life for it."

Pete laughed. Heshie said, "I'm tired. I'll go back and get your stuff loaded up, then I'm taking a nap."

Chuck hopped in his rickshaw. The pilot looked like fucking Quasimodo.

Pete stood on his tiptoes. The view spread waaay out.

Maybe a thousand stalk rows. Maybe twenty slaves per row. Low worker overhead: cot space, rice and beans came cheap.

Chuck and Heshie took off—dig that crazy rickshaw drag race.

Boyd said Mr. Hoover had a maxim: Anti-Communism breeds strange bedfellows.

They flew from Mexico to Guatemala. The Piper Deuce cruised sluggish—Chucky overstuffed the cargo hold.

With rifles, hate pamphlets, heroin, morphine, tortillas, tequila, Army surplus jump boots, Martin Luther Coon voodoo dolls, back issues of *Hush-Hush*, and five hundred mimeographed copies of a Guy Banister–circulated report culled from the L.A. FBI office, stating that even though Mr. Hoover knew full well that President John F. Kennedy was *not* playing bury-the-brisket with Marilyn Monroe, he kept her under intensive surveillance anyway, and duly noted that during the last six weeks Miss Monroe fucked Louis Prima, two off-duty Marines, Spade Cooley, Franchot Tone, Yves Montand, Stan Kenton, David Seville of David Seville and the Chipmunks, four pizza delivery boys, bantamweight battler Fighting Harada and a disc jockey at an all-spook R&B station.

Chuck called it "essential ordnance."

Pete tried to doze. Air sickness kept him awake. The training camp popped out of a cloud bank, right on schedule.

It loomed biggg. From the air it looked like ten Blessingtons.

Chuck cut his flaps and eased down. Pete puked out his window just shy of the runway.

They taxied in. Pete gargled tequila for a breath rinse. Cuban trainees hit the hold and off-loaded the rifles.

A case officer trotted up with supply forms. Pete got out and itemized them: guns, R&R booze, *Hush-Hush* anti-Beard propaganda.

The guy said, "You can eat now, or wait for Mr. Boyd and Mr. Stanton."

"Let me walk around a little. I've never seen the place."

Chuck pissed on the runway. Pete said, "Any word on a go date?"

The guy shook his head. "Kennedy's waffling. Mr. Bissell's starting to think we'll be lucky to go before summer."

"Jack will come through. He'll see that it's too sweet a deal to pass up."

Pete meandered. The camp was Disneyland for killers.

Six hundred Cubans. Fifty white men running herd. Twelve barracks, a drill field, a rifle range, a pistol range, a landing strip, a mess hall, an infiltration course and a chemical-warfare simulation tunnel.

Three launch inlets gouged out of the Gulf a mile south. Four dozen amphibious crawlers rigged with .50-caliber machine guns.

An ammo dump. A field hospital. A Catholic chapel with a bilingual chaplain.

Pete meandered. Old Blessington grads waved hello. Case officers showed him some good shit.

Dig Néstor Chasco—staging mock-assassination maneuvers.

Dig that anti-Red indoctrination workshop.

Dig the verbal abuse drills—calculated to increase troop subservience.

Dig the corpsman's amphetamine stash—pre-packaged pre-invasion courage.

Dig the action in that barbed-wire enclosure—peons flying on a drug called LSD.

Some of them screamed. Some wept. Some grinned like LSD was a blast. A case officer said John Stanton hatched the idea—let's flood Cuba with this shit before we invade.

Langley co-signed the brainstorm. Langley embellished it: Let's induce mass hallucinations and stage the Second Coming of Christ!!!!!

Langley found some suicidal actors. Langley dolled them up to look like J.C. Langley had them set to pre-invade Cuba, concurrent with the dope saturation.

Pete howled. The case officer said, "It's not funny." A drug-zorched peon whipped out his wang and jacked off.

Pete meandered. Everything sparkled and gleamed.

Dig the bayonet drills. Dig the spit-shined jeeps. Dig that rummy-looking priest dispensing outdoor Holy Communion.

Loudspeakers announced chow call. It was 5:00 and nowhere near dark—military types dined early.

Pete walked over to the lounge hut. A pool table and wet bar ate up two-thirds of the floor space.

Boyd and Stanton walked in. A large fucker blocked the doorway—resplendent in French paratrooper khakis.

Kemper said, *"Entrez, Laurent."*

He was jug-eared and plain huge. He had that frog imperialist swagger down pat.

Pete bowed. *"Salut, capitaine."*

Boyd smiled. "Laurent Guéry, Pete Bondurant."

Froggy clicked his heels. *"Monsieur Bondurant. C'est un grand plaisir de faire votre connaissance. On dit que vous êtes un grand patriote."*

Pete tossed out some Québecois. *"Tout le plaisir est à moi, capitaine. Mais je suis beaucoup plus profiteur que patriote."*

Froggy laughed. Stanton said, "Translate for me, Kemper. I'm starting to feel like a rube."

"You're not missing much."

"You mean it's just Pete trying to be civilized with the only other six-foot-six Frenchman on earth?"

Froggy shrugged—*Quoi? Quoi? Quoi?*

Pete winked. *"Vous êtes quoi donc, capitaine? Etes-vous un* 'right-wing crackpot'? *Etes-vous un* 'mercenary on the Cuban gravy train'?"

Froggy shrugged—*Quoi? Quoi? Quoi?*

Boyd steered Pete out to the porch. Spics double-timed through a chow line across from the drill field.

"Be nice, Pete. He's Agency."

"In what fucking capacity?"

"He shoots people."

"Then tell him to clip Fidel and learn English. Tell him to do something impressive, or he's just another frog geek to me."

Boyd laughed. "He killed a man named Lumumba in the Congo last month."

"So what?"

"He's killed quite a few uppity Algerians."

Pete lit a cigarette. "So tell Jack to send him down to Havana. And send Néstor down with him. And tell Jack that he owes me one for the Nixon-Hughes thing, and as far as I'm concerned, history's not moving fast enough. Tell him to give us a go date, or I'll boat on down to Cuba and whack Fidel myself."

Boyd said, "Be patient. Jack's still getting his sea legs, and invading a Communist-held country is a big commitment. Dulles and Bissell are keeping after him, and I'm convinced he'll say yes before too long."

Pete kicked a tin can off the porch. Boyd pulled his piece and unloaded it. The can danced all the way across the drill field.

The chow-line crew applauded. Big-bore reverb had a few guys clutching their ears.

Pete kicked at the shell casings. "*You* talk to Jack. Tell him the invasion's good for business."

Boyd twirled his gun on one finger. "I can't openly proselytize for the invasion without blowing my Agency cover, and I'm damn lucky to have FBI cover to be in Florida in the first place."

"That civil rights gig must be sweet. You just go through the motions and fly to Miami when the niggers start getting on your nerves."

"It's not like that."

"No?"

"No. I like the Negro people I work with just as much as you like our Cubans, and offhand I'd say that their grievances are considerably more justified."

Pete tossed his cigarette. "Say what you like. And *I'll* say this again. You cut people too much slack."

"You mean I don't let people get to me."

"That's not what I mean. What I mean is you accept too much weak shit in people, and for my money it's some condescending rich-kid quality you picked up from the Kennedys."

Boyd popped in a fresh clip and slid a round in the chamber. "I'll grant Jack that quality, but not Bobby. Bobby's a true judger and hater."

"He hates some pretty tight friends of ours."

"He does. And he's starting to hate Carlos Marcello more than I'd like him to."

"Did you tell Carlos that?"

"Not yet. But if things escalate a bit more, I might ask you to help him out of a scrape."

Pete cracked a few knuckles. "And I'll say yes, no questions asked. Now, *you* say yes to something."

Boyd aimed at a mound of dirt twenty yards off. "No, you cannot kill Ward Littell."

"Why?"

"He's got the books fail-safed."

"So I torture him for the pertinent information, then kill him."

"It won't work."

"Why?"

Boyd shot a rattlesnake headless.

"I said 'Why?,' Kemper."

"Because he'd die just to prove he could do it."

63

(Washington, D.C., 3/26/61)

His cards read:

> Ward J. Littell
> Counselor-At-Law
> Federal Bar Licensed
> OL6-4809

No address—he didn't want clients to know that he worked out of his apartment. No glossy stock or embossed letters—he couldn't really afford them.

Littell cruised the third-floor hallway. Indicted felons took the cards and looked at him like he was crazy.

Shyster. Ambulance chaser. Middle-aged lawyer on the skids.

The Federal courthouse did a brisk business. Six divisions and full arraignment docketing—all unaccompanied lowlifes qualified as potential clients.

Littell passed out cards. A man flicked a cigarette butt at him.

Kemper Boyd walked up. Beautiful Kemper—so fit and groomed that he sparkled.

"Can I buy you a drink?"

"I don't drink like I used to."

"Lunch then?"

"Sure."

. . .

The Hay-Adams dining room faced the White House. Kemper kept glancing out the window.

"... And my work entails taking depositions and filing them in Federal District Court. We're trying to insure that Negroes previously barred from voting aren't excluded on the basis of illegally levied poll taxes or constrained by literacy tests that the local registrars want them to fail."

Littell smiled. "And I'm sure the Kennedys will rig binding legal clauses to insure that every Negro in Alabama registers as a Democrat. You have to consider things like that in the early stages of building a dynasty."

Kemper laughed. "The President's civil rights policy isn't that cynically conceived."

"Is your application of it?"

"Hardly. I've always considered suppression ill-advised and futile."

"And you like the people?"

"Yes, I do."

"Your southern accent's back in force."

"It disarms the people I deal with. They appreciate it that a southern white man's on their side. You're grinning, Ward. What is it?"

Littell sipped coffee. "It occurred to me that Alabama is rather close to Florida."

"You were always quick."

"Does the attorney general know that you're moonlighting?"

"No. But I do have a certain sanction on my Florida visits."

"Let me guess. Mr. Hoover's supplying you with cover, and as much as he professes to hate him, Bobby would never do *anything* to upset Mr. Hoover."

Kemper waved a waiter off. "Your hatred's showing, Ward."

"I don't hate Mr. Hoover. You can't hate someone who runs so true to form."

"But Bobby—"

Littell whispered. "You know what I risked for him. And you know what I got back. And what I can't abide is that the Kennedys pretend to be better than that."

Kemper said, "You've got the books." He shot his cuffs and displayed a solid gold Rolex.

Littell pointed to the White House. "Yes, I do. And they're booby-trapped a dozen different ways. I filed instruction contingency briefs with a dozen different lawyers when I was drunk, and even I can't remember them all."

Kemper folded his hands. "With depositions on my Kennedy incursion to go to the Justice Department in the event of your death or prolonged disappearance?"

"No. With depositions on your incursion and depositions on astronomically lucrative Joseph P. Kennedy Mob-linked financial malfeasance to go to municipal PD gangster squads nationwide, and every Republican member of the House and the Senate."

Kemper said, "Bravo."

Littell said, "Thank you."

A waiter placed a phone on their table. Kemper placed a folder next to it.

"Are you broke, Ward?"

"Almost."

"You haven't expressed a word of rancor regarding my recent behavior."

"It wouldn't do any good."

"How do you currently feel about organized crime?"

"My current feelings are relatively charitable."

Kemper tapped the folder. "That's a pilfered INS file. And you're the best deportation-writ lawyer on God's green earth."

Littell's shirt cuffs were soiled and frayed. Kemper wore solid gold cufflinks.

"Ten thousand dollars to start, Ward. I'm certain I can get it for you."

"*For doing what?* For releasing the books to you?"

"Forget the books. All I ask is that you don't release them to anyone else."

"Kemper, what are you talk—?"

"Your client will be Carlos Marcello. And it's Bobby Kennedy who wants to deport him."

The phone rang. Littell dropped his coffee cup.

Kemper said, "That's Carlos. Be obsequious, Ward. He'll expect a certain amount of fawning."

DOCUMENT INSERT: 4/2/61. Verbatim FBI telephone call tran-
script: "TRANSCRIBED AT THE DIRECTOR'S REQUEST"/
"DIRECTOR'S EYES ONLY." Speaking: Director J. Edgar Hoover,
Attorney General Robert F. Kennedy.

RFK: It's Bob Kennedy, Mr. Hoover. I was hoping I could have
a few minutes of your time.

JEH: Certainly.

RFK: There were a few matters of protocol I wanted to
discuss.

JEH: Yes.

RFK: Communications, to begin with. I sent you a directive requesting carbons of all summary reports submitted by your Top
Hoodlum Program squads. That directive was dated February
17th. It's now the 2nd of April, and I've yet to see a single
report.

JEH: These directives take time to implement.

RFK: Six weeks seems like ample time to me.

JEH: You perceive an undue delay. I do not.

RFK: Will you expedite the implementation of that directive?

JEH: Certainly. Will you refresh my memory as to why you issued it?

RFK: I want to assess every scrap of anti-Mob intelligence the
Bureau acquires and share it where needed with the various regional grand juries that I hope to impanel.

JEH: You may be acting injudiciously. Leaking information
that could only have originated from THP sources might jeopar-
dize THP informants and electronic surveillance placements.

RFK: All such information will be evaluated from a security
standpoint.

JEH: That function should not be trusted to non-FBI
personnel.

RFK: I adamantly disagree. You're going to have to share
your information, Mr. Hoover. The simple cultivation of intelligence will not bring Organized Crime to its knees.

JEH: The Top Hoodlum Program mandate does not provide for
information-sharing to expedite grand jury indictments.

RFK: Then we're going to have to revise it.

JEH: I would consider that a rash and heedless act.

RFK: Consider it what you like, and consider it done. Consider the Top Hoodlum Program mandate superseded by my direct order.

JEH: May I remind you of this simple fact: you cannot prosecute the Mafia and win.

RFK: May I remind you that for many years you denied that the Mafia existed. May I remind you that the FBI is but one cog in the overall wheel of the Justice Department. May I remind you that the FBI does not dictate Justice Department policy. May I remind you that the President and I consider 99% of the left-wing groups that the FBI routinely monitors to be harmless if not outright moribund, and laughably inoffensive when compared to Organized Crime.

JEH: May I state that I consider that burst of invective to be ill-conceived and fatuous in its historical perspective?

RFK: You may.

JEH: Was there anything of a similar or less offensive nature that you wish to add?

RFK: Yes. You should know that I intend to initiate wiretap accountability legislation. I want the Justice Department to be informed of every single instance of wiretapping undertaken by municipal police departments nationwide.

JEH: Many would consider that undue Federal meddling and a flagrant abuse of States' Rights.

RFK: The concept of States' Rights has been a smokescreen to obscure everything from de facto segregation to outmoded abortion statutes.

JEH: I disagree.

RFK: Duly noted. And I would like you to duly note that from this day on you are to inform me of every electronic surveillance operation that the FBI engages in.

JEH: Yes.

RFK: Duly noted?

JEH: Yes.

RFK: I want you to personally call the New Orleans SAC and have him assign four agents to arrest Carlos Marcello. I want this done within seventy-two hours. Tell the SAC that I'm having Marcello deported to Guatemala. Tell him that the Border Patrol will be contacting him to iron out details.

JEH: Yes.
RFK: Duly noted?
JEH: Yes.
RFK: Good day, Mr. Hoover.
JEH: Good day.

64

(New Orleans, 4/4/61)

He was too late—by seconds.

Four men grappled Carlos Marcello into a Fed sled. Right outside his house—with Mrs. Carlos on the porch, throwing a fit.

Pete pulled up across the street and watched it happen. His rescue mission clocked in half a minute tardy.

Marcello was dressed in BVDs and beach flip-flops. Marcello looked like this low-rent Il Duce on the rag.

Boyd fucked up.

He said, Bobby wants Carlos deported. He said, You and Chuck get to New Orleans and snatch him first. He said, Don't call and warn him—just get there.

Boyd said bureaucratic jive would give them time. Boyd mis-fucking calculated.

The Feds took off. Frau Carlos stood on the porch, wringing her hands grieving-wife-style.

Pete tailed the Fed car. Early a.m. traffic got between them. He eyeballed the Fed's antenna and rode a purple Lincoln's back bumper.

Chuck was back at Moisant Airport, gassing up the Piper. The Feds were heading that way.

They'd fly Carlos out commercial or dump him on the Border Patrol. He'd be Guatemala-bound—and Guatemala loved the CIA.

The Fed car took surface streets east. Pete saw a bridge up ahead—toll booths and two eastbound lanes across the river.

Both lanes were hemmed in by guardrails. Narrow pedestrian walkways ran flush along the edge of the bridge.

Cars were stacked up in front of the booths—at least twenty per lane.

Pete hopped lanes and swerved in front of the Fed car. He spotted a squeeze space between the left-hand booth and the guardrail.

He accelerated in. A rail housing snapped off his outside mirror.

Horns blared. His left-side hubcaps went spinning. A toll taker looked over and doused an old lady with coffee.

Pete SQUEEZED past the booths and hit the bridge going forty. The Fed sled was stalled, way way back.

He made it to Moisant fast. His rent-a-car was dinged, chipped and paint-stripped.

He ditched it in an underground lot. He greased a skycap for airport information.

Commercial flights to Guatemala? No, sir, none today. The Border Patrol office? Next to the Trans-Texas counter.

Pete cruised by and loitered behind a newspaper. The office door opened and closed.

Men carried shackles in. Men carried flight logs out. Men stood outside the door and kibitzed.

A guy said, "I heard they popped him in his skivvies."

A guy said, "The pilot really hates wops."

A guy said, "They're flying out at 8:30."

Pete ran to the private-plane hangar. Chucky was perched on the snout of his Piper, reading a hate mag.

Pete caught his breath. "They've got Carlos. We've got to get down to Guatemala City ahead of them and see what we can work out."

Chuck said, "That's a goddamned foreign country. We're only supposed to bring the man back to Blessington. We've barely got the gas to—"

"Let's go. We'll patch some calls in and work something out."

Chuck got clearance to take off and land. Pete called Guy Banister and explained the situation.

Guy said he'd call John Stanton and try to rig a plan. He had short-wave gear out at Lake Pontchartrain and could radio in to Chuck's frequency.

They took off at 8:16. Chuck put on his headphones and cribbed flight calls.

The Border Patrol plane departed late. Their Guatemala City ETA was forty-six minutes behind them.

Chuck flew medium-low and kept his headset on. Pete skimmed hate pamphlets out of sheer boredom.

The titles were a howl. The ultimate: "KKK: Kommunist Krucifixion Krusade!"

He found a skin mag/hate mag combo under his seat. Dig that zaftig blonde with the swastika earrings.

Big Pete wants a woman. Extortion experience preferred, but not mandatory.

Dashboard lights flashed. Chuck bootjacked a plane-to-base message and transcribed it in his log.

> The Border Patrol guys are goofing on Carlos. They radio'd
> their HQ that they've got no lavatory on board & Carlos refuses
> to piss in a tin can. (They think he's got a little one.)

Pete laughed. Pete pissed in a cup and doused the Gulf from 6,000 feet.

Time dragged. Stomach flutters came and went. Pete chased a Dramamine with warm beer.

Lights flashed. Chuck rogered a Pontchartrain patch-in and transcribed the message.

> Guy got through to JS. JS pulled strings & got thru to Guat.
> contacts. We're cleared to land with no passport check & if we
> can get ahold of CM its set up to register him at G.C. Hilton under
> name Jose Garcia. JS says KB says to have CM call lawyer in
> Washington D.C. at OL6-4809 tonight.

Pete pocketed the message. The Dramamine kicked in to his system: good night, sweet prince.

Leg cramps woke him up. Jungle terrain and a big black runway hovered.

Chuck eased the plane down and cut the engines. Some spics rolled out a literal red carpet.

It was a bit frayed, but nice.

The beaners looked like right-wing toady types. The Agency saved Guatemala's ass once—some staged coup expunged a shitload of Reds.

Pete hopped out and stamped his legs awake. Chuck and the spics talked rapid-fire Spanish.

They were back in Guatemala—too fucking soon.

The talk escalated. Pete felt his ears pop-pop-pop. They had forty-six minutes to rig *something*.

Pete walked over to the Customs shack. He got this little Technicolor brain blip: Carlos Marcello needs to urinate.

The bathroom adjoined the passport counter. Pete checked it out.

It ran about 8 feet by 8 feet square. A flimsy screen covered the back window. The view featured more runways and a line of rattletrap bi-planes.

Carlos was stocky. Chuck was rail thin. He was all-around-huge himself.

Chuck walked in and unzipped by the urinal. "We got a big foul-up. I don't know if it's good news or bad."

"What are you saying?"

"I'm saying the Border Patrol's set to land in seventeen minutes. They've got to refuel here and fly to another airport sixty miles away. *That's* where Customs is set to pick up Carlos. That ETA I got is for the *other* goddamned air—"

"How much money have we got in the plane?"

"Sixteen thousand. Santo said to drop it off with Banister."

Pete shook his head. "We grease the Customs guys with it. We fucking inundate them, so they'll take the risk. All we need is a car and a driver outside that window, and you to push Carlos through."

Chuck said, "I get it."

Pete said, "If he doesn't have to piss, we're fucked."

The spics dug the plan. Chuck greased them at the rate of two grand per man. They said they'd keep the Border Patrol guys busy while Carlos Marcello took the world's longest whiz.

Pete loosened the window screen. Chuck stashed the Piper two hangars over.

The spics supplied a '49 Merc getaway car. The spics supplied a driver—a musclebound fag named Luis.

Pete backed the Merc up to the window. Chuck crouched on the toilet seat with last week's *Hush-Hush.*

The Border Patrol plane landed. A crew hustled out refueling pumps. Pete crouched behind the Customs shack and watched.

The spics zipped out the red carpet. A little geek brushed it off with a whisk broom.

Two Border Patrol clowns deplaned. The pilot said, "Let him go. Where's he gonna run to?"

Carlos tumbled out of the plane. Carlos ran to the shack, knock-kneed in tight BVDs.

Luis idled the engine. Pete heard the bathroom door slam.

Carlos yelled, "ROGERS, WHAT THE FUCK—?"

The window screen popped out. Carlos Marcello squeezed through—and snagged himself bare-assed in the process.

The run to the Hilton took an hour. Marcello blasted Bobby Kennedy nonstop.

In English. In straight Italian. In Sicilian dialect. In New Orleans Cajun French patois—not bad for a wop.

Luis detoured by a men's shop. Chuck took down Marcello's sizes and bought him some threads.

Carlos dressed in the car. Little window-squeeze abrasions bloodied up his shirt.

The hotel manager met them at the freight entrance. They freight-lifted up to the penthouse on the QT.

The manager unlocked the door. One glance said Stanton *delivered.*

The pad featured three bedrooms, three bathrooms and a rec room lined with slot machines. The living room was Kemper Boyd fantasy size.

The bar was fully stocked. A guinea cold-cut buffet was laid out. The envelope by the cheese tray contained twenty grand and a note.

Pete & Chuck,

I'm betting you were able to get ahold of Mr. Marcello. Take good care of him. He's a valuable friend to the Cause.

JS

Marcello grabbed the money. The manager genuflected. Pete showed him the door and slipped him a C-note.

Marcello snarfed salami and breadsticks. Chuck built a tall Bloody Mary.

Pete paced off the suite. Forty-two yards lengthwise—whoa!

Chuck curled up with a hate mag. Marcello said, "I really had to piss. When you hold a piss that long it pisses you off."

Pete snagged a beer and some crackers. "Stanton's got you a lawyer in D.C. You're supposed to call him."

"I've talked to him already. I've got the best Jew lawyers money can buy, and now I've got him."

"You should call him now and get it over with."

"You call him. And stay on the line in case I need you to translate. Lawyers talk this language I don't always get the first time around."

Pete grabbed the coffee table extension. The hotel operator placed his call.

Marcello picked up the bar phone. The long-distance rings came through faint.

A man said, "Hello?"

Marcello said, "Who's this? Are you that guy I talked to at the Hay-Adams?"

"Yes, this is Ward Littell. Is this Mr. Marcello?"

Pete almost SHIT—

Carlos slumped into a chair. "This is him, calling from Guatemala City, Guatemala, where he does not want to be. Now, if you want to get my attention, say something bad about the man who put me here."

Pete clenched up wicked bad. He covered his mouthpiece so they wouldn't hear him hyperventilate.

Littell said, "I hate that man. He hurt me once, and there is very little that I wouldn't do to cause him discomfort."

Carlos tee-hee-heed—weird for a bass-baritone. "You got my attention. Now, stow that ass-kiss routine you dropped on me before, and say something to convince me you're good at what you do."

Littell cleared his throat. "I specialize in deportation writ work. I was an FBI agent for close to twenty years. I'm a good friend of Kemper Boyd, and although I distrust his admiration for the Kennedys, I'm convinced that his devotion to the Cuban Cause supersedes it. He wants to see you safely and legally reunited with your loved ones, and I'm here to see that it happens."

Pete felt queasy. BOYD, YOU FUCK—

Marcello snapped breadsticks. "Kemper said you were ten grand's worth of good. Now, if you deliver like you talk, ten grand's just the start of you and me."

Littell came on servile. "It's an honor to work for you. And Kemper apologizes for your inconvenience. He was tipped off on the raid at the last second, and he didn't think they could pull it off as fast as they did."

Marcello scratched his neck with a breadstick. "Kemper always gets the job done. I've got no complaints against him that can't wait until the next time I see that too-handsome face of his face-to-face. And the Kennedys keestered 49.8% of the American voters, including some good friends of mine, so I don't begrudge him that admiration if it don't fuck with my life and limb."

Littell said, "He'll be pleased to hear that. And you should know that I'm writing up a temporary reinstatement brief that will be reviewed by a three-judge Federal panel. I'll be calling your attorney in New York, and we'll begin devising a long-range legal strategy."

Marcello kicked off his shoes. "Do it. Call my wife and tell her I'm okay, and do whatever you need to do to get me the fuck out of here."

"I will. And I'll be bringing some paperwork down for you to sign. You can expect to see me within seventy-two hours."

Marcello said, "I want to go home."

Pete hung up. Steam hissed out of his ears like he was Donald Fucking Duck.

They killed time. The jumbo pad let them kill it separately.

Chucky watched spic TV. King Carlos buzzed his serfs long-distance. Pete fantasized ninety-nine ways to murder Ward Littell.

John Stanton called in. Pete regaled him with the toilet-snatch story. Stanton said the Agency would cover their bribe tab.

Pete said, Boyd fixed Carlos up with a lawyer. Stanton said, I heard he's quite good. Pete almost said, Now I can't kill him.

BOYD, YOU FUCK.

Stanton said the fix was in. Ten grand would buy Carlos a temporary visa. The Guatemalan foreign minister was set to publicly state:

Mr. Marcello *was* born in Guatemala. His birth certificate is legitimate. Attorney General Kennedy is wrong. Mr. Marcello's origins are in no way ambiguous.

Mr. Marcello split to America—*legally.* Sadly, we have no records to corroborate this. The burden of proof now falls upon Mr. Kennedy.

Stanton said the minister hates Jack the K.

Stanton said Jack fucked his wife and both his daughters.

Pete said, Jack fucked my old girlfriend. Stanton said, Wow—and you *still* helped elect him!

Stanton said, Have Chuck grease the minister. And by the way, Jack's still dicking around on a go-date.

Pete hung up and looked out the window. Guatemala City by twilight—strictly the rat's ass.

They all dozed off early. Pete woke up early—a nightmare had him balled up under his sheets, gasping for breath.

Chuck was out on his bribe run. Carlos was on his second cigar.

Pete opened the living-room curtains. He saw a big hubbub down at ground level.

He saw a string of trucks at the curb. He saw men with cameras. He saw cables stretching into the lobby.

He saw people gesturing up.

He saw a big movie camera pointing straight up at them.

Pete said, "We're blown."

Carlos dropped his cigar in his hash browns and ran to the window.

Pete said, "The Agency's got a camp an hour from here. If we can find Chuck and fly out, we'll make it."

Carlos looked down. Carlos saw the ruckus. Carlos pushed his breakfast cart through the window and watched it bullseye down eighteen stories.

65

(Rural Guatemala, 4/8/61)

Heat shimmied off the runway. Blast-oven heat—Kemper should have warned him to dress light.

Kemper warned him that Bondurant would be there. He hustled Marcello out of Guatemala City three days ago and arranged for the CIA to play innkeeper.

Kemper added a postscript: Pete knows you've got the Fund books.

Littell stepped away from the plane. He felt woozy. His connecting flight from Houston was a World War II transport.

Propeller thwack boosted the heat. The campsite was large and dusty—odd buildings plunked down in a red clay jungle clearing.

A jeep skidded up. The driver saluted.

"Mr. Littell?"

"Yes."

"I'll drive you over, sir. Your friends are waiting for you."

Littell got in. The rearview mirror caught his bold new face.

He had three shots back in Houston. *Daytime* shots to help him rise to this one-time occasion.

The driver peeled out. Troops marched by in strict formation; cadence counts overlapped.

They pulled into a barrack's quadrangle. The driver stopped in front of a small Quonset hut. Littell grabbed his suitcase and walked in ramrod-straight.

The room was air-conditioned. Bondurant and Carlos Marcello stood by a pool table.

Pete winked. Littell winked back. His whole face contorted.

Pete cracked his knuckles—his old intimidation trademark. Marcello said, "What are you, faggots, winking at each other?"

Littell put his suitcase down. The snaps creaked. His surprise had the damn thing bulging.

"How are you, Mr. Marcello?"

"I'm losing money. Every day Pete and my Agency friends treat me better, so every day I end up pledging more money to the Cause. I figure the nut on this hotel's running me twenty-five grand a day."

Pete chalked up a pool cue. Marcello jammed his hands in his pockets.

Kemper warned him: the man does not shake hands.

"I talked to your attorneys in New York a few hours ago. They want to know, if you need anything."

Marcello smiled. "I need to kiss my wife on the cheek and fuck my girlfriend. I need to eat some duck Rochambeau at Galatoire's, and I cannot accomplish any of that here."

Bondurant racked up the table. Littell swung his suitcase up and blocked it off lengthwise.

Marcello chuckled. "I'm starting to detect old grief here."

Pete lit a cigarette. Littell caught the exhale full-on.

"I've got a good deal of paperwork for you to review, Mr. Marcello. We'll need to spend some time together and devise a story that details your immigration history, so that Mr. Wasserman can use it when he files his injunction to get your deportation order rescinded. Some very influential people want to see you repatriated, and I'll be working with them as well. I realize that all this unexpected travel must be exhausting, so Kemper Boyd and I are going to arrange for Chuck Rogers to fly you back to Louisiana in a few days and hide you out."

Marcello did a quick little shuffle. The man was deft and fast on his feet.

Pete said, "What happened to your face, Ward?"

Littell opened the suitcase. Pete picked up the 8-ball and cracked it in half barehanded.

Wood chunks snapped and popped. Marcello said, "I'm not sure I like where this is going."

Littell pulled out the Fund books. A quick prayer tamped down his nerves.

"I'm sure you both know that Jules Schiffrin's estate in Lake Geneva was burglarized last November. Some paintings were stolen, along with some ledgers rumored to contain Teamster Pension Fund notations. The thief was an informant for a Chicago-based Top Hoodlum Program agent named Court Meade, and he gave the books to Meade when he realized that the paintings were too well-known and recognizable to sell. Meade died of a heart attack in January, and he willed the books to me. He told me he never showed them to anyone else, and in my opinion he was waiting to sell them to somebody in the Giancana organization. There's a few pages that have been torn out, but aside from that I think they're intact. I brought them to you because I know how close you are to Mr. Hoffa and the Teamsters."

Marcello went slack-jawed. Pete snapped a pool cue in half.

He tore out fourteen pages back in Houston. He had all the Kennedy entries safely stashed.

Marcello offered his hand. Littell kissed a big diamond ring papal-style.

66

(Anniston, 4/11/61)

Voting rolls and poll tax reports. Literacy test results and witness statements.

Four corkboard-mounted walls dripping with paper—systematic suppression in typescript black-on-white.

His room was small and drab. The Wigwam Motel was not quite the St. Regis.

Kemper worked up a voting rights obstruction brief. One literacy test and one witness deposition formed his evidentiary basis.

Delmar Herbert Bowen was a male Negro, born 6/14/19 in Anniston, Alabama. He was literate, and a self-described "big reader."

On 6/15/40, Mr. Bowen tried to register to vote. The registrar said, Boy, can you read and write?

Mr. Bowen proved that he could. The registrar asked exclusionary questions, pertaining to advanced calculus.

Mr. Bowen failed to answer them. Mr. Bowen was denied the right to vote.

He subpoenaed Mr. Bowen's literacy test. He determined that the Anniston registrar fabricated the results.

The man said that Mr. Bowen could not spell "dog" and "cat." Mr. Bowen did not know that coitus precipitates childbirth.

Kemper clipped pages. The work bored him. The Kennedy civil rights mandate was not bold enough for his taste.

His mandate was gunboat diplomacy.

He grabbed a sandwich at a lunch counter yesterday. In the colored section—for the pure hell of it.

A cracker called him a "nigger lover." He judo-chopped him into a bowl of grits.

Shots zinged his door last night. A colored man told him the Klan torched a cross down the block.

Kemper finished the Bowen brief. He did it catch-up fast—he had to meet John Stanton in Miami in three hours.

Phone calls blitzed his morning and put him off-schedule. Bobby called for a deposition update; Littell called to drop his latest A-bomb.

Ward delivered the Fund books to Carlos Marcello. Pete Bondurant observed the transaction. Marcello seemed to buy Ward's convoluted cover story.

Ward said, "I made copies, Kemper. And the depositions on your incursion and Joe Kennedy's malfeasance remain fail-safed. And I'd appreciate it if you advised Le Grand Pierre not to kill me."

He called Pete immediately. He said, "Don't kill Littell or tell Carlos his story is bullshit." Pete said, "Credit me with some brains. I've been playing this game as long as you."

Littell finessed them. It was no severe loss—the books were always a moneymaking longshot.

Kemper oiled his .45. Bobby knew he carried it—and laughed it off as pretentious.

He wore it to the Inaugural. He found Bobby on the parade route and told him he cut Laura off clean.

He found Jack at a White House reception. He called him "Mr. President" for the first time. Jack's first presidential decree: "Find me some girls for later tonight."

Kemper rustled up two Georgetown coeds. President Jack told him to stash the girls away for late quickies.

Kemper stashed them in White House guest rooms. Jack caught him yawning and splashing water on his face.

It was 3:00 a.m., with Inaugural galas set to run past dawn.

Jack suggested a pick-me-up. They walked into the Oval Office and saw a doctor preparing vials and hypodermics.

The President rolled up one sleeve. The doctor injected him. John F. Kennedy looked positively orgasmic.

Kemper rolled up one sleeve. The doctor injected him. A rocket payload hit his system.

The ride lasted twenty-four hours. The time and place cohered around it.

Jack's ascent became his. That simple truth felt spellbindingly articulate. The time and place were beholden to one Kemper Cathcart Boyd. In that sense, he and Jack were indistinguishable.

He picked up one of Jack's old flames and made love to her at the Willard. He described the Moment to senators and cab drivers. Judy Garland showed him how to dance the Twist.

The ride sputtered out and left him wanting more. He knew that more would only vulgarize the Moment.

The phone rang. Kemper cinched his overnight bag and picked up.

"This is Boyd."

"It's Bob, Kemper. I've got the President here with me."

"Does he want me to repeat that update I gave you?"

"No. We need you to help us sort out a communications glitch."

"Pertaining to?"

"Cuba. I realize that you're only informally acquainted with some recent developments, but I still think you're the best man for this."

"For what? What are we talking about?"

Bobby came off exasperated. "The projected exile invasion, which you may or may not have heard about. Richard Bissell just dropped by my office and said the CIA's chomping at the bit, and their Cubans are just a bit beyond restless. They've got the key landing site picked out. It's some place called Playa Girón, or the Bay of Pigs."

It was NEW news. Stanton never told him that Langley picked a site.

Kemper faked bewilderment. "I don't see how I can help you. You know I don't know anybody in the CIA."

Jack came on the line. "Bobby didn't know the thing was this far advanced, Kemper. Allen Dulles briefed us on it before I took office, but we haven't discussed it since then. My advisors are split down the middle on the damn thing."

Kemper slipped on his holster. Bobby said, "What we need is an independent assessment of the exiles' readiness."

Kemper laughed. "Because if the invasion fails and it becomes known that you backed the so-called 'rebels,' you'll be fucked in the court of world opinion."

Bobby said, "Vividly put."

Jack said, "And to the point. And I should have taken Bobby into my confidence on this a few weeks ago, but he's been so goddamned busy chasing gangsters. Kemper . . ."

"Yes, Mr. President."

"I've been waffling on a date, and Bissell's been pressing me. I know you've been doing that anti-Castro work for Mr. Hoover, so I know you're at least somewhat . . ."

"I am somewhat conversant on Cuba, at least from a pro-Castro-group standpoint."

Bobby cracked the whip. "Cuba's always been a bit of a fixation for you, so go to Florida and make something positive out of it. Visit the CIA training camps, and take a swing through Miami. Call back and tell us if you think the operation has a chance to succeed, and do it damn fast."

Kemper said, "I'll leave now. I'll report back inside forty-eight hours."

John almost died laughing. Kemper almost called a cardiologist.

They sat on Stanton's private terrace. Langley let him upgrade to the Fontainebleau—hotel-suite living was contagious.

A breeze blew up Collins Avenue. Kemper's throat hurt—he repeated the phone talk replete with Jack's Boston bray.

"John . . ."

Stanton caught his breath. "I'm sorry, but I never thought presidential indecisiveness could be so goddamn funny."

"What do you think I should tell him?"

"How about, 'The invasion will guarantee your re-election.' "

Kemper laughed. "I've got some time to kill in Miami. Any suggestions?"

"Yes, two."

"Tell me, then. And tell me why you wanted to see me when you knew I was swamped in Alabama."

Stanton poured a short scotch-and-water. "That civil rights work must be vexing."

"Not really."

"I think the Negro vote is a mixed blessing. Aren't they easily led?"

"I'd call them slightly less malleable than our Cubans. And considerably less criminally inclined."

Stanton smiled. "Stop it. Don't make me start laughing again."

Kemper put his feet up on the railing. "I think you could use a few laughs. Langley's running you ragged, and you're drinking at 1:00 p.m."

Stanton nodded. "This is true. Everybody from Mr. Dulles on down would like the invasion to go off some time in the next five minutes, and I'm no exception. And to answer your initial question, I want you to spend the next forty-eight hours devising realistic-sounding intelligence on troop readiness to submit to the President, and I want you to pre-patrol our Cadre territory with Fulo and Néstor Chasco. Miami's our best source of street-level intelligence, and I want you to assess just how far and how accurately rumors pertaining to the invasion have spread within the Cuban community."

Kemper mixed a gin and tonic. "I'll get on it right away. Was there anything else?"

"Yes. The Agency wants to set up a Cuban 'government in exile,' to be housed at Blessington during the actual invasion. It's mostly cosmetic, but we've got to have at least a facsimile of a consensus-chosen leadership ready to install if we get Castro out within, say, three or four days of our go date."

"And you want my opinion as to who gets the nod?"

"Right. I know you're not too well versed on exile politics, but I thought you might have picked up some opinions from the Cadre."

Kemper faked deep thought. Steady now, make him wait—

Stanton threw his hands up. "Come on, I didn't tell you to go into a goddamn trance about—"

Kemper snapped out of it—bright-eyed and forceful. "We want far-right-wingers susceptible to working with Santo and our other friends in the Outfit. We want a figurehead leader who can maintain order, and the best way to re-stabilize the Cuban economy is to get the casinos operating on a full profit margin. If Cuba stays volatile or the Reds take over again, we've got to be able to draw on the Outfit for financial assistance."

Stanton laced his hands around one knee. "I was expecting something a bit more enlightened from Kemper Boyd the civil rights reformer. And I'm sure you know that the donations of our Italian friends only account for a tiny percentage of our legitimately funded government budget."

Kemper shrugged. "Cuba's solvency depends on American tourism. The Outfit can help insure that. United Fruit is out of Cuba now, and only a bribable far-right-winger will be willing to de-nationalize their holdings."

Stanton said, "Keep going. You're close to persuading me."

Kemper stood up. "Carlos is down at the Guatemala camp with my lawyer friend. Chuck's going to fly him to Louisiana in a few days and hide him out, and I've heard that he's getting more pro-exile by the day. I'm betting that the invasion *will* succeed, but that chaos will reign in-

side Cuba for some time. Whoever we install will fall under intense public scrutiny, which means public accountability, and we both know that
the Agency will be subjected to intense scrutiny that will limit our
deniability in all matters pertaining to covert action. We'll need the
Cadre then, and we'll probably need a half-dozen more groups as ruthless and autonomous as the Cadre, and *we'll need them to be privately
funded.* Our new leader will need a secret police, and the Outfit will provide him with one, and if he falters in his pro-U.S. stance, the Outfit will
assassinate him."

Stanton stood up. He looked bright-eyed verging on feverish.

"I don't have the final say, but you sold me. Your pitch wasn't as
flowery as your boy's Inaugural address, but it was a good deal more
politically astute."

AND PROFIT-MOTIVATED—

Kemper said, "Thanks. It's an honor to be compared to John F.
Kennedy."

Fulo drove. Néstor talked. Kemper watched.

They cruised Cadre turf in random figure-eights. Slum shacks and
housing projects zipped by.

Néstor said, "Send me back to Cuba. I will shoot Fidel from a roof-
top. I will become the Simón Bolívar of my country."

Fulo's Chevy was packed with dope. Powder puffed out of plastic
bags and dusted the seats.

Néstor said, "Send me back to Cuba as a boxer. I will beat Fidel to
death with bolo punches like Kid Gavilan."

Rheumy eyes popped their way—local junkies knew the car. Winos
pressed up for handouts—Fulo was a well-known soft touch.

Fulo called it the New Marshall Plan. Fulo said his handouts inspired
subservience.

Kemper watched.

Néstor stopped at drop sites and sold pre-packaged bindles. Fulo
backstopped all transactions with a shotgun.

Kemper watched.

Fulo spotted a *non-Cadre* transaction outside Lucky Time Liquors.
Néstor sprayed the transactors with .12-gauge-propelled rock salt.

The transactors dispersed every which way. Rock salt tore through
your clothes and made your skin sting like a mother humper.

Kemper watched.

Néstor said, "Send me back to Cuba as a skin diver. I will shoot Fidel with an underwater spear gun."

Street-corner rummies sucked down T-Bird. Glue fiends sniffed rags. Half the front lawns featured dilapidated jalopies.

Kemper watched. Cab calls squawked up the squawk box. Fulo drove from Darktown to Poquito Habana.

Faces went from black to brown. Incidental colors shifted and went more pastel.

Pastel-fronted churches. Pastel-fronted dance clubs and bodegas. Men in bright pastel guayabera shirts.

Fulo drove. Néstor talked. Kemper watched.

They passed parking-lot crap games. They passed soapbox orations. They passed two kids pummeling a pro-Beard pamphleteer.

Kemper watched.

Fulo glided down Flagler and traded cash for prostitute street talk.

One girl said Castro was queer. One girl said Castro had a 12" chorizo. All the girls wanted to know one thing: When's this big invasion gonna happen?

A girl said she picked up a rumor down at Blessington. Ain't that big invasion next week?

One girl said Guantánamo was gonna get A-bombed. One girl said, You're wrong—it's Playa Girón. One girl said flying saucers would soon descend on Havana.

Fulo drove. Néstor polled strolling Cubans up and down Flagler.

They'd all heard invasion rumors. They all shared them with gusto.

Kemper shut his eyes and listened. Nouns jumped out of run-on Spanish.

Havana, Playa Girón, Baracoa, Oriente, Playa Girón, Guantánamo, Guantánamo.

Kemper caught the upshot:

People were talking.

On-leave trainees were talking. Agency-front-group men were talking. The talk was innuendo, bullshit, wish fulfillment and truth by default— speculate on enough invasion sites and you'll hit the right one out of sheer luck.

The talk constituted a minor security leak.

Fulo didn't seem worried. Néstor shrugged the talk off. Kemper categorized it as "containable."

They cruised the side streets off Flagler.

Fulo monitored cab calls. Néstor talked up ways to torture Fidel Castro. Kemper looked out his window and savored the view.

Cuban girls blew them kisses. Car radios churned out mambo music. Street loafers gobbled melons soaked in beer.

Fulo clicked off a call. "That was Wilfredo. He said Don Juan knows something about a dope drop, and maybe we should go see him."

Don Juan Pimentel had a TB cough. His front room was littered with customized Barbie and Ken dolls.

They stood just inside the door. Don Juan smelled like mentholated chest rub.

Fulo said, "You can talk in front of Mr. Boyd. He is a wonderful friend of our Cause."

Néstor picked up a nude Barbie. The doll wore a Jackie Kennedy wig and Brillo-pad crotch hair.

Don Juan coughed. "It is twenty-five dollars for the story, and fifty dollars for the story and the address."

Néstor dropped the doll and crossed himself. Fulo handed Don Juan two twenties and a ten.

He tucked the cash in his shirt pocket. "The address is 4980 Balustrol. Four men from the Cuban Intelligence Directorate live there. They are terribly afraid that your invasion will succeed and that their supply from the island will be, how you say, removed. They have at the house a very large supply of single shots packaged to sell in order to make quick money to, how you say, bankroll their resistance to your resistance. They have over a pound of heroin ready to be sold in these small amounts where there is to be the, how you say, most profit."

Kemper smiled. "Is the house guarded?"

"I do not know."

"Who would they sell the stuff to?"

"Certainly not to Cubans. I would say to the negritos and the poor whites."

Kemper nudged Fulo. "Is Mr. Pimentel a reliable informant?"

"Yes. I think so."

"Is he strongly anti-Castro?"

"Yes. I think so."

"Would you trust him not to betray us under any circumstances?"

"Well . . . that is hard to . . ."

Don Juan spat on the floor. "You are a coward not to ask such questions to my face."

Kemper judo-chopped him. Don Juan clipped a doll rack and went down gagging for breath.

Néstor dropped a pillow on his face. Kemper pulled his .45 and fired through it point-blank.

His silencer ate up the noise. Blood-soaked feathers billowed.

Néstor and Fulo looked shocked. Kemper said, "I'll explain later."

REBELS RESCUE CUBA!
COMMIES PANDER POISON DOPE IN RAPACIOUS REVENGE!
HEROIN HOLOCAUST! PUSHER CASTRO GLOATS!
DESPERATE DICTATOR IN EXILE! DOPE DEATH TOLL MOUNTS!

Kemper printed the headlines on a dispatch sheet. Tiger Kab swirled all around him—the midnight shift was just coming on.

He wrote a cover note.

PB,

Have Lenny Sands write up Hush-Hush articles to accompany the enclosed headlines. Tell him to expedite it and to check the Miami papers over the next week or so for background details and call me if necessary. This, of course, pertains to the invasion, and my feeling is that we're very close to a go-date. I can't go into my plan in detail yet, but I think it's something you'd appreciate. If Lenny finds my orders confusing, tell him to extrapolate off the headlines in the inimitable Hush-Hush style.

I know you're somewhere in Nicaragua or Guatemala, and I'm hoping this pouch gets to you. And try to think of WJL as a colleague. Peaceful co-existence doesn't always mean appeasement.

KB

Kemper stamped the envelope: C. ROGERS/NEXT FLIGHT/URGENT. Fulo and Néstor walked by, looking befuddled—he never explained why he killed Don Juan.

Santo Junior had a pet shark named Batista. They drove to Tampa and dumped Don Juan in his pool.

Kemper pulled a phone into the men's room. He rehearsed his pitch three times, complete with pauses and asides.

He called Bobby's secretary. He told her to turn on her tape recorder.

She jumped to it. She bought his perfectly honed urgency.

He lauded. He gushed. He praised exile morale and combat-readiness. The CIA had a brilliant plan. Their pre-invasion security was water-tight.

He raved like a skeptic newly converted. He inserted New Frontier rhetoric. His Tennessee drawl oozed convert righteousness.

The woman said she'd rush the tape to Bobby. Her voice quivered and broke.

Kemper hung up and walked out to the parking lot. Teo Paez swung by and passed him a note.

W. Littell called. Said all is well with CM. CM's N.Y. lawyer says Justice Dept. agents are searching Louisiana for CM. W. Littell says CM should stay at Guat. camp or at least out of country for awhile.

Ward Littell in ascent—truly amazing.

A breeze kicked in. Kemper stretched out on a tiger-striped hood and looked at the sky.

The moon hovered close. Batista had bright white teeth the same color.

Kemper dozed. Chants woke him up. He heard GO GO GO GO GO—that one word and nothing else.

The shouts were ecstatic. The dispatch hut boomed like a giant echo chamber.

The invasion date was set. It couldn't be anything less than that.

Santo fed Batista steaks and fried chicken. His pool was an Olympic-sized grease spill.

Batista bit Don Juan's head off. Néstor and Fulo turned away.

He didn't. He was starting to enjoy killing more than he should.

67

(Rural Nicaragua, 4/17/61)

PIGS! PIGS! PIGS! PIGS! PIGS! PIGS! PIGS! PIGS! PIGS!

Six hundred men chanted it. The staging site shook behind that one word.

The men jumped into trucks. The trucks locked in bumper-to-bumper and headed down to the launch dock.

PIGS PIGS PIGS PIGS PIGS—

Pete watched. John Stanton watched. They jeep-patrolled the site and watched everything click into on-go status.

On-GO at the dock: one insignia-deleted U.S. troop ship. On board: landing craft, mortars, grenades, rifles, machine guns, radio gear, medical gear, mosquito repellent, maps, ammo and six hundred Sheik prophylactics—a Langley shrink foresaw mass rape as a victory by-product.

On-GO: six hundred Benzedrine-blasted Cuban rebels.

On-GO at the air strip: sixteen B-26 bombers, set to hammer Castro's standing air force. Dig their blacked-out U.S. insignia—this gig was non-imperialisto.

PIGS PIGS PIGS PIGS—

The abbreviation fit the destination. John Stanton got the chant going at reveille—that shrink said repetition built up courage.

Pete chased high-octane bennies with coffee. He could see it and feel it and smell it—

The planes neutralize Castro air power. The ships go out—staggered departures from a half-dozen launch sites. A second air strike kills militiamen en masse. Chaos spawns mass desertion.

Freedom fighters hit the beach.

They march. They kill. They defoliate. They link up with on-island dissidents and reclaim Cuba—weakened by dope and propaganda foreplay.

They were waiting for Bad-Back Jack to okay the first air strike. All the orders had to emanate from the Haircut.

PIGS PIGS PIGS PIGS PIGS—

Pete and Stanton jeep-patrolled the site. They had a short-wave set rigged to the dashboard—site-to-site communication made easy.

They had direct feeds to Guatemala, Tiger Kab and Blessington. They were radio contained at that level—only Langley direct-channeled to the White House.

The order came down: Jack says to send six planes out.

Pete felt his dick go limp. The radio man said Jack wants to move real cautiously.

Six from sixteen was a big fucking reduction.

They kept circuiting the site. Pete chain-smoked. Stanton fretted a Saint Christopher medal.

Boyd pouched a message three days ago—some cryptic *Hush-Hush* orders for Lenny Sands. He forwarded the information. Lenny said he'd write the stuff up quick.

Lenny always delivered. Ward Littell always surprised.

That Teamster book hand-off was superb. Littell's brown-nose job on Carlos was better.

Boyd had them lodged at the Guatemalan campsite. Marcello glommed a private phone line and ran his rackets biz long-distance.

Carlos liked fresh seafood. Carlos liked to throw big dinner parties. Littell had 500 Maine lobsters air-shipped to Guatemala daily.

Carlos turned crack troopers into salivating gluttons. Carlos turned said troopers into coolies—trained exile guerrillas shined his shoes and ran his errands.

Boyd was running the Marcello operation. Boyd gave Pete one direct order: LEAVE LITTELL ALONE.

The Bondurant-Littell truce was Boyd-enforced and *temporary*.

Pete chain-smoked. Cigarettes and bennies had him parched. His hands kept doing things he didn't tell them to.

They kept circuiting. Stanton sweated his clothes wringing wet.

PIGS! PIGS! PIGS! PIGS! PIGS!

They parked by the dock and watched troops climb the boarding plank. Six hundred men hopped on in just under two minutes.

Their short-wave set sputtered. The needle bounced to the Blessington frequency.

Stanton plugged in his headset. Pete lit his zillionth cigarette of the day.

The troop ship creaked and waddled. A fat Cubano puked over the stern.

Stanton said, "Our government-in-exile's in place, and Bissell ended up approving those far-right boys I recommended. That's good, but that fake-defector charade we cooked up backfired. Gutiérrez landed the plane at Blessington, but the reporters that Dougie Lockhart called in recognized Ramón and started booing. It's not a big thing, but a fuck-up's still a fuck-up."

Pete nodded. He smelled vomit and bilge water and oil off six hundred rifles.

Stanton unhooked his headset. His Saint Christopher was fretted shiny to dull.

They kept circuiting. It was gas-guzzling Benzedrine bullshit.

Please, Jack:

Send some more planes in. Give the orders to send the boats out.

Pete got wild-ass itchy. Stanton blathered on and on about his kids.

Hours took decades. Pete ran lists in his head to shut Stanton out.

The men he killed. The women he fucked. The best hamburgers in L.A. and Miami. What he'd be doing if he never left Quebec. What he'd be doing if he never met Kemper Boyd.

Stanton worked the radio. Reports crackled in.

They heard that the air strike fizzled. The bombers nailed less than 10% of Fidel Castro's air force.

Bad-Back Jack took the news hard. He responded in cuntish fashion: no second air strike just yet.

Chuck Rogers squeaked a call in. He said Marcello and Littell were still in Guatemala. He dropped some late-breaking stateside info: the FBI invaded New Orleans in response to fake Carlos sightings!

It was Boyd's doing. He figured erroneous phone tips would keep Bobby diverted and help cover Marcello's tracks.

Chuck signed off. Stanton clamped his headphones down and kept his ears perked for stray calls.

Seconds took years. Minutes took fucking millenniums.

Pete scratched his balls raw. Pete smoked himself hoarse. Pete shot palm fronds off of trees just to shoot *something*.

Stanton rogered a call. "That was Lockhart. He says our government-in-exile's close to rioting. They need you at Blessington, and Rogers is flying in from Guatemala to pick you up."

They detoured by the Cuban coast. Chuck said it added nil time to their flight plan.

Pete yelled, "Let's get low!"

Chuck throttled down. Pete saw flames from two thousand feet and half a mile out.

They swooped below radar level and belly-rolled along the beach. Pete jammed binoculars out his window.

He saw aircraft wreckage—Cuban and rebel. He saw smoldering palm groves and hose trucks parked on the sand.

Air-raid sirens were blasting full-tilt. Dock-mounted spotlights were pre-dusk operational. Pillboxes had been set up just above the high tide line—fully manned and sandbagged.

Militiamen crowded the dock. Dig those little geeks with Tommy guns and aircraft ID guides.

They were eighty miles south of Playa Girón. *This* stretch of beach was red-alert ready. If the Bay of Pigs was *this* fortified, the entire invasion was fucked.

Pete heard muzzle pops. Little chickenshit pepperings went bip-bip-bip.

Chuck caught on—they're shooting at *us*.

He flipped the Piper belly to backside. Pete spun topsy-turvy.

His head hit the roof. His seatbelt choked him immobile. Chucky rolled and flew upside down all the way to U.S. waters.

Dusk hit. Blessington glowed under high-wattage arc lights.

Pete popped two Dramamines. He saw redneck gawkers and ice cream trucks perched outside the front gates.

Chuck fishtailed down the runway and brought the plane to a dead stall. Pete hopped out woozy—Benzedrine and incipient nausea packed this wicked one-two punch.

A prefab hut stood in the middle of the drill field. Triple-strength barbed wire sequestered it. Unsynchronized shouts boomed out—a far cry from your snappy PIGS PIGS PIGS!

Pete stretched and worked out some muscle kinks. Lockhart ran up to him.

"Goddamnit, get in there and calm those spics down!"

Pete said, "What happened?"

"What happened is Kennedy's stalling. Dick Bissell said he wants a win, but he don't want to go the whole hog and get blamed if the invasion goes bust. I got my rusty old cargo ship all ready to go, but that Pope-worshiping cocksucker in the White House won't—"

Pete slapped him. The little shitbird weaved and stayed upright.

"I said, *'What happened?'*"

Lockhart wiped his nose and giggled. "What happened is my Klan boys sold the provisional government guys some moonshine, and they started arguing politics with some of the regular troops. I whipped up a crew and isolated the troublemakers with that there barbed wire, but that don't alter the fact that you got sixty frustrated and liquored-up Cuban hotheads in there biting at each other like copperheads when they should be concentrating on the problem at hand, which is liberating a Commie-held dictatorship."

"Do they have guns?"

"No sir. I got the weapons shack locked and guarded."

Pete reached into the cockpit. Right upside the dashboard: Chuck's fungo bat and all-purpose tool kit.

He grabbed them. He pulled out the tin snips and tucked the bat into his waistband.

Lockhart said, "What are you doing?"

Chuck said, "I think I know."

Pete pointed to the pump shed. "Let go with the fire hoses in exactly five minutes."

Lockhart hooted. "Them hoses will tear that prefab right down."

"That's what I want."

The sequestered spics laughed and yelled. Lockhart took off and hit the pump shed at a sprint.

Pete ran over to the fence and snipped out a section of coiling. Chuck wrapped his hands in his windbreaker and pulled down a big wall of barbs.

Pete scrunched down and crawled through. He ran up to the hut in a deep fullback crouch. One fungo bat shot took the door down.

His crash-in went unnoticed. The government-in-exile boys were preoccupied.

With arm wrestling, card games and shine-guzzling contests. With a baby-alligator race right there on the floor.

Dig the rooting sections. Dig the blankets covered with bet chits. Dig the bunks weighted down with moonshine jugs.

Pete choked up a bat grip. On-GO: that good old boot-camp pugel-stick training.

He waded in. Tight swings clipped chins and ribcages. The government-in-exile boys fought back—odd fists hit him haphazardly.

His bat shattered bunk beams. His bat shattered a fat man's dentures. The gators scurried outside while the getting was good.

The government boys got the picture: Do not resist this big Caucasian madman.

Pete tore through the hut. The spics made like a backdraft and got waaay behind him.

He tore out the rear door and swung at the porch-to-roof stanchions. Five swings left-handed, five swings right—switch-hitting like fucking Mickey Mantle.

The walls shuddered. The roof wiggled. The foundation shimmy-shimmied. The spics evacuated—Earthquake! Earthquake!

The hoses hit. Jet-pressure tore the fence down. Hydraulic force ripped the hut roofless.

Pete caught a spritz and went tumbling. The hut burst into cinderblock shingles.

Dig the government-in-exile:

Running. Stumbling. Doing the jet-spray jigaboo jiggle.

Call it *Hush-Hush* style:

WATER-WHACKED WETBACKS WIGGLE! BOOZE-BLITZED AND BESOAKED BASTION BOOGIE-WOOGIES!

The hoses snapped off. Pete started laughing.

Men stood up soaked and trembling. Pete's laugh went contagious and built to a roar.

The drill field was an instant prefab dump site.

The laughter went locomotive and shaped into a perfect martial cadence. A chant built off of it:

PIGS! PIGS! PIGS! PIGS! PIGS!

Lockhart dispensed blankets. Pete sobered the men up with bennie-laced Kool-Aid.

They loaded the troop ship at midnight. 256 exiles climbed on—hot-wired to reclaim their country.

They loaded weapons, landing craft and medical supplies. Radio channels stayed open: Blessington to Langley and every port-of-departure command post.

The word passed through:

Jack the Haircut says, no second air strike.

Nobody proffered first-strike death stats. Nobody proffered reports on coastal fortifications.

Those spotlights and beach bunkers went unreported. Those militia lookouts went unmentioned.

Pete knew why.

Langley knows it's now or never. Why inform the troops that we're in crap-shoot terrain from here on in?

Pete swigged moonshine to wean himself off the bennies. He passed out on his bunk midway through this weird hallucination.

Japs, Japs, Japs. Saipan, '43—in wide-screen Technicolor.

They swarmed him. He killed them and killed them and killed them. He screamed readiness warnings. Nobody understood his Québecois French.

Dead Japs popped back to life. He rekilled them barehanded. They turned into dead women—Ruth Mildred Cressmeyer clones.

Chuck woke him up at dawn. He said, "Kennedy came halfway through. All the sites launched their troops an hour ago."

Waiting time dragged. Their short-wave set went on the fritz.

Troop ship transmissions came in garbled. Site-to-site feeds registered as static-laced gibberish.

Chuck couldn't nail the malfunction. Pete tried straight telephone contact—calls to Tiger Kab and his Langley drop.

He got two sustained busy signals. Chuck chalked them up to pro-Fidel line jamming.

Lockhart had a hot number memorized: the Agency's Miami Ops office. Boyd called it "Invasion Central"—the sparkplug Cadre guys never got close to.

Pete dialed the number. A busy signal blared extra loud. Chuck nailed the source of the sound: covertly strung phone lines overloaded with incoming calls.

They sat around the barracks. Their radio coughed out strange little sputters.

Time dragged. Seconds took years. Minutes took solar-system eternities.

Pete chained cigarettes. Dougie Frank and Chuck bummed a whole pack off of him.

A Klan guy was hosing off the Piper. Pete and Chuck shared a reeeeealllly long look.

Dougie Frank jammed their wavelength. "Can I go, too?"

Diversionary dips got them close. They caught the Bay of Pigs in tight and ugly.

They saw a supply ship snagged on a reef. They saw dead men flopping out of a hole in the hull. They saw sharks bobbing at body parts twenty yards offshore.

Chuck swung around and made a second pass. Pete bumped the control panel. The extra passenger had them cramped in extra tight.

They saw beached landing craft. They saw live men climbing over dead men. They saw a hundred-yard stretch of bodies in bright-red shallow water.

The invaders kept coming. Flamethrowers nailed them the second they hit the wave break. They got flash-fried and boiled alive.

Fifty-odd rebels were shackled facedown in the sand. A Commie with a chainsaw was running across their backs.

Pete saw the blade drag. Pete saw the blood gout. Pete saw their heads roll into the water.

Flames jumped up at the plane—short by inches.

Chuck pulled off his headset. "I picked up an Ops call! Kennedy says, 'No second air strike,' and he says he won't send in any U.S. troops to help our guys!"

Pete aimed his Magnum out the window. A flame clap spun it out of his hand.

Sharks were churning up the water right below them. This fat Commie fuck waved a severed head.

68

(Rural Guatemala, 4/18/61)

Their room adjoined the radio hut. Invasion updates seeped through the walls uninvited.

Marcello tried to sleep. Littell tried to study deportation law.

Kennedy refused to order a second air strike. Rebel soldiers were captured and slaughtered on the beach.

Reserve troops were chanting "PIGS! PIGS! PIGS! PIGS! PIGS!" That silly word roared through the barracks quadrangle.

Right-wing dementia: mildly distracting. Mildly gratifying: a detectable rise in contempt for John F. Kennedy.

Littell watched Marcello toss and turn. He was bunking with a Mafia chieftain—mildly amazing.

His charade worked. Carlos scanned ledger columns and recognized his own Fund transactions. His indebtedness increased exponentially.

Carlos was accruing large legal debts. Carlos owed his safety to a reformed FBI crimebuster.

Guy Banister called this morning. He said he picked up some straight dope: Bobby Kennedy knows that Carlos is really hiding out in Guatemala.

Bobby applied diplomatic pressure. The Guatemalan prime minister kowtowed. Carlos would be deported, "but not swiftly."

Banister used to call him a weak sister. His phone manner was near-deferential now.

Marcello started snoring. He was drooping off his army cot in monogrammed silk pajamas.

Littell heard shouts and banging noises next door. He formed a picture: men slapping desks and kicking odd inanimate objects.

"It's a washout"/"That vacillating chickenshit"/"He won't send in planes or ships to shell the beach."

Littell walked outside. The troopers worked up a new chant.

"KEN-NEDY, DON'T SAY NO! KEN-NEDY, LET US GO!"

They bounced around the quad. They swigged straight gin and vodka. They gobbled pills and kicked apothecary jars like soccer balls.

The case officers' lounge had been looted. The dispensary door had been trampled to pulp.

"KEN-NEDY, LET US GO! KEN-NEDY IS A PU-TO!"

Littell stepped inside and grabbed the wall phone. Twelve coded digits got him Tiger Kab direct.

A man said, "*Sí?* Cabstand."

"I'm looking for Kemper Boyd. Tell him it's Ward Littell."

"*Sí.* One second."

Littell unbuttoned his shirt—the humidity was awful. Carlos mumbled through a bad dream.

Kemper picked up. "What is it, Ward?"

"What is it with you? You sound anxious."

"There's riots all over the Cuban section, and the invasion isn't going our way. Ward, what is—?"

"I got word that the Guatemalan government's looking for Carlos. Bobby Kennedy knows he's here, and I think I should move him again."

"Do it. Rent an apartment outside Guatemala City, and call me with the phone number. I'll have Chuck Rogers meet you there and fly you someplace more removed. Ward, I can't talk now. Call me when—"

The line went dead. Overtaxed circuits—mildly annoying. Mildly amusing: Kemper C. Boyd mildly flustered.

Littell walked outside. The chants were a good deal more than mildly pissed-off.

"KEN-NEDY IS A PU-TO! KEN-NEDY FEARS FI-DEL CAS-TRO!"

69

(Miami, 4/18/61)

Kemper mixed the dope. Néstor mixed the poison. They worked on two desks jammed together. They had the dispatch hut to themselves. Fulo shut down Tiger Kab at 6:00 p.m. and gave the drivers strict orders: Visit riot scenes and maim Fidelistos.

Kemper and Néstor kept working. Their hotshot assembly line moved slowly.

They mixed strychnine and Drano into a heroin-like white powder. They packaged it in single-pop plastic bindles.

They played their short-wave set. Awful death tallies sputtered in.

Hush-Hush went to press yesterday. Lenny called him for details. The piece described a resounding Bay of Pigs victory.

Jack could *still* force a win. The ODs would defame Castro, WIN OR LOSE.

They B&E'd the drop house two days ago—a little safety-first trial run. They found two hundred "H" bindles stashed behind a heating panel.

Don Juan Pimentel fed them straight information. His death eliminated witness testimony.

Néstor cooked up a shot. Kemper loaded a syringe and test-fired it.

A milky liquid squirted out. Néstor said, "It looks believable. I think it will fool the negritos who buy it."

"Let's go by the house. We have to make the switch tonight."

"Yes. And we must pray that President Kennedy acts more boldly."

. . .

A rainstorm pushed the riot action indoors. Prowl cars were double-parked outside half the nightclubs on and off Flagler.

They drove to a pay phone. Néstor dialed the drop pad and got an extended dial tone. The house was two blocks away.

They circled by it. The street was middle-class Cubano—small cribs with small front yards and toys on the lawn.

The drop pad was peach-stucco Spanish. It was late-night quiet and nonsecurity dark.

No lights. No cars in the driveway. No TV shadows bouncing out the front window.

Kemper parked at the curb. No doors opened; no window curtains opened or retracted.

Néstor checked their suitcase. "The back door?"

"I don't want to risk it again. The lock mechanism almost splintered last time."

"How do you expect to get in, then?"

Kemper pulled his gloves on. "There's a dog-access door built into the kitchen door. You scoot down, reach in, and pop the inside latch."

"Dog doors mean dogs."

"There was no dog last time."

"Last time does not mean this time."

"Fulo and Teo surveilled the place. They're sure there's no dog."

Néstor slipped gloves on. "Okay, then."

They walked up the driveway. Kemper checked their blind side every few seconds. Low-hanging storm clouds provided extra cover.

The door was perfect for large dogs and small men. Néstor scooted down and pulled himself into the house.

Kemper worked his gloves on extra-snug. Néstor opened the door from the inside.

They locked up. They took off their shoes. They walked through the kitchen to the heat panel. They took three steps straight ahead and four to the right—Kemper paced off exact measurements last time.

Néstor held the flashlight. Kemper removed the panel. The bindles were stashed in the identical position.

Néstor re-counted them. Kemper opened up the suitcase and got out the Polaroid.

Néstor said, "Two hundred exactly." Kemper shot a re-creation closeup.

They waited. The picture popped out of the camera.

Kemper taped it to the wall and held the flashlight on it. Néstor switched bindles. He duplicated the arrangement all the way down to tiny tucks and folds.

They sweated up the floor. Kemper swabbed it dry.

Néstor said, "Let's call Pete and see how things stand."

Kemper said, "It's out of our hands."

Please, Jack—

They agreed on a through-to-dawn car stakeout. Local residents parked on the street—Néstor's Impala wouldn't look out of place.

They slid their seats back and watched the house. Kemper fantasized Jack Saves Face scenarios.

Please come home and get your stash. *Please sell it quick to validate our hot-off-the-press propaganda.*

Néstor dozed. Kemper fantasized Bay of Pigs heroics.

A car pulled into the driveway. Door slams woke Néstor up wild-eyed.

Kemper covered his mouth. "Ssssh, now. Just look."

Two men walked into the house. Interior lights framed the doorway.

Kemper recognized them. They were pro-Castro agitators rumored to dabble in dope.

Néstor pointed to the car. "They left the motor running."

Kemper watched the door. The men locked up and walked out with a large attaché case.

Néstor cracked his window. Kemper caught some Spanish.

Néstor translated. "They're going to an after-hours club to sell the stuff."

The men got back in their car. The inside roof light went on. Kemper saw their faces bright as day.

The driver opened the case. The passenger unwrapped a bindle and snorted it.

And twitched. And spasmed. And convulsed—

GET IT BACK. THEY WON'T SELL IT NOW—

Kemper stumbled out of the car and ran up the driveway. Kemper pulled his piece and charged the dope car head-on.

The OD man spasm-kicked the windshield out.

Kemper aimed at the driver. The OD man lurched and blocked his shot.

The driver pulled a snub-nose and fired. Kemper fired straight back at him. Néstor ran up firing—two shots took out a side window and zinged off the roof of the car.

Kemper caught a slug. Ricochets ripped the convulsing man face-less. Néstor shot the driver in the back and blew him into the horn.

It went off AAAH-OOO-GAAAH, AAAH-OOO-GAAAH—LOUD LOUD LOUD.

Kemper shot the driver in the face. His glasses shattered and tore the pompadour off his toupee.

The horn blared. Néstor blew the steering wheel off the column. The goddamn horn reverberated LOUDER.

Kemper saw his collarbone push through his shirt. He weaved down the driveway wiping somebody's blood out of his eyes. Néstor caught him and piggybacked him to their car.

Kemper heard horn noise. Kemper saw spectators on the sidewalk. Kemper saw Cubano punks by the death car—boosting that attaché case.

Kemper screamed. Néstor popped a real "H" bindle under his nose.

He gagged and sneezed. His heart revved and purred. He coughed up some pretty red blood.

Néstor gunned the car. Spectators ran for cover. That funny-looking bone flopped out at a funny right angle.

DOCUMENT INSERT: 4/19/61. Des Moines Register headline:

FAILED COUP LINKED TO U.S. SPONSORS

DOCUMENT INSERT: 4/19/61. Los Angeles Herald-Express headline:

WORLD LEADERS DECRY "ILLEGAL INTERVENTION"

DOCUMENT INSERT: 4/20/61. Dallas Morning News headline:

KENNEDY BLASTED FOR "HEEDLESS PROVOCATIONS"

DOCUMENT INSERT: 4/20/61. San Francisco Chronicle headline and subhead:

BAY OF PIGS FIASCO REVILED BY U.S. ALLIES

CASTRO GLOATS AS REBEL DEATH TOLL MOUNTS

DOCUMENT INSERT: 4/20/61. Chicago Tribune headline and subhead:

KENNEDY DEFENDS BAY OF PIGS ACTIONS

WORLDWIDE CENSURE CRIPPLES PRESIDENT'S PRESTIGE

DOCUMENT INSERT: 4/21/61. Cleveland Plain Dealer headline and subhead:

CIA BLAMED FOR BAY OF PIGS FIASCO

EXILE LEADERS BLAME "KENNEDY COWARDICE"

DOCUMENT INSERT: 4/22/61. Miami Herald headline and subhead:

KENNEDY: "SECOND AIR STRIKE COULD HAVE SPARKED WORLD WAR III"

EXILE COMMUNITY HONORS LOST AND CAPTURED HEROES

DOCUMENT INSERT: 4/23/61. New York Journal-American headline and subhead:

KENNEDY DEFENDS BAY OF PIGS ACTION

RED LEADERS BLAST "IMPERIALIST AGGRESSION"

DOCUMENT INSERT: 4/24/61. Hush-Hush magazine article. Written by Lenny Sands, under the pseudonym Peerless Politicopundit.

COWARDLY CASTRATO CASTRO OUSTED!

RETREATING REDS WREAK RAT-POISON REVENGE!

His rancorous Red reign ran for a rotten two years. Shout it loud, proud and un-kowtowed: Fidel Castro, the bushy-bearded beatnik bard of bilious bamboozlement, was determinedly and dramatically deposed last week by a heroically homeland-hungering huddle of hopped-up hermanos righteously rankled by the Red Recidivist's rape of their nation!

Call it D-Day '61, kats & kittens. Call the Bay of Pigs the Caribbean Carthage; Playa Giron the Patriotic Parthenon. Call Castro debilitated and depilatoried—word has it that he shaved off his beard to dodge the deep and dangerous depths of revenge-seeker recognition!

Fidel Castro: the shabbily-shorn Samson of 1961! His deliriously delighted Delilahs: God-fearing, red, white & blue revering Cuban heroes!!!

Castro and his murderously malignant machinations: trenchantly terminated, 10-4, over-and-out. The Monster's maliciously maladroit maneuverings: still morally mauling Miami!!!!

Item: Fidel Castro craves cornucopias of cash—getaway gelt to felicitously finance future finaglings!

Item: Fidel Castro has cravenly criticized America's eminently egalitarian and instantly inclusive racial policies, reproachfully ragging U.S. leaders for their nauseously niggling neglect of Negro citizens.

Item: as previously posited, Fidel Castro and seditious sibling Raul sell homicidally hazardous Heroin in Miami.

Item: as the Bay of Pigs waggled and waxed as Castro's Waterloo, the mendacious mastiff's minor miscreant minions mined Miami's Negro section with rat-poison-riddled Heroin! Scores of Negro drug addicts injected these carcinogenic Commie cocktails and died doomonically draconean deaths!!!

Item: this issue was rushed to press, to insure that Hush-Hush readers would not be left hungrily homesick for our properly protectionist parade of Playa Giron platitudes. Thus we cannot name the aforementioned Negroes or offer specific details on their dastardly deaths. That information will appear in scintillatingly-scheduled subsequent issues, in courageous conjunction with a new ongoing feature: "Banana Republic Boxscore: Who's Red? Who's Dead?"

Adios, dear reader—and let's all meet for a tall Cuba Libre in laceratingly liberated Havana.

DOCUMENT INSERT: 5/1/61. Personal note: J. Edgar Hoover to Howard Hughes.

Dear Howard,

You must not be concerning yourself with Hush-Hush these days. If you'll glance at the April 24th issue, you'll see that it went to press at best precipitously and at worst with a certain amount of criminal negligence and/or criminal intent.

Did Mr. L. Sands perhaps possess some spurious foreknowledge of unforetellable events? His piece mentioned a number of Negro heroin overdoses in the Miami area, and my Miami police contacts tell me that no such overdoses occurred.

Nine Cuban teenagers, however, did die from injections of poisonous Heroin. My contact told me that on April 18, two Cuban youths stole an attache case containing a large quantity of toxic Heroin from a car involved in an unsolved shootout that left two Cuban men dead.

My contact mentioned the curiously prophetic (if historically inaccurate) Hush-Hush piece. I told him that it was merely one of life's odd coincidences, an explanation that seemed to satisfy him.

I would advice you to tell Mr. Sands to get his facts reasonably straight. Hush-Hush should not publish science fiction, unless it's directly in our best interest.

All best,
Edgar

DOCUMENT INSERT: 5/8/61. Miami Herald sidebar:

PRESIDENT CONVENES HIGH-LEVEL GROUP TO ASSESS BAY OF PIGS FAILURE

Calling the aborted Cuban exile invasion at the Bay of Pigs a "bitter lesson," President Kennedy today stated that it was also a lesson he intended to learn from.

The President told an informal gathering of reporters that he has organized a study group to delve into precisely why the Bay of Pigs invasion failed and to also assess U.S.-Cuban policy in the wake of what he called a "catastrophically embarrassing episode."

The group will interview evacuated Bay of Pigs survivors, Central Intelligence Agency personnel involved in high-level invasion planning and Cuban exile spokesmen from the numerous anti-Castro organizations currently flourishing in Florida.

The study group will include Admiral Arleigh Burke and General Maxwell Taylor. The chairman will be Attorney General Robert F. Kennedy.

DOCUMENT INSERT: 5/10/61. Personal note: Robert F. Kennedy to Kemper Boyd.

Dear Kemper,

I hate to trouble a wounded man with work, but I know you're resilient, healing nicely and looking forward to getting back to your Justice Department duties. I feel bad about sending you into harm's way, so thank God you're recovering.

I've got a second assignment for you, one that geographically suits your work in Anniston and your occasional Miami excursions for Mr. Hoover. The President has formed a group to study the Bay of Pigs mess and the Cuban question in general. We'll be meeting with CIA administrators, action-level case officers, Bay of Pigs survivors and representatives from many CIA-sponsored and non-CIA-sponsored exile factions. I'm chairing the group, and I want you to serve as my point man and liaison to the Miami-based CIA contingent and their Cuban charges.

I think you'll be good at the job, even though your pre-invasion appraisal of exile readiness turned out to be quite inaccurate. You should know that the President and I do not blame you in any way for the ultimate failure of the invasion. At this stage of assessment, I think the blame should be leveled at over-zealous CIA men, sloppy pre-invasion security and an egregious miscalculation of in-Cuba discontent.

Enjoy another week's rest in Miami. The President sends his best, and we both think it's ironic that a forty-five-year-old man who has courted danger all his adult life should be hit by a stray bullet fired by an unknown assailant at a riot scene.

Get well and call me next week.
Bob

DOCUMENT INSERT: 5/11/61. Identical airtel memorandums: FBI Director J. Edgar Hoover to the New York City, Los Angeles, Miami, Boston, Dallas, Tampa, Chicago and Cleveland Special Agents-in-Charge. All marked: CONFIDENTIAL 1-A/DESTROY UPON RECEIPT.

Sir—

Your name has been deleted from this airtel for security purposes. Consider this communique top secret and report back to me personally upon implementation of the following order.

Have your most trustworthy THP agents accelerate their efforts to install bug/wiretaps in known Organized Crime meeting places. Consider this your top priority. Do not communicate information pertaining to this operation within existing Justice Department channels. Conduit all oral and written reports and bug/tap transcripts to me exclusively. Consider this operation to be self-contained and void of superseding Justice Department sanction.

JEH

DOCUMENT INSERT: 5/27/61. Orlando Sentinel "Crimewatch" feature.

THE ODD ODYSSEY OF CARLOS MARCELLO

Nobody seems to know where the man was born. It is generally conceded that (alleged) Mafia Chief Carlos Marcello was born in either Tunis, North Africa, or somewhere in Guatemala. Marcello's earliest recollections are not of either location. They are of his adopted homeland, the United States of America, the country that Attorney General Robert F. Kennedy deported him from on April 4th of this year.

Carlos Marcello: Man Without a Country.

As Marcello tells it, the U.S. Border Patrol shanghaied him out of New Orleans and deposited him near Guatemala City, Guatemala. He said that he daringly escaped from the airport and hid out in "various Guatemalan hellholes" with a lawyer companion frantically seeking to legally return him to home, hearth, and his (alleged) three hundred million dollar a year rackets empire. Meanwhile, Robert F. Kennedy was following up on anonymous tips that placed the (alleged) Mob boss in numerous Louisiana locales. The tips did not pan out. Kennedy realized that Marcello had been hiding out in Guatemala, with Guatemalan government protection, since the very moment of his "daring escape."

Kennedy exerted diplomatic pressure. The Guatemalan Prime Minister bowed to it and ordered the State Police to begin a search for Marcello. The (alleged) Mafia sultan and his lawyer companion were discovered living in a rented apartment near Guatemala City. Both men were immediately deported to El Salvador.

They walked from village to village, ate in greasy spoon cantinas and slept in mud huts. The lawyer attempted to contact a Marcello underling, a pilot who might fly them to more amenable hideouts. The man could not be reached, and Marcello and his lawyer companion, ever fearful of another deportation action, kept walking.

Robert F. Kennedy and his Justice Department lawyers readied legal briefs. Marcello's lawyer companion wrote briefs and phoned them in to the (alleged) Mafia pasha's formal legal team in New York City. Marcello's pilot friend appeared out of nowhere, and (according to this reporter's confidential source) flew his contraband confreres all the way from El Salvador to Matamoros, Mexico, at treetop level to avoid radar detection.

Marcello and his lawyer companion then walked across the border. The (alleged) Mob maharajah turned himself in at the U.S. Border Patrol Detention Center in McAllen, Texas, confident that a three-judge immigration appeals panel would allow him to be released on bond and remain in America.

His confidence was justified. Marcello walked out of court last week a free man—albeit a man haunted by the awful specter of statelessness.

A Justice Department official told this reporter that the Marcello deportation matter could drag on legally for years. When asked if a suitable compromise might be reached, Attorney General Kennedy said, "It's possible, if Marcello is willing to give up his U.S. assets and relocate to Russia or Lower Mozambique."

Carlos Marcello's odd odyssey continues. . . .

DOCUMENT INSERT: 5/30/61. Personal note: Kemper Boyd to John Stanton.

John,

Thanks for the gin and smoked salmon. It beat the hospital fare hands down and was greatly appreciated.

I've been back in Anniston since the 12th. Little Brother does not respect the concept of convalescence, so I've been bird-dogging freedom riders and collecting statements for his Cuban Study Group. (We can thank N. Chasco for getting me into the hospital sans police notification. Nestor is excellent at bribing bi-lingual doctors).

The Study Group assignment troubles me. I've been around the Cause since its inception, and one loose word to Little Brother will destroy me with both brothers, get me disbarred as a lawyer and prevent me from ever obtaining any kind of police/intelligence agency work ever again. That said, you should know that I have deliberately sought out exile interviewees that I have not met before and that do not know that I am covertly Agency-employed. I am editing their statements to show the Agency's pre-invasion planning in as positive a light as possible. As you know, Big Brother has become virulently anti-Agency. Little Brother shares his fervor, but is also evincing a true enthusiasm for the Cause. This heartens me, but I must once again stress the absolute necessity of obfuscating all Outfit-exile-Agency links to

Little Brother, which now becomes more problematic, given his new proximity to the Cause.

I'm going to absent myself from my Agency contract work and concentrate solely on my two Justice Department assignments. I feel that I can best serve the Agency by working as a direct conduit between them and Little Brother. With the Cuban issue undergoing profound policy reassessment, the closer I remain to the policy shapers the better I can serve the Agency and the Cause.

Our Cadre business remains solidly lucrative. I trust the ability of Fulo and Nestor to keep it that way. Santo tells me that our Italian colleagues will continue to make sizable donations. Playa Giron gave everyone a taste of what could be. Nobody wants to stop now. Wouldn't our lives be a lot easier if Little Brother didn't hate Italians so much?

Yours,
Kemper

70

Tiger Kab featured a big indoor dartboard. The drivers tacked up Fidel Castro pix and shredded them into confetti.

Pete had his own private targets.

Like Ward Littell. Carlos Marcello's boy now—mobbed-up and untouchable.

Like Howard Hughes—his *ex*-bossman/benefactor.

Hughes fired him. Lenny Sands said the Mormons made him do it. The *Hush-Hush* fiasco helped.

Boyd was in the hospital then, plowed on morphine. He couldn't call Lenny and say, "Pull the issue." Lenny was incommunicado with some bun boy. He didn't know the invasion crapped out.

Dracula loved his Mormons. Boss Mormon Duane Spurgeon glommed some dope contacts. Drac could now fly Narco Airlines without a Pete Bondurant ticket.

The good news: Spurgeon had cancer. The bad news: Hughes scuttled *Hush-Hush*.

The Bay of Pigs/OD piece caught some embarrassing flak. Hughes kept Lenny on the payroll to write a *private* skank sheet.

The sheet would feature skank too skanky for public skank consumption. The sheet would be read by two skank fiends only: Dracula and J. Edgar Hoover.

Drac was paying Lenny five hundred clams a week. Drac was calling Lenny every night. Lenny was fed up with Drac and his "I want Las Vegas!" wet dream.

Hughes and Littell were strictly dartboard prelims. The main event was President John F. Kennedy.

Who:

Waffled, wiggled, weaseled, punked out and pulled out at Pigs.

Who:

Cringed, crawled, crapped his pants, cravenly crybabied and let Cuba stay Commie.

Who:

Shilly-shallied, sashayed, shook and shit his britches while eleven Blessington men got slaughtered.

He handed Jack the Hughes/Nixon loan dirt. *He* co-signed the cocksucker's White House mortgage. The Boyd/Bondurant casino percentage deal—about as au courant as Slippery Dick Nixon.

The Agency kept cloning exile hard-ons. Speedboat crews kept popping the Cuban coast. It was all fart-in-a-hurricane kid stuff.

Jack called a second invasion "quite possible." He wouldn't give a go date or commit beyond nebulous rhetoric.

Jack's chickenshit. Jack's a pouty, panty-waisted, powder puff.

Blessington was still capacity-booked. The Cadre dope biz was still flourishing. Fulo bought off the Boyd shootout witnesses—forty people got fat paydays.

Néstor saved Boyd's life. Néstor knew no fear. Néstor snuck into Havana once a week on the off chance that he might run into the Beard.

Wilfredo Delsol ran the cabstand. The kid was behaving solidly now. His pro-Castro dance was no more than a two-second tango.

Jimmy Hoffa bopped by Tiger Kab occasionally. Jimmy was Kennedy Hater Number One—for good fucking cause.

Bobby K. had Jimmy dancing to his beat: the old Nuisance Roust/ Grand Jury Blues. Jimmy got a wild bug up his ass—manifested by nostalgia for the Darleen Shoftel shakedown.

Jimmy said, "We could do it again. I could neutralize Bobby by getting at Jack. You got to believe that Jack still likes cooze."

Jimmy was persistent on the topic. Jimmy echoed the hate that the whole Outfit shared.

Sam G. said, "I rue the day I bought Jack Illinois." Heshie Ryskind said, "Kemper Boyd liked Jack, so we figured he had to be kosher."

Boyd was now some triple or quadruple agent. Boyd was a self-proclaimed insomniac. Boyd said rearranging lies kept him up nights.

Boyd was the Cuban Study Group liaison. Boyd was on Cadre sabbatical—a ploy designed to simplify his life.

Boyd fed Bobby pro-CIA distortions. Boyd fed the CIA Study Group secrets.

Boyd pressed Bobby and Jack. Boyd urged them to assassinate Castro and facilitate a second invasion.

The brothers nixed the notion. Boyd called Bobby more pro-Cause than Jack—but only up to some ambiguous point.

Jack said, No second invasion. Jack refused to grant whack-the-Beard approval. The Study Group cooked up an alternative called Operation Mongoose.

It was nifty long-range nomenclature. Let's recapture Cuba some time this century. Here's 50 million dollars a year—fetch, CIA, fetch!

Mongoose spawned JM/Wave. JM/Wave was the nifty code name for six buildings on the Miami U campus. JM/Wave featured snazzy graph rooms and the latest in covert study workshops.

JM/Wave was grad school for geeks.

Fetch, CIA, fetch. Monitor your exile groups, but don't act boldly—it might fuck with Jack the Haircut's poll standings.

Boyd still loved Jack. He was in too deep to see through him. Boyd said he loved his civil rights work—because there was no subterfuge involved.

Boyd had trouble sleeping. It's a blessing, Kemper—you don't want my claustrophobic nightmares.

71

(Washington, D.C., 6/61–11/61)

He loved his office. Carlos Marcello bought it for him.

It was a spacious three-room suite. The building was very close to the White House.

A professional furnished it. The oak walls and green leather nearly matched Jules Schiffrin's study.

He had no receptionist and no secretary. Carlos did not believe in sharing secrets.

Carlos brought him full circle. The ex–Chicago Phantom was now a Mafia lawyer.

The symmetry felt real. He hitched his star to a man who shared his hatreds. Kemper facilitated the union. He knew that it would jell.

John F. Kennedy took Kemper full circle. They were two charming, shallow men who never grew up. Kennedy sicced thugs on a foreign country and betrayed them when he saw how it looked. Kemper protected certain Negroes and sold heroin to others.

Carlos Marcello played the same rigged game. Carlos used people and made sure they knew the rules. Carlos knew that he would pay for his life with eternal damnation.

They walked hundreds of miles together. They went to mass in jungle towns and contributed extravagant church tithes.

They walked alone. No bodyguards or back scratchers walked with them.

They ate in cantinas. They bought entire villages lunch. He wrote deportation briefs on tabletops and phoned them in to New York.

Chuck Rogers flew them to Mexico. Carlos said, "I trust you, Ward. If you say 'Turn yourself in,' I'll do it."

He fulfilled that trust. Three judges reviewed the evidence and released Marcello on bond. The Littell writ work was considered audaciously brilliant.

Grateful Carlos set him up with James Riddle Hoffa. Jimmy was predisposed to fondness—Carlos handed the Fund books back to him and described the circumstances behind their return.

Hoffa became his second client. Robert Kennedy remained his sole adversary.

He wrote briefs for Hoffa's formal litigators. The results confirmed his brilliance.

July '61: A second Sun Valley indictment is dismissed. Littell writs prove the grand jury was improperly impaneled.

August '61: A South Florida grand jury is cut off at the knees. A Littell brief proves that evidence was obtained through entrapment.

He'd come full circle.

He quit drinking. He rented a beautiful Georgetown apartment and finally cracked the Fund book code.

Numbers and letters became words. Words became names—to track against police files, city directories and every financial listing in the public domain.

He tracked those names for four months straight. He chased celebrity names, political names, criminal names and anonymous names. He ran obituary checks and criminal record checks. He quadruple-checked names, dates and figures, and cross-referenced all salient data.

He tracked names linked to numbers linked to public stockholder reports. He assessed names and numbers for his own investment portfolio—and amassed a staggering secret history of financial collusion.

Among the Teamster Central States Pension Fund lendees:

Twenty-four U.S. senators, nine governors, 114 congressmen, Allen Dulles, Rafael Trujillo, Fulgencio Batista, Anastasio Somoza, Juan Perón, Nobel Prize researchers, drug-addicted movie stars, loan sharks, labor racketeers, union-busting factory owners, Palm Beach socialites, rogue entrepreneurs, French right-wing crackpots with extensive Algerian holdings, and sixty-seven unsolved homicide victims extrapolatable as Pension Fund deadbeats.

The chief cash conduit/lender was one Joseph P. Kennedy Sr.

Jules Schiffrin died abruptly. He might have sensed uncharted Fund potential—machinations past the grasp of the common mobsters.

He could implement Schiffrin's knowledge. He could put the full force of his will behind that one thing.

Five months stone-cold sober taught him this:

You're capable of anything.

Part IV

HEROIN

December 1961–September 1963

72

(Miami, 12/20/61)

gency guys called the place "Suntan U." Girls in shorts and halter tops five days before Christmas—no shit.

Big Pete wants a woman. Extortion experience preferred, but not mandat—

Boyd said, "Are you listening to me?"

Pete said, "I'm listening, and I'm observing. It's a nice tour, but the coeds are impressing me more than JM/Wave."

They cut between buildings. The Ops station was cattycorner to the women's gym.

"Pete, are you—?"

"You were saying Fulo and Néstor could run the Cadre business by themselves. You were saying Lockhart went off contract status to start up his own Klan in Mississippi and snitch for the Feds. Chuck's taking his place at Blessington, and *my* new gig is funneling guns to Guy Banister in New Orleans. Lockhart's got some gun connections I can tap into, and Guy's touting some guy named Joe Milteer, who's hooked into some guys in the John Birch Society and the Minutemen. They've got beaucoup fucking gun money, and Milteer will be dropping some off at the cabstand."

They hit a shady walkway and grabbed a bench out of the sun. Pete stretched his legs and eyeballed the gym.

"That's good retention for a bored listener."

Pete yawned. "JM/Wave and Mongoose are boring. Coastal harassment, gun running and monitoring exile groups is one big snore."

Boyd straddled the bench. College kids and Cuban hard-ons fraternized two benches over.

"Describe your ideal course of action."

Pete lit a cigarette. "We should clip Fidel. I'm for it, you're for it, and the only guys that aren't for it are your pals Jack and Bobby."

Boyd smiled. "I'm starting to think we should do it anyway. If we could develop a patsy to take the fall, the hit would probably never be traced back to the Agency or to us."

"Jack and Bobby would just figure they got lucky."

Boyd nodded. "I should run it by Santo."

"I already did."

"Did he like the idea?"

"Yeah, he did. And he ran it by Johnny Rosselli and Sam G., and they both said they wanted to be in on it."

Boyd rubbed his collarbone. "You got a quorum just like that?"

"Not exactly. They all like the idea, but it sounds like they'll need some more convincing."

"Maybe we should hire Ward Littell to whip up a few briefs. He's certainly the chief convincer of the moment."

"You mean you appreciate the way he snowed Carlos and Jimmy."

"Don't you?"

Pete blew smoke rings. "I appreciate a good comeback as much as the next man, but I draw the line at Littell. And you're smiling because your sissy kid brother finally started acting half-ass competent."

College girls walked by. Big Pete wants a—

Boyd said, "He's on our side now, remember?"

"I remember. And I remember that your friend Jack used to be."

"He still is. And he listens to Bobby like he listens to no one else, and Bobby's becoming more pro-Cause by the day."

Pete blew nice concentric rings. "That's good to know. Maybe it means we'll tap into our casino money about the time fucking Bobby himself gets elected President."

Boyd looked distracted. It could be shootout side effects—trauma fucked you up long-range sometimes.

"Kemper, are you listening to—?"

Boyd cut him off. "You were evincing general anti-Kennedy sentiment. You were about to start in on the President, even though he remains our best wedge to get at the casino money, and even though general CIA unpreparedness and *not* Kennedy cowardice was the major contributing cause of the Bay of Pigs disaster."

Pete whooped and slapped the bench. "I should have known better than to rag your boys."

"It's 'boy,' singular."

"I fucking apologize, although I still don't see what's so fucking thrilling about sucking up to the President of the United States."

Boyd grinned. "It's the places he lets you go."

"Like protecting niggers in Meridian, Mississippi?"

"I've got Negro blood now. That transfusion I got at Saint Augustine's came from a colored man."

Pete laughed. "What you've got is a Big White Bwana complex. You've got your spooks and your spics, and you've got this crazy notion that you're their southern aristocrat savior."

Boyd said, "Are you finished?"

Pete clicked his eyes off a tall brunette. "Yeah, I'm finished."

"Do you feel like rationally discussing a Fidel hit?"

Pete flicked his cigarette at a tree. "My one rational comment is 'Let Néstor do it.' "

"I was thinking of Néstor and two expendable backup shooters."

"Where do we find them?"

"We look around. You recruit two two-man teams, I recruit one. Néstor goes with the finalists no matter what."

Pete said, "Let's do it."

Dougie Frank Lockhart had the far-right South wired. Gun seekers knew the man to call: carrot-topped Dougie in Puckett, Mississippi.

Santo and Carlos kicked in fifty Gs apiece. Pete took the coin and went gun shopping.

Dougie Frank brokered the deals for a 5% commission. He procured A-1 hand-me-downs hot off the race hate circuit.

Lockhart knew his job. Lockhart knew the Dixie Right was reassessing its weaponry needs.

The Commie Threat had mandated major ordnance. Tommy guns, mortars and grenades fit the bill. Feisty niggers now eclipsed the Red Menace—and small arms handled them best.

The Deep South was one big loony yard sale.

Pete traded junk pistols for brand-new bazookas. Pete bought operational Thompsons for fifty scoots a pop. Pete supplied six campsites with half a million rounds of ammunition.

The Minutemen, the National States Rights Party, the National Renaissance Party, the Exalted Knights of the Ku Klux Klan, the Royal Knights of the Ku Klux Klan, the Imperial Knights of the Ku Klux Klan and the Klarion Klan Koalition for the New Konfederacy supplied him. He supplied six exile camps, full of expendable backup killers.

Pete spent three weeks gun shopping. He made five Miami–New Orleans circuits.

The fifty grand evaporated. Heshie Ryskind kicked in an additional twenty. Heshie was scared—his doctors diagnosed him with lung cancer.

Heshie whipped up a camp R&R tour to take his mind off his bum health. He brought in Jack Ruby and his strippers, Dick Contino and his accordion.

The strippers stripped and cavorted with exile trainees. Heshie bought entire campsites blow jobs. Dick Contino played "Lady of Spain" six thousand times.

Jimmy Hoffa showed up at the Lake Pontchartrain soiree. Jimmy ranted, railed and raved against the Kennedys nonstop.

Joe Milteer joined the party outside Mobile. He dropped ten grand on the gun fund, unsolicited.

Guy Banister called Old Joe "harmless." Lockhart said the old boy loved to torch nigger churches.

Pete auditioned backup triggers for the Fidel hit. He laid down his criteria with two simple questions.

Are you an expert marksman?

Would you die to set up Néstor Chasco's killshot?

He schmoozed up at least a hundred Cubans. Four men made the cut.

CHINO CROMAJOR:

Bay of Pigs survivor. Willing to detonate Castro with a strip-search-proof enema bomb.

RAFAEL HERNÁNDEZ-BROWN:

Cigar maker/gunman. Willing to slip the Beard a poison panatella and go up in smoke with the man who raped his tobacco fields.

CÉSAR RAMOS:

Former Cuban Army cook. Willing to whip up an exploding suckling pig and die at Castro's Last Supper.

WALTER "JUANITA" CHACÓN:

Sadistic drag queen. Willing to butt-fuck Fidel and go out orgasmic in exile crossfire.

Memo to Kemper Boyd:

Top my shooters—if you can.

73

(Meridian, 1/11/62)

emper snorted a coke-"H" speedball. It was precisely his sixteenth taste of dope.

It was his twelfth since the doctor cut off his medication. It averaged out to 1.3 *nonaddicted* tastes per month.

His head twirled. His brain revved. His shabby room at the Seminole Motel looked almost pretty.

Memo:

Go see that colored preacher. He's rounding up a group of voting rights complainants.

Memo:

See Dougie Frank Lockhart. He's got two would-be triggers lined up for you to audition.

The taste hit *all the way* home.

His collarbone quit throbbing. The pins holding it together meshed clean.

Kemper wiped his nose. The portrait above his desk took on a glow.

It was Jack Kennedy, photographed pre-Pigs. His post-Pigs inscription: "To Kemper Boyd. I guess we both caught a few bullets lately."

Taste #16 felt high-octane. Jack's smile was high-test—Dr. Feelgood shot him up before the photo session.

Jack looked young and invincible. The last nine months knocked a lot of that out of him.

The Bay of Pigs fiasco did it. Jack grew up behind a tidal wave of censure.

Jack blamed himself—and the Agency. Jack fired Allen Dulles and Dick Bissell. Jack said, "I'll smash the CIA into a thousand pieces."

Jack hates the CIA. Bobby doesn't. Bobby now hates Fidel Castro like he hates Hoffa and the Mob.

The Bay of Pigs postmortem was painfully protracted. He double-agented as Kemper Boyd, chaperone. He showed Bobby scores of sanitized exiles—the noncriminal types that Langley wanted him to see.

The Study Group called the invasion:

"Quixotic," "undermanned" and "based on specious intelligence."

He agreed. Langley disagreed.

Langley thought he was a Kennedy apologist. They considered him politically unsound.

John Stanton told him this. He silently agreed with the appraisal.

He vocally agreed: Yes, JM/Wave will prove efficacious.

He silently disagreed. He urged Bobby to assassinate Fidel Castro. Bobby disagreed. He said it was too gangster-like and inimical to Kennedy policy.

Bobby was a bully with strong moral convictions. His guidelines were often hard to gauge.

Bully Bobby set up racket squads in ten major cities. Their one goal was to recruit organized-crime informants. The move enraged Mr. Hoover. Independent Mob-busters might upstage the Top Hoodlum Program.

Bully Bobby hates Bully J. Edgar. Bully J. Edgar reciprocates. It was unprecedented hatred—the Justice Department seethed with it.

Hoover staged protocol slowdowns. Bobby trashed FBI autonomy. Guy Banister said Hoover placed illegal bug/taps in Mob venues coast to coast.

Bobby had no inkling. Mr. Hoover knew how to keep secrets.

So did Ward Littell. Ward's best secret was Joe Kennedy's Teamster Fund "malfeasance."

Joe had a near-fatal stroke late last year. Claire said it "devastated" Laura.

She tried to contact her father. Bobby prevented it. That three-million-dollar buyoff was binding and permanent.

Claire graduated from Tulane magna cum laude. The NYU law school accepted her. She moved to New York City and took an apartment near Laura.

Laura rarely mentioned him. Claire told her he was wounded by a "random gunshot" in Miami. Laura said, "Kemper and 'random'? *Never.*"

Claire believed his squeaky-clean version of the shootout. Claire zoomed down to Saint Augustine's the second the doctor called her.

Claire said Laura had a new boyfriend. Claire said he was nice. Claire said she met Laura's "nice friend," Lenny Sands.

Lenny violated his order and resumed contact with Laura. Lenny always played things indirectly—that *Hush-Hush* Bay of Pigs piece was filled with double-edged innuendo.

He didn't care. Lenny was extortable and long gone from his life.

Lenny dug up dirt for Howard Hughes. Lenny tattled certain secrets and quashed others. Lenny possessed circumstantial evidence on how badly Kemper Boyd fucked up in April '61.

Kemper sniffed another speedball.

His heart revved. His collarbone went numb. He remembered how last May compensated for last April.

Bobby ordered him to follow some Freedom Riders. He said, "Just observe, and call for help if Klansmen or whoever get rowdy. Remember, you're still convalescing."

He observed. He got up closer than reporters and camera crews.

He saw civil rights workers board buses. He tailed them. Hymns roared out of wide-open windows.

Shitkickers tailed the buses. Car radios blared "Dixie." He badged a few rock throwers off, with his gun arm still in a sling.

He stopped in Anniston. Some rednecks slashed his tires. A white mob stormed the depot and pelted a Freedom Bus out of town.

He rented an old Chevy and played catch-up. He zoomed out Highway 78 and caught a mob scene.

The bus had been torched. Cops, Freedom Riders and crackers were tangled up off the roadside.

He saw a colored girl batting flames off her pigtails. He saw the torch artist peel rubber. He ran him off the road and pistol-whipped him half-dead.

I take a few tastes now and then. It's just to help me keep things straight.

". . . And the best thing about what I'm proposing is that you won't have to testify in open court. Federal judges will read your depositions and my accompanying affidavits and go from there. If any of you are called to testify, it will be in closed session, with no reporters, opposing counsel or local police officials present."

The pretty little church was SRO. The preacher rounded up sixty-odd people.

Kemper said, "Questions?"

A man yelled, "Where you from?" A woman yelled, "What about protection?"

Kemper leaned over the pulpit. "I'm from Nashville, Tennessee. You might recall that we had some boycotts and sit-ins there in 1960, and you might recall that we've made great strides toward integration, with minimum bloodshed. I realize that Mississippi is a whole lot less civilized than my home state, and as far as protection goes, I can only say that when you go to register to vote, you'll have numbers on your side. The more people who offer depositions, the better. The more people who register and vote, the better. I'm not saying that certain elements will take kindly to your voting, but the more of you who vote the better your chance of electing local officials who'll keep those elements in line."

A man said, "We got a nice cemetery outside. It's just that none of us want to move in real soon."

A woman said, "You can't expect the law around here to jump on our side all of a sudden."

Kemper smiled. Two tastes and a two-martini lunch made the church glow.

"As cemeteries go, that one you've got is just about the prettiest I've ever seen, but none of us want to visit it until some time around the year 2000, and as far as protection goes, I can only say that President Kennedy did a pretty good job of protecting those Freedom Riders last year, and if those aforementioned white-trash, peckerwood, redneck-cracker elements turn out in force to suppress your God-given civil rights, then the Federal government will meet that challenge with greater force, because your will to freedom will not be defeated, because it is good and just and true, and you have the strength of kindness, decency and unflinching rectitude on your side."

The congregation rose and applauded.

". . . So it's what you call a sweetheart deal. I got my Royal Knights Klavern, which is basically an FBI franchise, and all I gotta do is keep my ear down and rat off the Exalted Knights and Imperial Knights for mail fraud, which is the only Klan stuff Mr. Hoover really cares about. I got my own informants subcontracted into both them groups, and I pay them out of my Bureau stipend, which helps to consolidate the power of my own group."

The shack reeked of stale socks and stale reefer smoke. Dougie Frank wore a Klan sheet and Levi's.

Kemper smashed a fly perching on his chair. "What about those shooters you mentioned?"

"They're here. They've been bunking with me, 'cause the motels around here don't differentiate between Cubans and niggers. 'Course, you're trying to change all that."

"Where are they now?"

"I got a shooting range down the road. They're there with some of my Royals. You want a beer?"

"How about a dry martini?"

"Ain't none of those in these parts. And any man asks for one's gonna get tagged as a Federal agitator."

Kemper smiled. "I've got a bartender at the Skyline Lounge on my side."

"Must be a Jew or a homo."

Kemper laid on some drawl. "Son, you are trying my patience."

Lockhart flinched. "Well ... shit, then, you should know that I heard Pete found his four boys. Guy Banister said you're still two short, which don't surprise me, given all the integration work you've been doing."

"Tell me about the shooters. Limit your extraneous comments and get to the point."

Lockhart wiggled his chair back. Kemper slid his chair closer to him.

"Well, uh, Banister, he sent them over to me. They stole a speedboat in Cuba and ran it aground off the Alabama coast. They robbed some gas stations and liquor stores and renewed an old acquaintance with that Frenchy guy Laurent Guéry, who told them to call Guy for some anti-Fidel work."

"And?"

"And Guy considered them too goddamn crazy for his taste, which is too crazy for just about anybody's. He sent them to me, but I got about as much use for them as a dog does for fleas."

Kemper moved closer. Lockhart backed his chair into the wall.

"Man, you are crowding me more than I'm used to."

"Tell me about the Cubans."

"Jesus, I thought we were friends."

"We are. Now, tell me about the Cubans."

Lockhart slid his chair sideways. "Their names are Flash Elorde and Juan Canestel. 'Flash' ain't Elorde's real first name. He just took it 'cause there's some famous spic boxer with the same last name as him who uses it as a nickname."

"And?"

"And they're both crack shots and big Fidel haters. Flash ran this prostitution slave trade in Havana, and Juan was this rape-o who got castrated by Castro's secret police, 'cause he raped something like three hundred women between the years 1959 and 1961."

"Are they willing to die for a free Cuba?"

"Shit, yes. Flash says that given the life he's led, every day he wakes up alive is a miracle."

Kemper smiled. "You should adopt that attitude, Dougie."

"Which means?"

"Which means there's a nice colored church outside Meridian. It's called the First Pentecostal Baptist, and it's got a beautiful moss-hung cemetery next door."

Lockhart pinched one nostril and blew snot on the floor. "So fucking what? What are you, some nigger church conno-sewer?"

Kemper milked his drawl. "Tell your boys not to touch that church."

"Shit, man, how do you expect a self-respecting white man to respond to something like that?"

"Say, 'Yes, sir, Mr. Boyd.' "

Lockhart sputtered. Kemper hummed the "We Shall Overcome" song.

Lockhart said, "Yes, sir, Mr. Boyd."

Flash sported a Mohawk haircut. Juan sported a big testicle bulge— handkerchiefs or wadded-up tissue filled the space where his nuts used to reside.

The range was a vacant lot adjoining a trailer park. Full-dress Klansmen shot tin cans and swigged beer and Jack Daniel's.

They hit one can out of four at thirty yards. Flash and Juan notched all hits from twice that distance.

They shot old M-1s in late-afternoon light. Better rifles and telescopic sights would make them invincible.

Dougie Frank circulated. Kemper watched the Cubans shoot.

Flash and Juan stripped to the waist and used their shirts to swat off mosquitos. Both men were torture-scarred from the hips up.

Kemper whistled and signaled Lockhart: Send them over, now.

Dougie Frank rounded them up. Kemper leaned against an old Ford half-ton. The bed was jammed with liquor bottles and guns.

They walked over. Kemper came on courtly and genteel.

Smiles and bows went around. Handshakes went down. Flash and Juan pulled their shirts on—a sign of respect for the Big Bwana white man.

Kemper cut the niceties off. "My name is Boyd. I have a mission to offer you."

Flash said, *"Sí, trabajo. Quién el—"*

Juan shushed him. "What kind of mission?"

Kemper tried Spanish. *"Trabajo muy importante. Para matar el grande puto Fidel Castro."*

Flash jumped up and down. Juan grabbed him and restrained him. "This is not a joke, Mr. Boyd?"

Kemper pulled out his money clip. "How much would it take to convince you?"

They crowded up to him. Kemper fanned out hundred-dollar bills.

"I hate Fidel Castro just as much as any Cuban patriot. Ask Mr. Banister or your friend Laurent Guéry about me. I'll pay you out of my own pocket until our backers come through, and if we succeed and get Castro, I'll guarantee you large bonuses."

The cash hypnotized them. Kemper went in for the close.

He slipped a hundred to Flash and a hundred to Juan. One to Flash, one to Juan, one to Flash—

Canestel squeezed his hand shut. "We believe you."

Kemper snagged a bottle out of the truck. Flash beat mambo time on the back fender.

A Klansman yelled, "Save some for us white men!"

Kemper took a drink. Flash took a drink. Juan chug-a-lugged half the bottle.

The cocktail hour segued into get-acquainted time.

Kemper bought Flash and Juan some clothes. They moved their gear out of Lockhart's shack.

Kemper called his broker in New York. He said, Sell some stock and send me five thousand dollars.

The man said, Why? Kemper said, I'm hiring some underlings.

Flash and Juan needed lodging. Kemper braced his friendly desk clerk and asked him to revise his WHITES ONLY policy.

The man agreed. Flash and Juan moved into the Seminole Motel.

Kemper called Pete in New Orleans. He said, Let's arrange a Whack Fidel audition.

They brainstormed.

Kemper set the budget at fifty grand per shooter and two hundred grand for general overhead. Pete suggested severance pay—ten Gs for each rejected shooter.

Kemper agreed. Pete said, Let's do the gig at Blessington. Santo can put Sam G. and Johnny up at the Breakers Motel.

Kemper agreed. Pete said, We need a spic fall guy—non-CIA/non-Cadre–connected. Kemper said, We'll find one.

Pete said, My boys are braver than your boys.

Kemper said, No, they're not.

Flash and Juan felt like drinking. Kemper took them to the Skyline Lounge.

The bartender said, They ain't white. Kemper slipped him twenty dollars. The bartender said, They are now.

Kemper drank martinis. Juan drank I.W. Harper. Flash drank Myers's rum and Coke.

Flash spoke Spanish. Juan translated. Kemper learned the rudiments of slave prostitution.

Flash kidnapped the girls. Laurent Guéry got them hooked on Algerian horse. Juan broke the virgins in and tried to perv them into digging random sex.

Kemper listened. The ugly things drifted away, compartmentalized and non-applicable.

Juan said he missed his balls. He could still get hard and fuck, but he missed the total shoot-your-load experience.

Flash raged against Fidel. Kemper thought: I don't hate the man at all.

The six wore starched fatigues and camouflage lampblack. It was Pete's idea: Let's turn our shooter candidates out scary.

Néstor built a range behind the Breakers parking lot. Kemper called it a jerry-rig masterpiece.

It featured pulley-mounted targets and chairs scrounged from a demolished cocktail hut. The audition weaponry was CIA-prime: M-1s, assorted pistols, and scope-fitted .30.06's.

Teo Paez fashioned straw-stuffed Castro targets. They were life-size and realistic—replete with beards and cigars.

Laurent Guéry crashed the party. Teo said he blew France *rápidamente.* Néstor said he'd tried to clip Charles de Gaulle.

The judges sat under an awning. S. Trafficante, J. Rosselli and S. Giancana—curled up with highballs and binoculars.

Pete played armorer. Kemper played MC.

"We've got six men for you gentlemen to choose from. You'll be funding this operation, and I know you'll want last say as to who goes in. Pete and I are proposing three-man teams, with Néstor Chasco, who you already know, as the third man in all cases. Before we start, I want to stress that these men are loyal, fearless and fully comprehend the risks involved. If captured, they will commit suicide rather than reveal who set up this operation."

Giancana tapped his watch. "I'm running late. Can we get this show on the road?"

Trafficante tapped his. "Move it, would you, Kemper? I'm due back in Tampa."

Kemper nodded. Pete cranked Fidel #1 fifty feet out. The men loaded their revolvers and assumed the two-handed combat stance.

Pete said, "Fire."

Chino Cromajor blew Castro's hat off. Rafael Hernández-Brown de-cigared him. César Ramos severed both his ears.

The reverberations faded. Kemper gauged reactions.

Santo looked bored. Sam looked restless. Johnny looked mildly nonplussed.

Juanita Chacón aimed crotch-high and fired. Fidel #1 lost his manhood.

Flash and Juan fired twice. Fidel lost his arms and his legs.

Laurent Guéry clapped. Giancana checked his watch.

Pete cranked Fidel #2 a hundred yards out. The shooters raised their obsolete M-1s.

The judges held up their binoculars. Pete said, "Fire."

Cromajor shot Castro's eyes out. Hernández-Brown lopped off his thumbs.

Ramos nailed his cigar. Juanita castrated him.

Flash blew his legs off at the knees. Juan slammed a cardiac bullseye.

Pete yelled, "Cease fire!" The shooters lowered their weapons and lined up at parade rest.

Giancana said, "It's impressive, but we can't go off half-cocked on something this big."

Trafficante said, "I have to agree with Mo."

Rosselli said, "You need to give us some time to think about it."

Kemper felt queasy. His speedball rush turned ugly.

Pete was trembling.

74

(Washington, D.C., 1/24/62)

Littell locked the money in his desk safe. One month's retainer—$6,000 cash.

Hoffa said, "You didn't count it."

"I trust you."

"I could've made a mistake."

Littell tilted his chair back and looked up at him. "That's unlikely. Especially when you walked it over here yourself."

"You'd've felt better walking over to my shop in this fucking cold?"

"I could have waited until the first."

Hoffa perched on the edge of the desk. His overcoat was soaked with melting snow.

Littell moved some folders. Hoffa picked up his crystal paperweight.

"Did you come for a pep talk, Jimmy?"

"No. But if you got one, I'm all ears."

"How's this. You're going to win and Bobby's going to lose. It's going to be a long and painful war, and you're going to win by sheer attrition."

Jimmy squeezed the paperweight. "I was thinking Kemper Boyd should leak a copy of my Justice Department file to you."

Littell shook his head. "He won't do it, and I won't ask him to. He's got the Kennedys and Cuba and God knows what else wrapped in tidy little packages that only he knows the logic of. There's lines he won't cross over, and you and Bobby Kennedy are one of them."

Hoffa said, "Lines come and go. And as far as Cuba goes, I think Carlos is the only Outfit guy who still gives a shit. I think Santo, Mo and the others are pissed off and bored with the whole notion of that rinky-dink goddamn island."

Littell straightened his necktie. "Good. Because *I'm* bored with everything except keeping you and Carlos one step ahead of Bobby Kennedy."

Hoffa smiled. "You used to like Bobby. I heard you used to really admire him."

"Lines come and go, Jimmy. You said so yourself."

Hoffa dropped the paperweight. "This is true. It is also fucking true that I need an edge on Bobby. And *you* fucking pulled the plug on that Kennedy wire job that Pete Bondurant was working for me back in '58."

Littell forced a wince into a smile. "I didn't know you knew that."

"That is obvious. It should also be fucking obvious that I forgive you."

"And obvious that you want to try it again."

"This is true."

"Call Pete, Jimmy. I don't have much use for him, but he's the best shakedown man alive."

Hoffa leaned across the desk. His trouser legs slid up and showed off cheap white sweat socks.

"I want you in on it, too."

75

(Los Angeles, 2/4/62)

P ete rubbed his neck. It was all kinked and knotted—he flew out in a coach seat made for midgets.

"I jump when you say 'jump,' Jimmy, but coast-to-coast for coffee and pastry is pushing it."

"I think L.A.'s the place to set this up."

"Set what up?"

Hoffa dabbed eclair cream off his necktie. "You'll see soon enough."

Pete heard noise in the kitchen. "Who's that poking around?"

"It's Ward Littell. Sit down, Pete. You're making me nervous."

Pete dropped his garment bag. The house stunk of cigars—Hoffa let visiting Teamsters use it for stag nights.

"Littell, shit. This is grief I don't need."

"Come on. Ancient history's ancient history."

Recent history: *Your* lawyer stole *your* Fund books—

Littell walked in. Hoffa put his hands up, peacemaker-style. "Be nice, you guys. I wouldn't put the two of you in the same room unless it was good."

Pete rubbed his eyes. "I'm a busy guy, and I flew overnight for this little breakfast klatch. Give me one good reason why I should take on additional fucking work, or I'm heading back to the airport."

Hoffa said, "Tell him, Ward."

Littell warmed his hands on a coffee cup. "Bobby Kennedy's coming down unacceptably hard on Jimmy. We want to work up a derogatory tape profile on Jack and use it as a wedge to get him to call off Bobby.

If I hadn't interfered, the Shoftel operation might have worked. I think we should do it again, and I think we should recruit a woman that Jack would find interesting enough to sustain an affair with."

Pete rolled his eyes. "You want to shake down the President of the United States?"

"Yes."

"You, me and Jimmy?"

"You, me, Fred Turentine and the woman we bring in."

"And you're going at this like you think we can trust each other."

Littell smiled. "We both hate Jack Kennedy. And I think we've got enough dirt on each other to buttress a non-aggression pact."

Pete popped some prickly little goosebumps. "We can't tell Kemper about this. He'd rat us in a second."

"I agree. Kemper has to stay out of the loop on this one."

Hoffa belched. "I'm watching you two humps stare at each other, and I'm starting to feel like I'm out of the fucking loop, even though I'm financing the fucking loop."

Littell said, "Lenny Sands."

Hoffa sprayed eclair crumbs. "What the fuck does Jewboy Lenny have to do with fucking anything?"

Pete looked at Littell. Littell looked at Pete. Their brainwaves meshed somewhere over the pastry tray.

Hoffa looked dead flummoxed. His eyes went out of focus somewhere near the planet Mars. Pete steered Littell to the kitchen and shut the door.

"You're thinking Lenny's this big Hollywood insider. You're thinking he might know some women we could use as bait."

"Right. And if he doesn't come through, at least we're here in Los Angeles."

"Which is the best place on earth to find shakedown-type women."

Littell sipped coffee. "Right. And Lenny was my informant once. I've got a hold on him, and if he doesn't cooperate, I'll squeeze him with it."

Pete cracked some knuckles. "He's a homo. He shanked this made guy in an alley behind some fruit bar."

"Lenny told you that?"

"Don't look so hurt. People have this tendency to tell me things they don't want to."

Littell dumped his cup in the sink. Hoffa paced outside the door.

Pete said, "Lenny knows Kemper. And I think he's tight with that Hughes woman that Kemper had a thing with."

"Lenny's safe. If worse comes to worse, we can squeeze him with the Tony Iannone job."

Pete rubbed his neck. "Who else knows we're planning this?"

"Nobody. Why?"

"I was wondering if it was common knowledge all over the Outfit."

Littell shook his head. "You, me and Jimmy. That's the loop."

Pete said, "Let's keep it that way. Lenny's tight with Sam G., and Sam's been known to go apeshit when people get rough with him."

Littell leaned against the stove. "Agreed. And I won't tell Carlos, and you won't tell Trafficante and those other Outfit guys you and Kemper deal with. Let's keep this contained."

"Agreed. A few of those guys hung me and Kemper out to dry on something a couple of weeks ago, so I'm not prone to tell them much of anything."

Littell shrugged. "They'll find out in the end, and they'll be pleased with the results we get. Bobby's been riding them, too, and I think we can safely say that Giancana will find whatever we had to do to Lenny justified."

Pete said, "I like Lenny."

Littell said, "So do I, but business is business."

Pete traced dollar signs on the stove. "What kind of money are we talking about?"

Littell said, "Twenty-five thousand a month, with your expenses and Freddy Turentine's fee worked in. I know you'll need to travel for your CIA job, and that's fine with both Jimmy and me. I've done wire jobs for the Bureau myself, and I think that between you, me and Turentine, we'll be able to cover all our bases."

Hoffa banged on the door. "Why don't you guys come out here and talk to *me*? This tête-à-tête shit is wearing me thin!"

Pete steered Littell back to the laundry room. "It sounds good. We find a woman, wire a few pads and fuck Jack Kennedy where it hurts."

Littell pulled his arm free. "We need to check Lenny's *Hush-Hush* reports. We might get a lead on a woman that way."

"*I'll* do it. I might be able to get a look at the reports Howard Hughes keeps at his office."

"Do it today. I'll be staying at the Ambassador until we get things set up."

The door shook—Jimmy had his tits in a twist.

Littell said, "I want to bring Mr. Hoover in on this."

"Are you insane?"

Littell smiled, kiss-my-ass condescending. "He hates the Kennedys like you and I do. I want to re-establish contact, leak a few tapes to him and have him in my corner as a wedge to help out Jimmy and Carlos."

Not *so* insane—

"You know he's a voyeur, Pete. Do you know what he'd give to have the President of the United States fucking on tape?"

Hoffa barged into the kitchen. His shirt was dotted with doughnut sprinkles—every color of the rainbow.

Pete winked. "I'm starting not to hate you so much, Ward."

Hughes' business office was marked RESTRICTED ACCESS now. Mormon goons flanked the door and checked IDs with some weird scanner gizmo.

Pete dawdled by the parking lot gate. The guard chewed his ear off.

"Us non-Mormons call this place Castle Dracula. Mr. Hughes we call the Count, and we call Duane Spurgeon—he's the head Mormon— Frankenstein, 'cause he's dying of cancer and looks like he's dead already. I remember when this building wasn't full of religious crackpots, and Mr. Hughes came in in person, and he didn't have this big germ phobia and these crazy plans to buy up Las Vegas, and he didn't get blood transfusions like Bela Lugosi—"

"Larry—"

"—and he actually talked to people, you know? Now the only people he talks to besides the Mormons are Mr. J. Edgar Hoover himself and Lenny the *Hush-Hush* guy. You know why *I'm* talking so much? Because I work the gate all day and pick up scuttlebutt, and the only non-Mormon people I see are the Filipino janitor and this Jap switchboard girl. Mr. Hughes can still wheel and deal, though, I got to say that. I heard he's pushed the TWA divestment price way up, so when he gets the gelt he can funnel it straight into some account he's holding, like some kind of zillion-dollar 'buy up Vegas' fund. . . ."

Larry ran out of breath. Pete whipped out a hundred-dollar bill.

"They keep Lenny's stringer reports in the file room, right?"

"Right."

"There's nine more of these if you get me in there."

Larry shook his head. "That's impossible, Pete. We got virtually an all-Mormon staff here. Some of the guys are Mormon *and* ex-FBI, and Mr. J. Edgar Hoover himself helped pick them."

Pete said, "Lenny's in L.A. full-time now, right?"

"Right. He gave up his place in Chicago. I heard he's writing *Hush-Hush* as some kind of restricted mimeo sheet."

Pete forked over the hundred. "Look up his address for me."

Larry checked his Rolodex and plucked a card. "It's 831 North Kilkea, which isn't that far from here."

A hospital van pulled up. Pete said, "What's that?"

Larry whispered. "Fresh blood for the Count. Certified Mormon-pure."

The new gig felt good, but strictly second-string. The main gig should be WHACK FIDEL.

Santo and Company quashed it. They acted bored, like the Cause meant jackshit.

WHY?

He cut his shooters loose. Kemper took his boys back to Mississippi.

Laurent Guéry went with them. Kemper tapped his own stock fund for Ops cash. Kemper was acting weirdly persistent lately.

Pete turned on to Kilkea. 831 was your standard West Hollywood four-flat.

The standard two-story Spanish-style building. The standard two units per floor. The standard beveled glass doors that your standard B&E guys drooled for.

There was no garage at the back—the tenants had to park at the curb. Lenny's Packard was nowhere in sight.

Pete parked and walked up to the porch. All four doors showed slack at the door-doorjamb juncture.

The street was dead. The porch was dead quiet. The mail slot for the left downstairs unit read "L. Sands."

Pete snapped the lock with his pocketknife. An inside light hit him straight off.

Lenny planned to stay out after dark. He could prowl the pad for four solid hours.

Pete locked himself in. The crib spread out off a hallway—maybe five rooms total.

He checked the kitchen, the dinette and the bedroom. The pad was nice and quiet—Lenny eschewed pets and stay-at-home bun boys.

An office connected to the bedroom. It was cubbyhole size—a desk and a row of file cabinets ate up all the floor space.

Pete checked the top drawer. It was one fat mess—Lenny jammed it full of overstuffed folders.

The folders contained 100% U.S. prime-cut skank.

Published *Hush-Hush* skank and unpublished skank tips. Skank logged in since early '59—the all-time Skank Hit Parade.

Boozer skank, hophead skank, homo skank. Lezbo skank, nympho skank, miscegenation skank. Political skank, incest skank, child molester skank. The one skank problem: the female skankees were too skankily well known.

Pete spotted some non-sequitur skank: a real skankeroo report dated 9/12/60. A *Hush-Hush* editorial memo was attached to the page.

Lenny,

I don't see this one as a feature or anything else. If it went to arrest & trial, great, but it didn't. The whole thing seems skewed to me. Plus, the girl's a nobody.

Pete read the report. Skewed?—no shit.
Lenny "Skank Man" Sands, verbatim:

I learned that gorgeous redhead singer-dancer Barb Jahelka (the lead attraction in her ex-husband Joey Jahelka's "Swingin' Dance Revue") was arrested on August 26th as part of an extortion scheme levied against Rock Hudson.

It was a photo job. Hudson and Barb were in bed at Rock's house in Beverly Hills when a man snuck in and managed to snap several pictures with infra-red film. A few days later Barb demanded that Hudson pay her 10 thousand dollars or the pictures would be circulated everywhere.

Rock called private detective Fred Otash. Otash called the Beverly Hills PD, and they arrested Barb Jahelka. Hudson then went soft hearted and refused to press charges. I like this for the 9/24/60 issue. Rock's a hot ticket these days, and Barb's a real dish. (I've got bikini pictures of her we can use.) Let me know, so I can formally write the piece up.

Skewed?—no shit, Sherlock.

Rock Hudson was a fruitfly with no yen for cooze. Fred Otash was an ex-cop Hollywood lapdog. Dig the skewed postscript: Freddy's phone number doodled right there on the report.

Pete grabbed the phone and dialed it. A man answered, "Otash."

"It's Pete Bondurant, Freddy."

Otash whistled. "This has to be interesting. The last time you made a sociable phone call was never."

"I'm not starting now."

"This sounds like we're talking about money. If it's your money for my time, I'm listening."

Pete checked the report. "In August of '60 you allegedly helped Rock Hudson out of a jam. I think the whole thing was a setup. I'll give you a thousand dollars to tell me the story."

Otash said, "Go to two thousand and throw in a disclaimer."

Pete said, "Two thousand. And if push comes to shove, I'll say I got the information elsewhere."

Funny noise hit the line. Pete ID'd it: Freddy tapping his teeth with a pencil.

"Okay, Frenchman."

"Okay, and?"

"Okay, and you're right. The setup was Rock was afraid of being exposed as a queer, so he cooked up a deal with Lenny Sands. Lenny brought in this number Barb Jahelka and her ex-husband Joey, and Barb and Rock got between the sheets. Joey faked a break-in and took some pictures, Barb made a fake extortion demand, and Rock fake called me in."

"And you fake called the Beverly Hills PD."

"Right. They popped Barb for extortion one, then Rock got fake sentimental and dropped the charges. Lenny wrote the thing up for *Hush-Hush*, but for some reason it never got published. Lenny tried to leak the story to the legit press, but nobody would touch it, because half the goddamn country knows Rock's a homo."

Pete sighed. "The whole caper went nowhere."

Otash sighed. "That's correct. Rock paid Barb and Joey two Gs apiece, and now you're paying me an extra two just to tell you the whole sorry tale."

Pete laughed. "Tell me about Barb Jahelka while you're at it."

"All right. My take on Barb is that she's slumming, but she doesn't know it. She's smart, she's funny, she looks good and she knows she's not the next Patti Page. I think she's from the Wisconsin boonies, and I think she did six months honor farm for maryjane possession about four or five years ago. She used to have a thing going with Peter Lawford"—

Jack's brother-in-law—

"and she treats her ex-husband Joey, who's a piece of shit, exactly the way he ought to be treated. I'd have to say she likes kicks, and I'll bet she'd tell you she likes danger, but my take is she's never been tested. If you're interested in her whereabouts, try the Reef Club in Ventura. The last I heard, Joey Jahelka was fronting some kind of cut-rate Twist show up there."

Pete said, "You like her, Freddy. You're an open book."

"So are you. And while we're being candid, let me heartily recommend that girl for whatever kind of shakedown you've got in mind."

The Reef Club was all driftwood and fake barnacles. The clientele was mostly college kids and low-rent hipsters.

Pete snagged a table just off the dance floor. Joey's Swingin' Twist Revue went on in ten minutes.

Wall speakers churned out music. Twist geeks flailed and bumped asses. Pete's table vibrated and shook the head off his nice glass of beer.

He called Karen Hiltscher before he left L.A. Sheriff's R&I had a sheet on one Barbara Jane (Lindscott) Jahelka.

She was born 11/18/31, in Tunnel City, Wisconsin. She had a valid California driver's license. She went down on a reefer beef circa 7/57.

She did six months County time. She was suspected of shanking a bull dyke at the Hall of Justice Jail. She was married—8/3/54–1/24/58—to:

Joseph Dominic Jahelka, born 1/16/23, New York City. New York State convictions: statch rape, flimflam, forging Dilaudid prescriptions.

Joey Jahelka was probably a slavering hophead. He'd probably drool for the Dilaudid he just copped back in L.A.

Pete sipped beer. The hi-fi blared jungle-bunny music. A loudspeaker blared, "Ladies and gentlemen, the Reef Club is proud to present for your twisting pleasure—Joey Jahelka and his Swingin' Twist Revue!!!"

Nobody cheered. Nobody applauded. Nobody stopped twisting.

A trio jumped on stage. They wore calypso shirts and mismatched tuxedos. Pawnshop tags dangled off their equipment.

They set up. The twisters and table crowd ignored them. A jukebox tune bled into their opener.

A high-school kid played tenor sax. The drummer was a bantamweight pachuco. The guitar man matched Joey's R&I stats.

The greasy little hump was half on-the-nod. His socks were de-elasticized way below his ankles.

They played loud, shitty music. Pete felt the wax in his ears start to crumble.

Barb Jahelka slinked up to the mike. Barb oozed healthy pulchritude. Barb was no show-biz-subspecies junkie.

Tall Barb. Lanky Barb. That sparkly red bouffant was no fucking dye job.

Dig that tight, low-cut gown. Dig the heels that put her over six feet.

Barb sang. Barb had weak pipes. The combo drowned her out every time she reached for a high note.

Pete watched. Barb sang. Barb DANCED—*Hush-Hush* would tag it HOT, HOT, HOTSVILLE.

Some male twisters stopped twisting to dig on the big rangy redhead. One girl poked her partner—You get your eyes off of her!

Barb sang weak-voiced and monotonous. Barb put out unique gyrations flat-out concurrent.

She kicked her shoes off. She thrust her hips out and popped seams down one leg.

Pete watched her eyes. Pete tapped the envelope in his pocket.

She'd read the note. The money would hook her in. She'd give Joey the dope and urge him to get lost.

Pete chain-smoked. Barb lost a breast and tucked it back before the Twist fiends noticed.

Barb smiled—oops!—dazzling.

Pete passed the envelope to a waitress. Twenty dollars guaranteed transmittal.

Barb danced. Pete shot her something like a prayer: Please be able to TALK.

He knew she'd be late. He knew she'd close the club and let him sweat for a while. He knew she'd call Freddy O. for a quick rundown of his pedigree.

Pete waited at an all-night coffee shop. His chest hurt—Barb twisted him through two packs of cigarettes.

He called Littell an hour ago. He said, Let's meet at Lenny's at 3:00—I think I might have found our woman.

It was 1:10 now. He might have called Littell just a tad premature.

Pete sipped coffee and checked his watch every few seconds. Barb Jahelka walked in and spotted him.

Her skirt and blouse looked half-assed demure. No-makeup did nice things to her face.

She sat down across from him. Pete said, "I hope you called Freddy."

"I did."

"What did he tell you?"

"That he'd never mess with you. And that your partners always make money."

"Is that all he said?"

"He said you knew Lenny Sands. I called Lenny, but he wasn't home."

Pete pushed his coffee aside. "Did you try to kill that dyke you shivved?"

Barb smiled. "No. I wanted to stop her from touching me, and I didn't want it to cost me the rest of my life."

Pete smiled. "You didn't ask me what this is all about."

"Freddy already gave me his interpretation, and you're paying me five hundred dollars for a chat. And by the way, Joey says, 'Thanks for the taste.' "

A waitress hovered. Pete shooed her away. "Why do you stay with him?"

"Because he wasn't always a drug addict. Because he arranged to have some men who hurt my sister taken care of."

"Those are good reasons."

Barb lit a cigarette. "The best reason is I love Joey's mom. She's senile, and she thinks we're still married. She thinks Joey's sister's kids are our kids."

Pete laughed. "Suppose she dies?"

"Then the day of the funeral is the day I say goodbye to Joey. He'll have to get a new girl singer and a new chauffeur to drive him to his Nalline tests."

"I bet that'll break his heart."

Barb blew smoke rings. "Over's over. That's a concept junkies don't understand."

"You understand it."

"I know. And you're thinking it's a weird thing for a woman to get."

"Not necessarily."

Barb stubbed out her cigarette. "What's this all about?"

"Not yet."

"When?"

"Soon. First, you tell me about you and Peter Lawford."

Barb toyed with her ashtray. "It was brief and ugly, and I broke it off when Peter kept pestering me to go to bed with Frank Sinatra."

"Which you didn't feel like doing."

"Right."

"Did Lawford introduce you to Jack Kennedy?"

"No."

"Do you think he told Kennedy about you?"

"Maybe."

"You've heard about Kennedy and women?"

"Sure. Peter called him 'insatiable,' and a showgirl I knew in Vegas told me some stories."

Pete smelled suntan oil. Redheads and bright stage lights—

Barb said, "Where are we going with this?"

Pete said, "I'll see you at the club tomorrow night and tell you."

Littell met him outside Lenny's building. Night-owl Lenny had his lights on at 3:20 a.m.

Pete said, "The woman's great. All we need is Lenny to front the introduction."

"I want to meet her."

"You will. Is he alone?"

Littell nodded. "He came home with a pickup two hours ago. The boy just left."

Pete yawned—he hadn't slept in twenty-four-plus hours. "Let's take him."

"Good cop–bad cop?"

"Right. Alternating, so we keep him off balance."

They walked up to the porch. Pete rang the bell. Littell screwed a crimped ugly look on his face.

Lenny opened up. "Don't tell me, you forgot—"

Pete pushed him inside. Littell slammed the door and threw the bolt.

Chic Lenny cinched his robe. Fey Lenny threw his head back and laughed.

"I thought we were quits, Ward. And I thought you only crawled around Chicago."

Littell said, "We need some help. And all you have to do is introduce a man to a woman and keep quiet about it."

"Or?"

"Or we hand you up for the Tony Iannone killing."

Pete sighed. "Let's do this civilized."

Littell said, "Why? We're dealing with a sadistic little faggot who killed a man and bit his goddamn nose off."

Lenny sighed. "I've been double-teamed before. This routine is nothing new to me."

Littell said, "We'll try to make it interesting."

Pete said, "Five grand, Lenny. All you have to do is introduce Barb Jahelka to another friend of yours."

Littell popped his knuckles. Lenny said, "Give it up, Ward. Rough-trade mannerisms don't suit you."

Littell slapped him. Lenny slapped him back.

Pete stepped between them. They looked ridiculous—two bloody-nosed pseudo tough guys.

"Come on, you two. Let's do this civilized."

Lenny wiped his nose. "Your face looks different, Ward. Those scars are soooooo you."

Littell wiped his nose. "You didn't seem surprised when Pete mentioned Barb Jahelka."

Lenny laughed. "That's because I was still in shock from the notion of you two as playmates."

Littell said, "That's not a real answer."

Lenny shrugged. "How's this? Barb's in the Life, and everybody in the Life knows everybody else in the Life."

Pete lobbed a change-up. "Name some hotels Jack Kennedy takes his women to."

Lenny twitched. Pete popped his thumbs double-loud.

Littell said, "Name some hotels."

Swishy Lenny squealed, "This is sooooo fun! Hey, let's call Kemper Boyd and make it a foursome!"

Littell slapped him. Lenny popped some tears—fag bravado, adieu.

Pete said, "Name some hotels. Don't make *me* get rough with you."

Lenny put on a lisp. "The El Encanto in Santa Barbara, the Ambassador-East in Chicago, and the Carlyle in New York."

Littell pushed Pete into the hallway—well out of Lenny's earshot. "Hoover's got standing bugs in the El Encanto and Ambassador-East. The managers assign those suites to whoever he tells them to."

Pete whispered. "He's put it together. He knows what we want, so let's close him."

They walked back to the living room. Lenny was guzzling high-test Bacardi.

Littell looked ready to drool. Hoffa said he had ten months off the sauce. Lenny's liquor cart was radioactive—rum and scotch and all kinds of good shit.

Lenny downed the juice two-handed. Pete said, " 'Jack, this is Barb. Barb, this is Jack.' "

Lenny wiped his lips. "I have to call him 'Mr. President' now."

Littell said, "When was the last time you saw him?"

Lenny coughed. "A few months ago. At Peter Lawford's beach house."

"Does he always go by Lawford's place when he's in L.A.?"

"Yes. Peter throws wonderful parties."

"Does he invite unattached women?"

Lenny giggled. "Does he *ever*."

"Does he invite you?"

"Usually, dear heart. The President likes to laugh, and what the President likes, the President gets."

Pete stepped in. "Who else goes to the parties? Sinatra and those Rat Pack guys?"

Lenny poured a stiff refill. Littell licked his lips and plugged the bottle.

Pete said, *"Who else goes to those parties?"*

Lenny shrugged. "Amusing people. Frank used to come, but Bobby made Jack drop him."

Littell stepped in. "I read that Kennedy's coming to Los Angeles on February 18th."

"That's true, dear heart. And guess who's throwing a party on the 19th."

"Were you invited, Lenny?"

"Yes, I was."

"Does the Secret Service frisk the guests or run them through a metal detector?"

Lenny reached for the bottle. Pete grabbed it first.

"Answer Mr. Littell's question, goddamnit."

Lenny shook his head. "No. What the Secret Service does is eat, drink and discuss Jack's protean sex drive."

Pete said, " 'Barb, this is Jack. Jack, this is Barb.' "

Lenny sighed. "I'm not an imbecile."

Pete smiled. "We're upping your fee to ten thousand, because we know you're way too smart to mention this to anybody."

Littell pushed the liquor cart out of his sight. "That specifically includes Sam Giancana and your Outfit friends, Laura Hughes, Claire Boyd and Kemper Boyd, on the extreme off-chance that you run into them."

Lenny laughed. "Kemper's not in on this? Toooo bad—I wouldn't mind rubbing whatevers with *him* again."

Pete said, "Don't treat this like a joke."

Littell said, "Don't think Sam will let you walk for the Tony job."

Pete said, "Don't think that Sam still likes Jack, or that he'd lift a finger to help him. Sam bought Jack West Virginia and Illinois, but that was a long time ago, and Bobby's been goddamn unfriendly to the Outfit since then."

Lenny weaved into the cart. Littell steadied him.

Lenny pushed him away. "Sam and Bobby must have *something* cooking, 'cause Sam said the Outfit's been doing some work to help Bobby out with Cuba, but Bobby doesn't know about it, and Sam said, 'We sort of think he should be told.'"

Pete caught a quick flash:

The Whack Fidel auditions. Three Outfit biggies, bored and noncommittal.

Littell said, "Lenny, you're drunk. You're not making any—"

Pete cut him off. "What else did Giancana say about Bobby Kennedy and Cuba?"

Lenny leaned against the door. "Nothing. I just heard two seconds of this conversation he was having with Butch Montrose."

"When?"

"Last week. I went to Chicago for a Teamster smoker."

Littell said, "Forget about Cuba." Lenny weaved and flashed the V-for-victory sign.

"Viva Fidel! Down with the U.S. imperialist insect!"

Pete slapped him.

Littell said, "'Barb, this is Jack.' And remember what we'll do if you betray us."

Lenny spat out some gold bridgework.

The combo played way off-key. Pete figured they were zorched on his Dilaudid.

The Reef Club rocked. Twist nuts had the floor shaking.

Barb danced close to chaste by her standards. Pete figured the potential gig had her distracted.

Littell commandeered a wraparound bar booth. Barb waved when she saw them walk in.

Pete drank beer. Littell drank club soda. Amplifier boom shook their table.

Pete yawned. He got a room at the Statler and slept through the day and half the evening.

Hoffa sent two grand to Fred Otash. Littell wrote a note to Hoover and sent it via Jimmy's FBI contact.

The note said, We want to install bugs and wiretaps. The note said, We want to fuck one of YOUR MAJOR ENEMIES.

Hoffa retained Fred Turentine. Freddy was set to tap phones and plant bugs where needed.

Pete yawned. Lenny's Bobby/Cuba pitch kept twisting through his head.

Littell nudged him. "She's got the looks."

"And the style."

"How smart is she?"

"A lot smarter than my last extortion partner."

Barb worked the "Frisco Twist" into a crescendo. Her junkie backup group kept playing like she wasn't even there.

She walked off stage. Twist clowns jostled her across the dance floor. A horny geek followed her and scoped out her cleavage close up.

Pete waved. Barb slid into the booth next to him.

Pete said, "Miss Lindscott, Mr. Littell."

Barb lit a cigarette. "It's technically 'Jahelka.' When my mother-in-law dies, I'll go back to 'Lindscott.'"

Littell said, "I like 'Lindscott.'"

Barb said, "I know. It fits my face better."

"Have you ever worked as an actress?"

"No."

"What about that charade with Lenny Sands and Rock Hudson?"

"I only had to fool the police and spend a night in jail."

"Was two thousand dollars worth the risk?"

Barb laughed. "Compared to four hundred dollars for three Twist shows a night, six nights a week?"

Pete pushed his beer and pretzels aside. "You'll make a lot more than two thousand dollars with us."

"For doing what? Besides sleeping with some powerful man, I mean."

Littell leaned toward her. "It's high risk, but it's only temporary."

"So? The Twist is temporary and boring."

Littell smiled. "If you met President Kennedy and wanted to impress him, how would you act?"

Barb blew three perfect smoke rings. "I'd act profane and funny."

"What would you wear?"

"Flat heels."

"Why?"

"Men like women they can look down to."

Littell laughed. "What would you do with fifty thousand dollars?"

Barb laughed. "I'd wait out the Twist."

"Suppose you get exposed?"

"Then I'll figure that you're worse than whoever we're shaking down and keep my mouth shut."

Pete said, "It won't come to that."

Barb said, "*What* won't?"

Pete fought this urge to touch her. "You'll be safe. This is one of those high-risk things that gets settled nice and quiet."

Barb leaned close to him. "Tell me what 'it' is. I know what it is, but I want to hear *you* say it."

She brushed his leg. The contact made his whole body flutter.

Pete said, "It's you and Jack Kennedy. You'll meet him at a party at Peter Lawford's house in two weeks. You'll be wearing a microphone, and if you're as good as I think you are, that will just be the start of it."

Barb took their hands and squeezed them. Her look said, Pinch me, am I dreaming?

"Am I some kind of Republican Party shill?"

Pete laughed. Littell laughed harder.

DOCUMENT INSERT: 2/18/62. Verbatim FBI telephone call transcript: "TAPED AT THE DIRECTOR'S REQUEST"/"DIRECTOR'S
EYES ONLY." Speaking: Director J. Edgar Hoover, Ward J. Littell.

JEH: Mr. Littell?

WJL: Yes, Sir.

JEH: Your communique was quite bold.

WJL: Thank you, Sir.

JEH: I had no idea you were employed by Mr. Hoffa and Mr.
Marcello.

WJL: Since last year, Sir.

JEH: I will not comment on the attendant irony.

WJL: I would call it manifest, Sir.

JEH: That is apt. Am I correct in assuming that the ubiquitous
and quite overextended Kemper Boyd secured you this
employment?

WJL: Yes, Sir. You are correct.

JEH: I bear Mr. Marcello and Mr. Hoffa no ill will. I have
viewed the Dark Prince's crusade against them to be ill-conceived
from the start.

WJL: They know that, Sir.

JEH: Am I correct in assuming that you have undergone an
apostasy concerning the brothers?

WJL: Yes, Sir.

JEH: Am I to assume that the promiscuous King Jack is the
target of your operation?

WJL: That is correct, Sir.

JEH: And the fearsome Pete Bondurant is your partner in this
endeavor?

WJL: Yes, Sir.

JEH: I will not comment on the attendant irony.

WJL: Sir, do we have your approval?

JEH: You do. And you, personally, have my astonishment.

WJL: Thank you, Sir.

JEH: Is the apparatus in place?

WJL: Yes, Sir. So far we've only been able to wire the Carlyle,
and until our plant makes contact with the target and facilitates
the affair, we don't really know where they'll be coupling.

JEH: If they couple at all.

WJL: Yes, Sir.

JEH: Your note mentioned certain hotels.

WJL: Yes, Sir, the El Encanto and Ambassador-East. I know that our target likes to take women to those hotels, and I know that the Bureau retains standing bugs at both locations.

JEH: Yes, although the Dark King now likes to cavort in the Presidential Suites.

WJL: I hadn't thought of that, Sir.

JEH: I'll have trustworthy Bureau men install the apparatus and monitor it. And I will share my tapes with you, if you forward copies of your Carlyle tapes to me.

WJL: Of course, Sir.

JEH: Have you considered wiring the first brother-in-law's beach house?

WJL: It's impossible, sir. Fred Turentine can't get in to install the microphones.

JEH: When will your plant meet the Dark King?

WJL: Tomorrow night, Sir. At the beach house you just mentioned.

JEH: Is she attractive?

WJL: Yes, Sir.

JEH: I hope she's wily and resilient and impervious to the boy's charm.

WJL: I think she'll do a fine job, Sir.

JEH: I'm quite anxious to hear her on tape.

WJL: I'll forward only the best transcriptions, Sir.

JEH: You have my admiration. Kemper Boyd taught you well.

WJL: You did, too, Sir.

JEH: I will not comment on the attendant irony.

WJL: Yes, Sir.

JEH: I know that in time you'll ask favors of me. I know that you'll keep me abreast of the transcriptions and ask your favors judiciously.

WJL: I will, Sir.

JEH: I misjudged you and underestimated you, and I'm glad we're colleagues again.

WJL: So am I, Sir.

JEH: Good day, Mr. Littell.

WJL: Good day, Sir.

76

Shots woke him up. Rebel yells made him dive for his gun.

Kemper rolled off the bed. He heard brake squeals down on the highway—non-Lockhart Klansmen or plain old rednecks popping rounds and running.

Word is out.

There's a Fed nigger lover in town. The Seminole Motel is packed with his spic/frog minions.

The shots were scary. The nightmare they cut off was worse.

Jack and Bobby had him under the hot lights. They said, J'accuse—we know you're Mob-CIA linked all the way back to '59.

The nightmare was literal and direct. The origin was Pete's phone call last week.

Pete talked up the Whack Fidel auditions. He said he developed a theory to explain why the Outfit nixed the hit.

Pete said Sam G. might be set to tell Bobby a secret. Hey, Mr. AG— the Outfit's been your Cuban Cause ally for three years now.

Pete picked up a lead that strongly suggested it. Pete thinks Sam might have someone spill the secret soon. Pete thinks Sam wants to embarrass Bobby into a Mob War cease-fire.

Pete said, I'll look into it.

Kemper got up and dry-swallowed three Dexedrine. Pete's theory speedballed and went personal.

Bobby wants *me* to show him JM/Wave some time soon. He thinks my CIA ties date from 5/61 on. JM/Wave is packed with my *pre-Pigs* colleagues—and Cuban exiles well acquainted with organized crime figures.

Kemper shaved and dressed. The Dexedrine kicked in fast. He heard thumps next door—Laurent Guéry pounding early morning push-ups.

John Stanton pulled strings. Laurent, Flash and Juan were granted INS green cards. Néstor Chasco moved to Meridian and joined the group. The Seminole Motel was now "Adjunct" Cadre HQ.

He cashed in twenty thousand dollars' worth of stock. Guy Banister donated matching funds. The Clip Castro Squad was now self-contained and totally autonomous.

He took voting rights reports by day. He staged assassination drills by night.

He won over quite a few local Negroes. First Pentecostal Baptist was now 84% depositioned.

Some crackers roughed up the pastor. He found them and broke their legs with a two-by-four.

Dougie Frank parceled off half his gun range. The Adjunct Cadre practiced seven nights a week.

They shot at standing and moving targets. They took recon tramps through the woods. Cuban infiltration runs would begin soon.

Juan and Flash had him close to Spanish-fluent. He could dye his hair and stain his face and go to Cuba as a covert Latin.

He could get close. He could shoot.

They all loved to talk. They drank post-practice moonshine and gabbed through half the night.

They worked up a three-language patois. They told gory campfire tales and passed around bottles.

Juan described his castration. Chasco talked up his Batista-ordered clip jobs.

Flash saw Playa Girón up close. Laurent saw the hushed-up Paris slaughter—gendarmes beat two hundred Algerians to death and dumped them in the Seine last October.

He could get close. *He* could shoot. The fair-skinned Anglo-Saxon could be Cuban.

The Dexedrine hit full-bore. Cold coffee provided a nice booster.

The date jumped off his Rolex. Happy Birthday—you're forty-six years old and don't look it.

DOCUMENT INSERT: 2/21/62. Partial microphone to mobile listening post transcript. Transcribed by: Fred Turentine. Tape/written copies to: P. Bondurant, W. Littell.

9:14 p.m., February 19, 1962. L. Sands & B. Jahelka enter house (target & entourage arrived at 8:03). Traffic noise on Pacific Coast Highway accounts for scrambled signal and large continuity gaps. B. Jahelka's visit clock synchronized & live monitored.

Initial code:

BJ—Barb Jahelka. LS—Lenny Sands. PL—Peter Lawford. MU1—Male Unknown #1. MU2—Male Unknown #2. FU 1, 2, 3, 4, 5, 6, 7: Female Unknowns #1–#7. JFK—John F. Kennedy. RFK—Robert F. Kennedy. (Note: I think MU #1 and #2 are Secret Service agents.)

9:14–9:22: garbled.

9:23–9:26: overlapping voices. BJ's voice comes through, mostly casual greetings. (I think she was being introduced to FU #1–#7. Note high-pitched laughter on tape copies.)

9:27–9:39: BJ & PL.

PL (conversation in progress): You stand out in this crowd, Barb.

BJ: My beauty or my height?

PL: Both.

BJ: You're so full of shit.

FU3: Hi, Peter.

PL: Hi, doll.

FU6: Peter, I just love the President's hair.

PL: Give it a tug. He won't bite you.

FU3, FU6: laughter.

BJ: Are they showgirls or hookers?

PL: The bleached blonde's a barmaid at the Sip n' Surf in Malibu. The others work the show line at the Dunes. You see the brunette with the lungs?

BJ: I see her.

PL: She plays skin flute in Frank Sinatra's all-girl band.

BJ: Very funny.

PL: Not funny, because Bobby made Jack drop Frank. Frank

put in a heliport at his place in Palm Springs so Jack could visit him, but that judgmental little shit Bobby made Jack give him the brush-off, just because he knows a few gangsters. Look at him. Isn't he a wicked looking little shit?

BJ: He has buck teeth.

PL: That never touch women.

BJ: Are you saying he's a fag?

PL: I have it on good authority that he only fucks his wife, doesn't go down, and only gives it to Ethel for purposes of pro-creation. Isn't he a wicked looking little shit?

FU2: Peter! I just met the President out on the beach!

PL: That's nice. Did you suck his cock?

FU2: You're a pig.

PL: Oink! Oink!

BJ: I think I need a drink.

PL: I think you need a lobotomy. Really, Barb. I just wanted you to sleep with Frank once.

BJ: He's not my type.

PL: He could have helped you. He would have kicked that wicked little shit Joey out of your life.

BJ: Joey and I have a history. I'll cut him loose when the time's right.

PL: You cut me loose too soon. Frank was deeply smitten with you, doll. He sensed that you were hiding things, and I have it on good authority that he hired a private eye to find out what those things were.

BJ: Did he tell you what he found out?

PL: Mum's the word, doll. Mum's the goddamn—

FU1: Oh God, Peter, I just met President Kennedy!

PL: That's nice. Did you suck his cock?

BJ, FU1, FU7: garbled.

PL: Oink! Oink! Oink! I'm a Presidential piglet!

9:40–10:22: garbled. Static quality indicates that Secret Service men installed and were calling out on private phone lines.

10:23–10:35: garbled. BJ (standing near hi-fi set) talking to: FU1, 3, 7. (She should have been told to avoid noisy appliances & record players.)

10:36–10:41: BJ in bathroom (indicated by sink & toilet sounds).

10:42–10:49: garbled.

10:50–11:04: BJ & RFK.

BJ (conversation in progress): It's just a craze, and you have to catch these things before they crest, and then bail out before they fizzle so you won't look like a loser.

RFK: Then I guess you could say the Twist is like politics.

BJ: You could. Opportunism's certainly the common denominator.

RFK: It sounds trite, but you don't talk like an ex-showgirl.

BJ: Have you met a lot of them?

RFK: Quite a few, yes.

BJ: When you were investigating gangsters?

RFK: No, when my brother introduced me to them.

BJ: Did they have a common denominator?

RFK: Yes. Availability.

BJ: I'd have to agree with that.

RFK: Are you going out with Lenny Sands?

BJ: We're not dating. He just brought me to the party.

RFK: How did he bill the gathering?

BJ: He didn't say, 'come join the harem,' if that's what you mean.

RFK: Then you noticed the high woman to man ratio.

BJ: You know I did, Mr. Kennedy.

RFK: Call me Bob.

BJ: All right, Bob.

RFK: I'm just assuming that since you know Peter and Lenny, you know how certain things are.

BJ: I think I follow you.

RFK: I know you do. I'm only mentioning it because I've known Lenny for a long time, and he seems sad and nervous tonight, and I've never seen him that way before. I'd hate to think that Peter put him up to—

BJ: I don't like Peter. I had a fling with him several years ago, and I broke it off when I saw that he was really no better than a toady and a pimp. I came to this party because Lenny needed a date and I thought it would be nice to spend a cool winter evening at the beach and maybe meet the Attorney General and President of the United States—

RFK: Please, I didn't mean to offend you.

BJ: You didn't.

RFK: When I get hornswoggled into evenings like this, I find myself checking out the anomalies from a security standpoint. When the anomaly is a woman, well, you see what I mean.

BJ: Given the other women here, it's good to be an anomaly.

RFK: I'm bored and two drinks over my limit. I don't normally get so personal with people I just met.

BJ: Want to hear a good joke?

RFK: Sure.

BJ: What did Pat Nixon say about her husband?

RFK: I don't know.

BJ: Richard was a strange bedfellow long before he entered politics.

RFK (laughing): Jesus, that's a riot. I'll have to tell that to—

Garbled (airplane flying overhead). Remainder of BJ–RFK conversation lost to static.

11:05–11:12: Hi-fi noise & car noise indicate that BJ is walking thru house & that people are leaving the party.

11:13–11:19: BJ talking directly to microphone. (Tell her not to do this. It's a security risk.)

BJ: I'm out on this deck overlooking the beach. I'm alone, and I'm whispering so people won't hear what I'm saying or think I'm crazy. I haven't met the Big Man yet, but I noticed him notice me and nudge Peter like he was saying, who's the redhead? It's freezing out here, but I dug a mink coat out of a closet, and now I'm nice and warm. Lenny's drunk, but I think he's trying to have a good time. He's schmoozing with Dean Martin now. The Big Man is in Peter's bedroom with two blondes. I saw Bobby a few minutes ago. He was eating out of the fridge like a starving man. The Secret Service men are looking through a stack of Playboy Magazines. You can tell they're thinking, boy, I'm sure glad stodgy old Dick Nixon didn't get elected. Somebody's smoking pot out on the beach, and I'm thinking hard to get's the way to play this. I'm thinking he'll find me. I heard Bobby tell one of the Secret Service men that the Big Man didn't want to leave until 1:00. That gives me some time. Lenny said Peter showed him my infamous Nugget Magazine foldout from November, 1956. He's about 6' or 6'1", so with flats on he'll have a few inches on me. I have to say that Hollywood trash aside, this is one of those moments that young girls write about in their diaries. Also, I declined three invitations to Twist, because I thought it might rip my microphone loose. Did you hear that? The bedroom door behind me just shut, and the two blondes snuck out, giggling. I'm going to shut up now.

11:20–11:27: silence. (Wave noise indicates that BJ has remained on the beach deck.)

11:28–11:40: BJ & JFK.

JFK: Hi.

BJ: Jesus.

JFK: Hardly, but thanks anyway.

BJ: How about, hello, Mr. President?

JFK: How about, hello, Jack?

BJ: Hello, Jack.

JFK: What's your name?

BJ: Barb Jahelka.

JFK: You don't look like a Jahelka.

BJ: It's Lindscott, actually. I work with my ex-husband, so I kept my married name.

JFK: Is Lindscott Irish?

BJ: It's an Anglo-German bastardization.

JFK: The Irish are all bastards. Bastards, cranks and drunks.

BJ: Can I quote you?

JFK: After I'm re-elected. Put it in the portable John F. Kennedy, next to 'Ask not what your country can do for you.'

BJ: Can I ask you a question?

JFK: Sure.

BJ: Is being President of the United States the biggest fucking blast on earth?

JFK (sustained laughter): It truly is. Your supporting cast of characters is worth the price of admission alone.

BJ: For instance?

JFK: That rube Lyndon Johnson. Charles de Gaulle, who's had a poker up his ass since the year 1910. That closet fairy J. Edgar Hoover. These crazy Cuban exiles my brother's been dealing with, 80% of whom are lowlife scum. Harold Macmillan, who defines the word—

MU2: Excuse me, Mr. President.

JFK: Yes?

MU1: You have a call.

JFK: Tell them I'm busy.

MU2: It's Governor Brown.

JFK: Tell him I'll call him back.

MU1: Yes, Sir.

JFK: So, Barb, did you vote for me?

BJ: I was on tour, so I didn't get the chance to vote.

JFK: You could have cast an absentee ballot.

BJ: It slipped my mind.

JFK: What's more important, the Twist or my career?

BJ: The Twist.

JFK (sustained laughter): Excuse my naivete. When you ask a silly question.

BJ: It was more like ask a candid question, get a candid answer.

JFK: That's true. You know, my brother thinks you're overqualified for this party.

BJ: He acts like he's slumming himself.

JFK: That's perceptive.

BJ: Your brother never won a dime at poker.

JFK: Which is one of his strengths. Now, what happens when this silly dance craze of yours wears itself out?

BJ: I'll have saved enough money to set my sister up in a Bob's Big Boy franchise in Tunnel City, Wisconsin.

JFK: I carried Wisconsin.

BJ: I know. My sister voted for you.

JFK: What about your parents?

BJ: My father's dead. My mother hates Catholics, so she voted for Nixon.

JFK: A split vote isn't too bad. That's a lovely mink, by the way.

BJ: I borrowed it from Peter.

JFK: Then it's one of the six thousand furs my father bought my sisters.

BJ: I read about your father's stroke. It made me sad.

JFK: Don't be. He's too evil to die. And by the way, do you travel with that revue Peter told me about?

BJ: Constantly. In fact, I'm leaving for an East Coast swing on the 27th.

JFK: Would you leave your itinerary with the White House switchboard? I thought we might have dinner if our schedules permit.

BJ: I'd like that. And I will call.

JFK: Please. And take the mink with you. You do things for it that my sister never could.

BJ: I couldn't.

JFK: I insist. Really, she won't miss it.

BJ: All right, then.

JFK: I don't normally raid people's closets, but I want you to have it.

BJ: Thank you, Jack.

JFK: My pleasure. And regretfully, I have to make some phone calls.

BJ: Until next time, then.

JFK: Yes. That's the way to look at it.

MU1: Mr. President?

JFK: Hold on, I'm coming.

11:41–12:03: silence. (Wave noise indicates that BJ has remained on the beach deck.)

12:03–12:09: garbled voices and hi-fi noise. (Obvious departures throughout.)

12:10: BJ & LS leave the party. Live tape feed close: 12:11
a.m., February 20, 1962.

DOCUMENT INSERT: 3/4/62. Carlyle Hotel bedroom microphone transcript. Transcribed by: Fred Turentine. Tape/written
copies to: P. Bondurant, W. Littell.

BJ phoned the listening post to say she was meeting the target
for "dinner." She was instructed to double open & shut the bedroom door to activate the mike. Active feed from 8:09 p.m. on.
Initial log: BJ—Barb Jahelka. JFK—John F. Kennedy.

8:09–8:20: sexual activity. (See tape transcript. High sound
quality. Voices discernable.)

8:21–8:33: conversation.

JFK: Oh, God.

BJ: Hmmm.

JFK: Slide over a little. I want to take some pressure off
my back.

BJ: How's that?

JFK: Better.

BJ: Want a back rub?

JFK: No. There's nothing you can do that you haven't done
already.

BJ: Thanks. And I'm glad you called me.

JFK: What did I get you out of?

BJ: Two shows at the Rumpus Room in Passaic, New Jersey.

JFK: Oh, God.

BJ: Ask me a question.

JFK: All right. Where's that mink coat I gave you?

BJ: My ex-husband sold it.

JFK: You let him do that?

BJ: It's a game we play.

JFK: What do you mean?

BJ: He knows I'm going to leave him soon. I'm in debt to him, so he takes these little advantages whenever he finds them.

JFK: It's a large debt, then?

BJ: Very large.

JFK: You've got my interest. Tell me more.

BJ: It's just grief from Tunnel City, Wisconsin, circa 1948.

JFK: I like Wisconsin.

BJ: I know. You carried it.

JFK (laughing): You're droll. Ask me a question.

BJ: Who's the biggest fuckhead in American politics?

JFK (laughing): That closet queen J. Edgar Hoover, who'll be retiring on January 1, 1965.

BJ: I hadn't heard anything about that.

JFK: You will.

BJ: I get it. You have to be re-elected first.

JFK: You're learning. Now, tell me more about Tunnel City, Wisconsin, in 1948.

BJ: Not now.

JFK: Why?

BJ: I'm tantalizing you, so we can prolong this thing of ours.

JFK (laughing): You know men.

BJ: Yes, I do.

JFK: Who taught you? Initially, I mean.

BJ: The entire adolescent male population of Tunnel City, Wisconsin. Don't look so shocked. The total number of boys was eleven.

JFK: Go on.

BJ: No.

JFK: Why?

BJ: Two seconds after we made love you looked at your watch. I'm thinking that the way to keep you in bed is to string out my autobiography.

JFK (laughing): You can contribute to my memoirs. You can say John F. Kennedy wooed women with room service club sandwiches and quickies.

BJ: It was a great club sandwich.

JFK (laughing): You're droll and cruel.

BJ: Ask me a question.

JFK: No. You ask me one.

BJ: Tell me about Bobby.

JFK: Why?

BJ: He seemed suspicious of me at Peter's party.

JFK: He's suspicious in general, because he's crawling around in the legal gutter with Jimmy Hoffa and the Mafia, and it's starting to get to him. It's some sort of occupational policeman's disease that he's developed. One day it's Jimmy Hoffa and land fraud in Florida. The next day it's deporting Carlos Marcello. Now it's Hoffa and the Test Fleet taxi case in Tennessee, and don't ask me what it means, because I'm not a lawyer and I don't share Bobby's need to pursue and eradicate.

BJ: He's tougher than you, isn't he?

JFK: Yes, he is. And as I told a girl several years ago, he's truly passionate and generous.

BJ: You're looking at your watch again.

JFK: I have to go. I'm due at the U.N.

BJ: Good luck, then.

JFK: I won't need it. The General Assembly is nothing but fuckheads. Let's do this again, Barb. I had fun.

BJ: So did I. And thanks for the club sandwich.

JFK (laughing): There's more where that came from.

Single door slam deactivates mike. Transcript close: 8:34 p.m., March 3rd, 1962.

DOCUMENT INSERT: 4/9/62. Carlyle Hotel bedroom microphone transcript. Transcribed by: Fred Turentine. Tape/written copies to: P. Bondurant, W. Littell.

BJ phoned the listening post at 4:20 p.m. She said she was meeting the target for "dinner" at 5:30. Active feed from 6:12 p.m. on. Initial log: BJ—Barb Jahelka. JFK—John F. Kennedy.

6:13–6:25: sexual activity. (See tape transcript. High sound quality. Voices discernable.)

6:14–6:32: conversation.

BJ: Oh, God.

JFK: Last time I said that.

BJ: This time was better.

JFK (laughing): I thought so, too. But I thought the club sandwich lacked pizzazz.

BJ: Ask me a question.

JFK: What happened in Tunnel City, Wisconsin, in 1948?

BJ: I'm amazed that you remembered.

JFK: It's only been a month or so

BJ: I know. But it was just a casual comment that I made.

JFK: It was a provocative one, though.

BJ: Thanks.

JFK: Barb.

BJ: All right. On May 9, I jilted Billy Kreuger. Billy got together with Tom McCandless, Fritzie Schott and Johnny Coates. They decided to teach me a lesson. I was out of town, though. My parents took me to a church fellowship convention in Racine. My sister Margaret stayed at home. She was rebellious, and she hadn't figured out that church conventions were good places to meet boys.

JFK: Keep going.

BJ: To be continued.

JFK: Oh, God. I hate unresolved mysteries.

BJ: Next time.

JFK: How do you know there'll be a next time?

BJ (laughing): I know what kind of interest I'm capable of sustaining.

JFK: You're good, Barb. You're damn good.

BJ: I want to see if it's possible to know a man in one hour, once-a-month increments.

JFK: You'll never make an untoward demand of me, will you?

BJ: No. I will not.

JFK: God bless you.

BJ: Do you believe in God?

JFK: Only for public appearances. Now, ask me a question.

BJ: Do you have somebody who finds women for you?

JFK (laughing): Not really. Kemper Boyd's probably the closest thing, but he makes me a tad uncomfortable, so I haven't really used him since the Inauguration.

BJ: Who's Kemper Boyd?

JFK: He's a Justice Department lawyer. You'd like him. He's wildly good-looking and rather dangerous.

BJ: Are you jealous of him? Is that why he makes you uncomfortable?

JFK: He makes me uncomfortable because his one great regret is that he's not a Kennedy, which is quite a tough regret to respect. He's been dealing with some of those lowlife exiles for Bobby's Study Group, and I think in some ways he's no better than they are. He just went to Yale Law School, latched onto me and proved himself useful.

BJ: Pimps ingratiate themselves with authority. God, look at Peter.

JFK: Kemper's no Peter Lawford, I'll say that for him. Peter's got no soul to sell, and Kemper sold his at a pretty steep price and didn't even know it.

BJ: How so?

JFK: I can't go into details, but he threw over the woman he was engaged to to curry favor with me and my family. You see, he came from money, but his father lost it all and killed himself. He's living out some unsavory fantasy with me, and once you recognize it, the man becomes hard to take.

BJ: Let's talk about something else.

JFK: How about Tunnel City, Wisconsin, in 1948?

BJ: To be continued.

JFK: Shit.

BJ: I like cliffhangers.

JFK: I don't. I hated movie serials when I was a boy.

BJ: You should install a wall clock here. That way, you won't have to sneak looks at your watch.

JFK: You're droll. Hand me my trousers, would you?

BJ: Here.

Single door slam deactivates mike. Transcript close: 6:33 p.m., April 8, 1962.

77

(Miami, 4/15/62)

The cop was late. Pete killed time doodling up dispatch sheets.

He drew little hearts and ar-rows. He wrote out words Lenny and Barb said and underlined them for emphasis.

The words were strong. Cabstand bustle washed over him like total fucking silence.

Lenny's words spawned a theory. The Outfit wants Bobby K. to know they've been helping out with Cuba. Bobby hasn't been told yet. If he knew, he would have fungooed Kemper Boyd. If he knew, he would have snipped all known Mob-CIA ties.

The Outfit knows that Bobby doesn't want a Fidel hit. They refused to fund the shooter team for just that reason.

His theory simmered for weeks. He ran guns to exile camps and Kemper worked his two gigs in Mississippi. Kemper was out to depila-tory the Beard—his lack of Mob sanction did not seem to bother him one bit.

Barb was out to trim Jack the Haircut.

The cop was late. Pete drifted into Barb Overdrive.

Her words were accumulating—on tape and in print. He had the best words memorized.

Fred Turentine was running the Carlyle bug post—an apartment off 76th and Madison. A Barb Fucks Jack tape/print library was now in the works. Littell's Hoover ploy succeeded. Feds wired the Presidential Suites at the El Encanto and Ambassador-East.

Mr. Hoover was their extortion colleague. Feds checked the Carlyle suite once a week—let's keep those bedroom mikes tucked out of sight.

Jack K. was a six-minute bed jockey. Jack K. was a big fucking loudmouth.

Jack called Cuban exiles "lowlifes." Jack called Kemper Boyd a pathetic social climber.

The cop was late. Pete drew more hearts and arrows.

He had a new theory. Dig it: Barb's talking to Jack and to ME.

Barb says she won't leave Joey Jahelka—"because he arranged to have some men who hurt my sister taken care of." Barb won't tell Jack the whole story.

Barb hints that big intrigue went down in May '48.

Barb knows *he'll* play the tapes and read the transcripts. Barb wants *him* to fill in the blanks. Jack won't press too hard for answers—she's just one of his three million steady fucks.

Barb knows *he's* an ex-cop. Barb knows *he* can find out.

He called the Wisconsin State Police. He had Guy Banister initiate Fed queries. The whole thing took forty-eight hours.

5/11/48:

Margaret Lynn Lindscott is gang-raped in Tunnel City, Wisconsin. She IDs her attackers: William Kreuger, Thomas McCandless, Fritz Schott, and John Coates. No charges are filed. All four boys have unshakable alibis.

1/14/52:

William Kreuger is shot and killed in Milwaukee. The "mugging-homicide" remains unsolved.

7/4/52:

Thomas McCandless is shot and killed in Chicago. The "assumed professional hit" remains unsolved.

1/23/54:

Fritz Schott disappears. A decomposed body is found near Des Moines—maybe or maybe not his. Three shell casings are discovered nearby. The "assumed gunshot homicide" remains unsolved.

John Coates is alive and well. He's a cop in Norman, Oklahoma.

Pete unlocked his desk and pulled out the magazine. There's Barb at twenty-five—a pulchritudinous Miss Nugget.

Barb seduced Mob-allied Joey Jahelka. Barb got him to finagle hits on the men who raped her sister.

John Coates was still alive. The Mob did not clip cops without big provocation.

Grateful Barb married Joey. Grateful Barb carried the debt.

The cop was late. Pete studied the foldout for the ten millionth time.

They airbrushed her breasts. They powdered her freckles. The picture didn't nail her smarts and je ne sais quoi.

Pete put the magazine away. Pete doodled up another dispatch sheet.

He called Barb once a week. He tossed out little love checks—You don't *really* dig Jack, do you?

She didn't. She dug the allure—but Jack was just a six-minute erection and some chuckles.

The shakedown was proceeding. Turentine flew out to L.A. and checked up on Lenny Sands. Freddy said Lenny was solid. Freddy said Lenny would never rat off the operation.

He played the Barb tapes over and over. He reran Lenny's blurt almost as much.

Three major Mob contributors abandoned the Cuban Cause. Littell said Carlos Marcello was the only Outfit big who still cared.

Why?

His guess was MONEY.

Pete kept his nose down for two months straight. His theory percolated.

He kept playing theoretical match-ups. He kept linking Cuban Cause and Outfit personnel. Last week he made a big theoretical jump.

November 1960.

Wilfredo Olmos Delsol is seen talking to pro-Castro agents. Wilfredo Olmos Delsol was *recently* seen:

Driving a new car. Wearing new threads. Showing off new women.

He hired a Miami cop to spot-tail Delsol. The man reported back.

Delsol met with hinky Cubans six nights running. Their license plates were fake number/fake tag counterfeits.

The cop tailed the men to their pads. The pads were rented under obvious fake names. The Cubans were pro-Castro agents with no visible means of support.

The cop glommed a phone-company snitch. He paid him five hundred dollars and told him to steal Delsol's recent phone bills.

The cop said his snitch succeeded. The cop was late with the goods.

Pete doodled. He drew little hearts and arrows, ad fucking infinitum.

Sergeant Carl Lennertz showed up a full hour late. Pete waltzed him out to the parking lot.

They exchanged envelopes. The transaction went down in two seconds flat.

Lennertz took off. Pete opened his envelope and pulled out two sheets of paper.

The Florida Bell man delivered. Delsol made four months' worth of suspicious phone calls.

He called Santo and Sam G. at their unlisted numbers. He called six pro-Castro front groups a total of twenty-nine times.

Pete felt his pulse go snap/crackle/pop.

He drove to Delsol's house. The puto's new-money Impala was parked on the front lawn.

He boxed it in with his car. He slashed the tires with his pocket knife. He wedged a porch chair under the front doorknob. He ripped a cord off an outside air cooler and balled it around his right fist.

He heard running water and music inside the house.

Pete walked around to the back. The kitchen door stood ajar.

Delsol was washing dishes. The geek was snapping his dishrag to a mambo beat.

Pete waved. Delsol waved soapy hands—Come on in.

A little radio was perched on the sink ledge. Perez Prado was cranking out "Cherry Pink and Apple Blossom White."

Pete walked in. Delsol said, *"Hola, Pedro."*

Pete sucker-punched him. Delsol jackknifed. Pete dropped the radio in the sink.

Water fizzed. Pete kicked Delsol in the ass and shot him into sink water up to his elbows.

He screamed. He pulled his arms out and cut loose with this godawful shriek.

Steam whooshed through the kitchen—dig that baby mushroom cloud.

Pete shoved the dishrag in his mouth. Delsol's arms were scorched bright red and hairless.

"You've been calling Trafficante, Giancana and some pro-Castro guys. You've been seen with some left-wing Cubans, and you've been spending money."

Delsol flipped him off. Dig that firecracker-red "Fuck You" finger.

"I think most of the Outfit's quits on the Cause, and I want to know why. You put all this together or your face goes into the water."

Delsol spat the rag out. Pete lashed his hands with the air-cooler cord and rabbit-punched him back into the suds.

He spun in sideways. Juiced-up water splashed all over him.

He screamed and pulled his arms out. Pete dragged him to the fridge and buried his hands in ice cubes.

Stabilize, fucker—don't go into shock.

Pete dumped loose cubes into a bowl. Delsol untied the cord with his teeth and wiggled his hands in.

The sink water bubbled and fizzed. Pete lit a cigarette to kill the charred-flesh stink.

Delsol slumped into a chair. His cardiac flush subsided—the puto radiated good resistance.

Pete said, "Well?"

Delsol hugged the bowl with his knees. Ice popped out and hit the floor.

Pete said, "Well?"

"Well, you killed my cousin. Did you think I would always stay loyal?"

His voice stayed just short of a whimper. Spics withstood pain with the best.

"That's not the answer I wanted."

"I thought it was a good answer for a man who killed his own brother by mistake."

Pete picked up a kitchen knife. "Tell me what I want to hear."

Delsol double-flipped him. Dig those two "Fuck You" fingers shedding skin down to the knuckle.

Pete stabbed the chair. The blade ripped a trouser seam half an inch from Delsol's balls.

Delsol pulled the knife loose and dropped it on the floor. Pete said, "Well?"

"Well, I suppose I must tell you."

"Keep going, then. Don't make me work so hard."

Delsol smiled. Delsol was exhibiting fucking epic machismo. "You were right, Pedro. Giancana and Mr. Santo have abandoned La Causa."

"What about Carlos Marcello?"

"No. He is not with them. He is still enthusiastic."

"What about Heshie Ryskind?"

"He is not with them either. I have heard he is very ill."

"Santo is still backing the Cadre."

Delsol smirked. Blisters started bubbling up on his arms.

"I think he will withdraw his support soon. I am certain it will happen."

Pete chained cigarettes. "Who else has betrayed the Cadre?"

"I do not consider what I did betrayal. The man you used to be would not consider it that, either."

Pete flipped his cigarette in the sink. "Just answer my questions. I don't want to hear your extraneous comments."

Delsol said, "All right. I am the only one in this."

" 'This'?"

Delsol shivered. A big blister on his neck popped and spritzed blood.

"Yes. This is what you thought it was."

"Explain it for me, then."

Delsol stared at his hands. "I mean that Mr. Santo and the others have gone over to Fidel. They are just pretending enthusiasm for La Causa, to impress Robert Kennedy and other powerful officials. They are hoping Kennedy will learn about their support and not try to hurt them so hard. Raúl Castro is selling them heroin very cheaply. In exchange, they have given him information on the exile movement."

Heroin was MONEY. His theory was confirmed straight down the line.

"Keep going. I know there's more."

Delsol did a little blank-face number. Pete stared at him. Pete held the stare and held it and held it—

Delsol blinked. "Yes, there is more. Raúl is trying to convince Fidel to let Mr. Santo and the others reopen their casinos in Havana. Mr. Santo and Mr. Sam promised they would inform Raúl on the progress at JM/Wave and try to warn them of any assassination attempts on Fidel."

More confirmation. More potential grief. Santo and Sam could force Boyd to disband his hit squad.

Delsol examined his arms. His tattoos were scorched into odd smudges.

Pete said, "There's more."

"No. There isn't."

Pete sighed. "There's your part. You were recruited because the pro-Castro guys knew the Cadre killed your cousin, and they figured you were vulnerable. You've got a part in this, and it's got something to do with heroin, and if you don't tell me, I'm going to start hurting you again."

"Pedro . . ."

Pete squatted in front of the chair. Pete said, *"Heroin. Tell me about it."*

Delsol crossed himself. The ice-cube bowl slipped to the floor and shattered.

"A Cuban shipment is coming in by speedboat. Two hundred pounds of it, uncut. Some pro-Castro men will be there to guard it. I am supposed to transmit it to Mr. Santo."

"When?"

"The night of May 4th."

"Where?"

"The Gulf Coast in Alabama. A place called Orange Beach."

Pete got the shakes. Delsol caught his fear instantaneously.

"We must pretend this never happened, Pedro. You yourself must pretend that you never really believed in the Cause. We must not interfere with men who are so much more powerful than we are."

Boyd took it cool. Pete steamed up the phone booth yelling.

"We can still make our casino deal happen. We can send in your team, have them clip Castro and create fucking chaos. Maybe things work out and Santo honors our deal, maybe they don't work out. At the very fucking least, we can snuff Fidel Castro."

Boyd said, "No. The deal is dead and the Cadre is finished, and sending in my men precipitously will only get them killed."

Pete kicked the door off its hinges—

"What do you mean, 'NO'?"

"I mean we should recoup our losses. We should make some money before somebody tells Bobby about the Outfit and the Agency."

The door crashed across the sidewalk. Pedestrians stepped around it. A little kid jumped on it and cracked the glass in half.

"The heroin?"

Boyd was calm. "There's two hundred pounds, Pete. We let it sit for five years and sell it overseas. You, me and Néstor. We'll make at least three million dollars apiece."

Pete went lightheaded. Dig it: that 9.9 earthquake is strictly internal.

DOCUMENT INSERT: 4/25/62. Carlyle Hotel bedroom microphone transcript. Transcribed by: Fred Turentine. Tape/written copies to: P. Bondurant, W. Littell.

BJ phoned the listening post at 3:08 p.m. She said she was meeting the target "for dinner" at 5:00. She was instructed to double open & shut the bedroom door to activate the mike. Active feed from 5:23 p.m. on. Initial log: BJ—Barb Jahelka. JFK—John F. Kennedy.

5:24–5:33: sexual activity. (See tape transcript. High sound quality. Voices discernable.)

5:34–5:41: conversation.

JFK: Shit, my back.

BJ: Let me help.

JFK: No, that's all right.

BJ: Stop looking at your watch. We just finished.

JFK (laughing): I really should have that wall clock installed.

BJ: And tell the chef to get with it. That was a lousy club sandwich.

JFK: It was. The turkey was dry and the bacon was soggy.

BJ: You seem distracted, Jack.

JFK: Smart girl.

BJ: The weight of the world?

JFK: No, my brother. He's on the warpath about my friends and the women I see, and he's acting like a colossal pain in the ass.

BJ: For instance?

JFK: He's on a witch hunt. Frank Sinatra knows some gangsters, so Frank had to go. The women Peter sets me up with are gonorrhea carrying tarts, and you're too polished and aware of your effects to be a Twist bunny, so you're suspect on general principles.

BJ (laughing): What's next? Can I expect to see FBI men following me?

JFK (laughing): Hardly. Bobby and Hoover hate each other too much to collaborate on anything that touchy. Bobby's overworked, so he's touchy, and Hoover's touchy because he's a Nazi faggot who hates all men with normal appetites. Bobby's running Justice, chasing gangsters and running point for my Cuban policy. He's up to his neck in psychopathic lowlife, and Hoover fights him on protocol matters every inch of the way. And I'm the one who takes the brunt of his frustration. Say, why don't we change jobs? You be the President of the United States and I'll Twist at, what's the name of that place you're appearing?

BJ: Del's Den in Stamford, Connecticut.

JFK: Right. What do you say, Barb? Shall we switch jobs?

BJ: It's a deal. And after I take over, I'll fire J. Edgar Hoover and order Bobby to take a vacation.

JFK: You're thinking like a Kennedy now.

BJ: How so?

JFK: I'm going to let Bobby be the one to give Hoover the sack.

BJ: Stop looking at your watch.

JFK: You should hide it from me next time.

BJ: I will.

JFK: I have to go. Hand me my trousers, will you?

BJ: They're wrinkled.

JFK: It's your fault.

Single door slam deactivates mike. Transcript close: 5:42 p.m., April 24, 1962.

DOCUMENT INSERTS: 4/25/62, 4/26/62, 5/1/62. Top Hood-lum Program wiretap outtakes: Los Angeles, Chicago and Newark venues. Marked: CONFIDENTIAL/TOP SECRET/ DIRECTOR'S EYES ONLY.

Los Angeles, 4/25/62. Placement: Rick-Rack Restaurant pay phone. Number dialed: MA2-4691. (Pay phone at Mike Lyman's Restaurant.) Caller: Steven "Steve the Skeev" De Santis. (See THP File #814.5, Los Angeles Office.) Person called: unknown male ("Billy"). Six minutes and four seconds of non-applicable conversation precedes the following.

SDS: And Frank shot his big fucking mouth off and Mo believed him. Jack's my boy, blah, blah. Jewboy Lenny told me he stuffed half the fucking ballot boxes in Cook County.

UM: You say Frank like you know the man personal.

SDS: I do, you fuck. I met him backstage at the Dunes Hotel once.

UM: Sinatra's a hump. He walks Outfit and talks Outfit, but he's really just a stupe from Hoboken, New Jersey.

SDS: He's a stupe who should pay, Billy.

UM: He should. Every time that rat prick Bobby comes down on the Outfit, Frankie should take a shot to the nuts. He should pay double for what that cunt Bobby's doing to Jimmy and the Teamsters, and triple for that stroll through Guatemala Uncle Carlos had to take.

SDS: The Kennedys should pay.

UM: In the best of all worlds they would.

SDS: They got no sense of fucking gratitude.

UM: They got no sense, period. I mean, Joe Kennedy and Raymond Patriarca go way back.

SDS: No sense.

UM: No fucking sense.

Non-applicable conversation follows.

Chicago, 4/26/62. Placement: North Side Elks Club pay phone. Number dialed: BL4-0808 (pay phone at Saparito's Trattoria Restaurant). Caller: Dewey "The Duck" Di Pasquale. (See THP file #709.9, Chicago Office.) Person called: Pietro "Pete Sap" Saparito. Four minutes and twenty-nine seconds of non-applicable conversation precedes the following.

DDP: What's worse than the clap and the syph is the Kennedys. They are trying to grind the Outfit into duck shit. Bobby's got these racket squads set up all over the country. These are cocksuckers who can't be bought for love or money.

PS: Jack Kennedy ate at my restaurant once. I should have poisoned the cocksucker.

DDP: Quack, quack. You should have.

PS: Don't start that duck routine with me, you hump.

DDP: You should invite Jack and Bobby and his racket squad guys to your place and poison them all.

PS: I should. Hey, you know my waitress, Deeleen?

DDP: Sure. I heard she plays skin clarinet with the best.

PS: She does. And she banged Jack Kennedy. She said he had this little piccolo dick.

DDP: The Irish ain't hung for shit. It's a well-known fact.

PS: Italian men have the biggest.

DDP: And the best.

PS: I heard Mo's hung like a mule.

DDP: Who told you?

PS: Mo himself.

Non-applicable conversation follows.

Newark, 5/1/62. Placement: <u>Lou's Lucky Lounge pay phone</u>. Number dialed: MU6-9441 (pay phone at <u>Reuben's Delicatessen</u>, New York City). Caller: Herschel "Heshie" Ryskind (See THP file #887.8, Dallas Office). Person called: Morris Milton Weinshank (See THP file #400.5, New York City Office). Three minutes and one second of non-applicable conversation precedes the following.

MMW: We're all sorry you're sick, Hesh. We're all pulling for you and praying for you.

HR: I want to live long enough to see Sam G. kick Sinatra's skinny bantamweight tuchus from here to Palermo. Sinatra and some CIA shitheel convinced Sam and Santo that Jack the K. was kosher. Use your noggin and think, Morris. Think about Ike and Harry Truman and FDR. Did they give us grief like this?

MMW: They did not.

HR: I know it's Bobby and not Jack that's the instigator. But Jack knows the rules. Jack knows you can't sic your rabid dogs on people who did you favors.

MMW: Sam thought Frank had pull with the brothers. He thought he could get Jack to call Bobby off.

HR: Frank was dreaming. The only pull Frank's got is with his putz. All Frank and that CIA guy Boyd want to do is suck the big Kennedy cock.

MMW: Jack and Bobby got nice hair.

HR: Which somebody should part with a forty-five caliber dum-dum.

MMW: Such hair. I should have such hair.

HR: You want hair? Buy a fucking wig.

Non-applicable conversation follows.

<u>DOCUMENT INSERT</u>: 5/1/62. Personal note: Howard Hughes to J. Edgar Hoover.

Dear Edgar,

Duane Spurgeon, my chief aide and legal advisor, is terminally ill. I need a replacement to go on retainer immediately. Of course, I would prefer a morally-sound lawyer with an FBI background. Could you recommend a man?

All best,
Howard

78

(Washington, D.C., 5/2/62)

Their bench faced the Lincoln Memorial. Nannies and small children scampered by.

Hoover said, "The woman is quite good."

"Thank you, Sir."

"She lures King Jack into provocative traps."

Littell smiled. "Yes, Sir. She does."

"King Jack has mentioned my forced retirement twice. Did you tell the woman to prod him in that direction?"

"Yes, Sir. I did."

"Why?"

"I wanted to increase your stake in the operation."

Hoover straightened the crease in his trousers. "I see. And I cannot fault your logic."

Littell said, "We want to convince the man to make his brother tone down his assault on my clients and their friends, and if they think you have copies of the tapes, it will go a long way toward convincing them to retain you."

Hoover nodded. "I cannot fault your logic."

"I would rather not go public with the tapes, Sir. I would rather see this resolved behind the scenes."

Hoover patted his briefcase. "Is that why you asked me to return my copies temporarily?"

"Yes, Sir."

"You don't trust me to keep them in cold storage?"

Littell smiled. "I want you to possess absolute deniability should Robert Kennedy bring in outside agency investigators. I want all the tapes kept in a single location, so that they can be destroyed if necessary."

Hoover smiled. "And so that, if worse comes to worse, Pete Bondurant and Fred Turentine can be portrayed as the sole perpetrators of the plot?"

Littell said, "Yes, Sir."

Hoover shooed a perching bird away. "Who's financing this? Is it Mr. Hoffa or Mr. Marcello?"

"I'd rather not say, Sir."

"I see. And I cannot fault your desire for secrecy."

"Thank you, Sir."

"Suppose public exposure becomes necessary?"

"Then I would go forward in late October, right before the congressional elections."

"Yes. That would be the optimum time."

"Yes, Sir. But as I said, I would rather not—"

"You needn't repeat yourself. I'm not senile."

The sun broke out of a cloud bank. Littell broke a slight sweat.

"Yes, Sir."

"You hate them, don't you?"

"Yes, I do."

"You're not alone. The THP has private taps and bugs installed in fourteen critical organized crime locales. We've been picking up a good deal of Kennedy resentment. I haven't informed the Brothers, and I'm not going to."

"I'm not surprised, Sir."

"I've compiled some wonderfully vituperative outtakes. They are hilariously colloquial and profane."

"Yes, Sir."

Hoover smiled. "Tell me what you're thinking."

Littell smiled. "That you trust me. That you trust me because I hate them as much as you do."

Hoover said, "You're correct. And my God, wouldn't Kemper be hurt if he overheard King Jack's assessment of his character?"

"He would be. Thank God he has no idea this operation exists."

A little girl skipped by. Hoover smiled and waved.

"Howard Hughes needs a new right-hand man. He asked me to find him someone with your qualifications, and I've recommended you."

Littell grabbed the bench. "I'm honored, Sir."

"You should be. You should also know that Howard Hughes is a very disturbed man with a rather tenuous hold on reality. He only communicates by telephone and letter, and I think there's a fair chance that you may never meet him face-to-face."

The bench shook. Littell folded his hands over one knee.

"Should I call him?"

"He'll call you, and I would advise you to accept his offer. The man has a silly, if exploitable, plan to purchase Las Vegas hotel-casinos a few years from now, and I think the notion has intelligence-gathering potential. I told Howard the names of your other clients, and he was quite impressed. I think the job is yours for the asking."

Littell said, "I want it."

Hoover said, "Of course you do. You've been hungry all your life, and you've finally reconciled your desires with your conscience."

79

(Orange Beach, 5/4/62)

They had 3:00 a.m. moonlight to work by. It was half a curse—*total* dark meant SURPRISE.

Pete pulled off the blacktop. He saw sand dunes up ahead—big high ones.

Néstor draped his legs across Wilfredo Delsol. Wilfredo the Mummy was duct-taped head to toe and stuffed between the front and back seats.

Boyd rode shotgun. Delsol wheezed through his nose. They kidnapped him at his pad on their way out of Miami.

Pete shifted to four-wheel drive. The Mummy lurched and banged Néstor's legs.

The jeep bounced between dunes. Boyd examined their track obfuscator—rake prongs attached to metal tubing.

Néstor coughed. "The beach is half a mile. I walked it twice."

Pete braked and cut the engine. Wave noise came on strong. Boyd said, "Listen to that. If we're lucky, they won't hear us."

They got out. Néstor dug a hole and buried Delsol in sand up to his nose.

Pete tossed a tarp over the jeep. It was light tan and sand-dune compatible.

Néstor rigged the rake gizmo. Boyd inventoried hardware.

They had silencer-fitted .45s and machine guns. They had a chainsaw, a clock bomb and two pounds of plastic explosive.

They slapped on lampblack. They loaded up their packs.

They walked. Néstor dragged the rake. Tire tracks and footprints disappeared.

They crossed the blacktop and hiked up to a parallel access road—about a third of a mile. The road-to-waveline sand strip was roughly two hundred yards wide.

Néstor said, "The State Police never patrol here."

Pete held up his infrareds. He spotted clumps 300 yards down the strip.

Boyd said, "Let's get close."

Pete stretched—his bulletproof vest fit tight. "There's nine or ten men just above the west sand. We should come up along the shoreline and hope the goddamn surf noise covers us."

Néstor crossed himself. Boyd filled his hands and his mouth—with two .45s and a Buck knife.

Pete felt earthquake tremors—9.999-fucking-9.

They walked down to the wet sand. They hunkered low and crab-crawled. Pete got this wild-ass notion: I'M THE ONLY ONE WHO KNOWS WHAT THIS MEANS.

Boyd walked point. The shapes took form. Smashing waves supplied audial cover.

The shapes were sleeping men. One insomniac was sitting up—check that glowing cigarette tip.

They got close.

They got closer.

They got very very close.

Pete heard snores. A man moaned in Spanish.

They charged.

Boyd shot the cigarette man. Muzzle flash lit a line of sleeping bags.

Pete fired. Néstor fired. Silencer thuds overlapped.

They had good light now—powder glare off four weapons.

Goose down exploded. Screams kicked in loud and faded into tight little gurgles.

Néstor brought a flashlight in close. Pete saw nine U.S. Army bags, shredded and blood soaked.

Boyd popped in fresh clips and shot the men point-blank in the face. Blood hit Néstor's flashlight and shaded the beam light red.

Pete heaved for breath. Bloody feathers blew into his mouth.

Néstor kept the light steady. Boyd knelt down and slit throats. He went in deep and low—windpipes and spinal cords snapped.

Néstor dragged the bodies out.

Pete turned the sleeping bags over and stuffed them with sand.

Boyd patted them into shape. It was good simulation—the boat men would see dozing men.

Néstor dragged the bodies down to a tide pool. Boyd brought the chainsaw.

Pete yank-started it. Boyd spread the stiffs out for cutting.

The moon passed by low. Néstor supplied extra light.

Pete sawed from a crouch. The teeth caught on a leg bone straight off.

Néstor pulled the man's foot taut. The teeth whirred through easy.

Pete sawed through a string of arms. The saw kept bucking into the sand. Skin and gristle pop-pop-popped in his face.

Pete quartered the men. Boyd severed their heads with his Buck knife. One swipe and one tug at the hair did the job.

Nobody talked.

Pete kept sawing. His arms ached. Bone fragments made the belt-motor skip.

His hands slipped. The teeth jumped and raked a dead man's stomach.

Pete smelled bile. He dropped the saw and puked himself dry.

Boyd took over. Néstor fed body parts to the tide pool. Sharks thrashed in to eat.

Pete walked down to the surf line. His hands shook—lighting a cigarette took forever.

The smoke felt good. The smoke killed the bad smells. DON'T THEY KNOW WHAT THIS MEANS—

The sawing stopped. Dead silence underscored his own crazy heartbeat.

Pete walked back to the tide pool. Sharks flailed and leaped halfway out of the water.

Néstor loaded the machine guns. Boyd twitched and fidgeted—high-pitched by Boyd cool-cat standards.

They crouched behind a shoal bank. Nobody talked. Pete got Barb on the brain wicked good.

Dawn hit just past 5:30. The beach looked plain peaceful. The blood by the sleeping bags looked like plain old wave seepage.

Néstor kept his binoculars up. He got a sighting at 6:12 a.m.

"I see the boat. It's about two hundred yards away."

Boyd coughed and spat. "Delsol said six men would be aboard. We want most of them off before we fire."

Pete heard motor hum. "It's getting close. Néstor, you get down there."

Néstor ran over and crouched by the sleeping bags. The hum built to a roar. A speedboat bucked waves and fishtailed up on shore.

It was a rat-trap double outboard, with no lower compartment.

Néstor waved. Néstor yelled, *"Bienvenidos! Viva Fidel!"*

Three men hopped off the boat. Three men stayed on. Pete signaled Kemper: ON for you/OFF for me.

Boyd threw a burst at the boat. The windshield exploded and blew the men back against the motors. Pete gunned his men down with one tight strafe.

Néstor walked up to them. He spit in their faces and capped them with shots in the mouth.

Pete ran up and vaulted onto the boat. Boyd circled around to the outboards and finished his three with single head pops.

The heroin was triple-wrapped and stuffed in duffel bags. The sheer weight was astonishing.

Néstor slapped the plastic explosive next to the outboards. The bomb clock was set for 7:15.

Pete off-loaded the dope.

Néstor tossed the sleeping bags and his three dead men on board.

Boyd scalped them. Néstor said, "This is for Playa Girón."

Pete rope-tied the wheel to the helm bracings and turned the boat around. The compass read south-southeast. The boat would stay on course—barring gale winds and tidal waves.

Boyd hit the motors. Both blades caught on his first pull. They jumped off the sides and watched the boat skid off.

It would explode twenty miles out to sea.

Pete shivered. Boyd tucked the scalps into his pack. Orange Beach looked absolutely pristine.

Santo Junior would call. He'd say, Delsol fucked me on a deal. He'd say, Pete, you find that cocksucker.

Santo would omit details. He wouldn't say the deal was Commie-linked and a direct betrayal of the Cadre.

Pete waited for the call at Tiger Kab. He took over the switchboard—Delsol never showed up for work.

Cab calls were backlogged. Drivers kept saying, Where's Wilfredo?

He's at a hideout pad. Néstor's guarding him. There's a pound of Big "H" in plain sight.

Boyd drove the rest of the dope to Mississippi. Boyd was stretched a wee bit thin, like he crossed some line with killing.

Pete felt the real line. DON'T YOU KNOW WHO WE FUCKED?

They'd watchdogged Delsol for two weeks running. He didn't betray them. The dope rendezvous would have been canceled if he did.

He's at his fake hideout. He's an instant junkie—Néstor shot tracks up his arms. He's zorched on horse—waiting for this goddamn phone call.

It was 4:30 p.m. They split Orange Beach nine and a half hours ago.

Cab calls came in. The phones rang every few seconds. They had pickups backlogged and twelve cabs out—Pete felt like screaming or putting a gun to his head.

Teo Paez cupped his desk phone. "Line two, Pete. It's Mr. Santo."

Pete picked up casual slow. "Hi, Boss."

Santo said the words. Santo came through right on cue.

"Wilfredo Delsol fucked me. He's hiding out, and I want you to find him."

"What did he do?"

"Don't ask questions. Just find him and do it right now."

Néstor let him in. He'd turned the living room into an instant junkie pigsty.

Dig the syringe in plain view. Dig the candy bars mashed into the carpet. Dig that white powder residue on every flat cutting surface.

Dig Wilfredo Olmos Delsol: dope-swacked on a plush-velour couch.

Pete shot him in the head. Néstor chopped off three of his fingers and dropped them in an ashtray.

It was 5:20. Santo wouldn't buy a one-hour search-and-find. They had time to reinforce the lie.

Néstor split—Boyd had work for him back in Mississippi. Pete tamped down his nerves with deep breaths and a dozen cigarettes.

He visualized it. He got the details straight in his head. He put his gloves on and did it.

He dumped the icebox.

He slashed the couch down to the springs.

He ripped the living-room walls out in a mock dope-search frenzy.

He burned cooking spoons.

He formed heroin into snort lines on a glass-topped coffee table.

He found a discarded lipstick and smeared it on some filter-tip butts.

He slashed Delsol with a kitchen knife. He scorched his balls with a wood-burning tool he found in the bedroom.

He dipped his hands in Delsol's blood and wrote "Traitor" on the living-room wall.

It was 8:40 p.m.

Pete ran down to a pay phone. Real live fear juked his performance.

Delsol's dead—tortured—I got a tip on his hideout—he was strung-out—dope everywhere—somebody trashed the place—I think he was on a toot with some whores—Santo, tell me, what the fuck is this all about?

80

Littell made business calls. Mr. Hoover gave him a tap scrambler to insure that his calls stayed private.

He called Jimmy Hoffa at a pay phone. Jimmy was profoundly tap-phobic.

They discussed the Test Fleet taxi fraud case. Jimmy said, Let's bribe some jurors.

Littell said he'd send him a jury list. He told Hoffa to have front men make the bribe offers.

Jimmy said, What's shaking with the shakedown?

Littell reported, ALL SYSTEMS GO. Baby Jimmy said, Let's squeeze Jack now!!!

Littell said, Be patient. We'll squeeze him at the optimum time.

Jimmy threw a goodbye fit. Littell called Carlos Marcello in New Orleans.

They discussed his deportation case. Littell stressed the need for tactical delays.

"You beat the Federal government by frustrating them. You exhaust them and make them rotate attorneys on and off your case. You try their patience and resources, and stall the hell out of them."

Carlos got the point. Carlos asked a truly silly goodbye question.

"Can I get a tax deduction on my Cuban bag donations?"

Littell said, "Regretfully, no."

Carlos signed off. Littell called Pete in Miami.

He picked up on the first ring. "This is Bondurant."

"It's me, Pete."

"Yeah, Ward. I'm listening."

"Is something wrong? You sound agitated."

"Nothing's wrong. Is something wrong with our deal?"

"Nothing's wrong. I've been thinking of Lenny, though, and I keep thinking he's too close to Sam for my liking."

"You think he'd spill to Sam?"

"Not exactly. What I'm thinking is—"

Pete cut him off. "Don't tell me what you're thinking. You're running this show, so just tell me what you want."

Littell said, "Call Turentine. Have him fly out to L.A. and tap Lenny's phone as an added precaution. Barb's out there, too. She's appearing at a place in Hollywood called the Rabbit's Foot Club. Have Freddy check on her and see how she's holding up."

Pete said, "This sounds good to me. Besides, there's other things I don't want Sam to make Lenny do."

"What are you talking about?"

"Cuban stuff. You wouldn't be interested."

Littell checked his calendar. He saw writ-submission dates running straight into June.

"Call Freddy, Pete. Let's not sit on this."

"Maybe I'll meet him in L.A. I could use a change of scenery."

"Do it. And let me know when the tap's in."

"I will. See you, Ward."

Littell hung up. The scrambler blinked and broke off his line of thought.

Hoover accepted him now. Their courtly moments were over. Hoover reverted to his standard curt behavior.

Hoover expected him to beg.

Please reinstate Helen Agee in law school. Please let my leftist friend out of prison.

He'd never beg.

Pete was nervous. He had a hunch that Kemper Boyd forced Pete into things he couldn't control.

Boyd collected acolytes. Boyd felt at one with Cuban killers and poor Negroes. Kemper's gloss seduced Pete. The Cuban mess pushed them far beyond their ken.

Carlos said they cut a deal with Santo Trafficante. Their potential profit made Carlos laugh. He said Santo would never pay them that much money.

Carlos embraced the Cuban mess. Carlos said Sam and Santo wanted to cut their losses.

Net loss. Net gain. Profit potential.

He had the Fund books. He needed to clear a stretch of time and develop a strategy to exploit them.

Littell turned his chair around and looked out the window. Cherry blossoms brushed the glass—close enough to touch.

The phone rang. Littell tapped the speaker switch. "Yes?"

A man said, "This is Howard Hughes."

Littell almost giggled. Pete told these hilarious Dracula tales—

"This is Ward Littell, Mr. Hughes. And I'm very pleased to talk to you."

Hughes said, "You should be pleased. Mr. Hoover has shared your impeccable credentials with me, and I intend to offer you $200,000 a year for the privilege of entering my employ. I will not require you to move to Los Angeles, and we will communicate solely by letter and telephone. Your specific duties will be to handle the writ work in my painfully protracted TWA divestment suit, and to help me purchase Las Vegas hotel-casinos with the profits I expect to accrue when I finally divest TWA. Your Italian connections will prove invaluable in this regard, and I will expect you to ingratiate yourself with the Nevada State Legislature and help me devise a policy to insure that my hotels remain Negro- and germ-free—"

Littell listened.

Hughes continued.

Littell didn't even try to respond.

81

(Los Angeles, 5/10/62)

Pete held the flashlight. Freddy replaced the dial housing. The work went down bite-your-nails nervous and slow.

Freddy fucked with some loose wires. "I hate Pacific Bell phones. I hate night jobs and working in the dark. I hate bedroom extensions, because the goddamn cords get tangled up behind the goddamn bed."

"Don't complain, just do it."

"My screwdriver keeps jamming. And are you *sure* Littell wants us to tap *both* extensions?"

Pete said, "*Just do it.* Two extensions and a pickup box outside. We'll stash it in those shrubs by the driveway. If you quit complaining, we can be out of here in twenty minutes."

Freddy gouged his thumb. "Fuck. I hate Pacific Bell phones. And Lenny don't have to use his home phones to rat us. He can rat us in person or rat us from a pay phone."

Pete gripped down on the flashlight. The beam wiggled and jumped.

"You fucking stop complaining, or I'll shove this fucking thing up your ass."

Freddy flinched and bumped a shelf. A *Hush-Hush* clipping file went flying.

"All right, all right. You been jumpy since you got off the airplane, so I'll only say it once. *Pacific Bell phones are the shits.* When you tap their lines, half the time the incoming callers can hear clicks. It's fucking unavoidable. And who's going to monitor the pickup box?"

Pete rubbed his eyes. He was nursing an on-and-off migraine since the night he killed Wilfredo Delsol.

"Littell can get some Feds to watch the box. We only need to check it every few days."

Freddy bent a lamp over the phone. "Go watch the door. I can't work with you standing over me."

Pete walked into the living room. His headache popped him right between the eyes.

He popped two aspirin. He washed them down with Lenny's cognac, straight from the bottle.

The stuff went down smooth. Pete knocked back a short refill.

His headache de-torqued. The veins above his eyes stopped pulsing.

Santo bought the charade so far. Santo never said *how* Delsol fucked him.

Santo said Sam G. got fucked, too. He didn't mention hijacked dope or fifteen dead men. He didn't say some big Outfit guys cozied up to Fidel Castro.

He said he had to cut the Cadre loose.

"Just for now, Pete. I've heard there's Federal pressure coming down. I want to extricate out of narcotics for a while."

The man just imported two hundred pounds of Big "H." The man was talking up extrication with a straight face.

Santo showed him a police report. The Miami fuzz bought the charade. They considered it one grisly dope killing—with assumed Cuban exile perpetrators.

Boyd and Néstor went back to Mississippi. The dope was stashed in forty safe-deposit boxes.

They resumed their Whack Castro training. They didn't care that the Outfit dug Fidel now. They didn't seem to know that there were men who could make them stop.

Their fear wasn't screwed on tight.

His was.

They didn't know you don't fuck with the Outfit.

He did.

He always sucked up to men with REAL power. He never broke the rules they set. He had to do what he did—but he didn't know WHY.

Santo swore vengeance. Santo said he'd find the dope thieves— whatever it cost, whatever it took.

Boyd thought they could sell the dope. Boyd was wrong. Boyd said *he'd* snitch the Mob-Agency links. Boyd said he could level out Bobby's rage.

He wouldn't do it. He couldn't do it. He'd never risk losing stature with the Kennedys.

Pete took another drink. His three shots killed a third of the bottle. Freddy lugged his tools out. "Let's go. I'll drive you back to your hotel."

"You go. I want to take a walk."

"Where to?"

"I don't know."

The Rabbit's Foot Club was a hotbox—four walls trapping smoke and stale air. Underaged Twisters ruled the dance floor—a big liquor-law infraction.

Joey and the boys played half on-the-nod. Barb was singing some dippy wah-wah tune. A single sad-ass hooker sat at the bar.

Barb spotted him. She smiled and fumbled some lyrics.

The only half-private booth in the room was occupied. Two Marines and two high-school girls—ripe for eviction.

Pete told them to shove off. They caught his size and did it. The girls left their fruity rum drinks on the table.

Pete sat down and sipped at them. His headache leveled off a bit more. Barb closed with a weak "Twilight Time" cover.

A few Twisters clapped. The combo dispersed backstage. Barb walked straight over and joined him.

Pete slid close to her. Barb said, "I'm surprised. Ward said you were in Miami."

"I thought I'd come out and see how things were going."

"You mean you thought you'd check up on me?"

Pete shook his head. "Everybody thinks you're solid. Freddy Turentine and I came out to check on Lenny."

Barb said, "Lenny's in New York. He's visiting a friend."

"A woman named Laura Hughes?"

"I think so. Some rich woman with a place on Fifth Avenue."

Pete toyed with his lighter. "Laura Hughes is Jack Kennedy's half-sister. She used to be engaged to that man Kemper Boyd that Jack told you about. Boyd was Ward Littell's FBI mentor. My old girlfriend Gail Hendee slept with Jack on his honeymoon. Lenny gave Jack speech lessons back in '46."

Barb took one of Pete's cigarettes. "You're saying this is all too cozy for words."

Pete gave her a light. "I don't know what I'm saying."

Barb tossed her hair back. "Did Gail Hendee work gigs with you?"

"Yes."

"Divorce gigs?"

"That's right."

"Was she as good as me?"

"No."

"Were you jealous that she slept with Jack Kennedy?"

"Not until Jack fucked me personally."

"What are you saying?"

"That I had a personal stake in the Bay of Pigs."

Barb smiled. Bar light twinkled off her hair.

"Are you jealous of Jack and me?"

"If I hadn't heard the tapes I might have been."

"What are you saying?"

"That you're not giving him anything real."

Barb laughed. "This nice Secret Service man always drives me back to where I'm staying. We stopped for pizza last time."

"You're saying that's real?"

"Only compared to an hour with Jack."

The jukebox fired up. Pete reached over and pulled the plug.

Barb said, "You blackmailed Lenny into this."

"He's used to getting blackmailed."

"You're nervous. You're tapping your knee against the table, and you don't even know you're doing it."

Pete stopped. His fucking foot started twitching to compensate.

Barb said, "Does our thing scare you?"

Pete jammed his knees down steady. "It's something else."

"Sometimes I think you'll kill me when all this is over."

"We don't kill women."

"You killed a woman once. Lenny told me."

Pete flinched. "And you cozied up to Joey so he'd buy hits on those guys who raped your sister."

She didn't flinch. She didn't move. She didn't show a fucking ounce of fear.

"I should have known you'd be the one to care."

"What are you saying?"

"That I wanted to see if Jack cared enough to do the checking that you did."

Pete shrugged. "Jack's a busy man."

"So are you."

"Does it bug you that Johnny Coates is still alive?"

"Only when I think of Margaret. Only when I think that she'll never let a man touch her."

Pete felt the floor dip.

Barb said, "Tell me what you want."

Pete said, "I want you."

They took a room at the Hollywood-Roosevelt. The Grauman's Chinese marquee blipped their window.

Pete tripped out of his pants. Barb pulled off her Twist gown. Loose rhinestones hit the floor—Pete gouged his feet on them.

Barb kicked his holster under the bed. Pete pulled the covers down. The stale perfume stuck to the sheets made him sneeze.

She raised her arms and unhooked her necklace. He saw the white-powdered stubble where she shaved.

He pinned her wrists to the wall. She saw what he wanted and let him taste her there.

The taste stung. She flexed her arms so he could have it all.

He felt her nipples. He smelled the sweat dripping off her shoulders.

She pushed her breasts up to him. The big veins and big freckles looked like nothing he'd ever seen. He kissed them and bit them and pushed her into the wall with his mouth.

Her breath went crazy. Her pulse tapped his lips. He slid his hands down her legs and put a finger inside her.

She pushed him off. She stumbled to the bed and lay down crossways. He spread her legs and knelt on the floor between them.

He touched her stomach and her arms and her feet. He felt a pulse every place he touched. She had big veins all over, pulsing out of red hair and freckles.

He jammed his hips into the mattress. The movement got him so hard it hurt.

He tasted her hair. He felt the folds underneath it. He made her pulse go crazy with little bites and nuzzles.

She buckled and thrashed off his mouth. She made crazy funny sounds.

He came without her even touching him. He shook and sobbed and kept tasting her.

She spasmed. She bit through the sheets. She lulled and spasmed, lulled and spasmed, lulled and spasmed. Her back arched and slammed the mattress into the box springs.

He didn't want it to end. He didn't want to lose the taste of her.

82

(Meridian, 5/12/62)

The air conditioner short-circuited and died. Kemper woke up sweaty and congested. He swallowed four Dexedrine. He started building lies immediately.

I didn't tell you about the links, because:

I didn't know myself. I didn't want Jack to get hurt. I only found out recently, and I thought it best to let sleeping dogs lie.

The Mob and the CIA?—it boggled my mind when I learned.

The lies felt weak. Bobby would investigate and trace his own links back to '59.

Bobby called last night. He said, "Meet me in Miami tomorrow. I want you to show me around JM/Wave."

Pete called from L.A. a few minutes later. He heard a woman humming a Twist tune in the background.

Pete said he just talked to Santo. Santo told him to hunt down the dope heisters.

"He said *find* them, Kemper. He said *don't kill them under any circumstances*. He didn't seem too concerned that I might find out the deal was Castro-financed."

Kemper told him to rig another forensic charade. Pete said, I'll fly to New Orleans and get started. Call me at the Olivier House Hotel or Guy Banister's office.

Kemper mixed a speedball and snorted it. The coke piggybacked the Dexedrine straight to his head.

He heard cadence counts outside. Laurent pushed the Cubans through calisthenics every morning.

Flash and Juan came up to his chest. Néstor could fit in his knapsack.

Néstor shanked a redneck yesterday. All the man did was nick his fender. Néstor had the post-heist screaming mimis.

Néstor fled. The cracker survived. Flash said Néstor stole a speedboat and headed for Cuba.

Néstor left a note. It said, Save my share of the stuff. I'll be back when Castro's dead.

Kemper showered and shaved. His little pick-me-up had the razor jumping.

Lies wouldn't come.

Bobby wore dark glasses and a hat. Kemper convinced him to tour JM/Wave incognito.

The AG with shades and a stingy-brim fedora. The AG as Rat Pack reject.

They strolled the facility. Bobby's getup inspired odd looks. Contract men walked by and waved hello.

Lies wouldn't come.

They toured at a leisurely pace. Bobby kept his famous voice to a whisper. A few Cubans recognized him and played along with the ruse.

Kemper showcased the Propaganda Section. A case officer rattled off statistics. Nobody said, Jack Kennedy is a vacillating sob sister.

Nobody dropped Mob names. Nobody dropped hints that they knew Kemper Boyd before the Bay of Pigs invasion.

Bobby liked the air recon plans. The communications room impressed him.

Lies wouldn't come. Details wouldn't mesh with any degree of verisimilitude.

They toured the Map Section. Chuck Rogers walked up, hale-hearty. Kemper steered Bobby away from him.

Bobby used the men's room and stormed out in a huff. Somebody scrawled anti-Kennedy remarks above the urinals.

They walked over to the Miami U cafeteria. Bobby bought them coffee and sweet rolls.

College kids carried trays past their table. Kemper forced himself not to fidget—the Dexedrine was surging especially strong.

Bobby cleared his throat. "Say what you've been thinking."

"What?"

"Say that coastal harassment and intelligence gathering aren't enough. Tell me we need to assassinate Fidel Castro for the three hundredth time and get it out of your system."

Kemper smiled. "We need to assassinate Fidel Castro. And I'll memorize your response, so you won't have to say it again."

Bobby said, "You know my response. I hate redundancy, and I hate this hat. How does Sinatra manage it?"

"He's Italian."

Bobby pointed to some coeds in short shorts. "Don't they have a dress code here?"

"The code is as little as possible."

"I should tell Jack. He could address the student body."

Kemper laughed. "I'm glad to see that you've become more accepting."

"More discerning, maybe."

"And more specifically disapproving?"

"Touché."

Kemper sipped coffee. "Who's the man been seeing?"

"Some fluff. And a Twist performer Lenny Sands introduced him to."

"Who isn't fluff?"

"Let's say she's mentally overqualified for some cheap dance craze."

"You've met her?"

Bobby nodded. "Lenny brought her to Peter Lawford's house in Los Angeles. I got the impression that she thinks a few steps ahead of most people, and Jack always calls me from the Carlyle to say how smart she is, which is not what Jack usually comments on in a woman."

Lenny, the Twist, L.A.—a puzzling little triad.

"What's her name?"

"Barb Jahelka. Jack was on the phone with her this morning. He said he called her at 5:00 a.m. L.A. time, and she still managed to come off smart and funny."

Pete called from L.A. last night. A woman was humming "Let's Twist Again."

"What is it about her that you disapprove of?"

"Probably just the fact that she doesn't behave like most of Jack's quickies."

Pete was a shakedown man. Lenny was an L.A. show-biz reptile.

"Do you think she's dangerous in some way?"

"Not exactly. I'm just suspicious because I'm the attorney general of the United States, and suspiciousness goes with the job. Why do you care? We've given this woman two minutes more than she deserves."

Kemper crumpled his coffee cup. "I was just steering talk away from Fidel."

Bobby laughed. "Good. And no, you and our exile friends cannot assassinate him."

Kemper stood up. "Do you want to look around some more?"

"No. I've got a car picking me up. Do you want a lift to the airport?"

"No. I have to make some phone calls."

Bobby took off his shades. A coed recognized him and squealed.

Kemper commandeered a vacant JM/Wave office. The switchboard put him through to LAPD R&I direct.

A man picked up. "Records and Information. Officer Graham."

"Dennis Payne, please. Tell him it's Kemper Boyd, long distance."

"Hold on, please."

Kemper scribbled up a scratch pad. Payne came on the line posthaste.

"Mr. Boyd, how are you?"

"I'm fine, Sergeant. You?"

"Fair to middling. And I'll bet you have a request to make."

"I do. I need you to check for a rap sheet on a white female named Barbara Jahelka, probable spelling J-A-H-E-L-K-A. She's probably twenty-two to thirty-two, and I think she lives in Los Angeles. I also need you to check for an unlisted number. The name is either Lenny Sands or Leonard J. Seidelwitz, and it's probably a West Hollywood listing."

Payne said, "I copy. You hold, okay? This might take a few minutes."

Kemper held. His pick-me-up was inducing mild palpitations.

Pete didn't state his L.A. business. Lenny was extortable and bribable.

Payne came back on the line. "Mr. Boyd? We've got two positives."

Kemper grabbed a pen. "Keep going."

"The Sands number is OL5-3980, and I got a felony marijuana possession on the girl. She's the only Barbara Jahelka in our files, and her DOB matches up to what you told me."

"Disposition?"

"She was arrested in July '57. She did six months and topped out two years of summary probation."

It was inconclusive information.

"Would you check for something more recent? FI cards or arrests that didn't go to arraignment?"

Payne said, "Will do. I'll check with the Sheriff's and our other local municipals, too. If the girl's been in trouble since '57, we'll know."

"Thanks, Sergeant. I appreciate it."

"Give me an hour, Mr. Boyd. I should have something or nothing by then."

Kemper disconnected. The switchboard patched him in to Lenny's L.A. number.

It rang three times. Kemper heard faint tap clicks and hung up.

Pete was a shakedown man. Pete was a bug/tap man. Pete's bug/tap partner was the celebrated Fred Turentine.

Freddy's brother owned a TV repair shop in L.A. Freddy worked there between wire jobs.

Kemper called Los Angeles information. An operator gave him the number. He fed it to the JM/Wave switchboard and told the girl to put him through.

The line hissed and crackled. A man picked up on the first ring. "Turentine's TV. Good morning."

Kemper faked a lowlife growl. "Is Freddy there? This is Ed. I'm friends with Freddy and Pete Bondurant."

The man coughed. "Freddy's in New York. He was here a few days ago, but he went back."

"Shit. I need to send him something. Did he leave an address?"

"Yeah, he did. Wait . . . let's see . . . yeah, it's 94 East 76th Street, New York City. The number's MU6-0197."

Kemper said, "Thanks. I appreciate it."

The man coughed. "Tell Freddy hi. Tell him his big brother says to stay out of trouble."

Kemper hung up. The office tilted in and out of focus.

Turentine was lodged near 76th and Madison. The Carlyle Hotel was on the northeast corner.

Kemper dialed the switchboard and gave the girl Lenny's number one more time.

She reconnected him. He heard three rings and three tiny tap clicks.

A woman answered. "Mr. Sands' residence."

"Is this Mr. Sands' service?"

"Yes, sir. And Mr. Sands can be reached in New York City. The number is MU6-2433."

Laura's number.

Kemper disconnected and redialed the switchboard. The girl said, "Yes, Mr. Boyd."

"Get me New York City, please. The number is MU6-0197."

"Please hang up, sir. All my circuits are busy, but I'll put your call through in a second."

Kemper leaned on the cutoff button. The pieces fit— circumstantially, instinctively—

The phone rang. He jerked the receiver up.

"Yes?"

"What do you mean, 'Yes?'? The operator placed *your* call to *me*."

Kemper wiped a line of sweat off his forehead. "That's right, she did. Is this Fred Turentine?"

"That's right."

"This is Kemper Boyd. I work with Pete Bondurant."

Silence stretched a solid beat too long.

"So you're looking for Pete?"

"That's right."

"Well . . . Pete's in New Orleans."

"That's right. I forgot."

"Well . . . why'd you think he'd be here?"

"It was just a hunch."

"Hunch, shit. Pete said he wasn't giving out this number."

"Your brother gave it to me."

"Well . . . shit . . . he wasn't supposed—"

"Thanks, Fred. I'll call Pete in New Orleans."

The line went dead. Turentine hung up dead finessed and dead scared.

Kemper watched the second hand circle his watch. His shirt sleeves were soaked clear through.

Pete would do it. Pete wouldn't do it. Pete was his longtime partner, which constituted proof of—

Nothing.

Business was business. Jack got between them. Call it the Triangle Twist: Jack, Pete and Barb what's-her-name.

Kemper dialed the switchboard. The operator redialed the LAPD.

Payne answered. "Records and Information."

"It's Kemper Boyd, Sergeant."

Payne laughed. "And an hour to the second."

"Did you find out anything else?"

"Yeah, I did. Beverly Hills PD arrested the Jahelka girl for extortion in August 1960."

Jesus God—

"Details?"

"The girl and her ex-husband tried to shake down Rock Hudson with some sex pictures."

"Of Hudson and the girl?"

"That's correct. They demanded some money, but Hudson went to the police. The girl and her ex were arrested, but Hudson retracted the charges."

Kemper said, "It stinks."

Payne said, "To high heaven. A friend of mine on the BHPD said the whole thing was some sort of ploy to establish Hudson as a pussy hound, when he's really some kind of homo. He heard a rumor that *Hush-Hush* was behind the whole thing."

Kemper put the phone down. His little palpitations almost cut his breath off.

LENNY—

He caught a 1:45 connector to La Guardia. He popped four Dexedrine and chased them with two in-flight martinis.

The flight took three and a half hours. Kemper shredded cocktail napkins and checked his watch every few minutes.

They landed on time. Kemper caught a cab outside the terminal. He told the driver to cruise by the Carlyle and drop him at 64th and Fifth.

Rush-hour traffic crawled. The Carlyle run ate up an hour.

94 East 76th Street was fifty yards from the hotel. It was an ideal apartment/listening-post location.

The cabbie swung south and dropped him outside Laura's building. The doorman was busy with a tenant.

Kemper ran into the lobby. An old lady held the elevator for him.

He hit "12." The old lady backed away. He saw his gun in his hand and tried to remember unholstering it.

He tucked it in his waistband. The old lady hid behind a huge handbag. The ride up took forever.

The door opened. Laura had redecorated the foyer—a complete French Provincial makeover.

Kemper walked through it. The elevator zoomed up behind him. He heard laughter on the terrace.

He ran toward the sound. Throw rugs snagged under his feet. He took the last hallway at a sprint and knocked over two lamps and an end table.

They were standing. They were holding drinks and cigarettes. They looked like they weren't quite breathing.

Laura, Lenny and Claire.

They looked funny. They looked like they didn't quite know him.

He saw his gun out. He saw the trigger at half-pull.

He said something about shaking down Jack Kennedy.

Claire said "Dad?" like she wasn't quite sure.

He aimed at Lenny.

Claire said, "Dad, please."

Laura dropped her cigarette. Lenny flicked his cigarette at him and smiled.

The tip burned his face. Ashes singed his suitcoat. He steadied his aim and pulled the trigger.

The gun jammed.

Lenny smiled.

Laura screamed.

Claire's scream made him turn tail and run.

83

(New Orleans, 5/12/62)

Bullshit flowed bilateral. Banister's office was submerged in right-wing rebop.

Guy said the Klan bombed some churches. Pete said Heshie Ryskind had cancer.

Boyd's Clip Castro Team was all-time elite. Dougie Frank Lockhart was one elite gun runner.

Pete said Wilfredo Delsol fucked Santo Junior on a dope deal. The fucker got fucked backed by fucker or fuckers unknown.

Banister sipped bourbon. Pete goosed the charade along. Say, Guy, what have *you* heard about this?

Guy said he heard bubkes. No shit, Sherlock—this line of talk is all shuck and jive.

Pete sprawled in a chair and played with a tall Jack Daniel's. He took little medicinal sips for migraine relief.

New Orleans was hot. The office sucked in heat. Guy sat behind his desk and peeled sweat off his forehead with a switchblade.

Pete kept drifting back to Barb. He couldn't hold a non-Barb line of thought for more than six seconds.

The phone rang. Banister dug through desk debris and caught it.

"Yeah? ... Yeah, he's here. Hold on a second."

Pete stood up and snagged the phone off the desk. "Who's this?"

"It's Fred. And don't you fucking lose your temper for what I'm gonna tell you."

"You just calm down, then."

"You can't calm down when you got a fucking concussion. You can't calm down—"

Pete walked the phone to the far end of the office. The cord stretched taut.

"Calm down, Freddy. Just tell me what happened."

Freddy caught his breath. "Okay. Kemper Boyd called the post this morning. He said he was looking for you, but I knew he was lying. Now, he came by—in person—an hour ago. He knocked on the door looking like a crazy man. I didn't let him in, and I saw him practically knock down an old lady and get into this cab she was getting out of."

The phone cord almost snapped. Pete stepped back and cut it some slack.

"And that's it?"

"Fuck no!"

"Freddy, what are you say—"

"I'm saying Lenny Sands came by a few minutes later. I let him in because I figured he knew what Boyd was up to. He brained me with a chair and sacked the place. He stole all the tapes and written transcripts and took off. I woke up after, shit—I don't know, half an hour. I went by the Carlyle and saw all these police cars out front. Pete, Pete, Pete—"

His legs dipped. The wall caught him.

"Pete, it was Lenny. He kicked the door in and trashed the Kennedy suite. He pulled out the microphones, and fucking escaped out a fire door. Pete, Pete, Pete—

"Pete, we're fucked—

"Pete, it had to be Lenny—

"Pete, I wiped down the post and moved out all my equipment and—"

The connection died—Pete twitched and jerked the cord out of the wall.

Boyd knew he was in New Orleans. Boyd would catch the first available flight down.

The gig was burned. Boyd and Lenny collided and fucked things up somehow.

The Feds knew by now. The Secret Service knew. Boyd couldn't go to Bobby to explain—his Mob ties compromised him.

Boyd would come here. Boyd knew he was staying at the hotel across the street.

Pete sipped bourbon and played every Twist song on the jukebox. A waitress swooped by with regular refills.

A cab would pull up. Boyd would get out. He'd intimidate the desk clerk and gain entrance to room 614.

Boyd would find a note. He'd obey the instructions. He'd carry the tape recorder over here to his booth at Ray Becker's Tropics.

Pete watched the door. Every Twist tune brought Barb back that much stronger.

He called her in L.A. two hours ago. He told her the gig was blown. He told her to drive down to Ensenada and hole up at the Playa Rosada.

She said she'd do it. She said, "*We're* still on, aren't we?"

He said, "Yes."

The bar was hot. New Orleans held the patent on heat. Thunderstorms hit and burned themselves out before you could blink.

Boyd walked in. Pete screwed a silencer to his magnum and placed it on the seat next to him.

Boyd was carrying the tape recorder in a suitcase. He had a .45 automatic pressed to his leg.

He walked up. He sat down across from Pete and put the suitcase on the floor.

Pete pointed to it. "Take the machine out. It's running on batteries, and there's a tape looped in already, so all you have to do is turn it on."

Boyd shook his head. "Put the gun in your lap on the table."

Pete did it. Boyd said, "Now unload it."

Pete did it. Boyd popped the clip out of his piece and wrapped both guns in the tablecloth.

He looked soiled and haggard. The ungroomed Kemper Boyd—a true first.

Pete slipped a .38 snub-nose out of his waistband. "It's compartmentalized, Kemper. It's got nothing to do with our other gigs."

"I don't care."

"You will when you play that tape."

They had a long row of booths to themselves. If it went bad, he could kill him and duck out the back door.

"You crossed the line, Pete. You knew the line was there, and you crossed it."

Pete shrugged. "We didn't hurt Jack, and Bobby's too smart to bring in the law. We can walk out of here and get back to business."

"And trust each other?"

"I don't see why not. Jack's the only thing that ever got between us."

"Do you honestly think it's that simple?"

"I think you can make it that way."

Boyd unlatched the suitcase. Pete laid the machine on the table and hit Play.

His tape splice rolled. Pete turned the volume up to cover the jukebox.

Jack Kennedy said, "Kemper Boyd's probably the closest thing, but he makes me a tad uncomfortable."

Barb Jahelka said, "Who's Kemper Boyd?"

Jack: "He's a Justice Department lawyer."

Jack: "His one great regret is that he's not a Kennedy."

Jack: "He just went to Yale Law School, latched onto me, and—"

Boyd was shaking. Boyd was ungroomed working on unhinged.

Jack: "He threw over the woman he was engaged to to curry favor with me."

Jack: "He's living out some unsavory fantasy—"

Boyd hit the tape rig barefisted. The spools bent and cracked and shattered.

Pete let him beat his hands bloody.

*

84

(Meridian, 5/13/62)

The plane fishtailed in and skidded to a halt. Kemper braced himself against the seat in front of him.

His head throbbed. His hands throbbed. He hadn't slept in thirty-odd hours.

The co-pilot cut the engines and cranked the passenger door open. Sunshine and steamy air blasted in.

Kemper deplaned and walked to his car. His finger wraps seeped blood.

Pete talked him out of reprisals. Pete said Ward Littell built the shakedown from the ground up.

He drove to the motel. The road blurred behind thirty-odd hours of liquor and Dexedrine.

The lot was full. He double-parked beside Flash Elorde's Chevy.

The sun hit twice as hot as it should. Claire kept saying, "Dad, please."

He walked to his room. The door jerked open just as he touched it.

A man pulled him inside. A man kicked his legs out. A man threw him prone and cuffed him facedown on the floor.

A man said, "We found narcotics here."

A man said, "And illegal weapons."

A man said, "Lenny Sands killed himself in New York City last night. He rented a cheap hotel room, slashed his wrists and wrote 'I am a homosexual' in blood on the wall above the bed. The sink and toilet were filled with burned-up tape fragments obviously taken off a bug installed in the Kennedy family's suite at the Carlyle Hotel."

Kemper thrashed. A man stepped on his face and held him still.

A man said, "Sands was spotted burglarizing the suite earlier in the day. The NYPD located a listening-post setup a few doors down. It was print-wiped and cleaned out, and obviously rented under a phony name, but the people running it left a large quantity of blank tape behind."

A man said, "You ran the shakedown."

A man said, "We've got your Cubans and that French guy Guéry. They won't talk, but they're going down on weapons charges anyway."

A man said, "Enough."

The Man: Attorney General Robert F. Kennedy.

A man pulled him into a chair. A man uncuffed him and recuffed him to the post at the foot of the bed. The room was packed with Bobby's pet Feds—six or seven men in cheap summer suits.

The men walked out and shut the door behind them. Bobby sat on the edge of the bed.

"Goddamn you, Kemper. Goddamn you for what you tried to do to my brother."

Kemper coughed. His vision shimmied. He saw two beds and two Bobbys.

"I didn't do anything. I tried to break up the operation."

"I don't believe you. I don't believe that your outburst at Laura's apartment was anything but an admission of your guilt."

Kemper flinched. The cuffs gouged his wrists and drew blood.

"Believe what you like, you chaste little piece of dogshit. And tell your brother that nobody ever loved him more and got back less."

Bobby moved closer. "Your daughter Claire informed on you. She told me that you've been a CIA contract agent for over three years. She said the Agency specifically instructed you to disseminate anti-Castro propaganda to my brother. She said that Lenny Sands told her you were instrumental in suborning organized crime figures into participating in covert CIA activities. I've taken all this into consideration and concluded that some initial suspicions of mine were correct. I think Mr. Hoover sent you over to spy on my family, and I'm going to confront him on it the day my brother forces him to resign."

Kemper made fists. Dislocated bones splintered. Bobby got up inside spitting distance.

"I'm going to sever every Mafia-CIA tie. I'm going to prohibit organized crime participation in the Cuban project. I'm going to expel you from the Justice Department and the CIA, I'm going to have you disbarred as a lawyer, and I'm going to prosecute you and your Franco-Cuban friends on weapons possession and narcotics possession charges."

Kemper wet his lips and spoke with a mouthful of spittle.

"If you fuck with my men or try to prosecute me, I'll go public. I'll spill everything I know about your filthy family. I'll smear the Kennedy name with enough verifiable filth to put a taint on it forever."

Bobby slapped him.

Kemper spat in his face.

DOCUMENT INSERT: 5/14/62. Verbatim FBI telephone call transcript: "TAPED AT THE DIRECTOR'S REQUEST"/"DIRECTOR'S EYES ONLY." Speaking: Director J. Edgar Hoover, Ward J. Littell.

WJL: Good morning, Sir.

JEH: Good morning. And you needn't ask me if I've heard, because I daresay I know more of the story than you do.

WJL: Yes, Sir.

JEH: I hope Kemper has money saved. Disbarment can prove costly, and I doubt that a man of his tastes could live comfortably on an FBI pension.

WJL: I'm certain that Little Brother won't file criminal charges on him.

JEH: Of course he won't.

WJL: Kemper took the fall.

JEH: I will not comment on the attendant irony.

WJL: Yes, Sir.

JEH: Have you spoken to him?

WJL: No, Sir.

JEH: I'd be curious to know what he's doing. The notion of Kemper C. Boyd without police agency sanction is quite startling.

WJL: I think Mr. Marcello will find him work.

JEH: Oh? As a Mafia back scratcher?

WJL: As a Cuban provocateur, Sir. Mr. Marcello has remained committed to the Cause.

JEH: Then he's a fool. Fidel Castro is here to stay. My sources tell me that the Dark King will most likely seek to normalize relations with him.

WJL: The Dark King is an appeaser, Sir.

JEH: Don't try to butter me up. You may have undergone an apostasy regarding the brothers, but your political beliefs are still suspect.

WJL: Be that as it may, Sir, I'm still not giving up. I'm going to think of something else. I haven't given up on the King.

JEH: Bully for you. But please be advised that I do not wish to be informed of your plans.

WJL: Yes, Sir.

JEH: Has Miss Jahelka resumed her normal life?

WJL: She's going to, Sir. At the moment she's on a Mexican vacation with a French-Canadian friend of ours.

JEH: I hope they don't procreate. They would produce morally deficient offspring.

WJL: Yes, Sir.

JEH: Good day, Mr. Littell.

WJL: Good day, Sir.

DOCUMENT INSERTS: Consecutively dated FBI wiretap out-takes. Marked: "TOP SECRET/CONFIDENTIAL/DIRECTOR'S EYES ONLY" and "NO DISCLOSURE TO OUTSIDE JUSTICE DEPARTMENT PERSONNEL."

Chicago, 6/10/62. BL4-8869 (Celano's Tailor Shop) to AX8-9600 (home of John Rosselli) (THP File #902.5, Chicago Office). Speaking: John Rosselli, Sam "Mo," "Momo," "Mooney" Giancana (File #480.2). Conversation nine minutes in progress.

SG: So fucking Bobby found out on his own.

JR: Which frankly, did not surprise me.

SG: We were helping him out, Johnny. Sure, it was mostly cosmetic. But the basic fucking truth of the whole thing was that we were helping him and his brother out.

JR: We were good to them, Mo. We were nice. And they kept fucking us and fucking us and fucking us.

SG: Some sort of fucking shakedown pre-pre-pre—what's that word that means set up?

JR: Precipitated, Mo. That's the word you want.

SG: Right. Some cocksucking shakedown precipitated Bobby finding out. The word is Jimmy and Frenchman Pete were in on it. Somebody got careless, and Jewboy Lenny killed himself.

JR: You can't fault Jimmy and Pete for trying to fuck the Kennedys.

SG: No, you can't.

JR: And it turned out Lenny was a faggot. Can you believe that?

SG: Who would have believed it?

JR: He was Jewish, Mo. The Jewish race has a higher percentage of homos than regular white people.

SG: That's true. Heshie Ryskind's no queer, though. He's had like sixty thousand blow jobs.

JR: Heshie's sick, Mo. He's real sick.

SG: I wish the Kennedys caught his fucking disease. The Kennedys and Sinatra.

JR: Sinatra sold us a bill of goods. He said he had influence with the brothers.

SG: He's useless. The Haircut kicked his guinea ass off the White House guest list. Asking Frank to plead our case with the brothers is useless.

Non-applicable conversation follows.

Cleveland, 8/4/62. BR1-8771 (Sal's River Lounge) to BR4-0811 (Bartolo's Ristorante pay phone). Speaking: John Michael D'Allesio (THP File #180.4, Cleveland Office), Daniel "Donkey Dan" Versace (File #206.9, Chicago Office). Conversation sixteen minutes in progress.

DV: Rumors are just rumors. You got to consider the source and take it from there.

JMD: Danny, you like rumors?

DV: You know I do. You know I love a good rumor as much as the next guy, and I don't particularly care if it's true or not.

JMD: Danny, I got a hot rumor.

DV: So tell. Don't be a fucking cock tease.

JMD: The rumor is J. Edgar Hoover and Bobby Kennedy hate each other.

DV: That's your rumor?

JMD: There's more.

DV: I hope so. The Hoover-Bobby feud is stale bread.

JMD: The rumor is Bobby's racket squad guys are turning snitches. The rumor is Bobby won't let Hoover near his fucking prospects. Furthermore, I heard the fucking McClellan Committee's gearing up to go into session again. They're getting ready to fucking keester the Outfit again. Bobby's working on turning this major informant. When the committee sessions start, this guy's supposed to come on as the starring fucking attraction.

DV: I heard better rumors, Johnny.

JMD: Fuck you.

DV: I prefer sex-type rumors. Haven't you heard any good sex-type shit?

JMD: Fuck you.

Non-applicable conversation follows.

New Orleans, 10/10/62. KL4-0909 (Habana Bar pay phone) to CR8-8107 (Town & Country Motel pay phone). Note: Carlos

Marcello (no THP file extant) owns the <u>Town & Country</u>. Speaking: Leon NMI Broussard (THP File #88.6, New Orleans Office) and unidentified (assumed Cuban) man. Conversation twenty-one minutes in progress.

LB: So you shouldn't give up hope. All is not lost, my friend.

UM: It feels as if it is.

LB: That is simply not true. I know for a fact that Uncle Carlos is still very much a believer.

UM: He is alone, then. A few years ago many of his compatriots were just as generous as he has remained. It is troubling to see powerful friends abandoning the Cause.

LB: Like John F-for-fuckhead Kennedy.

UM: Yes. His betrayal is the worst example. He continues to prohibit a second invasion.

LB: So the fuckhead doesn't care. I'll tell you this, though, my friend. Uncle Carlos does.

UM: I hope you are right.

LB: I know I am. I have it on very good authority that Uncle Carlos is financing an operation that could blow the whole Cuban thing to bits.

UM: I hope you are right.

LB: He's bankrolling some men who want to hit Castro. Three Cuban guys and an ex-French paratrooper. The leader's an ex-FBI/CIA man. Uncle Carlos said he'd die himself just to make the hit.

UM: I hope this is true. You see, the Cause has become scattered. There are hundreds of exile groups now. Some are CIA-financed and some are not. I hate to say it, but many of the groups are filled with crackpots and undesirables. I think direct action is needed, and with so many factions working at cross-purposes, this will be hard to accomplish.

LB: The first thing somebody should accomplish is cutting the Kennedy brothers' balls off. The Outfit was very fucking generous to the Cause until Bobby Kennedy went nuts and cut off all our fucking ties.

UM: It is hard to be optimistic these days. It is hard not to feel impotent.

Non-applicable conversation follows.

Tampa, 10/16/62. OL4-9777 (home of <u>Robert "Fat Bob" Paolucci</u>) (THP file #19.3, Miami Office) to GL1-8041 (home of <u>Thomas Richard Scavone</u>) (File #80.0, Miami Office). Speaking:

Paolucci and Scavone. Conversation thirty-eight minutes in progress.

RP: I know you know most of the story.

TS: Well, you know how it is. You pick up bits and pieces here and there. What I know specific is that Mo and Santo ain't talked to their Castro contacts since the heist.

RP: It was some heist. Something like fifteen fucking deaths. Santo said the heist guys probably ran the boat out to sea and blew it up. Two hundred pounds, Tommy. Can you estimate the fucking re-sale value?

TS: Off the graph, Bobby. Off the fucking graph.

RP: And it's still out there.

TS: I was just thinking that.

RP: Two hundred pounds. And somebody's got it.

TS: I heard Santo won't give up.

RP: This is true. Pete the Frenchman clipped that Delsol guy, but he was just the tip of the iceberg. I heard Santo has got Pete out there looking around, you know, sort of informal. They both figure some crazy spic exiles were behind the heist, and Pete the Frog's out there looking for them.

TS: I've met some of them exiles.

RP: So have I. They're all fucking crazy.

TS: You know what I hate about them?

RP: What?

TS: That they think they're as white as Italians.

Non-applicable conversation follows.

New Orleans, 10/19/62. BR8-3408 (home of Leon NMI Broussard) (THP File #88.6, New Orleans Office) to Suite 1411 at the Adolphus Hotel in Dallas, Texas. (Hotel records indicate the suite was rented by Herschel Meyer Ryskind) (File #887.8, Dallas Office). Conversation three minutes in progress.

LB: You always had a thing for hotel suites, Hesh. A hotel suite and a blow job was always your idea of heaven.

HR: Don't say heaven, Leon. You're giving me a pain in the prostate.

LB: I get it. You're sick, so you don't want to think about the thereafter.

HR: It's the hereafter, Leon. And you're right. And I called you to schmooze because you've always got your nose in other people's troubles, and I figured you could dish some gossip

on some of the boys with worse trouble than me and cheer
me up.

LB: I'll try, Hesh. And Carlos says hi, by the way.

HR: Let's start with him. What kind of trouble has that crazy
dago hump gotten himself into now?

LB: I gotta say nothing recent. And I also gotta say the deportation thing is hanging over his head and making him crazy.

HR: Thank God he's got that lawyer.

LB: Yeah, Littell. The guy's working for Jimmy Hoffa, too. Uncle Carlos says he hates the Kennedys so much that he'd probably work for free.

HR: I heard he's a red tape kind of guy. He just delays and
delays and delays.

LB: You're absolutely right. Uncle Carlos said his INS case
probably won't go to trial until late next year. Littell's got these
Justice Department lawyers fucking exhausted.

HR: Carlos is optimistic, then?

LB: Absolutely. So's Jimmy, from what I've heard. The trouble with Jimmy's troubles is that he's got eighty-six-fucking-
thousand grand juries chasing him. My feeling is that sooner or
later, somebody gets a conviction. I don't care how good a lawyer
this Littell guy is.

HR: This makes me happy. Jimmy Hoffa's a guy with troubles
approximating my own. Can you imagine going to Leavenworth
and getting shtupped in the ass by some shvartze?

LB: That is not a pleasant prospect.

HR: Neither is cancer, you goyisher shitheel.

LB: We're pulling for you, Hesh. You're in our prayers.

HR: Fuck your prayers. And give me some gossip. You know
that's why I called.

LB: Well.

HR: Well, what? Leon, you owe me money. You know I'm
gonna die before I collect. Give an old dying man the comfort of
some satisfying gossip.

LB: Well, I heard rumors.

HR: Such as?

LB: Such as that lawyer Littell's working for Howard Hughes.
Hughes is supposed to want to buy all these Las Vegas hotels,
and I heard—off the record, Hesh, really—that Sam G's dying to
work some kind of an angle on the deal.

HR: Which Littell don't know about?

LB: That is correct.

HR: I love this fucking life of ours. It is never fucking boring.

LB: You are absolutely correct. Think of the tidbits you pick up in this loop of ours.

HR: I don't want to die, Leon. All this shit is too good to give up.

Non-applicable conversation follows.

Chicago, 11/19/62. BL4-8869 (Celano's Tailor Shop) to AX8-9600 (home of John Rosselli) (THP File #902.5, Chicago Office). Speaking: John Rosselli, Sam "Mo," "Momo," "Mooney" Giancana (File #480.2). Conversation two minutes in progress.

JR: Sinatra's worthless.

SG: He's less than worthless.

JR: The Kennedys won't even take his phone calls.

SG: Nobody hates those Irish cocksuckers more than I do.

JR: Unless it's Carlos and his lawyer. It's like Carlos knows that sooner or later he'll get deported again. It's like he sees himself back in El Salvador picking cactus thorns out of his ass.

SG: Carlos has his problems, I've got mine. Bobby's racket squad guys are crawling up my ass like the regular Feds never did. I would like to take a ball peen hammer and cave Bobby's fucking head in.

JR: And his brother's.

SG: Especially his brother's. That man is nothing but a traitor masquerading as a hero. He's nothing but a Commie-appeaser in wolf's clothing.

JR: He made Khruschev back down, Mo. I gotta give him that. Khruschev moved those goddamn missiles.

SG: That is horseshit. That is appeasement with a sugar coating. A CIA guy I know told me Kennedy cut a side deal with Khruschev. Okay, he moved the missiles. But my CIA guy told me Kennedy had to promise not to invade Cuba ever fucking again. Think of that, Johnny. Think of our casinos and wave bye-bye for fucking ever.

JR: Kennedy's supposed to talk to some Bay of Pigs survivors at the Orange Bowl in December. Think of the lies he'll tell them.

SG: Some Cuban patriot should pop him. Some Cuban patriot who don't mind dying.

JR: I heard Kemper Boyd's training some guys like that to pop Castro.

SG: Kemper Boyd's a faggot. He's got his eyes on the wrong target. Castro's just some taco eater with a good line of bullshit. Kennedy's worse for business than he ever was.

Non-applicable conversation follows.

DOCUMENT INSERT: 11/20/62. Des Moines Register subhead:

HOFFA DENIES BRIBERY ACCUSATIONS

DOCUMENT INSERT: 12/17/62. Cleveland Plain Dealer headline:

HOFFA ACQUITTED IN TEST FLEET CASE

DOCUMENT INSERT: 1/12/63. Los Angeles Times subhead:

HOFFA UNDER INVESTIGATION FOR TEST FLEET JURY
TAMPERING

DOCUMENT INSERT: 5/10/63. Dallas Morning News headline and subhead:

HOFFA INDICTED

TEAMSTER BOSS HIT WITH JURY TAMPERING CHARGES

DOCUMENT INSERT: 6/25/63. Chicago Sun-Times headline and subhead:

HOFFA UNDER SIEGE

TEAMSTER BOSS ARRAIGNED IN CHICAGO ON SEPARATE FRAUD
CHARGES

DOCUMENT INSERT: 7/29/63. FBI wiretap outtake. Marked: TOP SECRET/CONFIDENTIAL/DIRECTOR'S EYES ONLY and NO DISCLOSURE TO OUTSIDE JUSTICE DEPARTMENT PERSONNEL.

Chicago, 7/28/63. BL4-8869 (Celano's Tailor Shop) to AX8-9600 (home of John Rosselli) (THP File #902.5, Chicago Office). Speaking: John Rosselli, Sam "Mo," "Momo," "Mooney" Giancana (File #480.2). Conversation seventeen minutes in progress.

SG: I am woefully fucking tired of this.

JR: Sammy, I hear you.

SG: The FBI's got me under twenty-four-hour surveillance. Bobby went over Hoover's head to order it. I'm out on the fucking golf course and I see fucking G-men skulking in the rough and on the fairways, and for all I know, they got the fucking sand traps bugged.

JR: I hear you, Mo.

SG: I'm woefully tired of this. So's Jimmy and so's Carlos. So's every made guy I talk to.

JR: Jimmy's going down. I can see the writing on the wall. I also heard Bobby turned a major snitch. I don't know details, but—

SG: I do. His name's Joe Valachi. He was a button man for Vito Genovese. He was in Atlanta, something like ten to life for narcotics.

JR: I think I met him once.

SG: Everybody in the Life's met everybody else at least once.

JR: That's true.

SG: As I was saying before you interrupted me, Valachi was in Atlanta. He blew his cork and killed another prisoner, because he thought Vito sent him down to clip him. He was wrong, but Vito did put out a contract on him, because the guy he clipped was a good friend of Vito's.

JR: This Valachi is one prime stupe.

SG: He's a scared stupe, too. He begged to go into Federal custody, and Bobby beat Hoover to him. They cut a deal. Valachi gets lifetime protection for ratting the Outfit en fucking masse. The word is Bobby's going to put him in front of the newly fucking revived McClellan Committee, like in September or something.

JR: Oh, fuck. Mo, this is bad.

SG: It's worse than bad. It's probably the worst fucking thing that's ever happened to the Outfit. Valachi's been a made guy for forty years. Do you know what he knows?

JR: Oh, fuck.

SG: Quit saying, oh fuck, you stupid cocksucker.

Non-applicable conversation follows.

DOCUMENT INSERT: 9/10/63. Personal note: Ward J. Littell to Howard Hughes.

Dear Mr. Hughes,

Please consider this an official business request, and one tendered only as a last resort. I hope that my five months in your employ have convinced you that I would never make an out-of-channels request unless I deemed it absolutely vital to your interests.

I need $250,000. This money is to be used to circumvent official processes and guarantee Mr. J. Edgar Hoover's continued tenure as FBI Director.

I deem Mr. Hoover's continued directorship to be essential to our Las Vegas plans. Please advise me of your decision as soon as possible, and please keep this communique in the strictest confidence.

Respectfully,
Ward J. Littell

DOCUMENT INSERT: 9/12/63. Personal note: Howard Hughes to Ward J. Littell.

Dear Ward,

Your plan, however obliquely stated, impressed me as judicious. The sum you requested will be forthcoming. Please justify the expense with results at the earliest possible date.

Yours,
HH

Part V

CONTRACT

September–November 1963

DOCUMENT INSERT: 9/13/63. Justice Department memorandum: Attorney General Robert F. Kennedy to FBI Director J. Edgar Hoover.

Dear Mr. Hoover,

President Kennedy is seeking to establish a normalization of relations plan with Communist Cuba and has become alarmed at the extent of exile-perpetrated sabotage and harassment aimed at the Cuban coastline, specifically violent actions undertaken by non-CIA sponsored exile groups situated in Florida and along the Gulf Coast.

These non-sanctioned actions must be curtailed. The President wants this implemented immediately and has mandated it a top Justice Department-FBI priority. Florida and Gulf Coast-based agents are to begin raiding and seizing weapons at all exile camps not specifically CIA-funded or vetted by established foreign policy memorandums.

These raids must begin immediately. Please meet me in my office at 3:00 this afternoon to discuss particulars and review my list of initial target sites.

Yours,
Robert F. Kennedy

85

(Miami, 9/15/63)

The dispatch hut was boarded up. The orange-and-black wallpaper was stripped into souvenir swatches.

Adios, Tiger Kab.

The CIA divested their half-interest. Jimmy Hoffa dumped his half as a tax dodge. He told Pete to sell the cabs and make him some chump change.

Pete ran the parking-lot clearance sale. Buyer-incentive TV sets were perched on every tiger-striped hood.

Pete hooked them up to a portable generator. Two dozen screens blasted news: a spook church in Birmingham got bombed an hour ago.

Four pickaninnies got vaporized. Kemper Boyd, take note.

Browsers jammed the lot. Pete pocketed cash and signed over pink slips.

Goodbye, Tiger Kab. Thanks for the memories.

Agency cutbacks and phaseouts dictated the sale. JM/Wave slogged on, minus mucho personnel.

The Cadre was disbanded. Santo said he was getting out of narcotics—an all-time epic lie.

The formal order came down last December. Merry Xmas—your elite dope squadron is kaput.

Teo Paez was running whores in Pensacola. Fulo Machado was on the bum somewhere. Ramón Gutiérrez was anti-Castroizing outside New Orleans.

Chuck Rogers was phased off contract status. Néstor Chasco was dead or alive in Cuba.

Kemper Boyd was still running his Whack Castro squad.

Mississippi got too hot for him. Civil rights grief was escalating and polarizing the locals.

Boyd moved his squad to Sun Valley, Florida. They took over some abandoned prefab pads. That old Teamster resort finally saw tenants.

They set up a target range and a reconnaissance course. They stayed focused on the KILL FIDEL problem. They infiltrated Cuba nine times—white men Boyd and Guéry included.

They took a hundred Commie scalps. They never saw Néstor. They never got close to Castro.

The dope was still stashed in Mississippi. The "search" for the heist men was still in sporadic progress.

Pete kept chasing fake leads. The fear got bad sometimes. He had Santo and Sam *half*-convinced that the heist men split to Cuba.

Santo and Sam harbored lingering suspicions. They kept saying, Where's that guy Chasco?—he split the exile scene post-fucking-haste.

He kept chasing fake leads. He synced the chase to Barb's road schedule.

Langley sent him out gun running. His circuits supplied good lead chase cover.

The fear got bad sometimes. The headaches came back. He popped goofballs to insure instant dreamless sleep.

He panicked last March. He was stuck in Tuscaloosa, Alabama—with Barb's local gig stone flat canceled.

Thunderstorms flooded the roads and closed down the airport. He hit an exile-friendly bar and tamped his headache down with bourbon. Two scraggly-assed spics got shit-faced. They started talking heroin, too loud.

He pegged them as skin poppers with a dime-bag clientele. He saw a way to close the fear out once and for all.

He tailed them to a dope den. The place was Hophead Central: spics crapped out on mattresses, spics geezing up, spics scrounging dirty needles off the floor.

He killed them all. He burned his silencer down to the threads shooting junkies in cold blood. He rigged the scene to look like an all-spic dope massacre.

He called Santo with his fear choking him dry.

He said he walked in on a slaughter. He said a dying man confessed to the heist. He said, Read the Tuscaloosa papers—it's got to be big news tomorrow.

He flew to Barb's next gig. The snuffs never hit the papers or TV. Santo said, "Keep looking."

The junkies died on the nod. Chuck said Heshie Ryskind was dying—Big "H" had him phasing out on a painless little cloud.

Bobby Kennedy cleaned house last year. He initiated a shitload of non-painless phaseouts.

Contract guys got fired wholesale. Bobby sacked every contract man suspected of organized crime ties.

He neglected to fire Pete Bondurant.

Memo to Bobby the K.:

Please fire me. Please take me off the exile circuit. Please phase me off this horrible search-and-find mission.

It could happen. Santo might say, Take a rest. Without CIA ties, you're worthless.

Santo might say, Work for me. Santo might say, Look at Boyd—Carlos has kept him employed.

He could beg off. He could say, I don't hate Castro like I used to. He could say, I don't hate him like Kemper does—because I didn't take the fall that he did.

My daughter didn't betray me. The man I worshiped didn't ridicule me on tape. I didn't transfer my hate for that man to some loudmouthed spic with a beard.

Boyd's in this deep. I'm treading air. We're like Bobby and Jack that way.

Bobby says, Go, exiles, go. He means it. Jack refuses to green-light a second invasion.

Jack cut a side deal with Khrushchev. He's phasing out the Castro War in not-too-provocative fashion.

He wants to get re-elected. Langley thinks he'll scrap the war early in his second term.

Jack thinks Fidel is unbeatable. He's not alone. Even Santo and Sam G. cozied up to the fucker for a while.

Carlos said the dope heist queered their Commie fling. The Castro brothers, Sam and Santo were now permanently Splitsville.

Nobody got the dope. Everybody got fucked.

Browsers walked through the lot. An old guy kicked tires. Teenagers grooved on the spiffy tiger-stripe paint jobs.

Pete pulled a chair into the shade. Some Teamster clowns dispensed free beer and soft drinks. They sold four cars in five hours—not good, not bad.

Pete tried to doze. A headache started tapping.

Two plainclothesmen crossed the lot and beelined toward him. Half the crowd sniffed trouble and hotfooted it off down Flagler.

The TVs were stolen. The sale itself was probably illegal.

Pete stood up. The men boxed him in and flashed FBI ID.

The tall one said, "You're under arrest. This is a non-sanctioned Cuban-exile meeting place, and you're a known habitué."

Pete smiled. "This place is defunct. And I'm on CIA contract status."

The short Fed unhooked his handcuffs. "We're not unsympathetic. We don't like Communists any more than you do."

The tall man sighed. "This wasn't Mr. Hoover's idea. Let's just say he had to go along. It's a standard, across-the-board order, and I don't think you'll be in custody that long."

Pete stuck his hands out. The cuffs wouldn't fit around his wrists.

The rest of the browsers vanished. A kid boosted a TV set and high-tailed it.

Pete said, "I'll go peacefully."

The booking tank was triple-capacity packed. Pete shared floor space with a hundred pissed-off Cubans.

They were crammed into a thirty-by-thirty-foot stinkhole. No chairs, no benches—just four cement walls and a wraparound piss gutter.

The Cubans jabbered in English and Spanish. Dig the bilingual gist: Jack the Haircut sicced the Feds on the Cause.

Six campsites were raided yesterday. Weapons were seized. Cuban gunmen were arrested en masse.

It was some sort of first salvo. Jack was out to ram all non-CIA-sanctioned exiles.

He was CIA. *He* got popped anyway. The Feds jerry-rigged a plan and went off half-cocked.

Pete leaned against the wall and shut his eyes. Barb twisted by.

Every time with her was good. Every time was different. Every place was different—two people always moving hooking up in odd locations.

Bobby never harassed her. Barb figured a fix was in. She said she didn't miss Two-Minute Jack.

She gave her sister her shakedown fee. Margaret Lynn Lindscott now owned a Bob's Big Boy franchise.

They met in Seattle, Pittsburgh and Tampa. They met in L.A., Frisco and Portland.

He ran guns. She fronted a cheap dance show. He chashed nonexistent dope thief/killers.

She said the Twist was burning out. He said his Cuban hard-on was, too.

She said, Your fear gets to me. He said, I'll try to tamp it down. She said, Don't—it makes you less frightening.

He said he did something very stupid. He said he didn't know why he did it.

She said, You wanted to force yourself out of the Life.

He couldn't argue.

Barb had a busy autumn pending. She had long club stints in Des Moines and Sioux City and a big Texas run through Thanksgiving.

She added lunch shows to her performance slate. The Twist was phasing out—Joey wanted to wring it dry.

He met Margaret in Milwaukee. She was meek and scared of just about everything.

He offered to kill the cop rape-o. Barb said no.

He said, Why? Barb said, You don't *really* want to.

He couldn't argue.

He had Barb. Boyd had hatred: Jack K. and the Beard as one fucked-up, pervasive thing. Littell had powerful friends.

Like Hoover. Like Hughes. Like Hoffa and Marcello.

Ward hated Jack on a par with Kemper. Bobby fucked them both—but they bypassed him to hate Big Brother.

Littell was Dracula's new Field Marshal. The Count wanted him to buy up Las Vegas and render it germ-free.

You could read Littell's eyes.

I have friends. I have plans. I have the Fund books memorized.

The holding tank smelled. The holding tank boomed with John F. Kennedy hatred.

A guard cranked the door and pulled men out for phone calls. He yelled, "Acosta, Aguilar, Arredondo—"

Pete got ready. A dime would get him Littell in D.C.

Littell could rig a Federal release writ. Littell could hip Kemper to the campsite raids.

The guard yelled, "Bondurant!"

Pete walked up. The guard steered him down the tier to a phone bank.

Guy Banister was waiting there. He was holding a pen and a false-arrest waiver.

The guard walked back to the tank. Pete signed his name in triplicate.

"I'm free to go?"

Banister looked gleeful. "That's right. The SAC didn't know you were Agency, so I informed him."

"Who told you where I was?"

"I was out at Sun Valley. Kemper gave me a note for you, so I went by the stand to deliver it. Some kids were stealing hubcaps. They told me the big gringo got arrested."

Pete rubbed his eyes. A four-aspirin headache started pounding.

Banister pulled out an envelope. "I didn't open it. And Kemper sure seemed anxious for me to make the transmittal."

Pete grabbed it. "I'm glad you're ex-Bureau, Guy. I might've had to stay here awhile."

"Don't fret, big fella. I have a hunch all this Kennedy bullshit is just about to end."

Pete caught a cab back to the stand. Vandals had stripped the tiger cars down to spare parts.

He read the note. Boyd cut straight to the point.

> Néstor's here. I got a tip that he was seen begging gun money in Coral Gables. My source says he's holed up at 46th and Collins. (The pink garage apartment on the southwest corner.)

The note meant KILL HIM. Don't let Santo get to him first.

He took bourbon and aspirin for his headache.

He took his magnum and his silencer for the job.

He took some pro-Castro leaflets to plant near the body.

He drove to 46th and Collins. He took this weird revelation with him: You might let Néstor talk you out of it.

The pink garage apartment was right there, as stated. The '58 Chevy at the curb looked like a Néstor-style ride.

Pete parked.

Pete got butterflies.

Go ahead, do it—you've killed at least three hundred men.

He walked up and knocked on the door.

Nobody answered.

He knocked again. He listened for footsteps and whispers.

He couldn't hear a thing. He picked the lock with his penknife and walked in.

Shotgun slides went KA-CHOOK. Some unseen party hit a light switch.

There's Néstor, lashed to a chair. There's two fat henchmen types holding Ithaca pumps.

There's Santo Trafficante with an icepick.

86

(New Orleans, 9/15/63)

Littell opened his briefcase.
Stacks of money fell out.
Marcello said, "How much?"
Littell said, "A quarter of a million dollars."

"Where'd you get it?"

"From a client."

Carlos cleared some desk space. His office was top-heavy with Italianate knickknacks.

"You're saying this is for me?"

"I'm saying it's for you to match."

"What else are you saying?"

Littell dumped the money on the desk. "I'm saying that as an attorney, I can only do so much. With John Kennedy in power, Bobby will get you all sooner or later. I'm also saying that eliminating Bobby would be futile, because Jack would instinctively know who did it and take his vengeance accordingly."

The money smelled. Hughes dredged up old bills.

"But Lyndon Johnson don't like Bobby. He'd put the skids to him just to teach the fucking kid a lesson."

"That's right. Johnson hates Bobby as much as Mr. Hoover does. And like Mr. Hoover, he bears you and our other friends no ill will."

Marcello laughed. "LBJ borrowed some money from the Teamsters once. He is well known as a reasonable guy."

"So is Mr. Hoover. And Mr. Hoover is also very upset about Bobby's plans to put Joe Valachi on TV. He's very much afraid that Valachi's revelations will severely damage his prestige and virtually destroy everything that you and our other friends have built."

Carlos built a little cash skyscraper. Bank stacks rose off his desk blotter.

Littell knocked them over. "I think Mr. Hoover wants it to happen. I think he feels it coming."

"We've all been thinking about it. You can't get a roomful of the boys together without somebody bringing it up."

"It can be made to happen. And it can be made to look like we weren't involved."

"So you're saying . . ."

"I'm saying it's so big and audacious that we'll most likely never be suspected. I'm saying that even if we are, the powers that be will realize that it can never be conclusively proven. I'm saying that a consensus of denial will build off of it. I'm saying that people will want to remember the man as something he wasn't. I'm saying that we'll present them with an explanation, and the powers that be will prefer it to the truth, even though they know better."

Marcello said, "Do it. Make it happen."

87

(Sun Valley, 9/18/63)

The squad shared turf with gators and sand fleas. Kemper called the place "Hoffa's Paradise Lost."

Flash set up targets. Laurent bench-pressed cinderblock siding. Juan Canestel was AWOL—with 8:00 a.m. rifle practice pending.

Nobody heard him drive off. Juan was prone to odd wanderings lately.

Kemper watched Laurent Guéry work out. The man could bench three hundred pounds without breaking a sweat.

Dust swirled up the main road. Teamster Boulevard was now a pistol range.

Flash played his transistor radio. Bad news crackled out.

There were no arrests in the Birmingham church bombing case. The revamped McClellan Committee was set to go to televised sessions.

A woman was found sash-cord strangled outside Lake Weir. The police reported no leads and appealed to the public for assistance.

Juan was one hour AWOL. Pete was missing for three days.

He got the phone tip on Néstor four days ago. The tipster was a freelance exile gunman. He gave Guy Banister a note to relay to Pete.

Guy called and said he delivered it. He said he found Pete at the Federal detention jail. He dropped hints that more FBI raids were coming.

A storm browned out their phone setup two days ago. Pete couldn't call Sun Valley.

Kemper drove to a pay phone off the Interstate last night. He called Pete's apartment six times and got no answer.

Néstor Chasco's death never made the news. Pete would have dumped the body in a newsworthy locale.

Pete would put a pro-Castro spin on the murder. Pete would make sure Trafficante got the word.

His morning Dexedrine surge hit. It took ten pills to kick-start the day—he'd built up a large tolerance.

Juan and Pete were missing. Juan was hanging out with Guy Banister lately—little Lake Weir drinking excursions every other day or so.

The Pete thing felt wrong. The Juan thing felt mildly hinky.

His amphetamine surge said, Do something.

Juan drove a candy-apple-red T-Bird. Flash called it the Rapemobile.

Kemper cruised Lake Weir. The town was small and laid out in a grid pattern—the Rapemobile would be easy to spot.

He checked side streets and the bars near the highway. He checked Karl's Kustom Kar Shop and every parking lot on the main drag.

He didn't spot Juan. He didn't spot Juan's customized T-Bird.

Juan could wait. The Pete thing was more pressing.

Kemper drove to Miami. The pills started to hit counterproductive—he kept yawning and fading out at the wheel.

He stopped at 46th and Collins. That pink garage apartment was right where the tipster said it would be.

A traffic cop walked over. Kemper noticed a No Parking sign on the corner.

He rolled down his window. The cop jammed a smelly rag in his face.

It felt like chemical warfare inside him.

The smell fought his wake-up pills. The smell might be chloroform or embalming fluid. The smell meant he might be dead.

His pulse said, NO—you're alive.

His lips burned. His nose burned. He tasted chloroformed blood.

He tried to spit. His lips wouldn't part. He gagged the blood out through his nose.

He stretched his mouth. Something tugged at his cheeks. It felt like tape coming loose.

He sucked in air. He tried to move his arms and legs.

He tried to stand up. Heavy ballast held him down.

He wiggled. Chair legs scraped wood flooring. He thrashed his arms and got rope burns.

Kemper opened his eyes.

A man laughed. A hand held up Polaroid snapshots glued to cardboard.

He saw Teo Paez, gutted and quartered. He saw Fulo Machado, shivved through the eyes. He saw Ramón Gutiérrez, powder-scorched from big-bore shots to the head.

The photos disappeared. The hand swiveled his neck. Kemper caught a slow 180 view.

He saw a shabby room and two fat men in a doorway. He saw Néstor Chasco—nailed to the far wall with icepicks through his palms and ankles.

Kemper shut his eyes. A hand slapped him. A big heavy ring cut his lips.

Kemper opened his eyes. Hands slid his chair around 360.

They had Pete chained down. They had him double-cuffed and shackled to a chair. They had the chair bolted directly into the floor.

A rag hit his face. Kemper sucked the fumes in voluntarily.

He heard stories filtered through a long echo chamber. He picked out three storytelling voices.

Néstor got close to Castro twice. You got to hand it to him.

A kid that tough—what a shame to put his lights out.

Néstor said he bought off some Castro aide. The aide said Castro was considering a Kennedy hit.. The aide said, What's with this Kennedy? First he invades us, then he pulls back—he's like a cunt who can't make up her mind.

Fidel's the cunt. The aide told Chasco he'd never work with the Outfit again. He thinks Santo screwed him on the heroin deal. He didn't know it was Néstor and our boys here.

Bondurant pissed his pants. Look, you can see the stain.

Santo and Mo were not gentle. And I got to say Néstor went out brave.

I'm bored with this. I got to say this waiting around is stretching me thin.

I got to say they'll be back soon. I got to say they'll want to put some hurt on these two.

Kemper felt his bladder go. He took a deep breath and forced himself unconscious.

•   •   •

He dreamed he was moving. He dreamed somebody cleaned him up and changed his clothes. He dreamed he heard fierce Pete Bondurant sobbing.

He dreamed he could breathe. He dreamed he could talk. He kept cursing Jack and Claire for disowning him.

He woke up on a bed. He recognized his old Fontainebleau suite or an exact replica of it.

He was wearing clean clothes. Somebody pulled off his soiled boxer shorts.

He felt rope burns on his wrists. He felt tape fragments stuck to his face.

He heard voices one room over—Pete and Ward Littell.

He tried to stand up. His legs wouldn't function. He sat on the bed and coughed his lungs out.

Littell walked in. He looked commanding—that gabardine suit gave him some bulk.

Kemper said, "There's a price."

Littell nodded. "That's right. It's something I worked out with Carlos and Sam."

"Ward—"

"Santo agreed, too. And you and Pete get to keep what you stole."

Kemper stood up. Ward held him steady.

"What do we have to do?"

Littell said, "Kill John Kennedy."

88

(Miami, 9/23/63)

1933 to 1963. Thirty years and parallel situations.

Miami, '33. Giuseppe Zangara tries to shoot President-elect Franklin D. Roosevelt. He misses—and kills Chicago Mayor Anton Cermak.

Miami, '63. A Kennedy motorcade is scheduled for November 18.

Littell slow-cruised Biscayne Boulevard. Every inch of ground told him something.

Carlos told him the Zangara story last week.

"Giuseppe was a fucking nut. Some Chicago boys paid him to pop Cermak and take the bounce. He had a fucking death wish, and he got his fucking wish fulfilled. Frank Nitti took care of his family after he got executed."

He met with Carlos, Sam and Santo. He bartered for Pete and Kemper. They discussed the fall-guy issue at length.

Carlos wanted a leftist. He thought a left-wing assassin would galvanize anti-Castro feeling. Trafficante and Giancana overruled him.

They matched Howard Hughes' contribution. They added one stipulation: we want a right-wing patsy.

They still wanted to suck up to Fidel. They wanted to replenish Raúl Castro's dope stash and effect a late-breaking rapprochement. They wanted to say, We financed the hit—now, will you please give us back our casinos?

Their take was too convoluted. Their take was politically naive.

His take was minimalistically downscaled.

The hit can be accomplished. The planners and shooters can walk. Bobby's Mob crusade can be nullified.

Any results beyond that are unforeseeable, and will most likely re-solve themselves in a powerfully ambiguous fashion.

Littell drove through downtown Miami. He noted potential motor-cade routes—wide streets with high visibility.

He saw tall buildings and rear parking lots. He saw Office for Rent signs.

He saw blighted residential blocks. He saw House for Rent signs and a gun shop.

He could see the motorcade pass. He could see the man's head explode.

They met at the Fontainebleau. Pete ran a wall-to-wall bug sweep before they said one word.

Kemper mixed drinks. They sat around a table by the wet bar.

Littell laid the plan out.

"We bring the fall guy to Miami some time between now and the first of October. We get him to rent a cheap house on the outskirts of down-town, close to the announced or assumed-to-be-announced motorcade route—*and* an office directly on the route—once that route is deter-mined. I cruised every major airport-to-downtown artery this morning. My educated guess is that we'll have plenty of houses and offices to choose from."

Pete and Kemper stayed quiet. They still looked close to shell-shocked.

"One of us sticks close to the fall guy between the time we bring him here and the morning of the motorcade. There's a gun shop near his of-fice and his house, and one of you burglarizes it and steals several rifles and pistols. Hate literature and other bits of incriminating paraphernalia are planted at the house, and our man handles them to insure latent fingerprints."

Pete said, "Get to the hit." Littell framed the moment: three men at a table and hear-a-pin-drop silence.

He said, "It's the day of the motorcade. We're holding our man hos-tage at the office on the parade route. There's a rifle from the gun-shop burglary with him, and his fingerprints are all over the stock and barrel housing. Kennedy's car passes. Our two legitimate shooters fire from separate roof perches in the rear and kill him. The man holding our patsy hostage fires at Kennedy's car and misses, drops the rifle and shoots the patsy with a stolen revolver. He flees and drops the revolver down a sewer grate. The police find the guns and compare them to the manifest from the burglary. They'll chalk up the evidence and figure they've got a conspiracy that tenuously succeeded and unraveled at the last second. They'll investigate the dead man and try to build a conspiracy case against his known associates."

Pete lit a cigarette and coughed. "You said 'flee' like you think getting out's a cinch."

Littell spoke slowly. "There are perpendicular side streets off every major thoroughfare that I've designated motorcade-likely. They're all freeway-accessible inside two minutes. Our legitimate shooters will be firing from behind. *They'll fire two shots total*—which will sound at first like car backfires or firecrackers. The Secret Service contingent won't know exactly where the shots came from. They'll still be reacting when *multiple shots*—from our fake shooter and the man guarding him—ring out. They'll storm that building and find a dead man. They'll be distracted, and they'll blow a minute or so. All our men will have time to get to their cars and drive off."

Kemper said, "It's beautiful."

Pete rubbed his eyes. "I don't like the right-wing-nut part. It's like we came this far and didn't play an angle that could help out the Cause."

Littell slapped the table. "*No*. Trafficante and Giancana want a right-winger. They think they can build a truce with Castro, and if that's what they want, we'll have to go along with it. And remember, they *did* spare your lives."

Kemper freshened his drink. His eyes were still bloodshot from chloroform exposure.

"I want my men to shoot. They've got the hate and they're expert marksmen."

Pete said, "Agreed."

Littell nodded. "We'll pay them $25,000 each, use the rest of the money for expenses and split the difference three ways."

Kemper smiled. "My men are pretty far to the right. We should downplay the fact that we're setting up a fellow right-winger."

Pete mixed a cocktail: two aspirin and Wild Turkey. "We need to get a handle on the parade route."

Littell said, "That's your job. You've got the best Miami PD contacts."

"I'll get on it. And if I find out anything solid, I'll start mapping out the hard logistics."

Kemper coughed. "The key thing is the patsy. Once we get beyond that, we're home free."

Littell shook his head. "No. The key thing is to thwart a full-scale FBI investigation."

Pete and Kemper looked puzzled. They weren't thinking up to his level.

Littell spoke very slowly. "I think Mr. Hoover knows it's coming. He's got private bugs installed in god-knows-how-many Mob meeting places, and he told me he's been picking up a huge amount of Kennedy hatred. He hasn't informed the Secret Service, or they wouldn't be planning motorcades through to the end of the fall."

Kemper nodded. "Hoover wants it to happen. It happens, he's glad it happened, and he still gets assigned to investigate it. What we need is an 'in' to get him to obfuscate or short-shrift the investigation."

Pete nodded. "We need an FBI-linked fall guy."

Kemper said, "Dougie Frank Lockhart."

89

(Miami, 9/27/63)

He liked to spend time alone with it. Boyd said he was doing the same thing.

Pete laid out bourbon and aspirin. He turned on the window unit and cooled off the living room just right. He leveled off his headache and ran some fresh odds.

The odds they could kill Jack the Haircut. The odds that Santo would kill him and Kemper, deal or no deal.

All the odds hit inconclusive. His living room took on a rather shitty medicinal glow.

Littell loved Dougie Frank's pedigree. The fuck was ultra-right and FBI-filthy.

Littell said, "He's perfect. If Mr. Hoover is forced to investigate, he'll put a blanket on Lockhart and his known associates immediately. If he doesn't, he'll risk exposure of all the Bureau's racist policies."

Lockhart was holed up in Puckett, Mississippi. Littell said, Go there and recruit him.

He strolled through the main MPD squadroom last night. He saw three prospective motorcade maps. They were tacked to a corkboard in plain fucking view.

He memorized them. All three routes ran by their gun shop and For Rent signs.

Boyd said he felt awe more than fear.

Pete said, I know what you mean.

He didn't say, I love this woman. If I die, I came this far and lost her for nothing.

90

(Miami, 9/27/63)

Somebody placed a tape recorder on his coffee table. Somebody placed a sealed envelope beside it.

Littell shut the door and thought it through.

Pete and Kemper know you're here. Jimmy and Carlos know you always stay at the Fontainebleau. You went down to the coffee shop for breakfast and were gone less than half an hour.

Littell opened the envelope and pulled out a sheet of paper. Mr. Hoover's block printing explained the surreptitious entry.

Jules Schiffrin died concurrent with your fall 1960 absence from duty. His estate house was ransacked and certain ledger books were stolen.

Joseph Valachi did extensive Pension Fund forwarding work. He is currently being questioned by a trusted colleague of mine. Robert Kennedy does not know that this interrogation is progressing.

The accompanying tape contains information that Mr. Valachi will refuse to reveal to Mr. Kennedy, the McClellan Committee, and indeed to anyone else. I trust Mr. Valachi to maintain his silence. He has been made aware that the quality and duration of his Federal relocation is predicated on it.

Please destroy this note. Please listen to the tape and keep it in a safe place. I realize that the tape has limitless strategic potential. It should be revealed to Robert Kennedy only as an adjunct to measures of great boldness.

Littell plugged in the machine and prepped the enclosed tape. His hands were butter—the spool kept slipping off the spindle.

He tapped the Play button. The tape splice sputtered and hissed.

Go over it again, Joe. Like I told you before, slow and easy.

Okay, slow and easy then. Slow and easy for the sixteenth goddamn—

Joe, come on.

Okay. Slow and easy for the stupes in the peanut gallery. Joseph P. Kennedy Sr. was the charter bankroller of the Teamsters' Central States Pension Fund, which loans out money to all kinds of bad people and a few good people at very high interest rates. I did a lot of the forwarding work. Sometimes I delivered cash to people's safe-deposit boxes.

You mean they gave you clearance to enter their boxes?

Right. And I used to visit Joe Kennedy's bank regularly. It's the main Security–First National in Boston. It's account 811512404. It's like ninety or a hundred safe-deposit boxes filled with cash. Raymond Patriarca thinks there's close to a hundred million dollars in there, and Raymond should know, 'cause him and Irish Joe go back a ways. I got to say the notion of Bob Kennedy as a racket buster makes me laugh. I guess the apple does fall pretty far from the tree, 'cause Joe Kennedy money has financed one whole hell of a lot of Outfit deals. I got to say also that old Joe's the only Kennedy that knows about that money. You don't tell people, I got a hundred million in cash put away that my sons the President and Attorney General don't know about. And now Joe's had this stroke, so maybe he's not thinking too clear. You would sort of like to see that money put to use and not just sit there, which it might if old Joe kicks off or goes senile and forgets about it. I should also mention that every big guy in the Outfit knows how dirty Joe is, but they can't shake Bobby down with the knowledge without putting their own tits in the wringer.

The tape ran out. Littell tapped the Stop button and sat perfectly still.

He thought it through. He assumed Hoover's perspective and spoke his thoughts out loud in the first person.

I'm close to Howard Hughes. I set Ward Littell up with him. Littell asked Hughes for money to help assure my FBI directorship.

Jack Kennedy plans to fire me. I've got private taps installed in Mob venues. I've picked up a great deal of Kennedy hatred.

Littell switched back to his own perspective.

Hoover possessed insufficient data. Said data would not lead him to extrapolate a specific hit.

I told Pete and Kemper, Mr. Hoover knows it's coming. I meant it in the metaphorical sense.

The tape and note implied specificity. Hoover called the tape "an adjunct to measures of great boldness."

He was saying, I KNOW.

The tape was a device to humble Bobby. The tape was a device to insure Bobby's silence. The tape should be revealed to Bobby before Jack's death.

Jack's death would explicate the purpose of the humbling. Bobby would thus not seek to establish proof of an assassination conspiracy. Bobby would know that to do so would forever besmirch the Kennedy name.

Bobby would assume that the man who delivered the humbling had foreknowledge of his brother's death. Bobby would be powerless to act upon his assumption.

Littell reassumed Hoover's perspective.

Bobby Kennedy broke Littell's heart. Kennedy hatred binds us. Littell will not resist the urge to maim Bobby. Littell will want Bobby to know that he helped plan his brother's murder.

It was complex and vindictive and psychologically dense Hoover thinking. A single logical thread was missing.

You haven't broken cover. Your financiers presumably haven't.

Kemper and Pete haven't. Kemper hasn't broached the plan to his shooters yet.

Hoover *senses* that you're pushing toward a hit. The tape's your "adjunct"—*if you get there first.*

There's a second plot in the works. Mr. Hoover has specific knowledge of it.

Littell sat perfectly still. Little hotel sounds escalated.

He couldn't lock the conclusion in. He couldn't rate it as much more than a hunch.

Mr. Hoover knew him—as no one else ever had or ever would. He felt an ugly wave of love for the man.

91

(Puckett, 9/28/63)

The geek wore a monogrammed Klan sheet. Pete fed him bonded bourbon and lies.

"This gig is you, Dougie. It's got 'you' written all over it."

Lockhart burped. "I knew you didn't drive out here at 1:00 a.m. just to share that bottle with me."

The shack smelled like a cat box. Dougie reeked of Wildroot Cream Oil. Pete stood in the doorway—the better to dodge the stink.

"It's three hundred a week. It's an official Agency job, so you won't have to worry about those Fed raids."

Lockhart rocked back in his La-Z-Boy recliner. "Those raids have been pretty indiscriminate. I heard quite a few Agency boys got themselves tangled up in them."

Pete cracked his thumbs. "We need you to ride herd on some Klansmen. The Agency wants to build a string of launch sites in South Florida, and we need a white man to get things going."

Lockhart picked his nose. "Sounds like Blessington all over again. Sounds also like it might be another big fuckin' buildup to another big fuckin' letdown, like a certain invasion we both remember."

Pete took a hit off the bottle. "You can't make history all the time, Dougie. Sometimes the best you can do is make money."

Dougie tapped his chest. "I made history recently."

"Is that right?"

"That's right. It was me that bombed the 16th Street Baptist Church in Birmingham, Alabama. That Communist-inspired hue-and-cry that's going up right now? Well, I got to say I'm the one that inspired it."

The shack was lined with tinfoil. Dig that Martin Luther Coon poster taped to the back wall.

"I'll make it four hundred a week and expenses, through to mid-November. You get your own house and office in Miami. If you leave with me now, I'll throw in a bonus."

Lockhart said, "I'm in."

Pete said, "Clean yourself up. You look like a nigger."

The ride back went slow. Thunderstorms turned the highway into one long snail trail.

Dougie Frank snored through the deluge. Pete caught newscasts and a Twist show on the radio.

A commentator talked up Joe Valachi's song-and-dance. Valachi dubbed the Mob "La Cosa Nostra."

Valachi was a big TV hit. A newsman called his ratings "boffo." Valachi was snitching East Coast hoodlums up the ying-yang.

A reporter talked to Heshie Ryskind—holed up in some Phoenix cancer ward. Hesh called La Cosa Nostra "a goyishe fantasy."

The Twist program came in scratchy. Barb sang along in Pete's head and out-warbled Chubby Checker.

They talked long-distance right before he left Miami. Barb said, What is it?—you sound frightened again.

He said, I can't tell you. When you hear about it, you'll know.

She said, Will it hurt us?

He said, No.

She said, You're lying. He couldn't argue.

She was flying to Texas in a few days. Joey booked them in for an eight-week statewide run.

He'd fly in for weekends. He'd play stage-door Johnny, straight up to November 18.

They hit Miami at noon. Lockhart dosed his hangover with glazed doughnuts and coffee.

They looped through the downtown area. Dougie pointed out For Rent signs.

Pete drove in circles. The house-and-office search had Dougie yawning.

Pete narrowed his choices down to three offices and three houses. Pete said, Dougie, take your pick.

Dougie picked fast. Dougie wanted to log in some sack time.

He picked a stucco house off Biscayne. He picked an office on Biscayne—dead center on all three parade routes.

Both landlords demanded deposits. Dougie peeled bills off his expense roll and paid them three months' rent in advance.

Pete stayed out of sight. The landlords never saw him.

He watched Dougie lug his gear into the house—this carrot-topped stupe about to be world-famous.

92

(Miami, 9/29/63–10/20/63)

He memorized Hoover's note. He hid the tape splice. He drove the three routes a dozen times a day for three weeks running.

He didn't tell Pete and Kemper that there might be another hit planned.

The press reported the President's fall travel schedule. They emphasized motorcades in New York, Miami and Texas.

Littell sent Bobby a note. It stated his affiliation with James R. Hoffa and asked for ten minutes of his time.

He considered the ramifications for close to a month before acting. His walk to the mailbox felt like his raid on Jules Schiffrin's house—multiplied a thousand times.

Littell drove down Biscayne Boulevard. He timed every signal light with a stopwatch.

Kemper burglarized the gun shop a week ago. He stole three sight-equipped rifles and two revolvers. He wore gloves with distinctive cracked fingertips—filched from Dougie Frank Lockhart.

Kemper surveilled the gun shop the next day. Detectives canvassed the area and technicians dusted for prints. Dougie's cracked-finger gloves were now a matter of forensic record.

The gloves were pressed all over surfaces in Dougie's house and office.

Pete let Dougie fondle the rifles. His fingerprints were pressed to the stocks and barrels.

Kemper stole three cars in South Carolina. He had them repainted and fitted with fake license plates. Two were assigned to the shooters. The third car was for the man assigned to kill Dougie.

Pete brought a fourth man in. Chuck Rogers signed on as their fall-guy impersonator.

Rogers and Lockhart had similar builds and similar features. Dougie's most distinguishing attribute was bright red hair.

Chuck dyed his hair red. Chuck spewed Kennedy hatred all over Miami.

He shot his mouth off at taverns and pool halls. He raged at a skating rink, a gun range and numerous liquor stores. He was paid to rage nonstop until November 15.

Littell drove by Dougie's office. Every circuit gave him a brilliant new embellishment.

He should find some rambunctious kids on the motorcade route. He should give them firecrackers and tell them to let fly.

It would wear the Secret Service escort down. It would inure them to gunshot-like noises.

Kemper was working up some Dougie Frank keepsakes. Lockhart's psychopathology would be summarized in minutiae.

Kemper defaced JFK photographs and carved swastikas on Jack and Jackie dolls. Kemper smeared fecal matter over a dozen Kennedy magazine spreads.

The investigators would find it all in Dougie's bedroom closet.

Currently in progress: Dougie Frank Lockhart's political diary.

It was hunt-and-peck typed, with printed ink corrections. The race-mongering text was truly horrific.

The diary was Pete's idea. Dougie said he bombed the 16th Street Baptist Church—a still-unsolved cause célèbre. Pete wanted to link the Kennedy hit and four dead Negro children.

Dougie told Pete the whole bombing story. Pete typed crucial details into the diary.

They didn't mention the bombing embellishment to Kemper. Kemper had a quirky affection for coloreds.

Pete kept Dougie sequestered at his house. He fed him take-out pizza, marijuana and liquor. Dougie seemed to enjoy the accommodations.

Pete told Dougie that his Agency gig had been postponed. He fed him a cock-and-bull story about the need to stay out of sight.

Kemper moved his men to Blessington. The FBI was raiding non-CIA campsites—housing his team at Sun Valley was risky.

The men bunked at the Breakers Motel. They test-fired .30.06's all day every day. Their rifles were identical to the rifles Kemper stole.

The shooters didn't know about the hit. Kemper would inform them six days before—in time to stage a full-dress Miami rehearsal.

Littell cruised by Dougie's house. Pete said he always came in through the alley and never let the neighbors see him.

They should plant some narcotics at the house. They should expand Dougie's pedigree to assassin/church bomber/dope fiend.

Kemper had a drink with the Miami SAC yesterday. They were old Bureau pals—the meeting wouldn't stand out as anomalous.

The man called the motorcade a "pain in the ass." He called Kennedy "tough to guard." He said the Secret Service let crowds get too close to him.

Kemper said, Any threats? Any loonies coming out of the woodwork?

The man said, No.

Their one risky bluff was holding. No one had reported the loud-mouthed pseudo Dougie.

Littell drove back to the Fontainebleau. He wondered how long Pete and Kemper would outlive JFK.

93

(Blessington, 10/21/63)

Training officers formed a cordon just inside the front gate. They wore face shields and packed shotguns filled with rock salt.

Refuge seekers slammed the fence. The entry road was jammed with junk cars and dispossessed Cubans.

Kemper watched the scene escalate. John Stanton called and warned him that the raids went from bad to godawful.

The FBI hit fourteen exile camps yesterday. Half the Cubans on the Gulf Coast were out seeking CIA asylum.

The fence teetered. The training men raised their weapons.

There were twenty men inside and sixty men outside. Only weak chain-links and some barbed wire stood between them.

A Cuban climbed the fence and snagged himself on the barbs at the top. A training man blew him down—one salt round de-snagged him and lacerated his chest.

The Cubans picked up rocks and waved lumber planks. The contract men assumed protective postures. A big bilingual roar went up.

Littell was late. Pete was late, too—the migration probably stalled traffic.

Kemper walked down to the boat dock. His men were shooting buoys floating thirty yards offshore.

They wore earplugs to blot out the gate noise. They looked like high-line, spit-and-polish mercenaries.

He moved them in just under the wire. They had free run of the campsite—John Stanton pulled strings for old times' sake.

Ejected shells hit the dock. Laurent and Flash notched bullseyes. Juan fired wide into some waves.

He told them about the hit last night. The pure audacity thrilled them.

He couldn't resist it. He wanted to see their faces ignite.

Laurent and Flash lit up happy. Juan lit up disturbed.

Juan's been acting furtive. Juan's been AWOL three nights running.

The radio reported another dead woman. She was beaten senseless and strangled with a sash cord. The local cops were baffled.

Victim #1 was found near Sun Valley. Victim #2 was found near Blessington.

The gate noise doubled and tripled. Rock-salt rounds exploded.

Kemper popped in earplugs and watched his men shoot. Juan Canestel watched him.

Flash made a buoy jump. Laurent nailed it on the rebound. Juan slammed three straight misses.

Something was wrong.

The State Police cleared the Cubans out. Black & whites escorted them to the highway.

Kemper drove behind the convoy. The line was fifty cars long. The rock-salt barrage blew out windshields and stripped convertible tops.

It was a short-sighted solution. John Stanton prophesied exile chaos—and hinted at much worse.

Pete and Ward called to say they'd be late. He said, Good—I have to run an errand. They rescheduled their meet for 2:30 at the Breakers.

He'd tell them Stanton's news. He'd stress that it was strictly speculative.

The car herd crawled—both outbound lanes were jammed up bumper-to-bumper. Two black & whites drove point to keep the Cubans boxed in.

Kemper turned onto a switchback. It was the only shortcut to Blessington proper—dirt roads straight in.

Dust kicked up. A light drizzle turned it to mud spray. The Rapemobile passed him, full-throttle on a blind curve.

Kemper hit his wipers. The spray thinned out translucent. He saw exhaust fumes up ahead—and no Rapemobile.

Juan's distracted. He didn't recognize my car.

Kemper hit downtown Blessington. He cruised by the Breakers, Al's Dixie Diner and every exile hangout on both sides of the highway.

No Rapemobile.

He grid-searched side streets. He made systematic circuits—three blocks left, three blocks right. Seven-come-eleven—where's that candy-apple-red T-Bird?

There—

The Rapemobile was parked outside the Larkhaven Motel. Kemper recognized the two cars parked beside it.

Guy Banister's Buick. Carlos Marcello's Lincoln.

The Breakers Motel faced the highway. Kemper's window faced a just-rigged State Police checkpoint.

He saw cops divert cars down an off-ramp. He saw cops force male Latins out at gunpoint.

The cops ran ID checks and INS checks. The cops impounded vehicles and arrested male Latins wholesale.

Kemper watched for one straight hour. The Staties busted thirty-nine male Latins.

They herded the men into jail trucks. They dumped confiscated weapons into one big pile.

He searched Juan's room an hour ago.

He found no sash cords. He found no perverted keepsakes. He saw absolutely nothing incriminating.

Somebody leaned on the doorbell. Kemper opened up quick to stop the noise.

Pete walked in. "Have you seen what's going on out there?"

Kemper nodded. "They were trying to break in to the camp a few hours ago. The head training officer called the Staties."

Pete checked the window. "Those are some pissed-off Cubans."

Kemper pulled the drapes. "Where's Ward?"

"He's coming. And I hope you didn't call us all the way down here to show us some fucking roadblocks."

Kemper walked to the bar and poured Pete a short bourbon. "John Stanton called me. He said Jack Kennedy told Hoover to turn up the heat. The FBI has raided twenty-nine non-Agency campsites within the past forty-eight hours. Every non-Agency exile in captivity is out looking for Agency asylum."

Pete downed his shot. Kemper poured him a refill.

"Stanton said Carlos put up a bail fund. Guy Banister tried to bail out some of his pet exiles, but the INS has put a deportation hold on every Cuban National in custody."

Pete threw his glass at the wall. Kemper plugged the bottle.

"Stanton said the entire exile community is going crazy. He said there's lots of talk about a Kennedy hit. He said there's a good deal of *specific talk* about a motorcade hit in Miami."

Pete punched the wall. His fist smashed through to the baseboard. Kemper stood back and talked slow and easy.

"Nobody on our team has broken cover, so the rumors couldn't have originated from there. And Stanton said he didn't inform the Secret Service, which implies that he wouldn't mind seeing Jack dead."

Pete gouged his knuckles bone-deep. He threw a left hook at the wall—plaster chunks flew.

Kemper stood *way* back. "Ward said Hoover sensed it was coming. He was right, because Hoover would have stalled the raids and sent out warnings to the old-boy network just to screw Bobby—unless he wanted to fuel the hatred against Jack."

Pete grabbed the bottle. Pete doused his hands and wiped them on the drapes.

The fabric seeped beige to red. The wall was half-demolished.

"Pete, listen. There's ways we can—"

Pete shoved him against the window. "No. This is the one we can't get out of. We either kill him or we don't, and they'll probably kill us even if we get him."

Kemper slid free. Pete slid the drapes back.

Exiles were jumping off the highway abutment. Cops were going at them with electric cattle prods.

"Look at that, Kemper. Look at that and tell me we can contain this fucking thing."

Littell walked past the window. Pete opened the door and pulled him in bodily.

He didn't react. He looked glazed and *hurt.*

Kemper shut the door. "Ward, what is it?"

Littell hugged his briefcase. He didn't even blink at the room damage.

"I talked to Sam. He said the Miami hit is out, because his liaison to Castro told him that Castro would never speak to any Outfit man ever again, under any circumstances. They've given up the idea of a rapprochement. I've always considered it far-fetched, and now apparently Sam and Santo agree."

Pete said, "This is all crazy." Kemper read Littell's face: DON'T TAKE THIS AWAY FROM ME.

"Are *we* still on?"

Littell said, "I think so. And I spoke to Guy Banister and figured something out."

Pete looked ready to blow. "So tell us, Ward. We know you're the smartest and the strongest now, so just tell us what you think."

Littell squared his necktie. "Banister saw a copy of a presidential memo. It passed from Jack to Bobby to Mr. Hoover, then through to the New Orleans SAC, who leaked it to Guy. The memo said that the President is sending a personal emissary to talk to Castro in November, and that further JM/Wave cutbacks will be forthcoming."

Pete flicked blood off his hands. "I don't get the Banister connection."

Littell tossed his briefcase on the bed. "It was coincidental. Guy and Carlos are close, and Guy's a frustrated lawyer himself. We talk from time to time, and he just happened to mention the memo. What it all ties in to is my feeling that Mr. Hoover senses there's a hit plan in the works. Since none of us have broken cover, I'm thinking that—*maybe*—there's a second hit in the planning stages. I'm thinking also that Banister might have knowledge of it—and *that's* why Hoover leaked the memo in his direction."

Kemper pointed to the window. "Did you see that checkpoint?"

Littell said, "Yes, of course."

Kemper said, "That's Hoover again. That's him letting the raids happen to keep the hate against Jack peaking. John Stanton called me, Ward. There's supposed to be a half-dozen or six dozen or two dozen more fucking plots in the works, like the fucking assassination metaphysic is just out there too undeniably—"

Pete slapped him.

Kemper pulled his piece.

Pete pulled his.

Littell said, "No," VERY SOFTLY.

Pete dropped his gun on the bed.

Kemper dropped his.

Littell said, "Enough," VERY SOFTLY.

The room crackled and buzzed. Littell unloaded the guns and locked them in his briefcase.

Pete spoke just shy of a whisper. "Banister bailed me out of jail last month. He said, 'This Kennedy bullshit is about to end,' like he had some kind of fucking foreknowledge."

Kemper spoke the same way. "Juan Canestel's been acting strange lately. I tailed him a few hours ago, and spotted his car parked next to Banister's and Carlos Marcello's. It was right down the road here, outside another motel."

Littell said, "The Larkhaven?"

"That's right."

Pete sucked blood off his knuckles. "How'd you know that, Ward? And if Carlos is in on a second hit, are Santo and Mo calling ours off?"

Littell shook his head. "I think we're still on."

"What about this Banister stuff?"

"It's new to me, but it fits. All I know for certain now is that I'm meeting Carlos at the Larkhaven Motel at five. He told me that Santo and Mo have handed the whole thing to him, with two new stipulations."

Kemper rubbed his chin. The slap left his face bright red.

"Which are?"

"That we reschedule out of Miami and work up a left-wing patsy. There's no chance at a truce with Castro, so they want to build the killer up as *pro*-Fidel."

Pete kicked the wall. A landscape print hit the floor.

Kemper swallowed a loose tooth. Pete pointed to the highway.

The cops were putting on full riot gear. The cops were running strip searches in broad daylight.

Kemper said, "Look at that. That's all Mr. Hoover's chess game."

Pete said, "You're crazy. He's not *that* fucking good."

Littell laughed in his face.

94

arlos arranged a liquor tray. The setting was incongruous— Hennessy XO and paper- wrapped motel glasses.

Littell took the hard chair. Carlos took the soft one. The tray sat on a coffee table between them.

"Your crew is out, Ward. We're using somebody else. He's been plan- ning his thing all summer, which makes it a better all-around deal."

Littell said, "Guy Banister?"

"How'd you know? Did a little birdie tell you?"

"His car's outside. And there's some things that you just tend to know."

"You're taking it good."

"I don't have a choice."

Carlos toyed with a humidor. "I just learned about it. The thing's been in the works for a while, which to my way of thinking increases the chance of success."

"Where?"

"Dallas, next month. Guy's got some rich right-wingers backing it. He's got a long-term fall guy, one pro shooter and one Cuban."

"Juan Canestel?"

Carlos laughed. "You're a very smart 'tend to know' guy."

Littell crossed his legs. "Kemper figured it out. And in my opinion, you shouldn't trust psychopaths who drive bright red sports cars."

Carlos bit the tip off his cigar. "Guy's a capable guy. He's got a Commie-type patsy with a job on one of the motorcade routes, two real shooters and some cops to kill the patsy. Ward, you can't fault a guy who came up with the same plan as you fucking independent of you."

He felt calm. Carlos couldn't break him. He still had the chance to maim Bobby.

"I wish it could have been you, Ward. I know you got a personal stake in seeing that man dead."

He felt secure. He felt inimical to Pete and Kemper.

"I wasn't pleased that Mo and Santo cozied up to Castro. Ward, you should have seen me when I found out."

Littell took out his lighter. It was solid gold—a gift from Jimmy Hoffa.

"You're building up to something, Carlos. You're about to say, 'Ward, you're too valuable to risk,' and offer me a drink, even though I haven't touched liquor in over two years."

Marcello leaned in. Littell lit his cigar.

"You're not too valuable to risk, but you're way too valuable to punish. Everybody agrees with me on that, and everybody also agrees that Boyd and Bondurant constitute another fucking matter."

"I still don't want that drink."

"Why should you? You didn't steal two hundred pounds of heroin and shit all over your partners. You took part in a shakedown that you should have told us about, but that's no more than some fucking misdemeanor."

Littell said, "I still don't want that drink. And I'd appreciate it if you told me exactly what you want me to do between now and Dallas."

Carlos brushed ash off his vest. "I want you, Pete and Kemper not to interfere with Guy's plan or try to horn in on it. I want you to cut that Lockhart guy loose and send him back to Mississippi. I want Pete and Kemper to return what they stole."

Littell squeezed his gold lighter. "What happens to them?"

"I don't know. That's not for me to fucking say."

The cigar smelled foul. An air conditioner blew smoke in his face.

"It would have worked, Carlos. We would have made it happen."

Marcello winked. "You always take business on its own terms. You don't do some regret number when things don't go your way."

"I don't get to kill him. That's a regret."

"You'll live with it. And your plan helped Guy set up a diversion."

"What diversion?"

Carlos perched an ashtray on his stomach. "Banister told some nut named Milteer about the Miami job, without naming no personnel. Guy knows Milteer's a loudmouth who's got a Miami PD snitch bird-dogging him. He's hoping Milteer will blab to the snitch, who'll blab to his handler, and somehow the Miami motorcade will get canceled and divert everybody's attention away from Dallas."

Littell smiled. "It's far-fetched. It's something out of 'Terry and the Pirates.' "

Carlos smiled. "So's your story about the Teamster books. So's the whole idea of you thinking I didn't know what really happened from the gate."

A man stepped out of the bathroom. He was holding a cocked revolver.

Littell shut his eyes.

Carlos said, "Everybody but Jimmy knows. We had detectives tailing you from the fucking instant you walked me over the border. They know all about your code books and the research you did at the Library of Congress. I know you got plans for the books, and sonny boy, now you got partners."

Littell opened his eyes. The man wrapped a pillow around his gun.

Carlos poured two drinks. "You're going to set us up with Howard Hughes. We're going to sell him Las Vegas and keester him for most of his profits. You're going to help us turn the Fund books into more legitimate money than Jules Schiffrin ever dreamed of."

He felt weightless. He tried to dredge up a Hail Mary and couldn't remember the words.

Carlos raised his glass. "To Las Vegas and new understandings."

Littell forced the drink down. The exquisite burn made him sob.

95

Heroin bricks weighed down the trunk and made the rear wheels drift. A simple traffic shake would net him thirty years in Parchman Prison.

He withdrew his bank-vault stash. Some powder leaked on the floor—enough to sedate rural Mississippi for weeks.

Santo wanted his dope back. Santo reneged on their deal. Santo let certain implications linger.

Santo might have you killed. Santo might let you live. Santo might tease you with some stay of execution.

Kemper pulled up to a stoplight. A colored man waved to him.

Kemper waved back. The man was a Pentecostal deacon—and very skeptical of John F. Kennedy.

The man always said, "I don't trust that boy."

The light changed. Kemper punched the gas.

Be patient, Mr. Deacon. That boy's got eighteen days left to live.

His team was out. Banister's was in. Juan Canestel and Chuck Rogers crossed over to Guy's crew.

The hit was rescheduled for Dallas on November 22. Juan and a Corsican pro would shoot from separate locations. Chuck and two Dallas cops were set to kill the fall guy.

It was Littell's basic plan embellished. It illustrated the ubiquitous Let's Kill Jack metaphysic.

Littell disbanded the team. Lockhart returned to his Klan gig. Pete flew straight to Texas to be with his woman. The Swingin' Twist Revue was scheduled to play Dallas on Hit Day.

Littell cut him loose. Some homing instinct drew him back to Meridian.

Quite a few locals remembered him. Some colored folks greeted him warmly. Some crackers gave him ugly looks and taunted him.

He took a motel room. He half-expected Mob killers to knock on his door. He ate three restaurant meals a day and drove around the countryside.

Dusk hit. Kemper crossed the Puckett town line. He saw a ridiculous sign framed by floodlights: Martin Luther King at a Communist training school.

The photo insert looked doctored. Someone drew devil's horns on the Reverend.

Kemper swung east. He hit the switchback leading out to Dougie Lockhart's old gun range.

Dirt roads took him right up to the edge. Shell casings snapped under his tires.

He killed his lights and got out. It was blessedly quiet—no gunshots and no rebel yells.

Kemper drew his piece. The sky was pitch dark—he couldn't see the target silhouettes.

Shells crunched and skittered. Kemper heard footsteps.

"Who's that? Who's that trespassin' on my property?"

Kemper tapped his headlights. The beams caught Dougie Lockhart head-on.

"It's Kemper Boyd, son."

Lockhart stepped out of the light. "Kemper Boyd, whose accent gets more syrupy the further south he gets. You got a chameleon quality, Kemper. Has anybody ever told you that?"

Kemper hit his brights. The whole range lit up.

Dougie, wash your sheet—you look awful.

Lockhart whooped. "Boss, you got me under the hot lights now! Boss, I gotta confess—it was me that bombed that nigger church in Birmingham!"

He had bad teeth and pimples. His moonshine breath was wafting out a good ten yards.

Kemper said, "Did you really do that?"

"As sure as I'm standing here basking in your light, Boss. As sure as niggers—"

Kemper shot him in the mouth. A full clip took his head off.

96

(Washington, D.C., 11/19/63)

Bobby made him wait.

Littell sat outside his office. Bobby's note stressed promptness and closed with a flair: "I'll give any Hoffa lawyer ten minutes of my time."

He was prompt. Bobby was busy. A door separated them.

Littell waited. He felt supremely calm.

Marcello didn't break him. Bobby was a relative child. Marcello bowed when he only took one drink.

The outer office was wood-paneled and spacious. It was very close to Mr. Hoover's office.

The receptionist ignored him. He counted down to the moment.

11/6/63: Kemper gives the dope back. Trafficante rebuffs his handshake.

11/6/63: Carlos Marcello calls. He says, "Santo has a job for you," but will not elaborate further.

11/7/63: Sam Giancana calls. He says, "I think we can find work for Pete. Mr. Hughes hates spooks, and Pete's a good narcotics man."

11/7/63: He conveys this message to Pete. Pete understands that they're letting him live.

If you work for us. *If* you move to Vegas. *If* you sell the local niggers heroin.

11/8/63: Jimmy Hoffa calls, elated. He doesn't seem to care that he's in very deep legal trouble.

Sam told him about the hit. Jimmy tells Heshie Ryskind. Heshie checks into the best hotel in Dallas—to enjoy the event close up.

Heshie brings his entourage: Dick Contino, nurses and hookers. Pete shoots him full of dope twice a day.

Heshie's entourage is baffled. Why uproot to Dallas when you're so close to passing away?

11/8/63: Carlos sends him a news clipping. It reads, "Klan Leader Murdered—Baffling Deep South Riddle!"

The cops suspect rival Klansmen. He suspects a Kemper Boyd gesture.

Carlos includes a note. Carlos says his deportation trial is going quite well.

11/8/63: Mr. Hughes sends him a note. Baby Howard wants Las Vegas like most children want new toys.

He wrote back to him. He promised to visit Nevada and compile research notes before Christmas.

11/9/63: Mr. Hoover calls. He says his private taps have picked up scalding outrage—the Joe Valachi Show is terrifying mobsters coast to coast.

Hoover's inside source says that Bobby is privately interrogating Valachi. Valachi refuses to discuss the Fund books. Bobby is furious.

11/10/63: Kemper calls. He says Guy Banister's "far-fetched" ploy succeeded: the Miami motorcade was canceled.

11/12/63: Pete calls. He reports more campsite raids and hit-plot rumors.

11/15/63: Jack parades through New York City. Teenagers and middle-aged matrons swarm his car.

11/16/63: Dallas newspapers announce the motorcade route. Barb Jahelka has a front-row seat—she's performing a noon show at a club on Commerce Street.

An intercom buzzed. Bobby's voice cut through static: "I'll see Mr. Littell now."

The receptionist got the door. Littell carried his tape recorder in.

Bobby stood behind his desk. He jammed his hands in his pockets and made no forward moves—Mob lawyers received cut-rate civility.

The office was nicely appointed. Bobby's suit was an off-the-rack sack cut.

"Your name seems familiar, Mr. Littell. Have we met before?"

I WAS YOUR PHANTOM. I ACHED TO BE PART OF YOUR VISION.

"No, Mr. Kennedy. We haven't."

"I see you brought a tape recorder."

Littell set it down on the floor. "Yes, I did."

"Has Jimmy owned up to his evil ways? Did you bring me some kind of confession?"

"In a sense. Would you mind listening?"

Bobby checked his watch. "I'm yours for the next nine minutes."

Littell plugged the machine into a wall outlet. Bobby jiggled the coins in his pockets.

Littell tapped Play. Joe Valachi spoke. Bobby leaned against the wall behind his desk.

Littell stood in front of the desk. Bobby stared at him. They stayed absolutely motionless and did not blink or twitch.

Joe Valachi laid down his indictment. Bobby heard the evidence. He did not shut his eyes or in any way discernibly react.

Littell broke a sweat. The silly staring contest continued.

The tape slipped off the spindle. Bobby picked up his desk phone.

"Get Special Agent Conroy in Boston. Have him go to the main Security–First National Bank and find out who account number 811512404 belongs to. Have him examine the safe-deposit boxes and call me back immediately. Tell him to expedite this top-priority, and hold my calls until his comes through."

His voice did not waver. He came on cast-iron/steel-plate/watertight strong.

Bobby put the phone down. The eyeball duel continued. The first one to blink is a coward.

Littell almost giggled. An epigram: Powerful men are children.

Time passed. Littell counted minutes off his heartbeat. His glasses started sliding down his nose.

The phone rang. Bobby picked it up and listened.

Littell stood perfectly still and counted forty-one seconds off his pulse. Bobby threw the phone at the wall.

And blinked.

And twitched.

And brushed back tears.

Littell said, "Goddamn you for the pain you caused me."

97

(Dallas, 11/20/63)

She'll know. She'll hear the news and see your face and know you were part of it.

She'll trace it back to the shakedown. You couldn't compromise him, so you killed him.

She'll know it was a Mob hit. She knows how those guys snip dangerous links. She'll blame you for bringing her so close to something so big.

Pete watched Barb sleep. Their bed smelled like suntan oil and sweat.

He was going to Las Vegas. He was going back to Howard "Dracula" Hughes. Ward Littell was their new middleman.

It was strongarm and dope work. It was a boilerplate commuted sentence: death for life imprisonment.

She'd kicked the sheets off. He noticed some new freckles on her legs.

She'd click with Vegas. He'd boot Joey out of her life and fix her up with a permanent lounge gig.

She'd be with him. She'd be close to his work. She'd build a rep as a stand-up woman who knew how to keep secrets.

Barb curled into her pillows. The veins on her breasts stretched out funny.

He woke her up. She snapped awake bright-eyed, like always.

Pete said, "Will you marry me?"

Barb said, "Sure."

. . .

A fifty-dollar bribe waived the blood test. A C-note covered the no-birth-certificate problem.

Pete rented a 52 X-long tuxedo. Barb ran by the Kascade Klub and grabbed her one white Twist gown.

They found a preacher in the phone book. Pete scrounged up two witnesses: Jack Ruby and Dick Contino.

Dick said Uncle Hesh needed a pop. And what's he so excited about? For a dying man, he sure seems keyed up.

Pete ran by the Adolphus Hotel. He shot Heshie full of heroin and slipped him some Hershey bars to nosh on. Heshie thought his tuxedo was the funniest fucking thing he'd ever seen. He laughed so hard he almost ripped his tracheal tube out.

Dick bounced for a wedding gift: the Adolphus bridal suite through the weekend. Pete and Barb moved their things in an hour before the ceremony.

Pete's gun fell out of his suitcase. The bellhop almost shit.

Barb tipped him fifty dollars. The kid genuflected out of the suite. A hotel limo dropped them at the chapel.

The preacher was a juicehead. Ruby brought his yappy dachshunds. Dick banged some wedding numbers on his squeezebox.

They said their vows in a dive off Stemmons Freeway. Barb cried. Pete held her hand so tight that she winced.

The preacher supplied imitation gold rings. Pete's ring wouldn't fit on his ring finger. The preacher said he'd order him a jumbo—he got his stuff from a mail-order house in Des Moines.

Pete dropped the too-small ring in his pocket. The Till Death Do Us Part pitch got him weak in the knees.

They settled in at the hotel. Barb kept up a refrain: Barbara Jane Lindscott Jahelka Bondurant.

Heshie sent them champagne and a giant gift basket. The room-service kid was atwitter—the President's riding by here on Friday!

They made love. The bed was flouncy pink and enormous.

Barb fell asleep. Pete left an 8:00 p.m. call—his bride had a gig at 9:00 sharp.

He couldn't sleep. He didn't touch the bubbly—booze was starting to feel like a weakness.

The phone rang. He got up and grabbed the parlor extension.

"Yeah?"

"It's me, Pete."

"Ward, Jesus. How'd you get this—?"

Littell said, "Banister just called me. He said Juan Canestel's missing in Dallas. I'm sending Kemper in to meet you, and I want the two of you to find him and do what you have to do to make Friday happen."

98

(Dallas, 11/20/63)

The plane taxied up to a loading bay. The pilot rode tailwinds all the way from Meridian and made the run in under two hours.

Littell arranged a private charter. He told the pilot to fly balls-to-the-wall. The little two-seater rattled and shook—Kemper couldn't believe it.

It was 11:48 p.m. They were thirty-six hours short of GO.

Car headlights blinked—Pete's signal.

Kemper unhooked his seat belt. The pilot throttled down and cranked the door open for him.

Kemper jumped out. Propeller backspin almost knocked him flat.

The car pulled up. Kemper got in. Pete punched it across a string of small-craft runways.

A jet whooshed overhead. Love Field looked otherworldly.

Pete said, "What did Ward tell you?"

"That Juan's loose. And that Guy's afraid that Carlos and the others will think he fucked up."

"That's what he told me. And I told him that I didn't like the risks involved, unless somebody tells Carlos that we helped him out and saved Banister from blowing the whole fucking hit."

Kemper cracked the window. His goddamn ears kept popping.

"What did Ward say to that?"

"He said he'll tell Carlos after the hit. *If* we find Canestel and save the fucking day."

A 2-way radio sputtered. Pete turned it down.

"This is J.D. Tippit's off-duty car. Him and Rogers are out looking, and if they get a spot on Juan, *we* go in. Tippit can't leave his patrol sector, and Chuck can't do anything that could fuck him out of showing up for the hit."

They dodged baggage carts. Kemper leaned out the window and popped three Dexedrine dry.

"Where's Banister?"

"He's flying in from New Orleans later. He thinks Juan's solid, and if something happens and they lose him, he'll move Rogers into his slot, and go out with him and the pro shooter."

They knew Juan was volatile. They didn't have him tagged as a possible sex killer. The job was fucked up and full of holes and reeked of amateur-night on-the-job training.

"Where are we going?"

"Jack Ruby's place. Rogers said Juan likes to dig on the whores there. You work inside—Ruby doesn't know you."

Kemper laughed. "Ward told Carlos not to trust psychopaths with bright red sports cars."

Pete said, "You did."

"I've had some revelations since then."

"Are you saying there's something I should know about Juan?"

"I'm saying I quit hating Jack. And I don't really care whether they kill him or not."

The Carousel Club was midweek listless.

A stripper was peeling on the runway. Two plainclothes cops and a hooker clique sat at ringside tables.

Kemper sat near a rear exit. He unscrewed the bulb on his table lamp—shadows covered him from the waist up.

He could see the front and back doors. He could see the runway and stage tables. The shadows made him close to invisible.

Pete was out back with the car. He didn't want Jack Ruby to see him.

The stripper stripped to André Kostelanetz. The hi-fi played off-speed. Ruby sat with the cops and spiked their drinks with his flask.

Kemper sipped scotch. It jump-started the Dexedrine. He got cozy with a new revelation: You've got a chance to toy with the hit.

A dog ran across the runway. The stripper shooed it off. Juan Canestel walked in the front door.

He was alone. He was wearing an Ike jacket and blue jeans.

He went straight for the whores' table. A hostess sat him down.

He'd enlarged his prosthetic bulge. Check that shiv in his left hip pocket.

A sash cord was bunched into his waistband.

Juan bought drinks all around. Ruby schmoozed him up. The stripper tossed a few hips his way.

The cops checked him out. They looked mean and full of hate for non-Anglos.

Juan always carries a gun. They might shake him on general principles.

They might book him on a weapons charge. They might rubber-hose him.

He might betray Banister. The Secret Service might cancel the motorcade.

Juan loved to drink. He might show up for the hit hung over. He might jerk the trigger and miss Jack by a country mile.

Juan loved to talk. He might arouse suspicion between now and noon on Friday.

The sash cord leaked out his *front* waistband.

Juan *is* a sex killer. Juan kills with his surrogate balls.

Juan chatted up the whores. The cops kept sizing him up.

The stripper bowed and walked backstage. Ruby announced last call. Juan zeroed in on a zaftig brunette.

They'll walk out the front door. Pete won't see them. Their combustion might affect Juan's hit performance.

Kemper popped the clip out of his piece and dropped it on the floor. He left one round in the chamber—let's toy with the hit a little more.

The brunette stood up. Juan stood up. The cops looked them over.

The cops huddled. One cop shook his head.

The girl walked toward the parking-lot door. Juan followed her.

The lot fed into an alley. The alley was lined with hot-sheet-hotel doorways.

Pete was just outside.

Juan and the girl disappeared. Kemper counted to twenty. A cleanup man started slapping tables with a rag.

Kemper walked outside. A light mist stung his eyes.

Pete was pissing behind a dumpster. Juan and the whore were strolling down the alley. They were moving toward the second doorway on the left-hand side.

Pete saw him. Pete coughed. Pete said, "Kemper, what are you—?"

Pete stopped. Pete said, "Fuck . . . that's Juan. . . ."

Pete ran down the alley. The second door on the left opened and closed.

Kemper ran. They hit the door together at a full sprint.

A center hallway ran back to front. Every door on both sides was closed. There was no elevator—the hotel was one story only.

Kemper counted ten doors. Kemper heard a stifled screech.

Pete started kicking doors in. He threw his weight left, then right— clean pivots and clean flat-heel shots sheared the doors off their hinges.

The floor shook. Lights snapped on. Sad old sleepy winos cringed and cowered.

Six doors went down. Kemper crashed through number seven with a shoulder snap. A bright ceiling light caught the face-off.

Juan had a knife. The whore had a knife. Juan had a dildo strapped to the crotch of his blue jeans.

Kemper aimed at his head. His one round in the chamber went way wide.

Pete pushed him out of the way. Pete aimed low and fired. Two magnum shots blew out Juan's kneecaps.

He spun over the bed rail. His left leg dropped off at the knee.

The whore giggled. The whore looked at Pete. Something passed between them.

Pete held Kemper back.

Pete let the whore slit Juan's throat.

They drove to a doughnut stand and drank coffee. Kemper felt Dallas ooze into slow motion.

They left Juan there. They *walked* to the car. They drove off law-abidingly slow.

They didn't talk. Pete didn't mention his toy-with-fate number.

This weird adrenaline had everything running in slow motion.

Pete walked over to a pay phone. Kemper watched him feed coins into the slots.

He's calling Carlos in New Orleans. He's pleading for your life.

Pete turned his back and hunched over the phone.

He's saying Banister fucked up. He's saying Boyd killed the henchman he never should have trusted.

He's pleading specifics. He's saying, Give Boyd a piece of the hit— you know he's a competent guy.

He's pleading for mercy.

Kemper sipped coffee. Pete hung up and walked back to their table.

"Who'd you call?"

"My wife. I just wanted to tell her I'd be late."

Kemper smiled. "It doesn't cost that much money to call your hotel."

Pete said, "Dallas is pricey. And things are getting more expensive these days."

Kemper laid on some drawl. "They surely are."

Pete crumpled his cup. "Can I drop you somewhere?"

"I'll get a cab to the airport. Littell told that charter man to wait for me."

"Back to Mississippi?"

"Home's home, son."

Pete winked. "Take care, Kemper. And thanks for the ride."

His patio looked out on rolling hillsides. The view was damn nice for a discount motel.

He requested a southern exposure. The clerk rented him a cabin apart from the main building.

The flight back was beautiful. The dawn sky was goddamn lustrous.

He fell asleep and woke up at noon. The radio said Jack arrived in Texas.

He called the White House and the Justice Department. Second-string aides rebuffed him.

His name was on some kind of list. They cut him off midway through his salutations.

He called the Dallas SAC. The man refused to talk to him.

He called the Secret Service. The duty officer hung up.

He quit toying with it. He sat on his patio and replayed the ride start to finish.

Shadows turned the hills dark green. His replay kept expanding in slow motion.

He heard footsteps. Ward Littell walked up. He was carrying a brand-new Burberry raincoat.

Kemper said, "I thought you'd be in Dallas."

Littell shook his head. "I don't need to see it. And there's something in L.A. I do need to see."

"I like your suit, son. It's good to see you dressing so nicely."

Littell dropped the raincoat. Kemper saw the gun and cracked a big shit-eating grin.

Littell shot him. The impact knocked him off his chair.

The second shot felt like HUSH NOW. Kemper died thinking of Jack.

99

(Beverly Hills, 11/22/63)

The bellhop handed over his passkey and pointed out the bungalow. Littell handed him a thousand dollars.

The man was astonished. The man kept saying, "You just want to *see* him?"

I WANT TO SEE THE PRICE.

They stood by the housekeeping shed. The bellhop kept checking their blind side. He said, "Make it quick. You've got to be out before those Mormon guys get back from breakfast."

Littell walked away from him. His head raced two hours ahead and locked in to Texas time.

The bungalow was salmon-pink and green. The key unlocked three deadbolts.

Littell walked in. The front room was filled with medical freezers and intravenous drip caddies. The air reeked of witch hazel and bug spray.

He heard children squealing. He identified the noise as a TV kiddie show.

He followed the squeals down a hallway. A wall clock read 8:09—10:09 Dallas time.

The squeals turned into a dog food commercial. Littell pressed up to the wall and looked through the doorway.

An IV bag was feeding the man blood. He was feeding himself with a hypodermic needle. He was lying buck cadaverous naked on a crank-up hospital bed.

He missed a hip vein. He jabbed his penis and hit the plunger.

His hair touched his back. His fingernails curled over halfway to his palms.

The room smelled like urine. Bugs were floating in a bucket filled with piss.

Hughes pulled the needle out. His bed sagged under the weight of a dozen disassembled slot machines.

100

(Dallas, 11/22/63)

The dope hit home. Heshie unclenched and eked out a smile.

Pete wiped off the needle. "It's happening about six blocks from here. Wheel yourself to the window about 12:15. You'll be able to see the cars go by."

Heshie coughed into a Kleenex. Blood dripped down his chin.

Pete dropped the TV gizmo in his lap. "Turn it on then. They'll interrupt whatever they're showing for a news bulletin."

Heshie tried to talk. Pete fed him some water.

"Don't nod out, Hesh. You don't get a show like this every day."

Crowds packed Commerce Street from curb to storefront. Homemade signs bobbed ten feet high.

Pete walked down to the club. He had to buck entrenched spectators every inch of the way.

Jack's fans held their ground. Cops kept herding avid types out of the street and back onto the sidewalk.

Little kids rode their dads' shoulders. A million tiny flags on sticks fluttered.

He made the club. Barb saved him a table near the bandstand. A lackluster crowd was watching the show—maybe a dozen lunchtime juicers total.

The combo mauled an uptempo number. Barb blew him a kiss. Pete sat down and smiled his "Sing me a soft one" smile.

A roar ripped through the place—HE'S COMING HE'S COMING HE'S COMING!

The combo ripped an off-key crescendo. Joey and the boys looked half-blitzed.

Barb went straight into "Unchained Melody." Every patron and barmaid and kitchen geek ran for the door.

The roar grew. Engine noise built off of it—limousines and full-dress Harley-Davidsons.

They left the door open. He had Barb to himself and couldn't hear a word she was singing.

He watched her. He made up his own words. She held him with her eyes and her mouth.

The roar did a long slow fade. He braced himself for this big fucking scream.

A Note About the Author

James Ellroy was born in Los Angeles in 1948. His *L.A Quartet* novels—*The Black Dahlia*, *The Big Nowhere*, *L.A. Confidential* and *White Jazz*—won numerous awards and were international best-sellers. He lives in Connecticut.

A Note on the Type

The text of this book was set in Cheltenham, originally designed by the architect Bertram Grosvenor Goodhue in collaboration with Ingalls Kimball of the Cheltenham Press of New York. Cheltenham was introduced in the early twentieth century, a period of remarkable achievement in type design. The idea of creating a "family" of types by making variations on the basic type design was originated by Goodhue and Kimball in the design of the Cheltenham series.

Composed by Creative Graphics, Allentown, Pennsylvania
Printed and bound by Quebecor Printing Fairfield,
Fairfield, Pennsylvania
Designed by Virginia Tan